A Choice of Treasons

A Novel of *The Treasons Cycle*

To save himself he first had to save two empires, but when he tried, he found his options limited to a choice of treasons.

by

J. L. Doty

A Choice of Treasons

A Novel of *The Treasons Cycle*

1

Interference

"MR. BALLIN, IS there a fight waiting for us or not?"

The bridge of the imperial heavy cruiser *Invaradin* was silent as everyone waited to hear York's verdict, but the silence was suddenly broken by the XO's voice blaring from allship, "Down-transition in ten minutes and counting."

York had spent the last twenty minutes trying to raise the imperial embassy on Trinivan, but had run into some suspicious interference. Ten minutes from down-transiting blind into a supposedly neutral system and Captain Telyekev wanted him to make the call.

"Mr. Ballin, is it Federals?"

"I'd be guessing, sir."

"Then take your best guess."

York couldn't prove anything one way or another, but his gut was telling him this was a trap, an ambush. "I haven't been able to pick up any kind of interference signature. Just broad spectrum." The interference shouldn't be there at all, though York kept that thought to himself.

"Any idea what's causing it?"

York turned away from his console, craned his neck to look through the maze of instrument clusters that crowded *Invaradin*'s bridge. He could see only Telyekev's head, a faint shadow in the darkened lighting, though the captain's eyes were bright sparks reflecting the dim glow of his console.

Telyekev stared at York and waited. Olin Rame, the XO, peered past one end of the navigation console, while Rame's two assistants peered around the other end. Anda Gant and her assistants at the scan console had turned almost completely around to look at him. At the weapons console Franklin Stara and Paris Jondee had also turned his way: Frank frowning intently, Paris with a one-sided grin. And Magdalena Votak, encased so completely in helm controls little of her could be seen by the rest of them—York wondered if she too was peeking through some little slit in the instrumentation that enclosed her. They were looking at their lifer: Senior Lieutenant York Ballin, their lucky charm, the man who was supposed to guess with clairvoyant certainty if they were going to live or die.

York looked Telyekev in the eyes, nodded. "It's got to be feddies, sir."

Telyekev seemed to shrink. "Thank you, Mr. Ballin. Sound General Quarters. Then contact *Nostran* and the *Diana* and tell them to cut drive and coast while we go in for a look-see."

"Aye, aye, sir." York spoke into his pickup. "Watch Condition Red."

In his implants the computer demanded, *Confirm status change.*

"Red status confirmed," York said.

A loud, irritatingly unpleasant horn burped once, was followed immediately by the steady clang of the alert klaxon. York switched his implants into allship and spoke precisely. "Watch Condition Red. All hands, this is not a drill. Repeat: this is not a drill." He repeated the message once more, recording it, then put it on continuous replay and switched his pickup to the exterior com. "*Nostran*, this is *Invaradin*."

"*Nostran* here, *Invaradin*. Our computer says you're on red. What's up?"

"Could be feddies, *Nostran*, but that's only a guess. We're going in fast for a look around. Telyekev instructs you and the *Diana* to cut drive and hold back until we're sure. Please advise the *Diana*."

"Consider it done, *Invaradin*. Good hunting."

"*Invaradin* out."

"*Nostran* out."

York put a combat status summary in the corner of one of his screens. By now it was a halflit patchwork of randomly placed black and green highlights superimposed over a schematic of *Invaradin*. He looked on intently as the remaining stations completed their precombat checks, and one by one the black highlights turned to green. But suddenly one lit up with a bright, demanding red. York touched it with a finger. "Turret three," he demanded. "This is com. What's wrong?"

"We've got an inoperative ordnance feed, com. We're looking into it now, but no estimate on repair time. We have eight rounds on turret."

"Thank you, Three," York said. "I'll advise Telyekev. Com out."

"Main Three out."

One of the defensive stations red-lighted with difficulty on their computer link. York tried a temporary routing through a nearby station. That cleared the link enough for him to green-light them, with a yellow flag for the computer to check into it later.

The last station reported in. The computer automatically cut the alert klaxon and a heavy silence descended.

York switched his implants into the bridge circuit. "All stations in, sir. Main Three reports an inoperative ordnance feed; eight rounds on turret and no estimate on repair time. All other stations are green, with one conditional yellow."

"Thank you, Mr. Ballin. Did you hear that, helm?"

"Yes, sir," Maggie Votak said. "Main Three. Eight rounds. If it gets hot, I'll favor starboard."

"Very good, Miss Votak. All ahead full."

"All ahead full, sir."

York tapped into Anda Gant's scan console, pulled up an outboard scan summary in the lower corner of one of his screens where it shared space with summaries from Olin Rame's navigation console and Frank Stara's weapons console. On it he watched the small blip of the destroyer *Nostran* and the larger blotch of the lumbering freighter *Diana* drop back as they cut drive power. Then Maggie firewalled *Invaradin*'s full drive and the two ships literally disappeared from York's screen. *Invaradin* was no longer limited to the slow crawl of the lumbering freighter she'd been assigned to escort.

"Navigation," Telyekev said. "What's our new ETT?"

"I'm computing now, sir," Olin Rame said, then York's timer flickered as it abruptly changed its reading. Rame spoke again. "Estimated time to transition is now two minutes, eighty-one seconds, sir."[1]

"Thank you, Commander Rame. Lieutenant Ballin, put me on allship."

York touched a switch as he spoke. "You're on, sir."

Telyekev paused, cleared his throat, then activated his pickup. "Attention," he said. "This is Captain Telyekev. You made it on station in ninety-three seconds, almost a full minute. That's atrocious, more than ten seconds off your best time. I'll expect you to do better in the future."

He cleared his throat again. "We're just under three minutes out from transition into the Trinivanian system. Two days ago, Fleet received an urgent message from the imperial embassy there. They need help and we're the closest warship, so we've got the job. We don't know any more than that, and we're having trouble making contact with the embassy, so we suspect there may be

---

[1] See Appendix: Some Notes on Time

Syndonese Federals involved. But remember, we only suspect. We don't know. So don't go off halfcocked—"

A red light on York's console pulled his attention to some problem down on Hangar Deck. He touched a switch. "You're red-lighted, Hangar Deck. What's wrong?"

One of York's screens lit up with the image of a young female officer named Krassille Doanne. She looked worried. "We found a steering malfunction in one of the drones during prelaunch check, sir. We're working on it, but it won't be ready at transition."

"Not acceptable," York growled. "Get me Nemkov."

Doanne frowned. "I'm sorry, sir, but Lord Nemkov gave me orders to—"

"I don't give a damn what he said. Get him here. Now. And tell him that's an order."

Doanne saluted. "Aye, aye, sir."

She disappeared from the screen. A moment later Nemkov replaced her, handsome, arrogant, angry. Nemkov started to speak but York cut him off, "What's this about a faulty drone, Lieutenant?" He refused to use Nemkov's title.

Nemkov's lips tightened. "It failed prelaunch check, something in its steering."

"And why did it wait until now to fail?"

"I wouldn't know. But you're welcome to come down and ask the drone yourself, Mr. Ballin."

"God damn it, Lieutenant, we need that drone."

"I know that. We're doing everything we can, but I'm no magician. If I send that drone out we'll lose her for sure. Then we'll only have four."

"We'll only have four if you don't send her out."

Nemkov's face darkened. "We'd have five if we could get replacements, six if we could get spare parts. Tell me why we can't get spares, Ballin."

"I don't know," York lied, trying not to think of an empire no longer able to maintain a war that had lasted for generations.

"Mr. Ballin!" Telyekev growled harshly. "Pay attention."

"Sorry, sir. Bad news from Hangar Deck. We've only got four drones on green, sir. No prognosis on the fifth. I'll keep you informed but it won't be ready at transition."

"God damn it!" Telyekev snarled. "How the hell do they expect me to fight a war without spare parts? Let me speak to hangar, Mr. Ballin, and keep an eye on that timer. I want a count down on allship starting at ten seconds."

"Aye, aye, sir." York made the connection. Then his attention turned to a red light from turret six: trouble with their local targeting computer. That was an easy one; he gave them priority to back up with *Invaradin*'s comp-central. He glanced again at his timer, then switched his pickup to allship. "Transition minus ten seconds and counting," he said, keeping his voice calm and even. "Nine . . . Eight . . . Seven . . . Six . . . Five . . . Four . . . Three . . . Two . . . One . . ."

His screens fluttered. An undefined tickle crawled up the back of his spine. He cut off all external communications and said, "Sublight."

The bridge went silent. Fresh out of transition, *Invaradin* was a blind target with no idea of what she'd dropped into until Anda Gant got them data.

"We're clear to a hundred thousand kilometers and expanding, sir," she finally said.

York's implants seemed to whisper with a long collective sigh of relief.

"Thank you, Anda," Telyekev said easily. "No surprises, then. Now let's see what's on long range. Drones out, Commander. Hold them at the limit of your short range scan."

A distant, ghostly clang sounded through the hull of the ship as the four drones shot out of their launch bays. "Drones out, sir," Gant barked.

York's scan summary compressed as the drones shot outward from *Invaradin*'s hull and their effective scan baseline broadened. At fifty thousand kilometers the drones shifted into a complex circular orbit about *Invaradin*, and the scan summary compressed even faster.

With one ear tuned to the bridge circuit York touched another switch on his console. "Hangar, this is com. Drone status."

Krass Doanne answered. "Parasitic demand is smooth. Response is strong. Still no word on number five."

"Thank you, Miss Doanne," York said. "Com out." He cut her out of the circuit.

"Clear to one million klicks and expanding," Gant announced.

"Excellent," Telyekev said happily. "Good job, Anda. Hold the drones at fifty thousand klicks. Go to extreme long range and start scanning. I want a full system map soonest. Mr. Ballin, get back on that com and see if you can raise Trinivan."

"Aye, aye, sir." York reopened an exterior com channel, confident now it wouldn't provide a homing beacon for a feddie warhead, and immediately, without any effort on his part, the signal came in clearly and strongly.

"Help! Please help! Whoever you are out there, we desperately need your help. Please answer."

York frowned suspiciously at his console as the message repeated itself. He touched a switch and a clear picture formed on one of his screens: a middle-aged man with unkempt hair dressed in a wrinkled tunic and several days' growth of beard.

York checked to see that the incoming signal was riding on an imperial encryption code. That was at least some sort of identification, so he touched another switch and broadcast his own picture on the same code.

At sight of York the man on the screen stopped speaking and his eyes widened. "Who are you?" he demanded.

York spoke precisely. "I'm Senior Lieutenant York Ballin of His Majesty's Ship *Invaradin*, Captain Lord Alexiae Telyekev commanding. Please identify yourself."

"Jerrik Lassen," the man said. "Thank God you've come. We'd almost given up—"

York interrupted him sharply. "Please identify yourself fully. Where are you and what's your function?"

The man frowned. "I'm a computer tech here at the embassy."

"Which embassy?"

"Why, the imperial embassy here on Trinivan, of course."

"Of course," York said. "Now, what's a comp-tech doing at a com station? And where's your com-tech?"

"He's dead, Lieutenant. A mob of locals literally tore him apart." Lassen shivered visibly. "I'm filling in."

"Who's in charge?"

"His Excellency, Lord Frederick Cienyey."

"Very good, Mr. Lassen. Now find Lord Cienyey and bring him here immediately. Captain Telyekev will want to speak to him."

"I'm sorry, Lieutenant," Lassen pleaded. "We haven't been able to find his lordship for hours, but Mr. Harshaw's somewhere about."

"Who's Harshaw?"

"He's the vice consul."

York nodded. "Then get him."

"Right," Lassen said. He tore off his headset and stepped out of view.

York switched to *Invaradin*'s command channel. "Sir, I've got Trinivan and it doesn't sound good."

"What happened to all that interference?"

"I don't know, sir. It's gone. My guess is the feddies are playing games with us."

"Or perhaps . . ." a new voice interrupted nastily, ". . . there aren't any Federals around here at all."

York cringed at the sound of third officer Commander Lord Mayhue Sierka's voice. Sierka had joined *Invaradin*'s crew less than a year ago, and taken an immediate dislike to York. "But I'm sure you'll have some excuse, won't you, Lieutenant?"

"The feddies are out there," York insisted. "You can bet on—"

"No more excuses, Lieutenant," Sierka interrupted. "You're going to have to—"

"Enough!" Telyekev barked. "And don't make excuses, York."

"But sir, those feddies are out there. I know it."

"We all make mistakes—you fewer than most—so don't worry about it. Now what have you got on Trinivan?"

York let it drop and spoke carefully. "A dead com-tech, sir. And a half-hysterical comp-tech filling in for him. Sounds like chaos down there."

"There you go, Sierka," Telyekev said, making excuses for York. "That damn comp-tech probably doesn't know a com from a weapons console. Probably caused that interference himself."

"No doubt Your Lordship is right," Sierka said.

A new face appeared on the screen carrying the signal from the embassy: probably Harshaw, an unattractive man, with a flat face and wideset eyes. Like Lassen's, his face showed fear.

York spoke. "I believe Vice-Consul Harshaw is ready for you, sir."

"Good," Telyekev said. "Put me on without introduction. And you stay in circuit."

York put himself and Telyekev on a split screen to Harshaw. Telyekev wasted no time. "I'm Telyekev, *Invaradin*'s captain. I assume you're Harshaw?"

Harshaw nodded. He seemed to know instinctively now was not the time to speak.

"We're standing on full alert status, Harshaw, and neither of us has a lot of time. So bring me up to date fast, and don't waste my time or yours with any bullshit."

For an instant Harshaw appeared offended, but he adjusted to the situation quickly. He swallowed once, then spoke carefully. "We're mixed up in a big power play on the part of some local politicos. For the last twenty years Trinivan's been neutral, which is just another way of saying its government is loaded with factions that include hard core supporters of both the Syndonese and us imperials, and of course everything in between. But the inbetweens have lately been drifting toward the Syndonese, and the imperial sympathizers are now badly out numbered. And this unscheduled visit of Her Royal Highness was like throwing fuel on an already hot fire. She—"

"Her Royal Highness?" Telyekev barked. "You have a member of the royal family down there?"

Harshaw frowned. "Why, yes. I thought you knew."

"I know nothing," Telyekev said. "Following standard procedure we down-transited two days ago to check in with Fleet. They told us you were in trouble and you needed help. That's all. Beyond that I am wholly unaware of the situation down there."

Harshaw nodded and visibly collected himself. "The emperor's daughter, Princess Aeya, arrived unannounced four days ago with an entourage of about fifty, apparently on a lark. Her arrival aggravated an already bad situation, though my intelligence sources suspect Directorate intervention here so I don't believe she alone is responsible for this. In any case, whoever's behind it started agitating shortly after she arrived and brought it to a head two days ago. With the active help of some local politicians, and the passive sanction of others, they whipped up a mob of several thousand supporters and stormed the embassy compound. They murdered about thirty of the embassy staff—literally tore them apart in front of our eyes—and ransacked most of the embassy. Those of us who are still alive are holed up in the top two floors of the main embassy building. The mob controls the bottom four floors. We've deactivated the lifts, and have about a dozen marines guarding the lift shafts and the two emergency stairwells at either end of the building. We have no food or water, no sanitary facilities, no medical supplies, and very little ammunition left for the few weapons we have. The situation is critical, and becoming more so by the hour. And the leaders of this mob started whipping it up as soon as you made transition, so they're obviously being fed data by someone in the local government with access to off-planet scanning equipment. Something's going to happen in the next hour, and when it does, we won't be able to hold out for long."

"What about feddies?" Telyekev asked. "Are they part of the mob?"

"Certainly there are Syndonese spies all over the place," Harshaw acknowledged, "competing with all the imperial spies, I have no doubt. But as for any direct intervention by the Syndonese, I couldn't say. We've been able to identify only a few of the mob's leaders, and they're all known locals with histories as empire haters."

"Mr. Ballin," Telyekev said. "Do you have any questions?"

"Yes, sir. I'd like to know if the mob is armed. And if so, with what kind of weapons?"

"They're not heavily armed," Harshaw said. "Not more than one in twenty, and their weapons are a mish-mash of knives, guns, and rifles of all sorts."

"Any Syndonese issue weapons?" York asked.

Harshaw shrugged. "I wouldn't know a Syndonese weapon from any other kind."

"You've got a noncom in charge of your marines, don't you? Ask him."

"Right," Harshaw said. "But he's a she, and it'll take a minute." He looked at Telyekev.

"Go ahead," Telyekev told him. "Lieutenant Ballin and I have to confer anyway."

York switched off the external audio. "We're offline, sir."

"Thank you, Lieutenant. Commander Rame. Compute a short transition hop into Trinivan nearspace."

"Aye, aye, sir. But it'll be difficult to be accurate. We're already within heliopause."

"Do what you can, Olin. Mr. Ballin, this is a job for your marines, don't you think?"

A cold knot formed in the pit of York's stomach. Several months ago *Invaradin*'s marine CO had taken a bullet in the face. Telyekev wanted an experienced officer in command of them, so he'd made York acting marine CO. York wanted to snarl that they weren't his damn marines, but instead he said politely, "Yes, sir."

"Very good, York. Mr. Sierka will relieve you at com." Telyekev looked at his screen. "I see Harshaw's back."

York switched on the audio. Harshaw needed no warning. "Corporal Elkiss says she's spotted several Syndonese issue weapons, though there aren't too many, and they've all been projectile weapons, no power weapons."

Telyekev shook his head. "Doesn't really sound like feddies, does it York?"

"No, sir."

Telyekev shook his head. "Any more questions, Lieutenant?"

"No, sir."

"Then you're dismissed as soon as Commander Sierka relieves you."

York's hands trembled as he punched in a call to the marine ready-room. Master Sergeant Mieka Palevi, looking quite bored, appeared on one of his screens. The marines didn't like regular navy, especially when they had to take orders from them, and the sergeant smiled with a special sneer he reserved for York.

"Sir," Palevi said flatly.

There was never any small talk between them. "One hundred marines," York said without emotion. "Full battle kit, plast-armor, and a fifty-fifty mix of radiation and projectile weapons. Short-term rations. Hazardous situation, nonhazardous environment. Both assault boats fully manned and armed. Orbital drop to planetary surface, high G, crash priority. Got all that?"

Palevi's look of boredom changed to a smile. "Of course, sir. Will there be anything else, sir?"

York couldn't put aside the fact that no one believed him about the feddies. "Bring along two portable mortars and a couple of portable rotary blast cannons. And have you got any antipersonnel gas that's unpleasant but nonlethal?"

Palevi's face broke into a broad grin. "Oh yes, sir. Some real nasty stuff, sir. How do you want it? Grenades, mortars, or sprayed from the boats?"

"All of the above. And scramble on it. I'll be down soonest."

"Aye, aye, Cap'm," Palevi said, granting him the marine equivalent of his naval rank, though, as was customary among the marines he carefully mangled the pronunciation to distinguish it from Telyekev's rank. The marines knew how much it bothered regular navy in general, and York in particular.

Sierka sat down in the seat next to York. "You're relieved, Lieutenant."

York lifted his hands off the console, acknowledged Sierka with a sloppy salute, stood and threaded his way through the darkened clutter of *Invaradin*'s bridge. He stepped into the personnel lift, cycled the lift hatch shut, and once alone he paused to retrieve a small container of pills from a sealed pocket in his fatigues. He crammed a half dozen phets into his mouth and swallowed hard.

He returned the container to his pocket and growled, "Hangar Deck, *One Bay*," and during the ride down he damned Telyekev a dozen times for making him acting-captain-of-marines. He was a ship's officer. He didn't belong in combat armor. Put him at a console, throw warheads at him that could crack a planet; that didn't bother him half as much as stepping personally onto the soil of some godforsaken rock so some idiot with a rifle could take shots at him.

The lift door slammed open and York stepped out into service bay *One*. He caught a momentary glimpse of one of *Invaradin*'s two assault boats, appropriately named *One*, then someone slammed his chest plate hard against his ribs. He would have fallen but someone else behind him let him stumble into his back plate. They spun him about dizzily, dropped him into his leg plates and boots, checked his joints and seals. It was a routine they'd rehearsed many times, for he, unlike they, was forced to post duty as both ship's officer and marine CO, and would never have time during an alert to stop by the ready-room for his gear. But it was more than that; it was a not-so-subtle reminder of who they were, and who he wasn't. It was an insultingly familiar pair of hands—male or female—touching him momentarily where they had no right to touch him, all under the guise of checking his seals. It was insult, bordering on insubordination, but never in such a way he could call them on it.

Someone slammed his helmet down over his head, and while they were checking his neck seals someone else snapped the heavy reactor pack into place on his back. That done, the marines stepped abruptly away from him.

The suit began its initialization sequence, flashing readings and diagnostic data on the inside of his visor. He flipped the helmet visor up as Palevi stepped in front of him. Like York's, his visor was up; he smiled and slapped a pistol into York's hand. "Yer sidearm, Cap'm," he said, grinning that special grin of his.

York suppressed a snarl, looked at the gun in his hand. Palevi had chosen a grav-gun for him. Its gravity field accelerated a small fragmentation shell up to something over Mach one. The shell would puncture armor, or flesh, then fragment. It frequently caused more damage than an explosive round.

York looked at the gun clipped to the sergeant's thigh plate, a bluish-black, chemically-powered, heavy-caliber slug thrower. Every time York saw that gun he thought of the previous marine CO, a desk jockey assigned to *Invaradin* with lots of rank and no experience. The marines had gotten into a pinch on some jerkwater planet and their new CO called *Invaradin* for fire support. Unfortunately he didn't know how to do so correctly, and *Invaradin* cut her own marines to pieces. After it was over the new CO was among the dead, though oddly enough no shrapnel had touched him. He'd been shot in the face by a chemically-powered, heavy-caliber slug thrower.

York gave his sidearm a quick once-over, snapped it into the clips on his thigh plate without fully inspecting it.

"You had a chance to check out the news yet, Cap'm?"

York looked at Palevi quizzically. When they'd down-transited the day before to check in with Sector, they'd received not only an urgent message to rendezvous with *Nostran* and the *Diana* and proceed with all haste to Trinivan, but also a standard transmission packet. York hadn't had time to review it personally, but it would contain mail, promotions, reassignments, transfers, and an up-to-date summary of every newsworthy occurrence since they'd gone out on patrol. "No, Sergeant, I haven't."

Palevi's grin broadened. "Darant bought the farm eight days ago somewhere in Orion. It's been confirmed."

York's armor grew very warm. "Who's the new Senior Drop Officer?"

"Sadeline," Palevi said. "She's on the *Lonesome Star* somewhere in this sector. You know, sir, with all your time on the clock, that moves you up to number two."

"No it doesn't," he growled. "I can't be SDO because I ain't no goddamn marine."

Palevi shook his head. "Don't worry about it, Cap'm. The closer you get to SDO the less likely you are to get shot. The way I figure it, them feddies don't wanna kill you until the reward's good."

"Shut up!" York snarled. "Visors down and seal 'em up, Sergeant. Short inspection and com check."

"But, sir, we've already che—"

"I don't give a damn. Do it."

Palevi saluted casually. "Yes, sir," he said, then shouted orders at his marines. They lined up quickly in front of *One*, their rifles held out for inspection, visors down. Palevi spotted something he didn't like, did more shouting.

Someone behind York cleared his throat politely. "Um. Lieutenant?"

York turned about slowly, found Canticle Thring dressed in the long, archaic robes of a churchman. York didn't have much use for the church; among crew he was not unusual in that. "What can I do for you, Canticle?"

The man seemed almost frightened of York. "I was wondering, Lieutenant, ah . . . if any of your people might care to be blessed before going into danger."

York shook his head, couldn't believe the man would ask such a stupid question. "Sorry. No time for that."

York turned back to Palevi and his marines, dropped his visor, felt his ears pop as his suit ran an automatic pressure check. A small square in the upper-right corner of the visor blackened and his suit computer displayed a stylized image of a suit of armor colored in green. A readout next to it told him they'd fully recharged the core of his reactor pack; he was carrying a capacity of well over fifty gigawatt-hours. "Computer," he said. "Status, physical, execute." The display on the inside of his visor changed to the silhouette of a naked man. The right knee and ankle were tinted a pale yellow; old wounds, old damage. The suit would keep the pressure seals around the knee and ankle slightly over-inflated to provide extra support, but short of having a new leg cloned it was the best he could do for now.

He shrugged inwardly, keyed his com. "Count off, Sergeant."

"Count off," Palevi shouted.

"One." "Two." "Three." "Four," came the reply, each word spoken in a different voice. The damn marines were a breed apart. The empire couldn't even keep them supplied in uniforms, but while their armor was patched and stained and blackened here and there, it functioned perfectly, like the marines themselves. They weren't much to look at—not much to like, either—but when needed they functioned, and they functioned well. York had to admire them for that, if nothing else.

The count reached one hundred. York keyed his com. "Sergeant, is Private Dakkart dropping with us?"

"Yes, sir. I worked out—"

"I thought we agreed she wouldn't drop again."

"We did, sir. But she's one of my best. I need her, so I made a deal with her."

"What kind of deal?"

"I'd rather not say, sir."

"I'll bet you'd rather not say! Anyone else I should know about?"

"Yes, sir. Private Stacy. New man, green as they come. This'll be his first hot drop."

"Both of them," York said. "Front'n'center."

Palevi shouted orders into his com. Two figures broke ranks and sprinted forward to stand rigidly in front of York. They flipped their visors up, held their rifles out for inspection.

York's ears popped again as he lifted his own visor, looked into the helmet of the shorter of the two. Female, not unattractive, with the fading remnant of a black bruise framing one eye. York kept his voice low. "You've got Palevi to thank for one more chance. But if you get into another brawl on this ship you'll never drop again."

She rightly said nothing.

York stepped sideways to stand in front of the new recruit. In the kid's helmet, York saw a young face with blond hair and blue eyes, and a chin that barely needed shaving.

"How old are you?" York asked.

"I'll be seventeen next month, sir."

Palevi leaned forward. "Excuse me, sir," he said politely. He turned to the boy, bellowed at the top of his lungs, "The cap'm did not ask you how old you will be, private. He asked you how old you are. And when you speak to the cap'm you'll address him properly. And I can't hear you. Is that clear?"

"Sir," the boy screamed. "Yes, sir."

Palevi stepped aside, spoke calmly to York, "Sorry about that, sir."

York nodded, looked at Stacy again. "How old are you?"

"Sir. Sixteen, sir," the boy screamed.

"Who are you buddied with?" York asked.

"Sir. Mackin, sir."

York shook his head. "Now you're buddied with Private Dakkart here."

Dakkart broke discipline. "But sir! I—"

Palevi shouted her down. "As you were, private."

Palevi, Dakkart, and Stacy all turned into statues of very silent stone as York said, "See to the details, Sergeant."

York's com came to life with Olin Rame's voice. "Stand by for transition." There was a pause, then Rame barked out a short countdown sequence. York felt *Invaradin* up-transit, then almost immediately down-transit. Another pause, then, "Stable orbit in two minutes."

York suppressed the panic crawling up into his gut. "Load 'em up, Sergeant."

Palevi shouted more orders. The marines split into two squads, Palevi in charge of one, and a female corporal named Tathit in charge of the other. Tathit double-timed her squad through an air lock to *Two Bay*. Palevi and his marines scrambled into *One*'s open hatch. York, the last to enter, took the commanding officer's position immediately aft of the hatch, a small recess that allowed him to be the first out in the drop zone. Like the rest of the marines, he sat down, strapped himself in place and waited.

"Cap'm," his helmet speaker said. "This is Pilot Corporal Hackla. Bridge reports weather over the embassy looks good. High G drop, right sir?"

York answered, "Crash priority. And give me a full exterior scan."

"Yes, sir. One moment, sir."

Hackla sent him a signal that blackened the inside of his visor, then showed the view forward of the gunboat: the open hatch of *One*'s now evacuated service bay, with just the edge of a blue-green globe showing in one corner.

"Stable orbit and ejection in twenty seconds . . . nineteen . . . eighteen . . ."

York stopped listening and spoke into his helmet without keying his com. "Computer. Hi-gee dosage, maximum. Execute."

He felt a pinch in his neck as one of his suit injectors fired: a mix of G drugs, phets, aggression hypes, and a few other things the marines wanted in their mood of the moment.

They cut gravity in *One Bay* and York's stomach rose up into his throat. A moment later Hackla activated *One*'s internal fields and his stomach dropped back into his bowels. A loud clang echoed through *One*'s hull as *Invaradin*'s docking boom pushed the boat gently out through the hatch.

"You all right, Cap'm?" Palevi asked.

York ignored him.

"Don't worry, sir, you'll make a good marine yet."

"Not if I can help it," York growled, then opaqued his visor, returning to the view forward of the boat. The bloated globe of a large planet now filled it almost completely.

Hackla's count reached zero. With the internal fields of the boat compensating, there was no sensation of acceleration, but a small readout superimposed in one corner of York's visor flickered and displayed a steadily rising number. After a moment it stabilized at thirty, and Hackla's voice said, "Shall I hold it at thirty G's, sir? Can't compensate beyond that."

"Take it to the limit," York growled, "Captain's orders."

A large, heavy hand pressed on York's chest, and the number on his display rose immediately to thirty-three. "Three G's internal, sir."

The number rose further. "Five . . . Eight . . . Ten . . . Holding at ten."

York instructed his suit to give him another dose of hi-gee, concentrated on breathing slow, steady, deep breaths. "Maneuvering," Hackla said. "Going to fifteen gravities internal."

York cursed.

"Eighteen G's. Twenty . . ."

York didn't actually black out. By that time he was so loaded on phets he couldn't lose consciousness, but he did drift off to a place where nothing seemed to matter, where he didn't care that he was a lifer, that the only perk in his retirement package was a free burial in space.

••••

His Majesty, Edvard the tenth, Duke de Lunis, King of the Nine Beasts, Commander-in-Chief of the nine fleets of the royal navy, guardian and protector of the people's faith, beloved emperor of the Lunan Empire, sat in the dark of his office and waited, feeling powerless and impotent.

He was much younger in years than his appearance, but the constant strain of ruling a crumbling empire losing a two-hundred-year-old war had etched deep lines in an almost boyish face. And as so many times before in his thirty-eight years of living, he wished again he was not king and emperor.

A soft knock at the door pulled him out of his dismal reverie. He rubbed his eyes and commanded the computer, "View." A display on his desk showed a tall and powerfully built man dressed in a naval uniform, unable to hide his impatience as he waited beyond the door.

"Admit," Edvard commanded the computer.

The door swung open instantly. The naval officer entered at a brisk walk, his back straight, and at first glance one might think him to be in late middle age, but a closer inspection revealed the signs of a much older man. He stopped before Edvard's desk, and holding a single piece of paper in his right hand he stood at rigid attention.

Edvard shook his head. "Please drop the formalities, Theodore. You have some news?"

Without relaxing the naval officer took the piece of paper in both hands and looked at it carefully. "*Invaradin* made transition into the Trinivanian system about an hour ago; they believe there are no Directorate ships in the vicinity. They've contacted the embassy and are trying to evacuate her personnel now, though the embassy reports approximately thirty dead so far. I've asked *Invaradin* to send us a complete list of casualties and survivors as soon as possible."

"What about *her*?" Edvard demanded.

The naval officer shook his head. "I don't know. I was afraid to ask about her specifically, don't want to draw attention to her. We can't afford even a hint of suspicion."

"I know," Edvard said, rubbing his eyes tiredly. "I know. Who's captain of the *Invaradin*?"

"Alexiae Telyekev. Old-line nobility. Fifth son of the Earl of Seegat. No inheritance prospects so he's made what he can of a commission. Basically a good man."

"Can he be trusted?"

Rochefort shrugged. "God knows, but I wouldn't risk it. If she's already dead, then he can't help, and if she isn't, then she's not likely to come to harm now that *Invaradin*'s on hand. And one never knows who's working for Admiralty Intelligence or the church. Don't forget AI reports only to the Admiralty, not through the normal chain-of-command. And those bastards do what they damn well please."

"Damn! How could it have gone so wrong? Years of careful planning, all for nothing."

"It's not over yet. *Invaradin*'s a good ship."

"What about Red Richard?" Edvard asked. "You told me yesterday he's been operating in that area. And there're rumors that he's working with the Syndonese."

Rochefort shook his head. "Richard's a Mexak, and pirates like easy pickings. I don't think he'll mix it up with *Invaradin*. I'm more concerned about the Syndonese. You know the riots on Trinivan began within hours of her arrival there."

"Coincidence?" Edvard asked.

"Not likely. Somebody was tipped off."

"Not from this side," Edvard said. "There are too few of us who know."

"It's possible the Trinivanians are working with the feddies. I suspect Telyekev's people are in a lot more danger than they realize."

2

Long Ago

"ATTEEUUN . . . SHUUUUUN!"

The shout startled York Ballin and he tried to assume the correct posture, but the manacles on his wrists and ankles prevented him from standing properly rigid with his hands at his sides. There was some sort of commotion near the front of the crowd, but York was only twelve years old and the forest of tall uniformed strangers surrounding him blocked his view. He glanced at the female marine standing guard over him, and, as if she sensed his gaze, she looked down at him, her face devoid of expression, her eyes cold and unsympathetic. "As you were," he heard someone say, and everyone relaxed.

"Spacer Apprentice York Ballin," someone barked. "Front'n'center."

The female marine nudged York unkindly.

He decided a look of simple innocence would be best. Edging forward among the elbows, he stepped out into the only clear space on Hangar Deck.

Behind a table sat three officers. York didn't know them, but guessed the woman in the middle was the captain. He threw his shoulders back, did his best to stand very proper and rigid.

The captain took no interest in him. Her hair was neatly trimmed, and she wore a freshly pressed uniform open at the collar. She glanced at a comp-tablet on the table before her, leaned to her right for a moment to consult privately with the sharp-eyed male officer seated next to her, then turned her attention to York. She had soft, pleasant eyes, and York hoped he might have better luck with her than with the marine. "At ease, Spacer Ballin."

York pretended to relax.

"I am Captain Jarwith, and this is captain's mast. Do you know what that means?"

York shook his head. "I'm sorry, ma'am, no."

She nodded. "Then I'll explain. Captain's mast is an informal proceeding convened for the purpose of disciplining enlisted personnel. It allows me to correct certain deficiencies in my crew without resorting to a trial or court-martial. Do you understand?"

"Yes, ma'am," York said. No trial; it appeared the old broad was going to be an easy touch after all.

"Good," she barked rather tersely. Again she looked down at the comp-tablet. "Now it's customary that a crewmember's civilian past is not held against him, but I'm free to consider it if I choose. Four months ago, while stealing an old woman's purse, you struck her on the head with a blunt object, causing her death. I don't mind telling you, if you were to commit such a crime while under my command, I'd keelhaul you out to an appropriate set of coordinates then vent you."

York didn't like the way her voice hardened as she spoke. "I'm not the one who hit her. And what's keelhauling?" he asked. "And what's venting?"

Her voice cracked angrily. "Pray you never learn.

"Because of your age the civilian courts chose not to execute you, even though you had previously been arrested god knows how many times. And for reasons I still don't understand, they pressed you into the navy instead of sentencing you properly, most unusual since the press gangs don't ordinarily take capital offenders. But be that as it may, you joined this ship on the planet Dumark and since that time have been a continuing disciplinary problem for my subordinate officers. You're conniving, deceitful and disobedient."

"But I try," York lied in a pleading voice.

"No you don't," she said. "Your civilian rearing has taught you if you can get beyond the moment, then you can repeat any offense you wish as often as you wish, and probably get away with it. But here that will not be the case. You committed an act of gross insubordination while this ship was on alert status. You disobeyed a direct order and struck the NCO in charge of your station."

"But she hit me first."

Captain Jarwith's eyes turned the color of steel. "Don't say anything more."

She paused, looked at him carefully for a moment, then barked out a sequence of staccato commands. "I sentence you to thirty days unflavored protein cake and water, and thirty days suspension of pay. During that time you will be given the dirtiest, filthiest, most dangerous jobs on this ship, and when not on duty you will be confined in the brig. Do you have anything to say for yourself?"

York stifled a sigh of relief. The punishment was a harsh one, but it evidently could have been worse. He tried to look deeply remorseful, thinking he could steal real food and wheedle his way out of the brig when needed. "No, ma'am," he said.

She frowned. "No doubt you think you can get around this punishment in some way. But you need to learn I have absolute power over your life, your very existence, and I will tolerate nothing less than absolute and instant obedience. And to teach you that lesson, I sentence you to fifty strokes of the lash."

York frowned. "What's a lash?"

Jarwith's eyes turned almost sympathetic, and there was no joy in her voice. "The lash is a strip of hardened plast two millimeters thick, one centimeter wide and two meters long. Its method of use is … well … it's really quite impossible to describe." She looked at the female marine guarding York and nodded. "Sergeant."

"Aye, aye, ma'am," the marine snapped crisply, then literally picked York up by the manacles on his wrists. He struggled but she cuffed him once across the jaw, then dropped him on his feet between the girders supporting two bulkheads. Two marines joined her and helped her manacle his wrists separately to the girders. York heard the unmistakable hum of a power knife as she cut away the back of his fatigues, then left him standing with his back bare and his arms spread wide.

An ominous figure stepped into York's now limited field of view. It was human in shape, but encased head to foot in mottled gray-black plast, with a face hidden behind the silvery glare of a helmet visor. It was the first time York had ever seen a marine in full-combat plast-armor. Someone had made judicious use of black tape to obscure all identifying insignia, as well as the name stenciled on the marine's chest plate.

The marine saluted Jarwith crisply. She returned the salute and handed him a long strap of transparent plast. He doubled it up in his right hand, then struck it against the armored gauntlet of his left. It cracked against the plast with a sharp snap, and York suddenly understood the lash.

The marine walked around him, behind him, out of his field of view. Jarwith remained in front of him, standing at arm's length, her eyes filled with sadness. That scared York even more than had the whip-crack of the lash against the marine's gauntlet.

"I'm sorry," he pleaded. "I didn't mean to do it. I won't do it again."

Jarwith shook her head and spoke without rancor. "Yes you did and yes you will, though I do believe at this moment you are truly sorry. But if I let you go now, you won't learn the lesson you need to learn."

She looked over York's shoulder, nodded at the marine. "You may proceed."

The metallic voice of the armored marine's helmet speaker answered her. "Aye, aye, ma'am."

There came an infinitesimal instant during which York had enough time to hope he was mistaken about the nature of this punishment. Then he heard a loud snap, and a pencil thin line of searing, white-hot fire etched itself with infinitely painful slowness across the back of his shoulders. His universe exploded, expanding like the fireball of a warhead in deep space, then shrinking again to that thin, narrow line of incandescent pain. He screamed and pulled violently at his restraints, had a nightmarish vision of his back splitting open to disgorge gouts of fire.

The instant ended, and the metallic voice of the marine's helmet speaker said, "One."

There came no delay now, no moment of respite. A second line of pain cut into York's back, burning its way this time across his ribs, and he disappeared for an instant into a gulf of black nothingness.

"Two," the marine barked.

The lash struck a third time, "Three," and a fourth, "Four." Each time the marine voiced the count, and each time the blackness of an unknowing vacuum swallowed York for a longer and deeper moment, while between the strokes he screamed and cried and begged for mercy. For a few strokes he screamed almost continuously, until finally he was unable to scream at all. Then the black gulf devoured him and he felt nothing more . . .

Awareness returned slowly. He still hung by the manacles between the bulkheads, too exhausted to whimper or cry. His back was a smoldering cauldron of fire, and he could no longer distinguish the pain of the individual strokes. In front of him the ship's doctor stood facing Jarwith, an injector in his hand. "That'll keep him conscious," the doctor said to Jarwith.

Jarwith nodded. "Any chance of permanent damage? It'd be a shame if he died."

The doctor shook his head. "He's young and strong. Probably be okay."

Again Jarwith nodded. "Thank you."

The doctor stepped out of York's field of view while Jarwith came closer and filled it completely. Her eyes were now deeply sad. "The count stands at twenty-three," she said. "I can't let you pass out. You have to feel every stroke for it to do you any good, and you have to know I'm a hard woman with a hard job to do. And I want you to understand in the depths of your soul that I will do it."

He could see lines of strain around her eyes as she looked at him, and he felt oddly sorry for her. She reached into a pocket, pulled out a length of some odd, brownish material about as big around as her thumb and a bit longer. "This is leather," she said. "Real leather, the kind you don't see any more, braided strips of treated cowhide. But then you probably don't know what a cow is, do you?"

Without another word she thrust the plug of material edgewise into York's mouth. It tasted strangely unfamiliar. "When the lash strikes again," she said, "bite down on that. Bite down hard. It helps a little. Not much, but a little." Then she turned her back on him, walked a few paces away, turned to face him again, and called loudly, "The count stands at twenty-three. Continue the sentence."

3

Confrontation

"CAP'M."

York came back from wherever he'd been.

"We're about two minutes out from the embassy, sir."

Without thought York said, "Computer, hi-gee antidote, execute." There came the all too familiar pinch in the side of his neck, then relief as the hi-gee antidote flooded his system. "Computer, status, global, execute." The inside of his visor flashed a detailed summary of his armor status: reactor pack levels and reserves; seal conditions; minor malfunctions flagged for repair at the next overhaul; maintenance status and schedules; his first aid reserves, which consisted primarily of drugs.

He put *One*'s outboard view on the inside of his visor, saw a large city sliding rapidly beneath *One*'s hull, a mix of old and new buildings. He keyed his com. "When you get to the embassy, circle it once at three hundred meters and give me a pan of the entire compound."

"Yes, sir."

Hackla kept them low, less of a target, skimming the rooftops of a semiresidential district. The tallest structure in the area appeared to be the main embassy building standing on the horizon dead ahead. The pilot banked to one side, began a turn while decelerating and lifting the nose to gain altitude. The view in York's visor suddenly shifted to a camera in the side of the craft, and as they rose above the city they circled the embassy slowly.

The embassy compound consisted of one large, square, six-story structure, several smaller buildings that were probably residential, what looked like a small barracks, and a large garage for surface craft. The whole was surrounded by a stone wall about three meters high, with wide avenues between buildings that had probably been spacious gardens, but now seethed with a mob that overflowed the compound wall and spilled out into the streets beyond, a sea of faces that swelled and rippled like the waters of some human ocean.

As Hackla banked *One* and began dumping altitude, a sharp ping reverberated through the gunboat's hull, some fool with a rifle taking shots at *impers*.

A small crowd of people were gathered on the roof of the tallest building waving frantically at *One* as it approached. Vents and climate control equipment cluttered the roof, but there were also several stretchers lined up. York keyed his com. "Sergeant. Are you watching this?"

"Yes, sir."

"Apparently our people control only the top two floors of that building. When we hit the DZ secure the roof and those two floors. There's also a member of the royal family down there—one Princess Aeya, daughter of the emperor. Find her. Put one of your best people on her. Tell him to stay with her no matter what, and to keep her alive."

"Think this is more than just a riot, Cap'm?"

"I'm not paid to think, Sergeant. Hackla, can you hover about ten centimeters above the roof?"

"You got it, sir."

York switched to the pickups on his helmet, which gave him the illusion of a transparent visor, though to someone facing him it would appear an opaque, shiny black. The boat's drive whined for a moment, then steadied to a low hum. "Cap'm, we're zoned for drop."

York popped the clips on his safety harness, stood, stepped up to the hatch. He slapped the hatch release, and with a hiss and outrush of air the hatch slid quickly into the bulkhead. He stepped out, dropped to the embassy roof, heard his marines fanning out behind him. Palevi and Tathit knew what to do without York's interference.

Harshaw stepped in front of him. "Lieutenant Ballin, you can't believe how happy we are to see you."

York flipped his visor up, and with it open the chant coming from the mob below was a deafening roar. Behind Harshaw a cluster of people were crowded about a single stretcher. "Who's on the stretcher?" York asked.

Harshaw looked over his shoulder. "Lady Sylissa d'Hart. She's—"

"Where's the princess?"

Harshaw flinched at the interruption. "She's the young one," he said, indicating a young girl in her midteens, wearing an unadorned coverall, kneeling beside the stretcher. She was crying.

York stepped around Harshaw to the stretcher. The princess looked up and stood to face him. Harshaw bowed deeply. York bowed too, but in the armor he was limited to a much shallower bow, and he saw the princess' eyes flash angrily at what she ignorantly considered an affront. She started to say something but stopped suddenly, and looking over York's shoulder she demanded angrily, "Where's it going?"

"*One* lifting," Hackla said on the com, "clearing for *Two*."

"There isn't room for two boats on the roof," York said, "not if it isn't absolutely necessary." As an afterthought he added, "Your Highness."

"But Syl's hurt," she pleaded, "badly. We have to get her up to your ship now, before she dies."

"I'm sorry, Your Highness. But I have to stabilize this situation before we can evacuate anyone. And we'll need both boats if a fight starts."

"Well, it's up to you to see to it a fight doesn't start. And Syl's dying. I command you to evacuate her instantly."

Clearly, logic would have little influence on her. He keyed his com. "This is Ballin. I want a medic on the roof immediately."

He stepped around the princess and bent over the woman on the stretcher. She was about York's own age—midthirties—and in obvious pain, clutching one arm tightly to her chest. Somehow she forced a smile to her lips, managed to choke out, "Sorry to be so much trouble."

York tried to give her a reassuring smile, though the way the phets chewed on his nerves it probably looked more like a snarl. At that moment, a female medic knelt down beside him.

"Lady d'Hart," York said politely. "May my medic examine your wound?"

The woman nodded, apparently finding speech too difficult.

The medic went to work immediately, cutting away the bandages the embassy people had improvised.

Palevi's voice spoke on York's command circuit. "Top two floors are secure, Cap'm. Where you want them mortars?"

"Here on the roof. I want to be able to target any place in the city."

"Yes, sir. Uh, one more thing, sir. It's real quiet down here all of a sudden. These fish are up to something. We'd better get the hell out of here, or start a fight."

"Captain!" the princess shouted at him. "Don't ignore me."

She was starting to get on his nerves. "I'm sorry, Your Highness. I'm not ignoring you, but this is a very unstable situation we're in and—"

"I don't care. I command you to take Lady d'Hart up to your ship. Now."

York looked at the medic. "How bad is the wound?"

"Fragment of a rifle slug, sir, just below the left breast about four centimeters under the skin. Didn't do much damage, just some bleeding, which I've already stopped. Want me to remove it?"

"Is she critical?"

"Nah," the medic said, shaking her head.

"Then don't bother. Field prep it, give her something for the pain and report back to your squad."

"Captain!" the princess shouted. "I demand that you obey me. Now."

"Aeya . . ." the injured woman groaned. "Let Captain Ballin do his job. I've been waiting for several hours. I can wait a few more."

"But Syl," the princess pleaded. "You're hurt, and in pain."

With the little snot distracted York took the opportunity to get lost. He grabbed Harshaw, growled, "Stay close to me, and show me how to get below."

A large hatch in the roof opened onto a stairway that led to a small storage room filled with janitorial supplies; no sign of the maintenance robot that should have been there. Harshaw led him out into a hallway jammed with people, many injured, some badly. York turned on Harshaw angrily. "How many people you got?"

"A little over a thousand."

"A thousand?" York demanded. "I was told less than two hundred."

"Imperial citizens, yes, Captain. The rest are Trinivanian locals who've—"

"Then start cutting out the locals."

"But the Trinivanians have to be evacuated too—"

"No locals," York growled. "Imperial citizens only."

That brought a mixed reaction from the crowd. On many of their faces the already visible fear turned to near panic, and anger.

"But Captain. You don't understand—"

"I said no locals."

"But that's a death sentence for these people." As Harshaw spoke, the princess stepped out of the janitorial closet behind him. "These people were part of the embassy staff. If we leave them behind that mob'll tear them apart. The Empire is responsible for their lives."

"We refuse to abandon them," the princess added. "Not one member of the embassy staff will board your shuttle if the Trinivanians are not included."

York looked at her carefully. She was just young enough to be just stupid enough to mean what she said, though at the look on Harshaw's face he wondered if the embassy staff felt as strongly about it as she. *Oh hell!* he thought. He could drag her onto one of the boats, but that would only get him court-martialed. "I have to ask my captain," he said, and without waiting for a reply he flipped his visor down and keyed *Invaradin*'s command frequency. "*Invaradin*. This is Ballin."

The wait was much longer than would have occurred had there been anyone else at the com console. "What do you want, Lieutenant?" Sierka demanded unhappily.

"We've got problems down here. I need to speak with the captain."

"Captain Telyekev is busy."

"Please tell him I wish to speak with him."

"He's too busy to be bothered—"

York interrupted him. "I'm asking you, the communications officer, to relay an urgent message to my commanding officer while we are on alert status." York had to quote regulations at Sierka to get anywhere. "Failure to do so at the earliest possible convenience can be construed as dereliction of duty in the face of the enemy."

There was a pause. "And you, Lieutenant, are insubordinate."

York didn't answer. He waited, and it took even longer to get a reply this time, but Telyekev finally came online. York explained the situation quickly, though through his visor he could see that, for Her Highness, it was not quick enough.

"She's right," Telyekev said. "They're our responsibility. What do you suggest?"

"I don't know, sir. Our assault boats are too small; we'd have to make too many trips. Take too long. Maybe the *Diana*. She's got to have a cargo shuttle big enough to carry them up in three or four trips. At the same time we can send imperial citizens up in the boats, and we marines can follow last."

"You've got it, Lieutenant. Anything else?"

"Yes, sir. That cargo shuttle can't hover over the roof like our boats. She'll have to put down on the lawn, and that means I have to secure the entire compound."

"I understand, Lieutenant. I'll have the *Diana*'s shuttle awaiting your orders. And try not to damage too many of the locals."

••••

A burst of automatic weapons fire erupted up the stairwell from below. York crouched against the wall on the fifth floor, watched the burst tear into the ceiling above, splattering chips of masonry across the debris strewn floor. In reply one of his marines slung the muzzle of his rifle blindly over the edge of the stair and cut loose with a burst of his own.

York keyed his com, tried to sound confident. "All set, Sergeant?"

"All set, Cap'm," Palevi answered.

York dropped his visor. His armor seals inflated and his ears popped. He keyed his com. "Visors down and seal 'em up. Tathit, check in."

Corporal Larwa Tathit was on the roof with Palevi's best sharpshooters. "We've got four of their ringleaders clearly identified, Cap'm. On your orders we'll burn them. Until then, standing by."

"*One* and *Two*?" York demanded.

"This is Hackla holding at three hundred meters, Cap'm. All systems are hot. Standing by."

"This is *Two*. We're go, Cap'm."

York made a mental note to ask someone the name of *Two*'s pilot. "Very good. Sergeant Palevi, count off."

Palevi barked some orders into the com and the marines repeated their count. York looked up the hall. Earlier, he'd had Harshaw move all the civilians up to the top floor and the roof, and now the fifth floor was empty except for York's marines.

They'd finally found Cienyey, the imperial ambassador, hiding in the com room, interfering with Lassen and pretending he was there to be on hand for any communications from *Invaradin*. York couldn't restrict a royal ambassador's movements so he'd assigned a marine to dog his heels. He also had marines dogging the princess and Harshaw.

The stairwell was a continuous shaft from the top floor to the basement, with a landing and a doorway on each floor, and an intermediate landing half way between floors. It was Palevi's idea to take only one of the building's two stairwells, leave the other on the opposite side open so the panicked mob could escape. Now all they had to do was panic the mob.

"All marines accounted for, sir," Palevi barked.

"All right," York said. "This is Ballin. Listen up. Remember, all we want to do is clear the compound, not take prisoners or do a lot of killing. Once the action starts, if they stand and fight, or come at you, do what's called for. When they turn and run, let them go. But go ahead and unload a few rounds at their heels, help them remember which way to run.

"Along those same lines, keep use of the A-P gas to a minimum. We're going to use it heavily in the stairwells, less so in the hallways and building proper, but outside I just want them uncomfortable and scared. If you overdo it and we end up with a lot of twitching, unconscious civilians, it's going to be you who'll have to carry them outside the wall and dump them in the street."

York looked at Palevi. "Anything you'd like to add, Sergeant?"

"No, sir."

"Tathit. Your snipers ready?"

"All set, Cap'm."

York looked down the hallway at his waiting marines: lined up, ready to file into the stairwell at his command. Oddly enough he was a little proud of them. They were good at what they did, and if nothing else, they were consistent. York unclipped his sidearm from his thigh plate, thumbed the safety. "All right, Sergeant. Let's go."

Palevi handed him a gas grenade, a cold, gray cylindrical canister with a readout on one face. "After you, sir," Palevi said.

York bent into a crouch, stepped onto the landing of the stairwell with Palevi behind him, thought he could imagine the grin on the sergeant's face.

York keyed his com. "Tathit. Take out those ringleaders. *One* and *Two*. Start gassing that mob. All units go!"

York triggered his grenade, dropped it over the edge of the landing. One second later it let out a loud *whoof*, followed by a cloud of green smoke wafting upward. Someone below responded with two pistol shots that chinged off the landing above them.

Using the smoke as cover York jumped to the intermediate landing in a single bound. Half a flight below he caught a glimpse of a lone figure partially hidden by the green haze. The man was turned away from him, clutching desperately at his eyes as he aimed a pistol blindly in the wrong direction and fired a single shot. York bounded down the half-flight of stairs, landed behind the man and kicked him out into the hallway on the fourth floor. The man staggered for a moment; York was about to follow him when he heard the unmistakable scream of a large rotary wind up to a firing rate of several hundred rounds per second. The hallway erupted with streamers of tracer fire crisscrossing from both ends.

Two rotaries, York realized as he watched the man cut to pieces by dozens of small shells. He started to back up the stairs, but before he'd moved a step the streams of fire converged on the open stairwell door; the stairwell walls exploded in York's face and he went down amidst the scattered rubble. He keyed his com, screamed, "They've got rotary emplacements at both ends of the hall."

York curled up in a tight ball as the two cannons tore at the wall, hurtling fist-sized blocks of masonry against his plast-armor and redlining his reactor pack. Over the com Palevi shouted, "Cap'm's pinned down. *One* and *Two*. Take out the southeast and southwest corners of the fourth floor. On the double."

The cannons continued to rip away at the wall for a few seconds, then York heard the *crump* of a large shell, felt the building shake, and one of the rotaries went silent. An instant later he heard another *crump*, the building shook again and the scream of the second rotary ceased.

"That changes the rules," Palevi growled over the com. "Advance with caution. And don't take chances."

York struggled to pull free of the rubble as several marines sprinted past him to take up positions at the gaping hole that had once been the stairwell door. He right leg was still stuck beneath a small piece of wall, and he was tugging at it when several gauntleted hands grabbed him by the armpits and hoisted him to his feet. "You all right, Cap'm?"

York shook his legs and arms. No pain; his suit status showed all green; no breaches. "I'm okay."

"Let's try 'er again, eh sir?" Palevi handed him a grenade and crouched by the hole in the wall leading to the fourth floor. York pressed his back against the wall on the other side of the hole. Small arms fire zinged and spattered up and down the corridor. Palevi smacked his grenade against the wall, tossed it up the hall at an angle. York followed suit, tossing his down the hall. Another *whoof*, more green smoke. A bullet zinged off his armor.

Palevi nodded at two of his marines, both carrying small, four-barreled, portable versions of the emplacement rotaries they'd just faced. The two marines jumped through the door, turned back to back, dropped to one knee, sprayed shot up and down the hall. The sound of their weapons made York think of a cutting machine grinding away at thick steel. Then abruptly they ceased fire, and on cue Palevi's top corporal, a man named Baddin Hyer, filed through the doorway between York and Palevi with forty marines behind him.

Palevi held out another grenade. "One more time, eh sir?"

York took the grenade, turned away from the fourth floor hall and back to the stairwell leading down to the third floor landing. He triggered the grenade, tossed it down, waited for it blow and waft the green smoke up, then jumped to the intermediate landing, saw something moving in the swirling, green mist below him. He took no chances this time, squeezed the trigger on his grav-gun. The bullet hit something, exploded with the muted thump of a fragmentation shell.

York took the stairs two at a time, halted at the door to the third floor hall and pressed his back against the wall. A stream of bullets spattered at the doorjamb.

Palevi and five marines joined him on the third floor landing. One of the marines handed him a grenade. "Careful, sir. That ain't gas."

York looked at the canister in his hand, a fragmentation grenade with a one-pound rating. At some time in the past he'd had to learn what a pound was, recalled only that it was some archaic measure of the weight of an archaic chemical explosive used to rate the yield strength of modern explosives. Someone called over the com, "One pound hot." A moment later the building shook, and he realized Tathit and her marines were using the same explosives on the floor above. York thumbed the timer for a two-second delay, touched the trigger, stepped against the wall again and tossed the grenade up the hall. He turned his back to the doorway and keyed his com. "One pound hot."

Out in the hallway his marines split up, half going to the front of the building and half to the back. They moved slowly, stopped at each doorway, tossed a fragmentation grenade through it, followed the explosion by spraying the room with rifle fire, cleared the room quickly, then moved on. They advanced steadily, herding the opposition before them, killing quickly and efficiently the few that tried to fight back.

Corporal Hyer's voice came over the com. "The side hall on the fourth floor is secure, Cap'm. We're moving out into the front and back halls now."

The two stairwells ran up the sides of the building, and on each floor opened out into a short hall that ran from front to back, connecting long hallways at the front and rear of the building. Like Hyer's marines above, York's were now moving out into the front and rear main halls, slowly working their way toward the stairwell on the other side.

"Hyer," York heard his com say. "This is Palevi. Ten imperials says we take the other stairwell first."

"You're on, Mieka," Hyer answered.

It was like a game to the marines, York realized: not a fun game, but at least a challenging game. Kill them and move on. He keyed his com. "Tathit, what's that crowd outside doing?"

"They're climbing all over each other trying to get away."

"Cap'm Ballin, this is Hyer. We've reached the other stairwell. Fourth floor is secure."

"Cap'm, this is Palevi. Third floor's secure. Total elapsed time: three minutes, eighty-one seconds. I owe ya ten, Bad."

"Make it ten drinks and you can help me finish them, eh Mieka?"

"Yer on, Corporal."

They took the lower floors with the same technique: Hyer and his platoon moving through the second floor while York and Palevi and their marines worked their way across the first. They ran into far less opposition, but they still moved slowly, checked out each room first before moving on. Hyer's squad swept the basement, and when they'd finished York stopped in the ground-floor entrance and surveyed the littered and chewed up embassy grounds. The only remnants of the mob were quite a few civilians sprawled haphazardly about, whether dead or wounded or overgassed, York couldn't tell. It had all been easy, he realized. Too easy.

4

Assault

"I'M NOT LEAVING until you have the last Trinivanian safely on his way."

York looked at the Princess and swallowed his temper. "Your Highness, Captain Telyekev has ordered me to evacuate the embassy staff first."

"I don't care about your orders. I'm not leaving until I'm satisfied you're taking proper care of these people."

York looked at the Trinivanians seated on the lawn, men, women, and children, huddled together in small groups, ringed by armed marines. To one side a smaller group of about three hundred had already been searched and was ready to leave.

A deep male voice behind York said, "You're treating them like criminals."

York turned around, faced another churchman. He wondered if they all made a habit of sneaking up on you that way.

"I'm Archproverb Rhijn, Her Highness' personal confessor. And you *are* treating these people like criminals."

York nodded deferentially to the churchman. "Your Eminence, we have no records on them, so we have to be careful."

"But do you have to search them like criminals?"

"Yes," the princess agreed. "Surely that's not necessary."

To the princess, he said, "We're just being thorough, Your Highness. The captain of the *Diana* has requested it, and rightly so. It would be disastrous if we allowed armed civilians aboard his ship."

"Don't be ridiculous. These people aren't armed."

York struggled to remain polite. "But quite a few of them are, or were. We've already accumulated a large collection of dangerous devices."

She scoffed, "*Dangerous devices!* What have you actually found, a few letter openers?"

"Yes, Your Highness," York said, "and we've also found several power knives, and one fellow even had a grav-gun much like my own sidearm, though his was Syndonese issue. We're giving him the benefit of the doubt and assuming he picked it off one of the dead rioters."

The princess sneered. "That's very big of you."

York shrugged. "In any case, Your Highness, I have my orders, and if you can convince my CO to change my orders, then I will, of course, obey. But short of that, there's nothing I can do."

The princess shook her head sadly, turned her back and, accompanied by Rhijn, walked away. But he heard her mumble under her breath, ". . . mindless automaton."

"Bitch," York growled under his breath.

"Cap'm," York's com said. "This is Palevi. We've cleared the last building. The compound is secure. With your permission I'd like to put most of my people around the wall, with a couple on the roof as lookouts."

"Very good, Sergeant."

Quite a number of dead locals littered the lawn, most trampled to death in the mindless stampede of the mob. The lower floors of the main embassy building were a much more grisly sight. It was astounding that unorganized civilians thought they could stand against armored, professional, disciplined, imperial regulars. And where the hell did they get rotaries?

A large shadow slid across the ground in front of York. He looked up, caught a glimpse of *One* disappearing into the heavens with the first load of embassy staff. *Two* came in from the other direction—York had learned the pilot's name was Blake—and slowed carefully as it approached the embassy roof.

"Ballin," his com said. "This is *Invaradin*. The *Diana*'s shuttle is about one minute out from you."

"Thank you, Commander Sierka," York said. He dropped his visor, programmed it to display a copy of *Two*'s overhead scan, used the blip displayed there to locate the *Diana*'s shuttle. *I hope we can get this done before nightfall,* he thought.

The shuttle had trouble setting down. It was much larger than the assault boats, had no hover ability and needed a short distance for landing. They were stretching its capabilities bringing it down in the embassy compound.

York had a few words with the shuttle's pilot. The loading went smoothly, and York relaxed a bit as he watched the ungainly cargo shuttle lift off the lawn.

"Cap'm. This is Palevi. I got something here I think you should see."

"I'm busy. Can it wait?"

"No, sir. I don't think so. Not this."

"All right. Where are you?"

"In the ambassador's residence. Private Stacy'll show you the way."

York turned around, found Stacy waiting behind him standing at a very rigid attention. "Lead on, private," he said.

The boy screamed, "Sir. Yes, sir," then he turned around and moved away at a trot.

"Slow down, private," York called after him.

Stacy led him to a one story, spacious, residential building, clearly the ambassador's residence. The mob had trashed the place, though it was clear the shattered furniture had once been rather lavish. Palevi and his marines were waiting in a hall toward the back of the building. "What is it?" York demanded as he stormed up to the sergeant.

"This," Palevi said without humor, then opened a door to a nearby room. The stench hit York like a slap in the face.

It had been a private bedroom, shared by two young girls, both still tied to their beds with their arms and legs spread. The two girls had died unpleasantly at the hands of the mob, with dried blood spattered throughout the room. York had to turn away, step out into the hall. Palevi followed him and closed the door.

York thought carefully; the list of missing or dead imperial citizens had not included two young girls. He dropped his visor so he wouldn't have to put up with the smell and reentered the room.

Both girls were locals. One about fourteen, the other about ten or twelve. York looked at the debris scattered about the floor, most of it broken beyond recognition, but it was the kind of paraphernalia found in most whorehouses.

He returned to the hall, closed the door again and flipped his visor back up. "Get me Harshaw," he barked angrily. "I want him here on the double, whether he likes it or not. And don't say anything about this."

Palevi barked orders into his com. York walked to the end of the hall and waited in sight of the front entrance to the residence. When the assistant consul arrived, escorted by two marines,

York could see his face as they directed him toward the hall, and his expression darkened. When he reached York, and saw down the hall where Palevi and his marines waited, he almost flinched.

York grabbed Harshaw's arm, bent it into an elbow lock, used it to push him down the hall. "Open the door," he shouted at Palevi as he hustled Harshaw toward the marines. Palevi moved quickly, had the door open before York reached it, and York literally threw Harshaw into the room.

Harshaw fell to the floor, started coughing and gagging. As he tried to rise, York grabbed his lapels and slammed his back against a wall, shoved one armored forearm under his chin and pressed hard enough to cut off his breathing. York kept the pressure on, and as Harshaw's eyes began to bulge he growled in his face, "What happened here?"

Between breaths Harshaw gasped out, "The mob must have killed them."

"I can see that, but why so brutal? And what the hell were they doing here in the first place?"

Harshaw closed his eyes for a long moment, then opened them and said, "Lord Cienyey's tastes . . . are . . . perhaps somewhat different than yours and mine."

York relaxed the pressure on Harshaw's throat. "Spell it out for me."

Harshaw nodded. "Lord Cienyey purchased the two young ladies as bond servants, though their duties were quite different from those of a servant. To the locals, whose mores are not as sophisticated as his Excellency's, the existence of this room was a constant source of irritation. In fact, this room probably had more to do with causing this riot than anything else. The rest—" Harshaw looked slowly about the room. "I have to assume the rioters vented their anger on these poor girls."

"Palevi," York growled. "Let's get Cienyey here."

Harshaw shook his head desperately. "Don't, Lieutenant. According to imperial law he did nothing illegal here, and if you press the matter you'll only get yourself in trouble."

"Best drop it, Cap'm," Palevi said.

York hesitated, and in that moment a voice on his com said, "Cap'm, Sarge, this is Tathit up on the roof. I think you two best come up here."

Palevi growled, "What is it?"

"There's something funny going on down in the city."

York let go of Harshaw, growled at him, "Get out." The assistant consul walked out of the room without a word.

York looked once more at the grisly mess, then keyed his com, "I'll come to the roof, Tathit. Palevi, stay with your marines on the wall."

••••

York headed for the main embassy building at a trot. The lifts were still out of commission so he had to use the stairs, and after six flights he staggered out onto the roof gasping for air. Tathit was waiting for him, visor down. York dropped his visor and they both walked out to the edge of the roof. As he looked out over the city he heard *One* lift off behind him.

Tathit pointed down into the city. York watched carefully for some seconds, then, for just an instant, he caught a glimpse of a dark figure as it darted between two buildings. He adjusted the magnification on his helmet pickups, watched the scene on the inside of his visor expand rapidly.

The figure moved again, and while York's glimpse was fleeting, it was enough to see the glint of armor and the hint of an insignia. A hard knot formed in the pit of his stomach.

He dropped the magnification back to normal and waited. Out in the city he saw another shadow move, then another, and another. He waited several seconds and saw a dozen more.

He and Tathit stepped away from the edge of the roof as he keyed his com to the open marine frequency. "This is Ballin. Visors down and seal 'em up. We've got armored feddie regs out there.

Looks like a full company of them. Palevi, you've got the wall. Act at your own discretion. I'll contact *Invaradin*."

York keyed his com to *Invaradin*'s command frequency. "*Invaradin*, this is Ballin requesting emergency com clearance."

There came no answer, Sierka again making him wait.

"*Invaradin*, this is Ballin. We are red down here."

Still he had to wait, but Sierka finally did acknowledge him. "What do you want now, Ballin?"

"We've spotted a company of Syndonese regulars moving in on us, sir. We're about to be hit hard."

"Syndonese regulars, Lieutenant. I seriously doubt that. There are no Directorate troops operating within thirty light-years of this system. Stop trying to justify your earlier errors in judgment by—"

"God damn it!" York shouted. "I know a feddie when I see one. And if we've got feddie troops down here, you've got a feddie warship up there somewhere."

York's com went silent. He switched com channels. "*One* and *Two*, dump your passengers and get the hell down here on the double. We need fire support and evac. And if either of you can get hold of anyone on the bridge, let them know we're being hit."

"Ready," he heard Palevi say. "On my command: two second burst . . . FIRE!"

The embassy compound filled suddenly with the scream of automatic weapons. A few of the darting shadows in the streets below were caught in the open; one literally burst into pieces in the crossfire between two power rifles. York drifted off into that half-dream world of adrenaline and fear where he oscillated between hysteria and panic.

The two second burst ended abruptly and the feddie troops began returning fire. "Three second burst," Palevi said. "Then fire at will . . . FIRE!"

The feddies were now returning a continuous stream of fire. York could see tracers from at least two emplacements skipping about through the compound. "Sierka, you son-of-a-bitch," he screamed into his com. "Where the hell are you? We're under assault. Now. We need fire support."

"Cap'm, this is Hyer. I got bad problems down here. The locals're out of control, crawlin' all over the *Diana*'s shuttle."

"Use your weapons," York barked.

"Can't, sir. The princess is with them. Probably hit her too. It's like she thought we was the enemy."

"Damn!" York snarled. "I'm coming down, and if anything breaks before I get there, your only responsibility is to keep her safe."

"Sir?" Hyer asked indignantly.

"You heard me. Just fucking do it."

York hit the stairwell at a run, taking the steps three at a time. His world narrowed to the next step, and the importance of hitting it squarely.

He reached the bottom, burst into the hallway there, realized he'd overshot by one floor and was down in the basement. He reversed his tracks, ran back up to the ground floor, then down the length of the first floor hall and out onto the embassy lawn.

The Trinivanian locals, swarming all over the *Diana*'s shuttle, looked like ants on a piece of rotted food. They spilled out of the open cargo bay, with people climbing desperately over one another in a panicked effort to save themselves. Some had wrapped their arms tightly about the shuttle's skids, hoping to ride out that way, never thinking what would happen when they reached the vacuum of space. And in the midst of it all stood the princess, shouting at everyone. York looked about quickly, spotted the churchman Rhijn standing far to one side out of danger.

"Cap'm," Hyer said. "Shuttle pilot wants to lift off. Says he's going whether you like it or not."

"The hell he will," York growled. "You tell him if he lifts one second before I give the word, we'll shoot hell out of him and leave him for the feddies.

"What about these locals? Did you finish searching them?"

"Only about half, sir."

York nodded unhappily. "I'm going into that mob to get the princess out. Cover me. And remember: her life has priority."

He walked into the mob with his hand resting on the hilt of his gun so no local could grab it. They took no notice of him at first. Frightened people ran about in front and behind him, but none blocked his path. He approached the princess from behind, reached out and gently took hold of her shoulder.

She jumped and turned to face him. "Who are you?" she shouted above the noise of the mob and the gunfire, unable to see his face through the blackened visor, and not thinking clearly enough to look at the name stenciled on his chest plate.

He activated his external speaker. "Ballin. Will you come with me please?"

"No," she said flatly, though without conviction.

"Cap'm. This is Palevi. We can't hold out much longer."

"Two minutes. I'm on the front lawn trying to get the princess out. I need two minutes."

There was an almost undetectable pause. "You got them, sir."

York switched back to his external speaker. The princess was shouting something at him. "Shut up!" he barked.

She started and her eyes narrowed angrily. "What did you say?"

"I said shut up. You're coming with me now if I have to carry you out. Is that clear?"

She put her hands on her hips. "I'd like to see you try."

"Listen to me," York said. "You can pound on me all day and my armor'll protect me. But you start that and this mob'll go crazy, and my marines will then protect you with some very powerful weapons and kill a bunch of these people. Or you can come with me nice-like. It's your choice, so make up your mind and do it now."

She said nothing, gritted her teeth and glared.

He grabbed her by the upper arm, gripping her hard enough to hurt. "Now walk beside me and try not to look forced."

Together they turned away from the shuttle and began walking. At first the crowd paid no attention to them and York thought they might get away with it. But then suddenly the mob stilled, a deathly silence descended, and with the sound of the weapons fire at the wall providing a deadly backdrop, the crowd began to close menacingly about them.

The mob's panic was gone. Fear still hung in the air but it no longer had the taste of many individuals. This was the fear of a single monstrous entity, cold, deadly, united. This mob would get foolishly brave now.

In that moment he almost halted, but he realized that to hesitate in any way would be a confession to them that he was not the one in control. He kept walking, taking long, great strides as if he would climb over anyone who got in his way, literally pulling the princess after him. His hand still rested on his grav-gun, and he knew how intimidating a faceless, black-visored suit of plast-armor could be.

The mob parted reluctantly, though one man was a little braver—or more foolhardy—than the rest and refused to step aside. York plowed into him, hit him under the chin with an armor-plated forearm and knocked him down. And then he was walking across open lawn, with Hyer standing not far away, a rifle in his hands. *We made it*, York thought.

Suddenly Hyer raised his rifle and screamed over the com, "Cap'm, behind you!"

York threw the princess to the ground and spun about as something zinged off his armor. A young woman stood a few meters away with a gun aimed at him.

Later, much later, when looking back on the incident, he could never remember pulling and aiming his sidearm. He remembered the fear, and he remembered that eternity of an instant when the gun in the young woman's hand kicked, spitting a puff of angry, gray smoke while he squeezed the trigger on his grav-gun, only then realizing that it was aimed at her abdomen, and that she was just a little girl, no more than ten or twelve years old, and that she was far more frightened than he, and that the signal from his brain to his trigger finger had already been sent, and the action irrevocably begun.

The bullet from her gun smashed into the center of his visor, splattered just in front of his eyes and slammed his head back painfully. He staggered with the force of the impact as his own gun kicked in his hand, barely managed to keep his feet.

"Hold fire," he screamed into his com, fearing a massacre if his marines lost control. "As you were." He glanced up at the telltale in his helmet: still green. His visor had withstood the impact of the bullet.

He didn't remember crossing the distance to stand over the Trinivanian girl. The single shot from his grav-gun had blown away most of her abdomen and pelvis. She was quite dead, and York felt nothing for her, only the letdown that followed the rush of adrenaline needed to react. His own cold, unemotional lack of reaction bothered him far more than the actual death of the poor girl.

"You bloodthirsty son-of-a-bitch!" the princess screamed. "You bloody butcher."

York turned on her angrily, felt his control slipping away. "She had a gun," he growled, "and I had to protect you. Those are my orders."

"Orders?" she screamed. "You animal. You monster! You maniac!"

Suddenly she was all over him, screaming and kicking and tearing at his armor. "Somebody give me a hand," he yelled.

"Incoming mortar!" someone screamed over the com.

York reacted instinctively, wrapped his arms around the screaming princess, let his knees buckle and fell on his back, pulling her down on top of him. She landed with an "oomph," lost her wind, and with his arms still locked tightly about her he rolled over and lay on top of her, trying to protect her from what he knew was coming.

The ground beneath them bucked like a wild animal. The shock wave hit with a loud *whomp* partially muffled by his helmet speakers as they cut out to limit the volume, and even York, protected within his shell of power-reinforced plast, was momentarily stunned while clumps of dirt and lawn rained down upon them.

York scrambled to his feet, took quick note of a large, smoking crater nearby. The next mortar round followed instantly, taking out a section of the compound wall. York keyed his com. "This is Ballin. Pull back to the roof. Double-time."

The princess picked herself up slowly, but her knees wobbled and she swayed from side to side like a drunkard as she tried to walk. York grabbed her by the back of her collar, swung her around and threw her at Hyer. She landed in a sprawl at the marine's feet.

"She's yours, Corporal," York shouted. "Get her to the roof and on the first available boat. And get her there alive."

Hyer pulled her to her feet. She started to struggle but the marine ignored her, threw her over one shoulder and ran unsteadily toward the main building. York and Hyer's squad turned toward the breach in the wall, started backing toward the main building and laying down a continuous barrage of cover fire.

The shuttle pilot begged for permission to lift without being shot down. "Go," York hollered.

"But what do I do about these fools hanging onto my skids?"

"Hell if I know," York shouted as he squeezed off several rounds at a gap in the wall. "You wanna stick around and figure something out that's your busi—"

The hand of some enormous god came out of nowhere and swatted him like a bug, left him dazed and sitting on the ground near another smoking crater. The *Diana*'s shuttle had already lifted several hundred feet in the air, ant-like humans still clinging to its skids. One of them lost hold, and in a last, frantic effort to save himself managed to take several of his friends with him when he fell.

York crawled to his feet and looked around groggily. The same godlike hand of the mortar had swatted his small squad, and two of them were not getting up.

Palevi and the rest of the marines had already reached the main building, were now laying down a heavy barrage of cover for York and his squad. Four of York's marines grabbed the two wounded by the ankles and started dragging them while York and the rest backed in behind them, spraying cover-fire indiscriminately. York keyed his com. "*One* and *Two*, where the hell are you?"

"On our way down now, Cap'm. High G drop—two minutes."

York thought of diverting one of them to the ground to pick him and his squad up there, but at dirt level the boat would be too good of a target for that mortar, and in two minutes the whole compound would be swarming with feddies. "*One*," he shouted, "go straight to the roof. *Two*, see if you can find that mortar and knock it out. And strafe the hell out of the feddies in the compound. When *One*'s full-up, trade places."

York and his squad reached the embassy building. "What's the count?" he asked Palevi.

"You were the last one in, sir. Rest are on the roof. All marines accounted for."

"What about the embassy staff?"

"Don't know for sure, sir. We got the princess, Cienyey, Harshaw, and about a hundred and fifty others."

"That'll have to do. Let's get the hell out of here."

"Right, sir." Palevi's next words came over the open marine frequency. "Pull it in, grunts. To the roof. Go! Go! Go!"

They hit the stairwell running. Palevi hollered something about keeping their eyes open for feddies in the building, but York was too busy counting the steps and each landing as he cleared it. He was on the fourth floor with his lungs burning and starting to slow down when one of the stairwell walls exploded in his face and slammed him to the floor. Everything came to a stop for an instant, then the floor crumbled beneath him. He scrambled to grab at anything, tumbled through the air with a dizzy view of the lawn far below, but landed instead one floor down on a pile of twisted ironwork and broken masonry. A wall collapsed on top of him, knocked him flat, then everything went still.

The first thing he checked was his telltale: still green; no suit breach, though he was half buried beneath a pile of broken masonry in the hall on the third floor. He could see blue sky through an enormous hole in the wall above and to one side of where the stairwell should have been. He thanked whatever gods existed the mortar hadn't hit the stairwell directly, then, with the aid of a lot of adrenaline, pulled free of the rubble.

He scrambled to his feet, saw the legs and hips of a suit of armor protruding from more rubble nearby. He grabbed the ankles, pulled with everything he had, and again, adrenaline did the job.

No stripes and the name Dakkart stenciled on the chest plate. Dakkart seemed to be in one piece, though badly stunned. York backhanded her visor with an armored fist. "Come on, Dakkart. Snap out of it."

No response so he slapped her again. "Come on, private. Any breaches?"

The woman shook her head. "No, sir. Telltale's green, sir."

The umbilical that connected Dakkart's rifle to her reactor pack disappeared in more rubble. York pulled on it and the rifle came free. He picked it up, slammed it against the marine's chest. "Take your rifle and let's get the hell out of here."

"Cap'm," Palevi's voice said in his ear. "There ain't much left of this stairwell; better head for the other one. We're coming down after you, so don't start shootin' until you're sure who you're shootin' at."

The building shook with the impact of another mortar round exploding somewhere. Dakkart was still groggy. York had to push her down the hall ahead of him, slapping the back of her helmet to keep her moving. They'd just rounded the first turn in the hall when York heard a groan over his com. He pulled Dakkart to a halt. "Palevi," he screamed. "What's your count?"

"We're missing you, Dakkart, and Stacy, Cap'm."

York had to think for a moment to recall Stacy: the new kid, the rookie on his first drop.

"And I'm missing Stacy," York snarled. He spun Dakkart about, pushed her down to one knee at the turn in the hall. "Cover me," he said. "I'm going back."

York ran back the way they'd come, conscious that feddies might come swarming up out of the broken stairwell at any moment, wondering if Dakkart might find it more convenient to let him take a feddie bullet. He dug through the rubble frantically until his eye caught the glint of a small piece of gray-green armor. More adrenaline helped him lift a piece of wall off the wounded marine and he had him free in seconds. He was still alive but unconscious.

York grabbed him by the ankles, started dragging him on his back down the hallway, trailing his small rotary on its umbilical. He was half way back to the turn in the hall when Dakkart screamed, "Cap'm, yer in my line o' fire."

York lifted his eyes and looked toward the broken stairwell, had one short instant in which to see a feddie there, and to understand he was looking straight down the muzzle of a rotary—

••••

The inside of a visor, blackened and scorched with a jagged line of a crack running down through the middle of it, spattered with flecks of blood. York stared at it for a long time before coming to the slow realization he was looking at the inside of his own visor. All of the lower half and most of the left half no longer functioned as a 3-D projection screen, and without power those areas had gone fully transparent. The telltale visible in the upper right corner of the visor still functioned, but only the upper half of the silhouette of the armored marine was visible, with the lower half cut off at the waist by an offshoot of the crack. The helmet and torso sections of the telltale were blinking an angry red at him, and his vision was oddly limited.

Beyond the visor he saw his chest plate; it too was blackened and scorched, with power arcing across a large crack like small bolts of lightning. His breathing came in shallow gasps, and any effort to breathe deeper punished him with excruciating pain.

Beyond his chest plate his legs were splayed out into the middle of the hall and tangled in Stacy's still form. York lay on his back in the hallway, his back and shoulders on the floor, his head propped up uncomfortably by the wall.

His com chattered incessantly with angry and frantic voices. For a moment his vision dimmed while he struggled to hold onto consciousness.

Suddenly a pair of armored feddie legs hurtled over Stacy then disappeared out of sight down the hall. York turned his head to the left carefully, and slowly, just enough to see the turn in the hall where a cluster of feddie regulars were huddled, staying out of sight of whatever lay beyond. York hoped it was Palevi and his marines that lay beyond.

Evidently he and Stacy had been taken for dead. Again he turned his head carefully and slowly, but now to the right. At the rubble-strewn entrance of what was left of the broken stairwell another cluster of feddies stood in the open, gesturing as they conferred about something. York guessed the situation was a temporary stalemate, though that wouldn't last long.

He looked about for a weapon of some kind, careful to keep his movements to a minimum. Stacy's rifle lay near his ankles, still attached to its umbilical, though whether or not it would function was academic since it was too far to reach quickly.

His eyes settled on a short, dark cylinder clipped to the boy's hip: a nuke, a big one. He kept his eyes on the feddies at the stairwell, had to gamble those at the turn in the hall were too busy with Palevi and his marines to pay attention to their backside. He inched his hand slowly toward the grenade, freezing whenever he thought someone might look his way. He reached the grenade, fumbled momentarily at the clips, panicked at the thought he might not get it free, but then it suddenly came loose and he had it in his hand. He kept it close to the floor, between him and Stacy, while he looked carefully at its face.

He wanted to cry. It had a forty-pound rating, and it wasn't adjustable. What he needed was a small two-pound chemical charge, not a forty-pound nuke. He swore that if he got out of this he'd kick Stacy's ass across Hangar Deck for carrying non-issue explosives. But now he had no choice, so he set the dial on its face for a ten-second delay, then keyed the arming sequence on its side. A small red indicator lit up.

"Computer," he said. "Kikker, execute." He felt the sting on the side of his neck as his suit flooded his system with a special mixture known as a combat kikker: adrenaline, phets, painkillers, anything that might help a badly wounded marine.

His thoughts cleared for a moment and he keyed his com, spoke into the middle of all the com chatter. "Palevi," he croaked.

His com grew suddenly silent, then everyone started shouting at once.

"Shut up," Palevi shouted. "Shut up, god damn it. Cap'm, is that you?"

"Ya. I'm gonna blow a forty-pound mininuke at the busted stairwell then hit the rest from behind with Stacy's rotary."

"We're ready when you are, sir."

York looked again at his chest plate. His suit computer had cut power from the area around the breach and the arcing had stopped. Otherwise it might short, and the energy available from his reactor pack could easily cook him alive in his suit. But without power to strengthen it, almost any weapon could punch through the plast.

He shrugged mentally. "I'm ready," he said. "Ten seconds." Then he pressed the stud on the grenade, released the arming safety. He started counting down from ten, and when he reached two he rolled over, pitched the grenade to his right as far down the hall as he could, then grabbed hold of Stacy and held on for everything he was worth.

There came a blinding flash and the walls lit up with an incandescent white glare. A shock wave traveled up the hall like the exploding powder in a gun barrel, and his ears popped as the force of it blew he and Stacy several meters up the hall. Then everything became suddenly still, silent.

York hurt everywhere but he ignored that and scrambled over Stacy, grabbed the kid's rifle, thumbed the settings to maximum muzzle velocity and fire rate, then rested the four-barrel rotary on Stacy's still form. He could see nothing through the clouds of dust in the hall, so he sighted blindly up its length and squeezed the trigger.

The rotary wound up to full firing rate and screamed with an angry, low-pitched whine, kicked and vibrated in his hands. Unlike his grav-gun it didn't fire fragmentation shells. Instead, with all four barrels spinning madly, it spit small, blunt projectiles with enough velocity, and in sufficient numbers, to deliver far more destructive energy than a grav-gun shell. He fanned it back and forth randomly, watched it light up the hall as the friction of the shells burned through the dust and debris in the air. And then suddenly it went silent.

He released the trigger and squeezed again. Nothing. He'd used up Stacy's weapons reserves.

He had nothing to lose now. He gave himself another dose of kikker, picked himself up with the intention of grabbing Stacy's ankles and dragging him down the hall again, but his bad knee gave way and his leg slipped out from under him. He fell flat on his butt and his right foot suddenly began to throb with enough pain to bring tears to his eyes. He looked down at it, realized his bad knee really wouldn't be giving him any more trouble since his right leg was missing from the knee down. His armor ended there in a jagged and bloody stump.

He passed out.

••••

York awoke weightless, stretched out on his back and strapped to something hard. It was dark, and he guessed he was in one of the assault boats since he could hear the cries of dying people all about him. He wanted to cry himself, to tell someone he didn't want to die, but he didn't have the strength.

Someone had cut away most of his armor. Bandages covered much of his head and face, and his ankle hurt like hell. One of the marine medics leaned over him working on his chest, and the sense of urgency in the medic's movements told York a great deal.

Palevi leaned over him, entered the field of view of his good eye. The sergeant had removed his own helmet and his head seemed disproportionately small protruding from his chest armor. And he wore that grin of his, though it was now strained and forced, and his eyes lacked the usual mirth. York reached up, tried to grab the sergeant's shoulder, but he failed and his hand fell back to the stretcher. Palevi took hold of it and lifted it with almost parental concern. "Don't try to move, sir. Yer in pretty bad shape."

If he was going to die, York had to know if it had all been for nothing. "The kid?" he asked, but the effort sent him into a fit of coughing that filled his mouth with blood and spewed globules of it all over Palevi and the medic.

"God damn it, Sarge," the medic cursed. "Keep him still."

Palevi nodded at the medic, looked at York. "Stacy'll be okay. But you gotta be still, sir. Yer chest is full of splinters from your chest plate."

"The . . . rest?" York demanded.

Palevi's face saddened. "Twelve dead, sir. Seventeen wounded. But we brought them all home, Cap'm."

York tried to relax, though his right foot was in agony and he couldn't stop shaking. He reminded himself his right foot was no longer there, but it didn't seem to care about that and still hurt like hell. The medic's actions became more frantic and he realized then that he was dying. He didn't want to die, not here, not this way: lying on a grav stretcher, his mouth filling over and over with blood, cries of the dying all about him. But at that moment he suddenly realized there was something far worse than death.

He struggled for one last instant of strength, managed to grip the open neck ring of Palevi's chest plate. He couldn't pull himself up, but he pulled the marine down to him. He knew what he had to say, and struggled to say the words, just a few simple words, the most important words in his life, "No . . . tanks."

"No tanks, sir?" Palevi asked. He looked at the medic.

The medic shook his head.

"Sorry, sir," Palevi said. "They may have to tank you to keep you alive."

A long ago memory climbed up out of his stomach and into his throat. York fought to hold onto consciousness long enough to speak. "Please . . . No tanks . . . The . . . *Vincent*."

"The *Andor Vincent*, sir?" Palevi asked. "Ah Cap'm, you shouldn't pay no attention to them ghost-ship stories. Just stories, that's all they are."

York shook his head frantically. He remembered all too well the voices, and the fear, and the pain, and now he had to make Palevi understand. He opened his mouth, pushed the words out with his last bit of strength, "I . . . was . . . on . . . the *Vincent*."

Palevi recoiled as if struck. His eyes opened and his jaw dropped, and for an instant the impenetrable wall of his self-confidence crumbled. The medic's reaction was no less dramatic, and he and Palevi looked at one another for a long moment.

York groaned, "Please . . ."

The medic gave one of those short, simple shakes of his head. At that, Palevi's face hardened. He nodded at the medic and looked carefully at York, paused for a long moment. "If you gotta go down, Cap'm, I'll personally see to it you go down clean. No tanks. You got my word on that, one marine to another."

York let go, relaxed completely, felt as if he'd been suddenly relieved of a great weight. Palevi would die before he'd break such an oath.

Something inside his chest turned a somersault and pain sent him to the edge of consciousness. He gasped, choked on a convulsion and his mouth filled again with blood. He coughed it out all over Palevi and the medic.

"Shit!" the medic swore. "He's goin' down." He started rifling desperately through his kit, but suddenly he stopped and turned to Palevi with a stricken look on his face. "Fuck, Sarge, I'm out of stass." The medic leaned back, looked up at the ceiling of the boat, shouted at the top of his lungs. "I'm out of stass, god damn it! Cap'm's goin' down and I'm out of stass. Somebody get me some fuckin' stass."

For York, reality became a distant, abstract thing, and a calm stillness settled into his soul. He was thankful his leg no longer hurt and the pain in his chest receded. Warmth washed over him with an enveloping softness, and then there was nothing.

5

Hunted

LIEUTENANT MAGDELENA VOTAK looked at the feddie warship on her screens, now an expanding fireball, and felt overwhelming relief. The enemy had been vanquished in the cosmic fires of thermonuclear fusion, and victory was *not* sweet. That was one of the first things she had learned as a young ensign: victory was never sweet; it was merely a relief.

"All stop."

She cut power to the sublight drive, felt the hull go free.

"A direct hit, sir," Anda Gant said. "One hundred megaton warhead; no survivors in that."

Maggie looked again at the ball of radioactive fire. "No," Telyekev said almost sadly. "No survivors. Let's pick up *One* and *Two*." Telyekev sounded tired. "Mr. Sierka, what's Palevi's casualty count?"

Maggie suddenly wanted to see something other than screens. She needed some human contact, needed to see Sierka look up from the com console, needed to watch him as he said, "Twenty-five, sir, counting civilians." But Maggie was denied that visual luxury, for in the helm cluster she could see next to nothing beyond the tiny world of her own console telemetry and implant feeds.

"Thank you, Commander Sierka. Mr. Rame, plot a course for Trinivan. Miss Votak, take it slow until we see how she's handling."

Rame's numbers appeared on Maggie's navigational screen and she spun *Invaradin* accordingly. She spoke without emotion, "Course is set at one quarter drive, which puts us about forty minutes out, sir."

She applied power gingerly to the sublight drive. The helm moved sluggishly, had a tendency to drift to starboard.

"How's she handling, Lieutenant?"

"Not too bad, sir," Maggie said. "The damage to the starboard drive is giving me a little trouble, but I've got room to compensate."

"What about full drive?"

"With your permission, I'd prefer to keep it at twenty-five percent, and we don't want to do any quick maneuvering."

"Very good. Do so."

The drive imbalance had begun to seem almost a personal, physical pain. She monitored it carefully until *Invaradin* was stable, then gave the computer partial control. Fatigue weighed heavily on her.

"I think it's time you took a break, Miss Votak. Lieutenant Moboow will relieve you."

Maggie wanted to protest. She was Telyekev's best pilot, and by comparison Geara Moboow was a novice.

"I relieve you," Moboow said.

Maggie stifled her protests, merely said, "Acknowledged. I am releasing . . ." she relaxed, keyed her implants out of the drive cluster, ". . . now."

She became instantly aware of Moboow's control: amateurish, indelicate. *Invaradin*'s keel wobbled momentarily as he adjusted to the damaged drive. To Maggie, with her senses still tied into the console, it was as if her own body was under his control. She felt she had almost become a part of *Invaradin*, and yet another part of her recognized *that* as the first symptom of a dangerous hallucination common to good pilots.

The helm cluster rose slowly, releasing her from its demanding grasp. For the first time in hours her eyes took in something besides scan readouts and navigational summaries. It brought home that she was not herself the ship; she suddenly became conscious of her own body, and how badly she needed to piss.

"Miss Votak," Telyekev said. "Mr. Nemkov's having trouble with the marines on Hangar Deck. Please go down there and take control."

Telyekev understood the need to get a pilot out of the cluster after a couple hours of combat. "Right away, sir," she acknowledged.

••••

Hangar Deck was a mess, dirtlovers wandering everywhere in a disorganized mob tainted by fear and confusion. For crowd control, Nemkov had brought in those marines who hadn't dropped to Trinivan. That was a double mistake: the marines didn't like taking orders from naval officers, and Nemkov wasn't good at giving orders to anyone, let alone a female marine sergeant with twenty years seniority on him. When Maggie stepped into Hangar Control, the first monitor she looked at showed a picture of young Lord Nemkov standing in the middle of one of the service bays screaming at the ranking marine noncom, a woman named Meciden Notay. There were civilians milling about freely, while Notay's marines stood idly by refusing to do anything.

Maggie leaned over the shoulder of one of the controllers, keyed her implants into the console there and activated the pickup. "Mr. Nemkov, Sergeant Notay," she growled, "report to Hangar Control immediately."

Nemkov stormed into the control room with Notay following casually behind him. He opened his mouth, started to shout something at Maggie but she cut him off. "Take charge of your controllers, Mr. Nemkov, while I speak to Sergeant Notay." Nemkov hesitated for a moment, looked into her face, then sat down at a console without speaking.

Notay came to attention and saluted carelessly. Maggie turned on Notay and lowered her voice to a soft growl. "*One* and *Two* are coming in with heavy casualties. They're your people, shot up pretty bad. Now get those service bays cleared so those boats can dock. And be careful. There are some very important people out there."

Notay's sloppy attitude disappeared. She shot out of the control room, barked orders at her marines, and they started herding the civilians like cattle. They were not easy on the first dirtlover to put up an argument, and after that everyone was careful to obey.

One came in nicely, but *Two* came in slewing to port and wobbling badly. Twisted and warped underbelly plates were dire evidence of a small rocket that had struck it just after takeoff. *Two*'s pilot managed to clear the main service bay seals, but at the last moment his braking jets failed, and *Two* came to rest in a slow motion of grinding and snapping plast and steel.

Hangar Deck crew was good. In seconds they had the service bays shut, sealed, gravved up, repressurized, and scanned for any residual contamination. When they sounded the all-clear the hatches of both boats burst open simultaneously and erupted with marines half stripped of their armor, carrying wounded comrades on grav litters and sprinting for the service lift.

Maggie left the control room looking for York. In the confusion of *One Bay* she caught glimpses of several wounded men and women with their features locked up in the rigidity of stass, their skin a bright, lobster red, their eyes open, unfocused, unseeing. She passed a wounded female marine lying momentarily abandoned on a litter. The woman had been stripped to the waist then wrapped in blood-soaked bandages, and one breast lay immodestly exposed. Maggie carefully draped a corner of the litter blanket over the breast.

Somewhere in the confusion Maggie heard a young woman shouting angrily. It took her a moment to spot her, the princess venting her anger at poor Palevi. Maggie intervened. "Excuse me," she said loudly as she stepped between the two. She bowed lightly from the waist. "I'm Lieutenant Magdelena Votak. May I be of some assistance, Your Highness?"

The princess spoke breathlessly. "Thank god there's someone here besides these marines!"

Maggie looked at Palevi. "Thank you, Sergeant. I'll take care of this." She scanned the crowd for York but saw no sign of him.

Maggie turned back to the princess, noticed a churchman behind the young noblewoman. His eyes were calculating and hard.

The churchman took up what seemed an almost defensive position behind the princess. "That marine refused to let me speak to your captain," the princess said. "I hope I won't have the same problem with you."

Maggie nodded deferentially. "If you'll come with me I'll try to arrange that." She herded the princess toward Hangar Control, the churchman following. "We've just come out of combat, and we took some damage, so Captain Lord Telyekev is very busy at the moment. Can you tell me what this is about?"

The princess halted, turned on Maggie angrily. "Captain Ballin murdered a defenseless Trinivanian woman, and I intend to press charges."

The princess had regained her composure. As for York committing murder, Maggie suddenly feared something like that was all too entirely possible. "That's a rather serious charge."

"It was a rather serious crime."

Maggie nodded. "Please follow me."

When they stepped into Hangar Control the princess spotted Nemkov and rushed to him. "Daka! What are you doing out here?" He in turn stood from his console and bowed deeply.

Nemkov had the princess occupied for the moment so Maggie quickly got hold of Telyekev and explained the situation. "Did she give you any details?" he asked.

Maggie shook her head. "No, sir. Nothing beyond the accusation that York murdered a defenseless woman."

"Damn it!" Telyekev swore. "What the hell has he done now?"

Maggie shook her head. "I don't know, sir. Have you spoken to him? I can't find him anywhere down here."

Telyekev flinched and his expression softened, and at the look on his face a hard lump formed in the pit of Maggie's stomach. "Mr. Ballin came in under stass on the A-list. Most of one leg missing, deep chest wounds, deep head wounds. He's in surgery now, listed as extremely critical. Yan thinks she may have to tank him, and even then he may not make it."

Maggie closed her eyes, tried to breathe evenly. "Not the tanks, sir. York wouldn't want that."

"God damn it!" Telyekev shouted. "I'm not going to let my best line officer die just because of some silly superstition about a ghost ship."

"It's not a superstition with York, sir."

Telyekev nodded, spoke more softly. "Ya, I know. And so does Miss Yan. She's doing everything she can, but she may have no choice."

Maggie nodded. "What should I do about Her Highness, sir?"

"Bring her up to my office immediately. Then talk to the marine noncoms and find out exactly what happened down there. And have anyone who might know anything report to Commander Joyson on the double. I want statements on record while their memories are still fresh."

"Aye, aye, sir," Maggie said mechanically.

Telyekev broke the connection.

Nemkov and the princess were still reliving old times. Maggie interrupted them politely. "Your Highness, Captain Telyekev has instructed me to escort you to his office immediately."

"It's about time," the princess snarled.

"This way," Maggie said, indicating the hatch to Hangar Control. The princess turned to leave and the churchman followed her. But before Maggie could follow them Nemkov grabbed her arm. He whispered quickly, "Is it true? Is Ballin dying?"

Maggie looked closely at Nemkov. The luck of a ship rode on the life or death of a lifer. She looked about and saw that everyone in Hangar Control was waiting on her words. "He's in pretty bad shape: deep chest and head wounds." She shook her head at Nemkov. "And you, Dak, are a real two-faced son-of-a-bitch."

Nemkov frowned angrily. "Just because I don't like the bastard, doesn't mean I want him dead."

The princess called out. "I'm waiting, Lieutenant Votak."

"Coming, Your Highness," Maggie said, then turned her back on Nemkov and the rest of Hangar Control.

••••

Theodore Rochefort, Lord Chancellor to His Majesty Edvard the Tenth, knocked softly on the door in front of him.

"Enter," the intercom said.

Rochefort grasped the heavy knob, pushed the door open and stepped through, then closed it carefully behind him. He had barely turned when the emperor asked, "Well?"

"She's alive," Rochefort said as he crossed the room. "And apparently unharmed."

The emperor let out a long, deep sigh. "Thank god!" he said. He buried his face in his hands, rubbed his temples and brow tiredly. When he looked up, years of worry had disappeared from his face. To Rochefort it was another reminder his king was still a young man. "What about Lady d'Hart?"

"She was hurt," Rochefort said, "but not seriously. For the time being they're both safe."

"Good," the emperor said. "For a while there I thought it was all over but the executions. But they're safe now, you say?"

"Yes, Your Majesty. They're aboard *Invaradin*. I took the liberty of ordering Captain Telyekev to head for Dumark, and about ten minutes ago they up-transited out of the Trinivanian system."

"Excellent, Theodore! Excellent! Did you warn my wife to expect them?"

"The message was sent, Your Majesty, though the Empress Cassandra has yet to acknowledge it."

"Is there something wrong there?"

Rochefort shook his head. "The message was coded, of course, and I placed no great priority on it. Again I felt we should avoid the possibility of unwanted attention. It will take her time to receive it, decode it, and reply. But she'll have ample time, since even at top speed, *Invaradin* will take at least a tenday to get there."

"Good," the emperor said. "Thank you, Theodore. I'll sleep better tonight than I've slept in a long time."

He was silent for a moment, then asked, "What about Aeya?"

"Your daughter too is safe," Rochefort said. "All three of them made it out alive."

"Good," the emperor said. He stared at his hands for a moment, then asked, "What about casualties? What did we pay for this little victory?"

Rochefort looked at the report he held. "*Invaradin* was forced to engage a Syndonese war craft. She was victorious, but she sustained damages. Her marines had to evacuate the embassy without fire support and under heavy fire from regular troops of the Syndonese Federal Directorate. Thirteen of *Ivaradin*'s marines, eight crew and four civilians died today, and another forty-one were seriously maimed and wounded."

The emperor's face aged while Rochefort spoke, and the young king said, "It's got to be worth such a price. It must be."

••••

Fleet Director Add'kas'adanna stepped into the committee chamber warily. Director General Kaffair already sat at the large, old table, tapping his fingers impatiently on the wood. Operations Director Zort sat next to him, equally as nervous, though if Add'kas'adanna knew Zort he was nervous only because he sensed Kaffair's mood. But Zort was always fearful of something or other. Zort eyed Add'kas'adanna carefully as she sat down, though neither he nor Kaffair spoke.

An instant later the door opened and Security Director Ninda stepped into the small room. "Well," Ninda said, taking control immediately and sitting down. "Let's get started."

Zort leaned forward. "Where's Theara?"

Ninda smiled. "Our esteemed Director of State is nowhere to be found. She has apparently disappeared, and not been heard from for more than a month. My people are this moment investigating the possibility of foul play."

Zort's ears perked up. "Is that why we're meeting?"

Ninda dismissed Zort with a wave of his hand. "Of course not. If she's been assassinated, then we'll make some effort to identify and execute the assassins, and we'll find another Director of State. If not . . . well, events are proceeding without her."

That was an invitation for someone to ask the obvious. "What events?" Zort demanded.

Kaffair spoke for the first time. "Obviously, this thing on Trinivan."

"Exactly," Ninda said.

"What thing on Trinivan?" Zort pleaded, looking nervously from one to the other, foolishly unable to see the battle lines being drawn between Kaffair and Ninda.

Ninda gave a fairly concise account of the events surrounding the evacuation of the embassy on Trinivan. From what Add'kas'adanna could tell, he injected only a few inaccuracies. He finished with, "We have yet to identify the Imperial warship involved."

Add'kas'adanna tossed out, "*Invaradin*—one of their heavy cruisers."

Ninda and Kaffair both looked at her sidelong. It would have been wiser to keep her mouth shut. These politicians wanted an obedient Fleet Director, one who kept her thoughts limited to executing their policies. They really didn't trust a Kinathin breed warrior, and Ninda, in particular, didn't like her to think for herself.

Zort saved her. "So what are we going to do about it?"

Ninda leaned forward. "We have an opportunity to capture a princess of the royal blood, the emperor's only daughter."

"And what would that buy us?" Kaffair asked. "I doubt she can provide us with any real information . . ."

Add'kas'adanna tuned Kaffair's words out, reached inside for the old training. She concentrated on the disciplines of thought construct, built the logical sub-mind carefully, then released it and experienced the odd sense of schizophrenia that accompanied the existence of a separate consciousness within her. It would view the proceedings distantly, allowing her to participate without the need to focus elsewhere, tallying subtle observations of breathing and gesture without the distractions inherent in being a participant.

The sub-mind focused on Ninda and Kaffair: their eyes, their hands, the tenor of their voices, the tempo, the rhythm. The two men argued back and forth, but there was a dispute here that had nothing to do with their words, a struggle between two old enemies concerning something neither was yet willing to reveal. Kaffair knew something—No! He was up to something, and Ninda was trying to block him. The imperial princess meant nothing, *Invaradin* meant nothing, but somehow they were keys in a power struggle between these two men. And until Add'kas'adanna knew more, she would be foolish to get involved.

"That's a waste," Kaffair argued.

"Not if we are successful," Ninda shot back. "I call for a vote."

That brought Add'kas'adanna back to the moment. "This is a military matter," Ninda continued. "And I propose we proceed as such."

"And I propose we let it alone," Kaffair said coldly.

They both looked at Zort, who, as always, immediately sided with Ninda. "We proceed," he said.

And then the three of them looked to Add'kas'adanna. Her vote was a foregone conclusion. In their eyes she would not dare oppose Ninda, for she was part of his power bloc, and a Kinathin dare not think for herself. But in fact it was none of that; it was *kith'ain*, which none of them understood.

She didn't yet know enough to oppose Ninda, and in any case, with Theara absent, it would only bring about a tie in the vote, a stalemate. And since the question was a military one, the decision would fall to her and she would have to declare herself, and she didn't know enough yet to do that. She nodded, did what was expected. "We proceed."

"It's done then," Ninda said, standing triumphantly. He looked at Add'kas'adanna. "You'll see to the details."

She nodded.

"Good. Then we are adjourned."

••••

Captain Jewel Thaaline, commanding officer of the *Pride of Altalane*, stared at one of her screens and swore silently to herself. She was a loyal officer with more than thirty-two years of service in the Federal Directorate of the Republic of Syndon, and she'd be damned if she would obey such orders without one hell of a good reason. Not now. Not ever.

"Captain," her first officer said. "I've got Subsector Operations on line. The CO there is Illcall Terman and he's—"

"I know," she growled. "Just give me the damn line."

"Yes, ma'am," Soe said coldly.

She'd hurt his feelings, she knew. She'd have to make it up to him later, but for the moment Terman was on her screen. "Jewel," he said happily. "What's the occasion? We haven't spoken in—"

"Cut the crap, Ill," she snapped. "You know goddamn well why I'm calling. I want to know what-the-hell kind of orders you're sending me?"

"Now calm down, Jewel—"

"Don't tell me to calm down. I'm damn mad and I'm going to stay mad—"

Terman interrupted her angrily. "Well, don't start barking at me. I was told to send in the nearest hunter-killer and you're it."

"Send someone else."

"Damn it, Jewel! I'm sending everyone else. The only ships I haven't sent in yet are the ships I can't communicate with because they're still in transition, but as soon as they down-transit they get the same orders as you. I've got my orders straight from Directorate Central Operations, and they say to divert every available warship into this. That means you and a lot of others."

Jewel's anger dissipated. "Why's DCO getting involved in Subsector Operations?"

Terman shrugged. "Hell if I know. Maybe something big. Late yesterday an imperial cruiser burned one of our destroyers off Trinivan, and DCO wants that cruiser bad. They don't have a positive ID but they think it was H.M.S. *Invaradin*. They'd like to take her intact, but they know that's impossible so they'll be happy if you just put a torpedo in her; a big one."

"But damn it, Ill," Jewel pleaded. "We've just spent a whole month drifting into position. We're right in the middle of the Cathan–Dumark shipping lane and the damn *impers* don't even know we're here. There's likely to be a big convoy along any day now. We could take out ten, maybe twenty million tonnes of shipping."

"I'm sorry, Jewel." Terman looked none too happy himself. "DCO didn't leave anything up to me. They think *Invaradin*'s headed for Dumark and they want you there."

"Two days," she pleaded. "Just give me two days."

Terman shook his head. "DCO's orders are quite specific. You move out now."

"Damn it! The *Pride*'s just a fifty-man hunter-killer. We can't take on an imperial cruiser."

Terman shook his head. "Now you're the one that's full of crap, Jewel. You've done it before. But in any case, you're the closest ship we've got to Dumark; you're behind their lines and well hidden. Just try to sneak into the Dumark system quietly and observe. See if you can be there before that cruiser arrives and get a positive ID on her. Then wait for some of our heavy stuff to show up."

"Why all the fuss over this damn cruiser?" she asked. "One of them burned one of us. So what? Happens every day. We'll burn one of them tomorrow."

Terman shook his head. "There's more to it than that, Jewel. But DCO's not talking, so your guess is as good as mine."

"Captain," Soe said urgently. "I've got a transition wake at about one light-year. Imperial patrol, I'd guess. Probably spotted some of our transmitter splash."

"Shit!" Jewel swore. "Are you sure they're coming this way?"

"No," Soe snapped angrily. "I'm not sure of anything."

"How much time have we got?"

"No more than half an hour."

She looked at Terman. "Looks like the game's up anyway. We'd better not be here when that patrol shows up."

Terman shrugged. "Sorry, Jewel. It was really out of my hands from the beginning."

"I know, Ill. I know. It's just a shame; a whole month of setting up this shot, wasted."

He smiled. "Good hunting, Jewel."

She smiled back. "Thanks, Ill. *Pride of Altalane* out."

6

Spies

"LIEUTENANT COLONEL JUESSIK."

Torrin Juessik looked at the young yeoman. She smiled pleasantly at him and said, "His Grace will see you now."

Juessik smiled back at her, then crossed the small room and stepped into the office of Admiral of the Imperial Fleet, Lord Bargan Abraxa.

The old man sat behind his desk, so Juessik crossed the room smartly and came to attention in front of it. He saluted and Abraxa returned the salute casually. "At ease, Mister Juessik."

Abraxa looked him over carefully, then tapped the folder sitting on the desk in front of him. "So. Rochefort personally intervened in the standing orders of a ship-of-the-line. He's done that before and he'll do it again. And he did it for a good reason: a member of the royal family. So why does a young lieutenant colonel of Admiralty Intelligence consider it a matter of such urgency that he'd bring it to my personal attention?"

Juessik spoke carefully. "When *Aeya arrived on* Trinivan, Your Grace, Directorate agents there broke cover almost simultaneously and began agitating openly for a riot. Their purpose, apparently, was to delay Her Royal Highness' exit until heavier forces could arrive. They succeeded, but in so doing they revealed their entire Trinivanian organization. The capture or death of the princess alone would not have warranted such costly action."

Abraxa looked at him narrowly, and after a few seconds nodded. "Go on."

"*Invaradin* successfully rescued Her Royal Highness and her entourage, as well as our embassy staff on Trinivan. Rochefort again intervened in Fleet Operations, this time to order *Invaradin* to Dumark."

It took a moment, but comprehension slowly appeared in Abraxa's eyes. "The Empress Cassandra is on Dumark, is she not?"

"Yes she is," Juessik said. "Traveling incognito. And so is the queen mother. Rochefort sent them a message after he left Fleet-Op."

"Very curious!" Abraxa said. "But why Trinivan? And why Aeya? She's nothing but a stupid, young girl, with obvious, but naïve, peacer sympathies. Not even Edvard is foolish enough to entrust her with something important."

"No," Juessik agreed. "But among Aeya's entourage is Sylissa d'Hart, and Edvard and Cassandra trust her implicitly."

Abraxa considered that for a long moment, then slowly began to nod. "Yes! They're up to something, aren't they? Do you have anyone in Aeya's entourage?"

"Yes," Juessik said. "But he's been rather ineffectual. Not his fault, actually. Whatever Edvard is up to, he's been exceedingly careful about leaks."

"We must have information," Abraxa demanded. "What's your next move?"

Juessik spoke carefully, for this was the key moment. "I had not intended to make a next move, Your Grace. My superior will not allow me to act on the matter."

Abraxa's face remained expressionless. "And your superior chose not to inform me at all of the matter."

Juessik shrugged. "Perhaps he feels it's unimportant."

"Or perhaps . . ." Abraxa added, ". . . he's withholding the information for his own purposes."

Juessik knew he had to speak carefully now. "I wouldn't know, Your Grace."

"Then why did you circumvent him? Why come directly to me? Are you not doing so for your own purposes?"

Juessik shrugged. "I would hope to be of some service, Your Grace."

"Of course," Abraxa said. He leaned back in his chair and smiled in a way that told Torrin Juessik his future was brightening. "Let us assume, Lieutenant Colonel Juessik, that I allowed you a free hand in this. What then would be your next move?"

"We need to let Edvard and Cassandra play their hand, so I would go personally to Dumark, under cover as an AI major, observe events and be ready to move at the right moment. I have an extremely reliable agent in Cassandra's entourage who'll be forewarned and on hand when they make their move, and hopefully we'll learn what they're up to."

"And if that fails?" Abraxa asked.

Juessik wanted to keep Abraxa as uninformed as possible, but he had to impress the fat old fart with something. "I have an option I would prefer not to exercise unless it's absolutely necessary, a certain leverage with the d'Hart woman, though she's not yet aware of that. If necessary I can induce her to aid us, albeit reluctantly."

Abraxa considered the matter carefully for some seconds, then nodded slowly. "Very well. I'll take care of your superior, and you may proceed without his interference."

••••

Abraxa sat for a moment without moving. It came as no surprise that Edvard and his women were up to something. Little by little, over the span of three generations, the emperor's power had declined while that of the Admiralty had grown, though Edvard and Cassandra still had influence and could cause difficulties. He'd have to be careful when he countered their move, but before he could do that he had to find out what their move was going to be.

Then there was the *Invaradin* thing. There was something he should remember about that ship, but nothing came to mind.

He turned to a small console built into the ornate desk, activated it, pulled up a description of *Invaradin*: an ordinary heavy cruiser. The ship and her captain had a distinguished record. Abraxa had even met him a few times: the youngest son of the Earl of Seegat. Perhaps that was it. No, there was something else he should remember, and it bothered him that he couldn't. But he was a patient man, and he was confident it would come to mind eventually.

••••

York slammed awake, sat up in bed, ignored the sideways tug of the gravity field of his cabin deck as it interfered with that of his grav bunk. He hesitated for an instant, wondering how he'd gotten back to his cabin, wondering why everything seemed so normal. Then he tore frantically at his shirt, exposing his bare chest. The skin there was pink and healthy.

He threw back the covers, found to his great relief that his right leg was still whole, with no indication it had ever been missing. He wiggled his toes and they felt fine.

It had all been a dream, an insane dream. Trinivan . . . the embassy . . . the chaos on Hangar Deck. It had all been just a dream.

He reached for the controls next to his bunk, cut the gravity field back to a few inches, and with years of practiced ease pivoted and landed on his feet as he dropped to the deck of his cabin. The field of the grav bunk held the covers pressed tightly against the wall.

He pressed a sensor on the opposite wall and a sink folded down out of the bulkhead. That was one of his few perks, a small fresher in his cabin. Not much to show for twenty-odd years of service. No toilet—he had to make command rank for that—but it was more than a typical junior officer's quarters. As a lifer he was more than a junior officer, less than a senior officer, and never to be promoted.

The sink settled into place with a soft click. York touched a sensor over the tap, and as the water flowed he touched another sensor to adjust the temperature to near scalding. He started to bend toward the sink, but before he got there he caught a momentary glimpse of his face in the mirror, and he froze half bent over the sink.

His left eye was a chrome-plated metal ball that reflected his own image back to the mirror, with a featureless black spot in the center that served as a pupil. On the skin surrounding the eye socket a starburst of bright, pink scars radiated outward in jagged lines; up his forehead, back along his temple, down his cheek.

He straightened up and looked again at his chest, still could find no trace of any scars there. He folded a chair down out of the wall, sat down and reexamined his right leg, discovered that if he looked closely he could just detect the last residues of scar tissue around his knee where his own skin joined that of the prosthetic. He wiggled his toes again; they felt like real toes.

It all came back to him now, though it seemed hidden behind a mist of confusion and drugs and fear. He had awakened in sickbay the day before, brought slowly out of electro-sedation by the technicians there. He had to struggle to remember what Alsa Yan had told him. "*. . . accelerated healing . . . rapid regrowth . . .*"

York closed his eyes, leaned back in the chair, listened to the water running in the sink. "You almost bought it, York. Your leg's gone just below the knee. Your knee was a mess too, but I managed to reconstruct most of it and regrow what I couldn't. Below that, however, the leg's a cyber-prosthetic, and I don't have the facilities to clone you another so you'll have wear it until we get to Dumark. But don't forget, the skin on that thing is as real as your own; it'll bleed if you cut it and it'll hurt, and it'll get infected."

"Dumark," York said aloud into the emptiness of his cabin. That would please the crew; they could get in some good R'n'R.

What else had Alsa said? ". . . That rotary shattered your chest plate and your visor, filled your head and chest with splinters and fragments of the rotary shells. I pulled your lungs and heart, stuck them in regrowth for a couple of days. They're pretty well healed now so I stuffed them back into you yesterday. I pulled the eye too and put it in regrowth, but it's scarring up on me. I think I'll be able to repair it, but it's going to take some time, so you'll have to be happy with the cyb I installed."

York looked in the mirror above the sink: the scars, the chrome-plated eye. ". . . I didn't have time for the cosmetic work. We can color match the eye and clear up the scars in a couple of hours. But I can't do it today, or tomorrow either. Talk to my floor nurse, see when she can schedule you in. And in any case, for the next few days you take it easy. It'll be at least that long before you're fully healed. Incidentally, Sergeant Notay scheduled you for therapy with the rest of the marines."

York remembered shaking his head, saying, "I don't want anything to do with those damn marines."

Yan had shrugged. "It's not up to you. The marine medics know their stuff as well as my own people, and Notay cleared it with me and the captain."

York looked in the mirror again, at the chrome-plated eye and the mess they'd made of his face.

••••

As Edvard entered the room the attendant at the door barked, "His Majesty, the King." Edvard smiled at the guests assembled there, and of course they all stopped whatever they were doing or saying and turned his way. Depending on station, or rank, some dropped to one knee, some bowed deeply, and a few, like Abraxa, and old Archcanon Bortha, merely bent at the waist slightly and lowered their eyes. Abraxa's bow had been getting shallower of late.

To dine with the emperor was an important privilege; a great honor, some thought. For Edvard these evenings were hard work, sometimes the only opportunity he had to meet informally with certain people under circumstances that weren't carefully orchestrated.

"Excuse me, Your Majesty," a rather nondescript man said, stepping casually in front of him. The man, while dressed rather simply, was actually a senior officer in Edvard's personal guard. He bowed carefully, then stepped in close, a small instrument in one hand. "We have a minor problem, sire," he whispered. He held the instrument out toward Edvard, paused at an appropriate distance, "May I, Your Majesty?"

Edvard nodded. "Certainly, Captain."

The man held the instrument, no larger than the palm of his hand, close to one of the buttons on the front of Edvard's coat. He looked at the instrument for a moment, nodded, touched something on the face of the instrument and pressed it against the button, nodded again, then discreetly put the instrument away in his own coat. "It's deactivated, Your Majesty."

"Thank you, Captain," Edvard said. "The press?"

The officer shook his head. "Not likely, Your Majesty. They're not usually that clumsy. Probably some branch of the military, or someone employed by one of the minor Houses. With your permission, we'll remove the button at the end of the evening and conduct a full investigation. At the least, someone on your staff has accepted a bribe."

The man disappeared into the small crowd. Edvard spoke for a time with the daughter of a minor Earl, a young girl bubbling over with excitement. But she'd been well trained and kept her enthusiasm appropriately damped, so Edvard enjoyed himself a bit. Next there were her parents. Her father's holdings had become somewhat strategic in an alliance between Houses de Vena and de Plutarr. All parties concerned were close to agreement on the terms of marriage between the young woman and the son of Andralla Schessa, the Duchess de Vena. The boy was a fool, careless and irresponsible, but by law he must inherit the properties of House de Vena. The girl was smart, though quite young, but given time and training and tutelage under Schessa herself, they could be sure the properties would be administered properly.

Edvard chatted for a time with old Bortha. The titular head of the church worked hard at presenting the image of a wise, old man in his declining years. It was quite a disarming act, but Edvard knew better than to succumb to the old churchman's guise. Bortha was a dangerous schemer.

Edvard was speaking with Andralla Schessa, second only to Abraxa on the Admiralty Council, when she said, "Since I've heard nothing more of Trinivan, Your Majesty, I assume Aeya is unharmed."

"Good of you to ask. She's quite all right, though I confess I'm a bit miffed at her for going to such a backward planet on nothing more than a lark."

"Was that all it was?" Schessa asked, and Edvard had the feeling she was testing him.

He shrugged. "I hope so. Better that than her peacer sympathies getting the best of her again."

Schessa changed the subject. "It's a shame about poor Colonel Eschmann's unfortunate demise."

Edvard nodded. He had no doubt Eschmann had stepped on the wrong toes and been eliminated. "Heart attack, wasn't it?" Edvard asked.

"Yes," Schessa said. "And alone, with no one to call for help. Could have easily been saved, I hear."

"Have you chosen a successor?" Edvard asked, knowing the answer.

Schessa said, "Young fellow named Juessik. He was Eschmann's second in command at AI, seems quite qualified. We'll be voting on confirmation in the Council tomorrow. I assume you'll see the paperwork shortly thereafter."

The evening proceeded nicely. From what Edvard could determine there seemed to be some suspicion about Aeya's activities, but no awareness of anything else. That was good.

••••

Driving steadily in transition there wasn't much to do on first watch, so York scanned the report on the engagement at Trinivan. The feddie destroyer had taken *Invaradin* by surprise, and the damage to turret six had come in the first instant of contact. Curious, York searched the log, found no mention, or recording, of his efforts to warn *Invaradin*, and he realized Sierka had done the unthinkable: he'd tampered with the official log. Without proof he dare not make any accusations. But someday, maybe someday, Sierka just might find himself standing next to York on the surface of some planet, with only marines for witnesses. Sierka would most likely die in combat that day.

At the end of first watch York headed for the officer's mess. With VIP's on board it was unusually crowded. York grabbed a tray full of food, didn't pay much attention to what was on it, had trouble finding an unoccupied seat, finally spotted an open place next to a bulkhead at a table full of civilians. But as he sat down all conversation at the table came to a sudden stop.

He peeled the lid off the tray, began eating in silence, heard someone whisper his name. Then one by one they stood and walked away, leaving York alone at the table. He sat there and concentrated on eating his lunch.

Maggie Votak and Frank Stara rescued him. They stood from a table across the room, lifted their trays, made a show of crossing the room and sitting down opposite him. As he sat down, Frank growled, "Damn dirtlovers! And they've got you to thank for saving their butts."

York shrugged. "They're just snobs. Or maybe they don't like the eye. Come to think of it, if the eye keeps the dirtlovers away, maybe I'll wait until we get to Dumark to have Alsa do the cosmetic work." He winked at Maggie.

She shook her head. "York! That's not very nice."

Frank grinned. "Who knows, York? You might discover a pretty, young civilian with a fascination for scars."

York grinned back at him. "Maybe she'll have a friend."

"That's all right for you, York," Maggie said, her eyes narrowing, "but if old Frankie-boy here discovers anything pretty besides me, all Fleet won't be able to protect him."

When she looked at Stara there was something in her eyes that caught York's attention. He frowned, looked carefully at them both for a second, then said to Maggie, "You finally accepted, didn't you?"

She smiled, blushed—rather unusual for Magdelena Votak. He reached across the table, aimed his open hand at Stara. "Congratulations, sucker. She's too good for you."

They shook hands, and York asked Maggie, "What made you change your mind? Old Frank here has asked you a dozen times. And Telyekev wouldn't have let you share Frank's cabin without contracts. And now, all of a sudden . . ."

"Well . . . I've been rotated back. It was in the contact packet we got before heading for Trinivan. And if we make it official then they'll let us stay together. And now . . ."

York knew the one fear she'd been hiding from them all. He finished her sentence for her. "And since you'd never been rotated back before, and you'd been out here for six years already, there was just the chance you were a lifer. But now you know you're safe, eh?"

She cocked her head slightly. "I'm sorry, York."

"Ah!" He shrugged it off. "We should do a little celebrating tonight."

Frank's attention suddenly shifted to someone behind York. York turned and saw Daka Nemkov heading their way with Lady d'Hart in tow. As they approached both he and Frank stood and bowed. "Please, gentleman," she said. "Sit down. I understand on ship we relax some of the formalities."

Nemkov greeted each of them with a nod. "Maggie. Frank. Ballin."

The noblewoman sat down, and York and Frank and Nemkov followed suit. She looked at York, nicely resisted the temptation to stare at his eye. "How are you feeling, Lieutenant? I hear you were rather badly wounded."

"I'm fine," York said. "They can fix us up pretty quick."

She smiled, was quite beautiful. "Well, we're all indebted to you for saving our lives."

Her words clearly didn't sit well with Nemkov. "Yes, Ballin, very heroic, unfortunately that one little incident seems to capture everyone's imagination best."

"Dak!" Maggie said angrily.

York stiffened. "What incident?"

Nemkov persisted. "I just want to know if it's true."

"If what's true?" York demanded.

"Daka," Lady d'Hart interrupted. "I've personally read the inquiry Captain Telyekev conducted, and Mr. Ballin was fully justified in his actions."

York demanded patiently, "What are we talking about here?"

"York," Maggie said softly. "We all realize we don't know what it's like to be in a drop zone, but we can guess."

"No you can't," York said.

"Well, we can try," she said. "And I think everyone knows what it's like to make split second decisions—"

York interrupted her. "What are you getting at, Maggie?"

She hesitated for a moment, and it was Nemkov who answered him. "There's a rather nasty story going around about a young Trinivanian girl . . ."

York's appetite disappeared as he thought of the dead young girl with most of her abdomen blown away. Maggie was saying something about the princess filing charges and Telyekev convening an official investigation. "You were exonerated of all charges, York."

From the looks on their faces it was clear there was more. "What are you not telling me?"

Nemkov grinned. "They've given you a nickname, Ballin."

York shook his head. "I don't think I want to hear this."

"*Butcher Ballin*," Nemkov said loudly. "They like to call you *Butcher Ballin*."

"God damn it," York snarled, not caring if he offended Lady d'Hart. "We were under assault. I'd like to see you do better with mortar dropping all around you."

Nemkov shrugged. "I'm no marine."

"No," York agreed. "You're not."

"Stop it, you two," Maggie said. "Why can't you get along?"

York looked at Nemkov. "Give His Lordship a year and he'll pull a Home Fleet assignment like all the rest. Then he can pretend he's an experienced line officer."

Nemkov shook his head. "I don't have to be a lifer to know what to do in combat."

"I've heard that expression before," Lady d'Hart interrupted in a blatant effort to change the subject. "What's a lifer?"

Everyone froze and looked at York, and as the silence drew out he answered her. "A lifer is an officer who never gets rotated off the front lines, and never gets promoted beyond the rank of lieutenant. He's forever a very senior junior officer, and his only break from combat duty is a few tendays of R'n'R here and there."

Lady d'Hart frowned. "Do you mean this goes on for his entire life?"

York shrugged and nodded. "Most don't live long."

"But that's terrible. How does such a thing happen?"

Maggie answered her, trying to put a positive spin on the rumors. "No one knows for sure. Lifers are rare. The rest of us get rotated on a random basis. Some after a year or two, but never more than six."

York added. "Unless you're a lifer."

Maggie tried to ignore him. "Rumor has it lifers are a glitch in the computer, an accident Fleet is unaware of."

"Some of us," Nemkov said, "think they have some character flaw that's hidden deep in their file."

"Lifers are valuable," Frank added, speaking for York's benefit. "They have enormous experience, and are considered good luck."

Lady d'Hart looked at him carefully, perhaps beginning to sense there was something more here than merely idle conversation. "Have any of you ever met a lifer?"

They all looked at York, then they realized what they were doing and looked away in embarrassed silence. Lady d'Hart frowned, then realization hit her and she looked at York. "Oh! I'm sorry, Lieutenant. I've stepped in it, haven't I?"

Behind him he heard Aeya growl, "Butcher Ballin." They hadn't seen her approaching.

York stood and turned to face her. She looked up at him, clearly intending to give him a piece of her mind. But then she saw his chrome eye and scarred face, and she stood there speechless.

York stepped around her and left the mess, thinking that maybe the chrome eye and scars weren't such a bad thing after all.

••••

The gathering was a small one. There wasn't that much room in the aft maintenance bay on Hangar Deck. Telyekev and his first officer Joyson, and York and Palevi, and the twenty-one flag draped bodies, and a couple marines and a few crewmembers. And of course Rhijn and Thring were there too. It was a shame Rhijn had chosen to supersede the young canticle's responsibilities. Thring took it all so seriously, even though most of his flock couldn't take him seriously.

York stared at the small puddle of clear fluid on the deck as Telyekev gave the command and the hull echoed with the emergency blow-down cycle of the aft maintenance hatch. For eight crewmembers it was over.

They recycled the hatch, then turned to the thirteen marines sealed in body bags and lined up on the deck. York had chosen, more out of respect for the dead than any allegiance to the living, to wear a marine tunic for this occasion. He'd had to borrow it from Palevi, have them mount captain's bars on it, and it felt odd to wear the dark blue with red piping and gold trim. He looked down at his chest, and as Rhijn started chanting his superstitious invocation over the dead, York couldn't take his eyes off the old-fashioned brass buttons that shone in the harsh artificial light.

Rhijn put on a good show, very formal, with much pomp and circumstance. But that wasn't appropriate here; better perhaps on the vids, or at court. It should have been Thring, York thought through the whole thing. It should have been Thring.

When Rhijn finished, it took York a moment to remember the next move was his, and though he intended to call out strongly, his voice came out barely above a whisper. "Sergeant, call the roll."

"Yes, sir." Palevi stepped forward carrying a list of names on an old-fashioned piece of paper. But as he called out the first name the paper stayed locked in his fist, unopened. "Private First Class Stanwell Sinscar."

"Here, sir," one of the marines called out loudly.

Palevi continued. "Private . . ."

Sinscar? York thought. He couldn't remember the man, and as Palevi called out each of the names, and as a marine answered symbolically for each, he realized he couldn't remember any of them. They were marines and he wasn't, so he'd never paid much attention to who they were. Now he felt ashamed that he'd thought so little of the people who died beside him.

The silence brought York out of his reverie, everyone waiting for him now that Palevi had finished. York nodded, and the marines of the grave detail began stacking the body bags into the maintenance hatch. A crewmember passed out small plast cups filled with a clear fluid. As they sealed the hatch York looked at the liquid in his cup: slightly diluted 'trate, very strong. He lifted the cup to his lips, and the others in the bay followed his lead. One sip, that was all, and the 'trate burned its way down his throat, then he held the cup out in front of him and spoke the time honored lament, "For them it's over. For us it goes on." He tipped the cup slowly and poured the rest of the 'trate onto the metal and plast of the deck where it spattered and splashed all over his boots. He waited until the rest had done likewise, then he called out, "Release them," and the hull echoed with the emergency blow-down cycle of the aft maintenance hatch.

7

Remembrance

YORK SAT DOWN on a bench against a bulkhead in the gym, breathing hard and soaked with sweat. The damn marines were pushing him too hard, wouldn't let him rest, and his leg was starting to ache. He looked around: nothing but marines, *Invaradin*'s entire complement of two hundred. The gym was filled with them, men and women all stripped down to the bare minimum with an immodesty that would have been shocking on the upper decks, grunting and sweating; exercise drills, hand-to-hand combat drills, physical therapy for the wounded.

Sergeant Meciden Notay stopped in front of him, tossed him a towel and put her hands on her hips. "Come on, Cap'm. One more set."

York caught the towel, wiped it across his face and looked at her carefully. She was actually rather good looking, if a little tough in appearance, but stripped down to shorts and a T-shirt he couldn't help noticing she was in pretty good shape. "Go to hell," York growled at her. He leaned over, began massaging his calf.

Notay squatted down in front of him. "Leg giving you trouble, sir?"

"You're damn right it's giving me trouble."

She stood up, shouted over her shoulder. "Kalee. Front'n'center. Cap'm's leg's acting up."

One of the marine medics slipped out of the crowd carrying a medical kit, squatted down in front of York and began rifling through the kit. It took York a moment to recognize him. "You're the one patched me up on the boat, aren't you?"

Kalee found what he was looking for. "Yeah, Cap'm. That was me."

"Thanks."

"Don't mention it, Cap'm." Kalee pressed a small, black box against the side of York's calf, threw a switch on it and York's leg went numb from the knee down. "Nothing to worry about, Cap'm. I just turned off your cyb. Need to make a few adjustments. That's all."

While the medic worked Notay sat down next to York, handed him a tumbler of cold water. York gulped at it greedily. "Glad you could make it this time, Cap'm."

York finished drinking, looked at the woman and shrugged, "The old man made it an order."

She smiled. "It's all for the best, Cap'm. We need to stress that new leg of yours a little, work the bugs out of it. Besides, you're a marine. It's only right, you working out with the rest of us."

York started to growl that he wasn't a damn marine, but instead he asked, "What kind of game are you playing, Notay? You and Palevi."

"Game, Cap'm?" She looked offended. "I don't understand."

"Of course you do. You marines treat me like shit, then all of a sudden you start acting like I'm one of you."

"But you are one of us, Cap'm. And we take care of our own."

"But I'm not. I'm navy, all the way."

She shook her head. "You went back for Stacy and Dakkart. Only a marine would'a done that."

"But I screwed it up."

"That doesn't matter, Cap'm. You went back. That's what counts."

The medic removed the little, black box from the side of York's leg and he could wiggle his toes again. "I dropped the gain back on the pain circuits, sir. I also checked the fit on the interface and the neural circuits. Shouldn't give you any more trouble."

York grinned unhappily. "Thanks. I appreciate it."

"Don't mention it, Cap'm."

"That's enough for me," York said. He stood, tested the leg for a moment. "I'm going back to my cabin, get cleaned up."

"Don't forget tomorrow, Cap'm," Notay reminded him. "Same time."

York turned for the exit. "Yeah," he said as he walked away.

He was only a few meters down the corridor outside the gym when someone called after him, "Cap'm."

He stopped, turned about, found Dakkart jogging down the corridor toward him. She stopped just in front of him, saluted crisply. He returned the salute. "At ease, private. What is it?"

The marine relaxed, and politely asked, "Can I speak frankly, sir?"

York nodded. "Sure."

"Well, sir, I just wanted to tell you I don't figure I owe you nothin' for coming back for me and Stacy. It was what you was supposed to do, so I don't consider it no favor." She finished with a defiant look.

York shook his head and ran a hand through his hair. "That's fine with me, private. Now leave me alone."

"Yes, sir," she shouted in his face, snapped to attention, saluted, then turned and jogged back toward the gym.

••••

"Captain's compliments," the yeoman said, "and Captain Telyekev wants you to report to his office immediately."

Even on a screen, York could see the tension in the yeoman's face. "Is Captain Telyekev aware I'm on bridge watch?"

"Yes, sir, he is. Commander Rame has been notified, and he's arranging your relief."

York nodded. "I'll be right down."

York logged off the system, cleared himself off the console. As he was doing so, Paris Jondee sat down next to him. "I'm here to relieve you, York old boy. Kind of funny, isn't it? Only an hour out from Dumark and captain, first officer, and third officer haven't even shown their faces on the bridge."

York shook his head. "You ask too many questions, Paris."

"Questions!" Jondee exclaimed. "I didn't ask any questions. Just thinking out loud, old boy."

York looked at Jondee carefully. "Well, do your thinking more quietly, eh?" He didn't wait for an answer, stood and stepped around the fire control console to stand beside Olin Rame at the command console. He saluted. "Request permission to leave the bridge, sir. Under orders of the captain."

Rame was busy. He didn't look up, threw a sloppy salute and said, "Permission granted."

As the captain's yeoman let York into Telyekev's office he whispered, "Watch out, sir."

York didn't need the warning. The tension in the room was palpable. Sierka stood at attention in front of Telyekev's desk, a bead of sweat running slowly down his brow. Telyekev sat behind his desk making no attempt to hide his anger. Commander Joyson, a calm counterpoint to the white-hot fury of her captain, sat comfortably on a nearby couch.

Not the time for sloppy manners, York snapped to attention beside Sierka and saluted crisply. "Lieutenant Ballin reporting as ordered, sir."

Telyekev growled, "At ease, Lieutenant."

York assumed the position, but there was no *ease* to be had in that room.

Telyekev was in no mood for small talk. "Tell me about Trinivan, Mr. Ballin."

York frowned. "Where would you like me to begin, sir?"

"From the moment you left this ship."

York told them about Trinivan. It was not the first time he'd told the story so he kept it brief, leaving nothing out, but hoping to avoid details. He didn't want to get caught in the middle of whatever was going on here. When he got to the part about his argument with Sierka, he merely said, ". . . so I contacted *Invaradin* to warn you of the danger and—"

"Then you did contact us prior to the attack?" Telyekev asked.

"Yes, sir. I followed standard procedure there, sir."

"Did you, now?" Telyekev asked. "And did you request fire support?"

"I believe so, sir."

"And what did Mr. Sierka say?"

This was getting nasty. "Well, sir, it's rather hard to remember. We were under fire—"

"Bullshit!" Telyekev shouted, standing and leaning forward on his desk. "I want to know exactly what was said."

Joyson intervened. "Now Alexiae," she said softly. "Don't take it out on poor Mr. Ballin." She looked carefully at York. "Lieutenant, we need to know exactly what happened."

York shook his head. "I'm sorry, ma'am. But I'd rather not make allegations I can't prove."

Joyson nodded resignedly. "I see you've already discovered portions of the ship's log have been erased."

York said unhappily, "It would just be my word, ma'am."

"His word against mine," Sierka added. "And I still don't understand why the both of you're so ready to side with him. He probably erased it to . . ."

Telyekev turned on Sierka with a sudden start, and Sierka's voice trailed off into silence as Telyekev stormed around his desk, his anger unchecked, his face slowly expanding into a mask of rage. When Telyekev spoke, his voice was even more frightening for the calm, cold menace it held. "I want you to listen to something, Commander."

Telyekev turned away from Sierka, leaned over his desk, touched a few keys on his console. York's voice came out of a speaker there, surprising both him and Sierka. ". . . Sierka, you son-of-a-bitch. Where the hell are you? We're under assault. Now. We need fire support—" His words were punctuated by the sounds of heavy weapons fire and exploding mortar rounds.

Telyekev touched another key and the sounds died. He turned toward Sierka, stopped with his nose only inches from the commander's face. "Apparently you weren't aware a copy of any marine transmission is automatically stored in the marine log, which is separate from the ship's log and its backup.

"I don't need to be told what happened. In fact I'll tell you. Mr. Ballin called com and told you about our feddie friends, and you ignored him. Not only that, you didn't bother to report the fact to me. And then, as if that weren't enough, you tried to cover up your actions by erasing the com recordings of the incident."

Sierka lifted his chin proudly. "You have no proof I destroyed any recordings—"

"Shut up," Telyekev shouted. For an instant, York thought he might hit him.

"Be careful, Alexiae," Joyson cautioned.

Telyekev made a visible effort to calm himself, but his voice still came out in a growl. "Don't you say another word, Sierka. I'm so mad right now, if you so much as squeak I'll have you vented on the spot and worry about covering it up later. You seriously endangered this ship. That feddie got the drop on us, nothing but a fucking destroyer and it managed to hull us. He could have burned us. Not only that, you left Mister Ballin and his people at the mercy of the enemy without the support they should have been able to expect from us. I don't give a damn what kind of difficulties you and he have between you. He and his marines are my people. Do you understand? *My people*. You don't double-cross them that way."

"It won't happen again, sir," Sierka said.

Telyekev shook his head and growled, "No. It won't. At least not on this ship. We're going to dock at Dumark Station shortly, and until that time you're confined to your cabin. You can take the time to prepare a request for transfer to dirtside assignment. Have it logged for my approval before we hit dock. And have your gear packed, because if you're not off this ship one minute after we break seal, I'll lock you up and vent you to space when we lift off again. You're dismissed."

Sierka was smart enough to know when to keep his mouth shut. He saluted, turned and left.

For a moment it seemed as if Telyekev had forgotten York. But then he glanced his way, looked him over for a second and said, "Get out of here."

••••

"Transition," York said on allship, simultaneously blanking all exterior transmissions as *Invaradin* went sublight in Dumark farspace.

"Drones out," Telyekev ordered.

Invaradin's hull echoed eerily as the combat drones launched. They waited in silence for Anda Gant to give her verdict, though on green status with little possibility of any feddies in the vicinity the atmosphere on the bridge was relaxed. York picked up an incoming transmission, switched it to his implants, heard the voice of a bored com-tech. "This is Dumark Station, requesting an identity check."

York examined the signal carefully. "Captain, I'm getting a request from Dumark for an identity check. It's properly encrypted and coded."

"Thank you, Mr. Ballin. Anda, what's the word?"

Gant's voice was calm. "Nothing in our immediate vicinity, sir. We're clear to a hundred thousand klicks. There's quite a bit of traffic near Dumark Station, but everything we've scanned so far seems to be ours."

"Olin?"

Rame sounded as bored as the station com-tech. "We're point-one lights out from Dumark's primary, well beyond nearspace. We can move fast if we have to."

York heard Telyekev take a deep breath. "Well, it looks like we're home. Mr. Ballin, open communications with Dumark."

York touched a switch on his console, activating a coded identity transmission. It also opened them up to receive their contact packet—news, mail, official business—and it transmitted a copy of their packet to Dumark for relay to Fleet, all in a fraction of a second. Then he switched in his voice pickup. "Dumark Station, this is H.M.S. *Invaradin* requesting docking clearance."

The com-tech's voice showed a little interest. "You people sure are cautious. How long you been out?"

"Six months," York said.

They made a short transition hop into Dumark nearspace. A big convoy was staging for transit to Cathan the following day. Dumark was a large agricultural concern out on the periphery of the empire, close enough that a feddie strike was unlikely, but far from the worlds of the inner empire. Cathan was two hundred light-years deeper in. York hadn't been that deep into the empire in ten years, and thinking of Cathan made him a little melancholy.

Invaradin waited in a holding orbit for three hours, though it would have been longer if the princess hadn't been on board. When the docking gantries clanged into place they slaved into Dumark Station's power, cut their power plant back to standby, broke seal, and were officially docked.

Anyone wounded on Trinivan was given immediate leave, while the rest remained on duty to get *Invaradin*'s repairs going smoothly. Back in his cabin York scrounged through his locker for a decent uniform, but everything was patched or badly worn. The best he could do was combine the trousers from his day blacks with the tunic from his grays.

York glanced in the mirror; there was nothing he could do about the chrome eye and scars. He'd put off the cosmetic work repeatedly, taken stubborn pleasure in the discomfort the sight gave the civilians. York got what he wanted: they'd avoided him with a vengeance. But he'd waited too long, and now Alsa Yan didn't have any time for him. "Maybe in a few days," she'd said.

The civilians on Dumark Station had the same reaction: some stared, most looked away. Even some of the military people had trouble looking him in the face. The ticket teller at the shuttle dock refused to look at him after doing so once. "Janston," York said. "It's on North Continent. Small agro coop."

"What's it near?" the teller asked.

York reached into his memory. He hadn't gone back there in twenty years. "Nearest big city is Bowenhead."

"Here it is," she said, reading data off her screen. "Population: ten thousand. And you say this Janstown is even smaller?"

"Janston," York corrected her. "And yes, it's small."

She scanned the data on her screen for another minute, finally said, "I can't find any reference to it. Best I can do is get you to Bowenhead. There's a shuttle leaving here in about two hours that'll drop you into Andermay. From there it's about a hundred klicks to Bowenhead via surface transit. Then you're on your own."

York thanked her, paid for his ticket, and six hours and half a world later was standing outside the transit depot in Bowenhead. It was a dingy, old place, badly in need of maintenance. There were no facilities for renting a vehicle, and only a few cabs, but none willing to take a passenger to the middle of nowhere. He finally found one fellow driving an old-fashioned, four-wheeled vehicle that coughed and spit obnoxious fumes. The vehicle's owner demanded double the round trip fare.

"What you want to go to Janston for?" the old man asked once they were under way. There was something vaguely familiar about him. "Ain't nothin' there for a big-shot officer like you."

The man's voice kept plucking at some memory. "Just want to look up some old friends," York said.

"I used to live in Janston, long time ago. What's their names? I might know how to find them for you."

It felt strange to speak the names of his foster parents after so many years. "Maja and Tollem Zoa."

"The Zoas, eh? Ya. Sure. I know them, or at least of them. Sour old Maja and her crazy old husband Toll."

The cab driver was right about Maja. But Toll? Good old Toll wasn't crazy. York wanted to hear what else the driver knew. "Didn't they have a foster son lived with them some years back?" he asked.

"Ya," the cab driver said. "Long time ago. Rotten kid. Always in trouble. No good. Come to a bad end, if I remember correctly. Tried to rob somebody. Fucked it up and killed her instead." The cab driver shook his head. "Ya. I'm remembering now. Judge sent him into convict labor, or into the navy, or something like that. Don't know which."

"He joined the navy," York said.

"Oh ya?" the cab driver asked. "How'd you know that?"

York didn't answer. The cab driver looked back at York and frowned at his uniform. Then he turned carefully back to face the road and they finished the trip in silence.

Janston was not what York remembered, though he didn't remember much more than a hateful old woman, and a friendly old man. The place was tired, run down and shabby. The cab driver stopped in front of a small agro supply store, said, "This is it."

York said, "I thought the Zoas were croppers."

The driver shook his head. "Not for ten, twelve years now. They never were much good at cropping, so now they run the supply."

York paid the driver and dismissed him, then stopped to look the place over. It needed paint, and repairs, and . . . He shook his head, pushed gingerly on the archaic, hinge-mounted door at the front of the store, stepped into a large, dimly lit room with racks and shelves half filled with supplies and equipment. A layer of dust coated everything. Evidently Maja and Toll were no better at managing an agro supply than they were at cropping.

He let go of the open door and a spring slammed it shut with a loud bang. "Be with ya in a minute," a female voice called. Some seconds later Maja appeared out of a back room. She was older now, but the sour and hateful expression on her face had not changed.

She looked at York suspiciously, though not with fear as any ordinary person would when looking into a face with scars and a chrome eyeball. "Good afternoon, yer lordship. What can I do for you?"

"I'm not a nobleman," York said.

"Right," she grunted. "I still need to know what you want. I can't guess what some highfalutin admiral wants here in a agro supply."

"I'm not an admiral either," York said. "Just a lieutenant."

"I still need to know what you want."

York didn't know what he wanted. He'd been on Dumark a dozen times in the last twenty years, and each time he'd thought about coming to see them, but always found some reason not to. He considered making up an excuse and leaving without identifying himself, but instead he blurted out, "I came to see you and Toll."

Her eyes narrowed. "What you want with us? We ain't done nothing wrong."

"No," York said. "You're not in any trouble. I just came to visit. I'm York Ballin."

She jumped as if stung, and her eyes narrowed even further. "The hell you say!" She stepped back warily, but leaned forward and squinted at him. After a moment she shook her head. "Well, I guess you are. What you come back for? We ain't got nothin' you can have."

"I don't want anything," York said. "I just came to visit."

"What for?" she asked. "Why now, after all this time?"

York shrugged and shook his head. "I just . . . thought I'd visit."

She squinted at him harder, dripping with suspicion, stood that way for what seemed an eternity, then suddenly nodded over her shoulder, spun about and walked toward the back of the store. "What the hell! Come on back. At least Toll'll like seeing you again. We're eating dinner. I suppose you want some for yourself. Probably still eat like a protein processor."

York followed her, stepping into a dark passage that led to the back of the store. They crossed through a small living room, littered and unkempt. Maja had never been much of a housekeeper.

In a tiny kitchen, Toll sat at a table that dominated the room, a plate of food in front of him, Maja's plate nearby. He, like Maja, was much older than York remembered: grayish-white hair, the skin of his face lifeless and fleshy. His attention was devoted to a portable vid sitting on the table in front of him, blaring something loud and noisy. He took no notice of York and Maja, stared blankly at the screen and giggled now and then at something, picked at the food in front of him.

Maja leaned over and shouted into his ear, "Look who's here."

He took no notice, continued to stare at the screen even as Maja grabbed a third plate and threw it onto the table with a crash. "Look who's here, you crazy old man."

She looked at York. "Sit down and eat."

York obeyed, feeling oddly like the twelve-year-old boy who, twenty-two years ago, had obeyed the same sour commands barked in the same harsh voice.

She threw some food on his plate, then, sitting down herself, she reached out and turned off the vid.

Toll whimpered and looked at her.

"York's here," she shouted at him.

Toll frowned. "York?"

"York Ballin. The boy, you old fool."

Toll's head turned toward York slowly, his face vacant and lifeless. York wanted to cry; strong silent Toll, able to withstand even Maja's strongest tongue lashing with an indifference York had always admired, reduced by the years to this whimpering old man.

"York?" he asked again.

"Hello, Toll," York said.

Toll started as recognition hit him. "York boy?" He smiled, and for an instant the old Toll was there, then just as quickly he was gone and the shabby old man returned. It was the shabbiness that bothered York most.

"Eat," Maja barked.

Toll obeyed.

York looked at the food. "I'm really not hungry."

"It's on your plate so eat it."

York ate. It was the lowest quality of protein cake and dark, bitter synthetic caff. It had almost no taste, but he ate it anyway.

They ate in silence, interrupted only by an occasional bark from Maja. When the meal was done she cleared the table, dropped the leftovers into the recycle processor and the dishes into the sterilizer, then left without a word. And York and Toll sat in silence.

After what seemed an eternity Toll finally moved. He reached out hesitantly, like a child afraid he might be slapped down, and touched the sleeve of York's tunic. He fingered the stripes there gently. "Navy boy," he said.

"Yes," York said. "I'm a lieutenant on the cruiser *Invaradin*. She's a good ship."

"Do you go see stars?" Toll asked.

York nodded. "Yes. Sometimes. But mostly we just fight feddies."

Toll nodded mechanically, looked at the silent vid longingly, then fearfully at the door through which Maja had disappeared. York understood now, as he and Toll had always understood one another. But he wondered if the old man could still understand him after all these years, especially with what he wanted to ask.

"Toll," he said tentatively, trying to get the old man's attention, reaching far back into the memories of a frightened, six-year-old boy, who, all those many years ago, had clutched desperately to the one familiar person in a world turned strange and foreign. It had been a man's hand he'd held so tightly that night. Not a father's hand, not someone he'd loved or longed for, but a face and a voice that was, at least, familiar when he'd needed familiarity most.

"Toll?" he asked. "Do you remember the man who brought me here? I was six years old at the time. That was twenty-nine years ago. I've tried to remember his name. It was something like *Matches*. Do you remember?"

"Matches?" Toll asked.

"Yes," York said eagerly. "Matches. Was that his name?"

Toll nodded. "Matches. Yes. Matches."

"Are you sure?" York asked. "It was a Lunan name—inner empire. Matches . . . or Mathis . . . or something like that."

"Yes," Toll said, nodding idiotically. "Mathis."

"What you asking him for?" Maja snarled, standing in the doorway. "He can't remember yesterday, let alone thirty years ago. And why you wanna know anyway?"

"I was just curious," he lied.

"Well, he don't remember."

"Do you?" asked York.

"O'course not. That was thirty years ago for me too. The man brought you. Said we was to tell everyone you was my dead sister's boy. Sent cash money every month. Said if we told anyone about him, or didn't raise you right, he'd take you away and the money would stop. Money stopped anyway once you went away to the navy." Her eyes narrowed as she looked at York angrily. "We needed that money. Bad we needed it. And that's all. There ain't no more to tell."

That night Maja fixed up a cot for York, but he didn't get much sleep. He lay awake most of the night, angry at himself for wasting his time on an idiotic quest for information thirty years dead. He managed to get a few hours of restless sleep near dawn, then got up quietly with the sun and decided to leave without saying good-bye. He was sneaking out through the store when he caught sight of the small comp terminal at the counter there, and on impulse he sat down and punched in a call to *Invaradin*.

Krass Doanne was on com watch and her face appeared on the screen. She was junior enough to obey most any order York gave her short of outright mutiny or treason. "Route me through ship's Central . . ." he said, ". . . into Dumark's central banking computer. And don't flag me as an indirect."

She looked at him narrowly. Such a request was highly improper, and only marginally legal. "Yes, sir," she said

Moments later he was in direct contact with Dumark Central. His access was limited, but they thought the call had originated on *Invaradin*. He requested access to Maja and Toll's banking and credit records, giving an access code that identified his request as a security matter. That, the apparent origin of the call, and Maja and Toll's status as nobodies, made it simple.

They were broke, he found, badly in debt and getting in deeper by the month.

He called up his own balance from *Invaradin*'s paymaster files. By Maja and Toll's standards he was rich. There wasn't much to spend your pay on when most of your life consisted of one deep space patrol after another: a couple of tenday leaves a year, a big binge now and then on a two day liberty, a luxury item or two aboard ship. And as the years had passed his money had just stacked up.

He withdrew half his account, paid off Maja and Toll's debts and had enough left to leave them a sizable sum in their own account.

"Why'd you do that?"

York jumped, turned about to find Maja looking over his shoulder. She was wearing an old dressing gown. "What for?" she demanded.

He shrugged. "I don't need the money. You and Toll do."

She thought about that for a moment, then she nodded and held out her hand. "Here," she said angrily, handing York a crumpled piece of yellowish paper.

He took it, opened it carefully. It was an old piece of paper, ready to disintegrate at the slightest misuse, and upon it, written in a tight and repressed hand, was a single name: *Collier Maczek*. "What's this?" he asked.

"You wanted his name," she said. "I wrote it down thirty years ago 'cause I thought I might need to remember it someday."

York's heart pounded as he looked at the piece of paper again. The name was there, *Collier Maczek*, written in a scrawl he guessed hadn't changed in all that time.

"Thank you," he said.

She shrugged. "I don't need the name. You do."

••••

"Transition flare!" Ducan Soe shouted. "Dead ahead."

Jewel Thaaline's heart skipped a beat. "Have we been spotted?"

Soe shook his head. "I don't know. We're still a good half light-year out. Maybe they picked up our transition wake. But we're running dead slow and awfully clean. They'd have to be good."

Jewel nodded. "Don't assume they aren't." She caught one of the scan-techs glancing at her fearfully. That wasn't what they'd wanted to hear.

"Damn," Soe swore. "Another flare, right on top of the first. They're coming at us in force."

"Can you see their wakes?" Jewel asked. "Are they fanning out, or coming at us straight?"

"I don't know," Soe said. "I can't see a damn thing."

"Then how the hell do you know they're coming at us?"

"I don't. I assumed—"

"Don't assume," Jewel barked. "I want hard data, not guesswork." She looked at Tac'tac'ah. "Mr. Tac'tac'ah, see if you can pinpoint those flares."

Tac'tac'ah wouldn't see much while they themselves were in transition, and not at this distance, just gross phenomena like transition flares and solar masses, and when they got in a little closer, planetary masses.

"There's another one," Soe said. His voice had calmed somewhat. "Right on top of the last."

That's better, Jewel thought. Soe was too experienced to be shouting excitedly.

Jewel glanced at Chief Innay. The old petty officer worked his console patiently, double-checking the data from his techs. He looked up and their eyes met, one corner of his mouth turning up just the slightest bit, the closest Innay had ever come to a smile.

"Well, Tac'tac'ah?" Jewel asked.

Tac'tac'ah's voice was also calmer. "Looks like it was about three hundred million kilometers out from Dumark's primary. Do you think they're coming after us, ma'am?"

Jewel shrugged. "Three hundred megaklicks? That could be Dumark herself. We're on line to Cathan; might be a convoy escort. We're too small to warrant three ships."

Soe gave her a sly look. The imperials had been jumpy lately, to the point where they just might send out three ships to intercept a lowly hunter-killer.

"Another flare," Soe barked. "That's four. Probably a convoy."

Jewel waited silently.

"There's another one. That's five."

Jewel started to breathe easier.

"Bam, bang, bam!" Soe yelled. "There went three of them, almost on top of one another. That's eight. She's a convoy, all right, and a big one."

"I've got a wake now, ma'am," Tac'tac'ah said. "Dead ahead at point-oh-nine-three lights and closing."

Jewel nodded. "Mr. Soe, sound General Quarters."

Soe slapped a switch on his console and the alert klaxon began pounding at their ears.

"Mr. Tac'tac'ah, back off to minimum transition drive, and rig for silent running. This close to all that flaring it's unlikely they'll spot our transition wake. I want that convoy escort to pass right over the top of us. But be careful. If you accidentally drop us into sublight we could flare enough for them to see us.

"Mr. Soe, how big is that escort now?"

"I've spotted fourteen flares so far. The last six were in rapid succession, and now nothing. I think that's it for the escort. We should see the main body flaring out any minute now."

"Fourteen, eh?" Jewel asked. "That's a big escort."

"That's a damn big convoy," Soe said. "And we're going to be right in the middle of it with their escort behind us." Soe cut the alert klaxon, then switched his voice pickup to another channel. "Standby forward launchers."

Innay ignored the order, waited for Jewel to confirm it.

"Belay that," Jewel snapped. "We pass it up this time."

"Pass it up?" Soe demanded. "This is the chance of a lifetime. We're going to be right in the middle of a big imperial convoy, with her escort out looking elsewhere. We could take out a couple hundred million tonnes of shipping before they knew what hit them, then transit out of here free as you please."

Jewel looked at him carefully before speaking. "This is a piece of incredible luck, all right. But it's luck we're going to use to help us carry out our mission, which is to slip quietly into Dumark nearspace. When that escort is past us I want full drive. I want to flare in right on top of that convoy as they flare out. They're going to mask our transition flare with theirs, and we're going to get closer to Dumark than could have been possible otherwise. And we'll *not* engage the enemy unless it's necessary to defend ourselves. *That* is an order."

••••

Archcanon Bortha led the procession out of the great cathedral on Luna. The ceremony celebrating the twentieth anniversary of the crowning of the present emperor had been tedious at best. Bortha watched Edvard and Rochefort walk away, huddled in some whispered conversation. "Lynna," he said, still looking at the back of the king.

His most trusted lieutenant stepped into his field of view. "Yes, Your Holiness."

"Have you learned anything yet?"

"Very little, Your Holiness. As you requested, I've made some discreet inquiries, but there's almost nothing of substance available. Apparently Aeya was present when a rather nasty riot erupted on a planet called Trinivan, and one of our warships had to evacuate the embassy there to get her out of it. Trinivan is far out on the fringes of the empire, an independent government, with no significant resources nor any strategic value to either us or the Syndonese."

Bortha turned toward the rectory, began walking briskly without the apparent age he carefully displayed in the presence of laymen. Lynna followed close on his heels. "Why was Aeya there?" Bortha asked.

"We're supposed to believe it was a lark," Lynna said.

"But you don't believe that, eh?"

"Lady d'Hart was on Trinivan with her. And they're being evacuated to Dumark, where Cassandra is waiting with the queen mother and Martin Andow."

Bortha nodded. "There is a pattern here, isn't there. Do we have anyone there?"

Lynna smiled, a rare occurrence. "Rhijn is Aeya's personal confessor."

"Rhijn?" Bortha asked. "Do I know him?"

"You've met him, Your Holiness, though that was some time ago and there would be no particular reason to remember him. But he is a man of undying faith and unquestioned fervor."

"You trust him, then?"

"Of course not, Your Holiness. But we can depend on him, especially if we offer him a Canonship if he does well."

"Very good, Lynna." Bortha nodded. He looked at the Canon, who always seemed to have trouble keeping pace with him. "Please continue to investigate. Edvard and his women are up to something, and the church must know what it is."

8

Condemned

YORK CLUTCHED MAJA'S piece of paper in his hand all the way back to *Invaradin*, though he didn't really need it because the name Collier Maczek was now etched deeply into his memory. And once back in his cabin he sat down immediately to dig into *Invaradin*'s data banks.

He had to believe Maczek was a man of some means, and there had to be some record of his existence. If Maczek was, or had been, a citizen of Dumark, there'd be local records on him, or if a citizen of another world, there'd be customs records of his entries and exits. York patched into Dumark's central computer, used his military status and security codes to gain as much access as possible, then ran a search on Collier Maczek, but the results came up negative.

"Damn you!" he growled. He tried again, looking for variations on the spelling, and after a long wait the computer responded with a list of 3238 names. "God damn it!" he shouted, slamming his fist painfully against the clear switch. The screen blanked.

He didn't remember much from his life before coming to Dumark at the age of six, just a kaleidoscope of images, a series of places where he must have lived, though he couldn't put them in any proper order. And he vaguely recalled a succession of people who shuffled him from one location to the next. The only constants were Maczek and a beautiful woman, though the years had blurred his memory of their faces. He'd always wondered if Maczek was his father, and the beautiful woman his mother.

His message light caught his eye, had been blinking for some time now, but he'd been too preoccupied to notice. He touched the acknowledge switch. The captain's yeoman appeared. "Good afternoon, Lieutenant Ballin. Captain Telyekev sends his compliments, and he'd like you to report to his office."

"I'll be right there," York said.

He blanked his console, took a quick look in a mirror and adjusted the snaps on his tunic, then stepped out into the corridor. With the repairs to *Invaradin* under way, crew traffic was heavy in the corridors.

The captain's yeoman was in a positively jovial mood, and as he ushered York into Telyekev's office he said, "Good luck, Lieutenant."

Telyekev sat behind his desk. York started to follow the usual formula, "Lieutenant Ballin reporting as—"

"At ease, York," Telyekev said, throwing a sloppy salute. "Sit down." He smiled and indicated a comfortable seat to one side. The sloppy salute was in character, the smile was not.

"How are your parents, York?"

That too was not in character. "They're okay, sir."

Telyekev nodded. Small talk with junior officers was not his forte. "I have some good news. You've been recommended for an Imperial Cross."

"For what, sir?"

"For the incident on Trinivan."

York shook his head. "Meaning no disrespect, sir, but that wasn't worth an Imperial Cross. Trinivan wasn't much more than a police action."

Telyekev nodded. "I suppose you're right, but visibility—being in the right place at the right time—can make all the difference. Her Majesty requested I make the recommendation, and under the circumstances, approval is almost a sure thing."

"Her Majesty?" York asked.

"The Empress Cassandra was waiting here on Dumark for Aeya, and in her mind you're the man most responsible for saving her daughter's life. And I don't doubt getting chewed up by a feddie rotary helped in the sympathy department."

Telyekev stood and crossed the room. York jumped to his feet, but Telyekev waved him back down. "Hell, York. Sit down and relax for a change."

York sat down. "Aye, aye, sir."

Telyekev shook his head as he opened a cabinet and pulled out a bottle. "That wasn't an order." He splashed an amber liquid into two glasses, capped the bottle, crossed the room and handed a glass to York.

Telyekev sipped at his drink. "Her Majesty has arranged a reception at the embassy tonight, and she'd like to present you with your decoration there. You're not exactly the guest of honor, but you're damn close to it. All you have to do is wear your best manners and be polite."

Telyekev was holding something back. York put the drink to his lips and swallowed the entire thing in one gulp. It burned like hell, and he almost coughed it back up. His eyes watered as he looked at Telyekev. "What's going on here, sir?"

Telyekev looked into his drink and swirled it around the edge of the glass. "*Invaradin*'s been ordered back for extensive refitting. The damage at Trinivan pushed us over the edge when it comes to operational readiness."

York knew the rest, always the same. He'd be reassigned to an outbound ship, newly outfitted and ready to go on patrol for years if need be. He shrugged it off. "What's my new ship?"

"You're to lay over here until H.M.S. *Miranda* arrives; about ten or fifteen days. She's a good ship, York. A hunter-killer with a good record."

York added, "And she's outbound for extended deep space patrol, right?"

Telyekev nodded. "But I think maybe this time there's an alternative."

"And what's that?"

"I've asked Her Majesty to intervene for you with the promotion board, to recommend a field promotion to lieutenant commander. She said she'd take the matter under advisement."

York suddenly felt cold all over. It had taken him years to accept his choices: desert and run, or spend the rest of his life on the front lines, his chances of surviving the next patrol diminishing with each year. At best, if by some chance he did survive, they'd probably retire him to some isolated rock bossing convict labor. And with just a few words Telyekev had washed away the carefully constructed emotional callus that protected him. Making it into the first level of command rank might open everything up for him again.

York stood, crossed the room, poured himself a healthy glass of Telyekev's booze without asking permission and gulped it down, ignoring the burn. He stood there for a moment, letting the whiskey take effect, then he spoke slowly, "Is there really any chance she'll actually do it?"

"I hope so," Telyekev said without emotion. "I hope so."

••••

York returned to his cabin, dug out a bottle of 'trate, poured himself a stiff drink, gulped it down, wanted another but didn't. If he had any chance with the empress, he'd kill it quickly by showing up drunk.

He showered, shaved again, then dug deep into his locker for his dress blacks, then remembered he hadn't owned a dress uniform in years. He did have one good pair of day blacks only slightly faded, with no patches. If he kept the tunic collar snapped tightly shut, he'd look passable.

He went stationside to catch a shuttle to the embassy and ran into Maggie and Frank and Paris waiting at the shuttle dock. They were in a party mood, and looking forward to some sort of spectacle surrounding the empress.

The shuttle was far from crowded, and once it got under way York leaned back, closed his eyes and recalled a lot of thoughts he'd long ago laid to rest. Telyekev already had two senior officers younger and less experienced than him. Anda Gant used to report to him, and now she was in charge of her own department, and he frequently reported to her.

Fleet would never let him quit, so his only real alternative was desertion. The navy was too busy to hunt him down if he did it right, and the war left enough chaos in its wake for someone like him to operate on the fringes of legality. But he'd need false papers and money. He'd have to start pulling cash out of his pay account now in small sums, stow it away somewhere safe. Maybe in a year or two he'd be ready.

The marines guarding the embassy gate were not at all happy with the tightened security procedures in effect that evening. Armed to the teeth, stuffed uncomfortably into their dress uniforms, they took great care to follow every regulation to the letter.

York, Maggie, Frank and Paris joined one of the many lines to have their identities checked. At the front of one of the other lines an older man in the uniform of a naval captain stood shaking an angry finger at the marine. The old man's voice rose steadily. "... preposterous ... personal friend of Commodore Berkma ..."

York didn't hear the marine's reply, but saw the apologetic shrug and guessed the rest: *I'm sorry, sir. But I have my orders.*

The old fellow's uniform was odd, nonregulation, improperly embellished with extra bits of gold filigree and piping, and little flashes added here and there to suit its wearer.

Jondee grumbled, "Damn marines!"

York said, "They've got the empress to worry about."

Jondee shook his head. "The real live fucking empress! What the hell is she doing out here anyway?"

"Rescuing her daughter."

Jondee laughed skeptically. "What the hell was a goddamn princess doing on Trinivan anyway? That's so far out on the fringes ..."

"Spoiled brat went on a lark."

"Bullshit! You believe that as much as I do, Ballin. Something's up, and you know it."

York leaned toward Jondee, kept his voice low. "Maybe so. But at least I'm not stupid enough to shoot my fuckin' mouth off around a bunch of strangers."

Jondee grinned, looked past York, ignoring him. He scanned the lines of people waiting to be admitted. "Looks like there's gonna to be a nice selection of pretty young things here tonight. I just might enjoy myself after all, old boy."

When York got to the front of the line the marine running the check noted his identity and said, "Cap'm Ballin. Nice to meet you, sir."

"Security tight tonight, huh?"

"Yes, sir. We got an AI major breathin' down our necks."

"Pain in the ass, eh?"

She nodded. "Name of Juessik. A real asshole too. I'd stay away from him if I was you, sir."

"Thanks for the warning."

The ballroom of the embassy took them all by surprise. Accustomed to small corridors, tight spaces, Spartan decor, none of them were prepared for the enormity of the place: high vaulted ceilings, gilt paint, heavy drapes and elaborate chandeliers. It could have swallowed *Invaradin*'s crew mess a dozen times over.

Invaradin's junior officers gathered far more than their share of attention, so York told them to split up and mingle. Paris took off with a hungry look in his eye, and Maggie and Frank went their own way. York decided to hunt down a drink, tried edging his way politely through the crowd.

"Bloody Butcher Ballin," someone said softly.

York froze, almost spun about to face his accuser, but realized that would just bring more attention. He moved on, conscious now of the unfriendly stares, conscious that his best uniform looked faded and worn in the presence of the noble and rich and that the chrome eye and scars made him stand out like a freak. He didn't belong here and he needed that drink badly.

He ran into Telyekev who introduced him to Commodore Berkma, a tall and good looking woman about Telyekev's age. She wore an expensive gown of some shimmering material, but discreetly sewn into the cuff were the insignia of her rank. York glanced for a moment in her eyes, and guessed she'd never seen a day of combat.

"Lieutenant," she said. "I'm told Her Highness owes you her life."

York shrugged. "There were a hundred marines that had a bit to do with it."

"Yes, I'm sorry to hear about your casualties."

For an instant her eyes focused on his face, then her attention shifted to a point somewhere behind York. "Ah, Alexiae. There's Martin Andow. I need to bend his ear a little. Come with me and I'll introduce you." She looked at York. "It was a pleasure meeting you, Lieutenant."

"Lieutenant Ballin."

The voice was female, young. York turned about carefully. A pretty, young lieutenant commander smiled up at him and said, "Good evening, Lieutenant."

York took in her uniform at a glance: crisp, new, good conduct and marksmanship ribbons on her chest, no campaign ribbons, no combat, no front line service, a Dumark Navy Yard pip on her collar. Age-wise she had to be somewhere between twenty and twenty-five. "Good evening, ma'am," York said.

She stuck out her hand. "I'm Hethis McGeahn. And you're York Ballin, aren't you."

York shook her hand. "Yes, ma'am."

She stared for a moment at his eye, then caught herself and focused on the ribbons on his chest. "Call me Hethis," she said. "I've been hoping to meet you. I've heard quite a bit about you."

"Good or bad?"

She threw her head back and laughed openly. "A little of both."

Behind her, far back in the crowd, a young officer looked their way suddenly, raised a hand and waved. "Hethis," he called. "Hethis McGeahn, is that you?"

At the sound of his voice she spun about, waved back. "Perra! Yes, it's me."

He wormed his way through the crowd, dragging a pretty little piece of civilian fluff behind him. The young man couldn't have been more than a year or two out of the academy, and yet he was a full commander. *Just kids*, York thought. *Goddamn kids, playing at soldier.*

"Hethis," the young commander said, hugging her, kissing her on the cheek. "I knew you were out here somewhere. Never dreamed I'd run into you my first night in."

"How was the trip out from Luna?" she asked.

"Terrible. Smallest cabin I've ever had. Even had to share it with another officer."

The young lady clutching his arm shook her head angrily. "You should have complained."

"Oh no!" he said. "Not proper to complain out here. We're roughing it, you know. But I did complain about the food. I mean there are limits, aren't there? And believe me, it was bloody awful, literally unpalatable."

"It's a pity you didn't travel with us," the young lady said.

"Had I known Cassandra was on her way out here, I certainly would have."

"I warn you, Perra," Hethis McGeahn said, "it's rough all the way around out here." She looked at York. "Oh! I've forgotten my manners. Perra, this is York Ballin of the *Invaradin*. York, this is Lord Perra Soladin, son of His Grace Johan, Duke de Satarna."

York bowed carefully. He was in the presence of the son of one of the most powerful men in the empire, one of the nine Dukes, and by that a member of the Admiralty Council.

Soladin looked at York as if to ask what kind of trash they were allowing in the embassy these days. He didn't offer his hand, acknowledged York with a simple, "Lieutenant," then introduced his friend, Lady Maree Sandre.

McGeahn threw out, "York's just in from the front."

Lady Sandre looked interested. "Really, Lieutenant. I hope you people can finally get around to doing something about these Syndonese torpedo ships. What do you call them?"

"Hunter-killers," York said. "And we have some of our own, you know."

"Well, they're making this war absolutely unbearable. Do you realize they've stopped spice shipments from Cathan?"

York lifted his eyebrows. "God forbid!"

"And the price of Tithian wine is sky rocketing."

York nodded. "We'll get right on it, Your Ladyship."

"Good for you, Ballin," Soladin said. "I say, Ballin, who did your face?"

York started, lost his composure and grew suddenly conscious of his eye and the scars. "My face?"

Soladin leaned forward, peered carefully at York. "Yes. It's interesting work. Bit savage looking, but then I suppose that's stylish out here. Perhaps I'll try something like that myself."

"Oh no, Perra," Lady Sandre pleaded. "You'd look atrocious." She looked suddenly at York. "Oh! No offense, Lieutenant."

McGeahn blushed with embarrassment. "They think it's cosmetic, done for effect. It's quite the rage on some of the inner worlds. Some people have scars applied and removed like makeup."

Soladin demanded, "Come now, Ballin. It'll literally drive my father insane if I show up wearing one of those. Who did the work?" He looked at York expectantly.

"A feddie," he answered. "With a rotary."

Soladin frowned.

"Perra," McGeahn said uncomfortably. "York was wounded in combat on Trinivan."

Lady Sandre blanched. Then her eyes filled with recognition. "You're the fellow that murdered that woman, aren't you?"

"What's this?" Soladin asked. "Killed a woman, did you, Ballin?"

"Oh yes, Perra," Lady Sandre said. "And she was just a girl too. Quite defenseless. Shot her without so much as a nod of his head, I hear."

"I say, Ballin," Soladin said. "Bad form. Why do such a thing?"

York thought of a hundred reasons why he'd killed her, but all he could really remember was the adrenaline and the fear. A small number of people nearby had paused and were waiting to hear his answer, and that made him angry. He pretended to think carefully for a moment. "I really don't remember killing one particular woman," he lied, finding it easy to keep his voice calm and even. "I mean, they all look pretty much the same when they're dead. You know, bits and pieces splattered all over hell, stinking to high heaven, making an absolute mess of your plast."

The shock on Lady Sandre's face was satisfying. He looked past her suddenly, pretended to recognize someone in the distance. "Ah!" he said. "I see an old acquaintance. If you'll excuse me." He stepped around Lady Sandre and started walking. It was time for that drink.

All he could find was a large punch bowl, filled with something colored a disgusting purple that contained very little alcohol.

"Lieutenant."

York looked over the rim of his glass, found a small, thin man standing squarely in front of him. The man wore dour, dark colors, and his face was completely devoid of expression, though as their eyes met, a nearly imperceptible smirk formed at the corners of his mouth. "You're Ballin, aren't you?"

York swallowed some of the punch, suppressed a nasty remark. "What can I do for you?"

"I wanted to meet you. I was one of the people you rescued on Trinivan. I heard you were injured. The eye?"

The smirk—York wasn't quite sure there had been a smirk—disappeared from the man's face. "And you're curious?" York said.

Now the man smiled openly. "Well, yes, a little, but mostly I wanted to thank you. I'm Arkan Dulell," he said proudly, waiting for York to react in some way.

"Nice to meet you, Mr. Dulell."

Dulell's mask of control returned and he shrank as if he'd been expecting York to recognize his name. "I'm the artist. Surely you've heard of me."

York felt awkward as he said, "I'm sorry, Mr. Dulell. I don't know much about art."

"Well, neither do my wealthy patrons," he said. "Please. Call me Arkan. And I'll call you York. That's a lot better than Butcher Ballin, isn't it?"

York tried not to react.

"Oh," Dulell said. "I see you're sensitive on that point. Well, you shouldn't be. They owe you their lives, and if they can't appreciate that then they're all petty fools."

York swirled the punch in his glass, looked at it unhappily. "Punch might as well be water."

Dulell nodded, looked about carefully, then reached into his coat and withdrew a small flask. He removed the lid, extended the flask toward York's glass, but York stopped him. "What is it?"

"It's just alc-trate," Dulell said, frowning. "I never attend one of these functions without it. Be careful, it's undiluted."

York tried to gauge the size of the flask. "Should be enough 'trate in there to get a dozen of them drunk."

"I try to be prepared."

"Thank you, but no," York said, shaking his head. "I have to stay sober."

Another voice interrupted them. "Are you sure you should do that?"

Sylissa d'Hart stepped out of the crowd like a phantom coalescing from the air, a disapproving look on her face. "Seriously, Lieutenant. Don't you think you should avoid that?" She nodded at Dulell's flask, which disappeared suddenly into his coat.

York wanted to tell her he'd turned the 'trate down, but he could see she'd already formed her opinion, so he let the incident pass without comment. He looked at her gown: it was very fashionable, touching the floor, clinging to her, must have cost half a year's pay. "Your gown is quite beautiful," he said. "Quite a change from shipboard fatigues."

It worked. She smiled and the tension disappeared. "Yes. Quite a change."

A splash of color in the crowd behind Lady d'Hart caught York's eye, a young woman dressed in a gown that clung so closely to her body she might as well be naked. And what little material she did wear was, for all intents and purposes, almost transparent.

York caught himself staring at the curve of the young woman's breasts, realized she was aware of his gaze and lifted his eyes to look into her face. She wore a many-colored mask, and her eyes seemed to be laughing at him. She crossed the few feet between them, stopped with her chin only inches from his chest. "You're Ballin, aren't you?" she asked in a sensual whisper.

York tried not to stare at her breasts, though he was exceedingly conscious of them in the press of the crowd. He looked instead at her face, and realized her mask was actually no mask at all, but carefully applied makeup, beginning around her eyes with radiating lines of color that extended down past her cheeks, neck, and shoulders, and ended on her upper chest and arms, blending with the low cut gown that only just covered her breasts.

York forced his eyes back to her face. "Yes I am. I don't believe we've met."

She spoke to Dulell, but she kept her eyes on York. "Arkan, sweetheart. Introduce us, please."

Dulell gave her an unpleasant smile. "Now Sabine, I've never been your sweetheart."

"Well, introduce us anyway."

Dulell nodded. "This is Lieutenant York Ballin. York, Lady Sabine Dubye."

"It's a pleasure," she said, smiling, sticking out her hand, and her breasts.

York took the hand, kissed it lightly, wanted to do the same to her breasts. "My pleasure."

"Sabine," Dulell said. "Your fangs are showing."

"Oh, Arkan! You say the naughtiest things."

"Only to the naughtiest people."

She stepped forward, pressing one of her breasts against York's arm. "We must talk later," she said in a whisper, "you and I. When you're not so . . . occupied."

She looked at Dulell, "Arkan," then at Lady d'Hart, "Sylissa."

Lady d'Hart smiled, though it looked forced, and as Lady Dubye walked away the smile morphed into a sneer.

Archproverb Rhijn, with poor Canticle Thring in tow, stopped next to Sylissa d'Hart and greeted each of them, "Lady d'Hart. Lieutenant. Dulell."

Rhijn leaned toward Lady d'Hart's ear and whispered a question York was not meant to hear. "Her Majesty is ready. Is he sober?"

York also heard her whispered reply. "I believe so. I've been keeping an eye on him."

Rhijn leaned away from her, stood up on his toes, looked across the room and raised two fingers in some sort of signal. The servant at the entrance to the ballroom struck a large, ornate staff loudly three times upon the floor, then paused while a hush fell over the crowd. When there was absolute silence he announced, "Her Majesty, Cassandra, Duchess de Lunis, Queen of the Nine Beasts, beloved empress of the Lunan Empire."

The main entrance to the ballroom opened onto a long cascade of stairs, and now, near the top of the stairs, a woman about York's age paused. Flanking and backing her were a number of elaborately dressed people, all of whom held the regal bearing of the noble, or the rich, or the influential.

York suddenly remembered his etiquette, dropped to one knee and bowed his head.

"Please," Cassandra said. "Rise. All of you. I've been looking forward to a respite from the formality of court, and I certainly didn't mean to bring it with me."

Slowly the individuals in the crowd stood and the murmur of conversation returned, though it was now somewhat subdued. The empress started down the stairway followed by Aeya—with the usual pout on her face—and a much older woman, probably the queen mother. Cassandra's descent, entourage and all, was a lesson in practiced informality. She paused on each step, spoke casually with someone waiting there, and suddenly York realized how carefully the situation had been choreographed, with no modicum of chance allowed to determine who might be on the stairs at that moment, nor on which step they stood.

The Lady d'Hart touched his arm. "You have a funny look on your face."

York spoke without looking away from the empress. "Nothing's been left to chance, has it?"

"Exactly."

"Including," he continued, "your presence here next to me, to make sure I don't screw up, eh?"

She frowned, looked uneasy, and lied. "You're imagining things."

The empress completed her descent of the stairs and moved carefully through the crowd. Rhijn and Dulell got into some sort of argument about the religious implications of direct church involvement in military matters. Thring kept his mouth shut for the most part, though Rhijn occasionally looked to him for support, and the young canticle always deferred to his superior.

The empress had a ring of sycophants surrounding her at all times, and of course there was the carefully chosen bodyguard of uniformed marines. But it was the plain-clothed AI goons that stood out most, perhaps because of their amateur attempts at appearing to be part of the crowd.

York drifted about, managed to lose Dulell and Thring and Rhijn, though the d'Hart woman never left his side. If he hadn't understood her true purpose, he might have believed she had some interest in him. He kept his distance from the empress, knowing that when the time was right for her to present his decoration, they'd see to it he was in the right place at the right time. But then after a couple of hours she excused herself and was gone.

Sylissa d'Hart then excused herself politely and left. York stood there alone, wondering why the change in plans.

Maggie, arm in arm with Dulell, approached through the thinning crowd. "York, this party's boring."

Dulell shrugged. "I could have told you to expect that, Miss Votak."

York demanded, "Where's Frank?"

Maggie waved a hand back toward the crowd. "He's taking care of Geara."

"What's wrong with Geara?"

"He got a little drunk."

York looked at Dulell. "I need a drink, something a lot stronger than this punch."

Maggie handed him hers. He took a sip and his eyes watered. He finished it in a single gulp.

"Making up for lost time?" Dulell asked.

Maggie swayed a little and York spotted Mayla Joyson crossing the room toward them. "Straighten up, Maggie, or you'll catch hell."

Joyson didn't try to hide her disapproval as she stopped beside Maggie. "Good evening, Mr. Ballin. Miss Votak. Mr. Dulell."

"Ma'am," York said stiffly.

Maggie tried to say something but fumbled it, wisely chose to say no more.

Joyson ignored her, said to York, "About Her Majesty . . ."

"We changed our minds, eh?"

That put Joyson off balance. "Ah, no. In fact, Her Majesty made it clear you would definitely receive the cross."

York respected Joyson, liked her, knew it was unfair to take it out on her but he couldn't stop himself. "But not from her hands, eh?"

Joyson sighed. "Her schedule has changed."

York shook his head. "You owe me better than that. She got worried about how it might look and talked herself out of it. Or someone else talked her out of it, right?"

At least Joyson met York's eyes. "Yes. That's basically right."

Joyson was suddenly all business again. "You're all on leave for the next three days. While you're here at the embassy keep your people somewhat sober. And you too."

"I am sober."

Joyson nodded, glanced side long at Maggie. "And her?"

"I'll take care of her," he said.

"See that you do, Mr. Ballin." Joyson turned, walked away.

A servant stepped in front of him, bowed and held out a small silver platter containing an even smaller piece of paper. "Sir, I have a message for you."

York took the piece of paper, unfolded it:

Lieutenant Ballin:

We've not met, but I believe we should.

Martin Andow

The seal of the imperial senate lay beneath the signature. The servant said, "You are to follow me, sir."

York looked at Dulell, had no one else at hand so he had to trust him He nodded at Maggie. "Take care of her."

Maggie protested, "I don't need taking care of."

Dulell smiled. "Of course."

York turned back to the servant. "Lead the way."

9

Damned

THE SERVANT LED York out of the ballroom through a nondescript side entrance. They passed down a long corridor, then up a flight of ornate stairs, down another long corridor with innumerable doors, and though each was indistinguishable from the last, the servant chose one, opened it, and waited for York to precede him. "If you please, sir."

York stepped into a small room with books along one wall—real books he noted, not readsheets and memcards—a couch along another wall, two straight back chairs and an unoccupied desk cluttered with equipment.

"Please wait here, sir."

The servant stepped around him, through another door on the opposite side of the room. York waited, felt the drink he'd just gulped starting to cut away the sharp edges of his anger.

"Sir."

The servant was back, holding the door open. "This way, sir."

York stepped into the next room, dimly lit by a single lamp on an enormous desk made of, what looked like, real wood. Behind it sat a man whose features were obscured by the shadows from the lamp, but York got an impression of black hair with salt-and-pepper gray at the temples; handsome, distinguished. The man stared intently at the screen of a compsheet in his hands, and he didn't look up as York entered.

Behind the man, and to one side, he recognized the queen mother. She sat in a large ornate chair, her features completely hidden in the shadows. And in some intuitive way he imagined her staring at him, glaring with a malevolence he couldn't explain.

The man behind the desk looked up from the compsheet. "You're Ballin?" he asked, not bothering to offer York a chair. He consulted the screen for a moment. "York Ballin? Lieutenant? 213596837?"

"That's me," York said. "And you're Senator Andow?"

The man nodded. "I assume you've heard of me?"

York had heard the name, though he knew nothing of the man himself. "Of course, sir."

"Good. That'll make things simple." Andow nodded at the screen in front of him. "I've been looking over your file. I'd like to discuss it with you."

"Certainly, sir. But may I ask why?"

Andow frowned at him as if he were impertinent. He spoke slowly. "Your captain asked Her Majesty to intervene for you with the promotion board at Fleet. Her Majesty, in turn, asked Her Highness and me to look into the matter in detail and recommend a course of action."

York had to assume that by *Her Highness*, Andow meant the old queen mother.

Andow's eyes returned to the screen, and without looking at York he said, "From what I see here, before joining the navy, you were essentially a juvenile delinquent with a police record of petty crimes, minor burglaries, and thefts. Then, at the ripe old age of twelve, you mugged an old woman and killed her. The king's bench gave you a choice between convict labor and the navy. I suppose you chose the navy for the obvious reasons?"

York had the feeling nothing he said would make this man happy. "I didn't choose. I wasn't given a choice. I was handed papers to sign and I signed them. They turned out to be enlistment papers and I was in the navy."

Andow touched a few keys on the terminal, flipping through York's file. "And for the next two years you had a spotless record. Were you so inspired by naval service that you gave up your life of crime instantly?"

"No, sir, I made some mistakes. But I was taught some rather harsh lessons, and I learned quickly."

Andow nodded. "I've heard justice on a deep space man-of-war can be quite cruel." He looked at York for a reaction, and when none came he continued, "So you served aboard the cruiser *Dauntless* for two years. What were your duties?"

"When I wasn't learning to be a pod gunner I scrubbed decks, shined boots, cleaned the head."

"I see," Andow said, keying through the file on the screen in front of him. "You were a lower deck pod gunner. Saw quite a bit of action too. And then—and this is quite amazing—you were on the cruiser *Africa* at the infamous battle of Sirius Night Star. The *Africa* took heavy damage; you were wounded and placed aboard the hospital ship *Andor Vincent.*"

For the first time, the old woman behind Andow moved. She leaned forward, the light caught her face and York saw her eyes: harsh and disapproving. "Wasn't that the ghost ship? I thought that was a myth, legend."

Andow turned respectfully toward her. "The *Vincent* is certainly legendary, but it did actually exist. When the Ninth Fleet was wiped out at Sirius Night Star, the *Vincent* was damaged and her crew killed, with Mr. Ballin here and a few hundred of his comrades suspended in her critical life support tanks. The *Vincent* was lost, her crew dead, but her tanks were still functioning and controlled by her central computer. To conserve power, the computer shut down everything but the tanks, and she might have drifted that way for centuries had not one of our ships, through sheer luck, discovered her two years after the battle."

Andow turned back to York and looked at him carefully. "About half the people in the tanks were still alive, Lieutenant Ballin here among them. A certain amount of legend, and a lot of stories, and quite a few rumors have developed around the survivors of the *Vincent*. I'll venture a guess few of Mr. Ballin's present friends know of his past."

Andow paused, apparently expecting a response from York. Again York said nothing, Andow looked at the screen and continued, "In any case, Mr. Ballin was the youngest of the survivors, and apparently there was some desire to observe him closely as he adjusted to the loss of two years of his life, so they stuck him in the Naval Academy at Mare Crisia on Luna."

Andow shook his head thoughtfully. "Life is truly amazing! A fifteen-year-old, juvenile delinquent, lower deck pod gunner, spacer first class, through a fortuitous set of circumstances, is enrolled in an institution that regularly turns down the sons and daughters of some of the most influential people in the empire." He looked at York. "What a stroke of luck. But you didn't make much of your luck, did you, Mr. Ballin?"

"I'm sorry, sir. I don't understand."

Andow looked at his screen. "You did rather poorly, graduated at the bottom of your class, barely graduated at all, in fact. A most undistinguished naval ensign. And since then you've had a mediocre career. You fought in most of the major battles of the last fifteen years, gained experience on just about every kind of ship we have, distinguished yourself a few times, but by and large you're just another officer. At least until the de Mercus thing. They wanted to hang you for that."

York tried to keep his voice even. "That was six years ago. And I only did what I had to."

"What were you thinking, Lieutenant, assaulting a superior officer, the son and heir of one of the nine ruling Dukes of this empire?"

York didn't like Andow, and for some reason he wanted to goad him a bit. "I thought the king ruled the empire."

Andow shrugged that off. "Answer my question, Lieutenant."

York kept all expression out of his face. "First, he was not a superior officer. He carried the same rank as I, so I was his superior by virtue of seniority. Second, he was incompetent. He would have gotten us all killed, let the feddies overrun us. Third, I didn't assault him. I merely prevented him from getting us all killed, and he later colored the events quite liberally."

Andow shook his head sadly. "I suppose that's the only thing that saved you. But you still drink too much, and you've developed a dependency on combat drugs."

"What are you trying to tell me, sir?"

Andow considered that question for a moment and the silence hung like a heavy weight about York's shoulders. "I've looked closely at your record, Lieutenant. For the most part you've served the empire well, but you've demonstrated no leadership capabilities, you've unwisely developed certain dependencies, at least once you were guilty of insubordination and assault on a superior— fellow—officer. All of that, combined with certain questions concerning the mental stability of the survivors of the *Andor Vincent*, preclude any possibility of your advancement to command rank."

There it was, the final sentence, pronounced with such ease. "Is there nothing I can say to change your mind, sir?"

York saw the answer in the senator's eyes before he spoke, because in Andow's mind York was nothing more than a thirty-five-year-old *juvenile delinquent, lower deck pod gunner, spacer first class*. "I'm sorry, Lieutenant."

"Just like that?" York asked. "You're going to trash my career just like that?"

"No," Andow said. "If your career has been damaged, you have only yourself to blame."

"Me?" York shouted. "I've been fighting feddies for this damn empire for twenty-two years, and—"

"Lieutenant!" Andow barked. "Control yourself."

York swallowed his anger, forced himself to speak calmly. "Will that be all, sir?"

Andow nodded. "You may go."

York slammed the door on his way out.

••••

York stormed through the room with the books and the empty desk, out into the corridor beyond. But there he came to a sudden and complete halt. Right or left? There was nothing to distinguish one direction from the other: a dark hall, a lot of closed, unmarked doors.

"Lieutenant," a soft feminine voice called from within the room at his back.

He spun about. The Dubye woman stood there proudly, and again the elaborate mask of makeup pulled his eyes down to her breasts. He wondered if she'd chosen the design for just that purpose. Certainly they were breasts worth the attention.

"Where's the servant?" he asked.

"I dismissed him."

He revised his opinion. Her voice was not soft, but husky and sensual. "How do I get out of here?"

"I'll show you the way."

"Okay," York said, forcing his eyes away from her breasts. She seemed disappointed that he succeeded. "I need a drink," he added. "Something strong. Not that garbage they're serving in the ballroom."

"Follow me," she said, a predatory smile on her lips. She stepped past him into the hall, purposefully brushed against him, and as he followed her he couldn't take his eyes off her hips. She led him into a corridor far different from the one they'd just left. Here, the lighting fell from ornate lamps suspended from the ceiling, rather than flat, dimensionless illumination panels. The carpet was thick and plush and the walls decorated with paintings.

She chose a door, pressed her hand against the lock. The door clicked open and she stepped through it, leaving it ajar. York followed her, closing the door behind him.

He stood still for a moment with his back to the door. He was in a lady's sitting room, decorated in soft muted colors. No doubt there was a bedroom attached to it, but the sitting room alone was larger than the largest captain's cabin on any ship he'd ever served.

"What's wrong?" she asked, dropping into an odd piece of furniture, half bed, half couch.

"This place is big," he said. "Is this your suite?"

She shrugged. "Part of it. Though this is rather Spartan compared to what I'm accustomed to."

He scanned the room. "Impressive."

"Of course. Appearances, Lieutenant. We here live by them. Status. One displays one's power, one exercises it, or one loses it. You wanted a drink?" She pointed to a small bar across the room. "Fix me one too."

York walked to the bar with the uncomfortable feeling she was inwardly laughing at him. "What would you like?"

"Whatever you're having," she said. "And like you, I want it strong."

York found a bottle of real Lunan gin, not 'trate, probably good stuff. He put some ice in two glasses and splashed the gin over it. The Dubye woman accepted hers with an inviting smile. She toyed with it, swirling the ice about with a finger. York gulped at his.

"Tell me, Lieutenant. What was Trinivan like?"

York was in no mood to mince words. "It was a bloody mess, especially with that bitch Aeya in the way."

"Ah yes," she said, laughing. "Her Highness can be . . . troublesome. But what about the people? Did you kill many?"

York thought about the hallways in the embassy on Trinivan, a memory that wouldn't fade. He gulped the rest of his drink. "It was slaughter, plain and simple."

"How many did you kill?"

York shrugged, returned to the bar for another drink. "Must have been three, four hundred. Those power rifles make a bloody mess."

He didn't bother with the ice; just poured the gin. "I don't understand how they ever thought they could stand against seasoned imperial regulars."

"How many did you kill? I mean you, personally?"

York turned about, looked at her carefully. A glint of excitement danced in her eyes. "What kind of question is that?"

She stood, crossed the room and positioned herself with her breasts almost touching his chest. "I'm just curious," she said, but he could see there was far more to it than curiosity. "I heard about the woman you killed."

"She had a gun," he growled defensively. "She put a slug right in the middle of my visor. So I blew her away, god damn it! And I'd do it again."

"I've heard about you marines," she said. "You have a reputation for being quite . . . bloodthirsty." Her face flushed with excitement, she reached up slowly, and with her fingertips gently traced the scars around his eye. Her voice came out in a tense and throaty whisper. "What's it like to be that close to death? To think you're going to die? What's it like to lie in your own blood?"

York stepped away from her, became conscious again of her breasts. And oddly, her nipples seemed more prominent beneath the filmy little gown.

She stepped toward him and her breathing quickened, shallow and hot on his face. "What's it like to kill someone face to face? Tell me about it. These others, they kill from inside a ship from vast distances. But you, you're there. You see the face of the person you're about to kill."

She took the last step and her breasts flattened against his tunic. He put his arm around her. "Tell me about it, please. Tell me what it's like in that instant before you kill them."

She pressed her pelvis against his thigh, undulating slowly. He kissed her; some of her makeup got on his tongue and it sent a charge through him, a mixture of anger and passion. He bent down, kissed one of her nipples through her gown, then bit it. She quivered, groaned. "Tell me, please. Does time slow? Do you see the fear on their faces? Can you feel the fear on your own?"

She dropped her drink and it crashed to the floor. He dropped his, pulled her gown down about her shoulders, and with his tongue traced a ring around her nipple. The makeup there had an odd taste to it, made his head swim.

"It's drugged, you know," she said, breathing heavily. "It'll give you uncontrollable desire. And stamina."

He bit her nipple hard.

She cried out. "It'll also make you very aggressive, and I like that."

He pulled her onto the couch, tugged at her gown. It came apart in his fingers, and beneath it the makeup ran the length of her body.

"Tell me about the killing," she demanded.

He bit the other nipple.

"Ah!" she screamed. "Do they know they're going to die? Do they? And do you hesitate? And then, finally, when your own fear takes over, do you kill? The act of ultimate power, ultimate control over a life. To take it. To destroy it. To end it."

She groped at his pants, pulled at them frantically. He licked at the makeup on her neck, down her chest, around her nipples. "Yes," she said. "Take it all."

He bit a nipple hard, tasted blood. She shuddered ecstatically and groaned. And yet somehow she was in control of the situation, and all he could do was follow as they both slid into an ecstasy of angry pleasure.

••••

York rolled off the couch; fell to his hands and knees on the floor. He crawled about until he found his clothes, pulled them on carefully over the bruises.

The Dubye woman, asleep on the couch, groaned and rolled over. They both wore some bruises. He was shaken; she was sated, and he wanted out before the sadomasochistic little bitch woke up.

He shook his head, the drugs doing his thinking for him. There'd been an aphrodisiac in her makeup—he was certain of that—and something else, something that fed on his anger, turned him into a willing and able partner for her kind of pleasure.

His pleasure too, he reminded himself, and that bothered him.

He staggered to the bar, splashed something into a glass and gulped it down. His emotions were all sharp edges and angry corners—the drugs again, probably aggression hypes. He poured another drink, gulped it like the first, hoping to blunt the effects of the drugs, poured another, took it with him while he searched the suite for a fresher.

He was a mess, even after he managed to wash the smeared makeup off his face and arms. He glanced at his watch: they'd been at it for a couple of hours, then slept for a few more. He combed his hair, still looked like hell. Mixed in with the aphrodisiac there must have been a powerful stimulant. He was shaking, and he had to force himself to unclench his teeth. He gulped down his drink, headed for the bar, poured another, gulped that down, then staggered out into the hall. He chose a direction at random, eventually found a servant to lead him back to the ballroom.

It was late. The crowd had thinned considerably, and what remained had spilled out into the neighboring halls where they'd broken up into small groups. A vaguely familiar voice called, "Ballin? Lieutenant Ballin, isn't it?"

A hand touched his shoulder and he turned about slowly. The old navy captain who'd made such trouble for the marine stuck out his hand, grabbed York's hand and started shaking it. "Armbruster," the old man said. "Captain Nathan Armbruster, retired navy." He kept shaking York's hand. "Glad to meet you, Lieutenant."

Hethis McGeahn and Perra Soladin, the Lady Sandre still hanging on his arm, joined Armbruster. McGeahn nodded pleasantly. "York."

Soladin acknowledged him with a flat, "Ballin," and a nod, while the Lady Sandre tried to pretend he wasn't there.

"We were just talking about the front," Armbruster said. "I hear you've had quite a bit of experience out there."

The drugs and the booze clouded York's judgment some, but not so much he didn't realize he should be polite. "Some," he said flatly, thinking that in any single year he'd had more experience than all of them put together, and yet they all outranked him.

"Perra and I hope to get posted there soon," McGeahn said eagerly.

"To the front?" York asked.

"Of course," Soladin said.

York felt hysterical laughter welling up in his chest, but he suppressed it, kept his voice flat, almost monotonic. "Why would you want to do that?"

"Why, that's where the war is," Soladin said. "The real war, not Home Fleet games."

"Ya," York said. "So?"

Soladin was offended, but McGeahn answered for him. "So it's our duty. It's a matter of honor."

"There's no honor out there," York said. "Besides, you're already at the front. All you gotta do is sit tight and I wouldn't be surprised if the war came right to you."

The Lady Sandre's eyes widened. "What do you mean?" she asked.

York felt anger rising up in his throat—probably the ag-hypes—but like the laughter he suppressed it. "The feddies ran us out of Trinivan. And that's just a quick jump from here."

"See here, Ballin," Soladin said angrily. "There's no need to upset the ladies. That's going too far."

York felt tired. "No. We mustn't upset Her Ladyship."

"Furthermore," Soladin continued. "If Hethis and I wish to learn the true test of our mettle, I think the least you can do is give us your support and respect."

. . . true test of our mettle! York thought.

Armbruster changed the subject quickly. "Perra here thinks Red Richard is working for the feddies."

York shook his head. "Red Richard's just a pirate. He's working for himself."

"That's what I say," Armbruster agreed.

Soladin put on his superior look. "Well, I don't mind telling you, at Fleet we've gotten some rather interesting intelligence reports about a connection between Richard and the Directorate."

York frowned, looked at the others standing beside Soladin. "Isn't that classified?"

"Oh, I shouldn't worry," Soladin said, lowering his voice carefully and looking around. "We all know each other here."

The Lady Sandre looked admiringly at Soladin. "Then Richard's working for the Directorate?"

York interrupted before Soladin could answer. "Richard might have some arrangement with the Syndonese, and it wouldn't surprise me if he had one with us too, but you can bet your ass when there's profit to be made, Richard is working for Richard."

York had had enough. He turned his back on them suddenly, staggered away, excusing himself by growling over his shoulder, "I need a drink."

He spotted Dulell right away, Frank standing next to him, Maggie hanging on his arm. The only senior officers present were holiday admirals like Armbruster and Soladin—wear a pretty uniform and impress the ladies, but by all means stay away from any of the actual fighting.

Maggie held her empty glass out toward Dulell. "Give me another hit of that 'trate, eh?"

Frank shook his head. "You've had enough."

Nemkov stepped up beside York, looked at her disapprovingly. "Votak," he said. "You drink too much."

"Not me," Maggie said, leaning heavily on Frank's arm. "York drinks too much. I drink just the right amount."

Dulell chuckled. Nemkov turned on York. "This is your fault, Ballin."

Maggie grabbed Nemkov's arm, spun him toward her. "Maggie Votak's a big girl," she said. "Maggie Votak can get herself drunk."

Nemkov pulled his arm out of her grip, grabbed her arm in turn. "You've still got a career, Maggie. Don't throw it away like—"

He didn't finish, but he didn't have to. "—like Ballin," York finished for him.

Nemkov shook his head, spun about angrily and stormed away.

York looked at Maggie and Frank. "That's probably good advice. But then that bastard can afford good advice. His father'll make sure he gets promoted and ends up in Home Fleet, attending little parties thrown by dukes and earls and emperors and empresses, while the rest of us spend our leaves drinking our brains out in some sleazy dockside bar on some godforsaken little rock of a planet."

"York," Frank said. "He's right about Maggie. And Geara too."

York nodded, looked around. "Ya, they're gonna blow it out, aren't they?" Maggie's eyes were starting to roll around. "Get her out of here," he said. "Get her out front. I'll try to find Paris and we'll meet you outside the gates."

Frank winked at him, hooked a forearm under Maggie's armpit, kept her upright as he pulled her out of the ballroom. York found Jondee out in the hall sitting in a chair, unable to even sit without swaying. Geara Moboow sat next to him in no better shape, with young Krass Doanne standing over them both, looking sober and worried. "I don't know what to do with them," she said.

"Grab Moboow," York said to her, happy one of them was sober enough to help, and Moboow was just small enough for the young woman to handle. "See if you can keep him upright. I'll take Paris."

A line of cabs waited outside the embassy gate. Frank had already flagged one down, stuffed Maggie into the back seat and was standing next to an open door waiting for them. He rushed over to help Krass with Geara. They got Paris and Frank in the back seat with Maggie, who was now unconscious, Krass and Geara into the front seat next to the cabby. And there was no room left for York. But he wasn't in any mood to go with them. Tonight he needed to strike out on his own.

"Check them into a hotel so they can sleep it off," York told Frank. "Wouldn't want the old man seeing them in this kind of shape."

"Aren't you coming with us?"

York shook his head. "I'm on my own tonight. Take care of them." He swatted the top of the cab. "Off you go."

The cabby lifted the vehicle up on its grav field, then slipped quietly off into the night. York took the next cab in line, stepped into the back seat. "You know where the strip is?"

The cabby nodded. "Course I do."

"Then get me there," York said. "And on the way stop someplace so I can buy a bottle. The real stuff. Not 'trate."

10

Old Friends

YORK BECAME CONSCIOUS of the rich, loamy scent of fresh soil. He smacked his lips, tasted both vomit and blood, and lay that way for some time, letting the realization sink slowly into his brain that he was on the ground, face down in the dirt.

He peeled open his eyelids, could see only the night, and a faint impression of plant life all about him. He rolled over carefully and sat up.

A fight! He'd gotten into a fight—with two spacers—or was it three. No matter. He wasn't in any shape to handle even one, and luckily for him they hadn't been much better off. Nothing felt broken. A split lip. His nose had bled for a while, though that had stopped and dried blood now caked his face. His ribs hurt, but not enough for concern; no sharp pains in his chest when he drew a deep breath.

He pulled himself to his feet, standing in a small park of some sort: plants and trees and grass and soil. Beyond the trees there was a great deal of light and activity and noise. The din told him he was not far from the strip, so he staggered in that direction.

He found a large fountain with water cascading down from some odd, surrealistic sculpture. He dipped his head into the water, made a half-hearted attempt to clean up. Then he sat down on a concrete bench at the edge of the park, and for a while the cold concrete felt good.

A row of cheap dives and honky-tonk bars lined the opposite side of the street, garishly lit signs, spacers staggering up and down the walk. It was late, and he guessed he'd already been through half the establishments there. But across from him now he saw a saloon with a big sign that flashed back and forth between two motifs: a bright display of shell bursts and rocket fire, armored marines blasting away at some unknown enemy; the other a sign reading *The Drop Zone*. York staggered to his feet, crossed the street, shambled past a couple of marines and through the doors of the big saloon.

He didn't make it to the bar. Someone spun him about violently, grabbed the front of his tunic, lifted him off his feet and slammed him against the wall. "What you think yer doin', navy?"

York shook his head to clear it, though that hurt more than it helped. A big hulk of a marine held him pinned to the wall. Over the hulk's shoulders, in the dark, smoke-filled air of the bar, York's eyes settled on two dancers undulating beneath a hazy blue spot light. They were high up on a pedestal, a man and a woman wearing almost nothing, doing something quite obscene.

The hulk slammed York up against the wall again. "I asked you what you was doin', navy?"

York couldn't focus his eyes close enough to look the hulk in the face. "Just wanted a drink," he said, still watching the dancers. A marine had joined the two entertainers, was kissing one of the woman's breasts while trying to get his pants off. Someone screamed out an encouraging epithet.

"Talk up, navy."

A small woman wearing sergeant's stripes approached the hulk from behind. "What ya got there, Meat?"

The hulk glanced over his shoulder at the small sergeant. "Got me some navy wants a drink, Terk."

Terk's brows shot up. "Navy wants to do his drinking in the Zone?"

York tried to say something. "I really didn't—"

The hulk bounced him against the wall a couple of times and his vision blurred for a moment. "Guess the fuckin' idiot don't know better."

"Seems not," Terk said. "I suppose we otta teach him a lesson."

The hulk drew back a fist the size of York's thigh. "You want me to bust him up a little, Sarge?"

Palevi appeared out of nowhere, put a hand lightly on the hulk's fist and said, "Hold on there, Meat."

The hulk looked at Palevi with a frown. "Wha' for, Sarge?"

"Wouldn't be right you mess up my CO."

"Yer CO?" Terk demanded. "This ain't no marine."

To York's right a woman's voice said, "You know the rules, Mieka." York snuck a look that way, saw a large woman standing behind the bar, the proprietress of the place. "Navy comes in here, Mieka, he takes his chances."

Palevi's eyes darkened. "I said he's my CO."

Terk shook her head. "He's wearing a navy tunic so he's fuckin' navy as far as I'm concerned." She looked at the hulk. "Go ahead, Meat."

The hulk's eyes lit up with pleasure, but before he could deliver the blow Palevi stopped them all short by bellowing out in his loudest drill sergeant, parade ground voice, "*Invaradin*, atteeuun . . . shuuuuun!"

There came a sudden crashing of tables and chairs as marines all over the place jumped to attention. The hulk froze. The music died slowly, disjointedly. The two dancers stopped. The marine that had joined them on their pedestal was one of those standing at attention, his pants down, his penis half erect.

With the convoy gone, the only other military ships around Dumark were *Nostran* and another small destroyer *Irriahm*, and clearly *Invaradin*'s marines had them badly outnumbered.

Palevi spoke softly, but in the silence his voice boomed. "Meat, the man you're about to lay into is Cap'm York Ballin. Now I don't care what kind of tunic he's wearing, me and the rest of his people won't take it kindly if you hurt him."

"Now, Mieka," the proprietress said. "Don't you go bustin' up my place."

Palevi looked hungrily at Terk, but he spoke to the proprietress. "Well now, Salley. That all depends on Terk here."

Meat looked at Terk. Terk looked at Salley as if she were an appropriate referee. Salley looked at Palevi. "He's really Ballin?" the proprietress asked.

Palevi nodded. "Look at his face."

They all looked for a moment at the scars on York's face, then they looked at Terk while she in turn looked carefully at each of them, then she shrugged. "Well, if Mieka says he's Ballin then I gotta believe it. Let him go, Meat."

Meat let York down. Salley waved at the band and the music started again. The dancers returned to their dance, if you could call it that, but not one of Palevi's marines moved so much as a muscle.

Salley pleaded, "Come on, Mieka."

Palevi looked at Terk, then at York. "Cap'm?"

It took York a second to realize Palevi was waiting for him. He nodded his permission, as if he were actually in control of his marines, and Palevi bellowed, "As you were." The Drop Zone exploded with a roar.

Terk stepped up to him, peered into his face without compunction and examined his eye and the scars. "You get that on Trinivan?"

York nodded. She stuck out her hand and he shook it. "Terk Yagell," she said. "Staff sergeant on the *Nostran*." She nodded toward Meat. "Corporal Jaspin Cleaver."

Meat stuck out a paw the size of both York's hands put together. York shook it warily. "Glad to meet ya, Cap'm. You can call me Meat like everyone else."

Salley grabbed York by an arm, pulled him to the bar. She reached behind it, dug out an old bar rag and handed it to him. "Put that on or you'll get yourself killed in here."

It was an old, faded marine tunic. York pulled off his navy tunic—it was torn and stained with dried blood anyway—discarded it and pulled on the old marine tunic. Salley pinned captain's bars on his shoulders, though they were crooked. "There," she said. "That'll do, Cap'm." She handed York a drink.

York reached into his pocket for script, but Salley shook her head. "Senior Drop Officer don't buy his own drinks here."

York frowned. Salley frowned back at him, looked at Palevi. "Mieka, I don't think he knows yet."

Palevi slapped York on the back. "Ain't you heard, Cap'm? Sadeline bought it fifteen days ago. Yer the new SDO. Look." Palevi pointed at a large board above the bar where someone had scrawled the name *Sadeline* along with a date. "It's been confirmed, Cap'm."

Beneath Sadeline's name was *Ballin*, with no date, but a string of meaningless numbers behind it.

York asked, "What're the numbers for?"

Palevi shrugged. "The odds, sir."

"What odds?"

"Odds on whether or not the new SDO'll make it through his first drop alive."

York nodded carefully, looked at the date behind Sadeline's name. "And that's the date Sadeline bought it?"

"That's right, sir."

"First drop?" York asked. "Not next drop?"

Palevi nodded. "First drop as SDO."

York asked carefully, "Can I bet on myself? And what kind of odds do I get?"

Palevi looked a little sheepish. "About twenty to one, sir. Not too many betting your way."

York looked at Terk. "You got any money down?"

"Ya," she said confidently, then reached into her pocket and pulled out a wad of script. "In fact—Salley, now I've met him, put me down for another hundred imperials against."

Salley took Yagell's wad of script, began counting it.

"Salley," York said. "How much to cover all outstanding bets?"

Salley, in the process of entering Terk's bet, looked up. Her eyebrows wrinkled. "About two thousand imperials. That's a lot, Cap'm."

"Whew!" someone whistled, and a crowd gathered around York.

York spoke confidently. "I'm good for it."

Salley shook her head. "No IOU's, Cap'm. Gotta be cash. I mean, if you lose, who's gonna pay off?"

"Okay," York said. "Bring me a credit terminal."

The crowd around him was building as Salley brought out a small electronic box, put it on the bar. York told her to enter the right amount, knowing his account would cover it, though just barely. She did so, and he thumb printed the transaction.

Salley shook her head. "That's a mighty big bet, Cap'm."

"I know," York said. He stuck out his hand. "Now pay up. I've won."

Someone said something unpleasant. Salley looked at York blankly. York pointed to the board and the date Sadeline had been killed. "Sadeline bought it the day before we made transition into

Trinivanian nearspace. So the drop on Trinivan was my first drop as SDO. I'm still alive, so pay up."

Palevi threw back his head and bellowed out a laugh. There was a short argument, but eventually they all agreed, though reluctantly, that York had won the bet. Salley brought out the credit terminal, transferred a considerable sum into York's account.

"Come on, Cap'm," Palevi said. "You're a fuckin' rich man, and we got a prime table other side of the room."

As they turned away from the bar, leaving behind the crowd gathered there, Palevi said the oddest thing. "By the way, Cap'm, thanks for not killing Meat back there."

York started, saw Terk frown uncertainly, realized Palevi had spoken for her benefit, and just loud enough for her to hear. York was about to say something to the effect that he couldn't have killed the big marine if he'd wanted to, but realized Palevi was playing with Terk. His marines were quite proud that their CO was the SDO, so he played along. "Just see to it he doesn't make that mistake again, Sergeant."

"Yes, sir."

They cut their way slowly through the dense crowd and became part of the roar, the din. They passed a crap table surrounded by marines. One of the bargirls was sitting in the middle of the table, her skirt haphazardly bunched about her thighs. Any undergarments she might have been wearing earlier were long since gone. As the marines placed their bets, throwing script out onto the table, she collected it eagerly. It would be winner take all.

A female marine stumbled in his way, a barboy on her arm, staggering toward an exit.

Palevi pulled York to a large table in the center of the crowd. Mec Notay sat there in a barboy's lap while he kissed her neck. Baddin Hyer, Larwa Tathit and the corporal from the Trinivanian embassy—York had to think carefully to remember her name, Elkiss—were in the middle of a poker hand. Next to them a young woman wearing second lieutenant's bars lay face down on the table, a motionless cascade of long red hair sprawled in spilled beer and whiskey. Next to her sat the newbie, Stacy, looking around the room with eyes the size of saucers. Palevi took in the table with a sweep of his hand. "NCO and officer's country, Cap'm."

York asked, "Then what's the kid doing here?"

Palevi shook his head. "Mother Hyer's watching over him."

Someone shoved a chair into the back of York's legs. He fell into it, spilled some of his drink. He nodded toward the young, unconscious, red headed officer. "Who's that?"

Yagell grinned. "That's Simorka, CO on the *Irriahm*, though she can't CO shit yet. Rookie, got a lot to learn, not too happy about being out here."

Elkiss looked up from the card game, grabbed her drink, nodded toward York's. "Drink up, Cap'm," she said, threw her own drink down in a gulp. York followed suit, almost blew it back up in their faces. It was 'trate, not sufficiently diluted, fire on the back of his throat.

Tathit leaned against him, threw an arm over his shoulders. "Rotten shit, ain't it, sir?"

York, still trying to hold the drink down, nodded. He had a long way to go to catch up with these people.

"Ya know, sir," Tathit said, having trouble focusing her eyes. "I didn't think you'd make much of a marine. But I gotta admit I was wrong. Fuckin right! Yer a fuckin' good marine." She looked at the rest of the table. "Ain't he?"

All agreed drunkenly that York was a *fuckin' good marine*.

Tathit turned back to York. "And yer kinda cute too, sir. You get tired of the hookers here, just let me know. I'll give you a good roll any time you want."

One of the bargirls dropped into York's lap, started rubbing the inside of his thigh, spoke in broken standard. "Meereen wanting good time?" she asked.

Palevi winked. "Don't worry, Cap'm. Salley imports her boys and girls, keeps them clean too."

York shook his head.

"Good job," she said in broken standard. "Meereen get good cheap."

"He said no," Tathit said, then gave her a shove that knocked her onto the floor.

She picked herself up, apparently unhurt, and dusted herself off. "You liking boys instead? We got young boys, old boys."

York shook his head again. "No boys. But maybe later—you."

She smiled. "Later costs more, meereen."

He shrugged. "Later."

A private first class with a familiar face, but a name York couldn't remember, leaned on the table heavily. "Welcome to the Zone, Cap'm," he said. He put a large glass of diluted 'trate in front of York, a handful of pills next to it. "Try these, Cap'm."

York looked at the pills, all kinds and colors. "What are they?" he asked.

The private shrugged and smiled. "I think some of them keep the 'trate from knocking you out so's you can drink more. And some of them lift you up, some of them crash you down. As for the rest, who the fuck knows? Who the fuck cares?"

York looked at the marine carefully, then he started laughing. At first it was just a chuckle, but it grew quickly. He threw a couple pills into his mouth, took a gulp of the 'trate to wash them down, and his laughter turned into loud bellows that brought tears to his eyes. Later he remembered laughing far into the night, beyond drunkenness, beyond sanity, beyond oblivion.

••••

York woke up basically sober, wishing he basically weren't, sprawled on his back on a bed, no clothes, his mouth open, his head pounding until he thought it might split and blow his brains all over the room. He rolled over, curled up and tried to return to unconsciousness.

"Wake up, meereen."

The whore screaming at him didn't help any. He ran his fingers across a three-day-old growth of beard, smacked his lips. His mouth was dry, and if the pounding got any worse it was going to squeeze his brains right out through his ears.

"Wake up, meereen," the whore screamed in his ear. She grabbed his shoulder, shook it.

He rolled over, took a blind swing at her and missed. "Fuck off."

"Wake up, meereen. Answering door."

York opened his eyes for a moment. The pounding got even worse so he closed them again, but an image of the whore remained etched on the back of his eyelids. She was standing with her back to the wall, naked, sagging breasts attached to a body that had seen better days.

"Answering door, meereen."

"You answer the door."

"No! Meereen answering door."

York slowly opened his eyes again. The whore had looked a lot better two nights ago.

He sat up carefully, swung his legs off the bed, gulped hard as his stomach turned a somersault, swallowed bile. But then the pounding started again, and the pain in his head took his mind off his stomach.

The pounding grew louder. He glanced around the whore's dingy little room, realized a lot of the pounding was coming from the door. "All right," he shouted. "I'm coming. Just cut the goddamn racket."

He stood unsteadily, staggered to the door and touched the lock mechanism. The door burst open in his face, knocked him across the room back onto the bed. The room filled quickly with marines carrying small guns.

York froze. The whore froze. The marines froze.

Palevi walked into the silence that followed, glanced about the room, bent down to York's uniform piled on the floor, picked it up and tossed it to York. "You're offline, Cap'm. Get back online, now."

York keyed his implants, heard, ". . . are canceled. You are ordered to report in immediately."

It was a recorded message. York waited for it to repeat. "Bridge *Invaradin* to all personnel. Watch Condition Red. All leaves are canceled. You are ordered to report in immediately."

York started pulling on his clothes while Palevi sent his marines back out into the hall with orders to "Seal the place up. Nobody in or out. Anyone opens a door—close it."

York keyed his implants as he pulled on his tunic. "Ballin reporting," he said.

The message in his implants ceased, was replaced immediately by the simple statement, "Stand by, Lieutenant."

York didn't think he could stand by long with his knees ready to buckle beneath him. But Kalee showed up, dug into his medical kit and produced an injector. "Clear your head, sir?"

York grunted, "Ya."

The medic casually pressed the barrel of the injector against York's throat, pulled the trigger. York heard the injector spit, felt a nasty sting on his neck. His head swam for a second, then the fog from the abuses of the past two days cleared, though he knew he'd pay later for this instantaneous relief.

His implants barked with Telyekev's voice. "Ballin, this is Telyekev. Where the hell have you been?"

"I was offline, sir."

"You were offline? You know damn well you stay online when you're off ship."

"Sorry, sir. It won't happen again."

"It better not. You're with Palevi and his marines, aren't you?"

"Yes, sir."

"Good. Get all your marines to the embassy on the double. You're authorized to commandeer any transportation you need. Use force if necessary and get there fast. We don't have much time."

"Pardon me, sir. But I don't understand."

"God damn it, York, we've got Federals transiting in all over the system. *Invaradin*'s already under way with *Nostran* and *Irriahm*, going to engage, buy you time. I had to scramble, left a lot of crew dirtside. We're telling everyone to head for the embassy. I want you and your marines there to protect them and the embassy staff, especially the royal family. Get there! On the double! Use your own discretion where necessary. Any questions?"

"Yes, sir. Then what do we do?"

"Berkma's working out some sort of evacuation plan. You'll have to find out what it is when you get there. Anything else?"

"No, sir."

"Good. Telyekev out."

York's implants went dead. He looked at Palevi, then at the small gun the sergeant held cupped in one hand. "Where'd you get that?"

Palevi grinned. "I don't go anywhere without something, Cap'm."

York nodded and started pulling on his clothes. "See if you can find me one. And did you hear the old man?"

"Yes, sir."

"How far to the embassy?"

"A good forty kilometers, sir."

"Ground transportation?"

"We ain't gonna get far on the ground, sir. Streets are jammed. It's a riot out there."

York froze with one leg in his pants. "A riot? Feddies?"

"Don't think so, sir. Just lots of civilians with lots of panic. Guess they figure when the warheads start falling they'd best be someplace else."

York continued pulling on his clothes. "Then how far to the navy yard?"

Clearly Palevi had already thought of that. "A little more than a klick, sir."

"Shuttles? Gunboats?"

"No gunboats, sir, but they've got two large shuttles and a small courier. Shuttles can each hold about a hundred of us packed tight. The courier—maybe ten."

"What's our count?"

Palevi grinned. "We got two hundred and forty-two actives, sir."

York sat on the bed, started pulling on his boots and asked, "We've got Yagell and her people?"

Palevi nodded. "Terk's a good marine, sir."

York got his boots on, stood too quickly and the room tilted crazily. Palevi reached out to steady him, then pushed a couple of pills into his hand. "These'll help, sir."

York looked at the pills and frowned a question at Palevi. The sergeant answered, "Nerve jackers."

York tossed the pills into his mouth, looked around quickly for something to wash them down with, found a half empty glass of 'trate near the bed. He took a gulp, fought to keep it down and barely succeeded.

"Staff meeting," he told Palevi, trying to breathe around the 'trate fumes. "All NCOs—" He tried to recall those he'd seen in the saloon. "—Notay, Yagell, Hyer, Tathit, Elkiss, Cleaver, and that second looey from *Irriahm*. The red head; what's her name?"

"Simorka, sir."

"Did I miss anyone?"

"No, sir."

They'd converted the ground floor of the saloon into an armed camp, with heavily armed guards posted at all exits. Most of the guards were toting rifles, and two were actually carrying rotaries. York nodded toward the guards. "Where'd we get the firepower?"

Palevi smiled. "Salley's ex-marine, keeps some stock on hand for emergencies."

York didn't comment on the legality of a civilian possessing such weaponry.

Most of the marines didn't look to be in any better shape than York. Simorka looked absolutely green. Elkiss was still drunk, or drugged, or both, and none of Kalee's instant remedies worked. York took her off the active list.

People and surface vehicles completely jammed the streets outside. Commandeering transportation would have been useless, so York decided to lead a squad of thirty on foot to the navy yard. He needed to get the two pilots, Hackla and Blake, to the shuttles so they could ferry marines to the embassy. With two hundred and forty-two marines present, The Drop Zone was nicely secure, and with a little over a kilometer of panicked civilians between there and the yard York decided to take Palevi, Notay, Hyer, and one of the rotaries as insurance. Nominally, Simorka would stay behind in charge of the saloon, but just before leaving York pulled the young lieutenant aside unceremoniously. "Between you and me," he told her, "you're in charge as long as you listen to Yagell and the other NCOs. You understand?"

Fear showed plainly in her eyes. "Yes, sir."

"Good. Just hold the place secure until we get back with the shuttles."

York marched to the main entrance of the saloon where Palevi had his squad lined up to one side of the door. He took his customary place in the front of the line. He looked at Palevi. "We all set?"

Palevi had on his grin. "As set as we'll ever be."

York switched his implants to the open marine frequency. He looked at the four marines guarding the entrance, nodded. They swung the doors open to reveal a sidewalk filled with confusion. York stepped through the doors, moved to one side and pressed his back to the outside wall of the saloon. Palevi was right behind him, took a position on the other side of the door. Ten marines followed on his heels and formed a tight semicircular perimeter the width of the sidewalk.

A half-dozen civilians, in the midst of a free-for-all, paused and suddenly took notice of them, and for a moment several of them seemed ready to turn their panic on the small group of marines. But then they took notice of the uniforms, the discipline, the weaponry—the rotary out in front— and any thought of attack disappeared quickly.

York barked into his implants, "Squad two, go," and again ten marines filed out of the saloon, but they moved to York's right, expanding the perimeter up the sidewalk. York followed them, at the same time calling out, "Squad three—go."

It went rather smoothly, leapfrogging by squad down the crowded streets to the navy yard, diligently maintaining their perimeter. On their way they picked up a number of *Invaradin* and *Nostran* crewmembers who'd been trying to make their way to the navy yard in small groups, and only once did they have any trouble with civilians: a large mob that outnumbered them so heavily it was not intimidated by uniforms or discipline. York had the rotary lay down a volley at their feet, and that discouraged them quickly. In all, it took them just over a half hour to get to the yard.

The yard was actually just a small shuttle port, with a junior officer in charge of a meager maintenance crew and a few marines for security. York and his marines swept past the gate and took charge of the place quickly. The two pilots went immediately to check out the shuttles while the rest of the marines found a small arms locker and started stripping it quickly of its contents. York spotted the young officer in charge of the yard having a difficult time trying to push his way through the marines. When he saw York he started waving frantically, shouted above the confusion, "Sir, Commodore Berkma wants to speak to you immediately." He waved a small handset above his head.

York sliced his way through the crowd of marines, took the small handset and put it to his ear. "Ballin here," he said.

"Ballin!" Berkma shouted. She was as close to panic as any civilian, and that confirmed what York suspected about her combat experience. "Where the hell have you been, Ballin? Why haven't I been able to contact you?"

"Sorry, commodore. Without a combat harness I had to lock my implants to the marine frequency while we made our way to the yard."

"Don't ever do that again."

"Yes, ma'am."

"Good." She calmed down a bit. "Where are you? We need your help. There's a riot going on here."

"I'm at the yard with thirty marines. I've got two hundred and forty-two actives, most holed up in a saloon about a kilometer from here. We've got two shuttles we'll use to ferry them over to you. Should have the first batch to you in less than half an hour."

Berkma's voice filled with relief. "Excellent, Lieutenant. Excellent!"

"Ma'am?" York asked carefully. "May I ask what the situation is?"

"So far we've had four feddie warships down-transit just beyond nearspace. But we've picked up transition wakes for another two out beyond that. It doesn't look good."

The gravitational well of a stellar mass made it difficult to maintain an accurate transition vector, so the feddie ships had down-transited just beyond nearspace to compute a course correction. They'd try to transit in as accurately as possible from there.

Telyekev was standing-to just beyond Dumark's nearspace, waiting for them to make that second short jump. The gravitational well of the planet would compound their inaccuracies, allowing him to ignore those with badly perturbed vectors. He'd target on the transition wakes of the rest while they were blind and nearly helpless in transition.

"Captain Telyekev said you were setting up an evacuation plan?"

Berkma's voice rose slightly, edging toward panic. "We're trying to reach *Cinesstar*. She's been parked in a synchronous orbit for the past two months going through systems checkout after complete overhaul at the station. Limited crew plus maintenance personnel, evidently with no one manning the com because we can't get a response. Any way you can get up there?"

"There's a courier ship here," York said, trying to formulate a plan as he spoke. "Should be able to get a few of us up there."

"You have my authorization to use any means you choose." Berkma switched off.

York keyed his implants. "Palevi. Notay. See if you can find any vac suits around here, then meet me at that courier."

They came up with seven standard issue vac suits, no plast or armor. The courier had seats for a pilot and four passengers, cramped, no air lock. York put Palevi in charge of the marines going to the embassy, decided to take Notay and five of her people with him. Kalee gave them all a good strong dose of hi-gee, and backed it up with nerve jackers.

They stuffed anything they could find as padding around the two marines who didn't have seats. York climbed into the pilot's couch, started throwing switches, felt the hum of the drive as it warmed up. He rested his hands on the controls, hesitated for a moment, realized he was just simply enjoying this. He had screens in front of him, could see the feddies transiting in, could see the positions of those already under drive to engage Telyekev, and he enjoyed the danger, the adrenaline, the fear, the drugs, the overload. It was an addiction: not just to the drugs but to the whole package. On leave he always felt empty, and only when he got back to the edge of death did he feel alive.

11

Desperation

BY THE TIME York reached *Cinesstar* there were five feddie warships standing-to just beyond nearspace, and more on the way. They were still too far out to target accurately on the planet's surface, but soon they'd make their second jump in-system and Telyekev would have his hands full.

York cut the courier's drive about three thousand meters from *Cinesstar*, let the small ship drift toward the larger one while he shook off the numbing effects of hi-gee. He threw a full visual on one screen, picked the ship out as a large, bright glint resting among the background of stars, turned his attention back to the navigational display.

He opened a secure hailing channel, broadcast a clearance request and received a coded denial response from *Cinesstar*'s computer. He repeated the request as he nudged the courier into place about fifty meters from the ship, but apparently there was no one manning her com. He keyed the com in his vac suit. "Notay. We're going to have to board her. Flush cabin pressure and get that hatch open while I get us in as close as I can."

"Yes, sir."

York glanced at the visual on his screen. *Cinesstar* was a heavy cruiser, even bigger than *Invaradin*, a blunted, spear-blade shape pocked with weapons turrets and gunnery pods.

Notay blew the courier's cabin seals, and as York's vac suit began to expand he nudged the courier sideways with her attitude jets, positioned her about twenty meters from *Cinesstar*'s aft personnel hatch.

"That's perfect, Cap'm. Hold her right there."

York locked the courier's autopilot onto *Cinesstar* so it would hold the relative position of the two vessels. He cut the courier's internal gravity, popped the release on his harness and floated free of the pilot's couch. By the time he got to the hatch, Notay and four of her marines had already jumped the gap between the two ships and opened *Cinesstar*'s hatch. The next marine made the jump while York test fired the small steam jet in each heel of his suit.

He'd positioned the courier with its hatch looking directly at *Cinesstar*'s personnel hatch. He triggered a quick, hard burst from his heel jets and the rim of the courier hatch fell away from him, suspending him in the vastness between the two ships.

At the halfway point he tucked his knees into his chest, rolled over backwards half a turn and pointed his heels at *Cinesstar*'s hatch, then fired his heel jets in a slow, gentle deceleration that brought him to a stop almost within the hatch. One of the two marines waiting there snagged him, pulled him into the airlock, closed the outer hatch and activated the pressurization cycle.

For a moment a blast of air buffeted him as the suit went limp. Then the inner hatch burst open and he and the two marines floated out into a maintenance bay. The fact that they were still floating free inside *Cinesstar*'s was not a good sign.

Notay and the other three marines had already stripped off their vac suits. York hooked his legs around the arm of a maintenance robot, got his helmet off, tossed it to one of the marines, pushed off toward the lift while trying to break the seals on his suit and barking orders over his shoulder. "Sergeant. Go below and check engineering, see if there's anyone down there who can get this bucket fired up. I'm headed for the bridge. Stay in contact."

The lift wasn't programmed to respond to his vocal commands and he lost precious moments breaking the seals on his gauntlets before he could manually punch in his destination. When the lift doors popped open, York pulled his way to the scan console and tried to fire it up: nothing. Without access codes he was locked out of the system. The com was at least open for general noncritical access, but the helm, damage control, fire control, and engineering consoles were all dead and locked up tight. Berkma had mentioned a limited crew. Where the hell were they?

He strapped down at the com, opened up an exterior channel, found that Telyekev had set up a command grid and was broadcasting a coded combat summary. He threw the summary up on a screen, flinched at what he saw—four more feddie warships had transited in at the edge of the system for a total of nine. One had tried to make a second jump to within targeting range of Dumark, had taken a direct hit in transition and was no longer a threat. Another four had moved more cautiously, transited in to a distance safely beyond *Invaradin*, *Nostran*, and *Irriahm*. The remaining four were scattered out at the edge of nearspace, probably setting up transitions at that moment to join their comrades. With those odds, the time Telyekev could buy them was minimal, but it might make the difference. It had to make the difference.

Telyekev's command grid also showed sixteen more transition wakes out beyond the system, all at distances of less than a light-year and converging on them rapidly, though only three were close enough to arrive before it was all over.

Notay's voice spoke from his implants, "Cap'm. We found a maintenance crew down here. Chief in charge, name of Cappik, wants to talk to you on ship's com."

York activated an interior com channel, and on one of his screens brought up the image of a middle-aged chief petty officer dressed in stained and smudged coveralls. Cappik spoke without waiting for York. "Your people tell me we're under attack."

York nodded. "That's right. Not specifically this ship, but the whole system. Where's *Cinesstar*'s crew."

"Crew?" Cappik asked. "There's no crew on this ship. We're the only ones here, and we're just running final systems checks before they install her access codes."

"No access codes?"

Cappik shook his head. "Just certain open access points so we can do our job. We've . . ."

York stopped listening. No access codes! None! Without access codes the ship was completely locked up. There was nothing he could do but gather up his marines and get the hell out of there, make a run for it, try to get back to the embassy without being targeted by a feddie warhead. The courier had no shields, not against that kind of firepower, and as those feddies got closer even a small ship under drive was a wonderful target—

York's thinking froze suddenly as Cappik's words hit him: ". . . certain open access points . . ." The man was still talking; York interrupted him. "When did they program these open access points?"

The man paused, thought for a moment. "About two months ago, just before they pulled her out of the station yard and put her in orbit."

That meant someone in the system had the ring-zero access code, and there was only one person the navy would trust with that. York looked carefully at Cappik. "If I get you access, how soon can you get me full combat status?"

"Combat status?" Cappik asked. "That'll take hours. We're on minimum idle, barely above complete shutdown. We'd likely—"

"We don't have hours," York growled. "I'll get you access and I want full combat status five minutes later."

Cappik frowned angrily, leaned toward the pickup. "Five minutes! You'll have to override every safety interrupt in the ship's systems. Do you realize the chances you'd be taking, the damage you could cause?"

A crewman questioning properly issued orders! Behind Cappik Notay stiffened, frowned, and something angry crawled up York's throat. "Do you realize the damage a warhead would cause if we don't have shields?"

Cappik shook his head. "This is all irrelevant. We're noncombatants, station personnel. This is a combat situation and we don't get involved in that."

"Don't get involved?" York asked.

"Exactly. We leave that to you people. My people and me are leaving, going back to the station."

"Chief," York asked carefully. "We need your help. We need this ship to evacuate the embassy, and without you we'll be a cloud of radioactive gas long before we can protect ourselves."

Cappik shrugged. "I'm sorry, you'll have to handle this yourself."

York nodded, and his voice came out low, calm, and hard. "Then I'm making it an order."

Cappik stiffened. "You don't give me orders."

"The entire system is on full alert," York said. "I've been properly placed in command of this ship, no matter how briefly, and you're on this ship. Failure to obey my orders constitutes a capital offense."

Cappik bared his teeth. "Don't give me that space lawyer bullshit. My crew and I are leaving. Now."

In the periphery of the screen York saw the man's people milling about behind him. A few were angry, most were scared, their attention more on Notay standing directly behind their leader than on the man himself, or on the rest of Notay's marines who'd quietly edged back a few steps and were now behind everyone else, their hands resting carefully on the weapons at their sides.

"You're refusing my order?" York asked.

Cappik growled, "Yer goddamn right."

"Ok," York said. He looked at Notay. "Sergeant, take Chief Cappik out and shoot him, vent him to space, then put his assistant in charge. Now!"

"Aye, aye, sir," Notay said calmly, and before Cappik could react she grabbed him by the back of his collar with one hand, pressed the muzzle of her sidearm under his chin with the other, and yanked him out of the pickup's range.

"Wait," Cappik screamed angrily. "You can't do this. You have no right." His people stood frozen, terrified, and the tone of Cappik's voice suddenly shifted. "This is insane. It's an outrage." York heard the sound of an opening hatch. "Wait! Wait! Stop. Stop. I'll do it. I'll do what you want."

York shouted, "As you were, Sergeant."

York heard the sound of scuffling off camera, then Cappik was thrown heavily against the pickup, blocking the view. He straightened slowly, stood upright, the collar of his coveralls torn half away, a trickle of blood at the corner of his mouth, his lips and hands trembling. Notay stepped into the picture behind him, gun in hand. Behind them all the other marines had pulled their sidearms.

York looked at Notay. "Notay, you and your people stay down there, keep an eye on them. When I give an order, if one of them hesitates for so much as a second, shoot them and replace them with someone smarter."

She smiled. "Yes, sir."

He looked at Cappik. "I'm going to have access shortly, so get ready to give me full combat status five minutes later."

He didn't wait for an acknowledgment, switched off the circuit, put in a call to the embassy. A com technician answered and York didn't have time to be polite. "Where's Berkma?"

"The commodore's in her office, though—"

"Put me through to her, now."

The tech didn't argue. There was a short delay, then Berkma appeared on York's screen. "Are you alone?" York asked.

"Yes," Berkma said, obviously unhappy with York's abruptness. "Why?"

"Because this ship is locked up tight. No access codes, and without access we can't do anything. You have the ring-zero access code, don't you?"

Berkma frowned. "Yes. I'll program access as soon as I get up there."

"And how long from now will that be? An hour? Two?" York looked at the readout on his console. "It's been thirty-seven minutes since I left the Yard. I don't know how things stand down there, but I'll guess you've got one load of marines and sent the shuttles back to the saloon for the rest." He could see in Berkma's eyes he was right. He looked again at the scan summary. There were now six feddie warships in a group confronting Telyekev and his three ships, both sides starting to take long-range shots with their transition batteries. Another feddie had transited in at the edge of the system, and soon there'd be more.

Berkma's eyes were filled with indecision.

York continued relentlessly. "You know the situation with *Invaradin*, *Nostran*, and *Irriahm*. By the time you get those marines into the embassy, then make four, maybe five, shuttle trips up here—long before then this ship'll be vapor and there'll be a big hole where the embassy used to be. Our only chance is for me bring this ship from cold stop to combat status in a matter of minutes, then set this ship down somewhere on the surface near you. And to do that I have to override every fail-safe procedure in the operating system. And I can't do that without ring-two access. That's captain's access or better. But you haven't programmed those access codes."

Berkma started shaking her head. "But ring-zero is Fleet Command level. I can't give you that. It's against regulations."

York shrugged. "Then we're all dead. The choice is yours."

Berkma shook her head for a moment, suddenly stiffened. "All right," she said. In the same instant she stood and disappeared from the screen.

She reappeared a few seconds later, sat down in front of the pickup with a file in front of her. She broke a seal on it, opened it and read for a moment, then looked unhappily at York and hesitated. She spoke carefully, "Three-C-Two-Nine-One-Nine-Alpha."

"Got it," York said. "Is there a large, open space nearby, a place to land? These ships don't like atmosphere and I'm going to need a lot of room."

Berkma spoke mechanically. "There's a park here in the embassy compound."

"Good. Tell Palevi this is a heavy cruiser. He'll tell you if your park's large enough. Tell him to clear it. And have him put one of our marines on your com. I need a landing beacon, but I don't want it switched on until I give the word, because it'll also make a nice homing signal for a feddie warhead. And get everyone ready to move fast."

York cut Berkma out of the circuit, cleared the com, locked out all external signals, activated vocal programming, then leaned back and tried to compose himself for a moment. He rubbed his temples, then spoke slowly.

"Computer."

Acknowledge, it replied.

"Log on. Access Three-Charlie-Two-Niner-One-Niner-Alpha."

The computer hesitated for an interminable second. *Please confirm access Three-Charlie-Two-Niner-One-Niner-Alpha.*

"Access Three-Charlie-Two-Niner-One-Niner-Alpha confirmed."

Again the computer hesitated. *Access Three-Charlie-Two-Niner-One-Niner-Alpha granted. Access priority is ring-zero.*

York almost jumped out of his seat. Ring-zero; godlike access. No one got ring-zero unless they were under the watchful eyes of armed AI. And afterwards it would be immediately erased.

He leaned forward, called up the emergency flags at ring-zero, had to dig for a few minutes to find the override for emergency ignition, found it, activated it, called down to the engineering section and told his recalcitrant CPO, "You're cleared. Five minutes. Do it! Now!"

••••

"Do we engage?" Ducan Soe asked.

Jewel Thaaline shook her head, though it was a useless gesture in the cramped confines of the *Pride*'s bridge. "No. We sit tight. We're a lot closer than anyone else, and they don't know we're here. This is developing into something weird, and I don't know what our real target is yet so I'm—"

She hesitated. Something new appeared on the near scan report. She demanded, "What's that?"

Innay answered. "A ship. Must have been in static orbit around Dumark, completely shut down, otherwise we'd have spotted it earlier. Not big enough to be a freighter, but showing a lot of power coming up fast, dangerously fast."

Jewel nodded to herself. "I think we might have found our target. Maybe everyone's target."

••••

York activated *Cinesstar*'s alert status since many of her systems operated differently otherwise. And just for himself, because he too operated differently otherwise, he let the alert klaxon blare in his ears while he started setting up access codes all over the ship, filling in random numbers and logging them into a file for later recall by whoever took command. That done, he killed the alert klaxon, then one-by-one activated each of the consoles, slaved each into the helm so he'd have limited control of all ship's functions from there. Then he sat down at the helm, adjusted the couch, and lowered the helm cluster.

It was an eerie feeling, having his senses completely cut off by the all-encompassing helm. It had been years since he'd piloted a real ship, and he'd forgotten how easy it was to succumb to the hallucination that he was the ship, especially when he was loaded on combat drugs.

The default programming for the helm cluster showed detailed scan reports both near, far, and system wide; engineering details on power demand, shield status and drive load. But he wouldn't have a commanding officer evaluating the combat situation and firing orders at him, so he replaced the system scan report with the combat summary coming off the System Command Grid. He'd have to do his own evaluations and make his own decisions.

Cappik's five minutes were up; York could feel the hum of the power plant in the hull and it gave him an odd sense of security. He placed a call down to engineering. Cappik answered, had to shout above the noise down there. "We just got the starboard chamber up to full status," he yelled. "Port and Centerline are almost there, but I think the ignition pile's going sour on us. Might go into meltdown."

York shouted back, "Jettison it if you have to. Can I get full drive?"

"Ya," Cappik shouted, "but you don't have enough power yet for that and shields."

"How long for shields?"

"Another minute, maybe two."

"Good," York shouted. "Hold this line open and stand by. We're going down."

He opened a com channel to the embassy, barked, "Who've I got down there on com?"

"This is Elkiss, Cap'm. Sarge said to tell you the park here at the embassy wasn't big enough, but we've got a large construction site nearby that'll work. Ground's just been cleared, nothing yet built."

York felt a pin prick in his neck. The helm cluster had determined that something in him needed adjusting. "I'm coming down, Elkiss. Give me that landing beacon just before I hit atmosphere, but kill it as soon as I hit dirt. ETA less than two minutes."

"Yes, sir."

York launched the drones so he'd have full scan capability, then spun the ship and firewalled the sublight drive. No carefully calculated navigational sequence. He was thirty-five thousand kilometers off the planet's surface. Accelerate at maximum sublight drive to the halfway point, forty-four seconds. Then flip her over and decelerate at full drive down to the planet's surface. And remember to err a little on the side of caution so he didn't slam into the planet like an oversized meteorite.

It was close. York got the shields up just before he slammed into Dumark's atmosphere. *Cinesstar* burnt a monstrous ionization trail through the stratosphere, would have disintegrated without her shields. As it was, he had to cut the drive and divert all power into the shields and structural support to hold the ship together, actually redlining the power plant for a few moments. The drones followed standard programming and went into simple low orbits evenly spaced around the planet.

At fifty kilometers he had enough reserve to bring the drive back up, though he didn't drop below Mach one until he was only three hundred meters from the surface. In atmosphere *Cinesstar* was like a beached whale, no maneuverability to speak of, vulnerable, out of her element. York followed the landing beacon and managed to set her down reasonably well.

He cut the drive back to idle, killed internal gravity, had the helm cluster rising up off him even before *Cinesstar* had settled fully on her rarely used landing supports. He stopped for a moment by the engineering console, opened all the access bays on Hangar Deck and keyed his implants. "Palevi, move 'em out. On the double. No time for niceties. We're a target now. Bring some pilots up in your first load and get *Cinesstar*'s boats into the act."

He glanced quickly at the power plant drain. *Cinesstar* wasn't designed to operate in a gravity well, so a lot of power was diverted into structural support that would normally be available for drive and weapons and shields.

He sat down at the fire control console, crammed on a headset since he couldn't key his implants into the console, activated *Cinesstar*'s defensive batteries and brought up a combat summary on one of his screens. With six drones orbiting and feeding him detailed information, he had an excellent chance of intercepting anything incoming.

The feddies and Telyekev's three ships were fully into it now, and a few of the Syndonese were in close enough to take long shots at the planet. York watched a feddie spit a warhead into transition; it covered several million kilometers in the blink of an eye, then dropped into sublight and detonated about ten thousand kilometers to one side of Dumark; a clean miss, its transition vector perturbed by the planet's gravitational field.

York activated several cameras on *Cinesstar*'s hull, started flipping through their views. Palevi was using the shuttles from the Yard like elevators, cramming as many people into them as possible, then lifting them the forty odd meters to the level of Hangar Deck and hovering at one of the open bays while they booted the civilians into *Cinesstar*.

The fire control console beeped at York, a warhead transiting in, no miss this time, though it would miss *Cinesstar* cleanly so he let it go. A large incandescent cloud blossomed on the horizon. *Atmospheric detonation*, the computer said. *Range: two hundred kilometers. Estimated yield strength: one megatonne.*

Outside everyone hesitated for a moment, looked toward the terrible light on the horizon. York switched on allship, growled into his pickup, "Don't waste time looking at it. There's more headed our way so get moving, god damn it."

The fire control console beeped at him again, another warhead. *Atmospheric detonation. Range: fifty-one kilometers. Estimated yield strength: fifteen megatonnes. Minimal shock wave expected.* Two more warheads followed in rapid succession, big ones, but still off the mark.

Palevi had gotten *Cinesstar*'s three gunboats into the act, along with the Yard's two shuttles. With warheads blossoming around them the civilians were getting frantic as the five boats dropped for another lift. "This should do it, sir."

The fire control console screamed a loud, angry note at York—a big warhead was arcing in directly overhead. He shifted into an odd, detached calm as he did a half-dozen things at once. He allocated the warhead as a high priority target to *Cinesstar*'s main transition battery, shouted over allship, "Incoming. Hit the deck," then confirmed target acquisition, fired an interceptor shot. The atmosphere above *Cinesstar* exploded with a bright red ionization trail from *Cinesstar*'s main batteries, and a new sun blossomed overhead. *Atmospheric detonation. Range: twelve kilometers. Altitude: thirty-one kilometers. Estimated yield strength: fifty-three megatonnes. Stand by for shock.*

York shouted over allship, "Brace yourselves. Shock wave incoming."

The marine pilots knew what to do. A civilian might have tried to ground his boat, but with no time to tie it down their best chance was to lift, get up into the atmosphere rather than be crushed against the ground. Unfortunately they spilled a few unlucky passengers as they lifted, and one of the shuttles was only a few meters off the ground when the shock wave hit.

Cinesstar shook, groaned under the impact, her power plant redlining as she diverted power to her structural supports. When it was over, one shuttle was down, nose crumpled and half buried in a giant divot of earth, badly injured people strewn about like dolls dropped by a petulant child. York's screen showed a dozen more warheads pounding into the planet, some so far off they were on the other side of the globe. The feddies had realized the other three imperial ships were trying to protect *Cinesstar*, were now making wild, desperate transition jumps, trying to get in close enough for an accurate shot.

York switched to the marine command frequency. "Palevi we're out of time. Load them up. Now! Do whatever you have to."

They landed a gunboat next to the crashed shuttle, started throwing bodies on the gunboat without checking to see if they were dead or injured. The marines on the other boats started herding the civilians like cattle, dealing out shoves to anyone who hesitated, harsher treatment for anyone who resisted. *Invaradin*, *Nostran*, and *Irriahm* had retreated in closer to the planet, were now each operating independently, trying to intercept any warheads they could and defend themselves at the same time.

"We're sealed up, Cap'm," York's headset shouted in Palevi's voice. "Let's get the fuck out'a here."

"I need help up here," York shouted. "Any line-officers down there, send them up on the double."

He put the fire control console on full automatic, all weapons and horizon-to-horizon saturation. It would target on anything that moved. He tore off his headset, vaulted around the fire control console, dropped into the helm couch, and even before the cluster was fully down he powered up the shields, slammed on internal gravity and firewalled the drive. He heard the fire control console go into action before they were out of Dumark's atmosphere, but he was too busy to pay attention and he had to trust it could do the job without his help.

Once clear of Dumark's atmosphere the drones took up circulating orbits around *Cinesstar*. The feddies, because of their wild transition jumps, had scattered themselves all around the planet. He couldn't head in toward the empire without becoming an easy target, his only escape a vector running parallel to the front with a heavy slant toward an enemy quadrant.

A hand touched his shoulder, startled him out of his wits, and at the same time his headset spoke in Maggie's voice. "I'm in the alternate helm cluster, York. I'm relieving you . . . now."

York let go, deactivated his cluster and as it started lifting off him he rolled out of the couch, saw uniforms all around him sitting down at *Cinesstar*'s consoles. He dropped down behind the captain's console, pulled on a headset and plugged it in, started barking orders. Frank was at fire control, Maggie at helm, Paris at com, Dak at engineering, Anda at scan. He was still barking orders when Olin Rame stepped onto the bridge, and he continued to bark orders as their eyes met. Rame nodded, a silent acknowledgement that York was in command, then sat down calmly at navigation.

"Commander Rame," York said. "We need transition, any way, anywhere, anyhow."

Rame glanced at his console as his hands danced across the keys. "It's going to be sloppy. We're barely twenty million klicks from Dumark. There'll be serious nearspace error."

"We'll take what we can get," York said, beginning to hope they might escape unscathed.

"Ballin." York flinched at the sound of Sierka's voice. "I'm taking command."

Sierka stood beside York next to the captain's console, Senator Andow standing behind him hunched uncomfortably beneath the overhang of an instrument cluster, and behind the instrument cluster stood the empress. "You can't," York said without thinking, realizing as he did so it was a mistake. Sierka was the most senior officer of command rank.

"I can't?" Sierka demanded, glancing toward Andow. "And why can't I?"

York couldn't give Sierka command. He hadn't gone to all this trouble only to let an incompetent idiot get them all killed. "But you don't know how. You don't have—"

"Don't know how, Lieutenant?" Sierka leaned forward angrily. "Are you questioning my authority? In combat? Under alert status?"

Andow leaned into the light from York's console. "It would be best if you did what he said, Lieutenant."

"I ah . . ." York didn't know what to say. He kept his mouth shut as he unplugged his headset and rose carefully from the captain's console, stepped aside. Sierka sat down, rubbed the edge of the console proudly and gave a contented nod.

York asked, "What station would you like me to take, sir?"

Sierka looked at him and grinned. "None. Just get off my bridge."

"But, sir, I—"

"Don't argue with me," Sierka screamed. "Off the bridge. Now!"

The captain's console beeped, and since Sierka didn't have a headset plugged in, Cappik's voice and the noise from engineering came out over a speaker. "Captain, I need to jettison the ignition pile. Now!"

Sierka touched a switch on the console. "Belay that."

"But, Captain, it's going—"

"Silence," Sierka screamed into the pickup. "Is everyone here insubordinate? Doesn't anyone obey orders?"

A telltale started blinking on the engineering console, then suddenly it flashed bright red and a horn blared. The computer barked, "Hazard warning! Low-level contamination; Engineering Section. Critical contamination in—"

York leaned over Nemkov's shoulder, plugged his headset into the engineering console. "Cappik, jettison the ignition pile. Now! That's an order."

York felt a tickle of premonition crawl up the back of his spine, as if he sensed a transition somewhere else, a warhead up-transiting. But that was impossible.

"Incoming," Gant shouted, "dead ahead."

Maggie changed course, and on Sierka's console the navigational readouts swung wildly. The power demand skyrocketed as a warhead flared nearby and the shields took priority. Sierka ordered, "Return to course, Miss Votak," and Maggie obeyed.

"A close one," Gant hissed. "Came out of nowhere. Must have been a long shot."

York turned, leaned over her shoulder, looked at the scan trace that remained.

"Ballin," Sierka screamed hysterically. "I told you to get off my bridge."

York started shaking his head, not at Sierka, but at what he saw, or didn't see, on Gant's console: no transition history for that warhead.

Sierka screamed, "Don't you argue with me. Get off this bridge now, or I'll have you arrested and shot."

The answer came to York so quickly he was moving before he realized it. He switched his headset to the command channel so they could all hear him. "There's a hunter-killer out there," he growled. "Running silent somewhere dead ahead. Maggie, take evasive action. Anda watch your scans closely, stand by to divert all power to the shields. Rame we need that transition."

"Shut up," Sierka screamed.

York had his back to Sierka.

Someone shouted, "York, look out."

Preoccupied with the scan readout he was slow to react, turned around just as Sierka swung a wrench at him and it slammed into his face just above his left eye. It wasn't a heavy wrench, but backed by Sierka's fist it knocked him against Gant's console, a small trickle of blood trailing down through the scars around his chrome eye. "Get off my bridge," Sierka screamed.

Rame called out, "Commander."

"You shut up too!"

York glanced down at Rame's console, saw the drone readouts swinging wildly as they approached transition.

"But Commander," Rame pleaded. "The—"

"Shut up. All of you."

Jondee's voice interrupted them all. "Transition in twenty seconds and counting. Nineteen . . . Eighteen . . ."

York shouted in Sierka's face, "He's trying to tell you you're going to lose the drones, you idiot."

Sierka froze, seemed unable to give the right order, unable to give any order. York leaned over the com console, slammed his fist down on a switch, shouted over the command channel, "Drones in."

"Eight," Jondee continued. "Seven . . . Six . . . Five . . . Four . . ."

"Drones are in," Gant acknowledged as the clang of the shutting drone bays echoed through the hull.

"Three . . . Two . . . One . . ."

York felt that strange sensation that always came at the moment of transition, the same feeling he'd felt when the hunter-killer had spit its warhead into transition.

"Transition. One-point-two lights and accelerating."

For a moment they all hesitated, breathed a collective sigh of relief as *Cinesstar* left the Dumark system behind.

"Mister Ballin, get off my bridge. Now! That's an order."

York turned slowly toward Sierka, looked at him carefully, wanted to kill him, but instead raised his hand to salute. "Aye, aye, sir."

Sierka didn't return the salute. "Get out of here."

York turned toward the lift, edged his way carefully past Andow and the empress, touched the sensor at the lift hatch and stepped through as it opened. Inside the lift he hesitated. He was still wearing the vac suit, minus the helmet and gauntlets, and he had to slide the seal ring at the end of the suit arm past his wrist to see his watch. Less than two hours ago he'd awakened in The Drop Zone, and now all the adrenaline and drugs and stress threatened to catch up with him. For a moment he thought he felt the hunter-killer make transition behind them, but realized he was hallucinating again.

They could probably use help in Engineering. He focused on that thought, used the action of programming the lift destination to bring him back to reality, and when, an instant later, the lift doors popped open in front of him, he had at least restored himself to the appearance of control.

••••

"Transition," Ducan Soe said calmly. "We're right in their wake, might be able to get off a good shot, maybe burn 'em."

Jewel Thaaline shook her head slowly. "Belay that," she said, looking at her console. "We're both in transition; we're blind; he's blind."

"But we have a pretty good idea where he is," Soe argued. "We can shove one up his ass and he won't even know what hit him."

Jewel continued to shake her head. "He knows we're here, behind him somewhere. He just doesn't know exactly where."

Soe looked up from his console angrily. "Impossible. We vectored that warhead so they'd think it was a long shot from somewhere else."

Still she shook her head. "That evasive action he took, just before transition. That was for us. He knows we're here. He's probably holding his crew on alert, waiting for us to try something, give away our position. And if we give him a nice accurate targeting vector, with the kind of firepower he's got, he'll squash us."

"But how could he know?"

That was bothering Jewel also; how could he know? She thought about that for a long moment, but it was Innay who gave her the answer. "He's one of us."

Jewel smiled and nodded. "Exactly. He probably served on an *imper* hunter-killer sometime. He knows our tricks."

"So what do we do?" Soe asked.

"We sit tight," Jewel said. "We hang on his tail, run clean and silent, don't give him anything to shoot at, wait for him to make a mistake. Maybe he'll have trouble. He's headed into the Directorate. He'll want to change that as soon as possible. Maybe he'll try a course change. And maybe he won't be patient enough to swing around slowly, and we'll catch enough flaring to really pin him down. Then we'll have a sure hit, and we'll take him. Clean, easy, neat."

12

Reality Lost

ADD'KAS'ADANNA NEEDED ALL of her training to contain her anger. It helped that Kaffair was doing the shouting for her, though he seemed unable to penetrate Ninda's smug demeanor. Zort could only stare, too frightened to say anything.

"That was insanity," Kaffair shouted. "A waste of ships and manpower and resources. And for what, to capture a princess worth nothing."

Kaffair looked at Add'kas'adanna, and she knew he blamed her as much as he did Ninda. He didn't know Ninda had given the orders, overridden her own command structure, had literally orchestrated the entire fiasco at Dumark. He hadn't wanted the princess at all, wanted something or someone else on that ship. And he was willing to throw every warship in the vicinity at that *imper* just to destroy whatever it was.

Kaffair demanded of Add'kas'adanna, "And what were the results? Did you destroy that ship?"

"*Invaradin*?" Add'kas'adanna said, controlling her voice. "No. *Invaradin* escaped, though badly damaged. But during the fighting it became obvious *Invaradin* and the other imperial warships were trying to protect another ship. We have no identification on her, but she too escaped. We can assume she was used to evacuate the princess."

"We can assume," Kaffair shouted, mimicking her. "Tell me, where is this ship now?"

Add'kas'adanna shook her head. "We don't know. We know her approximate heading when she up-transited out of the system—she's headed this way, by the way. And we believe some of our ships were able to follow, but we've had no contact from them so we're certain of nothing."

Add'kas'adanna was sure of one thing: whatever sort of opposing plots Kaffair and Ninda had hatched, the answer was on that *imper* ship.

"And are you diverting more ships from their regular patrols to capture this one ship?"

Add'kas'adanna looked at him coldly. "We don't have to. She's coming our way. We need only wait."

••••

York found utter chaos down in Engineering. The ignition pile had gone into meltdown before they'd jettisoned it. There'd been a minor explosion, rupturing a safety bulkhead and contaminating half the section. The explosion had also damaged a feed channel on one of *Cinesstar*'s three big power plants. Starboard was arcing badly, making an incredible noise, pushing the chamber into overheat and spilling more radiation into the section.

One marine and one of Cappik's people were badly contaminated. Notay had already gotten Kalee up from Hangar Deck to take care of the two injured men, and when York got there he pulled Notay aside, shouted above the noise, "How bad are they?"

Notay shouted back, "Don't know yet, sir."

"Can we get more help from Palevi?"

"If you order it, sir, but he's got his hands full down on Hangar Deck: a couple hundred civilians along with injured and wounded."

Cappik stepped between them, shouted above the noise, "Anyone here with time in a contamination suit?"

York nodded. "Me. Several hundred hours."

"Then get one and make yourself useful."

With York and his marines added to his crew, Cappik had thirty-one people and sixteen contamination suits. But there were only seven of them with enough experience to work in the hottest areas. Cappik put the less experienced to work cleaning up where they could, working in shifts and spelling one another when possible, while York and those with more experience spent the next twenty-seven hours sealed in their suits, working under varying degrees of exposure.

The worst of the contamination was around the damaged feed channel at the starboard chamber. Cappik had blown the evacuation seals around that chamber, so there was no air to conduct heat, but it had still melted through the deck, and it constantly threatened to do more. York paid particular attention to the constantly redlined readouts in his headgear. The flexible fabric of the suit also began to glow under the radiation bombarding it, and as the shielding imbedded in it demanded more power from his reactor pack, it began to hum with an unsettling whine. Twice his suit overheated, and he had to withdraw to let it cool down while others worked on.

After the first ten or twelve hours, Kalee kept them all jacked up on phets, though the drugs didn't do much for their tempers. More than once Cappik requested help from the bridge, but was told in no uncertain terms they also had their hands full up there. When they finally got the feed channel sealed and under control, York had spent the last four hours wedged into an access shaft trying to hold onto a cutting torch without taking off someone's arm. And when Cappik gave the all clear none of them had any energy left to do more than strip off the contamination suits and sit down in the first available spot.

York found a spot out of the way against a bulkhead in a maintenance closet next to a small robot, tried to relax and knew from experience the phets wouldn't let him sleep. A young woman stepped into the hatchway of the maintenance closet. She was one of Cappik's people, obviously as exhausted as York, and likewise showing the angry symptoms of the phets. She pointed a finger at York. "You got us into this, god damn it! If it hadn't been for you we'd all be safe on Dumark Station right now."

A few more of Cappik's people gathered behind her, some showing anger, others more cautious with the marines still about.

York closed his eyes, recalled the seconds immediately following their liftoff from Dumark. Mentally he'd been in combat mode, carefully filtering out anything that didn't pose a threat to his immediate responsibilities, though on a secondary level he'd been conscious of other events, like the warhead strikes on Dumark Station.

York opened his eyes. "You'd be dead."

Kalee stepped up beside her, pressed an injector against her arm. She flinched slightly as he pulled the trigger. She demanded, "What do you mean by that?"

Kalee stepped past her, leaned down and fired a dose into York's arm. York spoke calmly. "Dumark Station's gone, or if there's anything left it's just slag and vapor. She took several direct hits as we were lifting off—big warheads, in the one hundred megatonne range."

Kalee stepped out of the maintenance closet, started circulating among the small crowd behind the young woman, firing *phet* antidote into everyone he could find. York's revelation had taken the fire out of the young woman's anger, and stunned, she turned away as he closed his eyes.

The *phet* antidote was just beginning to take effect when Cappik leaned through the hatchway. "I got a man calling himself Lord Sierka on screen. Says he's the captain. He's madder'n hell. Wants to talk to you."

York picked himself up, staggered to the screen. As the phets wore off he felt a fog settling over his mind.

Sierka smiled as he demanded, "Where have you been?"

York shook his head groggily. "I was helping them clean up down here."

Sierka's eyes narrowed and the smile broadened into a grin. "I've been waiting for this for a long time, Ballin. You're under arrest. The charge is mutiny. Take yourself to the brig and confine yourself there until further notice."

York was too tired to challenge the charges, too tired to say anything other than, "Very good, sir."

A few minutes later, in a deserted security section on an all but empty ship, he picked out a cell, folded a chair down out of the wall, sat down for just a moment to pull off his boots. He fell asleep sitting there.

••••

"What happened?" Edvard demanded angrily, leaning heavily on Rochefort's desk. "What in God's name happened?"

Rochefort shook his head, shuffled through half a dozen reports in front of him. "I don't know. Information is too sketchy. Apparently Dumark's been hit, a major strike."

"What about her?"

Rochefort continued to shake his head, waved one of the reports at Edvard. "Her name doesn't come up. All this data's been thrown together hastily. Just summaries, and no one would think to mention a servant." Rochefort stopped shaking his head, frowned intently. "It doesn't make sense—a major strike on Dumark—not unless the Directorate knows everything."

Edvard shivered, turned away from Rochefort's desk and dropped tiredly into a seat. "What do we do now?"

Rochefort shrugged. "There's nothing we can do until we know more. I've got a man on Dumark. If he's still alive he'll get through to us shortly and we'll at least know what actually happened. In any case, Abraxa will send an AI team in without delay. I've also got a man in AI. I'll make sure he's part of that team. But beyond that, all we can do is wait."

••••

Canon Lynna bowed deeply as he entered Bortha's office. "Your Holiness, I have news from Dumark."

"Is it good?" Bortha asked.

Lynna shrugged. "That remains to be seen, Your Holiness."

Bortha stood, smiled and crossed the room to a small bar. "Join me in a glass of sherra, and we'll discuss it."

Lynna nodded humbly. The old pontiff was in a good mood today. "You honor me, Your Holiness."

Lynna waited patiently while Bortha poured a reddish brown liquid into two small, long-stemmed, crystalline glasses. He made a show of carefully eyeing the amounts, as if he were performing the ceremonial offerings of a high-church service. Then he turned and handed one to Lynna. They each took a small sip—the taste was quite pleasant, though Lynna was not accustomed to such expensive treats.

"Now," Bortha said as he returned to his desk and sat down. "You were saying?"

Lynna placed the glass of sherra on the edge of Bortha's desk, consulted his notes carefully. "I received a message from Proverb Serrin, prelate of the diocese of Dumark. He was able to confirm that the Directorate attacked Dumark with a massive strike force. The embassy, however, was evacuated by an unknown imperial ship. There ensued a heated battle between the ships defending Dumark and the Directorate strike force. Beyond that we know nothing."

Bortha frowned. "What of this unknown ship?"

Lynna stopped consulting his notes, retrieved his glass of sherra from the edge of Bortha's desk. "To the best of our knowledge the only imperial warships on or around Dumark Station were the *Invaradin*, the *Nostran*, and the *Irriahm*. And it has been confirmed none of them were this mysterious ship."

Bortha's frown deepened. "Then we know nothing?"

Lynna shrugged. "I suspect Abraxa knows more than we, or will shortly, but for the time being that information hasn't yet been intercepted by my sources. We must be patient, Your Holiness, though I think we'll not have long to wait."

Bortha smiled and stood. "Excellent, Lynna. I knew I could count on you. And tell that proverb on Dumark to continue to investigate, learn everything he can, and keep us informed."

Lynna took a breath and sighed deeply. "I fear that will not be possible, Your Holiness. Apparently Proverb Serrin suffered severe radiation poisoning, and will shortly be under the protection of the Divine Maker himself."

••••

Bargan Abraxa listened carefully to the pretty, young AI captain standing in front of his desk. "... *Invaradin* and *Nostran* were badly damaged, and *Irriahm* was lost with all hands. We've made direct contact with *Nostran*'s commanding officer, and from him we learned Cassandra and Lady d'Hart were evacuated on H.M.S. *Cinesstar* along with most of the embassy staff. *Cinesstar* was almost completely gutted in combat some months ago, then towed into orbit around Dumark, where she'd undergone complete refitting. She had no crew, but apparently one of *Invaradin*'s junior officers took command of her with a skeleton crew of some kind, and actually landed her on Dumark's surface to evacuate the embassy."

Abraxa allowed an eyebrow to rise slightly. "A bold move, and a dangerous one."

"Yes, Your Grace. In any case, while *Invaradin*, *Nostran*, and *Irriahm* fought a rear guard action, *Cinesstar* retreated in the only direction possible. When she made transition she was headed straight into Directorate territory, and there's been no contact with her since."

Abraxa leaned back in his chair, considered the situation carefully. "Do we know the name of this junior officer who took command of *Cinesstar*?"

The young AI captain consulted her notes for a moment. "*Nostran*'s captain wasn't sure about his last name: Barrin, Bayan, Ballyen—something like that. But he'd met him a few times and knew his first name was York. We're reviewing ..."

The young woman's voice trailed off at the reaction her words produced in Abraxa. He'd gone almost completely white, but he caught himself quickly and recovered. "Thank you, Captain," he said abruptly. "That'll be all."

She hesitated at the abrupt change in his interest, then snapped to attention, bowed deeply, and backed out of the office.

Abraxa turned immediately to his computer, brought up *Invaradin*'s roster, and there it was. It had been so long since he'd had to take any action on that matter he'd forgotten. He should have remembered the instant he'd heard the name *Invaradin*. How could he have been so stupid? The whore's brat was on that ship, with the empress, the queen mother, and God knew whom else. If anyone put the pieces together this could have catastrophic ramifications. He'd been reluctant to throw away such a convenient and possibly powerful pawn, but the time had come to end that meaningless little ploy.

Abraxa prepared a message that began with "My dearest son." To anyone who might intercept it, it would appear to be a letter from a loving mother to her only son serving aboard some ship somewhere. She told him about the farm, and the condition of the crops and the animals. His father's arthritis was acting up, but the doctors were recommending a minor operation that should eliminate his difficulties. Abraxa rambled on for more than a page, then carefully inserted the code phrase: *Winter was harsh this year, and the wildflowers are dying early.*

Abraxa rambled on for another page before finishing the letter, then he posted it through a phony box to the general distribution network for naval correspondence. The next time *Cinesstar* made transition near any kind of imperial facility and exchanged contact packets, that one little loose end would be appropriately terminated.

••••

York opened his eyes groggily, saw a hand reaching for his throat and struck out desperately, swatting the hand away.

He sat up, lifting most of his torso out of the field of the gravity bunk, almost fell out of it as the deck gravity pulled at him.

"Lieutenant!" Lady d'Hart said. "Be careful." She took him by the shoulders and helped him out of the bunk. He didn't tell her he could have done better without her help, but then, for her, getting in and out of a gravity bunk was probably a difficult feat.

He pulled a chair down out of the wall, didn't really care that she remained standing as he sat down, took a moment to orient himself. She reached out again toward his eye, and this time he saw the small handkerchief in her hand. "He shouldn't have hit you," she said. "It was all very unprofessional."

York closed his eyes while she dabbed at the dried trickle of blood on his cheek. He opened his eyes, looked at his watch, thought for a moment he'd only slept for an hour, then remembered waking seated in a chair and crawling half-conscious into the grav bunk. Apparently he'd slept through a full twenty hour day, and more. "You were there?" he asked. "On the bridge? I don't recall seeing you."

"I'm not surprised. You had your hands full, seemed to be doing quite well until Commander Sierka took over."

He smiled unhappily. "But then he's a nobleman, isn't he? So we all feel much safer now that he's in command."

She finished dabbing around his eye, stepped back to examine her work. "That's better. It really was a minor cut, but you should still have it looked at."

"By whom?"

"Your Lieutenant Yan is on board. I'm told she's quite a good physician."

"She's good. What about the damage down in Engineering?"

She frowned. "I wasn't aware there was damage down in Engineering."

"There's damage down there, all right. If I wasn't under arrest I'd go down there myself to help finish cleaning up."

At that she smiled. "But you're no longer under arrest. Senator Andow and Her Majesty had a brief word with Commander Sierka, and he's decided to drop the charges. You're free to go."

York shrugged, stood up and didn't feel too grateful. "That was real nice of them. Why are you here?"

"We seem to find ourselves again in your debt. I wanted to thank you . . . again."

York shook his head. "That's not what I meant. I mean why are you all the way out here, this far from Luna, this close to danger? Why is the empress out here too? And why do the feddies want to put a warhead into us so badly?"

She shrugged. "Aeya came out here on a lark. I came with her to keep her out of trouble. You rescued us on Trinivan and the empress came to Dumark to meet us. It's all very simple."

York looked her over carefully. She was feminine, beautiful, even dressed in plain, navy-issue coveralls. She was also a liar. "Too simple," he said. "Now if you'll excuse me, since I'm not under arrest, I should check the duty roster."

York left her standing there in the cell. No one had bothered to lock it; in fact the security section was still deserted. He stopped in the fresher there, splashed water on his face and ran some through his hair. He needed a shave, and a shower, but that would have to wait.

He used the console in the security section to check the duty roster, which listed a bare minimum of assignments. Sierka had made Soladin first officer, old Armbruster second, Rame third. Rame alone had more experience than the rest put together.

Rame was standing bridge watch at that moment, so York put in a call to him. He too hadn't shaved, and it was obvious he hadn't slept much either. When York asked him about his duty assignment, Rame shook his head. "I wouldn't know. I've been standing watch for the last ten hours."

"Can I help?" York asked.

Rame looked uneasy. "Not on the bridge. Commander Sierka has left orders you're not allowed on the bridge. You'll have to check with him."

"Thank you, sir." Both he and Rame cut the circuit.

He tried Armbruster next, who appeared on the screen in front of him seated at a desk piled with memcards and printouts. "Ballin," Armbruster said. "Good to see you."

"Captain," York said. "I'm—"

"Not captain," Armbruster interrupted. "Her Majesty has temporarily reinstated me at the rank of commander. Ah, my boy! It feels good to be back in the thick of it again."

"Congratulations, Commander. I was wondering if I had a duty assignment."

"A duty assignment?" Armbruster frowned uncomfortably. "I think you'll have to check with Lord Soladin. I believe Commander Sierka has put him in charge of the duty roster."

York tried Perra Soladin, found him in his cabin. "Commander, I'm trying to find out what my duty assignment is?"

Soladin's brows lowered impatiently. "Can't you see I'm entertaining, Ballin?"

Behind Soladin York caught a glimpse of the fluff who'd clung to his arm at the embassy. "I'm sorry, Your Lordship, but I thought, under the circumstances, I should get an assignment as soon as possible."

"Well, I suppose that's admirable, Ballin. But where have you been anyway? And stand at attention when you're addressed by a superior officer."

York straightened his shoulders slowly, raised his chin and tried not to let his anger show. Soladin was really only interested in clearing up the pecking order. "And answer my question."

York chose his words with care. "I'm sorry, sir. What question was that?"

"Where have you been, Mister Ballin?"

"I've been helping Chief Cappik clean up the damage in Engineering."

"Damage in Engineering?" Soladin asked. "There's no damage in Engineering."

"Yes, sir. If you say so, sir."

Soladin nodded. "That's better, Ballin. You've got to be more careful about your attitude."

"Yes, sir."

"I, for one, think you can make a valuable contribution to this crew, though I might add Mayhue and I disagree on that point."

"I'm grateful for your confidence, sir. Have you decided on a duty assignment for me, sir?"

"Yes, I have." Soladin appeared pleased with himself. "I've put you in charge of the marines."

York nodded slowly. "I'm a ship's officer, sir, not a marine."

"I'm aware of that, Mister Ballin. But there are a number of us here who can handle this ship quite nicely. You can contribute the most by taking control of those damned marines. That's an order."

"Aye, aye, sir," York said mechanically. "And my quarters?"

"Why, with the marines, of course."

"Of course, sir. Will that be all, sir?"

Soladin nodded, said, "Dismissed," then he cut the circuit.

York made his way down to the marine barracks. The marines had taken the place over easily, and though it was a bit crowded they'd settled in happily. As he walked through the barracks he passed a poker game and someone called out, "Evening, Cap'm. You look like hell. Here, this'll fix you up."

The marine held out a plast cup. York took it, took a sip: 'trate, properly diluted, but still 'trate, and it made his eyes water. He took a second gulp, handed it back to the marine and continued on. He was greeted in much that way several times before he reached Palevi's office.

"Cap'm," the sergeant said. "Glad to see you. I've got yer quarters all set."

He led York to the cabin reserved for the marine CO, a cabin nicer than any he'd ever had, with its own fresher, and he wasn't sure what else. He hadn't eaten anything but emergency rations for two days and he was hungry. He was in a bit of a daze as he showered, shaved and made himself generally presentable.

He found a new uniform laid out for him when he stepped out of the fresher, a crisp, clean, pressed, unused and never worn uniform. He picked up the tunic and shouted, "Palevi. Where the hell did you get this?"

Palevi stepped into the cabin and grinned. "Ship's stores, sir. This bucket's loaded with supplies like we ain't seen in years."

York couldn't remember the last time he'd worn something sharp and new.

"Sir? Will that be all?"

York nodded slowly. "Ya. Sure. Dismissed."

••••

Something about the new uniform lent a sense of unreality to the situation, as if somehow they'd all been transported far into the past. But it felt good, felt proud, and York held his head a little higher as he made his way up to the officer's mess.

There was a short line of people waiting outside, all civilians. In the navy, York had long ago learned the virtues of patience, so he took his place at the end of the line, and in only a few minutes he stood at the threshold of a darkly lit room with the soft strains of elegant music drifting on the air. A well-groomed, impeccably dressed maître d' stepped in front of him.

"Good evening, sir," the maître d' said, his lips breaking into an oily smile. "The name?"

"Uh . . ." York shook his head carefully, blinked several times, but the man didn't disappear. "Name?"

"Yes, sir," the maître d' said, and York wondered how he managed to speak without ever changing the shape or character of his smile. "Your name, so I can seat you."

Again York shook his head. "Ah . . . Ballin."

The oily smile disappeared, turned into a frown. "One moment, sir," the maître d' said as he leaned to one side and consulted a small screen set in the surface of a rostrum next to the entrance. The maître d' turned back to York, the oily smile returned. "Did you have a reservation, sir?"

"A reservation?" York forced himself not to shake his head a third time. "I'm a ship's officer. I just want some dinner."

"Of course, sir. I'll schedule you in." He leaned over the rostrum, pushed a few keys near the screen. "It looks like there'll be about a three hour wait, sir. Would you care to wait in the bar?"

"The bar?"

"Yes, sir. The bar. Right this way, sir."

The maître d' turned York over to an assistant, who led York down one side of the mess hall, though until his eyes adjusted to the dim lighting he had to feel his way carefully along a bulkhead. Small, carefully arranged tables filled the place, each covered by a white table cloth on which rested an intimate little lamp casting a faint glow. On impulse, York stopped at an unoccupied table, touched the surface carefully to reassure himself it was there. It was molded of rough plast, and to his amazement, under his touch, the table tilted slightly.

A waiter brushed past him carrying a large tray of food. "Sir?" the assistant maître d' pleaded. "This way, sir."

York shook his head. "It's not bolted down."

"Pardon me, sir?"

"The table. It's not bolted down."

"Of course not, sir."

"You'd better have someone see to it."

"Certainly, sir. This way, sir."

The assistant maître d' deposited York in another room that let off the main dining salon, left him standing just within the entrance. It was even darker there, though he could make out a bar along one wall. Not *wall*, bulkhead, he reminded himself.

"York."

That was Maggie's voice, calling from somewhere out of the dark.

"This way, York."

He spotted her at the bar waving at him, and as he crossed the room he saw Frank and Paris next to her. "Pull up a stool," Paris said. "And no, it's not bolted down."

York sat down, put his elbows on the bar, closed his eyes and began rubbing his temples, trying to convince himself this wasn't real. "What's your pleasure, York old boy?"

York looked at Paris. "What?"

"What do you want to drink?"

"Drink?"

"Anything you want," Frank growled with an angry edge to his voice. "They've got just about anything you could imagine."

"Booze?" York asked.

Maggie nodded. "They've got real whiskey, not just 'trate. Apparently Fleet was outfitting this ship for some big shot admiral, and he had it stocked with only the best, though it'll cost you an arm and a leg."

York shook his head, thought maybe he should stop doing that. He looked around. "Where'd this all come from?"

Paris shrugged. "The first thing Sierka did was get a damage control crew organized, then he put them to work remodeling this place so Her Majesty could have a decent place to dine."

"Damage control?" York asked. "What about the damage in Engineering?"

Frank looked up from his drink. "What damage in Engineering?"

York couldn't believe his ears. "We almost lost a power chamber, damaged feed channel, melted through one deck and nearly another. Had to shut it down to repair it. Contamination everywhere. We worked for almost two days straight, no rest, were told we couldn't get any help because everyone else was too busy. We assumed there was damage elsewhere."

Paris slapped him on the back. "We were busy, York, but it's a matter of priorities, like this dining salon, not something as insignificant as our power plant."

"Where the hell is Berkma?" York demanded. "She and Telyekev are old friends. And he was dumping Sierka on her. He wouldn't do that without telling her what kind of idiot he is."

Paris' smile disappeared. "Berkma's dead. She was in that shuttle that crashed during the evacuation, brains splattered all over the passenger compartment."

Paris' smile suddenly returned. "Well, Sierka's got his priorities, but right now my priority is another drink. I'm buying. What do you want?"

York looked at the bottles stacked behind the bar, thought to himself they should be secured. "I just want something to eat."

Paris asked, "How long is the wait now?"

York wanted someone to tell him he was dreaming. "Three hours."

Frank sipped at his drink. "It's going up. It was two when we got here."

"Come on," Maggie said. "Let's just go down to main mess. We can eat there."

Frank shook his head deliberately. "I'll be damned if I'm going to let them kick me out of my own mess. I'm waiting right here until I get a table, and then I'm going to eat, and I'm going to enjoy it."

"Bartender," Paris called.

The bartender turned away from a conversation with a young woman, walked the length of the bar and stopped in front of them. "What'll you have?"

Maggie, Paris and Frank placed their orders, then they looked at York, and suddenly it was all too much for him. "Do you have 'trate?" he asked.

The bartender shrugged. "I'm not sure. I'll have to see."

York leaned forward, grabbed him by the collar, pulled him half way over the bar and growled in his face, "Then go see right now. And make damn sure you find some, and put it in front of me, undiluted with a pitcher of water and an empty glass next to it."

The bartender nodded. York let go of him and he stood up, straightened his tunic and began rummaging beneath the bar. After a rather extensive search he produced a bottle of undiluted 'trate. It wasn't large, but there was enough there to get a dozen grown men very drunk. York poured some into the empty glass, then diluted it with water, only enough to be sure it wasn't lethal.

Maggie touched his sleeve. "Should you do that?"

York looked at her. "No. I shouldn't." Then he tossed the drink down.

••••

York came to slowly, just opened his eyes and lay in his bunk for a long time without moving, waiting for his hangover to go away so he could get up and get another drink. He and Frank and Maggie and Paris never did get that dinner. They'd waited more than six hours, with their reservations constantly pushed back, slowly drinking themselves into a stupor, until the usually cautious Frank was ready to start a fight. Maggie and York talked him out of it, dragged him back to his cabin and put him in his bunk. Then York staggered back to the marine barracks, pilfered an issue of emergency rations, sat down at a poker game and forced the rations down with more 'trate.

He didn't remember much of the poker game, though he had a vague recollection the marines had merely continued the party started in The Drop Zone. Even Salley was there. Being ex-marine, she'd understood right away the kind of attack coming down on Dumark, and she'd figured her best chances were off planet.

He rolled over, realized someone was lying next to him, though it took some effort to recall the pretty, young buck private, one of Yagell's people from the *Nostran*. He was on the high side of the gravity bunk, so he had to crawl over her to get out. He was clumsy about it, and she opened her eyes groggily while he straddled her. "Again?" she asked. "I'm too tired. Let me go back to sleep."

He didn't try to correct her.

He fell clumsily out of the gravity bunk, landed on his ass on the deck, threw up all over himself. Vomiting didn't make him feel any better. He needed something to eat.

He pulled on some pants, staggered out of his cabin, and what he found brought him up short. The place was a mess, the deck littered with spilled drinks, soggy cards, unconscious marines. The only movement in the entire barracks was the kid, Stacy, cleaning up something. He looked at York, a question on his face.

York walked unsteadily through the debris. He'd never seen such rotten discipline before. How could Sierka have let them come to this? What kind of commanding officer was he?

"Eh, Cap'm."

The voice startled York and he spun toward it, found corporal Elkiss lying in a corner trying to pour herself another drink. "Thanks fer the party, Cap'm," she said. "Ya know. Yer the best damn CO I ever had. A fuckin' good marine."

York stared at her, and wondered how he could have let them come to this, and what kind of a commanding officer he was. Elkiss held up her drink. "Join me, Cap'm."

York's head started to pound and he found it difficult to breathe. The distance between them was only a few paces, but it took forever to cross it, and when he got there his hand reached out of its own accord, swung out in a roundhouse arc and knocked the glass from her hand. It clattered across the room, making an awful racket and spilling 'trate over the deck. He leaned over and screamed in her face, "Get off your ass. Get off your fuckin' ass right now and stand at attention. That's an order."

Elkiss stumbled over herself trying to get up, and he kicked her once in the ass for her clumsiness. While she was trying to straighten up he caught movement out of the corner of his eye: another half-conscious marine sprawled on the deck, groggily demanding, "Wass all the racket?"

York jumped on the poor man, grabbed him by his tunic, lifted him to his feet, slammed him against a bulkhead and screamed into his face, "Attention, you idiot. That's what all the racket's about. I'm giving you a fucking order."

The marine turned several shades of green, but managed to stay on his feet, locked his knees to hold himself up. Next to him lay an unconscious marine, so York slapped and kicked him until he crawled to his feet. By that time there were a dozen of them awake, looking at him queerly. "I want everyone awake," he shouted at them. "On their feet and standing at attention."

They all hesitated for a moment. "That's an order," he screamed. "On the double."

That, they understood. They didn't move fast but they moved, and they got the job done. They woke up a dozen more, put them to work waking up more, and in that way it snowballed. At one point the pretty, young marine who'd been sharing York's bunk appeared in the hatchway to his cabin, wrapped in a blanket. He grabbed her by the arm, spun her violently toward a group of marines. She lost the blanket and he made her stand there at attention naked. She wasn't the only one.

York finally blew himself out, exhausted himself screaming and shouting and kicking until they were all conscious, standing at attention and distributed randomly throughout the barracks, most of them swaying a bit unsteadily. At some point Palevi had appeared from his cabin and gone about calmly helping York wake everyone up. And then, with all the marines standing at attention, the sergeant had thrown his own shoulders back and stood rigidly, and straight, and unwavering, though he didn't look to be in any better shape than the rest of them.

An eerie silence descended on the place, and for a long moment York didn't know what to do next. He was about to shout something else when he remembered the CO never shouted. If there was shouting to be done, he had NCO's for that. He looked at Palevi and spoke calmly, "Sergeant. I want this place cleaned up. And I want these people cleaned up. Full inspection in two hours. And post guards at the corridor."

Palevi smiled, not a sneer, nor his usual knowing look, but perhaps, this time, approval.

It took them three hours, not two. They were all too hungover to work efficiently, and it took everything they had to get the job done, but get it done they did. York helped—it wouldn't do for him to disappear into his cabin while the rest of them were suffering under his orders, especially since it was his own lack of discipline that had allowed them to get in such shape in the first place.

They really weren't ready when he started the inspection, but he went through the motions anyway, walked through it without actually inspecting anything closely, then he pulled Palevi into his office and shut the door. "Let them get some rest," he said tiredly. "Then go through it more carefully when I'm not around, make sure it's cleaned up so it'll pass a real inspection next time."

"Yes, sir. Will there be anything else, sir?"

York nodded. "Yes. I don't know who's got the 'trate still, and I don't care. Just see to it production's kept to an appropriate level from now on, with consumption limited to the right amount, the right time, and the right place."

Palevi grinned. "Yes, sir."

"Dismissed."

Palevi saluted, turned and stepped through the door. York went into the adjoining cabin, yanked off his uniform, collapsed into his bunk and was asleep in seconds.

13

Mistakes

ROCHEFORT CONSIDERED THE opening ceremony for the new senate a dreary exercise in tedium. It could have just as easily been handled by unlocking the damn doors and opening the place up. He thanked the gods of space he didn't have to be a part of it himself, could stand high in the galleries above and observe, while poor Edvard and Abraxa and Bortha sweated under the lights.

"Fascinating, isn't it?"

Rochefort looked back over his shoulder and nodded politely. "Canon Lynna." He turned, uncomfortable at having the little sneak at his back.

"Admiral," Lynna said politely, stepping forward so they could both look down at the senate floor. Rochefort felt better now that he could keep an eye on the fellow. "We're so dependent on our little ceremonies and traditions."

Rochefort nodded, keeping his eyes forward. "That we are."

"Why," Lynna continued, "I sometimes wonder if even this war of ours is merely a tradition. In a sense, a grand ceremony."

"I'd never thought of you as a philosopher."

Lynna laughed quietly. "No, my dear Admiral, I fear no one will ever think that of me. I'm much too practical. You'd be surprised how pragmatic I can be."

Now what did he mean by that? Rochefort wondered. *Some sort of hint?* "Don't say that too loudly, Canon. In your profession I would think a considerable amount of philosophy and doctrine, spiced with a bit of mysticism, was an absolute prerequisite."

"Well now, Admiral, as in many things in life there are certain requisite appearances that must be maintained. But even the church must be administered with a healthy dose of reality, and a careful eye on the practicalities of the temporal world."

Rochefort smiled. "And as Bortha's Chief of Security and primary source of intelligence it's your job to maintain that careful eye, eh?"

"Now, Admiral! Surely you've mistaken me for someone else. I am merely one of Archcanon Bortha's advisors." Lynna turned his face to Rochefort and pointedly grinned, and there was some sort of message there. "But that doesn't mean my loyalties are purely reserved for the Archcanon. That would be demagoguery. No, Admiral, my loyalties are devoted to a higher service."

Again that grin, and Rochefort thought, *Ya. Yourself.*

Lynna continued. "As any devout citizen should, I feel it my duty to serve the church and the crown."

That was an invitation for double-dealing if he'd ever heard one. And perhaps he could make use of this snake, even if doing so left him feeling soiled. Rochefort turned to Lynna. "Come, Canon Lynna. Join me for a small drink. It might be interesting to continue this discussion where we're less likely to be interrupted."

Lynna smiled, and they both turned and left the senate gallery.

••••

The intercom chimed. York looked up from the papers on his desk, touched his intercom screen and it came to life with Corporal Elkiss' image. "Yes?"

"Cap'm. Guard post at the corridor reports there's a churchman named Thring wants to see you. He's with a fellow named Harshaw."

York had been avoiding Thring all day. But what was Harshaw doing with him? "They're here?" York asked. "Physically standing in the corridor, waiting?"

"Yes, sir."

"Ok, let them in."

"The usual security procedures, sir?"

"Of course. Full security scans, but don't rough them up, eh?"

"As you wish, sir."

York stood, crossed his office and opened the door in time to see them crossing the ready-room. Oddly enough, Thring wore simple pants and shirt, rather than the usual flowing robes of a churchman, and he was gawking at the activity about them: marines cleaning their armor and equipment, a discipline detail polishing bright-work.

"Mister Harshaw," York said. "Canticle Thring. Come in. Sit down."

The two men seemed a bit surprised that he was congenial. "Thank you, Cap'm Ballin," Thring said. He and Harshaw sat down in the two chairs in front of York's desk, real chairs that didn't fold out of a bulkhead.

York sat behind his desk and spoke to Thring. "Not many civilians know enough to call me *cap'm*."

Thring smiled. "I try, Mr. Ballin."

Harshaw leaned forward. "It's often the little things that count most, the small symbolic gestures. Take you, for instance, Cap'm, wearing that old, patched and faded uniform when you could easily have a crisp, new one from ship's stores." York glanced down at one of his sleeves. He'd refused to wear the new uniforms once he'd started instituting discipline among his people. "I noticed your marines are imitating you. It separates you from the rest of the ship."

The intercom chimed again, Lieutenant Simurka. "Cap'm. You said you wanted to review the stock list when we got done inventorying spare parts."

"Thank you, Lieutenant. Have Palevi and Yagell join us—about a quarter of an hour from now—Sergeant Palevi's office."

"Very good, sir."

York cut the circuit, looked at the two men. Harshaw said, "You're obviously busy, so let me get to the point. Canticle Thring and I heard you believe we are being followed by a feddie warship."

York frowned. Once he'd sobered up the first thing he'd done was pull up copies of the scan reports from the time they'd left Dumark's atmosphere to about a half hour after they'd made transition out of the Dumarkan system. He'd spent a day going through the data, processing the information again and again to pull a faint trace out of a mess of noise. And he was certain he'd found the exact moment when each of four ships had made transition behind them. Comparing that with the much clearer data gathered before up-transition, he was confident he'd identified the second, third and fourth ships following them: a cruiser and two destroyers, all feddies. The first ship, however, had not appeared on the sublight reports, and, by all measures, shouldn't exist. That ship, he knew, was a hunter-killer.

Sierka wouldn't take any of his calls, so he'd shown the data to Maggie, though he'd had a difficult time convincing even her. But she decided to trust his judgment, had gone to Sierka with the data, and he'd blown his stack, refused to listen to anything.

But Maggie wasn't foolish enough to discuss such a matter with civilians. "May I ask," York said, "how you heard about this?"

Thring frowned. "Commander Soladin mentioned it at lunch yesterday."

"At lunch?" York asked.

Thring nodded. "It's public information, isn't it? Or rather, whether or not it was meant to be public, it is now."

York nodded. "In any case, without Commander Sierka's permission I'm not at liberty to discuss such a matter."

Thring's frown deepened, but Harshaw nodded. "Then it's true. I'm sorry, Cap'm, but anything short of denial is confirmation of the rumor. It also confirms my suspicion that young Soladin is a bit indiscreet." Harshaw stood. "We'll let you get back to your work."

Thring stood, but as they both left Harshaw said one last thing in an almost confidential whisper. "Be careful, Lieutenant."

The meeting with Simorka, Palevi, and Yagell lasted more than three hours, would have gone on even longer had they not been interrupted. "There's a Lady d'Hart and a Senator Andow here to see you, Cap'm."

York looked at Elkiss image on his console. "I'll be right there. And tell everyone to look sharp." York started to turn away from the screen, but he hesitated and turned back. "Oh yes, the usual security procedures, but don't let them know you're scanning them."

York met Andow and Lady d'Hart at the entrance to the barracks. He bowed carefully to the woman, then to Andow. "Your Ladyship. Senator Andow. To what do we owe this pleasure?"

Lady d'Hart smiled. "I've never seen a marine barracks before, thought if you had the time, you might show me around."

Andow added, "And I'm tagging along."

"Of course, I have the time," York said, though he didn't believe her explanation for a minute.

York showed them the armory, where a team of marines had three suits of armor broken down for maintenance. The marines started to jump to attention when York came into the room, but he barked, "As you were," and they returned to their chores.

Andow looked closely at one of the stripped down suits of armor. "This is new, isn't it?"

York nodded. "Yes. We found about three hundred new suits in ship's stores."

"But if they're new," Lady d'Hart asked, "why are you repairing them?"

"We're not repairing them. We're checking them out, making sure they work properly."

"But if they're new, you shouldn't have to do that either."

"If there's anything wrong with one of those suits, one of us dies. So we run each suit through an extensive checkout, then fit it to the marine that's going to wear it. And if that marine's smart, he'll then take the suit aside and run it through a complete checkout himself."

They moved on to ordnance supplies, where another group of marines had one of the heavy rotaries torn apart. "We test fired this weapon yesterday," York told his two guests. "It malfunctioned, so we're trying to find the cause."

Andow nodded. "You're being rather thorough, I see."

"Yes," Lady d'Hart said. "One would think half the Directorate was following us."

York looked at her closely, decided not to take the bait. He showed them through the barracks, then took them up one deck to Hangar Deck. They stopped in each of the service bays where York had crews checking out *Cinesstar*'s three gunboats. They were watching a crew working on *Three* when York's implants spoke. "Cap'm. This is Hyer in Hangar Deck control. I got Commander Sierka, and he ain't real happy. Wants to talk to you."

York keyed his implants. "Tell him I'll be right there."

York excused himself, left his guests in the gunboat bay, stepped into Hangar Deck Control, noticed that Hyer and a few marines were manning the stations there, that evidently no proper crew had been assigned to that duty. Hyer pointed to a screen. "There, sir."

York stepped up to the screen, activated it, and Sierka's face appeared. He immediately tore into York. "What's this I hear, Lieutenant? You're spreading rumors about feddie warships following us."

York shook his head. "No, sir. I've spoken to no one but Miss Votak about it, and that was strictly in an official capacity—"

"Then she's spreading the rumors, eh?"

"No, sir. I don't believe—"

"Don't argue with me, Lieutenant. I won't have you spreading false rumors and blaming other people for it."

"But they're not false, sir. There are four feddie warships following close behind us: a hunter-killer, a cruiser, and two destroyers. I was able to isolate their transitions in our scan reports from—"

"I've seen your data, Lieutenant, and it's a lot of meaningless, random scratchings on a screen. I won't have you needlessly exciting the crew and our passengers with your false conjecture. There are no Syndonese warships following us. Do you understand?"

York swallowed hard, decided to cut his losses. "Yes, sir."

"Good. Report to my office immediately. We're going to talk further about this."

"Yes—" York started to speak, but Sierka cut the circuit before he could finish.

York leaned forward on the now blank console and tried to compose himself. He turned about, found Andow and Lady d'Hart standing behind him. They and the marines had heard every word.

"You'll have to excuse me again," he said to his two guests. "I've been ordered to report immediately to the captain, and I mustn't delay. Corporal Hyer here will show you back to your cabins."

Lady d'Hart frowned. "So we're being followed by enemy ships?"

York shook his head. "You heard the captain. There are no Syndonese warships following us."

Andow's eyes narrowed. "But you disagree with him?"

Again York shook his head. "No, Senator. Commander Sierka has made it quite clear I was wrong."

Andow persisted. "But what if he's wrong?"

"Commander Sierka is the captain of this ship, and so by definition he's right, and if I disagree with him, then I'm wrong."

Andow considered him for a long moment. "Very well, then let's speak hypothetically. If there were four hypothetical enemy warships following us, and you knew where they were, could you target on them and eliminate them as a danger?"

York glanced at the marines in the control room, then lowered his voice carefully. "But I wouldn't know where they were. I would know where they had been at the moment they made transition behind us several days ago. I would also know that in transition they're as blind as we are, and neither of us can pinpoint the other with any accuracy."

"Why don't we just take a chance?" Sylissa d'Hart asked. "Fire on them, and perhaps get lucky?"

York shook his head. "Because it's highly unlikely we'd hit them. But in firing one of our transition batteries, we'd give them enough of a signal to target on us quite nicely."

Andow nodded. "I see. Stalemate. As long as we both do nothing, we're safe. But the first to make a move gives the other a significant advantage."

"You're only half right," York said. "Remember, anyone in sublight can spot our transition wake for a couple of light-years, if they're looking in the right direction. We're probably safe right now because we're in a region of space we've been fighting over for a long time, so we long ago blew the hell out of any permanent installations in the area, and no one wants to just sit around here in sublight unless they have to. But we're headed straight for the Directorate. Someone could spot us, take a few shots at us, and even if they miss, if we have to do anything to defend ourselves, we're going to become a very visible target. All hypothetically speaking, of course."

Andow nodded. "Of course."

York looked at his watch. "Now if you'll excuse me, I'm keeping the captain waiting."

They let him go without further delay and he headed straight for the lift. He was still not authorized to vocally program the lift, so he had to do so manually. Sierka was waiting for him with Soladin and Armbruster, and he'd managed to work himself up into a frenzy. York stood at attention in front of his desk for more than an hour while Sierka shouted at him, berated him, questioned his competence, his ethics, and his moral character. It took him that long to blow himself out, then he dismissed York with orders not to show himself above Hangar Deck again. "But, sir," York asked. "May I at least eat?"

"All right," Sierka growled. "You can go to the main mess for meals. But that's it. I don't want to see your face again."

On the way back, York programmed the lift incorrectly, accidentally stepped out on the crew deck, immediately noticed the locker room smell of stale sweat and realized his mistake. But the smell gave him pause, and he investigated further. A short distance down the corridor something had been spilled on the deck, then allowed to dry into a sticky stain. It looked as if it had been there for some days. He found several crewmembers lounging around one of the bunkrooms. They looked at him with obvious distrust when he asked, "Who's in charge here?"

They all frowned, looked back and forth at each other for a moment, then one fellow with chief's stripes on his sleeve shrugged and said, "Guess I am."

"What do you mean you guess? What's your duty assignment?"

The chief shrugged again. "I got no duty assignment." He looked at the rest. "Anyone here got a duty assignment?"

They all shook their heads.

Out of curiosity York took a walk through G-deck. They'd rescued about a hundred and fifty civilians from Dumark. Those without rank or station or wealth or power were barracked on G-deck, and like the spacers, were waiting for someone to take charge. Again, he noticed an unwashed smell to the place, and anyone he encountered viewed him with obvious suspicion.

He checked several more decks, found a lot of unmanned stations and no order.

••••

York looked up from his tray of food at Maggie and Frank who sat opposite him in the crew mess. They'd hunted him down there, and Frank had carefully posed an unsettling question. If he'd asked it in a slightly different way, it could be construed as *conspiracy to commit mutiny*, so York chose his reply just as carefully. "I can take no action on the crew deck, nor any concerning the civilians, without direct orders from Sierka. I recommend you discreetly take a census of those on board, then draw up a duty roster and give it to Armbruster or Soladin as a recommendation. But don't mention my name; they'll just pucker up—especially Sierka if he thinks it came from me."

York had intentionally chosen a seat with his back against a bulkhead facing the entrance, saw Daka Nemkov and Sylissa d'Hart step into the mess hall. Maggie was saying something, but York's attention focused wholly on the new arrivals as they paused and scanned the tables quickly. Nemkov's eyes locked on York, he said something to Lady d'Hart, and they both started toward him. Maggie and Frank were unaware of the newcomers closing in behind them, so York interrupted Maggie by standing suddenly. He bowed and said, "Lady d'Hart. Lieutenant Nemkov."

Maggie and Frank started to stand. "Please," Lady d'Hart said. "Don't stand. Continue with your meal."

They stood anyway and Maggie did a nice job of shifting gears. "Will you join us?" she asked.

Lady d'Hart smiled and said, "Yes, I'd like that." She sat down next to Maggie, and Nemkov sat down next to her, all four of them lined up opposite York.

"Actually," Lady d'Hart said, looking at York. "This isn't a coincidence. I asked Daka to help me find you." She looked at Maggie and Frank. "And I'm glad you two are here also. I wanted to ask you about the enemy ships following us."

Nemkov frowned. "There aren't any enemy ships following us."

"But Lieutenant Ballin maintains there are four Syndonese warships in transition behind us."

Maggie and Frank had suffered one of Sierka's tongue-lashings on that subject and looked at York uncomfortably, so York said, "I maintain no such thing. For me to do so would be in direct violation of Commander Sierka's orders."

"Surely you can disagree with him on a matter of opinion."

York shook his head. "On this subject he has given specific orders."

"Can't you even discuss them as a hypothetical premise?"

"Again, under the circumstances, such a pretext would be a violation of my commanding officer's orders."

Nemkov looked at her carefully. "He's right, Syl."

She didn't like being thwarted. "Then let's forget the Syndonese following us and talk about what we might do to get out of this."

York went back to eating as the four of them began playing with a number of ideas. York stayed out of it, determined not to be drawn into the discussion. But suddenly, at the edge of his senses, he detected the shift in the ship's fields indicative of the start of a hard maneuver. He reached out violently, grabbed Nemkov by his tunic and yanked him viciously across the table, dragging him through the food until their faces were only inches apart. His actions stunned everyone into silence. "We're maneuvering," he growled in Nemkov's face, "aren't we?"

Nemkov looked at him as if he were a madman. "Yes," he said coldly. "We do have a course change scheduled for some time this watch."

York shouted. "Don't you realize you're handing them a target signature?"

Nemkov started to say something, but before he could speak York pushed him back into his seat. Sierka had had him programmed out of the command channels so he couldn't reach the bridge with his implants. He shoved Nemkov aside into the d'Hart woman's lap, climbed up over the table scraping food out of the way with his elbows, landed on the other side and dove for a small intercom buried in the bulkhead near the entrance. He hit the intercom switch with his fist, "Bridge, emergency access."

The computer connected him instantly. "Bridge. Rame here."

"Shields up. General Quarters. Stand by for incoming."

"Incoming?" Rame asked. "Where the—"

"Don't ask questions," York snarled, praying Rame's reactions would take over, that he'd react before realizing he wasn't supposed to be taking orders from York. "That's an order."

The alert klaxon started to blare. York opened his mouth to shout another order, but the ship's superstructure echoed with the deep bass sound of a large warhead detonating nearby, and her gravity shifted sickeningly. The bulkhead containing the intercom became down, and a crushing force of several gravities slammed York into it. *Cinesstar*'s hull groaned and a rain of trays and food and dishes and human bodies slammed into the bulkhead all around him. Then another gravity wave pulsed through the ship and everyone and everything tumbled toward the deck overhead. A brief shock of pain shot through York's shoulder as he took most of the force of his upward fall on one side, then someone landed on top of him and knocked the wind out of him.

For a few moments he came close to losing consciousness, and it was some seconds before he was again fully alert, floating weightless amidst a confusion of bodies and debris, no gravity and dim emergency lighting, everything silent except for a few painful groans coming from somewhere. A sickening terror rose up in his chest as he realized the deep background sound of *Cinesstar*'s power plant had been silenced. Other than the groans he could hear, he had no way of knowing if anyone was still alive, and in any case, their lives were low on his priority list.

The debris and bodies floating in the mess hall, including him, were drifting slowly in random directions. He waited patiently for the few seconds it took to drift to a bulkhead, then grabbed a handhold, and ignoring the pain in his damaged shoulder he crawled from handhold to handhold to another intercom. He hit the switch. "Bridge. Emergency access. Ballin here."

No answer. "Bridge. This is Ballin. Is anyone there conscious? Answer me."

After a few seconds Anda Gant finally responded groggily. "Yes . . . Yes . . . I'm here."

"Who else up there is conscious?"

Another pause, then a slow, deliberate answer. "I don't know . . . Everyone I can see is out . . . don't know for sure."

"What's our status?"

There was silence for a few seconds and he prayed she hadn't passed out again. "All three chambers are down; no report on why. We're limited to emergency standby. No gravity, no shields, no weapons. We're sublight, coasting at just under point-nine lights. Dilation factor two-point-one. Near scan report is null to within one-point-three kilometers."

York asked, "Drones?"

There was a short pause, and again groans from nearby wounded punctuated the silence.

"I've got active status on three. Should I contact Hangar to check on the others?"

"No. Launch the three to twenty thousand klicks. Then get over to the weapons console and launch a mixed load of cluster and seeker mines. We don't need power for that. Concentrate them in our wake in a spread about three hundred kilometers wide. Dump half, wait ten minutes, then dump the other half. I'll check with Hangar, then get up to Bridge as soon as I can. In the meantime rig for silent running."

"Rig for what? That's a hunter-killer trick, isn't it?"

"Ya, but we can try it too. Shut down anything that might produce a detectable transition signal. Even critical systems if necessary. Stop feeding the drones power, run them static, and use only passive detection.

"We've got at least four feddies coming in behind us. Watch for their transition flares, record them, track them, and pinpoint them as accurately as you can. And especially watch for the first. It'll probably come sometime in the next five to ten minutes, and it'll be faint, almost undetectable. And if it doesn't come right away, then keep a close scan behind any other activity. There's a hunter-killer out there, and she'll likely try to use another transition flare or an exploding warhead to mask her own down-transition."

York cut the circuit, looked over his shoulder, saw Maggie hanging onto a handhold on a far bulkhead, shaking her head groggily, a smear of blood on her forehead. Nemkov was on another handhold nearby, looking alert and anxiously scanning the debris floating about. "Nemkov," York called, trying to keep his voice calm. "What are you doing?"

Nemkov called back with panic in his voice. "Where's Lady d'Hart?"

"Forget her," York said. "You've got more important things to worry about. Get down to Hangar and take command down there. We need drones."

Nemkov looked at him curiously for a moment, but York said calmly, "That's an order, Lieutenant."

Still Nemkov hesitated, but then he came to a decision and nodded. "Aye, aye, sir." He started crawling along the handholds toward the mess hall exit.

York hit the intercom switch again. "Ready-room. Emergency access."

"Palevi here, Cap'm."

"Sergeant, how many wounded?"

"I don't know about the rest of the ship, sir, but down here we got forty-two need patching up. Seven dead. I think we were lucky."

"Probably luckier than the rest of the ship. Take all your actives and comb the ship from stem to stern, help wounded get down to sickbay. Start with the bridge. Also look for damage and note it for damage control, if we have damage control. And have you got anyone who knows how to arm warheads, and how to operate a transition launcher?"

"I sure do, sir."

"Can you put together two crews?"

"No problem, sir."

"Good. Check the fore and aft launch rooms. If they don't have crews, and I doubt they will, make sure they're manned as soon as possible."

"Aye, aye, sir. Anything else, sir?"

"No. Ballin out."

York cut the circuit, crawled over to Maggie who was still sitting in a daze. He reached into a pocket, pulled out a disposable palm syringe he always carried, a small, gray, flat disk that easily fit in his hand. He pulled a little, red tab at its edge, tossed the tab into the rest of the debris floating about them. The disk changed color, flashed a bright red. He cupped it in the palm of his hand, grabbed Maggie by the upper arm with his other hand, then slapped the disk against the side of her throat. The disk pulsed once beneath his hand, and a second later Maggie shivered as the kikker took effect. Her eyes widened for a moment, then grew alert. "Shit," she swore, shaking herself violently. "I hate that stuff."

He shook her, said, "Listen up. All three power plants are down. We're sublight with four feddies coming at us real soon now."

He reached into his pocket, pulled out another palm syringe, handed it to her. "I need qualified officers. Now. See if you can find Frank. If you can bring him around fast, do so. If you can't, leave him. Either way, report to the bridge."

York found another intercom and hit the switch. "Engineering. Emergency access. Ballin here."

The answer came quickly. "Cappik here, Mister Ballin. Miss Gant says you're in command."

That was open to dispute, but York decided not to enlighten Cappik. "Status."

"We took a near miss, medium-size warhead, maybe twenty megatonnes. We were lucky it wasn't a direct hit, and someone got our shields up just before detonation. But it was close enough to overload all three chambers. Starboard went down first, of course, what with all that damage. But it pulled the other two down with it, might have damaged one of them also, though I don't know yet. Shouldn't have done that, but there's a bug in the programming somewhere we would've found if we'd had a chance to do a proper shakedown. Right now Starboard is the only one that's hot, and it's just barely at idle. Port and Centerline are in cold shutdown."

"How soon before we've got power?"

"Fifty minutes. Maybe an hour."

York glanced at his watch, did a quick mental calculation, then spoke carefully. "In about five minutes, maybe ten or fifteen, the feddie hunter-killer that just tried to burn us is going to make transition in our wake. She'll be the first of at least four Syndonese Federals strung out behind us, maybe more. We're too big for her to take on unless she's sure we're disabled, so my guess is she'll move cautiously, transit at extreme range in case we've still got teeth, sit back and let one of her buddies come at us first. That'll happen no sooner than fifteen minutes from now, no later than twenty-five. Do you understand?"

"Yes, sir. I do. Can you stand by for a moment?"

"Yes."

There was a short pause, then, "Sir. We'll have one chamber at half power in ten minutes, enough to grav up and do some maneuvering, make them think twice before coming at us. But it's that damaged chamber, so please don't put too much of a strain on her or we'll lose her. I'm going to use her to bootstrap the other two. Then I think I can have full combat status in a total of twenty minutes. I might be able to do better, but we're likely to blow ourselves to hell and back without the help of any feddies. Is that good enough, sir?"

"Thank you, Chief. That'll be just fine. I'm going to the bridge. Ballin out."

••••

Without gravity, it seemed that floating bodies and debris of one kind or another filled every compartment in the ship, and they all conspired to hinder York. He couldn't just push off one wall and launch across a room. Instead, he had to stay with the handholds on the bulkheads, pulling himself along at an agonizingly slow pace. He tried the main lift first, but it was down, so he made his way to the nearest maintenance access shaft, a narrow tunnel running parallel to the main lift that was always kept weightless. There were metal rungs on three sides of the shaft.

It seemed to take forever to crawl half the length of the ship, but he finally opened the shaft hatch on the bridge, floated out behind the fire control console. For some reason the thought came to him that if he ever needed to, he could probably use the shaft to sneak onto the bridge unnoticed.

Floating, he pulled himself around the console in time to see a small group of marines carrying away Rame and Sierka, both unconscious. York pushed himself through the weightless atmosphere, caught an edge of the captain's console, struggled into it and strapped himself in. Anda Gant peered through a narrow gap between instrument clusters, looked at him with relief as he yanked on a headset. "Status?"

"No sign of that hunter-killer," Gant said, "though I've got two transition wakes closing on us fast. We've got limited power, but I assume you want to keep running silent so I haven't done anything yet. We're awfully close to our own minefields. Should I pull away?"

"Negative," York said as he brought up a scan summary, looked it over quickly. Neither of the two transition wakes were the hunter-killer. Next he brought up a duty roster. Sierka and Soladin and Armbruster hadn't bothered to assign crews to most of the critical combat stations, but they had at least assigned bridge crews, and at that moment Jondee should be at the com. "Mister Jondee. Are you conscious?"

"Well now," Jondee's voice said in York's headset, "there are those who might dispute that fact, but I've always thought of myself as basically cognizant, and don't believe what you hear about my moral character."

"Shut up." York was in no mood for repartee. "And check on the fore and aft launch rooms, see if Palevi has crews there yet."

York glanced up from his screens and saw Andow floating over him. The senator's hair was a mess and his tunic badly torn, but he seemed unhurt. York pointed at one of the assistant's couches at the weapon's console. "Sit there," he said. "And strap yourself in. If we have any more gravity problems you'll be a lot better off."

Andow obeyed without question.

"And keep your hands off that console," York growled. "Don't touch anything."

"Sir, the aft launch room is manned, but Palevi's crew is having trouble getting forward."

"Lieutenant Commander McGeahn reporting for duty, sir."

York looked up and found the young woman he'd met at the embassy on Dumark. All he could think was that she had no combat experience. At least she was smart enough not to take command. He nodded at her. "Assist Miss Gant at the Scan Console."

Maggie and Frank showed up before McGeahn had herself strapped in. York gave Maggie the helm. Frank had a smear of blood on one cheek, and he looked groggy, but he had no one in any better shape, so he gave him fire control.

He made a quick call down to Alsa Yan in sickbay. "I need a med tech up here fast," he pleaded. "I've got wounded."

Yan shook her head. "Sorry, York, I've got wounded coming out my ears. Can't spare anyone until—"

"God damn it, Alsa!" York growled. "My wounded are sitting at critical combat stations, and we've got Federals closing on us."

Yan hesitated for a moment, then nodded. "What do you need?"

"Send me someone with stimulants: phets, ag-hypes, kikkers; I don't care what."

"Transition flare, sir," Gant shouted. "Dead astern. Range one hundred million kilometers and closing at point-eight lights."

McGeahn spoke, panic in her voice. "He's coming after us, sir. He can start targeting on us any moment now."

York needed McGeahn to remain calm. "Steady as she goes. He can't target on us if he can't see us. Everyone keep a close eye on our systems. I don't want anything to show on his screens. Miss Gant, any sign of that hunter-killer?"

"Nothing, sir."

York glanced at his Engineering summary. Cappik had one more chamber lit, though he was holding it barely above shutdown. McGeahn's nerves were ready to blow. York could feel it, and that meant everyone else could too. She needed something to do, and York needed someone to run the figures on a transition plan. "Miss McGeahn. Move over to the navigation console and compute a transition at ninety degrees to our previous course."

"Sir," Gant said. "That feddie in sublight is closing fast. And that second transition wake is coming in too."

York barked out orders. "Miss Votak, stand by. Miss McGeahn, we're going to need that nav run. Mister Jondee, check her figures. Mister Stara, instruct all weapons stations to stand by."

York paused, forced his voice into a low, even, calm tone. "All right, everyone. It's party time."

14

Illusion

"CAPTAIN," DUCAN SOE said calmly. "We've got one of our own destroyers climbing up our ass."

Jewel Thaaline glanced at Tac'tac'ah, her most inexperienced officer. The young man had a bead of sweat running down his brow as he concentrated on holding the *Pride* an infinitesimal degree above transition. "Tac'tac'ah," Jewel said. "You're doing just fine. Steady as she goes."

"I don't like this," Soe said. "We're about to ram that cruiser in front of us, and that destroyer behind us is about to overtake us, and we'll all be right on top of that damn *imper* at the same time. Let's down-transit now, stay back and let the big boys have him."

Jewel shook her head. "Negative. A single transition flare, without anything to mask it! That *imper* will pinpoint us as sure as I'm sitting here."

"I don't think he's that smart," Soe argued. "Only a real amateur would have given us a clear target signature like that. We hurt him. We hurt him bad."

Jewel shrugged. "Maybe." She looked over her shoulder at Innay, asked, "Andro?"

Innay shrugged and shook his head. "That was no amateur who set that ship down on Dumark."

Jewel agreed. "Let's play it a little cautious."

Tac'tac'ah interrupted. "Captain, here comes that destroyer behind us."

Jewel glanced at her screens. The transition wake of one of their own destroyers was closing on them fast, and they in turn were closing fast on one of their own cruisers in sublight in front of them.

"Transition flare," Soe barked. "Dead ahead. No, correct that. That was a detonation—ten megatonnes, maybe more." He flinched. "There's another one, right on top of the first. No sign of any transition launch. That fucking *imper* scattered mines."

It all fell into place, and Jewel knew what to do. "Chief Innay. Stand by with a warhead. Something big. Be prepared to target on any signal we pick up from that *imper*. If you get anything, transition to sublight and fire in the same instant."

"Here comes that destroyer," Tac'tac'ah said. "Ten seconds . . . Nine . . . Eight . . ."

Jewel struggled to remain calm. "Steady as she goes, Tac'tac'ah."

"Seven . . . Six . . . Five . . ."

Soe pleaded, "You know we're driving right into a mine field!"

"Four . . . Three . . ."

Jewel kept talking. "Take it easy, Tac'tac'ah. Don't let that destroyer's wake knock us into sublight."

"Two . . . One . . ."

••••

York let McGeahn cheer. She was still too inexperienced to understand that one feddie slamming into a mine was only the beginning. And that medic had just made the rounds, popping them each in the shoulder with an injector. McGeahn, like all the rest of them, was just getting over the initial rush of whatever the medic had given them. Then she quickly realized the veterans around her weren't joining in and she shut up.

"Captain," Gant said, her voice a monotonous calm. "I've got a second and third wake at extreme range, too far to guess on their make or type. But the next one's coming in now. I'd say it's a destroyer. Looks like he spotted those detonations, probably guessed we've trailed a mine field, now he's gonna try to run it in transition."

York took a quick glance at his console to make sure there were no surprises. "Mister Stara, tell the aft launch room to arm two ten-megatonne warheads and stand by."

York opened the command channel to Engineering. "Mister Cappik. Stand by for full combat status. We'll need gravity and shields first."

Gant glanced his way, frowned, didn't understand what he was doing. Like all the rest, she'd forgotten about that hunter-killer out there. "Miss Gant. I want all your scan activity recorded at highest resolution.

"Miss Votak. Stand by at the helm. Have you got your course yet?"

"Yes, sir, I do. And I checked it myself."

"Ranging," Gant barked. "Three hundred million kilometers and closing fast."

York felt a familiar calm wash over him. Everything seemed clear, concise, obvious. He knew what was going to happen now.

"I'll take command now."

York looked over his shoulder, found Soladin floating in the weightless atmosphere just above him and to one side. York shook his head. "Shut up and strap yourself down somewhere."

"What?" Soladin demanded. "You can't—"

"Perra!" Andow barked angrily. The senator looked like a scared, little man. He waved to the seat next to him. "Just do as he says, Perra."

"Two hundred million kilometers . . ."

York forgot Soladin, scanned his screens one last time. "Are you targeting, Mister Stara?"

"Not too well, sir. He's still on the other side of the noise from those mine detonations."

York spoke carefully. "Mister Stara and Miss Gant. We'll fire one warhead at that destroyer on my command. When that warhead detonates, whether we hit the destroyer or not, watch closely for a transition launch that'll seem to come from empty space just behind the detonation. Target on it, and fire the second warhead immediately without waiting for my command. Is that clear?"

They both looked at him oddly, but acknowledged the orders.

"One hundred million kilometers . . ." Gant said, then her voice suddenly shifted, lost its calm. "Fifty . . . He's into the mine field . . . and . . . he's through it, clear and clean."

"I've got him, sir," Stara shouted.

Gant's voice was almost hysterical. "Forty million kilometers . . ."

York tried to speak calmly. "Let's show them our colors. Mister Jondee—gravity and shields. Miss Votak—all ahead full."

York settled into his couch as gravity was restored. Maggie firewalled the sublight drive and *Cinesstar*'s hull groaned. York glanced at his readouts; they were accelerating at a right angle to the feddie's course, at just under ten thousand gravities, a dismal crawl compared to the feddie bearing down on them in transition. And they were now easily visible to anyone in sublight.

York watched *Cinesstar*'s power demand climb as Maggie fed more energy to the sublight drive. The shields drew no power as long as they took no hits.

"Thirty million kilometers . . ."

"Mister Stara," York said. "Fire one."

Frank flinched for an instant, and *Cinesstar*'s hull thrummed. "One away, sir," he said. "Detonation in three seconds."

York tensed. "All power priority to the shields."

He'd barely finished speaking when Frank shouted, "Direct hit, sir . . . My god!"

"Mister Stara," York growled. "Watch your defensive stations."

Frank shut up, turned back to his console and stared at his screens . . .

The drive power suddenly dropped back to zero and they went weightless again as the computer diverted all power to the shields. *Cinesstar*'s hull screamed and the readouts on York's screens shot off scale. A gravity wave pulsed through the ship and everyone's hair stood on end as the internal fields reached maximum. Frank slapped a switch on his console, the hull thrummed again and he barked, "Two away, sir."

"Miss Votak," York snarled, having trouble sounding calm. "Get us the hell out of here. I want transition—soonest."

"Detonation," Frank shouted. "Though I don't know what the hell we hit."

Soladin shouted, "What in God's name was that?"

York looked his way, saw Andow also anxiously awaiting an explanation. He spoke slowly, one eye on his screens, "That was a warhead from that hunter-killer. She waited for us to fire at that destroyer, used the flare from our transition launch to get an accurate fix on us. Then she down-transited and fired her own warhead at us, using the detonation of our warhead to mask her actions. It almost worked."

York's headset suddenly filled with noise, Cappik shouting in the background. "Captain, this is Cappik. I've got trouble down here." York looked at his screens. The starboard chamber had redlined even with no drain on the shields. "Permission to shut down Starboard?"

"Permission granted. And I'll try to get you some help."

York put in a call to Palevi, told him to send Cappik anyone experienced in a contamination suit.

"Ballin!" The voice was Sierka's, raised in a high-pitched scream. "I told you never to come on this bridge again."

York glanced back over his shoulder, spotted Sierka stepping out of the lift. It would take Sierka a few precious seconds to step around the nav console, then slip between fire control and com. York glanced at his screens. There were three feddie transition wakes headed their way, but too far to matter for the moment, and the expanding fireballs from the two feddies they'd burned. Somewhere there was that hunter-killer, running silent, all but invisible. But for all she knew *Cinesstar* was fully operational, and a hunter-killer was no match for a heavy cruiser, so she wouldn't give away her position by trying another shot. Maggie was pushing *Cinesstar* with everything she had, would make transition shortly. And Cappik had that chamber out of redline.

"Ballin, get off my bridge."

With a minimum of movement York touched a switch on the captain's console, opened a private channel to Gant, whispered into his pickup, "Anda. Continue to record all exterior activity at highest resolution as long as possible. Please."

"Ballin, get out of that couch."

York lifted his hand off the console, cutting the circuit to Gant, looked at Sierka, who stood next to him in a torn tunic, one arm in a sling, a smear of dried blood on his cheek. York nodded, pulled the headset off carefully. "Aye, aye, sir."

Sierka pointed at the lift. "Get out of here."

York lifted himself carefully out of the couch. It felt odd that he wasn't angry or upset, but he realized he was maintaining a delicate balance, that if he allowed Sierka's hysteria one instant of control, he would probably turn on the man and kill him with his bare hands.

He turned toward the lift, turned his back on Sierka without acknowledging him, slipped between fire control and com, Paris and Frank staring at him. Then he stepped around the nav console, into the lift, closed the lift doors, and once again he could breathe.

••••

"He sucker punched us," Soe snarled. "The son-of-a-bitch sucker punched us. Can we get in one more shot?"

"Negative," Jewel snapped.

"He set us up," Soe argued. "He suckered us into giving away our position, and I'll bet we didn't even touch him."

Jewel looked at Innay.

Innay shook his head slowly. "It was a good shot. We hurt him."

"And he hurt us," Jewel said. "Get me a damage report."

She closed her eyes, tried to think. "One moment he makes an idiot move, gives us a clean shot. Then the next he's one step ahead of us. It's as if he were two different men."

She turned carefully to Soe. "Mister Soe. We will, of course, follow. Are we close enough to track him in transition?"

Soe shook his head. "I don't know. Maybe. We won't know until we're in transition ourselves."

Jewel nodded thoughtfully. "We're not done with him yet. Not if I can help it."

••••

The lift doors opened on an intermediate deck to pick up a young woman. York stepped aside as the woman walked into the lift.

"Lieutenant Ballin," the young woman said. There was something familiar about her, though he couldn't place her. She put her hands on her hips. "Why, Lieutenant! I do believe you don't remember me."

She stepped aggressively toward him, literally backed him against the back of the lift with her tits. He knew only one woman who used her tits that way. "Lady Dubye."

She pressed a thigh into his crotch, rubbed it carefully from side to side. "I can't believe you'd forget."

He shook his head. "I didn't forget, just didn't recognize. The makeup. It covered most of your face that evening."

She grinned evilly. "Well then you're forgiven, though I do remember you removed most of that makeup with your tongue."

She didn't let up with her thigh, and York couldn't deny it was having an effect.

"I'm bored," she said. "Why don't you join me in my cabin?"

He shook his head. "I can't. I'm on duty."

She could tell it was a lie and she grinned. "We're a good match, you and I."

He continued to shake his head. "I've got responsibility for damage control."

"Oh yes!" she said, frowning, but still grinning. "We were attacked, or something like that?"

He nodded. "Something like that."

She put the palm of her hand on his chest. "Are you sure you can't join me?"

He was tempted. "I'm sure. Perhaps another time."

She stepped away from him. "That's a shame."

••••

York spent the next eight hours coordinating the marines from the ready-room. He wanted to put on a vac suit and help out himself, but the ready-room functioned as an excellent command center, and from there he had far greater control over operations.

Cappik had the highest priority down in Engineering, but his needs were specific and limited. They had to comb the rest of the ship, clearing out debris and an occasional body, checking for damage that didn't show up on the computer. The gravity wave that pulsed through the ship when the warhead hit them had caused a great deal of minor damage. But as their cleanup operation wound to a close, York began to breathe easier, for with the exception of the starboard chamber, there were no other serious problems. Just a lot of injured, and quite a few dead.

"Cap'm?"

York looked up from the command console at Corporal Tathit, who sat at the marine communications console.

"Cap'm, Lieutenant Yan wants a word."

York put Alsa Yan on one of his screens. She wore a bloody surgical gown, and leaned wearily toward the pickup, obviously exhausted.

York asked, "It was bad, huh?"

She shrugged, shook her head tiredly. "No. Not really. Mostly minor injuries. Just a lot of them. We've been cutting for ten hours straight." She closed her eyes and ran her fingers through her hair. "Listen, I've got something funny up here I'd like you to take a look at. It's important."

Yan was not someone to get overly excited about something trivial, and when York got to sickbay she pulled him into her office, closed the door and turned on him frowning. "Something came up, something real curious," she said, then hesitated. ". . . Shortly after that feddie blew us into transition . . . It was chaos here, injured people straggling in from all over the ship. We were swamped, stacking them up in the corridors, and then the empress shows up with two marines in tow, and they're carrying a servant of hers—woman, unconscious, nasty blow to the head."

Yan drifted off for a moment, preoccupied by her thoughts. "About the same time someone brings in the princess, half conscious, in quite a bit of pain. But the empress is nearly hysterical, wants the servant treated before anyone else. I mean even before her own daughter. A servant!

"Got my curiosity going. So I took care of the servant—just a bad concussion—then I took care of the princess—a broken arm—then the empress lets me know she's in pain, and I find out she's got four broken ribs.

"By this time my curiosity's jacked right through the ceiling, so I check them all into beds here and sedate them. Then when things quieted down I ran a full med profile on all three."

Yan turned to a console in her office and activated a screen. "Here. Look at this."

York stepped behind the console and looked over Yan's shoulder at the scan of a human skull. The image was a strange, unnatural mixture of computer-generated colors chosen to emphasize anatomical features. Yan rotated the image of the skull until they were looking at the back of the head, then she tilted it forward, and with her fingers dancing across the keyboard began peeling away layers of structure. York understood little of it, but as she peeled away the last few layers and got to the center of the skull he saw a device that, though he didn't know what it was, he did know damn well it didn't belong there.

"What the hell is that?" he asked.

Yan looked at him, grinned. "It's a small explosive device. They used chemicals so we wouldn't pick up a power device with a routine scan. It's not powerful, but since it's implanted adjacent to the brain stem it doesn't need to be."

"How would it be activated?"

"It's wired into the brain, probably activated by some specific thought sequence. It's a suicide device."

York shook his head. This all fit a pattern somehow, but one he couldn't yet discern. "Which one of them?" he asked.

"The empress and the servant; the princess was clean. But there's one more curious thing. The one in the empress' head was manufactured in the empire, and the servant's wasn't."

"A feddie?" York asked.

Yan shrugged. "I don't know if she's a feddie, but that device in her head isn't imperial hardware."

A strange connection: a feddie spy and the empress. "Why bring this to me, Alsa? Why not to Sierka? He's the CO."

Yan sneered at him. "Don't be ridiculous."

"All right. So what am I supposed to do about it?"

"God damn it, York. I don't know. I'm asking you what I should do about it."

"Who else have you told about this?"

"No one but you."

"Can you remove those devices?"

She shook her head. "Probably not without being detected. But I can disarm them."

He stared at her for a moment. "Good. Do so." He pointed at the image of the woman's skull on the screen. "And erase those spools. Destroy any records you've got of this, and keep your mouth shut."

He turned to leave, hesitated at the hatchway. "One more thing. Don't let anyone catch on, but I want you to run the same profile on everyone you can. Anyone who comes to sickbay for any reason—if you can get them under a scanner, do it."

Yan winked at him. "As you wish, sir."

On his way back to the marine barracks York had to wait an unusually long time for the lift, and while he was standing there he heard a group of spacers approaching from out of sight down another corridor. They were in the midst of a heated conversation—something about *asshole marines*—but when they turned into the corridor and saw York waiting there, the conversation died abruptly. They walked up to the lift in silence and stopped to wait.

Ordinarily York would have remained preoccupied with the facts surrounding the curious incident of the empress and her servant. Spacers didn't like marines; that was a fact of life. And more often than not they shut up in the presence of an officer. But what caught York's attention now was that two of the spacers were wearing sidearms, and they were not navy issue.

When the lift came York stepped in with the spacers. They programmed it for the spacer barracks, and out of curiosity York followed them. He took a quick walk through barracks deck; it appeared that about one in ten carried a weapon of some sort, there was no discipline, the whole deck stank, and the mood of the place was ugly.

There were two guards standing at the entrance to the marine barracks, and they snapped to attention as York approached. York stopped, looked at them carefully. In appearance they were unarmed. He asked one of them, "Are you armed."

The marine scowled. "Of course, sir."

York keyed his implants. "Sergeant Palevi."

"Palevi here, sir."

"Sergeant. I want the guards at the entrance to our barracks visibly armed with rifles and sidearms. And I want them to carry live ammunition. I also want the barracks on tight security at all times."

"Yes, sir. I'll take care of it right away, sir."

"Thank you, Sergeant. That's all."

••••

Torrin Juessik stood in the corridor and knocked softly on the hatch in front of him. When it opened, Arkan Dulell stood in the dark of the cabin framed in the light of the corridor. He'd obviously been sleeping, and it took him a moment to recognize Juessik, but when he did he lost his usual reticence for an instant.

"Hello, Torrin," he said coldly.

Juessik smiled. "Aren't you going to invite me in?"

Dulell considered that for a moment, said only, "I was sleeping."

Juessik stepped past him, palmed the light sensor and looked around the cabin. "These rooms are rather cramped, aren't they?"

Dulell shrugged. "It's sufficient."

"Ah Arkan, always the stoic."

"Why are you here?"

Juessik turned toward him. "I wanted to see you."

Dulell shook his head. "I don't believe that."

"Now Arkan. Don't be petulant."

"All right. You've seen me."

Juessik stepped close to him, leaned toward him, kissed him gently on the cheek, then on the side of the neck. "I've missed you."

Dulell closed his eyes. "No you haven't."

Juessik looked up and shrugged. "Well then, you've missed me."

Dulell said nothing as Juessik kissed him again, then added, "Yes. You have."

••••

"Where have you been?" Ninda shouted as Add'kas'adanna stepped into the Central Committee chamber. Ninda stood angrily, tried to face her down, but she was a Kinathin and she towered over him, and though there was never any real threat of physical violence, they all knew he stood no chance against her in a physical confrontation. And that knowledge thwarted his attempt at intimidation.

Ninda returned to his seat at the wide table, tried again from there. "Where have you been?"

She'd kept them waiting intentionally. She'd been monitoring the reports on the recent sighting and engagement of the *imper*. Using various erroneous excuses, she'd given her captains orders that none of Ninda's Security Forces stationed aboard their ships were to be allowed to communicate directly with DCO, forcing Ninda to activate the spies he'd placed among the her crews. She and her captains had identified most of them as they made contact in one fashion or another, though they'd take no action against them, would, in fact, pretend they didn't know who they were. But it was good to know your enemy.

Ninda, Zort, and Kaffair were looking at her, waiting for an answer. "I've been trying to assimilate the incoming reports. I've also been looking at the telemetry from the engagement, and attempting to correlate that with those same reports. I'm afraid it's a confusing mess, though I think I've begun to accumulate an accurate, if somewhat incomplete, picture."

It was half lie, but it calmed Ninda. "The captain of that *imper* is not stupid, though he fooled some of our people into thinking he was. We had five ships following him . . ." Privately, Add'kas'adanna suspected there was a sixth, but she kept that piece of information to herself. ". . . and he made an injudicious course change."

"Are you telling us we lost him?" Kaffair asked, and for an instant Add'kas'adanna thought she detected hope in his voice, as if he wanted the *imper* to escape.

Add'kas'adanna pulled out all her training, created and released the sub-mind and prepared herself to observe whatever reaction she could elicit from him. "No," she said bluntly, and there it was: Kaffair had wanted the *imper*—and its captain?—to escape. And Ninda, of course, wanted the imper dead, not captured.

She continued, "One of our ships got a targeting solution, took a shot. But the *imper* had his shields up, was ready for us, was apparently taking a calculated risk. He pretended to be hurt by the shot, down-transited, waited for the ships following him and burned the first two—no survivors." She looked at the faces of her fellow directors. They didn't care about survivors. They didn't care about her crews.

"The *imper* up-transited in a different direction before the last three ships could get there and engage him. They were, however, able to get a reading on his transition wake, so we have a good idea of the direction he's headed. They followed of course, though they're too far behind to effectively track him, and will undoubtedly lose him in a day or two."

Ninda shook his head unhappily. "So we *have* lost him."

Add'kas'adanna didn't mention the sixth ship she suspected was out there. She'd pored over the reports for hours, and obviously something was missing. Only when she assumed the existence of a sixth ship, probably a small hunter-killer, acting independently and maintaining transmission silence, only then did it add up. "Yes," she said. "It appears we have."

Ninda was angry with everyone, but he chose to take it out on her. "I think it best, Director Add'kas'adanna, if you go out there personally to lead the search."

Add'kas'adanna nodded, didn't tell him she wanted to do exactly that. "As you wish, Director Ninda." She bowed at the waist and left the chamber.

15

Choices

AS YORK LEFT the mess hall a short, overweight civilian man accosted him in the corridor. "Lieutenant Ballin. I'm Frederick Cienyey."

York nodded politely. "Your Excellency."

Cienyey gave York a smarmy smile. "I've wanted to meet you, to thank you for rescuing us from Trinivan, and again from Dumark."

"I was just doing my duty, Your Excellency."

"You're being modest, Lieutenant. In any case, you have my thanks, and . . ." Cienyey leaned close and dropped his voice to a whisper. ". . . there are some people in my cabin who'd like to thank you as well. Would you have a few moments?"

York didn't want to have anything to do with whatever plot Cienyey had cooked up, was about to lie, tell the man he had to report for duty, but the ambassador blurted out, "I checked the duty roster, just to be sure you'd have time."

York tried a different way out. "I'd love to, but except for meals, I'm not allowed above Hangar Deck, by order of the captain."

"Well then we're in luck," Cienyey said happily. "My cabin is on this deck." Cienyey took York by the arm and guided him down the corridor, prattling on about the opportunity to meet important people. Cienyey was certain that if York played his cards right, there was considerable advantage to be gained.

At the hatch to his cabin Cienyey knocked first, then touched the latch and the hatch clicked open. The interior was poorly lit, and the heavy smell of tobac rolled out into the corridor. Cienyey stepped aside and motioned for York to precede him. York did so warily.

Cienyey followed close behind him, closed the hatch, shutting out the light of the corridor. A woman's voice spoke out of the darkness, "Bring the lights up a bit, Frederick, so poor Lieutenant Ballin can see."

Cienyey touched the lighting control. They were in a small, cramped cabin with two other men and a woman. The men were both seated in chairs folded out of the bulkhead, while the woman occupied a small straight back chair, probably appropriated from ship's stores. One of the men put a small tube to his lips, sucked on it and exhaled a plume of smoke. The woman smiled at York pleasantly, though he had the impression the smile was just a courtesy. She looked at one of the men, the one not smoking. "Jandeer, get the lieutenant a chair."

Of the two men seated against the wall, the one smoking was small and wiry, while the other was large and powerfully built. The large one stood, offered York his seat, and everything about him said *bodyguard*.

"Thank you," York said, "but I'll stand."

The woman wore single-piece shipboard fatigues. Like everyone from the embassy, she'd probably been happy to escape with her life, and was dependent upon what she could draw from ship's stores. But it didn't matter what they wore; the aristocrats looked aristocratic, and the rich looked rich. But the woman in front of York, and the small wiry man seated next to her, radiated an aura of power.

The woman said, "I'm Sarra Fithwallen, and this," she indicated the small wiry man, "is Brentin Omasin." She looked at Cienyey. "You of course know Lord Cienyey, and next to him is my associate Jandeer Faiel." The large man nodded. York had heard of both Fithwallen and Omasin, though he couldn't recall where.

Cienyey blurted out, "Miss Fithwallen is the owner of Kordak Trading Industries, and Mister Omasin is the chief executive of the Darrien Concern."

There was a short, embarrassing silence. Obviously, Fithwallen and Omasin considered Cienyey excess baggage now that he'd run their errand. Omasin broke the silence. "We all owe you our lives. Once on Trinivan, and then again on Dumark."

York had heard of both outfits. They were big trading and merchant organizations, and he wondered why two such important people had been on a remote planet like Trinivan, one so close to potential Syndonese attack. "There were any number of people responsible for your rescue," he said.

The woman smiled. "Now my next comment should be something like, 'Oh Lieutenant, you're being modest.' "

York decided he liked her. "You know the script well."

She shrugged. "So I won't pretend to believe that you single-handedly rescued us. But when the man in command of this ship made an ill-conceived course correction four days ago, you were singularly responsible for keeping us alive. Is that not correct, Lieutenant?"

York shook his head. "We made a mistake. I happened to be the first one to spot it."

Omasin made a point of exhaling a large plume of smoke. "*We* didn't make a mistake, Lieutenant. Commander Sierka made a mistake. And when you realized what was happening, you understood the danger and tried to correct it. In fact, were it not for you, we wouldn't have had our shields powered when the first warhead struck, and we might not be here right now."

York looked at Omasin carefully. "You've done your homework."

Omasin nodded as if he'd gotten the answer he wanted. "You're experienced. You're a lifer, with more than—"

York interrupted him. "Yes! I'm good luck."

In the ensuing silence that followed he regretted the outburst. Omasin leaned back and sucked contentedly on his tobac. The bodyguard, Faiel, continued to lean patiently against the bulkhead, while Cienyey looked on expectantly. Fithwallen's eyes narrowed and she appeared to measure York before she said, "I try to concern myself with patterns of behavior, not single incidents. You, for instance, appear to be a bit unstable, on the surface. But you have a pattern of doing the right thing, especially under pressure. On the other hand, Commander Sierka is . . . perhaps a bit inexperienced in these matters. He has established a pattern, Lieutenant, and, though different, it's every bit as consistent as yours. Did you know that he's begun arming his officers?"

York couldn't help but frown. "I was aware some crewmembers were carrying non-issue weapons."

"And Sierka is issuing sidearms to his officers. They're carrying weapons at all times of the day and night. He's losing control."

York thought, *He never had control. Officers carrying sidearms! The situation was approaching critical mass.*

Omasin leaned forward. "Tell me, Lieutenant. What would you recommend we do?"

That was it! The conversation had turned in a direction that could get them all arrested and vented. "Do?" he asked, playing dumb. "Do about what?"

"This situation we're in," Omasin persisted. "The way we're headed right now, we're all likely to be killed."

York decided to leave before they crossed the line. He stood. "The best thing you can do, Mister Omasin, is to have faith in the officers and crew of this ship. They're trained and experienced and competent." York wasn't a good liar, but at that moment he was amazed at how easily he could spew such drivel. "I have to be going now," he said and turned toward the door, but he found it blocked by Faiel, who leaned casually in his way. York considered the big man for a moment. There was no threat in his posture, but too, he made no move to get out of the way. He was probably a professional, and York was no match for the man.

"Lieutenant Ballin," Fithwallen said.

York turned to face her.

She smiled pleasantly. "Mister Omasin and I are both powerful and influential people. If you were to have any suggestions on how our present situation might be handled better, we could support you in a compelling way, and of course we would be most grateful. In fact, when this is over I could use a good military liaison on my executive staff. The salary would be quite handsome, with considerable benefits and perquisites. And if there were any ensuing difficulties as a result of actions you might take now on our behalf, Mister Omasin and I could help the powers-that-be see the need for such measures, and extricate you from any entanglements in a most legal fashion."

In other words, York thought, *take over the ship, get us the hell out of this, and we'll make sure they don't execute you for mutiny.*

York said, "I really must be going now."

"Of course," she said. "Thank you for your time."

When York turned back to the door Faiel was no longer blocking it. Cienyey escorted him back to the lift, again prattling on about the importance of doing favors for important people, especially wealthy ones. When York got back to his cabin he pulled a chair out of the wall and sat down, and started shaking.

Mutiny! He sat there for several minutes before he could hold his hands steady.

••••

"Ballin," Sierka screamed, and York slammed awake. "Answer me. Now!" Sierka had used captain's access to override York's terminal, and was screaming a stream of profanity at him.

"Lights," York growled as he dropped out of his grav bunk.

He staggered groggily to his terminal, hit the receive switch and Sierka appeared on a screen, his face bright red, veins bulging on his forehead. Sierka saw York and hesitated, then, with spittle flying from his mouth, screamed. "Where have you been, you idiot?"

York opened his mouth to say he'd been asleep, but Sierka cut him off. "I'll have you up on charges for dereliction of duty. When I call, you answer. You're under arrest . . . No, forget that. The civilians on G-deck are rioting. Get your marines down there and stop it."

"Yes, sir, I'll—"

"You're a drunken incompetent. You'll never amount to anything . . ."

York tuned Sierka out. The fool wanted York to quell a riot on G-deck, but he needed to shout epithets and curses at him for ten minutes first. And he finished with, "You get those moronic marines of your down there, and kill anyone that resists. That's an order."

York scrambled the marines, told Palevi, "I need fifty marines in full armor. Nerve prods and riot gear, that kind of stuff. And tell them no lethal force unless absolutely necessary."

Palevi gave him a sour smile. "This ain't gonna be no fun."

While there would undoubtedly be some contraband weapons among the civilians housed on G-deck, there wouldn't be anything heavy enough to penetrate power-reinforced plast. So the best way to handle a riot was to send in invulnerable troops with orders to disable, but—and here York decided Sierka could go fuck himself—not kill anyone.

Just outside the main lift on G-deck a squad of AI had established a small perimeter, but were too badly outnumbered to take the rest of the deck. A young female AI second lieutenant marched up to York and said, "Glad you brought me reinforcements. Tell your people they're taking orders from me."

York hooked a thumb over his shoulder. "No. Get out."

Her face darkened, and as she spoke she rested a hand threateningly on her sidearm. "I gave you a direct order."

York grinned. "And I gave you an order."

She wasn't very smart. He outweighed her by a good thirty kilos, and she broadcast her move. He saw her muscles tense as she gripped her sidearm and started to draw it, so he simply reached down with his left hand, caught her wrist and halted it. Then with his right hand he grabbed her by the lapels, pulled her toward the lift and tossed her head-over-heels into it. She came up reaching for her gun again, but found herself staring into the barrel of Palevi's sidearm. She stopped and looked around quickly, realized she and her goons were badly outnumbered. She growled, "You haven't heard the last of this."

"Palevi," York barked. "Disarm these AI troops, and hustle them off this deck."

They hit G-deck at a run, let the few civilians with weapons ping shots of their armor as they charged straight at them, more often than not just slammed an armored forearm under someone's chin and knocked them on their butt, once or twice jammed a nerve prod in someone's gut. York didn't wear armor, just a light combat harness, let his marines sweep out in front of him and clear the way. But with his first step on G-deck a sense of foreboding settled in his gut, and his unease grew as they progressed. G-deck stank, not just the slightly unwashed smell of a locker room, but the rank overpowering odor of too many people crowded together without proper sanitary facilities.

"Cap'm." Palevi's voice in his implants. "We got a problem here. G-two-two-niner outboard."

"I'll be right there."

York checked the bulkhead number next to him, headed for Palevi. Five marines, Tathit in charge, stood guard over a clutch of civilians near G-two-two-niner. The civilians looked like they'd been roughed up, and as York approached, Tathit hooked a thumb toward a hatch, said, "In there, sir."

Palevi waited on the other side of the hatch with several marines in a large barracks. On the floor lay three AI troopers, in worse shape than the civilians outside. Palevi said, "Three still breathing, one not." He nodded toward a grav bunk on the wall. In it lay the remains of a fourth AI trooper, his pants down around his knees. The fellow had been beaten to death, his genitals mutilated.

York stepped through the hatch into the corridor and looked the civilians over more carefully. They were bloodied, beaten and angry, but they'd outnumbered the four AI troopers three to one.

York demanded, "What happened here?"

A young man, clearly the angriest of them all, tried to step forward, but a marine blocked his way. "They raped my wife," he snarled. "We stopped them, and we paid them back."

"Cap'm," someone shouted from down the corridor, another group of marines guarding another clutch of civilians. Salley, the ex-marine proprietress of The Drop Zone, blocked by one of York's marines, waved at him.

York keyed his implants. "Let her pass."

She brought with her an older fellow, a professor type, and introduced him as Joaha Sarvik. York guessed he held some sort of de facto leadership position among the civilians, and he looked tired. He said, "These rapes have to stop."

"Rapes?" York asked. "Plural?"

Salley said, "We call them rape squads, Cap'm. AI come down here quite regular, beat up some, rape some."

Sarvik said, "We can understand the limited food and water rations. I'm sure it's as hard on you as the rest of us, but—"

"Rations?" York demanded.

Sarvik frowned. "Yes. Limited food and water. No bathing. You have been on rations like the rest of us, haven't you?"

York wanted to lie, but Sarvik deserved the truth. "No."

Sarvik went from reasonable to angry. "What the hell is going on here?"

York spoke carefully. "I don't know. But it's going to end."

York turned to Palevi. "Throw those AI thugs in the brig. Yan can patch them up there. And set up regular patrols on this deck. Anyone wants to hurt someone, they get hurt first."

They secured G-deck quickly after that. Once back in his office, York told Palevi, "Can you do something to get that deck cleaned up? Teach them how to shower shipboard style, make sure they get a reasonable water ration and food."

Palevi smiled, not his usual grin. "Yes, sir."

York monitored the progress as Hyer and her squad conducted a search for contraband weapons on G-deck. About a half hour later he was thinking of returning to his bunk when he heard Thring pleading frantically with one of his marines, "Let me pass. I must see Lieutenant Ballin. It's a matter of life or death."

York called out, "Let him pass."

Thring stumbled into the room, his eyes wide with fear. "He's going to execute them."

York asked, "Execute who?" But before Thring spoke he already knew the answer.

"No trial," Thring pleaded. "No hearing. Nothing. Just plain murder."

York grabbed him by the front of his robe. "Where?"

"I think on Hangar Deck."

He tossed Thring aside, sprinted up the corridor, shouted back over his shoulder at the marine, "Tell Palevi I need backup."

Just as York reached Hangar Deck *Cinesstar*'s hull echoed with the hollow clang of the blow-down cycle of an air lock. *The drone service bay.*

He found the hatch to the Drone Bay wide open, and inside he came upon the AI major and his goons. Sarvik and a number of his people were on their knees next to a personnel hatch, their hands cuffed behind their backs, plast tongue gags jammed into their mouths. Salley, too, was cuffed and gagged, but she was laying on her side, one cheek swollen and her eyes puffy, blood trickling from her nostrils. A couple of the AI goons were in the process of recycling the hatch.

"What's going on here?" York demanded.

The AI major looked up unhappily. The stencil on his tunic read JUESSIK. "This is no concern of yours, Lieutenant."

York hesitated. There were admirals who would back down against an AI major. York shook his head and swallowed hard. "I'm the commanding officer of *Cinesstar*'s marine contingent, and as such I am Chief of Ship's Security. This is, therefore, my concern."

Juessik frowned and looked York over carefully. "Very well, Lieutenant. We're venting some mutineers."

York stuck his hand out. "May I see the execution order?"

The young, female, AI lieutenant York had tossed out of G-deck a few hours earlier stepped over to stand beside Juessik. "Is there some problem here, sir?"

Juessik looked at her. "I'm not sure yet, Lieutenant Darma." A dozen AI goons slowly surrounded York, and he hoped Palevi would hurry.

"The execution order," York said. "I have to see it before you can proceed."

Juessik shook his head. "That won't be necessary, Lieutenant."

"Look out, Cap'm!"

At Salley's warning York's reflexes took over. He spun and dropped to one side, but one of the AI goons caught him across the side of his head with a rifle butt. York hit the deck solidly, tried to climb up to his knees, but a boot slammed into his ribs, and another caught him in the back. He barely avoided another rifle butt aimed for his head, but something else hit him in the groin, and he curled up in pain as blow after blow landed all over his body . . .

For some odd reason the blows had stopped. There was a lot of shouting, and one of the AI goons suddenly landed face down on the deck in front of him, bounced hard. The bastard didn't get up, but lay there with blood trickling from his nostrils, his eyes closed and peaceful.

Someone rolled York onto his back. A marine medic leaned over him, and with Palevi standing above her she checked him with some sort of instrument. "He'll be all right," the medic said. "At worst, a couple broken ribs."

As consciousness returned, and with it a hard lump of pain in his left side, York looked around carefully. Palevi had arrived with overwhelming force; they'd disarmed the AI troops and rounded them up near a bulkhead. Several of them showed signs of a one-sided and rather nasty fight. York grabbed the medic's shoulder, and though his ribs and back complained painfully, he demanded, "Help me up."

He could barely walk, and they had to help him over to Juessik, who stood with his people behind him. York considered kicking him in the crotch or something, decided it wouldn't be worth it. "Major Juessik," York said. His lower lip was beginning to swell around a nasty cut. "I'm afraid I've been somewhat remiss in my duties as Chief of Security, and I've left you and your people without proper protection. I have almost three hundred marines under my command . . ." York emphasized the word *my*. ". . . and it seems only reasonable to provide for your safety."

York saw a little fear in Juessik's eyes, knew he'd have to be satisfied with that. "Sergeant Palevi," he said without looking away from Juessik.

"Sir."

"Sergeant. Assign four armed marines as a body guard for Major Juessik." York looked at the young AI lieutenant. "And four more for Lieutenant Darma here. Until further notice they are to accompany them everywhere. And no one will countermand these orders but me, and only me."

"Yes, sir."

"The rest of Major Juessik's people will be given proper quarters in the marine barracks, effective immediately."

York turned away from Juessik and Darma. Palevi was grinning as York pulled him aside and whispered, "I want to know everything Darma and Juessik do and say. And take the rest and lock them up."

Palevi's grin broadened. "Yes, sir. Happy to, sir."

York had Harshaw brought to his office, had to force himself not to vent his anger on the poor civilian. "I want to press charges against Juessik and his AI thugs: murder, rape, the works."

Harshaw shook his head sadly. "They report directly to the Admiralty, not through the normal chain-of-command. Even if *the empress* wanted to press charges, she'd have to file a complaint with the Office of the Admiralty and let them handle it. I'm sorry, Lieutenant, but there's nothing you can do."

At least he could bottle up the AI bastards so they could do no more harm. With his marines backing him, York set out to fill the brig.

16

Abandoned

"WE'RE GOING TO have to shut her down," the mechanic shouted above the noise in the engine room. "That *imper* hurt us."

"We can't," Jewel shouted back at him. They'd been limping along for days, trying to repair the damage from that imperial cruiser's lucky shot.

The mechanic shrugged. "Shut her down now for a couple hours, maybe a day, and we can repair her. Don't shut her down and we'll be dead in space fairly soon anyway."

"Damn!" Jewel swore. She shouted back at the mechanic. "I don't want to lose that *imper.*"

The mechanic shrugged. "You'll lose him no matter what if we don't do something to fix this boat."

Jewel shook her head. "All right. But let's transit easy, keep our flare to a minimum. I don't want that son-of-a-bitch to get a fix on us."

••••

The day after the civilians had their little uprising Sierka threw a fit about the way York had treated Major Juessik and his AI comrades. At least this time he didn't order York up to his cabin, but called him late that night and chose to rant and rave via com link. York turned the volume down, nodded politely now and then, and ignored most of it. Sierka did force York to release the AI goons he'd locked up and remove the escorts he had on Juessik and Darma.

When Sierka finished there was a message from Alsa. York called her on a screen. "I found another little surprise," she said. "The d'Hart woman. Same kind of device, buried at the base of the skull near the brain stem like the others."

York asked, "Federation or Imperial issue."

"Imperial."

"Anyone else?"

She grinned. "I decided not to wait for everyone to come to me. I told Sierka I should probably give every officer and VIP on ship a checkup after those gravity anomalies we went through. He gave me the nod, so I've been scheduling them one after the other. So far, in addition to the one's you already know about, I've run full profiles on Andow, Rhijn, Cienyey, Dubye, and all our officers—all negative."

"Does that include Soladin and his little piece of fluff?"

Yan frowned. "Soladin came out negative, but what little piece of fluff?"

York drummed his fingers on his console. "I can't remember her name; Lady Something-or-other. Try and get a complete passenger manifest, run profiles on anyone who's wealthy, powerful, royal, or of any kind of rank or stature whatsoever. Also anyone who's part of the entourage of any member of the royal family, and anyone who was on Trinivan, no matter how insignificant."

Her brow wrinkled. "That's a lot of work, York."

"I know. Just fit them in when you can. Oh, and make sure you check out Sarra Fithwallen, Brentin Omasin, and Fithwallen's bodyguard Jandeer Faiel."

"Whoa!" she said. "That's big money you're talking about. They're on board?"

"Yes they are. See what you can find out, but be careful. Remember: keep no records and tell no one."

She grinned. "Don't worry about me, York Ballin. You worry about you."

"I will," he said, and cut the circuit.

There was a message from Maggie. She wanted him to come up to the cabin she and Frank shared, said it was important, and not to worry about Sierka's orders that he stay below H-Deck. It was late and there wouldn't be anyone about.

Ordinarily York wouldn't have listened to her, but it would be good to get into a bottle and a game of cards with Maggie and Frank. But when Frank opened the hatch to their cabin, it was obvious he'd have no such luck.

There was a whole group of them packed into the small cabin. Frank and Maggie, Jondee, Nemkov, McGeahn, Gant, even Thring, and they all looked guilty, like a bunch of pubescent boys and girls caught showing one another their genitals.

"How about a drink?" Maggie offered.

York glanced around the room at each of them, and not one would look him in the eyes. "Ya," he said, leaning against a bulkhead. "Make it something strong. I think I'm going to need it."

No one moved or said anything as Maggie splashed something into a glass, then handed it to York. He took a sip, found it was real whiskey, not 'trate, was grateful for that luxury. "So," he said, looking at Maggie, and in no mood to beat around the bush. "You wanted to see me, said it was important." He looked around the cabin again. "And it's obvious this is not a social call. So, what's so hot?"

Again the silence, no one willing to meet his eyes. "Someone answer me. Now. Or I'm leaving."

He turned toward the hatch, and oddly, it was McGeahn who spoke. "Wait! Stay."

He turned back and leaned against the bulkhead again. "I'm listening. Someone start talking."

Again, McGeahn spoke. "How would you evaluate our present situation?"

York shook his head. "I wouldn't. How would you?"

"I don't know," she said, and she looked to the others for help.

Frank came to her rescue. "The situation is deteriorating steadily. The civilians and crew are all carrying contraband arms. Sierka has armed the officers in the hope of keeping control. No one trusts or respects him. There's no order, no discipline. He hasn't even bothered to issue duty assignments for most of the crew, and—"

Nemkov interrupted him. "Everyone's seen the way you've got your marines operating, a nice well-oiled organization. We need responsible leadership. We need authority and discipline from the top down."

York cut him off. "Sierka's the top. Go talk to him."

Nemkov shook his head. "He'd never listen."

"Maybe not. But that's the only course you've got."

"Please, York," McGeahn pleaded. "We're in a lot of trouble."

"Yes," York agreed. "If you've been in here hatching something, you're damn right you're in a lot of trouble."

Maggie blurted out, "Sierka's going to get us all killed."

"As captain, that's his prerogative."

"Damn it, Ballin," Frank demanded. "Help us here."

"Help you do what? You don't want me to help you. You want me to lead you in mutiny. Let's spell it out. *Mutiny* is the word. You're all talking about it, but not one of you has the guts to say it. And what the hell would that accomplish?"

Maggie shouted. "At least we won't get killed by some stupid mistake."

York shook his head. They didn't understand, and he knew he couldn't make them. "You bunch of idiots. You bloody, goddamned idiots." He sucked down his drink, swallowed the whole thing in a single gulp, looked at Maggie and Frank. "I thought you two were smarter than this." He looked around the room one last time. "You're all idiots."

He tossed his empty glass at Frank—didn't hear it shatter so he assumed Frank had caught it—and turned to the cabin door. Thring stood in the way, though he obviously had no intention of stopping York. But York grabbed him by the front of his church robes anyway, tossed him to one side. He palmed the lock on the hatch, stepped out into the corridor and slammed it behind him.

He got about five paces up the corridor when Soladin stepped out of Lady What's-her-name's cabin and they almost ran into one another.

"Ballin?" Soladin asked. "What are you doing here? This deck is off-limits to you and your kind. Answer me. And stand at attention when you're addressed by a superior."

York clamped down on his anger and pulled his shoulders back.

"Answer my question."

"What question was that, sir?"

"I asked you what you were doing here."

"I was walking down the corridor, sir."

Soladin's eyes widened. "Don't get smart with me."

"Yes, sir. Sorry, sir."

"I'm putting you on report. Now get below decks immediately."

"Yes, sir. Right away, sir."

York went back to his cabin and got drunk.

Early the next morning he was badly hung over when Sierka ordered him up to his office, had him stand in front of his desk for more than an hour while he shouted at him. Then, when Sierka let him go, York went down to the ready-room and shouted at Palevi and Yagell and Tathit and the marines for a while. It didn't make him feel any better.

••••

They floated York in on a grav stretcher: one arm, shoulder, and half his face blown away—the good half. The prosthetic eye with the scars radiating out from the socket was still intact, but the skin around it showed the pallor of death.

Alsa Yan leaned over him, shook her head sadly, mumbled something to one of her technicians about getting a body bag. The man left the examination room.

She peered into the side of York's head, noted that a good portion of the skull had been torn away by shrapnel. A fair amount of his brain was missing, and she could see shredded neural wiring where the interface to the prosthetic eye had been. Her job now was to retrieve all the prosthetic parts that had been installed in York over the years so someone else might make use of them, then wrap what remained in a body bag so Telyekev could give it a decent burial in space.

She set to work with grim determination. The arm that had been blown away had been his real arm. The one that remained was a prosthetic. She was mildly surprised that both legs were prosthetics, and when she popped his chest cavity she found that all of his internal organs had been replaced, one by one, with biomachinery and organo-synths. She worked steadily for a good hour, and when she finished pulling all the borrowed parts from York, she turned back to the table and was surprised to see there were only a few scraps left. The arm and the shoulder and the side of his head that had been blown away were basically all that had been left of the real York Ballin. And now, without them, all that remained was a bit of tissue, a piece of bone, a smear of blood.

The technician held out the open body bag. "I'll scrape him into it."

Alsa looked at what was left of York, shook her head. "That's not him. There's nothing left of him." She reached out, scraped the bits of tissue into a pan, turned toward the disposal can . . .

York slammed awake, sat up in his grav bunk and screamed, gasped for air and gripped the upper side of his bunk as the deck gravity field almost pulled him out of it.

He caught his breath slowly. "A dream," he said into the dark, trying to suck air into his lungs. "That goddamned dream."

He sat there trembling, beads of sweat dripping down his face, his chest, his arms. He lay back in the bunk and it took him quite a while to calm down. While he lay there he felt the ship make transition. Sierka had probably ordered it for some reason, and hadn't bothered to take any of the normal and reasonable precautions. That feddie hunter-killer would probably put a warhead in their side now.

York rolled over, drifted back to sleep, hoping it would happen fast and clean.

••••

Jewel Thaaline rolled out of her bunk, staggered across the deck toward her terminal. The alert klaxon wasn't sounding; rather it was just the terminal chiming softly at her, so she had to force down her combat reflexes and the rush of adrenaline that threatened to flood through her. But still, none of her crew would be stupid enough to wake her if it weren't important.

She hit the receive switch and Ducan Soe's face appeared on the screen. He didn't bother with any formalities. "We picked up a transition flare at extreme range, about ten light-years. Barely able to detect it—shouldn't have been able to detect it at all, if the fool had been smart enough to dump a little velocity before down-transiting. What kind of idiot's running that ship?"

Jewel tried to rub the sleep from her eyes and ignored Soe's question. "Any other activity?"

Soe shook his head. "Nothing that we can detect. He's just out in the middle of nowhere."

Jewel thought for a moment. "He probably needs a nav fix. And we'd better be sublight when he up-transits or we won't be able to track his new course."

Soe grinned. "I'm ahead of you, Jewel. Tac'tac'ah's powering us down now, bringing us down slow and careful. We're just about ready to down transit with almost no flare. I don't think he'll be able to fix on us at this range."

"Excellent!" Jewel said. "As soon as you're ready, go ahead and down-transit. I'm on my way up."

She cut the link, then pulled on coveralls, shot out of her cabin and scrambled up the ladder to the bridge. They down-transited just as she was sitting down at her screens. An instant later the *imper* cruiser up-transited and started picking up speed.

"Did you get that?" Jewel asked.

Soe was crouched over his console, working feverishly at his screens. "Shit!" he growled. "We missed him."

"Nothing?" Jewel pleaded.

Soe shook his head sadly. "I've got some data on his wake after he made transition, but that's not accurate enough."

The *Pride*'s bridge filled with silence, then Tac'tac'ah spoke. "Ma'am, I did happen to catch a fragment of a transmission. Maybe two transmissions, actually."

"Yes," Jewel growled. "What do you mean maybe?"

"One was that *imper* warship, clearly a transmission, heavily coded—nothing recognizable for us. The other was so faint I'm not sure it was a transmission. But if it was, it came from a system on a shallow diagonal from them, about six light-years from them, about eighteen from us, much too far out for us to receive it clearly."

"Do we have any information on that system?"

Chief Innay answered her. "It's the Anachron system, ma'am. One inhabited planet settled by agro-croppers. They're way out on the fringes, but still officially part of the Directorate, so there's a small garrison there."

There were any number of possibilities, but they were all irrelevant. The Anachron system was their only chance. "Mr. Tac'tac'ah, set course for that system. Maybe this game isn't over yet."

••••

When *Cinesstar* down-transited for a nav fix, they picked up a distress signal from *H.M.S. Dumayia*, an imperial hunter-killer assigned the mission of raiding Syndonese commercial shipping lanes.

Dumayia had torpedoed a convoy twelve days ago, but taken considerable damage from the convoy's escorts. Deep in enemy territory, she limped into the nearest solar system with a habitable planet, and her crew just barely managed to abandon ship before she disintegrated around them.

Fifty-two survivors had crammed themselves into a small boat meant to carry no more than twenty passengers, then crashed on the planet's surface: seven more crewmembers dead.

Shortly after down-transiting into Anachron farspace York got orders to put together a rescue mission. *Dumayia's* crew had dug-in about four hundred kilometers from Pare de'San, a coastal city with an estimated population of fifty thousand. *Dumayia's* captain, a woman named Straegga, reported that the garrison on Anachron IV had nothing of any danger beyond artillery and a few atmospheric fighters. And a long-range scan survey taken during their nav fix showed no feddie warships in the vicinity to hinder them. With fire support from *Cinesstar's* batteries, there was nothing to stop them from dropping a gunboat to the surface of the planet to rescue the *Dumayia* crew. Simple, easy.

York and Palevi had been called up to Sierka's office to brief him, Soladin, Armbruster and Rame on the rescue plan. "I'll take twenty marines in one boat," York told them, "and I recommend you hold *Cinesstar* at ten thousand kilometers. The only danger to us will be the atmospheric fighters, and *Cinesstar* can easily track an airborne target at that range. With that kind of fire support as a threat, I doubt the Syndonese'll try anything. And that way there'll be no need to unduly endanger the ship."

Sierka nodded and gave him an oily smile. "Excellent advice, Lieutenant. But take all three boats, and all of your marines. We won't need you up here, and you'll have all of your people as backup in case anything does happen."

York frowned. "But sir—"

"No, Lieutenant." Sierka waved a hand in polite dismissal. "I won't hear of anything else. You marines deserve some consideration here. In fact, it's an order. I won't hear any argument on the matter."

A few minutes later York and Palevi found themselves alone in the lift. Before giving the lift their destination, Palevi growled, "I don't like it, Cap'm."

York shook his head. "We shouldn't be stopping at all, not with half the royal family onboard."

Palevi grabbed York's arm, a horrible breach of military etiquette, but one York could forgive under the circumstances. "What's that bastard got up his sleeve, Cap'm?"

"I don't know," York lied, and he couldn't look Palevi in the eyes. "But I'm not taking any chances. Load those boats to the gills with everything we've got. Full combat armor, and all the rations and fire power we can carry. Also anything that'll help us hold a perimeter as long as we can."

Palevi looked at him narrowly, then as understanding hit him he nodded slowly. "We could just kill 'im, sir."

York shook his head. "We're marines, Sergeant. We obey orders."

Palevi looked at him, then slowly his face broke into a grin, but it was that nasty grin that York hadn't seen for a long time. "You're right, sir. We obey orders."

••••

When York and Palevi started shouting orders at everyone to load everything they could on the boats, the loading took on a solemn air as all of the marines slowly came to the realization something really wrong was about to happen. The drop really called for light combat harness, but York couldn't fit two hundred and thirty-seven combat troops, plus their equipment and full combat armor, in three assault boats without first stuffing most of the marines in their armor. For appearances sake, York and Palevi and a squad of twenty marines had their armor loaded separately on *Two*, and made the drop in light harness on *One*.

All the way down York stayed in touch with Straegga. Apparently, on and off for most of the three days they'd been down, the feddies had shelled them with surface artillery and made regular bombing runs with their fighters. But under threat of retaliation from *Cinesstar* all hostilities had come to a stop and they'd grounded the fighters.

On approach to the *Dumayia* crew York had the assault boats make a high altitude mapping run over Pare de'San and the forest between the city and the downed crew. And when *One* touched down at the edge of their camp he sent *Two* and *Three* on an expanding reconnaissance spiral around them.

York stepped out of *One*'s hatch, barked over his shoulder at Palevi, "Secure the perimeter, Sergeant. And have all three boats set up a four hundred meter electronic perimeter watch."

Straegga and another officer approached York, and the *Dumayia* crew gathered behind them. Straegga was a small woman, with short, blond hair, which, like her face and her torn uniform, was streaked with dirt. The officer next to her and the crew gathering behind her were in no better shape. She walked with a limp, but she had a big smile on her face. Most of them carried a weapon of some kind, and not far away the bombed out hulk of their small shuttle was a smoking ruin.

York saluted her smartly, but, as per drop zone etiquette, he did not drop his guard by snapping to any kind of attention. "Ma'am," he said, "I'm Lieutenant Ballin, acting Captain-of-Marines."

She reached out, shook his hand gladly. "Lieutenant, we're glad to see you." She looked at the marines spreading out into the forest around them. "And I appreciate your caution."

She introduced the officer next to her. "This is my number one, Lieutenant Jakobee."

York shook the young man's hand, and Jakobee said, "Ballin! Haven't I heard that name before?"

York shrugged. "I wouldn't know."

Mec Notay shouted from *One*'s hatch. "Cap'm. You better come and take a look at this."

Straegga's eyes narrowed as she caught the strain in Notay's voice. She followed close on York's heels as he turned and walked to the boat, stepped up through the hatch into the interior. Notay sat at the small command console used for coordinating assault troops. Straegga frowned oddly when she saw the sixty marines lined up in the boat in full armor, and as she and York leaned over Notay's shoulder her frown deepened.

Notay had the output of their telemetry-tap to *Cinesstar* on one of the screens, and it showed the cruiser accelerating at full sublight drive away from the planet. A few seconds later the screen filled with snow for a moment, then went blank. Notay touched a few switches on her console, shook her head and glanced over her shoulder at York. "*Cinesstar* cut our telemetry feed. I guess Sierka finally got rid of us, eh, Cap'm?"

Straegga could read the screens as well as York, and her jaw dropped as she looked at him angrily. York keyed his implants. "This is Ballin. Full alert status. Seal 'em up and unload. We're on our own, and as soon as those feddies realize that, they're gonna hit us. Palevi, use your own discretion at setting up perimeter defenses."

Straegga reached up and grabbed his arm angrily. "Lieutenant," she shouted. "What in hell is going on?"

York owed her the truth. "I'll explain fully after I've had a chance to set up our perimeter defense."

Straegga let go of his arm, leaned back against a bulkhead and ran the dirty fingers of one hand through her dirty hair.

"Commander," York said softly. "It's a good guess we're going to be under fire shortly, and I have work to do."

She looked at him, blinked her eyes, took a moment to orient herself. "Certainly, Lieutenant. I guess this is your show, eh?"

They dug in, literally. The boats were equipped with heavy diggers that could move a lot of earth in a short amount of time, as well as other heavy equipment for establishing an emergency perimeter. In less than two hours they cut a hundred-yard-wide swath of trees in a full circle around them, then mined it heavily.

They also dug four large pits for command bunkers, roofed them over with logs from the trees they'd cut from the perimeter, then covered them with about four meters of earth. They set up portable artillery all around the perimeter, as well as electronic counter measures, and they protected everything with electronic camouflage and shielding mesh. York was standing in the middle of the command center, watching the sun settle toward the horizon and wondering what he might have missed, when the first artillery barrage came in.

From the rate of fire it appeared the feddies had about a half dozen artillery pieces, and as many mortar emplacements. But the shells coming in were not smart shells; just casings with explosives, no on-board computer with tracking, homing, and trajectory adjustment.

The artillery barrage lasted through most of the night. It caused very little damage—in fact, one of the command bunkers took a direct hit, but it was buried so deeply the damage was minimal. For the most part *One*, *Two* and *Three* were able to track the incoming shells, predict their trajectories, and warn any station seconds before it sustained a hit. But the barrage served its purpose: it kept them up all night, stretched their nerves to the limit and reduced their effectiveness as a combat unit.

The fighters came in at dawn, their targets the three assault boats. They were using missiles guided by heat, light, and electronic emission. At high altitude the boats were no match for the fighters with their blinding speed and air-to-air strike capability. But the boats were each equipped with about thirty small drones, which, when released, provided a field of randomly shifting targets for any incoming missile by darting around the boat and broadcasting target emissions. So the boat pilots stayed close to the ground, darted in and out of the forest, made effective use of their drones and a boat's hover capability. And since the fighter pilots had to be constantly alert for small surface-to-air missiles from the marines, they were relatively safe.

At dusk on the second day York took stock of their casualties: three dead, eight wounded, one portable mortar destroyed, and they'd lost about a dozen of their ninety drones.

••••

Jewel shook her head, mumbled to herself, "What the hell is he up to?"

"Maybe it's a trap," Soe said.

Jewel glanced over her screens. They were about a tenth of a light-year out from the Anachron system, drifting slowly toward the planet. The *imper* was either a genius or a maniac, or maybe both, or just maybe schizophrenic. "What the hell is he doing in that system? Yesterday he transits out of there, and now he's coming back?"

Innay said, "He's got people down on the surface of number four."

Jewel shook her head. "I guess we'll just have to be patient, wait and see."

••••

In the distance, the *crump* of the mortar was followed by a burst of automatic weapons fire, all muffled by the dirt walls of the bunker. Each time a shell hit somewhere the walls shook and a soft rain of dust settled down through the shadows of the dim lamp overhead.

York sat down on a shelf of dirt next to Palevi, struggled at the neck seals of his helmet for a few moments. Palevi lent a hand, and when he finally lifted the helmet off his head the earthy smell of the bunker was a real pleasure. After three days in armor all of them had grown quite ripe. The armor kept them disinfected, but it couldn't replace a trip to the fresher, and the hot, steamy air rising up out of the neck ring of his armor warred with the smell of the bunker.

It was about an hour before dawn, and Straegga and Jakobee and Palevi and York had gathered to make some tough decisions. "What's our situation now?" Straegga asked.

Palevi pulled out a flask containing diluted 'trate, took a healthy swig and passed it to Straegga. She sniffed at the flask, then put it to her lips while Palevi spoke mechanically. "Fourteen dead, thirty-two wounded, one portable mortar destroyed, one rotary emplacement gone, and we're down to fifty-three drones."

York spoke, tried not to sound as mechanical but failed. "We've burned two of their fighters, and that sortie last night took out two of their artillery pieces. We've probably killed more of them than they have us, but we examined a few bodies last night and they're using amateurs—farmers, civilians, whatever. They're eventually going to wear us down just by the numbers, and as our fatigue increases, our effectiveness will steadily decline and our casualty rate will grow exponentially."

The flask came York's way. He put it to his lips, relished the burn of the 'trate as Straegga shook her head hopelessly. York had privately filled her in on the real situation with Sierka, so she had no fantasies about rescue. "We're equipped better than they are—you haven't seen any body armor, have you?"

York shook his head.

"Well then," Straegga asked. "Could we take that city, maybe just take the power plant?"

York and Palevi looked at one another. York shrugged. "Probably, but we can't hold it. Occupation troops need a strong supply line connecting them to their base of operations. We have no base."

Straegga sat silently for some seconds shaking her head. She looked odd in armor. "Well, that does it. I don't see any choice but to face reality and surrender. At least we can negotiate from a position of strength, get some terms." She looked at York. "I'll use the com tomorrow, try to set it up. I think it should be you and me, Mister Ballin."

York nodded. "Yes, ma'am."

Straegga dismissed him and Palevi. They helped each other back into their helmets, then crawled up the ladder into the darkness just before dawn. Palevi leaned close to York, and with both their visors up, he whispered, "Cap'm. Why don't you come with me? If you're goin' in among a bunch of feddies, you might as well take some insurance."

York grinned. "What have you got in mind?"

"Trust me, sir."

17

Escape

HACKLA BROUGHT *ONE* down slowly, held it hovering about twenty centimeters above the forest floor. York dropped his visor and sealed his armor. His suit said in his ear, "Minor hazard warning. Gauntlet breach. Decompression compensation activated."

His suit inflated an isolation seal around his left wrist, and he glanced up at the silhouette displayed on the interior of his visor. His left gauntlet was shaded red, a small tear in the flexible power mesh covering the palm of his left hand. He'd noticed it just after dawn, hadn't yet had time to repair it.

He stepped up to the hatch, hit the release and the hatch slid back into the skin of the boat. Outside stood about thirty feddies with rifles of various kinds aimed at him. He kept his hands well away from his sidearm as he stepped to the ground. Straegga followed him, wearing no armor. As a ship's officer, it would not be appropriate for her to wear armor to a truce conference. As a marine, under the circumstances, it would be out of character for York to wear anything else. The boat lifted off behind them and disappeared into the sky.

Even before the female feddie officer stepped forward, York noticed her standing among her troops. She wore the uniform of a Directorate sublegion, a rank equivalent to York's, but she stood easily ten centimeters above him and any man there, and while she probably outweighed most men, on that frame she looked thin and gaunt. Her skin was a deep olive hue, against which her pale blue eyes stood out like beacons. But the most striking feature was her snow-white hair, not yellow blond but bone-white, cut shoulder length and tied back in a utilitarian and unattractive way, though oddly enough she was quite beautiful.

When she stepped forward she walked like a predatory animal. In twenty years, York could count the number of times he'd been this close to a feddie on the fingers of one hand, but even had he met them regularly this would have been a rare exception. His suspicions were confirmed when she stepped forward, saluted Straegga, spoke standard with an accent. "I am Sab'ach'ahn, commander of all military forces of the Federal Directorate of the Republic of Syndon here on Anachron IV."

The name was the final piece of data York needed: a Kinathin breed warrior, an almost pure blooded descendent of a long-dead king's attempt to gene engineer the perfect warrior. The Kinathins were supposed to be the best.

Straegga introduced herself, surrendered her sidearm, and they shook hands. Then the Kinathin turned to York.

York reached up carefully, popped his visor. The feddies behind Sab'ach'ahn jumped, probably expected to find the face of a demon behind the visor. They definitely weren't expecting the chrome eye and scars. York and Sab'ach'ahn traded salutes, then he carefully reached for his sidearm while the feddies tensed. He unclipped it from his thigh plate, reversed it and surrendered it to Sab'ach'ahn. Then he paid the feddie a compliment by breaking his right wrist seal and removing the gauntlet to shake her hand. "Ballin," he said tersely. "Imperial marines."

Sab'ach'ahn frowned, and York hoped she didn't recognize his name. All he needed was for them to find out he was the SDO, with a million crowns on his head. But Sab'ach'ahn said nothing.

York put his gauntlet back on and Sab'ach'ahn said, "If you will follow me."

The feddies were cautious, perhaps expecting the *impers* to bring the boat down filled with assault troops. But more than two hundred years ago the rules of a civilized war had been drafted on a small planet that no longer existed on the charts. York and Straegga were going to be careful to follow the Treaty Accords of Sierah to the letter.

Sab'ach'ahn led them to a small bunker about two hundred meters away. Inside the bunker a single, middle-aged man waited with two armed guards, both feddie regulars by the look of them. Sab'ach'ahn turned to the middle-aged man and introduced him as "Planetary Governor Andleman."

Andleman stared at York and Straegga with a look of fanaticism and deep distrust. By the look of his clothes he was an amateur, and York wondered what chance they had of concluding any agreement with a fanatic farmer.

There was a small table in the bunker; Andleman motioned them to sit. They did so, then Andleman and Sab'ach'ahn sat down opposite them. Sab'ach'ahn gave their sidearms to Andleman, and the governor fingered them for a moment, then said, "So you're here to surrender."

Straegga shook her head. "We do wish to surrender, but we're here to negotiate terms before doing so."

Andleman looked closely at York's sidearm, a heavy weapon of dark metal that fired nonexploding shells at high velocity. "No terms. You surrender, and that's it."

Straegga looked across the table at Andleman for a long moment. "But if we surrender without terms, you can legally treat us rather badly."

"Exactly," Andleman said smugly. "You'll just have to trust me. You have no choice."

Straegga made an obvious effort to remain calm. "All we ask are simple terms guaranteeing us humanitarian treatment."

Andleman shook his head. "Like I said, you have no choice."

Straegga shrugged. "Certainly you outnumber us, and you have time on your side. But I have Cap'm Ballin here, and almost two hundred and fifty imperial marine regulars, all experienced combat troops in full combat armor, with assault boats, portable artillery, perimeter defense weaponry, and only God and Cap'm Ballin here know what else. So if you give us no better alternative than to continue fighting, you'll pay a dear price to defeat us."

Andleman continued to examine York's sidearm and shook his head. "Don't threaten me."

Straegga leaned back. "It was no threat, merely a statement of fact."

Andleman grinned. "You're full of shit!"

It went on like that for almost two hours. Andleman really had no intention of negotiating, but he went through the motions. Sab'ach'ahn seemed somewhat embarrassed by his style, tried to interject some reason occasionally. York kept his mouth shut, spoke up only when Straegga wanted support. And it might have gone on forever like that, but near midday York's helmet com came suddenly alive with a familiar voice. "Cap'm, Palevi here. Our telemetry tap to *Cinesstar* just opened up again. She's headed back this way, and she's sounding recall."

York almost flinched, and all he could do was wonder what Sierka was up to now. But it was not the time to question God-sent favors, so he reached over, touched Straegga's sleeve, interrupted her, and as he'd already done several times that morning, he leaned close to her ear and whispered, "I don't know why, but *Cinesstar*'s back to pick us up."

Straegga's face brightened. She looked at Andleman and said, "We don't seem to be able to converge." She lifted herself carefully to her feet. "Why don't we recess, see if we can continue this tomorrow. In the meantime, an extended cease-fire might be in order."

At that moment a guard burst through the door to the bunker and shouted, "An *imper* cruiser just transited into our farspace. And it looks like she's lining up to transit in close."

Andleman jumped to his feet, pointed York's sidearm at Straegga. "What is this? What's going on?"

Throughout that morning, York had kept his arms folded on top of the table, with his right hand resting casually on top of the access panel in his left forearm plate, his thumb resting over the catch that would open it. He sat motionless while Straegga answered Andleman honestly. "I don't know. But since these talks are going nowhere I'm exercising my prerogative to end them, and accordingly, Cap'm Ballin and I will withdraw peacefully."

Andleman shook York's gun at Straegga. "No you don't. You're staying here as my prisoners."

Straegga looked down the barrel of York's sidearm, then into Andleman's eyes. "No we are not. I'm calling these negotiations to an end, which I have a right to do per the Accords set down at Sierah more than two hundred years ago. As such, Cap'm Ballin and I are to be allowed to withdraw peacefully."

Andleman spit out, "Bullshit! We didn't sign any damn accords, so if you make one move I'll cut you down where you stand."

Sab'ach'ahn lifted herself slowly to her feet. "She is right, Your Excellency. This planet is a member of the Directorate, and as such is signatory to the Accords by association. You must allow them to leave, and failure to do so is a criminal act."

Andleman considered Sab'ach'ahn's words. "I don't give a damn about any accords. You're my prisoners, and you'll stay here whether you like it or not."

Straegga extended her right hand, palm up, not far enough out to reach Andleman, but obviously to ask for her sidearm. "If you'll return my—"

A bullet exploded from the barrel of the gun Andleman held. It caught her high in the chest and to one side and she dropped to the floor. Sab'ach'ahn shouted, "Stop!"

York slapped open the access plate on his forearm, rapidly hit a four button combination in sequence, and the reactor pack on his back suddenly whined ominously. But he was concentrating on the forearm panel, on getting his thumb pressed tightly over the proper switch, and he didn't see it coming when Andleman slapped him between the eyes with the barrel of his gun through the open face of his helmet.

York's head spun as he reeled back in his chair and almost fell over, but he concentrated on keeping his thumb pressed on the switch in his forearm plate. Andleman curled his fingers over the lip of the open face of York's helmet, yanked his head forward and jammed the barrel of the gun painfully up under York's chin. York kept his thumb on the switch while his reactor pack growled at them like an angry animal.

Andleman jerked the muzzle of the gun forward, pushed York's head back painfully. "What did you do? Stop whatever it is or I'll blow your brains all over the back of your helmet."

York could feel blood from a cut in his forehead dripping down between his eyes, past his nose to his chin. "If you do," he said, trying to keep his voice even, "you'll blow us all to fucking hell."

Andleman jerked the gun harder into York's throat, demanded, "What do you mean?"

York spoke slowly. "I mean that my reactor pack is wired to a dead man switch. If I release the switch I'm holding down with my thumb, or if my suit sensors detect serious physical damage to me, my reactor pack will overload and blow."

Andleman shook him. "This is a double-cross."

"No," York said. "You were the first to violate the truce statutes of the Accords, and from that moment we were free to use any means at our disposal to defend ourselves." He looked at Sab'ach'ahn. "Isn't that right, sublegion?"

Sab'ach'ahn looked into York's eyes. "He is correct, Your Excellency. But the reactor pack on imperial armor will not detonate in the way he implies."

York grinned, could sense that *don't give a damn* feeling coming on. "It does if you bypass its fail-safe circuitry, change its programming, specifically rewire it for that purpose, then give it a fifty percent overcharge. We estimate a yield well in excess of four kilopounds. It should leave a good sized crater."

Andleman looked at Sab'ach'ahn and demanded, "Is that possible?"

The Kinathin's eyes remained locked with York's. "Yes, Your Excellency. It may be."

Andleman looked from York to Sab'ach'ahn, then back to York. He jammed the gun harder into York's throat and growled, "You're bluffing."

York looked into Andleman's eyes, felt that *don't give a damn* feeling getting even closer. "Then pull the trigger," he said.

Sab'ach'ahn asked, "What is *bluffing?*"

Andleman shook his head. "He's lying, trying to fool us, trying to get us to give up when there's no need."

"Your Excellency," Sab'ach'ahn said. "Before you believe this *bluffing*, you should realize who you're dealing with. Cap'm Ballin is the most senior drop officer of all marines in the empire, the so called SDO, the man for whom the Directorate offers a standing reward of one million crowns, dead. His dossier states he has more than twenty years of almost continuous combat experience. He is reputed to be somewhat bloodthirsty, and a bit psychotic."

Andleman hesitated, and during that instant York had the oddest feeling that if Andleman didn't pull the trigger, his nightmare about Yan taking him apart bit by bit would someday come true. "Come on, damn it," York snarled. "Pull the trigger."

Andleman frowned.

"I said pull the trigger," York shouted. "You think I'm bluffing so pull the fucking trigger."

York rose up out of the chair, the barrel of the gun still pressed under his chin. "Come on, you stupid son-of-a-bitch. Pull the goddamned trigger."

He leaned forward over the table and almost climbed up onto it, pushing Andleman back. "Don't you understand?" he screamed. "This is probably the only chance I'll ever have to go out clean—pull the fucking trigger."

Andleman looked deep into York's eyes and he started to shake. York was thinking about reaching up, grabbing Andleman's hands and forcing him to pull the trigger, when a barely audible croak from Straegga filled the surrounding silence. "Ballin . . . Help me . . ."

York closed his eyes, thought about his dream, heard a faint click as Andleman activated the gun's safety, realized Straegga had robbed him of a clean end. He leaned back away from Andleman as the governor lowered the gun he was holding. Then York lifted his left hand palm up, careful to keep his right thumb pressed tightly on the switch in his left forearm panel. "Give me the gun."

Andleman lowered it carefully and put it in York's hand. York laid it on the table. "Sublegion Sab'ach'ahn," York said. "Tell your people one of our boats'll be coming to retrieve us, and that it's not to be fired upon."

Sab'ach'ahn touched her throat mic and issued the orders.

York keyed his com. "Palevi, this is Ballin. We need pickup. Bring *Two*, and be careful. Straegga needs a medic, and the *deadman* is alive."

"We're on our way, sir."

They waited in silence, York still concentrating on the deadman switch. Then he heard the sound of an approaching boat, heard it settle to the ground, heard a short bit of commotion, a few shouts and a couple of gunshots. By prior agreement, *Two* was filled with a squad of forty marines. The feddies guarding the bunker, without armor themselves, were no match for armored marines.

The door burst open and Palevi and four of his best filed into the room, quickly disarmed everyone. A medic dropped to one knee beside Straegga and started cutting away her tunic. York was still facing Andleman when Palevi stopped beside him and saluted. "The immediate vicinity is secure, sir."

York looked down at his forearm panel, held his thumb on the deadman switch while Palevi keyed in the deactivation sequence. The angry hum from his reactor pack died. "Sound recall, Sergeant. Let's get the hell out of here." York pointed at Sab'ach'ahn and Andleman. "And those two are under arrest. Cuff them."

"Arrest!" Andleman demanded. "You can't do that. What are the charges?"

York looked at Andleman and nodded toward the Kinathin. "Ask Sab'ach'ahn there. She can tell you."

Andleman looked at the sublegion. "War crimes," she said coldly. "As the most senior civilian and military officials here we are responsible for any violation of the Treaty Accords."

She turned away from Andleman, and it was as if he were long dead and forgotten. She said to York, "There is no need to restrain me. I accept the charges and will not resist. But tell me, were you . . . *bluffing*?"

He nodded toward Andleman. "Ask him. He knows."

True to her word, Sab'ach'ahn surrendered her sidearm without incident, and though York had her cuffed anyway, she marched calmly to the boat. Andleman, however, screamed and kicked until one of the marines slapped him with the butt of her rifle. Unconscious, he was much more cooperative.

Two headed back to the perimeter to help the other boats load up for recall. York was technically correct in arresting Andleman and Sab'ach'ahn, but that was really just a pretext for getting a few hostages. He wasn't confident they could depend on fire support from *Cinesstar*, and without that, if the feddies sent their fighters after them it would be tricky getting the boats off-planet. He had their military leader and their chief fanatic, and he hoped their subordinates would be confused long enough for the marines to escape. It didn't work.

They were half way back to the stronghold when *Two*'s pilot said excitedly, "Cap'm, I got two bogies coming in fast behind us. Looks like fighters."

York activated the command channel. "Heads up, everyone. We're being hit. All boats take evasive action. And give me a display, god damn it."

While the pilot launched *Two*'s target drones and dropped the boat down toward the trees, the lower half of York's visor flickered, then a console appeared in front of him. He had to squash the immediate reaction to reach out and start programming what was merely a virtual projection on the inside of his visor.

One of the screens showed two fighters coming in from behind, two more coming in from the left and already within targeting range of the perimeter where *One* and *Three* were loading up for recall. York had an instant to see the blips representing a salvo of rockets separate lazily from the fighters on his screen, then *Two* dropped below the treetops and for a moment the screen went blank.

The two fighters approaching from behind passed overhead, took out some of *Two*'s drones then started to swing around for another pass. Luckily the forest wasn't that dense and *Two*'s pilot was able to keep the boat below the tree line while zigzagging toward the stronghold.

"*Three*'s down," someone shouted over the com. "Rocket hit."

York keyed his com. "This is Ballin. How bad?"

"Yagell here, Cap'm, on the ground. She's still in one piece, about two hundred meters from me."

Counting the survivors of the *Dumayia* crew, they had almost two hundred and eighty people in combat armor. It would be impossible to fit that many into two boats, not in armor, and there was no time to strip down and abandon it. If they couldn't get fire support from *Cinesstar*, their only alternative would be to dig in and fight it out.

"*One* and *Two*," York shouted, "go in for support. Palevi, stand by for drop. Dig in around *Three* while we pull her people.

"*Two*. Get on the horn to *Cinesstar*, see if you can get us fire support. And give me a pan of *Three* as you come in."

One of the screens displayed on York's visor lit up with a nose view of the terrain in front of *Two*, a lot of trees and ground screaming past at low altitude. Then suddenly they lifted up over the trees, York got a momentary glimpse of the defensive perimeter they'd cut in the forest, then another glimpse of *Three*, sitting on the ground canted at an odd angle, a jagged hole ripped into the cockpit, a long furrow dug into the dirt where she'd plowed her way through about twenty meters of turf before coming to a stop, her landing skids torn away.

"Cap'm. *Cinesstar* says we've got orders to return to ship, on the double, but she can't risk coming in close enough to support us. We're on our own."

Palevi's voice came over the com. "Cap'm, we're zoned."

York hit the latches holding him clipped in his seat, scrambled to the hatch where Palevi was waiting with his marines lined up behind him. He hit the release and the hatch disappeared into the skin of the boat. *Two* was still moving so he hit the ground at a run, Palevi and his marines fanning out behind him. Fifty meters in front of him marines spilled out of the hatch of the damaged boat.

Palevi said, "She must have been low when she took the hit, sir, and not moving too fast. Otherwise she'd have broken up. Wonder if she'll still fly?"

"Dig in," York said. "But stand by to move out fast. I'm going to check her out."

One and *Two* took up defensive positions close to the ground, constantly moving and changing position, using their decoy drones and weaponry to hold off the fighters.

Three's nose had crumpled, though not badly, but the rocket had hit her right in the cockpit, leaving a large jagged hole of torn plast, tubing, and wiring. York climbed up over it, almost didn't have to crouch to get through the hole onto the deck of the cockpit.

Three's pilot was gone, though there were bits and pieces of her strewn on the ground in a semicircle in front of the boat. The copilot was still seated in his couch, at least the lower half of him was. The rocket had blown away the upper half, as well as the upper half of his couch. Not for the first time, York marveled at the fickle nature of a blast; the way it could, in this case, disintegrate the pilot, tear away the console and its screens along with the upper half of the copilot and his couch, but leave the lower half, including the copilot's two control yokes, completely intact.

York keyed his com. "Palevi, this boat may still fly. Stand by."

He edged his way past the remains of the copilot. The bulkhead separating the cockpit from the passenger compartment was badly warped, and York had to pry the auxiliary control panel loose with a piece of debris before it would fold down. It was completely dead until he hit the system switch. The auxiliary lighting dimmed for a second, a mortar round shook the ground in the distance, then miraculously the boat's operating system began flashing information on the screen above the keyboard as it ran through its emergency damage control sequence. It automatically shunted out the now nonexistent main console and the missing pilot's controls. It gave a warning message about the copilot's controls, recommended the boat be shut down for extensive repairs. York interceded and put the boat's system on red status, which redefined all of its safety protocols. He set it to take programming from one of his suit's com frequencies, programmed it to feed him a projection of the main console on the lower half of the inside of his visor, reprogrammed some of the most critical functions for access through his forearm panel, then ran it through a system check again. It finished with the message, *All functions accessible, but flight worthiness is unacceptable and flight operation is not advised.*

York turned to the remains of the copilot, and while he muscled the lower half of the man's body out of the couch he keyed his com. "Palevi, Ballin here. Load her up. And make sure you put people on her weapons stations. This boat's gonna fly if I have to flap my fucking arms to make it do so."

York tossed the remains of the copilot out through the hole in the front of the cockpit, snapped himself into the couch and used his forearm plate to bring up the boat's power. He sealed his armor. "Minor hazard warning," his suit said. "Gauntlet brea—"

He killed the message, tried not to think about what was going to happen to his hand if he was successful and got the boat out of the planet's atmosphere.

"Cap'm. Ten seconds, then we're ready to roll."

The fighters made another pass, took out some of the decoy drones and blew a few craters in the ground nearby. York counted slowly to ten, barked into his com, "Lifting!" then put power to the drive gingerly. "*One* and *Two* stand clear of me. I don't know how she's gonna handle."

With most of the front of the cockpit gone, it was an odd feeling to watch the ground drop away in front of him as the boat lifted straight up. It wobbled a little, had a tendency to drift to port, but he ignored that, tilted her forward and goosed the drive while watching his virtual screens for intruders. "Cap'm, this is Hackla in *One*. Me and *Two* are with you all the way."

The boat's aerodynamics were shot to hell, and as he started picking up speed the wind made an awful racket and pressed him back in the couch. At one hundred knots he lifted the nose, shouted over the com, "Let's go for it." His screens showed *One* and *Two* falling in behind him to cover him. When he reached five hundred knots she started to shake and jerk about and he had to drop back on the drive. It was then that he saw the four fighters appear on the edge of his screens.

He had the boat's nose almost straight up by then. *One* and *Two* dropped back to take on the fighters. York shouted into the com, "Do what you can to cover me, but don't go down with me. That's an order." They were marines. He hoped they weren't stupid enough to lose all three boats just to save one.

"Palevi, I can't coordinate fire. Do what you can with our gun turrets."

Palevi didn't acknowledge him, so he repeated the message, waited for a few long seconds, guessed the boat's relay circuitry was damaged, and without that the hull plating was blocking their suit transmissions.

An assault boat, with six weapons turrets, close to thirty decoy drones, electronic counter measures, air-to-air rockets and cannon, was a formidable opponent for the fighters. But the fighters had speed, and their pilots weren't stupid. It was obvious one of the three *impers* was damaged, so two of them kept *One* and *Two* busy while the other two went after the crippled boat.

York pushed the boat to the limit, kept it just below the velocity where it wanted to shake itself apart. The two fighters were climbing right up behind him. He kept his eyes on the console, watched the fighters overtaking him, waited until he saw the blips of their rockets, then fired a salvo of defensive interceptor rockets, dumped a load of chaff, launched *Three's* decoy drones.

The interceptor rockets took out half the salvo of feddie rockets, the chaff deflected more, and the decoy drones cut that number further. Four blips got through those defenses and Palevi's marines cut in with the gun turrets. York watched a blip disappear, and then there were three. Another salvo from the gun turrets, then there were two, then one. On his screen York saw it slowly converge with the tail of his boat.

The boat convulsed once, shuddered, lost all drive power, then careened wildly to one side. His status screen showed red lights all up and down the panel, the starboard drive pod had been blown away and the port pod lit up like a landing beacon for a moment, then shut down.

They still had plenty of velocity, but they were heading toward the top of a ballistic arc, and when they got there, without drive power, they'd start right back down to the bottom, and in the shape the boat was in he doubted he could bring it down dead-stick. He had one chance; he hit a three-switch combination on his forearm panel, and the boat's computer said in his ear, "Emergency launch pods activated. Ignition in twenty seconds and counting. Stand by for—"

"Override," York screamed. "Execute, god damn you, override and execute."

The emergency launch pods cut in without warning, slammed York back into the copilot's couch under about fifteen gravities. In seconds the boat went unstable and started to shake, and it took every bit of skill he had to keep it traveling in a straight line. He knew he had one hundred seconds before the disposable pods died, but by then they'd be traveling at close to three thousand meters per second and well beyond the planet's atmosphere, if the boat stayed in one piece and he could keep her nose aimed in the right direction.

"Major hazard warning," his suit reminded him. "Gauntlet breach. Decompression compensation increasing."

The isolation seal around his left wrist began to tighten painfully. Something tore away from the boat; it lurched badly to one side, almost went into a spin, but he got it straightened out and marginally stable again. His left hand started to throb painfully as the isolation seal got tighter. Again, the ship lurched badly as something tore away, but the shaking eased as the joints in his armor expanded. He took a chance, glanced at the console: no blips coming at him from behind, altitude just under fifty kilometers. They were almost there.

The copilot's couch really should have been able to take fifteen gravities, but then the rocket that opened up the front of the boat must have damaged it's mounting in some way. York was watching the boat's altitude, trying not to think about the pain in his left hand, but breathing easier because they were approaching an altitude of one hundred kilometers and moving beyond the range of the fighters, when the copilot's couch tore loose from its mounting. It was only about a half-meter drop from the back of the couch to the bulkhead behind it, but at fifteen gravities it was like falling better than seven meters. He slammed into the bulkhead and lost consciousness.

18

Murderous Need

YORK REGAINED CONSCIOUSNESS drifting weightless in a black and white world of bright glare and sharp shadows. He was still buckled in the couch, and a readout at the top of his visor told him he'd been out for less than ten minutes. His thoughts immediately settled on the intolerable pain in his left hand.

"*Three*, this is *One*. Do you read? *Three*, this is *One*. Do you read? Over."

York keyed his com. "Ballin here. Over."

"*Three*, this is *One*. Do you read? *Three*, this is *One*. Do you read? Over."

They weren't receiving him, and there was no console projection displayed at the bottom of his visor. His suit's connection to the boat's system was down.

He lifted his left hand; his suit had tightened the isolation seal around his wrist with crushing force and his hand had swollen to fill and distend the gauntlet. There was no feeling in the hand any more, not in the sense of manipulating the thumb and fingers, but there was plenty of feeling when it came to pain. As he looked at it a tiny drop of unhealthy looking yellowish fluid oozed out of the small tear in the mesh of the gauntlet, then dissipated quickly into the vacuum of space.

"*Three*, this is *One*. Do you read? *Three*, this is *One*. Do you read? Over."

He took a dose of kikker, then just for good measure added a couple of nerve jackers. The drugs accentuated the pain, but they cleared his head and he took stock of his situation.

He was floating near the hole in the cockpit, still buckled in the copilot's seat. When the seat had torn away it had taken both control yokes with it, pulling a couple of meters of shredded wiring out of the deck. If he hadn't been tethered to the boat by the wiring, he and the seat might have drifted out through the hole and floated away. With his good hand he released the straps buckling him to the seat, braced one foot against the deck and his hand against the bulkhead overhead, then used the other foot to kick the seat out through the hole. While doing that he felt a faint vibration in his hand and foot, as if someone was hammering on the frame of the boat.

"*Three*, this is *One*. Do you read? *Three*, this is *One*. Do you read? Over."

His suit was equipped with fifty meters of thin, plast safety line. He pulled out a few meters, clipped the end to a piece of tubing protruding from the wreck of the control console, yanked on it a couple of times to test it. He went back to the bulkhead at the rear of the cockpit, pressed the palm of his good hand against it, felt the vibration strongly there as a series of distinct, though seemingly frantic, blows. He wondered if the marines had some code of taps and clicks by which they could communicate. If so, they'd never taught it to him. He pounded on the bulkhead a couple of times and the hammering responded by picking up its pace.

"*Three*, this is *One*. Do you read? *Three*, this is *One*. Do you read? Over."

He turned to the backup console still folded out of the bulkhead, had difficulty programming it with one hand. He learned that when the control yokes had been ripped away the boat's computer had gone on autopilot, held to the simple program of maintaining course, and with the boat's nose straight up that was just what had been needed.

"*Three*, this is *One*. Do you read? *Three*, this is *One*. Do you read? Over."

A few more seconds and he had his suit tied back into the boat's system. He keyed his com. "Ballin here."

"Cap'm, Yagell here. Good to hear from you. We're having trouble locating you, not picking up any telemetry from your boat."

"Ya, she's a mess. I'll get a beacon going."

"Good. You do that and we'll be right there to help you, Cap'm."

"Negative," York said. "There's nothing you can do. We're dead in space. Just get your wounded back to *Cinesstar* and tell them to pick us up."

"You sure there's nothing we can do, sir?"

"Just get your wounded in, and tell *Cinesstar* not to waste any time."

"Right, sir. Yagell out."

York grabbed a twisted piece of plast with his good hand, closed his eyes for a moment. The pain from his hand made his head swim, but he couldn't chance the groggy side effects of a pain-killer. He tried to program another dose of kikker, but his suit warned him he'd had a dose less than five minutes before so he retracted the order.

It took him about ten minutes to get the emergency beacon going. He should have been quicker but the throbbing in his left hand dulled his senses. He programmed a few keys on the keyboard to give him crude control over the boat's attitude jets in case he needed to help *Cinesstar* during pickup. By that time his head was swimming and his hands were starting to shake from the pain pounding at his nerves. He paused again for a moment and closed his eyes . . .

The pounding on the bulkhead brought him back, and he realized he'd lost consciousness. He'd happened to float into a position where his helmet was touching the bulkhead, and the racket sounded as if there were a half dozen of them pounding away frantically. He looked at the readout on his visor, realized he'd been out for almost an hour. *Cinesstar* should have picked them up by now!

He took another dose of kikker. The boat's radar and scanners were shot, but he was getting a canned telemetry feed from *Cinesstar*. From that he had their positions. The wrecked hulk of *Three* had achieved escape velocity and was arcing away from the planet's surface. *Cinesstar* had picked up *One* and *Two* more than forty minutes ago, then taken up a position about fifty thousand kilometers from *Three*, was just sitting there, waiting.

The pounding on the bulkhead got more frantic. York had the boat's computer run a quick systems check, and there it was. The port drive pod had gone into overload, her power feed was pouring out heat and hard radiation. The back of the boat must be an oven. York keyed his com. "*Cinesstar*. This is *Three*. Mayday! Mayday! One of our drive pods has gone haywire. It's cooking us alive out here."

No answer, just silence. *Cinesstar* sat there and waited, and York realized Sierka was still trying to get rid of him. He'd been willing to sacrifice the entire marine contingent to do it. But for some reason he now needed them, and here was an opportunity to get most of them back, then sit back and watch York burn alive with the rest.

York looked frantically around the cockpit for something, anything, and spotted a small arms compartment. He hit the latch with his fist, tore the cover open: two rifles, two sidearms, and about a dozen grenades with various ratings. He grabbed two of the ten-pounders, forming a plan as he did so, and clipped them to his waist. He keyed his com. "Sierka, you son-of-a-bitch," he growled. "You can't kill me this easily. I'm coming back for you if it's the last fucking thing I do."

There was one chance. It wouldn't get them back on *Cinesstar*, but it might remove the immediate danger of the damaged pod and buy them some time. He reeled out twenty meters of safety line, guessing that to be length of the boat, then coiled it carefully, and crouching against the bulkhead he jumped out through the hole in the front of the boat, floated out until he reached the end of the safety line. It went taut, stretched a bit, then sprang him back toward the boat. It was an old trick, but it had been a long time since he'd done any real weightless work, and he missed a bit. If he'd done it right he would have come past the nose of the boat, swung around toward its tail, and when the line went tight a second time, he would have latched on to the aft end of the boat. As it was he careened off a gun turret, tumbled a bit, and when the line again went taut, through habit he reached out with his bad hand, tried to grab something, and that just shot pain up through his arm.

He ended up hanging onto the port gun turret, his line badly tangled, his arm a dead stump of pain, his lips growling a silent curse at Sierka. He played out more line, tried to ignore the pain and started crawling over the outside of the boat. Luckily, wherever a section of the boat's skin had been torn away he was able to find something to grip, but his suit started nagging him long before he got to the drive pod. "Radiation hazard. Limit exposure to five minutes."

Five minutes was enough for what he had to do.

Each drive pod was mounted to the rear of the boat by a large faring, one on each side. All that remained of the starboard drive pod was a stub of a faring that ended in a twisted, blackened mess of plast and steel. The port drive pod was still intact, though it was starting to glow a dull red.

"Radiation hazard. Limit exposure to one minute."

He might need more than a minute. He reeled out a few more meters of line and wrapped his good arm around the faring. But with his good arm holding him in place, the arm that remained was useless for the work at hand, so gritting his teeth against the torment, he wedged his bad hand between two supports; he almost lost consciousness, had to take another kikker.

He cursed and swore, tried to focus his anger on Sierka to remain conscious, pulled one of the grenades loose with his good hand, fumbled at it to set the timer for one minute, wedged it in place on one side of the faring. He repeated the process with the other grenade, placed it next to the first, then he armed them, and hit the detonation studs.

He pulled at his bad hand, and it wouldn't come loose. It was wedged too tightly, and it was too dead and useless to help him. He tugged at it, staring point-blank at the two grenades about to blow him to pieces, yanked on it with all his might, sending an excruciating jolt of pain up his arm with each pull. Then suddenly it came loose, and he careened away from the faring, floating helplessly. Floating free he swung his arms and legs about wildly, trying to connect with something, happened to be about ten meters from the two grenades and staring right at them when they blew . . .

••••

Critical hazard war . . . compress . . . and counting.

The agony at the end of his arm; he would have given anything to have Alsa cut it off at that moment. The hissing jet of air blowing out through the blackened crack in his chest plate didn't seem to bother him, though a piece of him knew it should.

Critical hazard warning, his suit said. *Torso breach. Terminal decompression in ten minutes and counting.*

He was a dead man. The grenades had blown away the bad pod. He could even remember the explosion, the soundless flash, an instantaneous glimpse of a big piece of debris hurtling straight at him. Either the blast itself, or the jet of air blowing out his chest plate, had spun him around the boat a few times like a rock on the end of a string. He'd finished up tied to the side of the boat twisted in the safety line. Soon his air would run out and there was nothing he could do about it.

Critical hazard warning. Torso breach. Terminal decompression in nine minutes and counting.

He triggered a dose of kikker and his mind started to race. There was an air line somewhere in the cockpit. There had to be. He reached for the power knife at his belt, a standard part of his kit, struggled for a moment before he found it and got it free.

Critical hazard warning. Torso breach. Terminal decompression in eight minutes and counting.

He wedged his bad hand beneath the outer skin of the ship where a section of plast had been torn away, and the agony became a distant ache as he flicked on the power knife and started cutting away the safety line.

Critical hazard warning. Torso breach. Terminal decompression in seven minutes and counting.

There wasn't time to favor his injured hand now. With no safety line to protect him against a chance misstep, with the blast of air blowing out through the crack in his chest plate threatening to jet him away helplessly into space, he needed four functional limbs if he was going to make it in time. He used his forearm panel to administer a heavy dose of painkiller, then triggered a triple dose of kikkers and jackers to counteract any drowsiness.

Critical hazard warning. Torso breach. Terminal decompression in six minutes and counting.

It worked. He was so blasted on painkillers and kikkers and jackers and pain itself, that it almost didn't hurt to use the dead stump of a hand as a climbing grapple: jam it into something convenient, move the good hand to another hold, tear the dead hand loose and lodge it into something else. No room for mistakes.

Critical hazard warning. Torso breach. Terminal decompression in five minutes and counting.

It almost didn't hurt; there was a schizophrenic piece of his mind that retreated from the reality of his actions, and took the agony with it. He controlled his motor functions nicely, while that other piece of him had taken control of his mouth and vocal chords, and was venting his torment by growling a vitriolic stream of curses aimed at Sierka.

Critical hazard warning. Torso breach. Terminal decompression in four minutes and counting.

His good hand reached the twisted edge of the hole blown in the nose of the boat. He crawled into the cockpit, pushed toward the warped bulkhead at the rear. The air line should be back there somewhere, hidden behind a panel of some sort.

The cockpit lighting had shut down completely, so he'd have to recognize the panel by feel through the mesh of his gauntlet. He started low, searching with his good hand, touching everything. He covered every centimeter of the bulkhead that was accessible. Nothing.

Critical hazard warning. Torso breach. Terminal decompression in three minutes and counting.

He was a fool. He returned to the console in the bulkhead, wasted no more than a second or two bringing up a repair schematic of the boat. A few more seconds and he had a blow-up of the cockpit. A few more and he'd found the air nozzle. It should be behind a small panel in the side bulkhead next to where the pilot's couch had been.

Critical hazard warning. Torso breach. Terminal decompression in two minutes and counting.

He scrambled over to the mess of wiring and twisted plast that had once been the pilot's console, found a large piece of warped wall plating concealing the panel. He reached around behind it, found the panel, touched its latch and it opened less than a centimeter before it came up against the plating bent over it. He couldn't even get a gauntleted finger behind the panel cover, let alone grab the air line and pull it out. He gave up on that approach, took hold of the edge of the bent plast, dug his heels into the deck and pulled. His eyes started to bulge and he almost passed out.

Critical hazard warning. Torso breach. Terminal decompression in one minute and counting.

He let go of the plast, pushed off to the arms locker, trying desperately to remain calm, to suppress the panic rising up his throat.

Critical hazard warning. Torso breach. Terminal decompression in ninety seconds and counting.

Still cursing at Sierka he rifled through the grenades in the small locker, found one with a two pound rating and pushed back across the cabin to the plate of bent plast.

Critical hazard warning. Torso breach. Terminal decompression in eighty seconds and counting.

He set the fuse on the grenade for three seconds, pushed it down behind the bent plast, wedged it between the plate of plast and the wall about half a meter to one side of the panel containing his only chance for survival.

Critical hazard warning. Torso breach. Terminal decompression in seventy seconds and counting.

He triggered the grenade, yanked his arm out from behind the plast, pushed away from the bent plate. He wasn't one for praying, but while he cursed at Sierka he silently prayed the blast wouldn't damage the tubing in the wall, nor the reel of hose, nor the valve on the end of it that he needed to connect it to his suit supply, nor . . .

Critical haz . . . breach . . . decompression in twenty sec . . .

The blast had blown him across the cockpit and he'd lost consciousness for a few critical seconds. It had also blown a hole through the sidewall and torn away the offending piece of plating.

Critical hazard warning. Torso breach. Terminal decompression in ten seconds and counting.

His ears popped and he was swimming on the edge of consciousness as he pushed toward the air line.

Nine.

The deck pitched and rolled in an effort to divert him.

Eight.

Tiny motes of death started to dance in front of his eyes and his ears started to hurt.

Seven.

He got hold of the line, yanked on it, pulled a couple meters out of the wall.

Six.

He fumbled for the nozzle on the bottom of the reactor pack on his back.

Five.

His fingers were going numb, his arm getting sloppy as if he'd slept on it wrong.

Four.

He found the nozzle just as he was blacking out.

Three.

It wouldn't connect, didn't seem to fit.

Two.

He cursed, pulled on the line, shouted an oath at Sierka.

One.

He struggled to connect the hose, his lips still feebly cursing Sierka, swearing he'd come back from the dead if need be . . .

••••

Frank Stara's hands were trembling with frustration and anger. York had accidentally left his com on and they'd all heard his ordeal, the desperate struggle to accomplish some task the purpose of which had something to do with keeping them from "cooking alive," the semi delirious curses, the explosion, the critical hazard warnings from his armor, the countdown to terminal decompression. The bridge had gone absolutely silent.

"Well, Mister Stara," Sierka demanded. "Answer me. Are there any signs of life?"

"No, sir," Frank said, struggling to contain his anger. "There was an explosion of some sort, and his suit telemetry reported a massive torso breach and terminal decompression. Then there was another explosion and we stopped getting any signal at all. He's dead. You killed him. You murdered him."

"What did you say?"

"I said he's dead, sir." Frank peered carefully over his shoulder. Sierka sat at the captain's console staring blankly at the screens, paralyzed with fear—mostly fear of York, it seemed. After the second explosion Sierka had ordered Maggie to move the ship to within a hundred meters of the crippled boat, and now they were sniffing around it fearfully, like a small animal frightened a large predator might come back to life at any moment.

"Sir," Olin Rame said carefully. "I recommend we retrieve that boat. Mister Ballin may be dead, but certainly there are others there in need of aid."

That was how they'd been getting Sierka to act, recommend the appropriate action, try to talk Sierka into doing the right thing, into doing anything, then all pretend it was he who was running the ship. "Yes," Sierka said. "Do it."

"Mister Stara," Rame said. "Open *Three Bay* and tell them to stand by for pickup. And warn Miss Yan we'll probably have more wounded for her.

"Miss Votak. Move us in slowly. I don't think that boat is going to be able to help you any, so you'll have to maneuver *Three Bay* around her."

••••

York's entire arm hurt now, right up to the elbow. As a sort of half consciousness returned to him he stared at the jet of air blowing out of the crack in his chest plate, pinning him to the bulkhead. Then his eyes followed the tangled mess of the air line that snaked between his reactor pack and the side wall of the craft. Slowly he came to the realization that he was alive.

Suddenly the harsh glare of the distant sun disappeared and everything went black. He looked out through the hole of what had once been a cockpit and he saw the bright lighting of one of *Cinesstar*'s service bays open to space like the mouth of a giant beast, seeming to grow as she drifted lazily toward the boat. He keyed his com. "Sierka," he said, the words coming out in a cracked and garbled growl. "I'm coming to get you, you son-of-a-bitch."

••••

Frank started at the sound of York's voice, but Sierka jumped as if he'd just heard from the dead.

"Shut that service bay," Sierka screamed. "Shut it, now."

Frank almost obeyed him, but finally he'd had enough. He put his hands flat on the com console and refused to move.

"Mister Stara, I gave you an order. Obey me, damn you. Obey me."

Frank sat dead still, refused to act, to speak, to even acknowledge the order.

"Miss Votak," Sierka screamed hysterically. "Get us out of here."

The ship didn't move. Maggie was hidden within the helm cluster so her act of defiance was less visible, but no less obvious.

Sierka crossed the distance to Frank, and he rammed the muzzle of a gun against the base of his skull. "This is an act of mutiny, Mister Stara. Now close *Three Bay* instantly or I'll execute you myself right here and now."

••••

York watched the open safety of *Three Bay* approaching, but then suddenly, with rescue no more than ten meters away, the bay doors started to close.

"No," York pleaded. "No. Please no!" He pushed off the bulkhead, but the jet of air forced him back against it. He reached down deep for the last bit of strength he had, slid along the bulkhead to the backup console, prayed that he remembered correctly the way he'd programmed the keys, hit three that should fire the right attitude jets.

Nothing happened for a moment, then the boat started to move with agonizing slowness. Ordinarily, in a docking procedure, you erred on the side of caution, gave the jets a tiny goose, let the boat drift carefully into place. But now York held the keys down and the boat picked up speed rapidly.

It almost worked nicely, but the bay doors were half closed, and the boat was a total wreck, and York was only conscious because he was close to overdose on kikkers and jackers, and it really wouldn't have been possible to exercise fine attitude control with a keyboard anyway. The boat clipped one of the bay seals on its way in, jackknifed around, tore off a good piece of its tail section on a large girder, entered the gravity field of the service bay, crashed to the deck and skidded to a stop in a grinding mess of twisted steel and plast.

York pitched forward through the hole in the cockpit, landed on his side on the deck, still tethered to the boat by the air hose, and the jet of air pinned him down.

Three Bay clanked shut with a crash that echoed through the hull, and the service crew brought pressure up in the bay. As the air pressure around him rose, the jet of air slowly stopped blowing, York's suit depressurized the isolation seal around his wrist, and that increased the agony he was trying to contain. He triggered a kikker, rolled over and tried to struggle to his feet.

Someone helped him up, half dragged him to a bulkhead and sat him down against it. The bay was filling quickly with service crew and marines from the other boats, all starting to swarm over the wreck of *Three*. York popped his visor, filled his lungs with the clean, fresh air from the bay, looked up, found Maggie and Frank standing over him. He tugged at his helmet, growled, "Help me get this thing off. And what the hell are you doing here?"

While they struggled with the neck seals on his helmet Maggie and Frank explained. When Sierka had abandoned York and his marines he'd almost had a mutiny on his hands among his junior officers, but Maggie had reminded them all of York's own words about such idiocy. But when the AI had resumed their rape squads, the mutiny had come about anyway, a mix of civilians, the enlisted ranks, and some of the NCO's.

"Well, not exactly a mutiny," Frank said. "More like another riot. We've sealed them in E, F, and G decks."

Maggie grimaced, lifted York's helmet slowly off his head. "Sierka tried to arm the officers, but even armed we're too heavily outnumbered by the mutineers, so he needs your marines. And in any case, the empress ordered him to come back and pick you up." She looked at his face. "What the hell happened to you?"

York touched his face, felt the dried blood from the cut on his forehead where Andleman had struck him with the barrel of his gun, a fresh trickle of blood from his nose due to the near-terminal decompression of his suit. "Forget me. Why aren't you two on the bridge?"

Maggie and Frank looked at each other, grinned. Maggie shrugged. "Frank and I aren't getting along well with His Lordship. We've been relieved of duty, we're under arrest, and we're supposed to report to the brig. I guess we'll get there eventually."

There was a crowd of marines and technicians gathered around *Three*'s small airlock, and it was starting to bother York that neither that nor the main hatch were open yet, that no marines weren't spilling out of the boat carrying wounded to sickbay.

He stood up carefully. His left arm and hand were an intolerable torment, the gauntlet still distended and rigid. His legs trembled and he wanted to collapse, but the kikkers and jackers kept him conscious and moving. He marched over to the crowd at the airlock, got there just as they forced the outer seal.

It spilled open and four, half-naked bodies spilled out, marines stripped of their armor, their wounds wrapped in blood soaked bandages, their skins the blue of carbon dioxide asphyxiation.

"What happened?" Maggie asked.

Each of the four marines had one or more bandages on their head, neck, or torso, and York understood, but Yagell answered her. "They must have lost pressure in the main compartment. If you got a limb breach you just lose an arm or leg, but a torso or helmet breach is a death sentence. So they stripped them and stuffed them into the airlock, hoping it would hold pressure. Would have worked, Cap'm, if you'd got picked up faster. But they ran out of air."

One of the technicians looked at a readout on the inside of the airlock. "Pressure's equalizing inside, air's leaking back in."

York backed away from the four bodies, and Yagell's words kept echoing through his thoughts . . . *if you'd got picked up faster . . .*

The inner seal on the airlock popped loudly when they finally opened it, and the marines inside poured out carrying their wounded. York couldn't take his eyes off the four, blue skinned casualties, and even when Soladin approached him and barked an order at him, he still could hear only Yagell's words . . . *if you'd got picked up faster . . .*

Palevi stopped beside him, popped his visor, sucked fresh air into his lungs, looked down at the four dead marines. "What happened, Cap'm? Why'd it take so long to get picked up?"

. . . *if you'd got picked up faster* . . . York felt something rising up within him, something akin to hatred, but colder, with a hard knife-edge of purpose attached to it.

"What happened, Cap'm?"

"Ballin," Soladin shouted. "Are you listening to me? I'm giving you an order, and it comes directly from Commander Sierka."

. . . *if you'd got picked up faster* . . . York turned to Soladin, saw the young nobleman as if through a strange, distorted haze.

Soladin shouted, "Answer me, or I'll—"

York backhanded him with the closed fist of his good hand. Soladin landed on his back in a sprawl, bounced once and came to a stop. He groaned, rolled onto his side and curled up. There were two AI goons with him, armed with sidearms and rifles. They backed away warily, but made no hostile moves.

York looked down at the empty clips on his thigh plate, couldn't remember where he'd lost his sidearm. He turned back to Palevi, looked at him through that distorted atmosphere and held out his good hand palm up. "Sergeant, may I borrow your sidearm."

Maggie grabbed him by his bad arm, and the resulting pain cleared his head even further. "What are you going to do, York?"

He didn't look at her as he answered. "Something I should have done a long time ago."

Palevi unclipped his sidearm from his thigh plate, an old-fashioned, heavy-caliber revolver. He popped it open, checked the load, closed it, reversed it, laid it carefully in York's hand. "Eight rounds, sir."

York growled like a wild beast, "I'll only need one."

"York," Maggie pleaded. She tugged on his bad arm and he was thankful now for the pain. "Please! What are you going to do?"

York shook her off, turned away from her toward the lift and stepped over Soladin who was trying to get to his feet. As he marched to the lift there was a certain peace that came over him now that he knew what to do. He could even ignore the throbbing agony that had once been his left arm, and he thought that perhaps the four dead marines from the boat's airlock were a fair price to pay if it got him to finally do the right thing.

"God damn it, Ballin!" Maggie shouted. She caught him from behind by his bad arm, and again he was thankful for the pain. She spun him about to face her, screamed in his face, "What are you—"

He backhanded her like Soladin, but this time his hand was carrying the weight of Palevi's gun and she went down like a rag doll. He stood over her, screamed at the top of his lungs, "I'm gonna blow Sierka's fucking brains all over the goddamned bridge. That's what I'm gonna do."

Three Bay was dead silent as he turned back to the lift. But Soladin had regained his feet, and with the AI goons, was now blocking his path. The young nobleman backed away a step, and behind him the AI goons backed with him. "You're under arrest, Ballin."

Even York couldn't believe the sound that crawled up out of his throat. "Get out of my way, or I'll kill you too."

Soladin backed up another step, pointed a finger at York, shouted at his two AI goons, "Shoot him. That's an order."

York stood there without moving and the two AI goons hesitated uncertainly, so Soladin started fumbling at the gun holstered to his side.

An odd sound came from behind York. It began with a single click and the sound of a reactor pack whining up to combat status. Then a second click, and a third, more reactor packs whining up to status, safeties snapping off, a cacophony of weapons cocked and brought to bear that blended together into a single, drawn-out roar that rose almost tediously into a deafening crescendo, then died slowly into a silence broken only by the hum of a multitude of weapons ready to kill.

The effect on Soladin was extraordinary. He froze with stark terror on his face, his gun only half drawn from the holster, his mouth so wide open you could park a gunboat in it.

York froze too, his arms slack at his sides, Palevi's gun pointing at the deck. He turned slowly about to look at what had so dramatically transfixed Soladin. About a hundred weapons were all fixed on the poor nobleman standing in the lift. Every marine in *Three Bay* stood statue still, some upright, some on one knee, but each in a textbook combat stance for firing a weapon with maximum accuracy. Even Stacy, the kid, had leveled his rotary and powered up his reactor pack, though he looked more scared than angry or determined. One nod from York and they'd disintegrate Soladin and his two AI goons. Then York could go up and murder Sierka. Then he and his marines could murder anyone else they felt like murdering. Then what?

He turned slowly back to Soladin, who hadn't moved a muscle, and he spoke in a soft voice, almost a whisper. "Holster your gun."

Soladin's eyes considered a useless act of idiotic heroism, but York shook his head calmly and said, "Don't. You won't even clear the holster."

Soladin hesitated for a moment, then he carefully pushed the gun back down into its holster. A wave of pain washed up York's arm as he turned back to Maggie, and now he was not thankful for the torment. She lay still with Frank crouched over her. York called for a medic, though he didn't have to shout, and one scrambled across the deck, dropped to her knees beside Maggie and started to work. York looked at Palevi, tossed him the sidearm, then crouched down beside Frank.

Maggie was blinking groggily, a nasty cut below her right eye. York reached out with his good hand, brushed hair out of her eyes and said, "I'm sorry."

Her eyes focused and she grinned painfully. "No way to treat a lady, York."

York looked at the medic. "You broke her cheek, Cap'm. Nothing more serious than that."

Again York said, "I'm sorry." He stood, marched back to Soladin and said, "You wanted to see me?"

Soladin was still transfixed, still staring back over York's shoulder. York turned around slowly. The reactor packs were still whining and the marines still frozen with their weapons aimed at the poor nobleman. Even Palevi had raised the gun York had just tossed him, was now sighting down the barrel. "Put your weapons down," York said.

There was a click or two, and one or two reactor packs went silent, but the rest didn't move. York looked at Palevi, looked down the barrel of his gun, past it, looked him in the eyes. "Put your gun down, Sergeant. That's an order."

A few more reactor packs wound down, a few more weapons lowered, but still Palevi hesitated. Then finally his hand moved and the gun dropped in a slow arc to his thigh where he clicked it into place. One by one the rest of the marines followed his example, shut down their reactor packs and lowered their weapons.

York turned back to Soladin.

"The captain wants to see you," Soladin said, his arrogance gone. "In his office. Now."

York marched toward the lift, forcing Soladin and his two AI goons to step aside as he stormed past them. They stepped in behind him, scrambled to keep up.

••••

Sierka had a guard outside his office, but the man took one look at York and stepped timidly aside. With Soladin following close on his heels, York pushed his way into Sierka's office and Sierka nearly jumped out of his skin. "I'm still alive," York announced, refusing to follow the normal formalities of salute and acknowledgment.

Sierka had a small gun sitting on the desk in front of him. Sweat glistened on his face and his breathing came in short desperate gasps. But after a few seconds, he realized York wasn't going to kill him and he recovered.

York turned upon Soladin. "Get out," he shouted.

Soladin started to say something but York cut him off. "I said get out. And close the fucking hatch behind you."

Soladin backed carefully out through the hatch and closed it.

York turned his attention back to Sierka. "What do you want?"

Sierka toyed with the small gun. "You're . . . insubordinate."

"So what? Execute me!"

Sierka looked at him carefully. "I have a certain . . . security situation you need to take care—"

"I know," York said. He leaned on Sierka's desk. "You've got a mutiny on your hands on E, F, and G decks. You've screwed things up so fucking badly the rest of your crew is ready to join them, and now you want me to clean things up for you. I'll clean your mess up, but then you're going to start doing things right around here. You're going to set up a proper crew, and you're going to captain this ship like the man-of-war it is, or so help me God I'll . . ."

As York hesitated Sierka responded with a broad grin. "That's it, Lieutenant, isn't it? You'll what? You can't even say it. Well, I'll say it. You must either kill me and take over the ship, or do what I command. And right now I command you to squash the mutiny that's threatening us all."

York raised his good hand over his head in a fist, brought it down on the desk with an incredible crack, sending papers and debris scattering in all directions. Sierka's confidence disappeared and the fear returned to his eyes, and York was thankful for even that small victory. He turned and stormed out of the office. Out in the corridor he felt *Cinesstar* make transition.

••••

It was a fairly simple matter to squash the mutiny on E, F, and G decks. They'd disarmed most of G-deck after the riot, but E and F were crew, with a lot of contraband weapons. York gathered his marines, didn't bother to get new armor—he wouldn't need it—started on E deck with a hand com piped into the deck allship. "This is Cap'm Ballin. I have more than two hundred marines in full combat kit. We have orders to take this deck and restore order. If you surrender without resistance, you have my word no harm will come to you. If you don't, then we will be quick, efficient, and ruthless.

"Lay down any weapons you have, then lay down on your stomach with your hands locked together on the back of your head, and I personally guarantee your safety."

It worked, probably because the mutiny had no leadership and had degenerated into just another riot. There was only one incident, on F deck. They'd cleared about half of it when a young woman jumped out into the middle of the corridor, and with a hysterical scream started swinging a small handgun wildly about, pulling the trigger. The marines dove for cover as bullets ricocheted up the corridor, and they started to bring their weapons to bear, but York screamed, "Hold your fire. As you were. That's an order."

Above all, the marines were disciplined. They let her stand in the corridor screaming and pulling the trigger on the gun. It was a small grav gun, with a magazine of nonexplosive projectiles and a reactor pack in the grip. When she'd fired all the projectiles the gun shut down, though she remained there screaming and pulling the trigger. York stood, stepped into the corridor, and at sight of him her screams died, became a whimper, though she continued to pull the trigger on the now empty weapon. York walked slowly up the corridor, the only sound the click, click, click as she repeatedly pulled the trigger. He walked up to her until she could press the barrel of the gun against his chest at point-blank range, the trigger clicking into the silence around them. He raised his hands, cupped them around the gun and carefully pulled it out of her grip. She buried her face in her hands and broke into sobs.

York spoke into the hand com. "Get a medic here and sedate her."

That set the tone for the cleanup operation, and the marines were careful to kill no one.

When it was over, York reported to Soladin and his two AI goons. "Very good, Mister Ballin," Soladin said. "Now. I have orders from Commander Sierka. You're under arrest for attempted mutiny. These two men will escort you to the brig."

York allowed the AI goons to escort him to a cell, noted with an oddly disconnected sense of reality that prisoners of one sort or another occupied many of the other cells. As they locked him in he said, "I need medical attention."

The two goons looked at each other and grinned. "Sure you do," one of them said.

"I need treatment," York said. "Please have a marine medic or someone from Doctor Yan's staff come here as soon as possible."

Their grins broadened and they turned away without comment. York folded a seat out of the wall and sat down. His left hand was so badly swollen the gauntlet was rigid, with a steady stream of ooze drizzling out of the tear in the mesh. He tried to get his armor off, managed to pop the seals on his right shoulder, but either the armor was too badly damaged, or he was too exhausted to succeed. What he needed now was rest, so he flopped into the lowest of the grav bunks in his armor and had no difficulty passing out.

••••

"Did you get it?" Jewel demanded.

Soe looked up from his screens, craned his neck to look past the fire control console with a big grin on his face. "We got him. I got his transition vector clean and precise. We won't miss him this time."

"Excellent," Jewel said. "Let's follow. Mr. Tac'tac'ah, set us up for transition."

"Aye, aye, ma'am."

••••

Abraxa looked at the report in front of him, wondered what in God's name *Cinesstar* was doing on Anachron IV. The information from their informant there was sketchy, but there was no doubt it had been *Cinesstar*. Whoever the fool was commanding her, he'd given away their position to everyone.

Abraxa brought a star chart up on one of his screens. *Where would they go next?* he wondered. The sector headquarters at Aagerbanne was the largest base near them, but the subsector headquarters at Sarasan was closer. Which one would they make for? It was imperative that he guess correctly.

And what were they up to, Edvard and Rochefort and Cassandra and Sylissa d'Hart? What little plot had their scheming hatched?

19

Another Choice

ALSA YAN CRAWLED out of her bunk in no mood to be awakened from a sound sleep. "Lights," she said angrily, and the computer brought her cabin lights up. She threw on a robe, hit the door lock and opened it. A civilian stood in the corridor outside her cabin, a man she'd noticed about the ship a few times. "What do you want?" she growled before she noticed Sylissa d'Hart standing next to him. "Your Ladyship, I didn't mean to . . ."

The noblewoman shook her head. "It's we who should apologize. I know you've been working late with the wounded, but I felt this was important enough to wake you. May we come in?"

Alsa stepped back. "Certainly. What can I do for you?"

The man stepped aside, let the noblewoman precede him, followed her in and spoke. "Let me introduce myself. I'm Thomas Harshaw, late the imperial vice consul on Trinivan. At the moment, however, I'm acting as Lieutenant Ballin's legal counsel."

Alsa frowned. "Legal counsel. Why does he need legal counsel?"

"Commander Sierka has charged him with mutiny, gross insubordination, and a number of other serious crimes."

"That's bullshit!" Alsa snapped, then remembered Lady d'Hart. "Umm . . . sorry, but York would get us all killed before he'd commit mutiny."

Lady d'Hart smiled. "Have you heard what happened on Hangar Deck?"

Alsa shook her head. "All I know is I got swamped with wounded, spent a day and a half cutting, then came here for some rest."

Harshaw shrugged. "Apparently Mister Ballin threatened to kill Commander Sierka."

Alsa laughed bitterly. "I don't blame him. Sierka dumped him and his people."

"Nevertheless," Harshaw continued. "Commander Sierka intends to convene a court-martial tomorrow morning. I've been appointed to represent Lieutenant Ballin, and been given until then to prepare his case."

Alsa ran her fingers through her hair. "What do you need me for?"

Harshaw shook his head. "I went down to see Lieutenant Ballin in the brig and I found him comatose and apparently quite ill. I tried to get him to tell me what was wrong, he mumbled something barely intelligible about a . . . breach wound, whatever that is. I asked the guards to summon medical help, but they refused and just laughed at me. I appealed to Lady d'Hart here, and she recommended we seek your help."

Alsa nodded. It was just like the AI to refuse a prisoner medical aid. "Please wait out in the corridor while I put on some clothes."

Harshaw and Lady d'Hart stepped out of her cabin. Alsa threw off the robe, pulled on a pair of medical coveralls, grabbed her bag and joined them.

Down in the brig the AI sergeant in charge refused to let her pass. "I'm the chief medical officer on this ship," she said angrily, "and I have a report you have a seriously ill man in one of these cells. Now let me pass."

The sergeant asked, "How did you get this report?"

Alsa said, "Mister Harshaw here—"

"He's a lawyer type," the sergeant interrupted her. "What's he know about sick?"

They argued a bit longer, but finally Alsa gave up and tried a different tack. She called Sierka, but he refused to take her call. She tried to explain to Armbruster, but the old man was too frightened to act on the matter. Finally, she put in a call to Palevi, and the sergeant answered with a grin that bothered her.

"What can I do for you, ma'am?" he asked politely.

"You can help me get in to see your CO."

Palevi shrugged. "Sorry ma'am. I got no authority there. The captain has him locked up and sealed away."

"I know that," Alsa said. "Sierka won't let anyone in to see him but his legal counsel, Harshaw. And Mister Harshaw here informs me Lieutenant Ballin is suffering from a breach wound. Did you know about that, Sergeant?"

That got a reaction out of Palevi. "No, ma'am. Breach wound?"

"Well, apparently he picked it up leaving that planet. And apparently he's gone for almost two days now without treatment. And apparently he's in pretty bad shape. And apparently those AI bastards aren't going to let me in to treat him unless you can convince them to. So get your ass down here, Sergeant, with about two dozen of your best to back me up."

Palevi nodded, and by the look on his face Alsa suddenly felt sorry for the AI guards. "Yes, ma'am. Right away, ma'am."

It was simple with Palevi's help. He and his marines, all wearing sidearms, filed into the guard station down in the brig before the AI guards could react. The marines didn't even need to draw their weapons. They just stood there with their hands resting on their guns while Alsa quoted chapter and verse of the regs concerning her right to examine the physical wellbeing of any person onboard ship. And anything she wasn't sure about, she made up.

She and Palevi and Harshaw and Sylissa d'Hart and two marines marched down the cellblock to York's cell. While she stood outside the cell with Palevi barking orders into his com, what she saw of York was not good. He was laying up against the wall in a grav bunk, still wearing his armor, which had a large crack down the middle of the chest plate. He didn't have his helmet on, and his face was white and pasty, with a greasy-looking sheen of perspiration beading around a five-day growth of beard. There was an obvious cut in the middle of his forehead, and dried blood smeared over most of his face. His eyes were open, staring blankly, and they had a yellow, rheumy appearance. Alsa growled, "Get that goddamned cell open!"

As the plast bars slid aside Alsa crossed the cell yanking her portable med console out of her kit. She knelt down beside York's bunk, plugged it into the med tap on his suit and switched it on. It instantly started screaming a high-pitched whine. "Stand back, all of you," she shouted. "He's hot. Fuck he's hot!"

She herself didn't back away, but the rest of them did. She tapped keys on her console, learned that she could put up with about an hour of exposure without having to go through anything more than mild chemotherapy. York, though, was going to have to go through one hell of a lot more than that.

His armor was a mess, had completely shut down, wasn't even giving her vital signs. She finally managed to access his telemetry log, started scanning it. "Breach wound," she announced, finding what she was looking for. "He had a left gauntlet breach before he left the planet's surface."

She turned around, barked at Palevi. "Contact sickbay. Tell them I want a grav stretcher down here on the double with a contamination shield. And I want a contamination team here for cleanup. And get in here and help me strip off this armor."

While Palevi and two marines started popping York's armor seals, Alsa brought out a power scalpel, dialed it up to maximum, started cutting away the plating of his left gauntlet. She peeled a section back and the stench that hit their noses made them all wince. "Shit," one of the marines swore, "what the hell is that?"

Alsa nodded carefully. "Gangrene. By now his whole system's septic. At a minimum he's going to lose the arm. And he's in no shape for cloning or a transplant."

The grav stretcher arrived. They bundled York into it, sealed him behind the contamination shield. As they were about to leave, Harshaw stopped Alsa. "Is it safe to say that my client is not physically capable of standing trial at this time?"

Alsa was getting tired of Harshaw. "What the hell does it matter? It's safe to say your client may not live to stand trial."

••••

Alsa looked sadly at her handiwork. All that remained of York was a bit of tissue, a piece of bone, a smear of blood.

The technician held out the open body bag. "I'll scrape him into it."

Alsa looked at what was left of York, shook her head. "That's not him. There's nothing left of him." She reached out, scraped the bits of tissue into a pan, turned toward the disposal can . . .

York slammed awake, sat up in his bunk, struggled for long seconds while mentally he flipped back and forth between the two realities: Anachron IV had been dream. No it wasn't . . . yes it was . . . no it wasn't . . . This time he wasn't going to be fooled. Not by any of them. Anachron IV was real, the body bag dream was a dream, and the whole world swam around him as he examined his left arm carefully, found the seam where the real arm ended and the prosthetic began. He started crying with relief. It wasn't a dream. They'd cut off his arm and it wasn't a dream. He wasn't insane. No, he was insane, but that was all right, as long as Anachron IV was real. He understood it all now, so he lay down again and slipped back into sleep.

••••

For York, his court-martial was an odd sort of dream, though through the whole thing he was less concerned with whether he was dreaming, and far more concerned with his ability to distinguish the dream parts from the real parts. If he could keep those two straight, he'd be satisfied.

Harshaw coached him rather extensively beforehand. "Sierka was going to hold a closed hearing and allow only those witnesses he wanted. But Her Majesty asked to be allowed to observe, and of course he dare not refuse her. So you keep your mouth shut. We don't need your testimony, but we do need you to sit there quietly and look smart and disciplined and wounded and victimized."

York didn't understand. He couldn't even remember where it was that he and Harshaw had had their conversation: the brig, his cabin, maybe sickbay? Nor could he remember how long the court-martial lasted. Sierka sat as chief jurist, with Soladin as his second and Armbruster as his third. They called in witnesses, questioned them, and the evidence was quite clear: York had threatened to kill Sierka and there was no denying it. There were also implications of excessive use of the suit's combat drugs, and questions concerning York's judgment and competence. In York's defense Harshaw called only Alsa Yan.

"Doctor Yan," Harshaw began. "When you first saw Lieutenant Ballin after he had returned from Anachron IV, what condition was he in, medically speaking?"

Alsa shrugged. "He was a wreck, close to death . . ." She went on to describe York's condition in considerable detail.

"And how did he come to be in such shape, Doctor Yan?"

"It began with a breach in his left gauntlet down on the surface of the planet—"

Soladin objected at that point, claiming she couldn't know the details of what had happened on the planet's surface. Sierka sustained his objection, said he would allow no further discussion of events prior to the alleged mutiny attempt. But the empress asked if she could ask a question or two of her own. Of course Sierka granted her request, and she asked about marine armor.

Alsa went into considerable detail concerning the time-stamped telemetry and medical logs kept by a suit's computer. From those she had been able to determine exactly when the breach had occurred, and exactly how long York's hand had been under vacuum. She also knew the dosages and timing of all the drugs he'd taken. "Lieutenant Ballin was knocked unconscious no less than three times, resulting in a concussion and a certain amount of disorientation. He was suffering from an extended breach wound of the left hand, an excruciating injury at best. He had also been exposed to a lethal dose of hard radiation, which would certainly affect his ability to function, though since his suit alarms were damaged and inoperative, he was probably not aware of it. And yet he managed to save the lives of his people and return them to this ship. Certainly his capacity was diminished by his condition, and the drugs he'd taken in the line of duty."

"The drugs," Harshaw said, nodding thoughtfully. "In your professional opinion, Doctor, how would you evaluate Mister Ballin's judgment in self-administering combat drugs?"

"In my professional opinion, given the wounds he'd suffered, Lieutenant Ballin used the drugs effectively to remain conscious and sufficiently alert to save the lives of nearly sixty members of this ship's crew. I believe his judgment was impeccable, and his reasoning sound."

Harshaw was finished then. Sierka adjourned the court-martial and a couple of AI goons hustled York back to his cell. All he could do was wait while Sierka met with Armbruster and Soladin in closed session to decide how to execute him.

He pulled a chair out of a bulkhead, sat down under the weight of sheer exhaustion, raised his left arm and examined it carefully. Alsa had cut off his arm just below the elbow, done a neat job of attaching the prosthetic. He wiggled the fingers, and like the toes on his false foot, he wouldn't have known by feel that they were plast and circuits wrapped in skin from a clone culture.

He looked up at his bunk, wondered if he had the strength to climb into it, knew he'd need another twenty hours of sleep before he'd be rid of the side effects of Alsa's speed healing treatments . . .

Harshaw woke him sitting there. York had trouble bringing his mental processes up to any kind of reasonable speed, looked at his watch. He'd only been out an hour.

"You've been acquitted of all charges," Harshaw said happily. He reached down, lifted York's hand and shook it.

York looked at him and shook his head. "Sierka acquitted me? Just like that?"

Harshaw grinned. "Well, not just like that. Apparently the empress felt that *closed session* didn't exclude her. I don't know what went on in there, but you've been acquitted."

York stood unsteadily. "Am I free to go?"

"Yes, you are." Harshaw leaned close to him, whispered softly, "But Her Majesty would like to see you in her cabin."

York looked at him carefully for a moment, couldn't read anything in his face. The side effects of the speed healing were still weighing on him heavily, and if there was some meaning hidden between Harshaw's words he couldn't fathom it. York turned away from him, walked out of the cell, called over his shoulder, "Later. After I get some sleep."

"But . . ." Harshaw said. "But Lieutenant, she said now. You can't . . ."

••••

When York got back to his cabin the chime on his terminal was sounding steadily. He debated ignoring it but decided he might as well answer it.

He touched the receive switch on the terminal and a rather officious looking woman in the uniform of the royal guard appeared on the screen. "Ah!" the woman said, looking a bit perturbed. "Finally! Where have you been, Lieutenant?"

York blinked and shook his head. "In jail. I just got out."

Her look shifted to impatience. "Well, it's about time. If you'd answered your terminal earlier you'd have more time now, but as it is you'll just barely be able to make it up here."

She was starting to irritate him, and he knew that too was a side effect of the treatments, as well as her attitude. "Up where?" he asked, trying not to sound angry.

"The empress suite, of course. You mustn't keep her waiting. I'll tell her five minutes—"

"The empress wants to see me?" York asked. All he wanted to do was go to sleep.

The woman could no longer contain her impatience. "Well, what else would this be about?" she demanded.

"What for?" York asked.

She stopped short, frowned angrily. "Pardon me?"

"I asked what for."

Her frown deepened. "I'm sure Her Majesty will discuss that with you—"

"No. You discuss it with me now."

"I'm afraid I don't know. You'll—"

"Then find out. And when you know, call me back." He hit the blank switch.

He leaned against the console, shook his head. He was a damn fool, he knew. But he was so tired, and all he wanted to do was sleep.

He folded a seat out of the bulkhead and sat down, almost too tired to make it to his bunk . . .

The chime on his terminal woke him again. He'd fallen asleep sitting up with his head cocked to one side. He checked the time, found he'd been out for about ten minutes.

The chime sounded again, so he stood, leaned over the terminal, touched the receive switch, and the officious looking guardswoman appeared again, though the expression on her face was quite different now. "Lieutenant Ballin," she said. "I'm Major Dewar of Her Majesty's Guard, and I would like to express my apologies for my rather abrupt behavior a few minutes ago. I was not aware that you had recently suffered some rather serious injuries, and Doctor Yan informs me you're still in need of time to sleep off the effects of the speed healing medications. Again, my apologies, but this is an important matter that cannot wait."

Someone had given her hell: *be nice, if you have to, but get the idiot up here.* She was still abrupt, but now she was at least polite, though York had to struggle to avoid biting her head off anyway. He closed his eyes, couldn't think of any better way of calling a truce than to say, "Apology accepted. I was a bit short myself."

"Thank you, Lieutenant," the woman said. "Her Majesty cordially requests your presence, at your convenience, in her suite. May I convey your reply?"

Someone had really come down hard on this woman. "Certainly," York said, trying to come up with something better than *Ya, sure.* "Tell her I would consider it an honor, though I need about twenty minutes to make myself presentable."

She smiled. "Thank you, Lieutenant. Twenty minutes then."

York took a quick, cold shower, shaved, put on a clean uniform, though, out of a recently acquired habit, the last thing he did before leaving his cabin was slip a small gun into his belt hidden beneath his tunic. By the time he reached the empress' suite he was starting to get hungry, and he realized he hadn't eaten real food in days.

He tapped on the door politely and Daka Nemkov opened it, stepped aside to let York enter. The room inside was crowded. Besides Nemkov there was Olin Rame, Alsa Yan, Armbruster,

Straegga, and Maggie. York was glad to see Maggie there. Nemkov and Armbruster looked guilty, Rame looked determined, Alsa looked confused, and Maggie looked like she wanted to warn York about something. Straegga marched right up to York, took his hand and shook it. "Lieutenant, this is the first chance I've had to thank you for saving my life, though I wish you'd told me beforehand you were going to booby-trap your reactor pack that way." She grinned. "Andleman wasn't at all pleased, was he?"

Straegga held a cup of caff in one hand and the smell of it made York's mouth water. "Do you think I could get a cup of that?"

Armbruster jumped. "Let me do the honors, Lieutenant." He crossed the room to some sort of bar, and York wondered if they had any 'trate, though he didn't voice that thought.

The room seemed overly large. He knew *Invaradin* from stem to stern, and there were no cabins on her of this size. *Cinesstar* wasn't much larger than *Invaradin*, and a luxury the size of this cabin didn't belong on her. It took him a moment to understand they'd cut away a bulkhead between two cabins to make a large sitting room for the empress. It was connected to another cabin beyond that, where he wouldn't be surprised to find they'd cut away another bulkhead to make a large bedroom. He wondered if they'd gotten the starboard chamber repaired first.

Armbruster shoved a cup of steaming hot caff into his hands. York stepped back out of the center of the room, put his back to a bulkhead and took a sip. Alsa cornered him there, reached up without ceremony, peeled back the eyelid on his real eye and peered into it carefully.

"Alsa?" he whispered. "What's going on here?"

She whispered, "I don't know any more than you. They called me up here about an hour ago, asked about your condition, and wouldn't let me leave after that. Against my recommendation they woke you up early, said it was important. I think Maggie knows what's going on, but they won't let me near her. Be careful, York. You're still short about twenty to forty hours of sleep before you're done with the side effects of the healing. You're going to be tired and on edge, so don't bite anyone's head off."

She produced an injector, pressed it against his thigh and pulled the trigger. He heard a faint puff and it stung a bit. "That'll give you a little energy. No drugs, just synth-nutrition concentrates."

"It was bad, eh?" he asked her.

She looked him in the eyes. "You almost bought it again. That's twice now in as many months. Be more careful, eh?"

"Yes, Lieutenant, you should be more careful."

Alsa spun about quickly and stepped aside. The empress approached, saying, "We need you, Lieutenant. Please take care of yourself. We'd hate to lose you, though that was a brave thing you did, willingly suffering a breach wound and exposing yourself to lethal radiation to save your people."

York knew protocol required him to bow, or drop to one knee, or something. Probably drop to one knee, but he didn't have the strength to get up again if he did that so he opted for a deep bow. "Your Majesty." York thanked all the gods of space she didn't hold out her hand.

Behind the empress stood Sylissa d'Hart, Martin Andow, Sarra Fithwallen, the old queen mother with her usual sour expression, and of course Major Dewar. "Doctor Yan tells me you're still a bit tired after your ordeal, so why don't we dispense with the formalities. Let's find a comfortable place to sit and chat."

She led York to a small couch on the other side of the room, and when she sat down everyone else followed suit as if it had been rehearsed, leaving him and Alsa standing, both a little confused. The empress nodded toward an empty seat facing her. "Please, Lieutenant."

York felt every eye in the room tracking him as he carefully sat down.

The empress smiled. "Tell me about your condition, Lieutenant. Are you feeling better?"

York shrugged. She had something she wanted to say, but she was going to take her own time saying it. "I'm just tired, and a bit confused."

"Confused?" she asked. "About what?"

He lied. "It's always confusing when you wake up after healing."

"Ah!" she said. "Yes, that must be unpleasant, though there hasn't been much on this voyage that has been pleasant."

If that was an opening he wasn't going to take it. "This is a warship. And warships aren't meant to be pleasant."

He decided to throw a joker into the deck, see if he could get any reaction. He looked around the room, said, "Nice place you have here."

The empress smiled. "Yes. Commander Sierka has been most accommodating, though I'd really be quite content with something more Spartan, under the circumstances."

York shrugged. "If I were you I'd check to see if anyone ran any simulations on the structural integrity of this section of the ship before they cut out those bulkheads. If you find they didn't, then I'd recommend you shore up the deck above your heads before it collapses. When it collapses, and it will, it could start a chain reaction and take the entire ship with it."

Doubt registered on her face and she glanced worriedly about for an instant. But she recovered quickly, said, "I'm sure it's been taken care of. But tell me. You have quite a bit of experience to draw upon. If it were up to you, how would you get us back to the empire?"

York shook his head. "But it's not up to me, Your Majesty, and I wouldn't attempt to second-guess my captain."

Her eyes narrowed, and she gave him a knowing little smile. "No, you wouldn't, at least not publicly. But you almost committed mutiny. Or rather, you were almost driven to mutiny, and your people were ready to follow you, to push you into it, from what I've heard. And while you didn't allow yourself to be drawn into open rebellion, I have to assume you have some thoughts on how this ship might be better run. Please. This is a private conversation. Anything you say here will be held in the strictest confidence."

York looked around slowly. Other than him, there were eleven people in the room. So much for *private conversations*. He shrugged again. "I suppose I might try to get us back to the Sector Headquarters at Aagerbanne. But we have no idea where the lines are in this sector so we'd have to move cautiously."

Andow laughed. "Lieutenant, you're a master of understatement. Let me ask you a question. What do you think our chances are of getting back to the empire under the present command?"

There it was, York thought, taking care to remain expressionless. They finally wanted to replace Sierka, and with his marines close to mutiny, they wanted to know if he'd support Sierka's successor. He hoped they were smart enough to pick Rame, or even Straegga. "It would not be appropriate for me to guess at such chances." He looked at Andow and couldn't resist a little gibe. "Especially since the present command was specifically put in place by your orders and the passive consent of the crown."

Andow nodded and grinned. "Touché, Lieutenant. But let's be frank with one another. We all know Sierka is incompetent, and we're also well-aware of your feelings on the matter."

York tried not to feel anything at the moment. "My feelings are irrelevant. You will do what you will do." He looked at the empress. "And if you replace Sierka, I and my subordinates will serve his successor with the same loyalty we've always shown the rightfully appointed commanding officer of this ship. I hope there is no question of that."

"Oh, Lieutenant!" the empress said. "No one here questions your loyalty. We only question Commander Sierka's competence. But we need someone with the strength and resolve to take action. And we want you to know we'll support you in whatever you choose to do, regardless of the ramifications."

Now that was an odd thing to say. He had to roll that around in his head a few times. It sounded as if they weren't going to replace Sierka, probably didn't want to admit officially he was an incompetent fool. And while he was in command their chances of getting back to the empire were diminishing with every second.

York glanced around at the faces in the room. They were all looking at him, waiting for him to say something, though Maggie seemed to be biting her tongue, and Alsa had a look of incredulity on her face. She understood what they were talking about, and her disbelief was conspicuous. And then suddenly York also understood.

He looked at the empress, realized his own face must mirror Alsa's. "You can't mean—" he started to say, but the empress lifted a hand and cut him off.

She said, "I meant only what I said."

York shook his head. The idiots were playing games like children. "No, you didn't," he said, unable to contain his anger. "You meant a lot more than that."

He stood up, looked around at them all, finished by looking last at the empress. "You meant you don't want to dirty your hands fixing the mess you created."

Nemkov jumped up. "See here, Ballin. You can't speak that way to—"

York turned on him. "Shut up, Nemkov, and sit down." He turned back to the empress. "You meant that you'd like me to clean it up for you. You'd like a nice little mutiny, one you could disclaim all knowledge of. Have Ballin clean up your mess, then when it's all done you can hang him and make noises about what kind of a monster he was."

Maggie jumped up. "I told them you wouldn't buy it, York."

York threw his hands up. "Well, thank god there's someone here with an ounce of sanity."

The empress stood. "Mister Ballin, we need your help."

"You need my help?" York asked. He thought of his dream. "You don't want my help, you want my blood." The deck beneath his feet seemed unsteady. He pleaded with the empress. "I've been fighting this war for more than twenty years, and every year they shoot up a little bit more of me. And I'm afraid that when the day comes, there won't be anything left of me to put into the goddamn body bag."

"I told you he's psychotic," Nemkov shouted.

York wheeled toward the hatch and growled, "I've had enough of this."

He almost made it, but Nemkov stepped in his way just as he reached the exit. "You haven't been dismissed, Ballin."

York and Nemkov were about the same size, but they both knew York was too weak to resist Nemkov. What Nemkov didn't know, what none of them knew, was that York had stopped with his hand just beneath the hem of his tunic resting on the gun in his belt. "Get out of my way," he said with a calm, deadly edge to his voice.

Nemkov shook his head arrogantly, grabbed a handful of York's tunic and pulled him forward so their faces were almost touching. "You're not leaving until you're dismissed."

York jammed the muzzle of the gun up into Nemkov's gut, thumbed the safety off, and the gun's power pack hummed ominously for a moment as it came to life. They all heard it, and Nemkov turned white. York shoved the muzzle of the gun up harder into Nemkov's gut until he knew he was hurting him. "Get out of my way," he growled like an animal, "or I'll blow you out of my way." He heard some motion behind him and he called over his shoulder, "Dewar, stay where you are, unless you want a junior officer with his guts blown up into his brains."

No one moved. Nemkov stood there for a moment and started to tremble. He really wasn't a bad sort, but for some reason York wanted to kill him, wanted to kill someone. And he might have killed Nemkov then and there, but Maggie stopped him. "York, don't."

Nemkov glanced to one side, trying to think of how to stay alive, how to get out of York's way. He started to edge in that direction so York gave him a hand, actually an elbow. Nemkov landed across the back of a chair, York palmed the latch on the hatch and shoved it open. He stepped into the corridor, closed the door softly behind him.

When he got back to his cabin he pulled out a bottle of 'trate and decided to get drunk. He poured a glass, barely diluted it, looked at it for a moment and realized he really just wanted to go to sleep. He put the 'trate down untouched, pressed the intercom switch on his terminal.

"Corporal Tathit here. What can I do for you, Cap'm?"

"No calls," York said. "No visitors, no nothing. I don't care who it is. I don't care if it's the fucking emperor himself. I'm going to get some sleep."

••••

As the hatch to the empress' suite closed following York's exit, Maggie could no longer contain herself. "I knew it wouldn't work. I told you—"

"Be silent, young woman," the old queen mother commanded. "You will not speak—"

Suddenly everyone started shouting. "Please," the empress said. "Please," she repeated several times. She spoke calmly, didn't shout commands or issue orders. "Let's have some sanity here. Everyone please be silent for a moment."

The room became still, filled slowly with a terrifying calm. The empress turned to Maggie, met her eyes squarely and said, "Miss Votak. I believe you were trying to say something. Please continue."

Maggie bit her lip, glanced quickly at the old queen mother; saw only anger and disapproval there. She looked at the empress and said, "It was nothing."

Cassandra took a slow, deep breath and let it out with a sigh. "You said you knew it wouldn't work. Why wouldn't it work?"

Maggie wasn't sure whom she could trust. She hesitated, but realized there was no way to be certain. All she could do was chance it, so she began cautiously. "He doesn't trust you."

The room exploded with a dozen people speaking at once. Again the empress silenced them with a calm voice and a patient wave of her hands. Again she turned on Maggie. "Why doesn't he trust us?"

Maggie shook her head. "He doesn't trust *you.*"

The empress raised an eyebrow. "He doesn't trust . . . *me*? Why doesn't he trust me?"

Maggie shrugged. "I thought he explained himself rather clearly. You'd like him to take command of this ship by force. But you don't understand that even he can't hold this ship together if he's just another criminal. He doesn't trust you, because you don't trust him."

The empress' eyes narrowed sharply. "And do you trust him?"

"With my life," Maggie said. "And with your life."

20

More Choices

WHEN THE KNOCK on the door came, York realized he'd been awake for some time, lying in his bunk staring at the bulkhead in his cabin. He slid out of his bunk, though he moved like a tired, old man. He hit the latch on his cabin door angrily and tossed it open. Palevi stood there, rigidly at attention. "Cap'm. I—"

"I told you not to bother me," York snarled.

"But Cap'm! It's the empress. She—"

"So tell her I'll call her back when I'm damn good and ready."

"But she didn't call, sir. She's here, now, in person. I know you said no visitors, but sir . . ."

"Here? Now?"

"Yes, sir. I put her in your office, sir."

York shook his head. "Tell her I'll be right there."

"Yes, sir." Palevi saluted, turned, and marched away.

York splashed some water on his face, ran more through his hair. He found the empress seated in a small chair in his office. She didn't stand as he entered, and he still didn't know what he was supposed to do. Bow? Drop to one knee? He bowed awkwardly.

She smiled skeptically. "Let's forego the formalities. You're not very good at it anyway. By the way. You were right about my cabin. They're installing all sorts of beams to shore up the deck. It's a mess."

He shrugged, didn't know what to do with his hands so he crossed them behind his back. "A lucky guess."

"No, no guesswork in you, Mr. Ballin. And we do have a mess on our hands, one created by, as you so aptly put it, royal edict." She grinned.

York shrugged and said nothing.

She laughed, and without warning stood. "Do you have anything to drink around here?"

A bottle of 'trate in his desk, but nothing around fit for an empress. He shook his head. "Nothing, Your Majesty."

"Oh come now, Lieutenant. You have this wondrous reputation for boozing. You must have something. What do you call that concentrate you drink . . .'trate?"

York raised his eyebrows skeptically, but turned to his desk, palmed the latch on the bottom drawer, lifted out a bottle and a plast cup. He retrieved another cup from the fresher, poured a small amount into each. As he returned to the fresher for some water the empress called after him, "And I've heard it's customary to drink it only partially diluted."

He diluted it about ten-to-one, roughly the equivalent of straight alcohol, not as strong as it might be, but still stronger than recommended. He returned to his office, handed her a cup.

She looked at him for a moment, then lifted her cup and said, "To the mess I've got us into . . . and to the only man who can get us out of it."

He sipped at the 'trate, watched her over the lip of his cup as she sipped at hers. She flinched a little at the first sip, then took another. "Tell me," she said. "Haven't you ever wondered why Fleet sent you to the academy?"

He took another sip of 'trate. "What you mean, I believe, is why Fleet sent a half-literate, juvenile delinquent, lower deck pod gunner to the academy?"

"Yes. I guess that's what I mean."

He shrugged. "Certainly not just so he could rub elbows with rich kids. Andow believes it's because I was the youngest survivor of the *Andor Vincent*."

"And you don't believe that?"

"I don't disbelieve it."

"Have you ever wondered about your parents?"

He finished the 'trate, wanted more. "I know my father's name was Collier Maczek—"

If he hadn't been watching her at that moment he would have missed it, the most important moment in his life would have slipped right past him. She flinched at the name, hesitated for an instant, then regained her composure without losing her stride, though she gave him one quick look to see if he'd noticed. *She knew the name! She knew the son-of-a-bitch!* "My stepmother recently told me his name. But she knew nothing about my true mother."

He wanted to ask a hundred questions, was certain she knew something, but he was just as certain she'd reveal nothing. "What do you want from me?"

She looked into her cup, swirled the liquid there for a moment before speaking. "Why haven't you taken command of this ship already? Your marines want you to, most of the officers want you to, I want you to. Sierka is patently incompetent, and has betrayed you time and again. He doesn't deserve your loyalty, so why do you insist on giving it to him?"

He had to make her understand. "I'm not loyal to him. I'm loyal to the position he holds. And some day when he's not holding it, I'm going to kill him. But for now he's in command of this ship, and a ship is made of discipline, and tradition, and custom. If I take command from him illegally, then all of that's gone and we no longer have a ship. We only have a mob, and a mob won't get us out of this."

Her brow wrinkled thoughtfully and she nodded. "After you left my cabin, Miss Votak and Commander Rame said something similar."

"Why were you out here in the first place?" he demanded bluntly, trying to shock a reaction from her.

He watched her consider her answer carefully, consider lying to him, but she said, "Wouldn't you like to see this war end?"

"Does it matter?"

"Of course it matters."

"It does? Why? It's just the war. It's there. It's always been there. We fight it. That's all."

"But it's destroying us. Don't you see that?"

He shrugged. "Right now they're winning and we're losing. Maybe in ten or twenty years we'll be winning."

She shook her head violently. "But they're not winning. They're in worse shape than we are. All of our intelligence indicates their borders are shrinking faster than ours, that their warships are having even more difficulty getting supplies. This war is destroying us both. Don't you hate it? All the killing, the waste?"

"I don't know. When I'm out here it's all so clear. I know what's to be done, and how to do it, and I'm good at it."

"Aren't you afraid of dying?"

He had to consider that for a moment. "I think I'm more afraid of dying wrong."

Oddly enough, trying to recall what he hated about a firefight also recalled what he liked. "It's funny," he said, "but I feel most alive when someone's trying to kill me." He laughed. "As long as they don't succeed."

He turned toward her, made a point of looking at her carefully. "So you think you know how to end this war?"

"Yes, I do."

"And you want me to help you?"

"I want you to get us back to Luna. Leave the rest to me."

She put her cup down on his desk, crossed the room and stopped in front of his console, touched a switch and activated it. She tapped at the keys for a moment, then said, "Come here, Captain."

He ignored the mistake about his rank, looked over her shoulder at the screen she'd brought to life. On it was a warrant promotion to the rank of captain and the orders giving him command of *Cinesstar*. Both were issued by her hand, and under her seal. She nodded at the screens with satisfaction. "Miss Votak told me this was what I'd have to do if I wanted to give you any chance of success. I sought Mister Harshaw's advice to be certain of its legality. All I need to do is enter these in the ship's log for transmission back to Fleet, and you'll be in command of this ship."

He didn't want such a command. "You'll regret that. I'll do things you won't understand, and you'll want to intervene, and I won't let you. You'll think I'm cruel, and brutal, and thoughtless. You may even want to rescind those orders, put someone else in command, and I won't let you do that either. These orders, at least until we're back at Luna, or dead, are irrevocable."

She looked at him for a long moment, and for just an instant he saw beneath the mask. She didn't know what she was doing any more than he did. "Well, I thank you for being honest with me. And so I'll be honest with you. I have no choice. You're my last hope. You've got to get us back to Luna alive. There are millions of lives at stake."

She turned back to the console and reached toward it, but his hand shot out instinctively and caught her wrist. "Don't," he said. "Not yet. Who knows about this?"

"Only Mister Harshaw."

York looked at the two screens. "The moment you enter this into the log Sierka'll know about it. And I'd like to make certain preparations before that moment comes."

She smiled. "My confidence in you, Captain, is growing."

York keyed his implants. "Sergeant Palevi, please assemble all officers and NCO's in my office immediately."

"Yes, sir. Right away, sir."

It seemed only mere seconds before his office door opened and Elkiss, Palevi, Tathit, Hyer, Hackla, Notay, Yagell, Cleaver and Simorka filed into the room. They all bowed rather clumsily to the empress, then stood stiffly at attention, waiting for York to say something. "At ease and relax," he said, and pointed at the screen on his console. "Each of you file past those screens, read them, read every word on them."

Palevi stepped up first, and as he read the promotion and orders his face broke into that grin York hated, though this time it mirrored his own feelings. And when they'd each taken their turn there were a number of grins present. York picked on Cleaver. "What are you grinning about, Corporal?"

The grins disappeared. "Nothing, sir."

"That's better," York said. "Her Majesty has chosen not to log this until a more opportune moment. So keep your mouths shut until I say so." He looked at Palevi. "Sergeant, I want all actives in light harness with riot gear and sidearms. For backup, put two squads in full combat armor, keep them out of sight, and have them carry some of that AP gas just in case, though it and they will be used only as a last resort. Is that clear?"

"Yes, sir."

"And as soon as you're in harness, I'd like you and three of your best to accompany me to the bridge. That is all."

"Yes, sir."

Palevi barked orders at the rest of them and they marched out of the office. York blanked the screen on his console, and by the time he and the empress left his office Palevi was waiting for them.

Sierka had sealed off access to the bridge in case the anticipated mutiny actually came about. But there was only a skeleton crew on duty at the moment, with Frank at the com. At the empress' request he cleared the lock on the lift. Frank was surprised to see York, Palevi and the three marines accompanying Her Majesty. "York," he hissed. "I didn't know you were . . . I called Sierka as soon as Her Majesty . . . He's on his way up. He won't like this."

York edged his way around fire control to the com, retrieved the screen containing his promotion and orders. He pointed at it. "Read that."

Frank skimmed it quickly, and like the marines his face broke into a grin. York gave him a moment, then said, "Mister Stara. Her Majesty would like to register those orders into the log. Please set it up."

Frank couldn't get rid of his grin as he said, "Aye, aye, sir." Frank worked at his console for a moment, then stepped away and bowed to the empress. "You'll have to log it yourself, Your Majesty."

She stepped up to the console, tapped in her own private command code.

The lift doors popped open and Sierka called out, "What's going on here?" as he stepped around the fire control console. He was wearing a gun, and when he saw York put his hand on it. The marines behind him tensed. He looked back and thought better of it. "It's mutiny now, eh?"

The empress shook her head. "Captain Ballin is obeying my orders, Commander. I've put him in command of this ship."

"You can't do that."

"Of course I can."

For a moment Sierka looked as if he might do something desperate. "Sergeant," York said, "relieve Commander Sierka of his weapon."

Sierka froze while Palevi stepped up behind him and carefully pulled the sidearm from his holster.

"Commander Sierka will also be taking new quarters on the officer's deck. Please find him something appropriate, and have two of your people escort him there immediately. And for his own protection, have them remain as bodyguards."

Sierka's eyes pinched together with undisguised hatred. "You're going to regret this, Ballin."

York ignored him, turned to Frank, "Mister Stara. Sound General Quarters."

Frank frowned and hesitated for a moment. But then he nodded and said, "Aye, aye, sir." He sat down at the com console and a moment later the alert klaxon began blaring throughout the ship.

York sat down at the captain's console, brought a station status summary up on a screen and waited. The marine ready-room green-lighted in less than a minute, but it was more than three minutes before the next station checked in. Someone had at least assigned a crew to the forward main turret, though York was not ready to assume they were any good just because of that. During the next five minutes several officers showed up on the bridge, but York didn't look up to see who, and a jumbled mix of stations green-lighted sporadically, until the status readout showed about twenty percent active. As the klaxon blared on, Soladin stopped next to the captain's console and demanded, "See here, Ballin. What do you think you're doing?"

Apparently, every officer on board had decided to report to the bridge, as well as Andow, the queen mother, Lady d'Hart, Aeya, Fithwallen, and just about anyone else of any consequence. They were all crowded in and around the bridge's consoles and instrument clusters.

"Mister Stara. Cut the alert klaxon and put a copy of our new orders on every screen on this ship."

The silence that descended was eerie. While Frank went to work, York looked at Soladin. "Commander Soladin, Her Majesty has put me in command of this ship."

Soladin looked stricken. He turned to the empress. "Your Majesty, that's a horrible mistake. This man can't—"

York interrupted him. "Be that as it may, Commander, I'm now this ship's lawful captain. You may debate the subject at your leisure, but not here on the bridge."

York picked out the officers he wanted. "Commanders . . . Rame and Gant, Lieutenants Stara, Votak, Jondee, and Nemkov, and Sergeant Palevi, please remain here with me. The rest of you, please report to your cabins and remain there until further notice."

Soladin shouted, "This is an outrage. I won't—"

"Lord Soladin," the empress snapped, cutting him off sharply. York had never heard her speak with the sharp edge of command before, and it had a dramatic effect on Soladin. "I have asked Captain Ballin to take command of this ship. And now it would behoove us all to obey his orders."

Slowly, reluctantly, they left the bridge in groups small enough to fit in the lift. But long before they were gone York was organizing his bridge crew. Rame would make a good first officer. And with Gant in charge of the scan console, Maggie at the helm, Frank at fire control, Jondee at com, and Nemkov in charge of Hangar Deck, he had the skeleton of a command. Straegga had been among those on the bridge a few moments ago, and no doubt she was quite competent. But he didn't know her so he'd integrate her into the crew once he had a basic organization put together.

York sent Nemkov down to Hangar Deck to evaluate the situation there, then contacted Cappik down in Engineering for a quick status report. Besides sporadic fluctuations in the output of the damaged chamber, there was nothing out of the ordinary there.

York knew he had to take control decisively. "Mister Stara, close off all air-tight seals."

Cinesstar's hull echoed repeatedly as Frank sealed off each station on the ship, limiting everyone's movement. "Sergeant."

Palevi materialized beside his console, snapped a rigid salute. "Sir."

York threw a casual salute at him. "I want you to search this ship from stem to stern and confiscate all weapons. Also, I want you to take a census of everyone aboard her: name, rank or civilian occupation, present location on the ship, anything else you can think of. Lock anyone who resists you in the brig. And if there's anyone wandering about aimlessly, lock them up too. And lock up the AI regulars, and put guards on the empress, Aeya, Lady d'Hart, Andow, the queen mother, Rhijn, McGeahn, Soladin and his piece of fluff, Armbruster, Juessik, Cienyey, Harshaw, Fithwallen and her bodyguard, Dulell, Dubye, Omasin . . . Did I miss anyone?"

"No, sir. I don't believe so, sir."

"Good. They're all confined to their quarters until further notice. You have four hours. Dismissed."

Palevi disappeared, but York called after him, "And I want no violence. Do you understand?"

"Yes, sir. No violence, sir."

York put his bridge crew to work checking *Cinesstar*'s systems while he dug into the damage log. But damage reports had not been properly logged, if they'd been logged at all.

"Mister Stara, get me Sergeant Palevi, Commander Straegga, and her first officer . . . what's his name?"

"Lieutenant Jakobee, sir."

"Thank you, Mister Stara. Miss Gant, I want a complete navigational report soonest, with a proposed transition plan for Aagerbanne."

Frank was quick. "Sir, I've got Palevi, Straegga, and Jakobee."

York switched on his com. "Commander Straegga and Lieutenant Jakobee, our damage log is incomplete. Sergeant Palevi is making a sweep of the ship. I'd like both of you to accompany him and prepare detailed damage control reports on anything you find. Sergeant, have your people keep their eyes open and report anything they find to the commander and the lieutenant. Any questions?"

"None, sir," Palevi barked. Straegga and Jakobee probably had a dozen questions but they were smart enough to save them for later.

It took Palevi more than six hours to complete the sweep of the ship. But long before then York took the ship off alert, pulled everyone but Frank off the bridge into the captain's office, which served as a decent, but cramped, conference room. Palevi was feeding names and the pertinent data concerning them into the computer. At the same time, York and his officers were assigning each person appropriate quarters and a duty station. When they were finished they had a basic command structure and better than eighty percent of what constituted a full crew.

York, Maggie, Rame, Gant, Jondee, Straegga, Jakobee and Palevi were enough to nearly fill the captain's office. But now he needed a much larger place. He put a call in to Frank on the bridge. "Mister Stara. Contact all station commanders and tell them to report to the officer's mess immediately. Miss Votak will contact you from there and pipe the meeting up to your console so you can be part of it."

Through years of conditioning York hesitated, waiting for the ranking officer to move first, but they were all waiting for him. He stood slowly and marched to the door. Gant got there before him, opened it for him, held it, waiting for him to pass, and they all filed into the corridor behind him.

The maître d' at the officer's mess brought him up short, stepped in front of him and blocked the entrance, curled his lips upward in an oily smile. "Good afternoon, sir. Do you have a reservation?"

"No," York said, trying to contain his anger.

"Must have a reservation, sir."

York turned slowly about and sought out Rame. "Commander Rame. We'll meet this time in the officer's mess. But please see to it that it's completely shut down immediately afterwards. And until further notice everyone will dine in the main mess."

Rame nodded. "As you wish, sir."

Rame stepped around him, took the maître d' by the arm and politely pulled him aside. York stepped past them into the dim lighting of the mess hall. "Someone bring up the lights. And clear these tables out of the way. We can stand."

The officers that accompanied York moved quickly to obey while York looked the place over. The atmosphere of a secluded restaurant disappeared as he stood there. He watched them toss the impeccable, white tablecloths into a pile and stack the tables and chairs to one side.

Palevi appeared in the entrance a bit out of breath and carrying a small bundle. He jogged across the room to Maggie, saluted and handed her the package. "Sorry it took so long, ma'am. Had to convince a few crewmembers things have changed."

Maggie took the package, stuffed it under one arm and marched over to York. She saluted him. "Sir. I need to speak with you privately. It won't take but a minute, and it's a matter of utmost importance."

Maggie was up to something. They stepped into the kitchen, startled a few civilian cooks. Maggie hooked a thumb over her shoulder and said, "Get out."

One of them started to argue, but she turned on the man, spoke in a flat tone. "I said get out, and I'm not willing to debate the matter. Now get out, or I'll have the marines get you out the hard way."

The cooks disappeared like so much air released into vacuum. Maggie tore open the package and handed York a flight suit with captain's stripes on it. "Please put this on, sir."

York brushed her off. "I don't need that bullshit."

"God damn it, yes you do! You're the one who did all the shouting about tradition and custom. And you know as well as I do you can't pull this crew together just by giving the right orders. You can't just walk, talk and act like the captain, you have to look like him too. Now put it on."

She was right, of course. As he stripped down, Maggie noticed the small gun tucked in the holster at his waist. "Do you really need that?"

He shrugged. "Old habit."

"You never packed a gun before, not on board ship."

"All right, it's a new habit. But it's still not going away." He stuffed the gun into a pocket on one thigh.

The stripes on his sleeves drew his attention, scared him a bit.

"Here," Maggie said. "Put this on too."

She handed him a small cap with gold filigree smeared all over the bill. He put it on carefully, set it on his head straight and square. She shook her head sadly. "York, sometimes you're the most boring turd I've ever known." She suddenly shifted her weight, squared her shoulders and saluted him smartly. "But I wouldn't have anyone else for a CO, Captain."

York didn't know if he deserved her trust. He squared his own shoulders, returned her salute carefully, then nodded toward the mess hall. "Let's go do this, eh?"

The station commanders were waiting for him nervously, and as he stepped into the officer's mess Palevi barked out in his best parade ground style, "Captain on the deck."

He caught York by surprise as much as he caught the rest. There was a sudden flurry of motion as everyone snapped to attention, followed by a complete and tense silence.

York marched business-like through the middle of them, threw a casual "As you were," over his shoulder, headed straight for the bar at the far end of the room. There was a small raised area around the bar, and he'd decided to speak from there. He stepped up onto the platform, turned around and clasped his hands behind his back.

There was a rustle of movement, the hiss of hidden conversations and unasked questions. He waited statue still, and slowly the noise and the bustle died. He waited until the last sound was gone from the room, then he waited further, allowed the silence to grow pregnant and uncomfortable. "I assume you've all seen the orders issued by Her Majesty that put me in command of this ship. If not, they're in the public log of this ship."

He saw a lot of distrust on the faces there. "You've each been assigned duty as the commander of a station or department on this ship. Each of you will shortly be given a list of the people that report to you. Some are stationside personnel with no shipboard experience. Some are civilians we are conscripting into service by order of Her Majesty. You'll have one hour to make sure each of them knows the locations of his or her quarters and duty station. Don't bother with anything beyond that; you won't have time. Some of them, by the way, you'll find in the brig for minor offenses. As of this moment I'm dropping all charges against them, but they won't be discharged until you sign their release and escort them back to their quarters."

He scanned the faces again: no change. "At the end of that hour we'll hold our first combat drill. It is then that you'll have the opportunity to begin training your people."

Still the faces hadn't changed. "That is all. Dismissed."

A hand shot up in the middle of the crowd. "Sir. May I ask a question?"

York shook his head. "No questions. Dismissed."

He didn't wait for a response, but cut a path through the middle of them as he made his way to the door. Behind him he heard Palevi bark, "Atteeuun . . . shuuuuun!" but he was gone before they had a chance to react.

21

Old Memories

THE FIRST DRILL taxed York's patience to the limit. He let the klaxon hammer away at them for more than ten minutes before finally shutting it down. And even then only a little over seventy percent of the stations had reported in.

At that point he put the station commanders to work running a succession of simple combat simulations while Palevi ran another sweep of the ship to herd up lost sheep. Anyone merely lost or confused was given directions or a guide to their station. Anyone who resisted or refused to comply with orders—and there were a few—was thrown in the brig. Finally, when York once again knew that every soul on the ship was properly on station or in the brig, he took the ship off alert status.

He allowed himself a moment to think of that feddie hunter-killer out there. He had to assume they were still tracking *Cinesstar*, couldn't afford the luxury of doing otherwise. But this crew couldn't yet take on a small gunboat, let alone an experienced warship. He'd have to bide his time, hope he could get them trained before they had to face a real fight.

Gant and Rame sat down with York in his office to brief him on options for a transition plan. Gant said, "We're about twenty light-years behind the lines, or at least where we knew the lines to be about a month ago. Sarasan is another thirty beyond that. On a direct line of sight from our present position Aagerbanne is sixty-two light-years distant. But if we drive straight to her we'll slant diagonally through the lines, spend a lot of time in danger of attack from pickets on either side. I recommend we parallel the lines for about thirty light-years, then cut straight across toward Aagerbanne. It'll take us longer, a total of sixteen days, but it'll be safer." She looked at York for comment.

York asked Rame, "You like her plan?"

"We worked it out together."

"Then do it," he said as he looked at his watch. A half hour had passed since he'd released his new crew from their stations. "Commander Rame. Sound General Quarters."

Rame issued the order to the bridge through his implants, and the alert klaxon started blaring immediately. Rame and Gant looked at York, he nodded his permission and they shot out of the room. He stood there for a moment, let the noise wash over him and tried not to think about what would happen if they had to actually engage an enemy warship. Then he turned and headed calmly for the bridge.

••••

York ran them back and forth for almost a full day. He put the ship on alert, ran a few simulations, stood down to a skeleton watch, then repeated it. Each time he went on allship to tell them their time to station, and the third time they made it in just under four minutes, so he told them he'd let them rest when they got it under two minutes. He lost count of the number of times he cycled them on and off watch. They got down to two minutes, thirty-one seconds, but then began to deteriorate. "It's the fatigue factor," Maggie said, looking over York's shoulder at the data on his console. "They're exhausted now, probably won't be able to do any better until they get some rest."

Fatigue weighed on all of them. "Give me allship," he said.

Frank murmured, "Channel three."

York touched a switch on his console. "You made it on station in one minute, ninety-eight seconds," he lied. "You still have to do better, but for today that'll do. You now have a five-hour rest period, after which I'll be holding captain's mast. Attendance is mandatory."

He cut the circuit. "Mister Stara, Watch Condition Green. Commander Rame, set up a skeleton crew for mast. I want everyone there. Miss Votak, you're in charge of the arrangements for mast. Attendance is also mandatory for the civilians, so make sure they show up. If anyone gives you any trouble let me know and I'll get help from Her Majesty."

York stood, headed for his cabin, the captain's cabin. He should go over the damage control estimates with Rame and Cappik, but he needed rest before mast. This would be the turning point. If it went well the crew would support him. They wouldn't like him, and some would fear him, but they would leave mast confident someone was now in command.

••••

York looked up from the table where he and Maggie and Rame sat, while the spacer standing in front of them bowed his head remorsefully. The three of them put their heads together for a whispered conference. "Shall we give him the benefit of the doubt?" he asked.

As Maggie and Rame debated the virtues of the poor fellow, York scanned the crowd. Most of the civilians were present only because the empress had made it known that attendance was mandatory. There were thirty-two cases concerning minor infractions before the captain, and grinding through them was tedious at best. He was powerless to do anything about the atrocities the AI had committed. It was probably illegal to keep them locked in the brig, but York didn't care.

Rame was saying, ". . . we can't let them question the orders they're given. But he's a dirtlover, a stationside spacer. He just needs to learn it's different out here."

The three of them broke up their little conference. "Spacer Second Class Phaeda," York announced loudly, drawing everyone's attention. "Apparently you felt the assignment your station commander gave you was beneath you, so you chose to debate the issue. To help you understand that no assignment is beneath you, I sentence you to a tenday of the most degrading tasks we can dig up. Hopefully, you will learn that when your superior gives you an order, you will obey it, then and there. That is all."

The man was intelligent enough to keep his mouth shut, square his shoulders and salute smartly. York returned the salute; the man did a textbook about-face and marched away.

"Twenty-seven down," Maggie said tiredly. "Five to go."

The next case, another stationside spacer, stepped in front of York, looked at him defiantly, threw her chin out and stood righteously forth to plead her case. York didn't like the look of the situation.

"The charges?" Maggie asked.

A middle-aged woman stepped forward. "Chief Petty Officer Therma reporting as ordered, ma'am. I'm preferring charges against Spacer First Class Jayna Dyte for insubordination." The NCO's upper lip was badly swollen, a fact they all wanted to ignore.

"Yesterday," Therma continued, "at about twelve hundred hours, Spacer Dyte refused a direct order."

Maggie frowned. "Did she refuse the order, or merely misunderstand it?"

"She refused to obey it, ma'am, with considerable profanity."

Maggie shook her head. "Please be more specific, Chief Therma."

Therma frowned, glanced uncomfortably toward the empress and spoke reluctantly. "She told me to fuck myself with a neural prod, said she'd suck feddie cock before she'd take any orders from me."

York closed his eyes and rubbed his temples. There was a lot more to this than Therma was telling them. She clearly wanted to handle it quietly on her own, and he hoped she'd be allowed to do so.

"Spacer Dyte." Maggie looked at the angry young woman. "Did you understand the order given to you by Chief Therma?"

Dyte lifted her chin even higher. "O'course I did. I was—"

"Thank you, Spacer Dyte. Chief Therma, did—"

"Wait a minute," Dyte interrupted. "You haven't even asked what the order was. No one gives me that kind of—"

"The specific order," Maggie said, "is irrelevant—"

"And she assaulted me," Dyte continued, "grabbed me by my tunic, lifted me right out of my seat. No one touches me that way. No one, do you hear me? She was lucky I only hit her once. If she'd tried anything else—"

Dyte suddenly froze in mid-sentence. Without realizing it, York had stood, shoving his chair back with his legs and leaning forward on the table. At the unexpected action from him everything had come to a sudden standstill, though Dyte shrank away from him.

"You struck your station commander?" he asked, though it came out in a growl.

"I ah . . . I was . . . just defen . . ."

"God damn it!" York shouted. "I asked you a question. Did you strike your station commander?"

Dyte hesitated, suddenly unsure of herself. "I don't allow anyone to touch me that—"

"Did you strike her?" he shouted.

She shrank further. "Well, yes I did. But you have to—"

"Shut up," York shouted as he sat down. He had to think carefully. "Chief Therma. What was ship's status at the time of this incident?"

Therma cleared her throat uncomfortably. "Watch Condition Red, sir."

"We were on alert?"

"Yes, sir."

Dyte had forced his hand, shot off her big mouth with no concept of what she was getting into. "Spacer Dyte," he said. "Do you deny Chief Therma's allegations that you refused to obey a direct order?"

"No, but I—"

"And do you admit you struck Chief Therma while this ship was on alert?"

"Yes, sir, I do. But she had no right—"

Maggie jumped up. "Shut up, you idiot!"

Dyte started shouting. Maggie shouted back at her. During the commotion York keyed his implants. "Sergeant Palevi, I need an executioner up here, on the double."

Maggie and Dyte shouted at one another until Rame shouted them both down. "Miss Votak," York said. "Please sit down. Commander Rame, thank you for injecting some sanity into this proceeding. And Miss Dyte . . ." He looked carefully at the woman spacer. "Please be silent until you're invited to speak."

York hesitated for a moment. "You committed a serious breach of naval regulations, and under naval law your actions constitute a capital offense."

No one missed those words and the crowd began to grumble. Rame shouted, "Silence."

York continued. "But under captain's mast I can show you some leniency. You're sentenced to fifty strokes of the lash, sentence to be carried out immediately."

Dyte lunged forward suddenly, shaking her head and pointing an accusing finger at York. "You have no right. I know what the lash is, and you can't do this to me without a trial. I demand a proper trial." She looked around the deck for support.

York stood and faced her squarely. "You do have the right to such a trial—a court-martial, actually—if you so choose. But if you do, I'll have to prefer formal charges against you, and I'll be forced to follow the prescribed procedures. But at captain's mast I can exercise some . . . discretion."

"I want the trial," she shouted. "I'm not going to let you beat me senseless."

York felt very tired as he said, "Lieutenant Votak, please explain to Spacer Dyte the ramifications of a court-martial."

Dyte glowered at Maggie as she spoke carefully. "If you persist in your demands, then we must try you for the charge of assaulting a superior officer, which, under alert, is a capital offense."

For the first time a hint of uncertainty appeared on Dyte's face. "Capital offense?"

Maggie continued. "Captain Ballin will be required to convene the court-martial as soon as possible. It will be his responsibility to choose the three jurists who sit in judgment upon you. I assume that because of the magnitude of the offense, he will sit as chief jurist . . ." She glanced at York and he nodded, then she looked back at Dyte. "He will also appoint prosecution and defense councils. You and your council will be given a few hours to prepare, after which time the court-martial will convene. And because of your admissions here during the last few minutes, you'll be found guilty. The punishment for such a crime is death, and I assume the sentence will be carried out at dawn tomorrow morning by venting you alive to space. Are there any questions, Spacer Dyte?"

Her confidence had disappeared completely. At that moment the lift doors clanged open and a marine in full combat armor stepped out of it. His rank, insignia, and name stencil were hidden beneath black tape and he carried a length of lash. Dyte shook her head, looked at the marine with the lash and mumbled. "Death? You're insane. You have no right . . ."

"But we do," York said calmly. "This ship is a deep space man-of-war isolated behind enemy lines. And the rules here are different from what you're used to. Everything Lieutenant Votak has just described to you is not only legal, it is required, if you persist in your demands."

York looked at the empress, expecting to see disapproval in her eyes, but instead there seemed to be a curious sort of understanding there. On the other hand, Aeya and several others looked on with contempt and denial.

"What choice do I have?" Dyte whispered into the silence.

York couldn't hide a grimace. "You can be tried by a court-martial, and executed, or you can waive that right and accept the judgment of this mast. Do you still want a court-martial?"

Dyte just stood there, shaking her head almost imperceptibly. She opened her mouth for a moment, couldn't seem to find the strength to speak.

"Answer me."

She shook her head violently. "No."

"Then do you waive your right to a formal hearing?"

She mumbled something.

"Speak up. Say it."

"Yes."

"Yes, what?"

"Yes, damn it!" she shouted. "I waive my right to a hearing."

York had almost hoped she wouldn't agree. A quick death in the vacuum of space might even be preferable to the lash. He looked at Palevi and said simply, "Sergeant."

Palevi bellowed out a couple of names and two marines hustled forward, almost picked Dyte up by her armpits. They half carried her to an arch between two plast girders, cuffed her wrists to a couple of girders in an all too familiar position, then cut away the back of her coveralls with a power knife. As York watched he could feel a bead of sweat rolling down his back.

He owed Dyte one thing, the same thing Jarwith had given him. He would look her in the eyes through every stroke of the lash. It was a debt he also owed Jarwith.

He crossed the deck, stepped beneath one of Dyte's extended arms, stopped a few paces in front of her and turned to face her. Her face was flushed, and there was a wild, animalistic look in her eyes. Behind her he could see the mixed crowd of civilians and crew looking on with horror. Dyte grimaced at him. "Please," she said.

When everything was ready the marine in the armor uncoiled the lash, let one end of it drop to the deck, then waited for York's command. Another bead of sweat rolled down York's back as he looked at the marine and gave a slight nod of his head. "Proceed."

The first stroke of the lash was over and done with, the sound of the crack echoing in York's ears, and etched in his memory was an image of Dyte as she exploded toward him, her back arching, her wrists tearing frantically at the cuffs, her face contorting with anguish and pain. As her scream settled down among them all York thought he could almost feel the searing line of pain on his own back. "One," the marine said.

The lash struck again, and again Dyte screamed and tore at the cuffs. "Two."

Each stroke seemed to cut deeper into York's memory. "Three."

Dyte struggled, screamed and pleaded, begged for mercy. "Four."

And he wanted to show her mercy, to call a halt to the whole thing, but he didn't know how. "Five."

It was then York noticed Aeya and many of the civilians had closed their eyes, turned their faces away from the grisly sight. "Six."

That made York mad, for this was their punishment as much as Dyte's. "Seven."

"Halt," he shouted, and the marine froze.

Dyte's cries faded slowly to a whimper. "Doctor Yan," York said as he marched past Dyte. "Please take a look at Spacer Dyte."

York was past Dyte and approaching Aeya, who was only now opening her eyes. She saw him approaching and grimaced angrily. He stopped in front of her and a silence descended about them that not even Dyte's sobs could penetrate. "Your Highness," York said, finding it strangely easy to stay calm. He looked past her and scanned the faces of those around her as he spoke. "It's imperative you watch this proceeding, as unpleasant as it may be. So I cannot allow you to close your eyes and look away."

She shook her head, leaned forward and growled in his face, "You can't stop me."

"No. I can't. However, if you, or anyone here, looks away during a stroke of the lash, then that stroke will not count as part of Spacer Dyte's sentence. If we have to stand here all day and beat the poor woman to death until you see a full fifty strokes, then we will."

Aeya opened her mouth, but her jaw just hung there, a look of horror and loathing in her eyes. Behind her the empress kept her part of their bargain, and there was nothing to be read in her face. Lady d'Hart, though, seemed to have the opposite reaction, as if she had thought of York as a monster when the beating had begun, but now she understood its real purpose.

"That applies to all of you," York said, again scanning the faces in the crowd. "If any one of you looks away, then Spacer Dyte will have to suffer that stroke again."

He didn't wait for a reaction, spun around and saw Dyte's back for the first time, the red welts etched there, the first few trickles of blood beginning to well forth. He ducked beneath one of her arms and stopped in front of her.

She hung by the cuffs, no longer able to support herself on her feet, Alsa Yan standing beside her. "She's strong and healthy," Yan said. "She'll survive with nothing more than memories."

York nodded. "Thank you. Dismissed."

Yan backed away as York looked into Dyte's eyes. "Please," she said.

"I'm sorry," he said, suddenly conscious of the plug of leather suspended from a plast string around his neck, and he realized he'd been gripping it through the material of his coveralls through each and every stroke of the lash. He'd kept it with him all these years, though no longer even aware that it existed. But there it was, as if he'd subconsciously carried it all these years for just this moment. He reached into his coveralls, and though it was a bit awkward to do he lifted the loop of string over his head and held the plug of leather in his hand for a moment, looking at it. He could still see the faint traces of his own teeth marks.

Without warning he thrust the plug of leather between Dyte's teeth. She looked at him, surprised by the strange action. "Someone gave me that a long time ago," he told her. "It's made from the skin of a cow, though I don't know what a cow is. But that doesn't really matter, does it? When you feel the lash strike, bite down hard on it, bite down with everything you've got. It helps . . . a little. I know."

She frowned at him, and maybe she even understood a little.

He backed away a few paces, planted his feet squarely with his hands gripped behind his back and gave the order, "Proceed."

The crack of the lash rocked Dyte forward, though now the plug of leather muffled her screams. "Eight."

She and York locked their eyes together, and he couldn't look away as the lash returned relentlessly to her back. York felt the fire of each stroke, almost as if it were cutting away the flesh of his own back. And slowly both she and he settled into the rhythm of the ordeal: the whip-crack sound of the lash as it struck her back, the strange sort of delay between that moment and the actual onset of the pain, followed by the toneless voice of the marine as he announced the count.

Dyte wasn't conscious through the last ten or fifteen strokes. York let the sentence proceed nevertheless. If nothing more, he could show poor Dyte that much mercy.

When it was done the marines unlocked the cuffs on Dyte's wrists, lowered her carefully to a grav stretcher. The silence surrounding them all was complete.

Yan, who'd been standing behind York, stepped up carefully and whispered in his ear, "York. Your back is bleeding through your tunic. Adjourn the mast; tell them you'll consider the remaining cases tomorrow. Then you and I can slip out quietly to my office."

York glanced down at his hands. There was a bloody ring around each wrist where more than twenty years ago the manacles had cut into the flesh as he'd struggled under the lash, and suddenly he felt twelve years old again.

••••

Abraxa smiled at Archcanon Lynna, watched him smile back, bow, turn and leave. Lynna was pleased with himself, thinking he'd just struck a deal with the most powerful man in the empire. But Lynna, ordinarily an astute and cunning man, had been clumsy in this instance.

Abraxa touched a switch on his terminal and spoke softly, "Why don't you join me now, Your Holiness?"

A panel in the wall opened and Bortha stepped out. He was livid, unable to maintain his usual air of wizened understanding. Abraxa, for no other reason than that he was enjoying the old hypocrite's loss of control, decided to bait him. "Archcanon Lynna is a cunning and dangerous man, is he not, Your Holiness?"

Bortha actually turned red. "Archcanon Lynna is a dead man," he shouted. "I'll personally have that conniving, little sneak strangled in his own vestments. That little . . ." Bortha suddenly got hold of himself, realized he was giving Abraxa too much of a show. With force of will, and an obvious effort, he forced a veneer of calm on his features, smoothed his robes and sat down, though he was speechless for several seconds.

"May I recommend," Abraxa said, "that, as yet, you take no action against him?"

Bortha's forced calm broke again. "No action? No action! He as much as offered to betray me to you. He probably thinks he can have the Archcanonship, if he's a clever little sneak."

"No doubt he does," Abraxa agreed. "It took a considerable amount of confidence to approach me that way. So much so, that I don't doubt he's approached others. We could turn this to our advantage, you know?"

Bortha frowned and looked at Abraxa. "What do you mean?"

Abraxa stroked his chin and spoke absentmindedly, as if he were thinking out loud. "Perhaps I should encourage him, see if I can't strengthen our ties. And if we're careful, and we watch him closely, we may learn a great deal, not only from him, but from anyone else he's struck a deal with."

Bortha nodded. "Yes," he said. "Yes. I should have thought of that myself." He smiled and leaned back in the chair.

Abraxa continued. "And when we've learned everything, then you can kill him."

22

Gunner's Blood

"WELL?" JEWEL DEMANDED angrily, craning her neck to get a look at Soe leaning forward over his console, shaking his head unhappily.

"I think we lost him," he said. "He's too damn cautious, taking two whole days to swing through a turn like that."

Jewel pulled up a star chart on one of her screens. "There's only two places he could be going: they've got a sector headquarters at Aagerbanne and a subsector headquarters at Sarasan. Sarasan is closer, but Aagerbanne's bigger, better equipped." She drummed her fingers on her console for a moment and came to a decision. "If we down-transit, can you get a fix on his vector?"

"Well, I'm damn well not going to get anything here in transition."

Chief Innay's voice came on the line. "If we down-transit we'll give away our position."

"Yes," Jewel said. "I know. But we've got no choice. We'd better play it safe, though, just in case he decides to take a shot at us.

"Mr. Tac'tac'ah, stand by for sublight transition. Mister Soe. Sound battle stations."

••••

At the sound of the chime York touched a switch on his console and said, "Yes."

His yeoman said, "Commanders Soladin and McGeahn are here to see you, Captain. They have an appointment."

York made a mental note to ask Maggie the name of his yeoman. "Thank you. Send them in."

A few seconds later the yeoman swung the door open and held it for Soladin and McGeahn. The two officers stopped in front of York's desk; Soladin saluted him casually while McGeahn gave proper care to form and technique. As York returned their salutes his attention was drawn to the gold piping and decorative stitching on their uniforms, all nonregulation. "At ease. Sit down."

They both dropped into chairs. McGeahn said, "Thank you for making time available, sir."

Soladin suppressed a yawn. "Yes, Ballin, good of you."

York didn't tell them his yeoman was responsible for that. "Certainly. What can I do for you?"

Soladin took the opening. "Well now, Ballin. You've done a nice job of getting this crew organized."

"Yes," McGeahn added. "You've transformed the entire ship. The crew look like professionals again."

"Thank you," York said. "But they have a long way to go before they'll be ready to take on a feddie warship."

McGeahn nodded. "Let's hope that's not necessary."

"But that's why we're here," Soladin said. "Hethis and I have no crew assignments, and our experience shouldn't be left untapped. As senior officers we can help you whip these amateurs into shape."

York looked Soladin over carefully, and not for the first time wondered if the man had any idea how ridiculous he sounded. McGeahn seemed a bit embarrassed. York asked, "Have either of you got any combat experience?"

"Certainly," Soladin said.

McGeahn shook her head. "Just simulations."

"Commander," York asked Soladin. "Where and when did you get your experience?"

Soladin puffed up. "I've spent the last two years as a senior line officer with Home Fleet."

York nodded and rubbed his chin. "To my knowledge, Home Fleet hasn't seen combat for more than fifty years, so I assume you've never been part of a crew that actually engaged the enemy."

"See here, Ballin." Soladin rose from his chair and leaned forward over York's desk. "What does that matter? You know how realistic the simulations are. One can't tell the combat isn't real."

"But you still *know* it isn't real. And that's where it counts." York pondered the two officers for a moment. "Let me at least offer you the opportunity to gain that experience the same way every officer on this ship has, the traditional way, as a rank ensign. If you'll accept a voluntary demotion, I'll assign you a duty station and—"

"Absolutely not!" Soladin shouted. "I've never heard of such a thing. I'm an experienced officer. In fact, I can't understand why Her Majesty didn't put me in command, rather than you. There certainly is a clear distinction between the two of us. I must assume you're here only because of some implied threat from you and your marine ilk—"

"Enough!" York shouted. He rose to face Soladin, and as dictated by etiquette McGeahn also stood. "Commander, I have work to do. If you don't care to accept my offer, then you're dismissed. Now."

The last word hung in the air while Soladin glared angrily at York. "Ballin, there are no conceivable circumstances under which I would accept such an offer." He spun about and stormed out the door, leaving it open.

York turned on McGeahn. "Well?" he demanded. "What are you waiting for?"

She scrunched up her courage, then said, "I'd like to take you up on that offer . . . sir."

He looked her over carefully. "No guarantees."

She nodded and grinned. "No guarantees, sir."

"Wipe that grin off your face," he growled, spun toward his console and slapped the intercom switch. "Get me Lieutenant Votak," he barked into the pickup. "On the double."

They only had to wait a few seconds before Maggie's voice exploded from the speaker. "Captain, Lieutenant Votak reporting as ordered."

"Miss Votak, Lieutenant Commander McGeahn has volunteered to accept a demotion to ensign. Please execute the paperwork immediately."

York scanned the station assignments quickly, found a lower deck pod-station running sims to make up for low scores on the last drill. He called the NCO in charge. "I have a new ensign for you. She'll be reporting to you immediately. Start her at the bottom. And if she's not there in two minutes, put her on report."

The chief grinned, nodded. "Aye, aye, sir."

McGeahn frowned worriedly. "Two minutes, sir?"

"That's right. You'd better hurry." He looked at the embellishments on her uniform. "And you're out of uniform. Ask your station commander for a new one."

"Yes, sir," she said, throwing a salute at him. "Aye, aye, sir."

He returned the salute. "Dismissed."

She turned and shot out of the room. After several seconds York's yeoman peered uncertainly through the open door. "Sir? Would you like the door open or closed?"

York growled, "Close it."

York sat down to review the damage reports. The starboard chamber was still acting up, and they couldn't properly repair it without the facilities of a navy yard. An aft bulkhead had buckled badly when the hunter-killer threw that warhead at them, though that had been repaired, along with the weakened structures in the empress' stateroom. The officer's mess was still closed, would probably remain that way for some time to come. He couldn't justify fixing it when there were so many more things to do that—

The alert klaxon suddenly started blaring. York's first thought was that it was a bit early for the drill he'd scheduled, then Stara's voice bellowed out of allship, "Battle stations! All hands, this is not a drill. Battle stations. This is not a drill."

York scrambled around his desk, into the captain's private lift, shouted, "Bridge," at the computer. The lift door slammed open and he stepped out.

"Captain on the bridge."

York keyed his implants as he dropped down behind the captain's console, hit a switch to log his station into the computer. "Captain, this is Commander Gant. We picked up a transition flare dead astern. Looks like that hunter-killer, probably down-transited to get a fix on us, maybe take a shot. You've got a summary."

The summary on York's screens showed a transition flare about half a light-year behind them. Gant had immediately activated *Cinesstar*'s shields, but the feddie was just sitting there, receding in their wake, too far out for a shot. York scanned all of the screens on his console; everything seemed as it should. "Frank. Give me allship."

"Channel three, sir."

York activated his pickup. "This is Captain Ballin. This was not a drill. The feddie hunter-killer on our tail was losing us, so they down-transited to get a fix on us. They've got it, but now they're too far behind to take an accurate shot.

"You made it on station in one minute and nine seconds. I still want to see you under one minute, but that's your best time so far so let me congratulate you on a job well done.

"We had planned an advanced training drill to begin in the next hour, but since we're already on station we'll go ahead with it now." York cut the circuit.

Maggie's voice mumbled in his implants. "What's that feddie up to?"

York thought that if he ever had a chance to meet the captain of that feddie he'd probably like her, even as they tried to kill each other. "I don't know. But she's good, doubt she'll give up that easily. I don't think we're done with her yet."

••••

"Did you get it?" Jewel demanded.

Soe frowned. "I got it. I don't know what it means, but I damn well got it."

"What the hell do you mean by that?"

"Look at your console."

Jewel looked at the data on her console. Soe had managed to get them an excellent fix on the *imper*'s position and vector. But the *imper* was headed for neither Aagerbanne nor Sarasan. If it had been Sarasan, he'd be cutting straight across the lines, if Aagerbanne, a diagonal through them. Instead, he was running parallel to the lines.

"What's that damn *imper* doing?" Soe pleaded.

Innay said easily, "He's playing it safe."

And then Jewel saw it herself. "Of course. He's going to Aagerbanne. But he's going to run parallel to the lines until he's directly opposite Aagerbanne, then make a straight run for it."

"We've lost him then," Tac'tac'ah groaned.

"Yes we have," Jewel said, nodding calmly. "If he's really going to Aagerbanne. But he just wants us to think that. We've been hitting Aagerbanne pretty hard lately, and it might not be a wise place to go. Now, if he's really going to Sarasan, and this is just a feint, we could be there waiting for him when he gets there."

••••

York watched the empress and Lady d'Hart as Maggie and Rame argued over station assignments. The empress had insisted that the two of them be allowed to sit in on York's staff meetings, and one did not say no to an insistent empress, though York had extracted a promise from her to just observe, and not interfere.

They'd been drilling the crew mercilessly for a tenday and they'd shown considerable progress. But some imbalances had surfaced, and it was time to redistribute the crew a bit. Maggie and Rame could argue like drunken spacers on leave, but York had learned to let them have at it. And sure enough, they quickly converged on a solution that both could endorse.

They looked at York and he said, "Do it."

He stood, and all but the empress and Lady d'Hart stood with him. "Thank you. Dismissed."

He turned and stepped through the door to his office. He was anxious to see the results of the program he'd left running during the staff meeting and he sat down immediately behind the terminal at his desk. On the screen were the words:

Abort threshold exceeded, search discontinued.

Success correlation: 10%

Items matched: 231

He shook his head sadly, touched a key and the first of the two hundred and thirty-one names appeared on the screen: KALLEAR MATCHEK.

Perhaps old Maja had merely guessed at the spelling of the man's name, so he'd refined the search to include names phonetically similar to Collier Maczek. And he could make a reasonable guess at the man's age, and there had to be some sort of record of him on Dumark. York had slowly put together a complicated search filter, but even that resulted in too many names for him to review with any kind of alacrity. So during stolen moments he took them in small groups, pulled up each name and reviewed what was known—which often was almost nothing. Most of the names he flagged as solid rejects, and a few he retained as possibilities, usually because there was not enough known to properly eliminate the man.

It helped that he had ring-zero access. He could do almost anything at that level, for there were no restrictions. Under normal circumstances, when it became necessary to insert new code with that access, some unknown number of programming teams reviewed it first and ran it through several simulations. Opening a ring-zero portal normally required the presence of the emperor and all nine admirals, watching each other closely—probably with considerable distrust; they'd open the portal, insert the new code, then shut it down immediately. Only in that way could they insure that no one created a backdoor. That's the procedure that would have been followed with *Cinesstar*, had the feddies not changed the circumstances.

"That's curious," a soft voice said.

He started, looked up and back, found Sylissa d'Hart looking over his shoulder. At his reaction she straightened up quickly. "I'm sorry, Captain. I didn't mean to startle you."

He blanked the screen, stood up and faced her, tried not to look guilty. But she was visibly embarrassed. "I'm sorry," she said again. "You left the door open. And I wanted a word with you. And when I looked in you were so engrossed with your work I thought I'd step in and wait until you were ready to be interrupted. And then I caught a glimpse of the name on your screen and it reminded me of a man I once knew, though the spelling was different . . ." She suddenly stiffened, straightened, resumed the cold, impersonal persona of the Lady d'Hart. "I didn't mean to pry."

He lied. "I was just reviewing the files of a crewman." Had she recognized the name somehow? "But you say you know him?"

She shook her head. "No. I knew another man a long time ago, when I was a little girl. The spelling of his name was different." She quickly spelled out the name, and it was the spelling old Maja had given him. For some reason she felt the need to explain her intrusion, and as York's heart raced he dared not stop her. "Actually, I didn't know him. I just saw him a few times about the old palace. I was young, and romantic, and he was a loyal servant to a beautiful woman named Francesca Ballinov . . ."

York felt giddy, to search so hard, and then to have it suddenly dropped in his lap like this.

"Are you all right, Captain?"

Lady d'Hart looked at him oddly, and he realized he must have let something show. "How did you say his name?" he asked.

"Collier Maczek."

At that point they both retreated, and he knew he'd get no more out of her without arousing suspicion. He bent over his desk, retrieved the bottle of 'trate from the bottom drawer. He held it up in trembling hands. "Can I offer you something to drink? It's only 'trate. I wish I could offer you better, but this is all I've got."

She lifted an eyebrow and seemed about to disapprove, but then she shrugged, laughed at herself a little, and the stiff persona disappeared again. "Why not?"

He mixed them two drinks and handed her one. As she sipped at hers he asked, "You wanted a word with me."

She grinned and tossed down the last of her drink. "You and your officers always refer to the captain of that hunter-killer as *she* or *her*. Why not *he* or *him*?"

"I hadn't thought about it. It just seems right."

"Does it give you more confidence to think you're in a battle of skills with a woman?"

"No. She's good, too good for me to feel a lot of confidence."

"But you're certain it's a woman?"

"I'm not certain of anything."

She nodded, grinned and looked him over carefully. "Thank you, Captain."

"For what?"

"For letting me know you're human." She turned and quietly left him there.

When she was gone he stood there for a moment, knowing he'd missed something, but not really caring because, without knowing it, she'd given him the name of his mother.

••••

The alert klaxon woke Meekl Donohae from stim-sleep, the lights in her coffin flashed to full brightness, and the voice of that handsome young officer blared over allship, telling them to report to battle stations. "Coffin" was what the veterans called a sealed bunk compartment, and she remembered not to sit up immediately and slam her nose against the ceiling only centimeters above her face. The bloody nose she'd gotten before her first drill had been a supreme embarrassment.

She was the rookie on the J-deck, niner station pod crew, and was therefore assigned the top bunk, which meant she had to wait longest for her coffin to cycle out of storage. She tried to calm herself, to slow her racing heart, because she desperately wanted to make a good showing. Her simulation scores were improving rapidly, and she was hoping during the next drill, this drill . . .

It was then that the young officer's words hit her. ". . . This is not a drill. I repeat: this is not a drill . . ."

She didn't hear anything else until her coffin suddenly cycled into the bunkroom and her reflexes took over. She sat up and at the same time killed the grav field in her bunk, let the deck gravity start her into a fall toward the deck. By hooking one hand on the edge of her bunk, she spun herself so she landed on her feet like a veteran with dozens of kill chevrons cut into the skin of her arm.

She hit the deck in panties and bra, a one-piece coverall tucked in her left hand, took only a few seconds to get her legs into it, then sprinted up the corridor trying to get her arms into the upper half. She got it in place just as she reached her station.

Chief Syda glanced over his shoulder at her, gave her an approving nod as she dove for her pod hatch. She scrambled up the zero-G tube toward the outer skin of the ship, slipped into the couch in her pod with practiced ease, tore on her headset, wished she had implants like the officers and the more experienced crew, strapped herself in place and threw the switch that sealed the pod.

Comp was already running her pod through precombat check. She scanned the readout, watched closely as the status check ran its course, and the instant it was complete she slapped the active switch. She was on station.

She scanned her screens: guidance and ballistic control, ordnance, fire control, three tracking screens . . . A chill ran up her spine; there was a large yellow blip on her tracking screens about three hundred million kilometers distant. Through sheer bad luck they'd tripped over a feddie warship on patrol. No simulation, but a real enemy that could throw a warhead at them large enough to split a small moon. And as she looked on, the yellow blip spit out a smaller yellow blip: a transition launch, aimed at *Cinesstar*, aimed at her. The shooting had already begun, no time for reassuring words from the old man, no time to think herself into a calm. She started to tremble, and almost lost control of her bladder.

Cinesstar's hull thrummed with the sound of one of the main turrets slamming a barrage of shells into transition, and a small green blip appeared on her screens headed for the enemy ship. More yellow blips from the enemy ship, one after the other; more green blips from *Cinesstar*, with the hull starting to sound like a giant reverberation chamber. And then suddenly one of the yellow blips turned red, her targeting computer began tracking, her firing console lit up like a field of landing beacons on a dark night, and a timer on her screen started counting down from five. She'd been allocated a target, and she had five seconds to kill it, five seconds in which to confirm the computers firing sequence or to override and track it herself, five seconds before it killed them all . . . and she froze.

At the last instant the hull thrummed with a more intense beat as one of her station-mates took the target. She began hyperventilating and wanted to cry, and then Chief Syda's voice came over her headset, calm and easy, no derision, no judgment. "Calm down, Meekl. It's no different from a drill. Keep your head, stay cool, and try again."

On her next allocated target she overrode the computer and fired immediately, missed, and fired again, and again. She lost count of the number of rounds she wasted, didn't hit a thing, still needed one of her station-mates to take the target.

On her third target she only wasted two rounds, though one of the other stations took it out. But on her fourth target she held on, let the computer track it and monitored the trajectory closely. It was a miss, so she let it go, didn't waste anything.

Without warning the hull screamed at her, and a shock wave passed through the ship. It took her a few seconds to realize *Cinesstar* had taken a hit. She switched her com to damage control for a moment, heard something about minor damage aft, then switched back to the station. She got another target with a six-second trajectory. The computer was targeting for a close-in shot, but she decided to try a long shot, overrode and fired. She didn't hit it; not a real kill, but the detonation of her pod-shot deflected it. One of her station-mates broke into her com line, "Atta girl, Meekl," and she flushed with pride.

The battle turned into a chase. The enemy was a smaller ship with just a bit less range in her main batteries, though she managed to sting *Cinesstar* a few times. But she was outgunned and she took to her heels and ran, and *Cinesstar* followed. Twice Meekl had more than one target to deal with, and she came close to panicking again. But she didn't, and with help from her station-mates they took care of the targets.

The enemy warship took a hit from one of *Cinesstar*'s main batteries, and then they started to sting her regularly. And then suddenly the enemy blossomed into a bright orange flower on Meekl's screens, and the battle was over. And they were alive. She was alive. The order came from the bridge to go to Watch Condition Yellow, and she started to cry.

She was still crying when the old man's voice came over allship. "This is Captain Ballin. We took some minor damage aft and amidships. There are some casualties but we don't have a full count yet."

He paused, and she could imagine him leaning over his console deep in thought, that strange steel eye of his staring with such intensity at his screens. "You fought valiantly," he continued. "You burned that feddie so she couldn't give away our position and call half the Directorate down on us. I'm proud of you. Every last one of you."

A shiver ran up Meekl's spine. The old man seemed to be done, but then, as if it were an afterthought, "Oh yes! You beat one minute. You were on station in ninety-eight seconds. Congratulations. A new record. Next time we'll try to beat ninety."

••••

It was a victory celebration, or at least that's what the rookies and the civilians thought. York had ordered that a limited crew of seasoned veterans man all stations, and that everyone else, crew and civilians and nobility alike, eat at the same time in the main mess, a rather crowded banquet. He'd had the seating carefully arranged, with a select group seated at the captain's table, the empress on his right, then Olin Rame, then Princess Aeya, then Maggie, then Lady Dubye, then Frank, then Sarra Fithwallen. Sylissa d'Hart was on his left, then Straegga, then the old queen mother, then Gant, then Andow, then Nemkov, then Brentin Omasin.

Sierka and the AI Major were seated with the other officers, though not at the captain's table. Even the feddie breed warrior Sab'ach'ahn and Governor Andleman were there, under guard. It was all carefully done by rank, with some help from Lady d'Hart to insure that the nobility were seated properly. There had been only a little juggling for York's preferences, and a little more to insure every civilian and rookie sat close to a veteran.

Dinner was pleasant. Even Aeya managed to avoid baiting York. As dinner came to an end the Dubye slut was making her moves on poor Frank, while Maggie visibly ignored the situation. Sylissa d'Hart asked York, "Where are we now, Captain?"

York nodded toward Gant. "Anda, you're probably better able to answer that."

Gant glanced at her watch, thought carefully for a moment. "Right now we're about six light-years short of the front lines, about two days at our present drive. We could move faster, but we're being cautious, running silent, slow, and careful. We'd like to avoid interception by pickets on either side."

Andow asked, "Are we likely to have to fight our way past any more Directorate warships."

York nodded slowly. "Hopefully the ship we engaged this morning was sublight to get a navigational fix, just pure luck. In transition they'd never have spotted us."

"You said *hopefully*?"

Nemkov answered him. "There's a good chance Anachron IV alerted the Directorate to our position. They could then order all ships in the vicinity to down-transit and sit in sublight, waiting and watching for us. If they did that, then it wasn't luck, and we'll run into more."

The festive atmosphere that had lasted through dinner disappeared. York said, "That's partly the reason we ran parallel to the lines for almost ninety light-years. I wanted to get out of the vicinity of Anachron IV. We also ran a bit off course for Aagerbanne. And it's likely that feddie warship reported our position before engaging us. So we've changed course again, and are going to run parallel to the lines for a few more light-years before turning to cross. And I don't know how often we may have to repeat that process. A crossing directly opposite Aagerbanne or Sarasan would be too obvious."

The conversation at the table broke up into small groups. Sylissa d'Hart leaned toward York, pointed to the small plast cup at the top of her place setting, whispered, "Tell me, Captain, what's that cup for? I've noticed there's one like it for each and every one of us. And I've also noticed that, quite a number of times this evening, when anyone reaches for that cup, someone seated next to them politely tells them not to touch it." There was a small, almost unnoticeable grin on her lips, and a glint in her eyes. "What are you up to?"

In his other ear, the empress whispered, "Yes, Captain. What are you up to?"

York glanced around the table, then around the mess hall, and with few exceptions everyone had finished dinner. He rose to his feet. The other officers at the table started to stand. "As you were," he said quietly, and they lowered themselves back into their seats.

The moment he stood Palevi appeared in the mess hall entrance on cue, and at the same time several mess orderlies began moving among the tables, pouring a small amount of 'trate into each cup. Several rookies and civilians started to reach for their cup, but a nearby veteran stopped them. Most of the crew had instantly stopped speaking; the civilians and some of the rookies were a little slower to react, and several seconds passed while the background murmur slowly died.

One of the orderlies handed Palevi a cup, poured some 'trate into it. Then they served themselves, and last they served York, filling his cup generously.

York let the final, complete silence fall among them all, and then he let it draw out until it was thick and heavy with anticipation. Then he reached forward and picked up the cup, looked at the clear liquid swirling within it. He scanned the room slowly, then said, "Today two of our comrades died. But previously there were a number of others, and while they have been buried at space, it has come to my attention they have not been properly laid to rest.

"In the plast cup at your place is a small amount of 'trate. By custom it was made in a still on this ship while in deep space, not on another ship, and especially not on the surface of a planet. Also by custom it's strong, only slightly diluted."

York looked again at the fluid in his cup, then at Palevi. He gave the sergeant a slight nod.

Palevi snapped to attention so rigidly his entire body quivered like spring steel. Then he bellowed in his loudest parade-ground voice, startling quite a number of those present, "Atteeuun . . . shuuuuun!"

The veterans in the crowd shot to their feet instantly. The rookies were slower to react, and they moved with some hesitation, but eventually every crewmember stood and tried to imitate Palevi's spring-steel rigidity. Most of the civilians remained seated. York looked around slowly. "Please," he said. "All of you. Please stand."

Lady d'Hart and the empress stood without hesitation, and one by one the others followed suit.

"Sergeant," York called.

"Sir," Palevi bellowed back.

"Have the names been inscribed on the hull of the ship?"

"Sir, yes, sir."

"Very good, Sergeant. Then call the roll."

"Aye, aye, sir." Holding the cup in one hand, the marine held up a piece of paper in the other. He read from it.

"Spacer Apprentice Andis Bannaer."

"Here, sir," one of the veterans called out.

"Private First Class Misorrdah Coemak . . ."

Slowly, one by one, he called out each name and someone responded. And each carried its own message, until eventually an unhappy sorrow settled over them all. Sometimes those who knew a particular name winced, and occasionally someone shed a tear or two, but for the most part it was merely farewell. And when Palevi finished the last name a silence descended that seemed oddly devoid of the sorrow that gripped them moments earlier.

York looked at the clear liquid in his cup, then lifted it to his lips. One small sip, and the 'trate burned its way down his throat, almost bringing tears to his eyes. Then he held the cup out in front of him at arm's length, and in a loud voice he spoke the words, "For them it's over. For us it goes on."

Slowly, carefully, he tipped the cup to one side. The liquid drizzled over the edge in a small, steady stream, spattering widely as it hit the plast tabletop. It spattered all over York's uniform, all over Sylissa d'Hart and the empress, all over those near them. To the credit of the rest of them, Aeya was the only one to cringe away from the spattering, trying to protect herself behind her napkin.

When York was done the table was a mess. Without lowering his hand he opened his fingers and let the cup drop and clatter loudly to the tabletop. Olin and Maggie and Frank and the rest of the officers at the table reached out and lifted their cups. The veterans in the crowd did likewise, leading those less familiar with the ceremony, taking a small sip, then in a disharmonious unison they all echoed York's words, "For them it's over. For us it goes on." Then they held out their cups, poured the remaining 'trate on their tables, and with a loud, disjointed crash dropped their cups.

Before York could proceed the empress reached down, picked up her cup, took her sip, followed the formula and poured the remainder on the tabletop, said, "For them it's over. For you—it goes on." There was a tear in her eye.

York waited for the silence to return, then said softly, "Release them," and for the two who had died that day the hull echoed with the emergency blow-down cycle of the aft maintenance hatch.

When the sound finally died York said, "Dismissed," and backed away from the table, was out in the corridor headed for the bridge.

But Sylissa d'Hart called after him. "Captain . . . York . . ."

He stopped and turned about. She rushed up the corridor and caught up with him. "That was another lesson, wasn't it? As much for us as for your novice crewmembers."

He shrugged. "We have a lot to learn if we're going to get out of this alive."

"But must everything be a lesson? Don't you ever let up? Don't you ever relax?"

He thought about it for a moment. "I'll make a deal with you. If I get you and the empress and your friend out of this . . ." His veiled reference to the empress' servant, the only other person on the ship with a suicide device, had the desired effect. She frowned uncertainly as he continued, "If I do that, then when this is all over I'll give you a chance to show me how to relax properly."

He left her standing there with a frown on her face.

••••

It was late, and down on the lower decks the corridors were all but deserted. York hesitated outside the pod gunners' barracks, wondering if he was doing the right thing. He wore a one-piece coverall, no rank insignia, the sleeves cut away just above the elbows, all according to custom. His presence, however, required a broad interpretation of tradition, and it could backfire, have the opposite effect of what he wanted.

He knocked on the closed hatch. Except under alert it would normally be open, but this was a special occasion, even if it was officially illegal.

The hatch opened a crack and an old chief petty officer peered out at him. The man recognized York instantly, opened the hatch enough to stand in it at attention, though he was careful to block York's view of anything within. "Sir," he said nervously, and started to salute.

"As you were," York said calmly. "May I come in?"

"Uhhh! Well, Captain," the chief said uncomfortably. "Certainly, sir . . . Uhhh . . . but officers don't usually come down here . . . uhhh . . . sir."

York grinned. "Especially not for this occasion. But I'm not an officer tonight." With his right hand he reached up and slid his left sleeve up to his shoulder, exposing a dozen scars in the skin of his upper arm. Each was in the shape of a chevron. York asked the chief, "Tonight there's only one kind of rank here, isn't there? And isn't attendance mandatory for all blooded gunners?"

The chief's lips slowly broke into a grin. He considered York for a moment, then nodded and stepped aside. "Come on in, sir."

York stepped through the hatch. The lights were dim, though York could see there were quite a number of spacers present. He rolled up his sleeves so they'd stay that way, noticed the chief had more chevrons than him, which was good. He didn't want to be the senior gunner tonight.

The chief announced, "Gunner York Ballin. Twelve chevrons. Someone get 'im a beer."

Someone stuck a cup of black beer in York's hand. He could see the word spreading fast. *The captain's here and he's got gunner's stripes on his arm.*

All of the pod gunners had gathered for the ceremony called *gunner's blood.* They were crowded into the barracks, some sitting on the deck up against a bulkhead. As York crossed the barracks they got out of his way, and at the far end someone who had a chair started to get up. York turned away from him, edged into a spot between two gunners sitting on the deck with their backs against a bulkhead. One was a pretty, young girl, perhaps nineteen or twenty. York stuck out his hand. "York Ballin," he said.

Her mouth hung open as she extended a limp hand.

He grinned. "Pick yer jaw up off the deck and tell me your fuckin' name."

She closed her mouth, opened her eyes just as wide to make up for it. "Uhhh! Meekl Donohae . . . uhhh . . . sir."

"Nice to meet you, Meekl. You drawing blood tonight?"

Her face filled with disappointment. "No, sir. No kills today, sir."

The man seated next to her chimed in, "I'm her station chief, sir. And you can bet yer ass she did just fuckin' fine, sir, even though it was her first time out. Didn't get any goddamn kills, but I saw her take a real nice long shot at about a hundred million klicks, had to override the computer to do it, deflected a big fuckin' warhead, as good as any kill, sir."

York nodded, tried to look impressed. Tradition called for excessive profanity and too much beer, so he said, "Well, goddamn, Meekl! I froze up through the whole fuckin' engagement, first time in a pod. You'll do just fine."

She grinned like a child, then York remembered she basically was a child.

"Listen up," the ranking chief shouted. "I want the following front'n'center immediately." He read off a list of names, no rank, and as each was called a young spacer shot forward accompanied by loud jeers and crude epithets, along with a steady stream of accusations concerning their ancestry and their sexual preferences—usually something to do with certain exotic animals. Each had full-length sleeves on their coveralls.

Hethis McGeahn was one of the names. She jumped up like all the rest, no insignia on her coveralls. Buck ensigns were the one exception to an officer's presence at *gunner's blood,* though it was quite rare for one to actually earn a chevron. McGeahn looked as excited as the rest at the prospect of getting the coveted scar.

One by one each candidate was escorted to the center of the room, their station chief recounted the particular kill that had earned the scar, usually with some flair and a certain amount of embellishment, and of course accompanied by a lot of crude cheers and shouts. Then they cut away the candidate's sleeves, and an old, steel knife was used to make a half-chevron cut in the skin high up on the arm. It was important the wound bleed nicely, that blood stream down the arm all the way to the fingertips and onto the deck. Then they washed the blood into the deck with a splash of the black beer, and the next candidate stepped forward.

When the new bloods had been properly initiated, the old bloods who had added a kill or two to their records took their turn. Each got another half-chevron scar added to those for past kills. York enjoyed the event thoroughly, contributed quite nicely to the profanity and the cheering, and drank his share of beer. Little, awe-struck Meekl would probably have given him anything he wanted, and he was tempted to take her up to his cabin. But then she'd miss her first *gunner's blood*, and that wouldn't be right. And once the ceremonies were done, for York to stay longer would just put a damper on things. It was time for him to exit before he got in the way.

He shook a few hands, downed another black beer, then left so they could have their fun.

••••

Add'kas'adanna looked at the sightings she'd plotted. Many were obvious mistakes; otherwise the *imper* would have had to be in two, sometimes three places at once. Anachron IV was the last unquestionable sighting. There were a few others with enough substantiating data to indicate a reasonable probability it was her *imper* and not some other, or some commercial vessel, or a stray pirate, or anything else for that matter.

The *imper* was probably headed down-sector, though that was, as yet, only an educated guess, could be headed for Aagerbanne or Sarasan, or one of the other planets with a large *imper* installation. He could even be headed for a small installation. Now that would be a crafty move.

At least she was on a ship again. She much preferred life aboard ship, wondered often if the purity of her honor had become soiled over the years by the crafts of statesmanship she'd learned in the halls of the Directorate.

She looked again at the plot of sightings, decided to amass a large fleet in the neighborhood of Sarasan and Aagerbanne. It wouldn't hurt to have them on hand, and she might need them.

23

Betrayal Upon Betrayal

YORK STARED AT the image of the tall Kinathin breed warrior. He struggled with his memory for a moment, trying to compare the officer he'd met on Anachron IV with the woman before him now. Back then she'd stood erect, eyes alert, conscious of every movement and sound around her. But the woman York saw now had grown distant, appeared ignorant or uncaring of her surroundings. Her uniform was wrinkled and unkempt, and she'd removed all insignia and badges of rank or station, leaving it with a number of small, dark patches where the emblems had prevented the material from fading. Her snow-white, lank hair now hung so that it almost covered her face as if she would hide behind it. She seemed even thinner than before, perhaps wasn't eating, and might not even be bathing.

"There!" Maggie shouted, standing up and pointing at one of the frames on the large wall screen. "She flinched just as Sab'ach'ahn was brought into the room. Right there. Back it up and play it again."

York kept his eyes glued to the screen, though he could hear Alsa's fingers dancing over the controls. It had been his idea to let Maggie in on it. Alsa had completed her medical survey of the crew and passengers, and still only the empress, Lady d'Hart, and the one servant had turned up with suicide devices. Alsa and York had carefully orchestrated the seating for the banquet the night before. Then he'd had the breed warrior escorted in and seated opposite the servant.

He and Alsa had gone over the vids a dozen times, and as Sab'ach'ahn sat down neither she nor the servant had shown the slightest reaction to the other's presence. It was Maggie who went back and reviewed the recordings from several other cameras, caught the servant flinch just as Sab'ach'ahn was escorted into the mess. The servant went through an obvious transformation as she steeled herself to not react to the presence of the breed.

"It's pretty clear, isn't it?" Maggie said. "The servant's a feddie."

"All right," Alsa said. "So she's a feddie. But why would the d'Hart woman bring a feddie disguised as a servant into the empress' entourage?"

"Assassination?" Maggie asked. "The empress?"

Alsa shook her head. "No. The empress knows she's a feddie too."

"She's going to assassinate someone else then, and the empress is in on it."

York said, "That's too pat. If the empress wants someone assassinated she doesn't need to go to all this trouble. I mean, Lady d'Hart goes to Trinivan to connect with a feddie spy and bring her into the empire disguised as one of the empress' servants. What's the reason?" York didn't tell them about his conversations with the empress and Lady d'Hart, both of whom exhibited blatant peacer sympathies. He had the uneasy feeling anyone who knew too much about this was going to be in some sort of danger.

He and Maggie and Alsa hashed around several ideas for a good hour, but nothing added up. In the end they tossed down a few drinks, then adjourned, though once Maggie and Alsa were gone York replayed the recording of Sab'ach'ahn, and wondered what had brought about such a dramatic change in so strong a woman.

••••

York bowed carefully to the empress, then turned and left, closing the hatch cautiously. He'd come to her hoping to learn a little about the plot she and Sylissa d'Hart were hatching. Not to confront her directly, but to probe subtly. It hadn't worked because he wasn't good at that kind of subterfuge, and she now understood he knew something.

"Captain!"

At the sound of Martin Andow's voice York turned about. "Senator."

"Captain, this is opportune. I've wanted to speak with you. Will you join me in my cabin?"

York could almost see the wheels turning behind Andow's eyes. York would rather stay clear of him, but he was far too powerful to be ignored. "Certainly."

Andow led York to a hatch just down the corridor, opened it and indicated York should precede him. York stepped into a dark cabin. Andow stepped past him, sat down at a small desk against one wall and turned on the desk lamp, leaving everything in darkness but a small sphere of light around the desk. To one side, seated in the shadows, the old queen mother shifted her weight. The cabin was considerably smaller than the office where the three of them had met in the embassy on Dumark. But Andow and the old woman had almost exactly recreated the setting of that meeting.

Of course there was no large high back chair where the old woman might sit as if on a throne, but she had placed a small chair at the back of the cabin where the lighting was dimmest, and it was difficult for York to see her face. And there was no ornate desk behind which Andow could sit and shuffle papers while he questioned York. Nor was the desk in the middle of the room, but then he had contrived to position a chair to one side of it, the side opposite York, and so in a subtle way he was seated in the position of the inquisitor, while York was forced to stand beneath the revealing light of the accused.

Andow smiled his insincere smile. "Well now, Captain. Won't you be seated?" He indicated the small chair.

"I'll stand. What was it you wanted to discuss?"

The skin around Andow's eyes tightened, and when he spoke he did so cautiously. "Tell me, Captain, what do you intend to do with this ship?"

York decided to make Andow work for whatever he was after. "I intend to avoid getting burned by a feddie warhead."

That wasn't the answer Andow wanted. "I assume you have a destination in mind?"

"Aagerbanne."

"Why Aagerbanne? Sarasan's closer."

"Aagerbanne's bigger, better equipped. But most importantly, Aagerbanne's less obvious. We've been spotted too many times in the quadrant opposite Sarasan, so that's the obvious choice. And in this game, it's important we never do the obvious. We can afford the time, so we'll take the long way."

Andow shifted in his seat. "How does the empress feel about this?"

The question surprised York. Andow was obviously speaking for two of them. York had assumed the empress consulted regularly with her husband's mother, but that was clearly not the case. "Her Majesty has expressed concern about the danger, but nothing beyond that."

"And have you discovered why she was out here in the first place?"

There it was, York realized. Whatever Cassandra and Sylissa d'Hart were up to, Andow and the old woman were not in on it. "I must assume," York said, trying to put a touch of skepticism in his voice, "that she was out here to retrieve her recalcitrant daughter."

Andow shook his head. "Do you really believe that?"

"What I believe is irrelevant."

Andow nodded slowly, his eyes boring into York. "Tell me, Captain, what happens after Aagerbanne?"

"I don't have the vaguest idea," York said flatly. "I think it's safe to say I'll no longer be CO of this ship. You once made it quite clear I'm not fit for command, and I'm well aware I'm in charge now only because you and the empress have no choice—at the moment. You, or Fleet, or someone else, will determine what happens to you after that."

The old woman leaned forward, almost dipping her face into the light. "But what happens to you, Mister Ballin. What'll you do then?"

That was a strange question. York answered it warily. "I'll do what I've always done. I'll obey orders, though I have no idea what those orders'll be."

The old woman grinned. "Can you guess?"

She was leading up to something, but York felt no inclination to help her get there. "I'd rather not."

"Then let me guess for you. You'll be transferred to another ship, one going back out to the front lines. And when that ship is returning for some kind of lighter duty, whether a month from now or a year from now, you'll be transferred to another ship going out to the front lines. The pattern is clear, Captain, and you're powerless to break it."

She let that statement hang in the air for a long time, then she added, "But we are powerful people, and if we were inclined to do so, we could intervene. We could break that pattern for you."

They wanted him to spy for them, and in return, they could give him the one thing he wanted. York was tempted, but he had nothing to give them, and he really didn't like either of them, nor did he trust them.

"We can be generous to those who help us," the old woman continued. "You could be free of the navy, with enough money to support yourself for the rest of your life. You could go back where you came from, find your family, do whatever you please."

York smiled, nodded, though he wanted nothing to do with these two. But maybe he could get something out of this after all. He was curious to see if they'd known his father. "I have no family," he said. "My father is dead. Perhaps you've heard of him, a man named Collier Maczek?"

The old woman flinched, and York decided to press the advantage. "And apparently my mother is dead also. Her name was Francesca Ballinov?"

The old woman took a deep, unhappy breath, though in the shadows it was difficult to gauge her reaction. Clearly, she knew both names. "No," she lied. "I don't believe I've ever heard either name."

"Well, Captain," Andow said, breaking the spell. He stood. "Thank you for making time for us, Captain. We know how busy you are."

He escorted York to the small cabin hatch. "I see no reason we can't be of mutual benefit, so we should consider ourselves allies."

Once York was gone and the cabin hatch closed, Andow returned to his seat while the old woman sat in silence. "Now that was interesting," Andow said. "So he's the whore's brat. After all these years he's turned up alive. Amazing! Who would have thought?"

The old woman added, "And he thinks Maczek was his father."

"Yes," Andow said. "But we know better, don't we?"

The old woman turned on him. "What do you mean?"

Andow grinned and shrugged. "It's obvious. You can see his father in his face, in the bone structure, in the eyes. I can see his brother in his face."

"I don't know what you're talking about."

Andow frowned, clearly enjoying her discomfort. "Oh you don't! Well, all you have to do is look at how old he is, then remember who her lover was at that time. Add that to that face, and it's obvious."

The old woman stood and marched to the hatch. "You don't know what you're talking about," she snarled as she opened it.

"Just one thing," Andow said quickly. She paused halfway through the hatch and looked back at him angrily. "Don't have him assassinated. At least not yet. Not until he gets us out of this mess."

She said nothing, closed the hatch and was gone.

••••

They floated York in on a grav stretcher: one arm, shoulder, and half his face blown away—the good half. The prosthetic eye was still intact, and the scars radiating out from the socket were unchanged, but the skin around it showed the pallor of death.

Alsa Yan leaned over him, shook her head sadly, mumbled something to one of her technicians about getting a body bag. The man left the examination room.

She peered into the side of York's head, noted that a good portion of the skull had been torn away by some sort of shrapnel . . .

The alert klaxon brought York awake almost instantly, and he felt far from bright and alert. The hull thrummed with a deep, eerie chime—one of the main transition turrets firing a shot. York got his legs into a one-piece coverall then stepped into his private lift. As he stumbled onto the bridge the yeoman barked, "Captain on the bridge." He dropped down at the captain's console with the coverall half on, activated the console, keyed in his implants.

Maggie had the watch, was seated at the first officer's console barking orders into her com. "All stations stand by. Down-transition in two minutes and counting. Someone took a shot at us. We're still analyzing the transition data—no fix on him yet—so be ready for anything . . ."

York left Maggie in command for the moment. She knew her stuff, had the situation under control, while he didn't know enough yet to give a sound order. A damage control report was scrolling up on one of his screens: minor damage aft from a near miss. He glanced at the navigation summary: they were out in the middle of nowhere, cruising at about a third of what *Cinesstar* was capable, making only about two light-years a day, in the hope of keeping their transition wake down to a minimum and lessening the chance of discovery. It hadn't done much good though. They were averaging better than one contact or false alarm per watch, four a day. They'd had to fight their way out of a corner five times, almost been hulled once, and York had lost count of the number of times some ship sitting in sublight had taken a shot at them as they passed by. No one on ship had gotten more than two or three hours sleep at a stretch for the past six days, and the strain was beginning to show on all of them.

"Down-transition in one minute and counting. Velocity is down to one hundred lights and slowing."

It was time for York to take command. "Miss Gant, have we got a fix on that feddie yet?"

"Yes, sir, but our accuracy's questionable. It was a long-shot; he was so far aft we were able to spot the wake of the incoming round."

"Then belay transition," York said. "Hold at one hundred lights. You had the watch, Maggie. What do you think?"

"I think everyone out here is really trigger-happy. That long-shot was stupid. And I also think we're running in to too many contacts. The question is: are they after us, or is there something big going on in this sector—or both?"

York shrugged mentally. "Let's don't waste our time. That feddie is too far behind us to matter. Take her up to one thousand lights and stand down to Watch Condition Yellow. We'll hold on yellow until we put a little more distance between us."

Not really a false alarm—but still, he needed to get his crew off watch as soon as possible, get them back to their bunks. Twenty minutes later they stood down to Watch Condition Green.

••••

Lynna looked odd in the beggar's robes, though Rochefort had to admit the disguise worked rather well. The beggar fit right in among the patrons of the seedy, little bar where they sat at a small table in a nicely dark corner. Rochefort had chosen common attire, which fit nicely in the whorehouses and bars in this section of Luna.

"Abraxa and Bortha are both curious," Lynna said.

A marine and a spacer on the far side of the establishment started a fight. One of the bouncers broke it up quickly and the normal din of the place returned.

"You chose this place well," Lynna said.

"It'll do for our purposes." By unspoken agreement neither of them used names or ranks. "So they're curious. What have they learned?"

"They know Aeya's lark to Trinivan was just an excuse to get d'Hart there."

"Any fool could surmise that. Tell me something that's not obvious."

"They're worried. The presence of the whore's brat bothers them. They're wondering how you managed to locate him."

Rochefort wondered who the hell the whore's brat was, but he dare not ask outright. Lynna was fishing, had assumed this unknown person was part of their plot.

The back door to the bar opened and three figures stepped quietly into the establishment. Entrance via the back door wasn't that uncommon, but in this instance it drew Rochefort's attention because two of the three wore the black uniform of AI troops, and the third wore the scarlet and green livery of the Incalla, the church guard. The three stood at the door, blocking it.

Rochefort ignored Lynna and looked slowly toward the main entrance of the establishment. There were more Incalla and AI filing in, and as the rest of the patrons began to notice, an ever-expanding silence slowly replaced the din of the place. Rochefort looked at Lynna and growled, "Why you dirty, little sneak."

Lynna had finally noticed the intruders, was staring at them wide-eyed and open-mouthed, and Rochefort realized the man was terrified. "They'll kill us both," Lynna said.

Rochefort nodded and whispered, "Every man for himself."

Without moving quickly he stood. The place was crowded and it was easy to blend in to the crowd, to put distance between him and the churchman. It was probably just a simple raid of some sort, though the presence of the Incalla and AI made that unlikely. But still it was best to play it safe.

Lynna wasn't so smart. He panicked, made a rush for the back door and pulled a gun. Several muzzle flashes lit up the dark, smoky haze of the place, accompanied by ear-splitting shots. Rochefort thought he saw the Incalla officer at the back door drop, and Lynna too, but he couldn't be sure because the crowd panicked and surged to the exits. Rochefort decided to help, pulled his own gun, raised it over his head, fired two shots into the ceiling and shouted, "They're killing everyone"

The mob went insane. There were more shots, even a burst or two of automatic weapons fire. But the place was too crowded, the mob and the Incalla and the AI goons too tightly packed, and it all happened quickly. The mob burst from the exits into the streets, carrying Rochefort safely with them.

He controlled his adrenaline, didn't let it take hold. He was too old for this sort of thing, had to pace himself carefully, ran down the street for a good distance at an easy jog, then cut into a side street, taking care to avoid alleys. He slowed to a quick walk, turned down another street and slowed further to an easy walk. He was now just another of hundreds of people wandering the streets. He glanced up at the rock ceiling of the street, knew he had to get back up to higher levels before AI started a full sweep.

An armored AI carrier rolled up the street with its siren blaring. He stepped into the shadow of a doorway as it shot past headed in the direction of the riot. It was then that he noticed something odd about a man on the other side of the street. The fellow lifted one hand furtively to his mouth and rubbed his chin. But Rochefort could see his lips moving, knew he was using a small com, had to be either Incalla or AI, though he wore clothing appropriate for the area. That also lay to rest any doubts about why they'd raided the bar where Lynna and he were meeting.

The man was calling for help, so Rochefort had to move. He stepped out of the shadow into the street and crossed the street at a brisk walk. His tail followed at a discreet distance.

Rochefort walked past several alleys until he found just the right one, a dark tunnel with only the far exit visible because of the streetlights there. He stepped into it, moved a few paces down the alley, slipped into the darkness along its sides and thumbed the safety on his gun. This had to be quick and clean.

He waited, waited far too long, then three figures stepped into the alley, pressed themselves into the same darkness at its sides. At the far end of the alley more of them stepped into the light there, using lamps to light up every shadow. Damn, he thought. His tail had been smart, had waited for reinforcements.

Rochefort sprinted for the nearest end of the alley, squeezed the trigger on his gun, firing rounds into the darkness where the three had hidden. His only chance was to get them to react instinctively for just an instant, get them to duck first before firing back. And in that instant he had to be out of the alley. But as the first bullet struck him in the back all he could think about was that he was just too old for this. He slammed into the pavement thinking he would have made it a few decades ago.

He rolled over quickly, feeling no real pain, fired two more rounds, never really felt the grav-gun shell that blew away most of his upper torso.

••••

"Five lights and holding," Tac'tac'ah hissed breathlessly.

Jewel tried to sound calm. "Steady as she goes, Mr. Tac'tac'ah. Drop back to four lights. Mister Soe, what's our range?"

"Point-oh-one light-year, ma'am."

"Four lights and holding."

Jewel took a good look at her screens. They were approaching Sarasan farspace and she could feel the tension on the bridge. Below ten lights the *Pride* should broadcast almost no wake, but there was always a chance they might drive right over the top of an *imper* picket. "Three lights, Mr. Tac'tac'ah."

Tac'tac'ah looked at her nervously. He was always nervous during a close approach, but was also just plain, damn good—maybe because he was nervous. "Three lights and holding."

"Range, Mister Soe?"

"Five hundred and sixty thousand astronomical units, ma'am."

This was looking good. "Hold steady to five hundred thousand AUs."

"Aye, aye, ma'am."

Jewel leaned back, watched her screens, watched the minutes tick by.

"Ranging at five hundred thousand AUs, ma'am."

Jewel sat up straight. "Mr. Tac'tac'ah, two lights."

"Two lights, ma'am. She's starting to show some instability."

Jewel switched her pickup to allship. "All hands, stand by for transition." She switched back to the bridge circuit. "Mr. Tac'tac'ah, down-transit."

There was a momentary delay, then Tac'tac'ah shouted, "Sublight! Point-eight lights."

They waited and the tension built. Then Innay spoke calmly, "Clear to one thousand klicks."

"Drones out."

Pride of Altalane's hull reverberated with the hollow sound of the drone launch. "Drones out, ma'am."

It took a few minutes, but as the drones began to fill in details on the Sarasan system the tension died. They were a bit under five hundred thousand AUs out from the Sarasan primary, coasting inward at point-eight lights, running silent and no sign they'd been detected. It would take them three and a half days to coast into the middle of the system.

That was cutting it close, but it had worked. Ordinarily, a hunter-killer like the *Pride* would play it a lot safer, perhaps take up to a month to set up such an approach. But under the circumstances they had to take chances.

"I've got an approach plan, ma'am."

Jewel looked at her screens where Innay was displaying a summary plan for close approach—a slight course correction now would bring them closer to Sarasan's primary. To avoid detection they'd use just the smallest amount of drive power, then use the star's gravity to divert them into the plane of the ecliptic and out to a large planet on the edge of the system. There, a swing around the planet would help by killing some velocity and aiming them back at the primary. After two or three such cycles they could then swing toward Sarasan at a much more workable velocity. And then they would wait.

"Excellent, chief. Thank you.

"Mister Soe. Is there a relay transceiver anywhere in this sector? We're far enough out—we ought to be able to transmit without being detected, if we're careful. I should report this to DCO."

••••

The night before they were due to transit into Aagerbanne York and the crew got a good night's sleep. There had been no contacts or alerts for more than a day, and Aagerbanne suddenly seemed within reach.

That morning he took his time showering, was a bit extravagant with his water ration—a prerogative of the captain. He ate a nice leisurely breakfast in the main mess where he noticed everyone's spirits were up. So close to their objective it was impossible not to be optimistic. He then made his way up to the bridge about two hours before they were due to down-transit into Aagerbanne farspace.

"Captain on the bridge."

York sat down at his console, logged in and started reviewing a status summary. The mood on the bridge was almost festive. They were about a fifth of a light-year out from Aagerbanne, driving cautiously at six hundred lights and decelerating slowly. In another hour they should encounter Aagerbanne's pickets: challenge, reply and counter-challenge. Since their recognition codes were clearly out of date they would be instructed to down-transit for boarding and verification. And then, with the passengers they were carrying, they'd undoubtedly get a high priority for docking at Aagerbanne Station. It would all be over.

York wondered what ship Fleet would assign him to this time. At a major facility like Aagerbanne there should be plenty of available posts on outbound vessels. He wondered if he could influence the selection any by signing on to a good ship before the computers spit out their choice.

"There's a lot of transition activity near Aagerbanne," Olin Rame said.

Rame had the watch. York glanced his way, could just see him between fire control and navigation. Rame didn't seem to share the happy mood of the rest of the crew. Jondee took the bait. "Sector headquarters—big facility—should be lots of activity."

Rame nodded slowly. "Lot of clustering in the transitions too. I suppose traffic control might be getting a little sloppy."

"Those boys and girls are always sloppy," Jondee said.

York expanded his navigation summary for a detailed report, and keeping one eye on the live data flowing in he began playing back the navigation log.

In transition they were fairly nearsighted, couldn't really see anything until they were within about one light-year of the source, and then they were only able to pick up gross phenomena like the transition flare of a large ship. As expected, starting from about one light-year out, the navigation log showed a history of fairly dim and indistinct data. And as they'd gotten closer the data had grown stronger and clearer until they were finally able to distinguish just about any transition flare in Aagerbanne nearspace.

When several ships traveled in a group it was customary to make transition a few minutes apart, spread out and avoid any possible side effects from the flares of nearby ships. But avoiding clustered transitions was really just a precaution, and not practical under certain circumstances, like under hot pursuit, or in really large convoys. Still, some effort was usually made to break up the clustering. But, as Rame had observed, the Aagerbanne traffic control operators were getting sloppy.

Gant interrupted York's thoughts. "We're point-oh-eight light-year out, sir. About one hour at our present velocity."

York nodded, commented to no one in particular. "Should be challenged any minute now." He thought about down-transiting, taking a good look from a distance, but a flare out there all by themselves might make them too good of a target if there was a feddie nearby stalking the shipping lanes into Aagerbanne. And as long as they kept their transition velocity down their transition wake was minimal. A little more caution might be wise. "No exterior transmissions without my authorization. Passive scan and navigation only."

"Aye, aye, sir," Gant said.

Jondee couldn't help a comment. "Getting awfully cautious, aren't we?"

"Captain," Rame said tentatively. "I'm picking up some interesting data here."

York was looking at the same data: raw traces from their navigational scans. There was something odd about it. He looked up from his console, saw that Rame had moved over to the navigation console, decided to join him there. Looking over Rame's shoulder he stared at the traces while Rame began trying to clean up the data.

It was an odd sort of data, small, randomly spaced pulses of noise in the transition spectra. Rame tried to isolate it, pull it up out of the noise, while York leaned back and just stared at it. It had the oddest ring of familiarity, and he struggled to recall some phantom memory. He watched the odd pulses of data grow stronger as they got closer and it made him uneasy. "What's our ETT?" he demanded, sounding more concerned than he'd meant to.

"About a half hour, sir. We're about twenty-five hundred astronomical units out, and closing at six hundred lights."

"And no challenge yet," he mumbled to no one in particular. "Decelerate to three hundred lights. Watch Condition Yellow. We're going in slowly, just to be safe."

Gant said, "New ETT is ninety-seven minutes, just under an hour, sir."

York returned to the captain's console, sat down and stared at the data Rame was processing. On his screen he watched a pulse appear, then another, then a rapid staccato of overlapping pulses, one on top of another—then a pause, then more individual pulses at random intervals. It was the tempo, the pace and spacing and timing of the pulses, that haunted him. There was something familiar about it, something he should recognize, but just couldn't identify.

Time ticked slowly by and the signal grew stronger, but still its meaning eluded him. He looked at the navigational report on his console. They were three hundred astronomical units out and scheduled for down-transition in eleven minutes.

"Decelerate to one hundred lights."

"Aye, aye, sir. New ETT is thirty-five minutes."

"Could be a little unstable," Maggie said, standing behind him. She had been looking over his shoulder while he stared at the data. "This ship wasn't designed to run that slow in transition."

York looked at her carefully. "Then please keep an eye on the helm yourself. I don't want to inadvertently down-transit."

She looked at him carefully, and under normal circumstances might have made some sort of remark. But she simply nodded, "Aye, aye, sir." She edged her way around fire control to the helm.

York looked around the bridge, at Gant, Stara, Rame, Jondee, their various assistants. The cheerful mood of a few hours ago had vanished.

"It's the beat," Rame said, staring intently at his data. "The way it comes in little bursts, then pauses, then comes again all of a sudden . . ." He gazed at it for another moment, then jerked upright and snarled, "Shit! Those are flares from transition batteries. That's heavy bombardment."

Now that Rame had identified it York could see it too. "Watch Condition Red. Warn engineering we may need shield power and stand by for transition."

Nothing happened for a moment as they all peered around their consoles and stared at him in horrified disbelief. "Move, god damn it," he shouted. "The feddies are hitting Aagerbanne. That's a major engagement down there, and we're stumbling right into it."

Jondee was the first to react. He slapped the alert switch on his console and the blare of the alert klaxon broke their paralysis.

York barked, "Decelerate to eighty lights, and rig for silent running."

"Sir," Maggie said. "We may not be able to keep from down-transiting at eighty lights."

He spoke carefully. "Miss Votak, take the helm yourself. Decelerate to eighty lights and do not down-transit. That's an order. Do you understand?"

She didn't hide her vexation. "Aye, aye, sir."

He was going to try an old hunter-killer trick. The more velocity they had when they down-transited, the bigger the flare. But also each change in velocity dumped energy into the transition spectrum around them, energy an enemy could spot. The trick was to dump the energy in little increments then transit only when you had to.

"Holding at eighty lights, sir," Maggie acknowledged.

"Thank you, Miss Votak," York said. "Decelerate to sixty lights and do not down-transit. Jondee, get me Cappik."

"You've already got him, sir."

Jondee had anticipated him. Cappik's face was staring at him out of one of his screens. "Chief Cappik, stand by to cut all power: gravity, shields, the works. When I give the command I want us all the way back to minimum idle. No exterior transmissions, no emissions of any kind. But be ready to give me shield power instantly."

Cappik gaped at him for a second, but he didn't flinch or hesitate. "You got it, sir. Just give me the word."

"Holding steady at sixty lights, sir."

"Very good, Miss Votak. Decelerate to.fifty lights. And do—"

"I know, sir. *And do not down-transit.*"

Jondee, on allship, warned everyone to stand by for weightless maneuvering. *Cinesstar*'s hull started to groan and creak. "Holding unsteadily at fifty lights, sir. We're starting to experience discrete gravitational instability on some of the lower decks."

"I understand," York said. "Decelerate to forty lights. And do everything you can to keep us from down-transiting for as long as you can. But if she does go into transition, hold as much sublight velocity as possible. Don't broadcast our position by dumping energy. Mister Stara, tell your weapons stations to be ready for anything. But they're not to fire without specific orders from you or me."

York's stomach crawled up into his throat as a gravity wave rolled through the bridge. The drive started to thrum erratically, and the hull's groans turned into shrieks.

"Holding at forty lights. Serious gravitational . . . No . . . She's transiting . . ."

"Transition," Gant screeched.

"All stop," York shouted. "Cappik, shut us down. Drones out on passive."

The deck gravity suddenly disappeared and York floated up in his straps. The hull echoed with the sound of the drone launch.

"Miss Gant, I want a situation map soonest."

"We're two hundred and fifty-three astronomical units out, sir. Coasting at point-nine-three lights and closing. Dilation factor two-point-seven. We're scanning our own nearspace now, sir."

Everything came to a sudden and complete halt, and they waited. York caught himself holding his breath so he exhaled slowly.

"Clear to a hundred thousand klicks, sir."

York spoke calmly, though it wasn't easy. "Very good. Go to long range."

That was an order he didn't need to give. Gant and her assistants were already pulling in every bit of data they could, and as the time passed they all watched a frightening picture unfold on their screens.

They'd blundered into a full assault on a major imperial installation by a Directorate armada. The Syndonese had come in with at least two hundred ships, and Fleet had met them with a like number.

York had seen it before. It was impossible to marshal a force large enough to take an installation like Aagerbanne without detection. So it wasn't uncommon for the enemy to be waiting for you with a like force. When that happened you could just withdraw, hope for a better chance on another day, or you could do what the feddies had done in this case, try to fight it out. *Cinesstar* had already missed the preliminary rounds: a little sparring for a few days while both sides tried to gauge the strength and determination of their opponents.

The Syndonese clearly outnumbered the imperial forces, even with support from Aagerbanne. It appeared *Cinesstar* had arrived just in time to see the real action. At the moment, York and his ship were in no danger. But at their present sublight velocity it would take them just under two days to coast right into the middle of it, and all they could do was pray the Directorate finished the job before then.

24

Aagerbanne

WHEN THE GUARDS brought in her prisoner, Add'kas'adanna lifted her head slowly and looked into his eyes. They'd met only via the screens in their various command centers, and then only for a few brief minutes while they negotiated the terms of surrender. And he had shown no surprise that the Fleet Director herself had led the assault on Aagerbanne. He should have been surprised.

His uniform was torn in places, burned in others, splotched with grime, but he threw his shoulders back and saluted her smartly, and all the while his eyes burned into her.

She stood from her desk, returned the salute and looked him over carefully. This man was very much the imperial officer, a man who commanded troops and fought in battles, not one of their foppish holiday soldiers. When it had become clear Aagerbanne would fall, their effete noblemen had evacuated the system, leaving this warrior to surrender.

Add'kas'adanna pointed to a chair and spoke without malice. "Please, Admiral Sayalla. Sit and rest."

Sayalla nodded and sat down wearily. Add'kas'adanna turned to her guards. "You may go."

The guards saluted crisply and left.

From a drawer in her desk Add'kas'adanna retrieved a bottle of slaeka, the whiskey made on her home planet. She poured some of the reddish liquid into two glasses, stepped around her desk and handed one to Sayalla. He nodded his thanks and sipped at it carefully. She put hers to her lips, and as was customary for the first sip, she took a healthy gulp. Then she returned to her desk and sat behind it.

"You and your crews fought well," she said.

Sayalla shrugged. "Not well enough. We lost."

"You were heavily outnumbered. You couldn't have fought better."

Sayalla's eyes brightened. "But we could have, if I'd been allowed to fight my own battle."

Add'kas'adanna knew well what he meant, for even in her position as the Supreme Commander of Directorate naval forces her superiors constantly hampered her. Ninda and Kaffair wanted an obedient Fleet Director, one who kept her thoughts limited to military matters. Neither of them trusted a Kinathin breed warrior enough to bring her into his confidence. Ninda certainly didn't want her to think for herself, to wonder why he had sent her with an entire armada just to hunt down an *imper* man-of-war. She smiled at Sayalla's remark. "But we are soldiers, and that's our lot in life. And like even the most common of soldiers, sometimes we can only wonder at the reasoning behind our orders."

Sayalla grinned. "Yes, though right now I'm wondering more about your orders than mine."

Add'kas'adanna looked at him carefully and took the bait. "For instance?"

"Well now, I wonder why you chose Aagerbanne—we aren't that significant, at least not militarily. We're just big, and well equipped. And why send the Fleet Director herself? I'm sure you have better things to do."

He was baiting her, though there was no reason to conceal her purpose so Add'kas'adanna spoke openly. "I am, of course, here to find the ship *Cinesstar* and destroy her."

Sayalla nodded calmly, though he should have started, showed some surprise. "Of course," he said flatly. "Though I wish we could have gotten her first."

Add'kas'adanna considered his words carefully. He hadn't said, ". . . gotten *to* her first," as if he wanted to rescue her. He had said, ". . . gotten her first," as if he too had orders to destroy her.

"Hmmm!" Sayalla continued. "The Directorate wants *Cinesstar* so bad they're willing to send their highest military officer with an armada to get her. I don't suppose you'll tell me what you and my superiors have got cooked up?"

Did Sayalla believe the Directorate Central Committee and the Imperial Admiralty were conspiring in some way to do away with a single ship? Add'kas'adanna decided not to enlighten him. As long as he thought she knew more than she did, he might tell her something she didn't know. In answer to his question she shook her head slowly. "That would not be appropriate, though I will confess I've not seen the exact wording of your orders."

Sayalla shrugged. "*Shoot on sight*—simple, straight from Admiralty Intelligence. You all want her bad, don't you? Has her captain gone renegade?"

Add'kas'adanna ignored his questions. "And you say you have no knowledge of her whereabouts?"

"If I did," Sayalla said, "I'd be going after her with everything I could muster. There's probably a healthy promotion in store for the man who gets her, and certainly a nice reward."

Add'kas'adanna retreated into her thoughts. This was interesting and valuable information. She'd have to think carefully how to use it. Perhaps, with a little luck, and a deft hand, she might be able to learn why everyone wanted *Cinesstar* so badly. If Sayalla was telling the truth, then *Cinesstar* was nowhere near Aagerbanne, and to push further into the empire would only cost her needed ships and crews.

She looked at Sayalla. "I will, of course, have to test you to insure that you're speaking the truth. Nothing barbaric, mind you. Just some drugs, and a deep neural probe operated by a highly skilled technician. You should feel no pain."

"Thank you," Sayalla said. "I appreciate the courtesy."

••••

Ninda was a hard, unpleasant man, who made no effort to hide his distrust of Add'kas'adanna. Oddly enough, she reflected, when she had first begun working for him he could have trusted her implicitly. In accepting the appointment to his staff, *kith'ain* dictated she support him, even if she did not agree with him, even if she must compromise her honor. She had served him well through the years, and he had carefully advanced her through the ranks until finally—more through covert manipulation than anything else, she had later discovered—he had won for her the appointment to Fleet Director. She had been quite proud the day she became one of the five most powerful people in the Republic of Syndon, a member of the Central Committee of the Federal Directorate. But her pride was badly misplaced.

She quickly learned the role he had chosen for her was that of a lackey, one who must support him in all things, without question, blindly. He used her as a goad to frighten those such as Zort: support me, Ninda implied to all who might oppose him, or I'll turn the Kinathin loose on you. In that, he had cost her great honor, and by doing so he had broken the implicit pact between them, and she was free to seek her own honor, independent of his. It was ironic that his distrust of her had forced her to become an untrustworthy associate.

"Yes, yes," Ninda said impatiently. "Abraxa wants them to succeed no more than we do."

Ninda should have been surprised at that information, so Add'kas'adanna was in a mood to take a slight risk. "But why does the empire want them dead?"

Ninda shook his head. "Not the empire. Just those old men and women in the Admiralty."

"Then why does the Admiralty want them dead?"

"Because they might end this war, and that's something none of us want, is it, Fleet?"

"Of course not," she said, but only because that was expected of her. "But how can one, lone ship end the war?"

Ninda tone was insultingly condescending. "Ah, you Kinathins! You can see no solution but the military one, can you?"

Ninda had always believed that about her, and she had never had reason to correct him. In answer she shrugged. "Shall I continue searching for this imperial ship?"

"Yes," Ninda said, nodding his head thoughtfully. "I doubt they've managed to cross into imperial territory yet. So it's probably best if you keep up the pressure. I'd rather *we* caught them anyway, and we'll consider the imperials insurance just in case they do slip through."

"As you wish." Add'kas'adanna cut the circuit.

She considered the blank screen for a moment. She wanted that ship, but not to destroy it. She wanted to question the ship's occupants. She wanted to know how one, single ship could stop an interstellar war that had lasted generations.

She looked at her screen, at the map drawn there, at the sequence of pinpoints indicating probable sightings of the imperial ship. Her captain had obviously been trying to break through the lines and get to Aagerbanne. And the timing of the most recent sightings made it clear he should be only days away from approaching the system.

She had a large number of ships assembled right in the path of that imperial ship. And there were reliable methods for finding a needle in a cosmic haystack.

She came to a decision and keyed her implants. "Commodore Martak."

The reply came instantly. "Yes, Your Excellency."

"Tell the Fleet Captains there'll be a command summit on my flagship in . . ." She glanced at her watch. ". . . one hour."

"Yes, Your Excellency."

••••

York floated into the brig and grabbed a handhold. Notay had the brig watch, with Stacy assisting her, and when York appeared she somehow stood up, locking her ankles under the console to keep from floating off the deck. She saluted slowly—in zero-G they were all careful to avoid sudden movement. "Good afternoon, sir."

The kid tried to imitate her and screwed it up badly, ended up spinning in the air near her.

York threw a salute back at her. "Mec. I'd like to see the feddie breed warrior."

"The weird one, eh?" she said as she plucked Stacy out of the air and helped him to a handhold.

"What do you mean by that?"

Notay shrugged. "She's weirdin' out, sir. Don't eat much. Don't bathe. Gettin' more fucked up every day. You better stay away from her, sir."

York nodded toward the cellblock. "I want to see for myself."

Notay was nervous. They were all nervous. They'd been coasting toward the battle for the last day and a half, watching both sides throw a lot of nasty stuff at each other, and not daring to use any energy to divert their course or slow their advance. York had watched from the captain's console as the feddies took the outer reaches of the system, burning one imperial ship after another and advancing steadily. *Cinesstar* was just touching the edge of Aagerbanne's nearspace when the battle turned to a route. The feddies gutted Aagerbanne Station with several large warheads, then systematically took out all military installations on the planet's surface. After that, most of the imperial fleet withdrew, retreating to the subsector headquarters at Sarasan. And *Cinesstar* coasted into the middle of an armada of Directorate warships.

With so much sublight velocity left from their down-transition they should have passed right through the system in a couple of hours. But as luck would have it, their vector drew them into the gravity well of a large planet. *Cinesstar*'s velocity prevented the planet from capturing them, but it swung them around into the plane of the ecliptic and killed a lot of their speed. They'd swung in close to the primary, lost more velocity there, and were now headed for the gravity well of another planet out near the edge of the system. According to Gant's calculations they were going to lose more velocity in their swing around that planet, and get slung right back toward the center of the system. She wasn't sure if they'd get caught again, or pass on through and out the other side. But at any time a feddie warship might detect the hot spark of their power plant, even though they were holding it to a bare minimum. The one thing they had going for them was the mess that remained around them. The battle had scattered hot debris all over the system, and there were hundreds of detectable fragments that would appear little different from *Cinesstar* on a scan report.

Notay wasn't exaggerating about Sab'ach'ahn. The breed warrior had lost significant weight, and while she probably outweighed most full-grown men, on such a tall frame the weight loss had taken her from gaunt to emaciated.

She sat in a corner of the cell, her legs crossed haphazardly, her back against a bulkhead, one hand tucked absentmindedly into a handhold to keep her from floating away in zero-G. She'd torn the sleeves off her tunic, and to hold back her matted and unwashed hair she'd tied a strip of cloth around her head like a bandanna. She'd painted the upper and lower eyelids of her left eye with some sort of dark, reddish-brown paint. The air around her held a faintly pungent and oddly foreign smell of stale sweat. Her eyes were distant, unseeing, lost in some other universe of thought, or escape.

York held onto a small girder, floating directly in front of her cell. Still she seemed unaware of him and stared right through him. He spoke softly, "Sublegion."

The Kinathin didn't move, and her eyes still remained focused on a spot far past York. York tried a different tack. He kept his voice steady and level, and he spoke as if she were one of his subordinates. "Sublegion Sab'ach'ahn."

Her shoulders shifted slightly, then her eyes came into focus. She didn't move other than to blink once, and a small fleck of the dark reddish-brown paint around her left eye broke loose and floated away from her cheek. York realized it was dried blood.

"Captain Ballin," she said, her voice flat and lifeless. "What may I do for you?"

"Tell me what you're doing to yourself."

She lifted one of her own hands, looked at the dark skin of the fingers, considered it for a moment and lowered it again. "I have done nothing."

York shook his head. "You're not eating, not bathing, not taking care of yourself." York had used the ship's library files to learn what he could about the Kinathins. Most of what the empire knew was speculation and rumor, sometimes legend, but it appeared they had strict rules concerning their own code of conduct and honor. "I am responsible for you. I have asked you a question that does not require you to betray your comrades, so you must answer."

She looked at him carefully for the first time since Anachron IV. "I am in disgrace," she said flatly.

"Why are you in disgrace?"

"I broke the contract of truce between us."

"Andleman was the one who violated the truce."

"But he was my responsibility."

"And so you're going to starve yourself to death?"

She didn't answer, and while he was trying to think of another approach his implants came to life. "Captain, this is Gant on bridge watch. I think that Syndonese armada is getting ready to leave. They're lining up for transition out system. This could be it, sir."

York keyed his implants. "I'll be right up."

York growled one last order at the Kinathin. "You're my prisoner and my responsibility. You will eat, and you will bath, and you will take care of yourself. That is an order."

He didn't have time to argue with her, or to wait for her to reply, or to even confirm that she'd heard him and not slipped back into her trance. He turned and started pulling his way from one handhold to the next, heading for the bridge.

It took the Syndonese armada more than two hours to form up into seven wings and begin driving out of the system. By that time, *Cinesstar* was deep into her swing around the planet at the edge of the system. When the ships in the armada started up-transiting, *Cinesstar* was already coasting back in toward the center of the system. An hour later Gant declared, "There goes the last one, sir."

York stared at his screens carefully. Maggie said, "I think we're all alone here. I think those feddies pulled out completely, took all the imperials they could find as prisoners."

"York, old boy," Jondee said, breathing a sigh of relief for all of them. "I sure wish I had your luck. But I guess I'll have to be happy hanging around the edges of it, picking up magical emanations from the wondrous glow."

"Funny transition vectors, though," Maggie said.

York nodded. "Ya."

Rame's voice was almost a ghostly whisper. "All spread out. Fanning out, heading back into Syndonese territory, transiting in all directions."

The feddies were going back the way they'd come, not pursuing the defeated imperial fleet— good news for *Cinesstar*. For all intents and purposes, that feddie fleet defined the front line in this sector—which meant *Cinesstar* was back in imperial territory—heavily disputed, but still imperial territory.

Jondee asked, "But why would they fan out like that?"

It was Gant who gave them the answer. "They're looking for someone."

"They're looking for us," York said, "probably think we haven't gotten here yet and are fanning out to intercept us before we do."

"I wonder if that's why they were here in the first place," Jondee speculated, mirroring York's own thoughts. "Do you think they were looking for us all along, and they sent an entire armada to take a goddamn sector headquarters just for us?"

For York it was all coming together now. "And they didn't find us here, so they're searching their back-trail. But that's a stroke of luck for us. We're clear now."

Rame asked, "Shall I instruct engineering to give us some power, sir?"

York shook his head. He still felt uneasy. "Belay that. Anda, what's our present course? Are we going to yo-yo back into the system again?"

York's caution killed their relief. "No, sir. We're headed into the system, but we won't be passing near enough to any planets to be deflected by more than a few degrees. We should be well out the other side in about four hours."

"Then steady as she goes," York said. "Once we pass through we'll be headed roughly in the direction of Sarasan. We won't have to do a lot of maneuvering to line up for transition. So we'll just sit tight for the time being, make sure they didn't leave anyone behind running silent and waiting for us. Then when we're through the system we'll drive like all hell straight for Sarasan."

••••

An hour passed, and an eerie silence descended over the Aagerbanne system, matched by the hush on the bridge of *Cinesstar*. "Sir," Jondee whispered. "Her Majesty would like admittance to the bridge."

"There's no need to whisper, Mister Jondee," York said, though by comparison his voice boomed. "And yes, admit the empress."

Straegga, Lady d'Hart and Andow accompanied Cassandra, with all three of the civilians fumbling a bit in zero gravity, though the women had had the presence of mind to abandon their gowns in favor of less fashionable but far more practical coveralls. York had found it necessary to assign Straegga to the empress almost as a combat station. The ex-hunter-killer captain could read a console and keep the empress informed and off York's back during any tense situations.

"Captain," Cassandra said.

York turned toward her. "Your Majesty, if you don't mind, the usual rules."

She grinned. "Strap down, keep our mouths shut and our hands off the instruments."

Gant was constantly mapping the system, isolating anything that might be a concealed enemy, then using every trick she and the rest of them knew to learn what they could.

"Why are we waiting?" the empress whispered over the command circuit. She too had succumbed to the hush that held them all.

"Because it won't do us any harm. At worst we'll waste a few hours coasting quietly through the system. At best, if there are any hidden dangers we won't advertise our presence until we're well out of reach."

"Ever cautious, eh?"

"And still alive."

Gant continued to sweat over her instruments, but suddenly Jondee started and jumped. "I've got a distress signal," he said excitedly. He listened further, ". . . H.M.S. *Dominant*, imperial registry. Heavy damage on all decks . . . life support failing on some . . . an open request for aid . . ."

"Miss Gant, what's her range?"

"About eleven astronomical units, sir."

York needed to hear this. "Put it on the bridge channel, Mister Jondee."

A strange voice spoke in York's implants. ". . . Mayday. Mayday. This is H.M.S. *Dominant* requesting emergency aid . . ."

Jondee asked, "Shall I answer, sir?"

"Negative," York snapped.

The empress had leaned heavily to one side to see past the fire control console. "But Captain," she said. "Those are our comrades. Surely there's no danger in aiding them?"

"Which is more important, Your Majesty, getting you and the people with you back to safety, or taking a chance we might step into a trap? How important is your mission?"

She hesitated for a moment, and that told York that whatever she was up to, it was important enough for her to consider abandoning some of her subjects to certain death. "But there should be no reason we can't do both. We should be able to do . . ."

York reached down to the controls on his console, intending to open a private channel between them, to remind her of her promise not to second guess him, but Gant suddenly shouted, "I've got a ship powering up. Way out on the edge of the system, a good thirty astronomical units out. Looks like something in the destroyer class, though I've got no recognition sequence on her. She's not showing any colors."

A situation summary appeared on one of York's screens. The unidentified ship was obviously powering up for a short jump through transition. They all watched and waited for a few moments, then Gant called, "Transition flare."

The unidentified ship quickly accelerated to better than a thousand lights, was in transition for thirty-four seconds, then, "Down-transition," Gant said excitedly. "Big flare. They dumped most of their velocity, trying to match velocity with *Dominant. Dominant* isn't responding, probably dead in space."

"Well, that solves our problem," the empress said. "Help is on the way, and we can leave with a clear conscience."

York said nothing, but wondered why the unidentified ship had lain quietly in wait. The voice of the com officer on *Dominant* echoed hauntingly in York's ear. "This is H.M.S. *Dominant* to the unknown ship approaching us. Please identify. Please identify."

The unidentified ship remained silent, refused to answer his request. He repeated it again and again as the ship approached and matched velocities with *Dominant*, and though he was obviously disciplined, a hint of fear began to show in his voice at the continued silence. The unidentified ship took up a position about a hundred kilometers off *Dominant*'s bow, then released a small shuttle.

"This is H.M.S. *Dominant* to the unknown ship approaching us. Do not approach further until you identify yourself. Please identify. If you don't we'll assume hostile intent and—"

A loud crash in the background interrupted the com officer. He grunted, demanded, "What the hell—" Another crash and an explosion interrupted him again.

Gant shouted, "That ship's firing on *Dominant*."

Cassandra asked, "What's happening?"

"It's a raider," York said. "A pirate. They're on a scavenging run. They'll blow *Dominant*'s bridge, try to board her, kill anyone who's alive, then strip her for ordnance, weapons, anything they can find."

"Mayday! Mayday! Someone help us. Please—" Another crash in the background.

"Do something," Cassandra pleaded. "I don't care about anything else. We can't leave them at the mercy of those animals."

Andow and Cassandra both started shouting at York. Lady d'Hart stared at him silently through a gap in the instrument clusters. She was like his crew in that, leaning awkwardly to one side to get some faint glimpse of him between consoles and displays, but smart enough to keep her mouth shut.

"Mayday! Mayday! We've been—"

"Ah to hell with it," he said. "Mister Jondee. Cut that audio circuit, sound General Quarters, Watch Condition Red, and tell engineering to stand by for full combat status."

"Aye, aye, sir," Jondee yelled a little too enthusiastically, and the alert klaxon started screaming at them.

York drifted into that odd, schizophrenic state of mind where he could isolate his fear in an almost separate personality, leaving the cold-blooded killer he needed free to do the work at hand. "Power up," he ordered. "Gravity up. Shields up." He settled into his seat under his own weight.

"Anda, where are the drones?"

Gant consulted one of her screens. "They've been drifting outward at about five hundred meters an hour. They're presently out at seventeen kilometers."

"Go fully active and take the drones out to one thousand kilometers. And compute a short transition hop to the nearspace of that raider—soonest."

Maggie applied power to the drive and for the first time in days York felt the comforting pulse of *Cinesstar*'s main engines.

"Stand by forward main batteries."

Straegga's ex first officer was working with Stara at the fire control console. "Standing by, sir."

The raider shuttle had already docked with *Dominant*. "Mister Stara," York said. "We're going to need a boarding party for that raider, and another one for the *Dominant*. You and Elkiss take thirty marines in *One* and board that raider after we loosen him up a bit. Tell Palevi and Simorka to take fifty marines in *Two* and board *Dominant*. Full combat armor all."

York had done the same thing to Frank that Telyekev had done to him. He needed an experienced officer as CO for the marines, though Frank was no happier about it than York had been. Frank stood up from the fire control console, left Jakobee in charge and disappeared into the lift.

"Transition in ten seconds and counting, sir. That raider's spotted us, started to run, leaving his shuttle behind."

"Mister Jakobee. Put a shot across his bow."

"Aye, aye, sir. Fire one!"

Cinesstar's hull drummed as one of the big turrets spit a shell into transition.

"Transition in four seconds, sir."

The shot flared just in front of the raider. "Mister Jakobee. Watch your defensive stations for incoming."

The raider would be fast, certainly faster than *Cinesstar*, but nowhere near as heavily armed. And *Cinesstar* had the jump on him, was already close to transition, while the raider would have to build speed.

"Three seconds . . ."

The raider ignored the warning shot. "Another shot across their bow, Mister Jakobee."

"Two seconds. Drones in, sir."

"Fire two, sir."

"One . . ."

On one of his screens York watched the second shell explode in front of the fleeing raider. "Transition," Jondee shouted, and York's screens froze as they went blind.

"Ten seconds to down-transition."

York growled, "Maggie, take evasive action. He's going to try to hit us now. And dump all our velocity when we down-transit. Anda, drones out immediately on transition. Mister Jakobee, kill-target that raider as soon as you—"

The power plant red-lined as *Cinesstar*'s shields sucked power for a near miss. The raider had taken his shot.

"Two seconds, sir."

The power plant red-lined again, the hull creaked and whined.

"Transition," Gant screeched. "Drones out."

"Incoming," Jakobee said much more calmly. "Defensive stations responding. I've got acquisition, sir. Ranging at thirty-one million kilometers and closing rapidly."

"All forward main batteries, Mister Jakobee . . . fire!"

Cinesstar's hull groaned and shook as all four forward turrets slammed shells into transition. An instant later one of the shells flashed by the raider harmlessly, but two more tore off a small piece of his bow, and the fourth punched a hole amidships. The raider went dead in space.

"All stop," York ordered. "But stay alert, don't trust that raider's dead yet. Mister Jondee, see if you can raise him. Also see if you can raise *Dominant*."

Cinesstar swung past the raider, and it took close to a half hour to swing back and match velocities with the two stricken ships. Gant worked nervously, keeping an eye on the rest of the system for any activity, but their fears proved to be groundless.

The raider captain was nothing like York expected. He sat at his console ramrod straight, humorless, with an almost military demeanor, reminding York that such men were often deserters from one side or the other. "Captain," he said. "I'm Captain Duart. I must protest this unwarranted attack on a legitimate salvage operation. I and my men—"

York cut him off. "Are pirates. You fired on a disabled vessel, and we fired on you. You can state your case before an Admiralty Court. Stand down and prepare to be boarded. You're under arrest."

Duart hesitated, considering his options. "We should discuss terms."

York shook his head. "Surrender and you'll not be tortured or subjected to inhuman treatment. Don't, and I feed you a warhead. No terms beyond that."

Duart nodded precisely. "Very well, Captain. We surrender."

York made Duart remain on the screen while he dispatched the two boats. To be safe he held *Cinesstar* three hundred thousand kilometers off the raider's stern, and a similar distance from the wreckage of *Dominant*. It was basically point-blank range for *Cinesstar*'s weapons systems, but far enough away to give her automatic defenses a fraction of a second to kick in if the raider tried something. It took the two boats nearly half an hour to cover the distance. York watched Duart on one screen, and Frank's boat approaching him on another. Frank and Elkiss and their marines were about one hundred kilometers from the raider when suddenly Duart's picture disappeared from his screen, and *One* blossomed into a white-hot globe of incandescent fire.

York stared at his screen for a long second, waiting for someone to tell him there was something wrong with his scan summary, but instead he heard, "That son-of-a-bitch burned them."

"Captain, the raider's running."

"Small warhead, estimated yield strength fifty kilotonnes."

There would be no survivors in that, York knew. In fact, there wouldn't even be debris to speak of, just vapor—Frank, Elkiss, his marines. York looked toward Maggie, but she was encased in the helm cluster and he could see nothing of her.

"Captain, the raider's running. What should we do?"

York looked at his screens. The raider was running at about ten thousand gravities, would be able to make transition in five or ten minutes. They could put a warhead into him, but that was too easy, too clean of a way to die. "Miss Votak. All forward main batteries."

"It's done, sir." York heard the strain in her voice.

"Mister Jakobee, at this range you should be able to target nicely on his drive and power plant."

"Targeted, sir."

"Very good, Mister Jakobee. All main turrets, fire one volley."

"Fire one, sir."

Cinesstar's hull echoed loudly with the thrum of the transition batteries firing in unison. All eight shells tore into the raider's aft end, scattering debris behind him. The raider went dead in space.

"That debris is really dirty, sir. Picking up a lot of hot stuff in it. I'd say we blew his power plant."

"He's broadcasting a surrender flag, sir, requesting aid."

York nodded, thinking of Frank, and Elkiss. "Mister Jakobee. Target amidships."

"Targeted, sir."

"Very good. All main turrets, fire one volley."

"Fire one, sir."

The second volley literally cut the raider in two.

"Captain, I have Duart on channel three. He wants to surrender."

"I'm sure he does," York said. He put Duart's picture on one of his screens, turned the volume down, plugged his own audio into the channel so the raider could hear the orders he gave. "Mister Jakobee, line up for a broadside and target all forward main batteries on the forward half of that raider, and all aft main batteries on the aft half of that raider. On my command they're to commence firing at will. Tell them the first set of turret crews, fore versus aft, who reduces their respective half of that raider to pieces of debris no larger than one cubic meter, will receive an extra water ration and light duty for the next tenday." Duart's eyes flashed visible fear, exactly what York wanted to see.

"Captain," the empress shouted. "You can't do that. That's murder."

"Captain," Jakobee said. "Targeted and standing by."

York swallowed hard. "Very good, Mister Jakobee. Commence firing."

York reflected that there were probably quite a few people on *Cinesstar* who had never before heard a continuous fire barrage. It was an eerie sound, much like that of a deep bass drum, beginning with the first loud beat as all of the turrets fired in unison on the initial command, but quickly breaking up into randomly spaced beats as the turret crews competed with each other for speed and accuracy.

On his screen, Duart pleaded with York, alternating between demands that York recognize his obligation to treat prisoners properly, and begging for mercy. Cassandra and Andow shouted at him to show reason. York saw the helm cluster rising up from the combat configuration, caught a momentary glimpse of Maggie staring numbly at her screens. Finally the empress unstrapped and floated across the bridge, reached out, took York by the shoulders and shook him violently. She must have leaned into the field of view of the camera in York's console, because Duart's eyes suddenly flashed with recognition, and for an instant he looked past his own console at someone not visible on the screen. He said, "Captain, they've got the empress."

He replayed Duart's words in his own mind: *Captain, they've got the empress.* Who was Duart speaking to? And if Duart wasn't the captain of the raider, then who was?

"Cease fire," York shouted.

••••

They'd cut the raider into several pieces. York let the raider crew wait while they rescued *Dominant*'s survivors: no officers, a few NCO's, and about thirty enlisted men and women. Then he put an engineering crew aboard the wreckage with orders to strip her of anything that might be of use: ordnance, weapons, vac suits, spare parts.

York then had armored marines board the largest pieces of the raider and arrest the surviving crewmembers. There were about fifteen of them.

"I want to see them," York told Palevi. "Assemble them on Hangar Deck."

"Olin," he said, standing. "You have the watch. Get us out of here soonest, on a course to Sarasan." He stood and left the bridge.

When York stepped out of the lift, Palevi shouted, "Atteeuun . . . shuuuuun."

Palevi and Yagell had the pirates lined up in a row with a half dozen heavily armed marines watching over them. The marines had just lost thirty of their comrades, and hadn't been kind with the pirates.

The surviving raiders were an undisciplined lot, no uniforms to speak of, some rather garishly dressed, some not, some clean-shaven, some not. Duart stood out among them. Taller than the rest, he looked more like a naval officer than a raider captain. *But he's not the captain.*

York stuck his hand out toward Yagell and said, "I need your sidearm."

Yagell's weapon of choice was a large caliber grav gun. She put it in York's hand and grinned at him.

York marched straight to Duart, said, "Do you know who I am?"

The question confused the man so York helped him out. "I'm Ballin, marine SDO."

Duart's eyes told York he understood, so York stepped back and shot him in the foot.

Duart crumpled to the deck, screaming in agony. York let him writhe for a few seconds, then stepped in, grabbed him by the hair, pulled his head back and jammed the barrel of the gun in his crotch. Duart froze, gasping and sweating, but he no longer screamed and his eyes locked on York.

"You killed some people in that boat that were important to me. And I know you're not the captain. So if you don't tell me who is, I'm going to blow your balls off, and order my marines to stand here and watch you die slowly, make sure no one helps you. Should take you a couple days to die."

Duart grimaced in pain, pointed at one of the pirates. "The dumpy little guy." Only one of the pirates fit that description.

York turned toward the real raider captain. He stopped in front of him, raised the pistol and put the muzzle between the man's eyes. He thought of Frank—not enough left of him to stuff into a body bag—and Maggie, her chance at happiness blown to vapor.

"Now Cap'm," the little man said, backing away, bastardizing York's rank through sloppiness rather than because of any marine custom. "Let's be reasonable men here," he said with a heavy accent.

York snarled, "I don't feel reasonable." He advanced on the man.

"But shootin' me'll be murder, Cap'm."

"Ya," York said, grinning. "Murder, plain and simple."

"Wait, Cap'm," the man pleaded, raising his hands. "Wait. I'm too valuable to you alive."

"And why is that?"

There was sudden triumph in the little man's eyes. "Don't ya be askin' yerself why go to so much trouble to hide me identity?"

The man had a point. "Spit it out."

"I'm Richard, Cap'm. The redman, the most famous pirate what ever lived. I'm Red Richard."

Through the years, York had read reports on Red Richard's activities, and he'd scanned a few security briefings upon occasion. Richard was reputed to be short, dumpy, with black hair, a scar over the right eye, and a heavy, uncultured accent. This fellow fit the description, and he and his men had gone to some trouble to conceal his identity.

"I know all sorts of things, Cap'm. Things real valuable to a skipper bein' hunted by every ship in a hundred light-years."

York raised the muzzle of the pistol until it pointed at the deck overhead and considered the little man carefully. He came to a decision, clicked the gun's safety, turned to Yagell and tossed her the gun. The marine caught it casually, snapped it into the clips on her thigh. "Interrogate them all," York said to her. "Confirm without doubt that he's Red Richard. And I want to know everything they know about anything that might be useful." York looked at the pirate as he finished, "And I don't care what condition they're in when you're finished with them."

The grin on Richard's face disappeared. York got some satisfaction in that.

••••

Cinesstar up-transited out of the Aagerbanne system shortly after midnight. Sarasan was their best hope; it wouldn't have anywhere near the facilities that Aagerbanne had had before being destroyed, but the defending imperial fleet had retreated in that direction, and the feddie fleet had withdrawn the other way. What better escort for the empress than an entire fleet, even if it had been badly mauled.

Sarasan was twenty-one light-years distant; at *Cinesstar*'s top speed of better than two thousand lights they could make it in four days. She was running nicely, no one on her tail. There was a little instability in the damaged power chamber, but the two good chambers could handle the load without difficulty, and they were basically back in imperial space now, so York gave Cappik permission to shut Starboard down for a day and see what he could do about repairs. York scanned his screens one more time, decided *Cinesstar* could do without the guidance of her captain for a few hours.

Maggie was in her cabin. When he knocked on the door she didn't answer at first, but after repeated efforts her voice came out of the speaker above the door in a garbled mumble, "Enter."

He found her sitting in the dark, one elbow resting on her desk, a half-empty drink in her hand, her eyes staring blankly at the opposite bulkhead. When York closed the door the room went completely dark. "Mind if I bring up the lights," he asked.

"Sure," she said. "But not too bright."

"Computer," he said. "Lights. Very dim."

The cabin filled with a faint glow, enough for them to see each other. He pulled another chair out of the bulkhead and sat down opposite her at the desk. "How ya doin', girl?"

She shrugged with her eyebrows. "Not too good. I keep trying not to think about him, but the harder I try the more I do." She looked at York seriously. "No chance he's alive?"

She knew the answer to that before she saw it in his eyes, but she'd needed to ask it anyway. Her eyes returned to the drink. "Fuck 'em. Fuck 'em all—the navy, the empire, the feddies, the whole goddamned war." Her voice trailed away with her thoughts. "Fuck 'em."

He sat there in silence for a while, then reached out slowly and placed his hand on her wrist. Her face remained blank, but then a tear rolled down one cheek. "Why him?" she pleaded, and her voice broke.

York shook his head. "Why any of them?"

She fought for control. He could see her struggling, but slowly her face screwed up, her lower lip curled outward and started to tremble. "Why couldn't we have made it? Frankie and me had such plans. Why did the bastards have to take him away from me?"

She started to sob. York stood, stepped around the desk, lifted her up and took her in his arms. He squeezed her tightly and let her cry. "We were going to make babies, you know?"

"No. I didn't know that."

"Ya. We were. We were going to get out of the navy somehow, even if we had to desert. Find someplace where they couldn't find us."

Her body shook with deep, uncontrolled sobs. "I miss him so much. He's only been dead for a few hours and I miss him already. Just knowing he's dead . . . I'm never going to see him again . . . I just can't . . ."

She started sobbing again, and he held her like that for a long time, neither of them speaking, while slowly her grief dwindled to a quiet whimper. After a time, he felt her weight leaning heavily on him, and he knew she was half-asleep with exhaustion. He let his arms relax a little but she clutched at him desperately. So he picked her up, marveled for a moment at how small she seemed. He expanded the field on her grav bunk, laid her down gently in it. But she wouldn't let go of his hand, so he lay down beside her and wrapped his arms around her.

"You come with me," she said. "You and me. We can go make babies somewhere, someplace where they'll never find us. We can live normal lives, not wonder every moment if today is our last day alive. Will you do that with me?"

He nodded, realized she couldn't see the gesture, though with his cheek resting against hers perhaps she could feel it. "Ya, I will."

"Promise?"

"Ya, I promise."

After that she slept, though it was fitful and she whimpered a little from time to time. The empire cared nothing for people like him and Maggie. If they survived this, they'd both end up on another warship going out to fight in what he now acknowledged was a pointless war. He slept a little too, but mostly he lay awake and made plans. He planned how he and she would desert as soon as he could figure out a way. He knew more about these things than her. He had a considerable amount of pay in his account and he knew how to withdraw it slowly over a period of time so it wouldn't draw any suspicion. A bribe here, a bribe there, steal a small courier ship and get lost out on the fringes where, rumor had it, there was no war.

But first, he had to get the empress back in one piece.

He whispered softly, "Ya, Maggie, I promise."

25

Sarasan

"MORNIN', CAP'M."

York stood outside Richard's cell, looked the fat, little pirate over carefully. Richard grinned at him. "There are certain advantages for a pirate who don't look like a pirate, Cap'm."

"So you're admitting to piracy now, not legitimate salvage operations?"

Richard's grin broadened. "Well now, Cap'm. Just between us girls, it wouldn't do me no good to deny it, would it? But don't be expectin' me to be so free and easy in a court o' law."

York shook his head. "Admiralty Court, not court of law."

"Aw, Cap'm! Can't you cut a poor down-and-out fella a break?"

"You killed my friends."

Richard shrugged. "And you killed most of me crew."

"Were any of them your friends?"

Richard winked. "Touché, Cap'm. But you and me could be friends, you know? We're a lot alike, you and me."

"You don't know anything about me."

"Well now, Cap'm." Richard leaned back in his seat, raised a hand and started ticking off points on his fingers. "You're Ballin—*Butcher Ballin*. I could use me a nickname like that. Good for the image, if yer a pirate. Yer also a marine, and the SDO—the most bloodthirsty son-of-a-bitch of an *imper* anyone's ever heard of. Yer a lifer, and you've managed to survive for more'n twenty years out here. That's a rare commodity, Cap'm. You don't have no prospects for the future: we both know they're gonna take yer command away from you as soon as you get Her Nibs back to His Nibs. And then that little twat of a princess'll probably have you up on charges. Have I got it right so far, Cap'm?"

York's crew had obviously been rather talkative, though Richard was probably good at wheedling information. It occurred to York he could have Richard and his crew tanked; then no one could talk to him, but he was reluctant to do that even to the likes of him. "Go on," he said.

Richard stood, crossed the small cell and faced York through the plast bars. "When you go back they're gonna take this fine ship away from you, Cap'm. And then they'll treat you no better'n they're gonna treat me. But you don't owe them nothin'. Nothin' at all . . ."

Richard let that hang for a long moment. York prompted him, "And?"

The pirate waved a hand, indicating the ship around them. "Look at yer opportunities here, Cap'm. You got a beautiful ship—a fightin' ship like no freebooter ever dreamed of. You don't owe them nothin'. In fact it's them what owes you—after you been fightin' for 'em for so long." Richard leaned close and spoke just above a whisper. "You don't have to go back, Cap'm. You don't have to let them treat you like shit, after all you done for them. You just don't have to."

"And what are my alternatives?"

Richard shrugged, looked about carefully to insure no one else could hear. "Come with me to Andyne-Borregga. I could show you the way, Cap'm. With this ship and crew, and with the cargo you're carryin', you could buy yourself a good captaincy in the Mexaks. Start workin' for yourself for once."

York stepped back from the cell. Richard had caught him completely off balance. The infamous free port of Andyne-Borregga—center of operations for the Mexaks, the shadowy and notorious league of pirates about which even AI knew only a little. Borregga was a haven for smugglers and pirates, the center of commerce for contraband weapons and drugs whose location was allegedly a well-kept secret. York knew better; it was impossible to keep secret the location of a major center of commerce, even if the commerce in question was mostly illicit and illegal. York didn't doubt that it could be found and taken by a large and determined fleet. But Borregga was rumored to be well protected by its inhabitants, and even if it was destroyed, the illicit traffic would just crop up elsewhere in short order. So the empire and the Directorate tolerated its existence because it served a basic purpose and it wasn't worth the trouble. Some effort was made to limit access; its location had never been on any charts that York had seen. And, of course, the Borreggans themselves wouldn't tolerate the presence of an imperial cruiser, unless someone like Richard could help them gain entry.

"Cargo?" York asked. "What cargo do I have that would be of any value to the Mexaks?"

"Come on, Cap'm," Richard said, tapping the side of his head. "You got to start thinkin' creatively. Her Royal Sweet Ass'll command a high price anywhere, especially from the feddies. And that little bitch of a princess and the rest of them are gravy, free and clear. What a team we'd make, eh Cap'm, Red Richard and Butcher Ballin?"

That left a bad taste in York's mouth, not because of what Richard suggested, but because York was tempted to accept the pirate's proposition. He didn't say anything, just turned on his heels and marched out of the brig.

"Hey, Cap'm," Richard called after him. "Where ya goin'? I thought we had a deal."

York called Alsa Yan from the terminal in his office. "Tank Richard and his entire crew. Tell Palevi it's my orders."

Yan frowned and said, "Very good, sir," but York could see the question she didn't ask mirrored in her face.

"I don't want him communicating with anyone on this ship. He's tricky and dangerous."

"Yes, sir," Yan said skeptically, then switched off her terminal.

York had lied to her. He really didn't want Richard communicating with him.

••••

"Damn!" Add'kas'adanna swore, looking at her screen. "Damn, and damn again!" She activated her com. "Martak, come in here immediately."

"Yes, ma'am. Right away, ma'am."

Add'kas'adanna shook her head, looked at her screen again. It had become almost a morning ritual—splash a little water on her face, get a cup of hot caff, and then, before anything else, sit down and pull up the map of probable *Cinesstar* sightings. But that morning it had been different. She'd become so used to looking at the same unchanging map of sightings she recognized the difference immediately. At first she'd been excited, thinking a recent sighting had been logged while she'd slept. But then she pulled up the full report—filed hastily nine days ago by Captain Jewel Thaaline of *Pride of Altalane*, then misfiled for god knew how long before being properly routed to Add'kas'adanna's intelligence officer.

Thaaline had been tracking *Cinesstar* since Dumark, actually engaged the *imper* once, took some damage, was forced to give up the chase temporarily and lost the trail. But Thaaline had finished by recording her own hunch that, while *Cinesstar's* trail appeared to be headed for Aagerbanne, she thought it was a ruse, and the *imper* was actually headed for Sarasan.

Add'kas'adanna looked at her screens again. She had new data, new sightings, much more information than Thaaline, and it was obvious the *imper* was headed for Aagerbanne. But Thaaline's confirmed sightings made it clear which of the other sightings were false, and which were real, and that gave Add'kas'adanna a much clearer picture. The *imper* should have reached Aagerbanne at about the same time the shooting had started, had probably transited right into it, for all she knew. He couldn't have reached Aagerbanne before that—her neural interrogation of Sayalla had confirmed the *impers* still hadn't located *Cinesstar*. So the *imper* had probably waited for her to withdraw, and when she'd done so, she'd passed right over the top of him.

Her intercom bleeped and her yeoman announced, "Commodore Martak is here, ma'am."

"Send him in," Add'kas'adanna barked.

Before Martak even sat down she was throwing orders at him. "Reposition the entire fleet. I want a small strike force—ten of our fastest ships—under my personal command. We'll drive straight for Sarasan. I want the rest of the fleet spread out between Aagerbanne and Sarasan. He's out there somewhere, and we're going to catch him."

••••

"Captain, I've got a hot one here."

Jewel looked up from her screens, made eye contact with Soe in the cramped confines of the *Pride*'s bridge. "It came in on general broadcast, coded *top priority, for your eyes only*. I don't even have the cipher key to decode it."

Jewel nodded. "Send a copy down to my cabin terminal. I'll look at it there."

Now what, she thought. They were in a good position—approaching Sarasan at a reasonable velocity. They had options now: they could throw warheads at the *impers* if they wanted to, or sit tight if that seemed the right thing to do. As long as DCO didn't mess it up for them.

Jewel stood stiffly, turned to the ladder at the back of the bridge, tossed over her shoulder, "Mister Soe, you have the bridge."

Down in her cabin the coded, top priority message was waiting for her. She punched in the cipher key, waited a few seconds for the computer to decipher the message and bring it up on one of her screens.

The picture showed Illcall Terman seated at his console, a trickle of blood streaming down his cheek from a cut over his right eye, more blood drizzling out a nostril, running past his lips and dripping off his chin. The left shoulder of his tunic showed the unmistakable signs of a flash burn, the kind caused by something exploding nearby.

As the recording began, a choking cough racked his entire frame, and that brought up a mouthful of blood. Jewel heard pounding in the background and muffled shouts.

The coughing stopped, Terman looked into her eyes and she had to remember it was only a recording. "I don't have much time, Jew. They'll be in here any minute—"

He started coughing again, and Jewel wanted to shout, *Who'll be in there any minute?*

"You've got to trust me on this one, Jew. I don't have time to explain, but the *impers* want to burn that *imper* cruiser as much as we do . . . But we don't . . . I mean he's gonna end the war. He's gonna end the damn war . . ."

There was an explosion in the background—Terman's picture shook and a chunk of debris barely missed taking off his head. "Don't let them burn that *imper*," he shouted into the pickup. "Just trust me, Jew. Don't let—"

Terman's head exploded in a shower of bone and brains; his body rocked forward, slammed against the console only inches from the pickup, then everything went still.

Jewel waited, looking at Terman's open, dead eyes for an eternity. Then a dim, shadowy figure approached him carefully from behind, and, finally assured that Terman no longer posed a threat, stood erect. Terman's corpse still blocked most of the figure, but then it pulled him clumsily out of the way by the collar of his tunic and dropped him to one side.

"What was he up to?" the figure asked someone.

"Hell if I know," the someone answered.

"Look!" The figure pointed at something on the console, a finger only inches from the pickup. "He was broadcasting something."

"Shit! Still is broadcasting. Kill it."

The figure reached out, slapped at the console and the picture went blank.

Jewel stared at the blank screen for several minutes. Terman was an old friend. She could count the times they'd met face-to-face on the fingers of one hand, but they'd met by screen hundreds of times over the years.

She wanted to know who killed him. But she hadn't seen their faces, just a glimpse of a uniform, and that had been unmistakable. The killer had been wearing the uniform of DCO Security.

••••

"It's a whole fleet. It's got to be, a whole, goddamned fleet. I've already picked up close to thirty transition wakes, all within one light-year."

Jewel looked at her screen.

Soe continued. "And I'm sure some of those wakes are multiple ships, clustered so close together I can't resolve individual wakes."

"Steady as she goes," Jewel said, trying to affect some semblance of calm. "Anything you can identify?"

Soe shook his head. "A wake is a wake, some bigger, some smaller."

"Andro. Any activity from Sarasan Station?"

Innay shook his head. "Nothing. Business as usual. Shields are probably up, but that's normal. No activity in the outer defenses, no movement from her orbital weapons platforms."

That told her what she needed to know. Sarasan had undoubtedly detected the approaching wakes, and if they were unidentified, or clearly Federals, the Station Commander would be bringing all her defenses up to battle readiness. So the approaching ships had to be an imperial fleet, and from their transition vectors they were coming from their sector headquarters at Aagerbanne.

"Steady as she goes," Jewel said calmly. "That's an *imper* fleet coming in. We're going to be right in the middle of them. But with all the transition noise they're making there's not much chance they can detect us. So let's just sit tight."

••••

"Fifty lights and holding, sir. Range: point-one-three light-years."

York scanned his screens, could feel a bead of sweat running down his back inside his tunic. As they approached Sarasan farspace the entire ship filled with anticipation. Their journey was almost over; safe harbor was within easy reach, but York was spoiling it for them.

Assume nothing, he'd told them. *We're going in with extreme caution. Hunter-killer approach; battle stations; the works.*

He glanced at the helm cluster and wondered about Maggie. After the night of tears in her cabin she'd gone stoic on him. He knew she had more tears to shed, and thought it would be healthier if she did so.

"Forty lights," he ordered.

"Forty lights," Maggie responded. "Serious gravitational instability all over the ship . . . but she's holding."

The last time they'd tried this *Cinesstar* had dropped into down-transition at forty lights. Maggie was getting better at this. "All right, Maggie. Start easing her back slowly until she drops into transition, and when she does, hold onto all the velocity you can. Keep our flare to a minimum."

York waited, tried to watch all his screens at once, couldn't ignore the tumbling in his stomach as a cluster of gravity waves rolled through the ship. Maggie got *Cinesstar* down to thirty-one lights before she dropped into transition. Cappik cut the deck gravity instantly and they floated free.

They all waited for Gant. York wanted to bark at her to hurry up, but he knew better. Finally, she cried out, "Clear to a hundred thousand kilometers."

York let out his breath. "Drones out—passive."

The hull echoed with the clang of the drone launch. Jondee acknowledged, "Drones out."

Gant started filling in the details. "We're point-one-two light-years from Sarasan farspace, coasting at point-nine-three lights, dilation factor two-point-seven. Preliminary scan shows no activity between here—" Her voice shot up an octave. "Wait! Contact. Dead ahead. Ranging at point-oh-five lights."

"Us or them?" York demanded. "And are they closing."

"They're headed this general direction, but I can't tell more than that. With the drones passive I don't have enough of a baseline for the resolution I need. Whoever they are they're driving hard in sublight, or I wouldn't be able to pick them up. But I can't get a good vector on them, no possibility of a targeting solution, and I certainly can't resolve a recognition profile."

Whoever was out there was driving hard, and that had to mean they'd been spotted. "Tell Mister Cappik to stand by with full power for the shields. Let's power up and have a look."

York felt the weight of gravity in his bones again, and Gant started to smile as her drones spread out under power.

"Incoming," she suddenly shouted. "Extreme long-range transition shot."

"Hold your fire, Mister Jakobee," York growled, "unless it's actually targeted on us."

The shot flared about one million kilometers in front of them—a shot across the bow—the standard calling card of a deep space picket. Gant confirmed York's suspicion. "It looks like one of ours, sir."

"Mister Jondee. Send them an imperial recognition code, but don't identify us."

York waited for several seconds, then, "I'm getting a reply, sir, but I can't decode it. Our codes must be out of date."

"Resend the recognition code until they reply in kind."

Jondee had to broadcast the code eight times before the captain of the distant ship decided to communicate with them in a code they could decipher.

"Captain," Jondee said. "You'd better take this."

The image of a middle-aged woman in an imperial uniform with commander's pips on her collars appeared on one of York's screens. York knew her, had met her somewhere, though he couldn't recall her name, or the circumstances under which they'd met.

She spoke immediately, "Your codes are out of date. Identify yourself and . . ." Her eyes narrowed.

Good, York thought. *She recognizes me too.*

"York Ballin," York said. "Late of *H.M.S. Invaradin*. Presently commanding *H.M.S. Cinesstar*."

She flinched, frowned, an odd reaction. York continued, "And you are?"

She considered his image for a long moment, then nodded. "Commander Vilnay. Commanding *H.M.S. Australis*, attached to the Third Fleet. Please excuse me for a moment."

York gave her a nod and she blanked her screen. He looked at the empty screen, began to feel uneasy. She should have asked for more information, should have paid deference to certain courtesies, should have expected him to return those same courtesies in kind.

York's screen suddenly flashed back to life, but now it was split, with Vilnay occupying one half, and an older man with admiral's stripes and scrambled eggs all over the bill of his cap on the other. There was something about the look in the man's eyes, as if he expected absolute, unquestioned obedience. Vilnay said, "Captain Ballin. May I introduce His Grace, Sergai Leonavich, Duke de Neptair."

Shit! York thought, almost said it aloud. He managed an appropriate bow of his head and said, "Your Grace. I'm honored."

Leonavich didn't have to pay deference to any courtesies. "We're sending you a transition plan for a short jump into Sarasan nearspace. Execute it immediately. That's an order."

No mention of the empress. No request for assurances that she was all right. No request to speak with her. York bowed again. "Very good, Your Grace. Can you clear us for contact exchange? With updated codes we'll be able to set it up a lot easier and faster." Only a small half-truth.

"Sure," Leonavich said almost angrily. "Do it, Vilnay. It won't do any harm."

It won't do any harm. An odd thing to say. That phrase made York think back to the look on Vilnay's face when she'd first heard him identify *Cinesstar*.

Australis' computer set up a link with *Cinesstar*'s computer. The two ships exchanged contact packets in an automated process each had gone through hundreds of times, and in minutes *Cinesstar*'s codes were up-to-date and she could tie into Third Fleet's command grid.

It won't do any harm.

York looked at the plan Vilnay had fed them: a short transition hop into the Sarasan system, but nowhere near Sarasan herself. They were receiving data from Third's command grid now and York could see the deployment of all the elements of the fleet. The plan would have them down-transit in the midst of a cluster of cruisers and destroyers. It was safety, of a sort, having your friends all about you, but not as safe as having *Cinesstar* transit deep into the system well behind the protective armaments of the fleet. York made a slight adjustment to the plan that put them close to, but not in the midst of, the cluster of fighting ships.

"But sir," Gant said. "Duke Sergai's orders—"

York growled at her, "You just worry about my orders."

It was an easy jump. They barely had time to accelerate before down-transiting. York had his crew set up the down-transit without any deceleration. They were close to two thousand lights, and the resultant flare was excessive, would be momentarily blinding to any targeting computer trying to compute a solution on them.

••••

"That's it," Tac'tac'ah shouted. "Big flare. That's our *imper*."

"He's close enough for a solution," Soe added. "We've got him now."

Jewel looked at the system summary on her screen. "I want solutions on all of them," she said.

She should be elated. Their *imper* had come right to them, was almost asking to be burned. And yet she couldn't erase the image of Illcall Terman's dead eyes staring at her from the recording he'd sent. In a way, it was his last will and testament, something he'd felt was important enough to die for. That image, and his last words, had haunted her dreams, had kept her awake at night.

"Funny thing," Innay said. "His friends are closing about him like he was one of us, like they didn't trust him."

"I want targeting solutions on all of them," Jewel repeated. "All of them."

••••

Leonavich was on one of York's screens immediately. "What kind of sloppy vectoring is that, Ballin?"

"I'm sorry, Your Grace," York lied. "We have a damaged drive chamber; it threw us off a bit."

Leonavich's ships were moving quickly to close about *Cinesstar*. It wasn't the action of a friend welcoming an ally home after a long and dangerous journey.

It won't do any harm. And the look on Vilnay's face, the look that now settled on Leonavich's face: distaste, as if confronted with the need to perform an unpleasant task.

"Your Grace," York said. He tried to get Leonavich to meet his eyes, but the Duke looked away under some pretext. One of the nine most powerful people in the empire, Sergai, Duke de Neptair, couldn't meet the eyes of a former *juvenile delinquent, lower deck pod gunner, spacer second class.* York pleaded with him, "What's going on here, Your Grace? Please."

Leonavich finally met his eyes. The Duke's eyes were angry, and tired, but mostly they were sad, and they were hardened, as if reluctantly accepting the need to do something unpleasant.

"Captain!" Jondee's voice intruded. "Captain, I just got us tied into their command grid, and there's been some sort of mistake here."

York's eyes remained locked on Leonavich's. He flipped a switch on his console so Leonavich couldn't hear Jondee, then he asked, "What kind of mistake, Mister Jondee."

"Well, I don't see how it happened, or maybe I'm just reading this wrong, or maybe we've got com problems, or—"

York grew impatient. "Spit it out."

"Yes, sir." It was rare for Jondee to be so respectful. "Sir, we've been allocated as a target on Third's command grid. I know it's not possible, but—"

Now it made sense, or at least the actions of Leonavich's ships made sense, if they were trying to close on an enemy and cut off all possibility of escape. *But why?* The *why* of it didn't make sense.

To Leonavich, their eyes still locked, York said, "Your Grace. I don't know why you're doing this, but there's no need. I'll surrender, without terms. I'll surrender myself and my ship and all aboard her, and trust to your honor to judge us fairly for whatever it is you think we've done. I'll lower my shields, cut my drive, go fully static, whatever you require."

Leonavich nodded sadly. "Then do so now. Drop your shields."

York saw no lessening of the hard intent in Leonavich's eyes. He asked, "Will you accept my surrender, take proper care of my people?"

Leonavich hesitated, almost lied to him, but at the last instant he seemed unable to stomach whatever motivated his actions, and all he said was, "I'm sorry, Captain . . ."

York's hand shot out almost involuntarily and hit a switch on his console, killing Leonavich's picture.

"Shields up. Full combat status. Mister Jondee, cut all external transmissions. Pull us out of their command grid, but we've got the codes to decipher their command transmissions so feed their command grid into our targeting computer. And I want a copy on my screens.

"Miss Votak, hard astern. Take us out of the plane of the ecliptic. I want to make transition soonest."

"Captain," someone shouted, "we've got incoming."

"Mister Jakobee, target on anything out there."

"But they're our ships, sir!"

Maggie and Paris responded nicely, and Rame too, but Jakobee and a few others were staring at York slack mouthed. "I know they're our own goddamned ships," he shouted at them as the ship rocked under the impact of a hit taken somewhere. "But they're going to burn us if we don't fight back."

A report flashed on one of York's screens: *Minor damage amidships.*

That pulled them out of their stupor. "Sir," Jondee barked. "It'll take too long to set up a feed from Third's command grid to our targeting computer."

More than once York had awakened late at night, lay awake reviewing the disconcerting facts of their situation, chided himself for his paranoia. But paranoid he'd been, and the only way he could get back to sleep was to satisfy his paranoia by thinking through a contingency plan and programming it on the computer.

Cinesstar took another hit as York heard the comforting echo of her transition and defensive batteries go into action.

"Mister Jondee," he shouted above the noise. "You'll find such a program already set up in library *Ballin*, hidden and protected sublibrary *Ballinov*, password *paranoia*, program name *endgame*."

"Got it."

Leonavich hadn't gotten them completely englobed. He could only bring about twenty of his ships to bear on *Cinesstar*. Jakobee was starting to fight back, manually using the data from Third's command grid to pinpoint targets. *Cinesstar*'s hull thrummed as its transition batteries went into action, but between the echoes of their own weapons came the occasional crash of a hit taken. Too many hits taken.

"Paris," York shouted. "Try broadcasting into their command grid; allocate a few of them as targets on their own goddamned grid."

Heavy damage aft. Hull breach.

"Maggie, get us out of here."

••••

"Holy shit!" Soe swore. "Those *impers* just went crazy. They're shooting at each other. It's a free-for-all out there. And they're coming right at us."

Jewel shook her head. She hadn't told them about the transmission from Terman. "No," she said. "Not a free-for-all. They're after the same *imper* we are. But he's smart. He's got access to their command grid and he's using it against them."

"Here's our chance at the son-of-a-bitch," Soe shouted happily. "They're headed this way."

Jewel nodded. "Stand by all stations."

••••

Minor damage on decks A through D, H, and K through M.

Heavy damage amidships—hull breach deck E, starboard.

Turret 7 inactive. Crew status unknown.

The noise was incredible. The recoil from every round they fired sent a deep, bass note echoing back and forth through the hull. And every round that tore into *Cinesstar*'s shields, whether it penetrated the hull or not, struck a louder, harsher note.

Cinesstar rocked violently. It shouldn't have rocked at all; her computer should have compensated all motion with her internal gravity fields. But she rocked hard enough to send most of them to the edge of consciousness, and the readings on the port chamber redlined for an instant, then dropped to flat nothing.

"Captain," Cappik screamed at York from one of his screens. "Port chamber just blew. Blew a hole right through the fuckin' hull. And Starboard's gonna take a shit on me any minute."

York kept his voice calm. "Miss Votak, get us into transition any way you can, in any direction possible—now."

"No can do, sir. We've got too many ships too close to us, too much transition static, we—"

"Don't argue with me," York shouted. "Just do it."

York hit a switch on his console, cutting his implants out of the bridge command circuit, suddenly filling his ears with relative quiet, and he got an odd sense of detachment from the chaos around him. Rame screamed something at him, but he couldn't hear it and he ignored him.

York spoke into his pickup. "Computer."

Acknowledged, the computer said.

"Access library *Ballin*, sublibrary *Ballinov*, password *paranoia*, program name *Desperate*."

Program Desperate access acknowledged.

Another program York had written during a sleepless night, something he couldn't have done without ring-zero access. He hadn't intended to use it against imperial ships, so it didn't really belong under the password *paranoia*. But that was as good a place as any. *Desperate* was a complex program. It systematically removed all of *Cinesstar*'s fail-safe procedures, nullified whatever protection there was against an inappropriate or improper transition, then attempted to put *Cinesstar* into up-transition regardless of the circumstances. It was a dangerous program, and so aptly, if unimaginatively, named. *Cinesstar* could disintegrate, could simply and rather undramatically break up into small pieces. Or she could turn very dramatically into a small nova.

"Load program *Desperate*."

Program Desperate loaded.

York felt Maggie unsuccessfully try to take *Cinesstar* into transition.

"Execute program *Desperate*."

Program Desperate executing . . .

Maggie had turned *Cinesstar* toward Leonavich's thinnest clustering of ships—two cruisers and two destroyers. It was hopeless, but it was their best chance. The four ships knew *Cinesstar* had sustained serious damage, were matching her pace, hammering away at her, tenaciously holding on until they could make the kill.

York felt the computer try to take *Cinesstar* into transition, felt the computer fail.

Unable to effect transition. Excessive gravitational mass and nearby transition noise make such—

"Override, goddamn you," York screamed. "Override . . . override . . . override."

Suddenly one of the ships in front of them flared into an incandescent ball of fire—a direct hit from a large warhead out of nowhere. York looked at the transition trail of the warhead mapped on one of his screens. It had no origination, and with a smile he realized the feddie hunter-killer was still with them. Another of the ships flared into incandescence, and *Cinesstar* tried again to make transition.

York was slammed painfully forward against his restraints. A piece of bulkhead shot past him, cut a crewwoman in two.

The computer said calmly, *Transition.*

His eardrums burst, his eyes bulged from their sockets as the air was torn from his lungs. He was dying, he knew. But he had one consolation: at least he was going out clean, not piece by piece—no indefinite, never-ending, nondeath in the tanks . . .

26

Tank Dreams

EVERY TIME EDVARD thought about old Theodore he wanted to cry. He was so lonely with-out Rochefort. There were few people he truly trusted: Cassandra, certainly, perhaps Sylissa d'Hart, and of course Theodore. The old man had been like a father to him, had been more of a father than his own father. The old king had been more concerned with his mistress, his *true love*, had even favored her over Edvard's mother, a woman chosen as the king's bride for reasons of state, not love. And after the mistress had died, when Edvard was still a young boy, the old king had with-ered, shrunk, grown suddenly old and frail, until he died a few years later, making Edvard a very young king and emperor.

He wasn't sure if he'd ever really loved his father, wasn't sure if his father ever loved him. But Theodore had loved him, and that was all he needed. Now Theodore was gone, and his loss brought up so many painful memories.

His intercom sounded and he answered it mechanically. "Yes."

"Your Majesty, Duke Abraxa and Archcanon Bortha have arrived."

Edvard nodded, brought the lights of his study up a bit. "Please show them in."

When the door opened, old Bortha shot across the room with his robes trailing behind him. "My son. How terrible you must feel."

The old man rounded Edvard's desk with a flourish, put a friendly hand on his shoulder. "I know how close you were to Theodore. How terrible that he should die at the hands of common thieves!"

Edvard wanted to strike the old churchman, to ball up his fist and hit the old hypocrite in the nose. Theodore was to have met Lynna in some sleazy part of Luna. There were rumors of a com-bined AI-Incalla raid somewhere there, and Lynna was now missing. Edvard was no fool.

Abraxa waddled into the room. He'd gained even more weight since the last time Edvard had seen him, had long ago surpassed obese. "Yes. Truly a tragedy."

Abraxa didn't have the flair for the dramatic that Bortha enjoyed, but Edvard wanted to hit him no less. He was tempted to at least say something, but he suppressed the urge. Now was not the time for a confrontation.

He stood, crossed the room to a small bar recessed into the wall, poured a stiff drink and gulped at it. It was something to do, something to keep him from blurting out his anger.

He turned around to face them, realized they were watching him closely for some reaction and fought to show nothing. "Yes," he said coldly. "A tragic loss. He was an excellent servant. I shall miss his advice and counsel."

Bortha frowned, obviously surprised at the passionless statement from a man he had assumed would be distraught with grief. *Cat and mouse*, Edvard thought.

"Your Majesty," Abraxa said. "We are saddened by your loss, but we've come here with a purpose beyond expressing our sympathies. We have some distressing news we felt you should hear from us, and not from some servant."

Abraxa paused, while Edvard wondered what blow he would strike now. "The ship *Cinesstar* has been destroyed with all hands. Apparently there were no survivors."

"Cassandra?" Edvard asked. "Aeya?"

"They were both aboard her. I'm sorry, Your Majesty, but there is no hope they survived."

Now Edvard could show grief. He'd lost his wife and daughter in this pointless war, and realized now that he was merely suffering the same pain millions of others had gone through. He gulped at his drink, tried not to think, tried to empty his mind of all thought. Any thought that would come could only be painful. Bortha was prattling on about something, again laid a supposedly comforting hand on Edvard's shoulder. Edvard interrupted him. "How?"

Abraxa shrugged. "Apparently, *Cinesstar* made her way back to Sarasan, obviously hoping for protection from the subsector headquarters there. At the same time, the Third Fleet was regrouping there after their defeat at Aagerbanne while a Directorate strike force was moving in to finish the job. From what we can determine, *Cinesstar* down-transited into the middle of the ensuing battle. We don't know how many warheads she took, but apparently she was completely destroyed. We're searching now for anything, but there's little hope we'll find even wreckage, let alone survivors."

Edvard just stared at his drink. Bortha said, "I'm sorry," and Edvard could even see that he meant it. But Edvard could still find no liking for the old churchman.

"Thank you," he said. "Please leave me now. I need some time alone with this."

After the two old men had left and were alone in a shielded ground car, with armed escorts accompanying them front and rear, Bortha asked, "Why did you have Rochefort killed? We could be questioning him now."

Abraxa shook his head. "That was a mistake—a fresh AI patrol, new on the scene, answering an all-points bulletin, unaware they were to take him alive. The watch commander for that district has paid for that mistake dearly."

Bortha nodded and leaned back in the cushioned seat. "Well, at least it's over. They're all dead, aren't they?"

Abraxa shrugged. "I think so. I've had my best people going over the telemetry data from the fight—can't really call it a battle. *Cinesstar* took a direct hit from a big warhead—big enough that we can be confident there were no survivors."

Bortha shook his head. "Then why don't you sound confident."

Again Abraxa shrugged, as if trying to say he was unconcerned. "*Cinesstar* had, at that moment, launched a few large warheads of her own. One destroyed a nearby ship of ours, another detonated in space not far from *Cinesstar* herself. And there were a lot of small warheads being detonated by *Cinesstar*'s defensive batteries, and a lot of transition wash everywhere. So the data was somewhat obscured. And when the surrounding space cleared, there was nothing left. Just a lot of debris, mostly metal and plast slag, none of it large enough to be specifically identified as having come from *Cinesstar*. But that warhead was large, and it detonated close enough to her to leave no possibility she could have escaped."

"You still don't sound confident."

Abraxa suddenly turned on him violently and shouted, "Well, I'm as confident as I need to be, churchman." With a visible effort he forced an outward calm. "In any case we're not taking any chances. We're searching the system carefully to be sure, though I doubt we'll find anything more than we already have."

••••

Meekl Donohae thought about a lot of things as she crawled slowly back to consciousness. On Dumark she had been a stat clerk in the embassy—no status in that. But here, she was a pod gunner. Maybe she didn't have much experience, but she was nevertheless a good pod gunner, damn good, with a full chevron cut into her arm as proof of her first two confirmed kills.

That made her think of the old man, and the night he'd sat next to her at *gunner's blood*. He'd had a whole string of chevrons, must have been a gunner for quite some time. It was good to have a captain who knew what it was like to be a gunner. She hoped he was all right. In a way, she felt like she owed her newfound status to him.

Then suddenly it occurred to her that at the moment her *newfound status* just might not be so healthy. She turned her head groggily, found that every muscle hurt.

There was no gravity in her pod, no light either. It was pitch dark, not even the flicker of the telltales on her console, and dead silent. She realized she'd never heard such silence before, and it frightened her. *Don't panic*, she told herself.

She explored the console by touch, tried to reboot the pod system and got no response. Finally, she cut the pod's master switch, manually switched the pod system to her local emergency power reserve and tried again.

The pod's operating system only made it about halfway through the boot sequence before detecting major problems with its hardware, then the system locked up. She tried four times, got the same response each time, finally went back to the main switch box and tried cutting out each major subsystem before attempting a reboot. It worked, though she'd had to cut out fire control, gravity, exterior scan, and her connect to comp central. But she had information now, and from that she finally understood she might not get out of this alive.

No gravity, enough standby power to run the gauges for a few hours. Enough local oxygen reserves for about a day. So, all she had to do was open the hatch on her pod, crawl down the access tube to the inner hull of the ship, open the hatch there, and climb back into the ship. But her gauges showed there was no air in the access tube. This section of the ship had been hulled—certainly, the confines between the inner hull and the shield hull were under vacuum, and apparently the access tube had also taken some damage and it too was under vacuum.

She tried pounding on the hatch for a while. Her efforts sent a faint echo through the ship, but she got no reply so she started to think. That's what Chief Syda always told her, "Think, girl, think. Use your head. That's what'll save yer life."

So Meekl thought long and hard and finally decided to kill the power to the system and get some sleep. Perhaps, in a few hours she might get a response to her pounding.

It was while she was sitting there in the dark, finding it impossible to sleep, that an idea began to grow in her mind. If the access tube was only damaged, not completely blown, it might hold air for a short period of time, enough for her to crawl to the hatch on the inner hull and get back into the ship. She had enough air to fill the tube and her pod several times over. If the tube would hold air at all, she'd only have to deal with a nasty drop in pressure. She knew she could survive just fine at fairly low pressures, and in any case, if the tube wouldn't hold air at all, the veteran gunners had told her she could survive vacuum for a short period of time, hopefully enough to close the hatch again and repressurize her pod. What she'd do after that—she'd worry about that if and when the time came.

She programmed her computer to let the pod pressure drop, even if it went all the way to vacuum. If it did, she didn't want the computer trying to protect her, blowing air into the pod and preventing her from closing the hatch.

Luckily the pod hatch opened outward, so she wouldn't have to fight the pressure in the pod. She made sure her restraint harness was secure—when she blew the hatch it wouldn't do to have her sucked out through it—then she overrode the safety interlocks on the hatch, paused for a moment of indecision, and blew the hatch.

It made an awful racket, her ears popped painfully, and at the rapid drop in pressure a dense fog suddenly condensed in the air around her. But the pressure stabilized at a tolerable level, and out in the access tube she heard the whining, screaming sound of a high-pressure leak. The pressure started to drop further, quickly, but not instantly. Good!

She tapped the keys on her console, instructing the computer to start feeding air into the pod. *Critical hazard warning,* the computer said. *Terminal decompression in seventeen minutes and counting.*

"Good," she said aloud to no one, popped the buckles on her restraints and pushed out into the access tube.

No lights, except for the telltale on the hatch on the inner hull. That was good too.

Crawling in the dark she discovered by touch that the tube had buckled about halfway to the inner hull, and there she could feel a strong breeze, and the scream of the air leak was deafening. She crawled past it carefully, got to the inner hatch, checked the gauge there and almost cried aloud when she saw there was air pressure on the other side.

In the background she heard her computer issuing another warning, though the scream of the air leak drowned out the message. She overrode the safety interlocks, palmed the hatch release, and pushed. Nothing!

She realized the problem instantly. The hatch opened away from her, but the pressure on this side of the hatch was about half an atmosphere. She was pushing against a couple of tonnes of pressure. Somehow she had to equalize the pressure on both sides of the hatch.

She crawled quickly back into the pod, instructed the computer to run the pod pressure up as high as it could—with the leak it wouldn't be able to get far, but it would try. *Critical hazard warning,* the computer said. *Terminal decompression in three minutes and counting.* This had better work, she realized.

She crawled back down the tube to the hatch on the inner hull. The pressure differential was less now, but still not enough. She pushed, strained desperately, cursed at the hatch.

She crawled back up the tube into the pod again, started tearing at the cushion on her seat, pulled it loose—it was made to be detached for maintenance. *Critical hazard warning,* the computer said. *Terminal decompression in one minute and counting.*

She crawled back into the tube to the leak, stopped there, and in the dark slid the cushion along the wall of the tube until it suddenly stuck in the hole, and the scream of the leak changed pitch.

Her ears popped, and at the far end of the tube she saw a thin sliver of light as the inner hatch cracked open spontaneously. She moved quickly, knowing once the pod reserves ran out the pressure would drop and the hatch would close again.

The hatch was wide open now, but just as she reached it her ears popped again, and the hatch started to close. She shouted, kicked at it with all her strength, forced it open and spilled out into her station, floating in zero-G toward a console, tumbling wildly head over heels. The hatch on the inner hull slammed shut with a thump as the pressure on the other side dropped. She slammed into the console, caught hold of it and hung onto it for several long seconds to catch her breath.

She spotted a big crease in the plating of the deck; a wrinkle actually. She held onto the console to keep from floating away and traced the crease with her eyes. It ran across the deck, up one bulkhead, back across the deck overhead, then down the other bulkhead. Just before they'd lost power, *Cinesstar*'s internal gravity must have given out in that section of the ship. One side of the crease had been subjected to a lot of acceleration, while on the other side *Cinesstar*'s internal fields had compensated the gravity nicely. Even if the effect had lasted for just a moment, she was probably alive only because her pod had compensated the fields around her. She'd heard about unlucky crewmembers who'd—

Her stomach suddenly climbed up into her throat. There was a big mess strapped in a couch at a far console—from where she stood she could make out the chevrons on one sleeve, realized the mess was what remained of Syda. She vomited all over the console in front of her, and in zero-G the contents of her stomach floated about and started sticking to everything.

Poor Syda! She didn't want to go any closer—but she decided then she was going to make someone pay for this. They'd been double-crossed, betrayed by their own side, and someone was going to pay.

But the first step was to see what was left of *Cinesstar*. There had to be other gunners in her station who were still alive, and maybe she could help rescue them. And then somewhere someone had to be organizing the crew. Somewhere, someone.

••••

York ran down the corridors of the ship, cut through walls and ran out into space. But this time there were no big people running madly about with him, screaming at everyone and everything, tearing at themselves, crying and sobbing, pleading for mercy. He was lost and alone and there was no place to go, and he just knew he was going to spend forever searching for a way home.

"York."

He jumped at the sound of his name, turned, found one of the big people towering over him. One of her arms was missing at the shoulder, one leg at the hip, a big, ugly gash in the side of her head. She floated in front of him, and he cringed away from her.

"Don't be afraid," she said. "It's me—Maggie. I won't hurt you."

He did recognize her, but he didn't know from where.

"Come," she said. "Let's talk. It's not as bad as it looks. And I think I can help you. But you can't be twelve years old anymore." She held out her hand. "Come with me."

••••

Alsa Yan snapped awake, peered blindly into the darkness, curled her fingers reassuringly around the grip of the small gun, hugged a girder tightly to keep from floating away in zero gravity. Something had awakened her, probably one of those fucking marines trying to get at him again. She waited, tried not to hold her breath, tried not to make any noise by breathing either. The marines were better at this than her.

There he was—or maybe she—a shadow, moving slowly and carefully across sickbay. Alsa waited in her shadow, waited until the other shadow was within arm's reach, then reached out carefully with the gun and pressed the muzzle softly against the back of the shadow's head. "It didn't work," she said. "You can't have him."

The shadow spoke in a woman's voice, "We promised him. We gotta keep that promise."

Alsa didn't see it coming—a big, meaty hand grabbed her by the back of the neck, and another deflected the gun upward. She squeezed the trigger anyway, the small grav gun kicked and a slug pinged off the deck. She struggled, but there were marines all over her, most of them a lot bigger than her, and a lot better at this kind of thing than her. They didn't even hurt her.

Someone flicked on the lights—Palevi. "You can't have him," she said. "He's still alive."

Palevi shook his head. "Is he really alive, or are you just guessing?"

"Statistically the odds are—"

"Fuck statistics," Palevi growled. "I made him a promise."

"You bloodthirsty son-of-a-bitch!"

The muscles in Palevi's jaw tightened. "We ain't animals, ma'am. We could have taken you a long time ago, but you were a friend of his and we know he wouldn't want you hurt. So we did it the hard way, without hurting no one."

"But you're going to hurt him."

Palevi flinched, and she realized how hard this was for him. "No, ma'am. I ain't gonna hurt him. You've got him sealed up in one of them tanks, and I promised him I wouldn't ever let that happen. I'm just going to let him die clean like he wanted."

"Does he have to die at all?" a new voice interjected. The empress floated into the room and the marines backed away from her, gave her a clear path, probably the only person in the universe to whom they would pay such deference. "If there's a chance he's still alive, then he's the only person who can get us out of this."

Palevi shook his head. "I ain't leaving him in the tanks."

"I'm not suggesting you do." The empress looked at Alsa. "I'm suggesting the good doctor here bring him out of the tanks, bring him back to us as a healthy and whole leader."

Alsa shook her head violently. "I can't. He's a mess. You don't realize how bad it is. And with the facilities I have here he might not survive. Regrowth might not take; he's had so much of it lately. Speed-healing might not work; he's had a lot of that too."

The empress nodded calmly. "I understand. But the fact remains that if you don't, then these marines will most certainly see to it that he dies. And even if they didn't force your hand, he's the only man who has any chance of getting us back to a place where you would have the proper facilities."

Alsa closed her eyes and buried her face in her hands. She had no choice. "Fuck!"

••••

York slammed awake, sat up in bed, ignored the sideways tug of the gravity field of his cabin deck as it interfered with that of his grav bunk. He hesitated for just an instant, wondering how he'd gotten back to his cabin, wondering why everything seemed so normal. Then he tore frantically at his shirt until he could see his bare chest. The skin there was pink and healthy.

He threw back the covers, found to his great relief that his right leg was still whole, with no indication it had ever been missing. He wiggled the toes, they felt fine.

It had all been a dream, he realized, an insane dream . . .

••••

Alsa looked sadly at her handiwork. All that remained of York was a bit of tissue, a piece of bone, a smear of blood.

The technician held out the open body bag. "I'll scrape him into it."

Alsa looked at what was left of York, shook her head. "That's not him. There's nothing left of him." She reached out, scraped the bits of tissue into a pan, turned toward the disposal can . . .

York slammed awake, sat up in his bunk, struggled for long seconds while mentally he flipped back and forth between the two realities: it was a dream. No it wasn't . . . yes it was . . . no it wasn't . . . This time he wasn't going to be fooled. Not by any of them. It was real, the body bag dream was a dream, but this was real. He started crying with relief. It wasn't a dream. He wasn't insane. No, he was insane, but that was all right, as long as it was real . . .

••••

York could see that Alsa was tired. She could barely hold herself up as she described all the miraculous work she'd done to him: regrowing his eardrums, one artificial lung—the list went on and on. When she finished York just said, "Thanks, Alsa. Go get some sleep."

Alsa stood to leave, but York stopped her with an afterthought. "Tell Olin and Anda and Maggie I want to see them."

Alsa nodded tiredly. "Rame's in sickbay, hardly better off than you, certainly no better at being a patient, been running damage control from sickbay. Gant's all right; I'll tell her . . ." Alsa hesitated, then blurted out, "Maggie's dead."

York closed his eyes. "Who else?"

Alsa spoke mechanically. "Paris, Straegga, the Dubye woman, a lot of others."

"What about d'Hart, and Cassandra, and that servant of the empress?"

"They're okay."

York nodded. "Tell my officers, meeting in my office in half an hour."

Alsa shook her head. "Your office is under vacuum, along with the bridge and most of officer's country."

York said. "Then tell them we'll meet in the marine CO's office. I'll use that as a command post until further notice."

York hesitated. It was time to have a pointed talk with the empress. Etiquette required that he go to her, but . . . "Fuck that," he said, and Alsa's eyebrows rose. "Bring the empress to me there."

••••

York waited in the marine CO's office, trying to contain his anger. He wanted to shout at someone, but he was going to be speaking to an empress, and he doubted that shouting at her would do any good.

At the knock on the door he spoke through his implants. "Enter."

Palevi opened the door, stepped through with parade-ground etiquette and held it for the empress. She stepped through uncertainly and said, "You wished to see me, Captain?"

He stood and said, "Yes, Your Majesty, please have a seat."

She sat down in the same chair she'd used when she gave him command of the ship.

"Will there be anything else, sir?" Palevi asked.

"No, Sergeant, you may go."

Palevi closed the door quietly and York stood staring at it for a moment. Behind him, the empress said, "I know you—"

York spun toward her and said, "Don't talk."

She paused with her mouth open, then closed it carefully and gave him a dubious look.

"Don't talk unless you're going to tell me what this is about. Don't talk unless you're going to tell me why you and your empire just murdered a third of my crew."

She looked down at the floor, wouldn't meet his eyes. "I'm sorry about your crew, but I can't tell you what this is about. There are too many lives at—"

"You can't tell me? You're killing my people and you can't tell me why?"

"They're my people too."

"Then start acting like it, god damn it."

There, he'd shouted at an empress, though it didn't make him feel any better.

She stood, making no attempt to hide her anger. "Whether you believe me or not, Captain, I am working to achieve something that will benefit the greater good for generations. I am saddened by those deaths, and had I anticipated how far certain factions in the empire would go, I would have warned you. But I did not, and I truly regret that."

She walked past him, opened the door and stepped out into the corridor, then closed it with a soft click.

••••

Cinesstar was a mess. While York was in the tanks, and then under the knife, his officers had organized damage control teams, cataloged and analyzed the extent of the damage, even begun repairs. They showed him vids of the interior and exterior of the ship. Apparently, his special little computer program hadn't been able to put them into transition all by itself. It had tried several times, come close, would have failed, except for the last try when, apparently, right in the middle of diverting all of *Cinesstar*'s power into a transition attempt, she took a direct hit from a large warhead—estimated yield strength two hundred megatonnes. It should have disintegrated *Cinesstar*, but it turned out to be just the extra kick needed to blow her into up-transition. *Cinesstar* left the destructive force of the warhead behind, though before doing so she'd had a big piece of her bow blown away, and even more melted.

They weren't in transition long, traveled only a short distance across the Sarasan system before *Cinesstar* shut down completely and spontaneously down-transited. What remained of Third Fleet— hurt badly at Aagerbanne, then further by *Cinesstar* and the feddie hunter-killer—withdrew from the system some hours later.

Rame finished the briefing with, "We're close enough to monitor Sarasan's transmitter splash, and apparently no one knows we're here. They're not completely sure we were destroyed, but they think we were. Highest probability kind of thing."

They were meeting in the wardroom used for marine briefings. "What about that feddie hunter-killer?" York asked.

"That's real curious," Gant said. "I reviewed the scan log of the battle—that feddie could have burned us easily, but she didn't. She kept taking on more difficult targets, actually helped us quite a bit, though I doubt she meant to. In the end she took a big one herself, went out with all hands."

Cinesstar's computer systems were a mess, but actually quite repairable. Almost every unit had sustained some radiation damage, but by scavenging circuitry from some units, they could make others operable. Without access to more spare parts they'd be operating below the margins neces- sary for combat, but Cinesstar wasn't going into combat anytime soon.

"My crew?" York asked. Clearly Alsa was functioning on chemicals to stay conscious.

"Thirty-two percent dead. Almost all of the survivors injured in some way, half seriously."

"I need all survivors functional, even if they are wounded. Do what you can."

Alsa just nodded.

"Structural integrity?"

Nemkov answered. "We lost about thirty meters off the bow, but what's left is in fairly good shape, structurally. Of course we've been hulled in . . ." He consulted his terminal, ". . . twenty- seven places, and half the ship's under vacuum, but we can patch most of that. With only two ex- ceptions, which we're fixing now, we're structurally sound. She won't fall apart under drive."

"Drones?"

"That's the good news. Since we didn't launch them we didn't lose any. Some minor damage here and there, but we should have them all active in a matter of hours."

"Good," York said. He looked at Gant. "As soon as we're done here launch those that are functional on passive. I want you to start monitoring everything around us—this system, the inter- stellar space around it, the works."

She nodded.

"Weapons and shields?"

Jakobee was now in charge of fire control. "We've got about thirty percent of our ordnance reserves left. Turret one went with the bow, and of course we've got no shielding there so we're vulnerable to frontal attack. Turret seven's a wash; we're scavenging it for parts. Varying amounts of damage to turrets three, four, and eight, all of it repairable. The aft launch room is undamaged and fully operational, though we don't have enough power to put a warhead into transition. Defen- sively, with the exception of the bow, the pods and shielding are in good shape; ninety percent effectiveness there. Providing power so they can work is another matter."

York nodded. They were all looking at him for answers, but all he could give them was a knowing look and an authoritative nod. They needed to think he knew what he was doing. "What if we had the facilities of a small navy yard?"

Jakobee frowned, answered carefully as if the question were purely a hypothetical one. "Well, sir, we could probably mount some moderately effective shielding on the bow, certainly repair turret seven, all depending on the size of the yard and its facilities."

York looked at Cappik. "Power? Drive?"

"Transition drive's shot . . ." He raised an eyebrow, reluctantly playing along with York's fantasy. ". . . though with the facilities of a decent repair yard we could fix her. Sublight drive took some damage, but not so much we can't repair her here on our own. Power plant's the problem. Port chamber's a total loss, hardly even good for spares. Starboard's no worse off than she was before, which ain't saying much. And Centerline's nonfunctional, though repairable with access to a yard."

Cappik leaned forward. "Starboard's all we got, Captain. She'll put out enough power for sublight drive, but we'll be limited to about a thousand gravities. And no way in hell we'll make transition. Certainly no power for combat: no shields—except a little for small debris deflection. And of course no real weapons; we won't be throwing anything at anyone with our transition batteries."

Cappik let that hang, basically a death sentence. Without transition capability they were stranded in the Sarasan system, at the mercy of the next warship to come along. But there was a chance, a faint chance, even if the rest of them didn't see it. All he had to do was discard all his values, betray every quality he held dear, abandon his sense of honor, his code of justice, his convictions, his principles, his ethics. And then he had to convince them to do the same.

York looked them over carefully, asked, "If I got us access to the Sarasan Navy Yard, could you make this ship transition-worthy, combat-worthy?"

For the first time, they realized he was serious, and Cappik spoke cautiously. "I'm not familiar with the facilities at Sarasan, but she's only a subsector base, so I'll guess we can do something with Centerline, maybe get enough out of her to make transition, with the help of Starboard." He shook his head. "We need a full-sized yard to really repair Starboard, and Port needs to be replaced. Probably all we can do with Sarasan's facilities is patch them enough to get out of here."

An uncomfortable silence followed, until Cappik finally asked the question all of them wanted to ask. "But, Captain, you can't just get on the horn and ask Sarasan for permission to use their facilities. We're under a shoot-on-sight order. They'll burn us before you say word one."

York nodded, gave Cappik a look he'd seen Telyekev use, a look that said York didn't approve of stupid questions. It was unfair of him to do that to Cappik, but for what he was about to tell them, he wanted no argument, no discussion, no debate. "That's true, Mister Cappik," York said without emotion. "But then I don't intend to ask their permission."

They looked at him as if he'd just told them he was going to be the next emperor. "Now to do that, Mister Cappik," he continued, "we have to take Sarasan. And to take Sarasan I need sublight drive and as much of this ship operational as possible." He looked at his watch. "I expect all repairs complete in twenty hours."

He looked at Rame. "I need bridge crew, so get McGeahn up here, if she's still alive. I think she's in one of the pod crews. We'll see if she's any good as an officer."

Now for the clincher. He looked at Alsa. "Red Richard's in the tanks, if I remember correctly. Thaw him out. I want to talk to him."

That had the desired effect.

••••

York took a tour of the ship. He didn't need to; he could see everything on vids and damage control reports. But what the crew needed most now was to see him, healthy, whole, in command, giving knowing nods and authoritative looks. He knew of the rumors: *the old man was going renegade, maybe go pirate*. There was no help for it, since their own comrades had double-crossed them anyway. But still, it needed much discussion, and they needed to see that he wasn't half-insane with grief or injuries. They needed to see the purpose in his eyes, the cold-blooded intent and the will to survive. And to give them that he needed to avoid thinking about Maggie, and Frank, and Paris, and the others.

Half way through the tour Rame pulled him to one side, held a small com out to him and said, "Captain, Commander Gant. She says it's important."

York took the com and held it to his ear. "Yes, Commander?"

"I've got some funny data here, Captain. We've picked up indications of scattered, but heavy, fighting about three light-years from here. It's all in free space, not near any system. At this range we can't really tell who's who. All we can pick up are a lot of up and down-transitions and some big warhead detonations. Indications are that there are somewhere between fifty and two hundred ships mixing it up pretty heavily. The funny thing is—it's all coming from the direction of Third Fleet's withdrawal. They must have run into something unpleasant. Sorry to disturb you, sir, but I thought you should know about it."

"Thank you, Commander. Please continue to monitor the situation closely. I'd like regular updates, and let me know immediately of any changes."

••••

York slammed awake, sat up in bed, caught himself before slipping into any hallucinations about dreams and reality. Maggie had come to visit him in his dreams, or maybe nightmares, he didn't know what to call them.

Maggie! And Paris! They hadn't been laid to rest properly, he realized. He unstrapped from his bed, controlling reflexes long accustomed to a grav bunk, wishing he had a grav bunk. They'd gotten pressure back in his cabin—though they were still working on the bridge—and under zero-G the captain slept strapped to a regular bed.

York pulled up the disposition reports for Maggie and Paris. Paris was in cold storage in the aft isolation locker, and Maggie was . . .

Maggie was . . .

Maggie was . . . in tank one-two-six.

. . . tank one-two-six . . .

••••

"You lied to me," York screamed as he floated into sickbay.

Alsa looked up from her desk, blinked groggily at him.

"You lied to me. She's alive, god damn it! She's alive and you stuck her in a fucking tank."

Alsa shook her head, blinked at him, then understanding showed in her face. "Ya. I lied. But I—"

"Get her out of there," York screamed. "Get her out of there and let her die clean."

Alsa shook her head. "I'll do no such thing."

York started to shout epithets, but she cut him off, said, "Shut up and listen to me." She lifted a hand and raised one finger. "First. Statistically, she's dead anyway. Less than a one percent chance of recovery."

"I don't care. I want her out of there."

Alsa raised another finger. "Second. It doesn't matter what you want. Maggie gave me specific permission to tank her if it ever came to this. She said as long as there was a chance, she wanted to go on fighting. So that's all there is to it; her personal preferences happen to be quite different from yours. I'm sorry I lied to you, but I knew you wouldn't be able to handle it. As for Maggie, don't waste your breath arguing with me. Those were her wishes. Period."

York kept having dreams about Maggie, and as long as she was dead he could chalk them up to dreams. But if she was in the tanks, maybe half-alive—

No! Alsa said she was dead. York repeated that all the way back to his cabin.

27

The First Treason

YORK WOULD RATHER be wearing marine armor than a standard vac suit, but for the show they were about to put on that wouldn't look at all right. Without station-based heavy equipment they'd been unable to repressurize the bridge, along with a good twenty percent of the rest of the ship—but that would make it look even better.

They'd replaced Maggie at the helm with a spacer named Eldinow from Cappik's original shipyard crew. He'd been qualified on helm controls years ago so he could shuttle big vessels in and out of the repair docks at Dumark station, and he had quite a few hours logged—he'd never piloted in transition or under combat, but Cappik swore he was smart and kept his head when things got dicey.

McGeahn had replaced Paris at the com. Her pod had taken a hit, and she'd almost bought it, was missing one leg at the knee, swore it didn't matter, though it looked odd to see the empty leg of her vac suit distended under pressure. Her station commander gave her good marks under fire, though she was showing some of the bravado of a rookie who'd just survived her first nasty one.

"Miss McGeahn," York said. "Put me on allship."

"Aye, aye, sir. Channel three, sir."

"And tell Cappik to stand by."

York made a small speech to the crew. He didn't say anything worth listening to, was careful not to include any facts. Red Richard was conscious now and probably listening to every word. York hadn't spoken to Richard yet, needed Richard to form his own opinion of what was going on. With Palevi's help he'd carefully chosen Richard's cell so it was close to the brig guard office. Then for brig watch he and Palevi had chosen marines known to gossip a lot. By now they'd talked over the whole situation, Richard had probably overheard most of it, and was nicely up-to-date. And he'd probably reached the same conclusion as everyone else. It was imperative Richard believe the right things, or he'd never cooperate the way York needed.

York finished his little speech, switched off allship and opened a line to Engineering. "Are you ready, Mister Cappik?"

"Yes, sir. I got a fire lit in Starboard and I'm ready to light up Centerline. Soon as you give me the word I'll goose 'em both. It'll look a bit like a flare, especially with all the shit we'll start spewing all over the system, and you'll have sublight capability."

"Very good, Mister Cappik. Thank you."

Cappik grinned. "Captain, if they don't blow us to hell and back they're going to court-martial us for sure."

York grinned back at him. "They gotta catch us first."

"Right you are, sir. I gotta tell you, sir. It's been one hell of a ride."

"It's just starting, Mister Cappik." York looked at his screens then glanced around the bridge. They were all watching him, waiting for him to give the nod, trusting his judgment that they had a good and proper excuse for *high treason*. York looked at Cappik one more time and nodded, "Execute."

"Aye, aye, sir. Powering Starboard, sir."

The readings on the starboard chamber rose quickly and the feel of the ship returned—she was alive again. When Starboard reached the maximum power Cappik was comfortable with, the engineer threw a switch and dumped a big pulse of energy into the Sarasan system. To a casual observer it would appear to be a transition flare. Immediately, the readings on the centerline chamber started to rise.

"Gravity up," York barked. "Helm, you've got the drive plan; execute."

The readings on Centerline leveled off at something above a large trickle. The chamber was too badly damaged to sustain ignition, but by feeding some power into it from Starboard they could, as Cappik had put it, ". . . spew shit all over the system," and hopefully look like a ship in serious trouble.

Gant read off their status casually. "Range: point-six-seven AUs. Velocity: point-one-five lights. Deceleration: just over one thousand gravities. ETA at Sarasan Station: one point-oh-three hours."

They were close; thanks to the coordinates Leonavich had fed them. Their little transition hop had hardly changed that, though it had left them in a fairly eccentric orbit around Sarasan. It was important that Sarasan not have a lot of time to think about the data they were getting. York had also chosen to make his move when Sarasan was on night watch, which might help in some small way.

"Sir," McGeahn shouted. "I'm getting a demand for a recognition sequence."

"Ignore it," York barked. "We have to time this right."

••••

"I can't read their signature, Lieutenant. It's a mess. They're throwing radiation all over the system. They gotta be in some kind of bad trouble."

Lieutenant Steela looked over the technician's shoulder. She could see that the unidentified ship was in serious trouble. She keyed her implants. "Com, any response from that bogie?"

"No, ma'am."

Steela stared at the data on the technician's screen. "Why didn't we pick up his transition wake long ago?"

The technician shrugged. "In the shape he's in he probably came in at a crawl, not much wake to read."

Plausible, but Steela still didn't like it. "Bring station defenses to Watch Condition Yellow. Tell Power we may need shield reserves without warning. And wake Commodore Quae."

The technician looked at her and grimaced. "You sure you want to do that, Ma'am?"

Quae's temper was well known, but under the circumstances she had no choice. "I'm sure. And after that, put a couple of interceptors on standby."

Steela paced back and forth in Sarasan Station's command center, stopping behind each seated technician, looking over the tech's shoulder at the screens on his console. The station's defenses were fully operational, and combined with Sarasan's orbital weapons platforms, no single ship could harm them. But still, Steela didn't like this at all.

"Lieutenant, the commodore wants to talk to you. And he ain't happy."

Steela went to her own console, sat down and took the call. Quae's unhappy face appeared on one of her screens. "I'm told we're not under attack, Lieutenant. So why was I awakened in the middle of the night?"

"I'm sorry to inconvenience you, sir. But we have an unidentified ship on close approach. We're—"

"Well then follow standard procedures. There's no need to wake me for that."

"Yes, sir, but we haven't been able to get a response from them." Out of the corner of her eye she caught one of the technicians waving at her. To Quae she said, "Excuse me, sir. Something's happening." Quae nodded and she switched circuits quickly.

The technician said, "I just got an identification sequence, Lieutenant. *H.M.S. Wolf's Blood.* A medium cruiser. She was listed as missing in action in sector four about two months ago. Her cipher codes correspond to those in effect at that time."

"Thank you," Steela said to the technician, then switched back to Quae and relayed the information to him.

"Well, there you have it," Quae said angrily. "Follow standard procedures. Board her and confirm the identification. It's simple, Lieutenant, and there was no need to wake me in the first place. Now I'm going back to bed." Quae cut the circuit without waiting for a reply.

Steela tried to remain calm. The technician shook his head sympathetically, and gave her an I-told-you-so look.

••••

Commodore Meelas Quae sat up groggily in response to the unpleasantly demanding chime coming from his terminal. He glanced first at the time, then cursed out loud. That idiot woman had awakened him again. He hit the receive switch, and as her image appeared he shouted, "What is it now?"

"I'm sorry to awake you again, sir. But the captain of that ship refuses to allow us to board her. And he now demands to speak to you personally. I tried to——"

Quae cut her off. "There was no need to wake me for this. You can tell whatever his name is that I'm sleeping."

Steela nodded. "Very well, sir. I'll tell Admiral Lord Leukoy you are not to be disturbed."

Quae's heart skipped a beat as Steela reached for the receive switch on her console. "Wait! Wait, Lieutenant. Admiral? Lord?"

"Yes, sir. Rear Admiral Lord Leukoy."

It wouldn't do his career any good to anger a member of the nobility, especially an admiral. "Put him through immediately."

"Yes, sir."

Quae gasped, flinched away from the terminal as the monster appeared on his screen, and it took him a moment to realize he was looking at the faceless visage of a vac suit helmet, not that of some bug-eyed creature out of a nightmare. Other than the two camera pickups on either side, spaced much wider than human eyes, there were no features on the face of the helmet, and it was disconcerting to carry on a conversation with something so inhuman. Even the opaqued visor of marine armor gave more semblance of humanity.

The faceless helmet leaned toward the pickup and spoke quite calmly. "Commodore. I regret we have to meet under these circumstances. However, I must beg your indulgence. We have serious difficulties here, and any help you can provide to expedite our arrival would be most appreciated."

Quae relaxed. The man seemed most reasonable. "Certainly, Your Lordship. What can I do?"

The helmet nodded. "You can instruct that overzealous, young lieutenant of yours to waive the normal board-and-identify requirements. That would save us considerable time—and lives."

Quae wanted to accommodate the man, but then the station log would show he had personally authorized a violation of standard security procedures. "Well now, Your Lordship, that's difficult to do. Lieutenant Steela and I are only following the procedures required by——"

Quae jumped as the image on his screen shook violently. And while he had never served on a ship-of-the-line, he knew the ship's internal gravity fields should compensate for any motion involved, and the fact that it didn't was an indication of dire circumstances.

The admiral forgot Quae, slapped a switch on his console, though in his preoccupation with his difficulties he forgot to switch Quae out of the circuit. *Heavy damage aft*, someone shouted into the circuit. *Starboard just blew. Radiation hazard on decks G through K. Twelve missing, presumed dead.*

The admiral shouted orders into the circuit, though the transmission was garbled and to Quae his commands were unintelligible. Quae saw hurried activity behind the man, then the admiral switched the link out of the circuit and returned his attention to Quae.

The admiral leaned slowly toward the pickup, his shoulders hunched. Quae could easily imagine the expression on his face, and when he spoke it came out little better than a growl. "Listen to me, Quae. I've got two chambers down, and only one chamber left operating at half power, and it's flooding us all with a lethal dose of radiation. Our tanks are going bad on us, and they're already overflowing with critically wounded. I've got wounded laying in the corridors, at least in what corridors I've got left to put wounded in. I've lost thirty meters off my bow, half my ship's under vacuum, including critical operating stations like the goddamned bridge. We've run out of vac suits and we're losing life support in the rest of the ship. And every minute you delay me costs me more lives. Now I want clearance to dock, and I want it now, or I swear to you, Quae, by whatever gods exist, I'll personally preside at your court-martial. Do you understand me?"

The admiral's voice had risen slowly until the last had come out in a frightening shout. Quae's career was on the line here, and there was no doubt the admiral could, and would, carry out the promised threat. "Well, Quae," the admiral demanded. "I'm waiting."

Quae gave him a slight, but respectful, bow. "I'll instruct my subordinates to allow you to proceed immediately to an appropriate dock." Now, Quae thought, if there was any blame to be had he needed to shift as much as possible away from himself. "And please don't blame poor Lieutenant Steela. She's young, and not terribly creative, and she was just following standard procedures."

"Of course," the admiral barked. "Just get me that docking clearance, and tell your medical people to be ready for us. We're going to overload your facilities."

Quae nodded. "As you wish, Your Lordship."

Quae put in a call to Steela, instructed her to waive the standard procedures and allow the ship to dock.

"But, sir," she pleaded. "There's something funny about this whole situation. We should have detected them long before this, but they registered no incoming transition wake and—"

"God damn it!" Quae shouted. "I don't want any argument out of you, young woman. I'm giving you an order, and I expect you to obey it now, without hesitation. Is that clear?"

The young woman's jaw muscles clenched. "Of course, Commodore. I didn't mean to—"

Quae interrupted her again, then berated her for several minutes. He only let her go when he realized he had little time left to prepare for Admiral Leukoy's arrival. It wouldn't do to greet the admiral improperly attired. Quae decided that something functional was appropriate—he should look like a working station commander—though his uniform should be clean and newly pressed.

Quae put on a fresh uniform, combed his hair, glanced in the mirror, and made it up to station command just as Leukoy's ship entered the main dock.

"Shit!" one of the technicians said. "Look at her. She's a mess."

Looking at the image of the crippled ship on the screen, Quae felt no need to reprimand the man for his language. The docking gantries locked the *Wolf's Blood* in place, then the station crew went to work coupling to her main air lock. Quae decided to meet Admiral Leukoy at the lock. He left station command, walked quickly to the lock and waited patiently for it to be sealed and opened.

The word *Clear* came out of a speaker over the lock, Quae heard it cycle through pressure equalization, then the doors burst open and he was almost overrun by combat marines in plast armor.

"Out of our way," one of them shouted. "We've got wounded here."

Of course! The admiral would think of his wounded first. Quae stood to one side while the marines hustled several grav stretchers past him, each covered by a contamination shield. He waited until the marines were well past him, turned to look after them, noticed that one group had stopped at the end of the corridor and cycled open the contamination shield.

"Sir?"

Quae turned toward the voice: a marine in combat armor, with sergeant's stripes stenciled on his arms. "See here, Sergeant," Quae said to the man. "Is that safe, opening a contamination shield in an unprotected corridor?"

The sergeant motioned for Quae to step into the air lock. Quae did so, and asked again, "But is that safe?" He turned once more to look back.

With the contamination shield open, Quae now saw that the stretcher contained not a wounded crewmember, but portable assault weapons.

To Quae's credit, he made the connection almost instantly. *The corridor cameras!* he thought. But the marines had chosen their position well, a blind spot at the intersection between two corridors. And Quae had been drawn into another blind spot just inside the air lock. He turned desperately back toward the marine sergeant, only to look down the muzzle of a large gun.

••••

Steela looked unhappily at her screen, and it hit her like a slap in the face. Quickly she pulled up the data on *H.M.S. Wolf's Blood.* A *medium* cruiser, it said. "That's no medium cruiser out there."

She turned to one of the technicians and shouted, "We've been boarded. Watch Condition Red. Seal off all—"

She never finished the last order; the control room hatch exploded inward and a piece of shrapnel took off most of her head.

••••

Seated at his console in the marine CO's office, York felt helpless as he listened to the *crump* of heavy weapons reverberating through the hull of the station. His conscience told him he should be in the thick of it, risking his life along with his people; but as captain he no longer had that luxury. His conscience also reminded him they were killing their own comrades, under his orders.

"Captain," Yagell shouted over the command circuit. She was in Sarasan's main command center. "They got her onto red too quick. We've got control of the command center and most other vital functions, but they've still got the main power plant. We're going to have to take her the hard way."

York spoke into his com. "They've got to have an auxiliary Station Command down there, and from there they can take control of a lot of the station's resources. Self-destruct the orbital weapons platforms before they think to use them against us, and blow the transition transmitter before they get a call out for help."

It turned out that Yagell, even from the command center, couldn't induce such self-inflicted damage on the station without some high-level clearance codes. But the two command centers were not designed to war with one another, so Yagell jammed up the station's operations, disabling her transition batteries and weapons platforms and transmitter long enough for the marines to go out in *Cinesstar's* assault boats and do the job manually. One of the assault boats went over the outer hull of the station, shot up each of its transition batteries in turn, while the other boat rendezvoused with each of the four big weapons platforms, planted charges, then detonated them from a distance. That part of the job took less than an hour, the rest took a lot longer.

In the end, the station was neither prepared nor equipped to defend itself against an assault from within, especially against two hundred fully-equipped, seasoned marine regulars. But the fighting was ugly, and it wasn't until four hours later that they took Sarasan's core power plant. Even before that, York put Cappik to work on *Cinesstar*'s repairs.

••••

"That fighting's moved a lot closer, sir," Gant said, looking at York from one of his screens. "It's within a light-year now."

York heard the faint thud of a heavy recoilless as somewhere the marines cleared out a pocket of resistance. It made him sick to think of the lives he was expending, the people he was murdering. They were probably good comrades all, many of whom he might have fought beside at one time or another, and whose only crime now was to be caught on the opposite side of a web of intrigue about which he didn't even know enough to give them a reasonable explanation as to why he was betraying them.

"We've also spotted an incoming transition wake, range a little under two light-years, coming in from the direction of Aagerbanne, ETA about a day and a half, no information as to size or type of ship."

They'd hardly begun repairs and were already running out of time. "Very good, Commander. Keep me informed."

No sooner had York cut the circuit than his terminal chimed, and when he answered his yeoman said, "He's here, sir."

York nodded. "Send him in."

The door to his office opened and, escorted by two marines, Red Richard sauntered in. York had given Palevi instructions to leave Richard uncuffed and unrestrained. York told the marines, "Go."

The marines saluted crisply, turned and closed the door behind them. York opened the bottom drawer of his desk, pulled out a bottle of 'trate, looked at Richard and asked, "Join me?"

Richard smiled expansively. "Most certainly, Yer Excellency."

"I'm no *Excellency*," York said. "Captain will do."

"As you wish, Cap'm."

York handed Richard a healthy shot of diluted 'trate. Richard lifted his glass. "To yer health, Cap'm. And to success in the ventures yer plannin'."

They both took a gulp, then York asked, "And why would you think I'm planning any ventures?"

Richard shrugged, looked around at the walls as if they were all the proof he needed. "Well now, Cap'm. Seems to me you'd best be plannin' somethin'. 'Cause what yer superiors got planned fer you ain't too healthy a career move."

"You've been listening to rumors."

Richard shook his head in a friendly, conspiratorial way. "I don't have to listen to rumors, Cap'm. I just got to look at this bucket yer sittin' in, and what they did to her. And I just got to listen to all the artillery yer exercising in this here station. I suppose a quick look at the body count for the station would be pretty interesting too, wouldn't you say?"

"Yes. I suppose it would."

"You got yerself into some interesting circumstances, Cap'm."

"Yes, interesting."

"Let me see now." Richard ticked points off on his fingers. "The empire double-crossed you, even though you had her nibs on board." York wondered if he was the only one who understood the empire double-crossed them precisely *because* they had the empress on board. Richard continued, "They tried to burn you, killed a third of yer crew, blew bloody hell out of yer ship. But they made one mistake, Cap'm."

Richard paused for dramatic effect, expecting York to prompt him, so York obliged. "And that was?"

Richard grinned. "They didn't finish the job, Cap'm. Butcher Ballin, the marine SDO, a man with a million crown price on his head, more'n twenty years of combat experience—now Cap'm, I'd say yer one hell of a survivor. And if I decided to kill you, I'd be smart enough to make sure I did a full and complete job of it, 'cause yer one man I wouldn't want comin' back from the dead. I just got one question. Tell me, Cap'm. Are you out fer revenge, fer retribution? Or are you out to survive?"

Until that moment York hadn't thought about that carefully. "I don't know exactly where I'm going from here. But I do intend to survive. The dead are dead. The only thing we can be certain of is there'll be more dead tomorrow."

Richard thought about that carefully and nodded. "Good, Cap'm. Good. I think you and me can work together."

York lifted an eyebrow skeptically. "Really? Why would we want to work together?"

Richard laughed. "Come on, Cap'm. Why else did you thaw me out? And by the way, that wasn't a very hospitable way of treatin' a future comrade. No, Cap'm, you need me fer somethin', or I wouldn't be standin' here now. So what is it?"

Richard was no fool, so York nodded and spit it out. "I need you to get me into Andyne-Borregga. Me and this ship."

Richard sucked air through his teeth. "By the gods of space, Cap'm. Now that I would'a never guessed. Yer going pirate, are ya?"

York shook his head. "I just want access as an independent ship to the free port of Andyne-Borregga. With the facilities here at Sarasan we can only make temporary repairs. We need access to a major shipyard. And I think we can both imagine what'll happen to an imperial cruiser that just transits into the farspace of Borregga and asks politely to use her yard facilities."

Richard pleaded. "But this here's the chance of a lifetime. Why, with the ransom on the princess alone you could buy yerself a seat in the Mexak league and pay fer repairin' this ship. And a ship like this—oh, Cap'm! There ain't a freebooter aspace could touch her when she's in fightin' trim. And yer reputation. Let's don't ferget yer reputation: *Butcher Ballin, the meanest, fightinest, bloodiest, murderinest man ever to captain a fightin' ship*."

York grimaced. "I don't have that kind of reputation."

"Well, no, Cap'm, o'course not. At least not yet. Yer name ain't that familiar. But let's not forget you just took Sarasan Station single-handed. There ain't no one ever done nothing like that before. And with a little careful press, and the right rumors started in the right places, you could be really famous. Butcher Ballin! What a name. Why I almost like that better'n me own."

York didn't like it at all. "Let's just take it one step at a time. Right now, with the facilities here, we can repair *Cinesstar* enough to get to Borregga. At Borregga, I need access to her shipyard. After that, I'll consider my options."

"Fair enough," Richard said. "I can get you into Borregga without gettin' yer ass shot off. But yer gonna pay, Cap'm. Yer gonna have to pay me fer gettin' you into Borregga, and yer gonna have to pay the League and the Yard Authority fer using the yard. And none of us come cheap."

"Okay," York said. "I'll pay a fair price. You, for instance, get your life. Because unless you and I strike an agreement you're headed for a low gravity gallows. So in return for your help I'll give you your freedom. You'll be released at Borregga. As to any yard fees, you let me worry about that." York didn't add that he didn't have the faintest idea how he'd come up with hard currency. The only thing the ship carried was script.

"All right, Cap'm. You got a deal. Me life fer me help."

They didn't shake hands on it. This wasn't an agreement as much as recognition of mutual need. As soon as the need ended, so would their alliance.

York called the marines back in, but as Richard was leaving he had a nasty thought, and his curiosity got the best of him. "Richard," he said, stopping the pirate half way through the hatch. "How much ransom would the princess bring?"

Richard just threw his head back and laughed.

28

Chaos

YORK WOKE TO an urgent call from the bridge, though as his heart stopped pounding he was thankful it wasn't the alert klaxon. As he settled down behind his console Gant started feeding him information. "Three ships broke off from the fighting near Third Fleet, are headed this way under full drive. If they don't change course, they'll be here in under six hours." She gave him a moment to absorb that, then added, "You should also take a look at this, Captain . . ."

They'd put the drones in wide orbit around Sarasan so they could monitor the surrounding space—the station's facilities were a mess. York looked down at his screens where Gant was feeding him a scan summary. "We've got those three ships coming in from Third Fleet, arriving in five or six hours. Then in the opposite direction we've got that lone wake coming in from Aagerbanne. She'll be here in about fourteen hours. And finally there's this . . ."

York didn't need Gant to interpret the scan report for him. There was a big cluster of wakes at extreme range, ten or fifteen ships, driving hard and fast for Sarasan, clearly coming from feddie space. "A small fleet," he said, "or a large strike force. Have you got an ETA?"

"Yes, sir. They'll be here first thing tomorrow morning—maybe twenty hours from now."

York put in a call to Cappik. The chief answered on audio, meaning he wasn't near a console. York guessed he was out somewhere on the hull of the ship in a vac suit. "Cappik here, sir."

"Chief. Can you get us out of here in something under twenty hours? We need to be transition worthy."

"Ah, Captain, no way! We're in the middle of major work here on Starboard and Port. You can shoot me at dawn, if you want, but I can't get this ship into transition in under twenty hours. We need at least two days."

"Chief, we've got a feddie strike force headed our way, ETA twenty hours, and we have no station defenses."

Cappik said nothing for several seconds while everyone fidgeted nervously, then he finally spoke, but hesitantly. "Sir, I got an idea. We can get the heavy work done in fourteen or fifteen hours. After that we'll be rewiring and reprogramming, then we've got to align the fields in the chambers. That takes a while, but it can be done in space just as easily as on station. We'll get the heavy work done here, then let's go out into a stable orbit and we'll do the light work out there, do one of them hunter-killer tricks of yers where we run silent, and those feddies can do whatever they damn well please with this station. When we're done, we'll just sit and wait them out."

Cappik was not known for his creative thinking, but at that moment York could have kissed him. "You're to discuss this plan with absolutely no one," York said. "But when this is done, I'm going to buy you the tallest drink I can find."

"Thank you, sir."

••••

A soft tap on the door! Alone in her cabin, Sylissa d'Hart looked up cautiously. "Identify," she said, and the computer threw a picture of Torrin Juessik on her screen, waiting impatiently outside her cabin.

She touched a switch on her terminal. "Major Juessik. What can I do for you?"

Juessik started. "Lady d'Hart," he said with an ingratiating smile. "I . . . need your help. May I come in?"

She didn't like him much—no one really did—but it would be foolish to needlessly insult even a middle-ranking AI officer. "Enter," she said, and the computer unlocked her door.

Juessik stepped in carefully and glanced over his shoulder before closing the door. She rose to greet him, but he ignored her, stepped quickly past her and programmed the screen on her terminal to display the image from her door pick-up—the corridor outside was empty. Satisfied now that he was safe from some unknown danger, he turned his attention to her.

"Forgive me for being blunt," he said, "but I don't have much time. I need your help. Ballin is rounding up those of us he considers undesirables, including all the civilians he can't recruit into his little crew. No doubt, he intends to leave us behind when the rest of you depart Sarasan Station, which I believe will happen shortly."

She frowned, opened her mouth to speak, but he waved a hand impatiently at her and said, "Be silent. There's no time for foolish questions."

He reached into his tunic, retrieved a small, rectangular device just big enough to fit in the palm of his hand. "Ballin's smart, and no doubt he'll escape again." He showed her several buttons on the face of the small device in his hand. "When the time comes, and you'll know when that is, press these three buttons in sequence, then speak your own name. It's programmed to recognize your vocal signature, so only you can activate it. That's all you have to do—"

A knock on the door interrupted him. The terminal screen showed two marines standing outside her cabin.

"What is it?" she demanded.

He looked at the terminal, ignored the marines and spoke rapidly. "It's a small transmitter. Its range is limited, but it'll activate a larger device hidden elsewhere in this ship and capable of broadcasting a signal recognizable by any imperial warship. The signal will identify this ship and provide information on its location so Ballin can't sneak up on us. But you must be within one-tenth light-year for the signal to be received."

She couldn't believe her ears. "You want me to betray this ship to the people who have already tried to murder us once, and will certainly do so again if I do this?"

One of the marines outside rapped on the door loudly. "Lady d'Hart," he said. "We're looking for Major Juessik. We know he's in there—we've got a psyche-tracer on him. Open the door immediately or we'll override the lock ourselves and come in anyway."

She opened her mouth to give the computer the order, but he cupped a hand over her mouth. "Wait until you see everything," he said mysteriously.

As he removed his hand from her mouth she demanded, "What makes you think I would help you in any way?"

He reached into his tunic again, retrieved a small card and laid it next to the transmitter. "Read this," he said, "before committing yourself one way or another." Then he turned to the computer and said, "Enter."

The door clicked open and the two marines stepped in.

"Ma'am," one of them said to her, "What's he doing here?"

"Being unpleasant, as always," she said, though she didn't mention the small transmitter sitting on her desk, nor the card next to it. Juessik looked at them and grinned.

"Sir," one of the marines said. "Captain Ballin would like you to accompany us."

Juessik smiled. "Of course." He turned back to d'Hart. "Good day, Lady d'Hart." Then he turned and stepped out into the corridor.

When they were gone, she looked at the small transmitter and the card next to it. She picked up the card, inserted it into a slot on her terminal and a picture of Juessik sprang to life on the screen. "Lady d'Hart," he said. "Before you choose to disobey me, you need to see this."

Juessik's picture disappeared, the screen was blank for a moment, and then her heart leapt as a picture of her son replaced him. "Andrew," she said involuntarily.

"Mother," he said, making it almost a question. "They told me this message would be sent to you." He stood there proudly, trying to pretend he wasn't frightened. "I'm all right. They came last night and took me away. I don't know where I am, but I'm all right."

The picture went suddenly blank and Juessik's image appeared again. "As you can see, Lady d'Hart, we knew where you were hiding your son, and now the brat is in my custody. If you want him to remain alive and healthy, you'll do as I say."

The picture went dead.

"You bastard!"

••••

When the three ships from Third Fleet down-transited into Sarasan farspace, it came as a considerable surprise when they started shooting at each other, two of them chasing the third.

"Try to make contact," York barked at McGeahn. "And remember to pretend we're Station Command."

York watched a heated dog-fight develop until McGeahn interrupted his thoughts, "Sir. I've got Captain Zackrowski, *H.M.S. Black Star*."

"Give him to Rame. And remember our story."

McGeahn introduced Rame to Zackrowski as Commander Rame, Acting Station Commander. York listened to the conversation.

"Acting Station Commander?" Zackrowski demanded. "What the hell happened to Quae?"

Rame did a beautiful job without really acting. He said only, "Commodore Quae is dead. I'm now in command of the station. Why are you shooting at an imperial ship?"

"It's a goddamned traitor. Whole crew's gone traitor. In fact, half of Third Fleet's gone traitor—they didn't like that business with *Cinesstar*. Didn't like it much myself, blowing a ship with the empress aboard and all, but I know when to obey orders and keep my mouth shut. We're under orders to take them alive if we can—turn them over to you."

Now York understood why Third Fleet had pulled out of Sarasan nearspace so quickly. Leonavich had been faced with a mass uprising, had tried to isolate his fleet so he could deal with it.

Rame shook his head at Zackrowski. "We can't take them. We were hit by a feddie strike force just after you pulled out, barely managed to drive them off. The station's a total loss—a complete wreck. Those feddies went for reinforcements, are on their way back here now. Have your scan crew look out-system—there's a strike force out there coming in to finish the job. We're abandoning the station, going to get the hell out of here. I'd recommend you let that traitor go his own way, get the hell out of here yourself."

It worked. Zackrowski and the captain of the other loyal ship turned about quickly, started accelerating for transition back to Third Fleet. The traitor never did make contact, just went off in another direction, probably thankful for the reprieve.

The lone transition wake that came in eight hours later was an imperial hunter-killer returning from deep space patrol. The same lie worked on them, though with the added variation that the fighting in the distance was Third Fleet heavily engaged with a feddie fleet. After months on patrol, with his supplies and ordnance reserves marginal at best, the captain of the hunter-killer wisely chose not to join the fighting. Rame sent them off in another direction. Two hours later, Cappik was ready to disengage from the station.

York had kept Juessik and his AI goons and Sierka and several others isolated so they'd get no hint of his plans. The marines herded them into the barracks with the prisoners from Sarasan Station, left them with plenty of food and water, made sure the station's life support systems were in good shape and that none of her transmitters were operational. Then *Cinesstar* disengaged from the station and settled into a high static orbit around Sarasan. Four hours later, the feddie strike force down-transited into Sarasan nearspace.

••••

York watched them come in on his screens, a classic swift-strike approach. Coming in at full drive, well in excess of two thousand lights, they knew their wakes were easily visible, could be targeted by pickets properly positioned along their course.

At three-tenths light-year one feddie down-transited, launched its drones, began broadcasting detailed scan data to the rest of the strike force still in transition. In that way the strike force was not blind while it attempted a close approach.

At one-tenth light-year the strike force began to spread out, and another feddie down-transited and took over the job of feeding it scan data. As they got closer the data grew considerably more accurate.

A classic approach, allowing the strike force to drive deep into Sarasan's nearspace with minimum probability of blindly taking warheads. If an enemy vessel threw anything at the strike force, the ship that had down-transited could lock onto the transition launch and provide accurate targeting data to the main force.

Cinesstar was running silent in the same high orbit as the blown orbital weapons platforms, difficult to find among all the hot debris, even if anyone knew to look for her there.

••••

Add'kas'adanna was rarely surprised. As the commander of Directorate naval forces many lives and ships were usually lost if she were surprised. But she was surprised now at what they found in the Sarasan system.

A small cloud of debris surrounded Sarasan Station, the type of wreckage that resulted from heavy fighting close in to the station, and the station was completely inert. The station's primary means of defense, the large orbital weapons platforms orbiting the planet Sarasan, would ordinarily make even a full fleet move cautiously. But they too had been destroyed.

Add'kas'adanna chewed that over for a while. She was not aware of any recent attack on Sarasan, and she would be aware of such an attack by Directorate forces, or heads would roll.

"Your Excellency, we've detected a number of transition wakes in the distance, and a considerable amount of transition activity and fighting in one particular direction."

Add'kas'adanna reviewed the data: one lone wake headed outward parallel to the lines, another lone wake headed in the opposite direction, but also parallel to the lines, and finally two wakes headed toward a considerable force engaged in some heavy fighting.

As the strike force got closer to Sarasan Station, some odd facts became apparent. The station, while completely inactive, had not been hulled by any large warheads, was, in fact, basically whole, though her weaponry had been shot out and she was now defenseless.

"Keep us at a reasonable distance," she said, "while we send in a boarding party. Commodore Martak, you'll lead the boarding party."

Like all commanders, she hated the waiting most, waiting for the boarding party to get organized, waiting for the gunboats to shuttle them down to the station, waiting for them to set up a secure perimeter in the station then expand the perimeter and cautiously investigate every possible danger. She was surprised when she received a sudden call from Martak much earlier than expected. "Your Excellency, we've found a large group of imperials, evidently abandoned here after the station was taken. One of them—a Commander Mayhue Sierka—is quite talkative. He has an interesting story to tell."

From the moment she set eyes on Sierka, Add'kas'adanna didn't like the man. He was too willing to betray his former comrades, too lacking in honor to fight his own battles, and she herself felt no honor in having captured him. After filtering out Sierka's vehemence and obviously colored opinions, the events were clear. Ballin had been betrayed by his superiors, had responded by taking Sarasan, had gotten his stricken ship repaired sufficiently to escape, and had done so only hours before Add'kas'adanna's arrival. As Sierka glared at her from the screen and told his story she realized he was hoping to use her to exact some sort of revenge on the captain of *Cinesstar*, and it left a bad taste in her mouth to realize her duty compelled her to aid him in Ballin's destruction, even if only indirectly.

"Confirm everything under deep neural probe," she told Martak some minutes later. "And don't be gentle with him," she added out of pure spite. Martak came as close as he ever did to a smile.

Cinesstar had transited out of the Sarasan system only hours before. She looked at the scan reports on her screen; the renegade *imper* was alone so the double wake was not her prey. One of the two lone wakes, headed outward in opposite directions, had to be *Cinesstar*. This was her chance.

She split her strike force into three small units: her two slowest ships would stay behind and coordinate, while four of her fastest would chase one of the two *impers*, and four more would go in the opposite direction after the other. It galled her that, until she knew which of the two ships was *Cinesstar*, it would be a mistake to go herself after one while the chance existed it might be the other.

The two four-ship groups headed out using a classic chase strategy. In each group all four ships would drive at maximum transition velocity. They'd be blind in transition, but Add'kas'adanna's flagship, sitting still in the Sarasan system, could give them accurate navigational data for two to three light-years. Then, as soon as the range grew too extreme, the slowest of the four ships would down-transit, go static, and start providing accurate navigational data for the remaining three. Then a few light-years later the slowest of the three would down-transit and navigate for the remaining two. Then the slower of the two would do the same for the last and fastest of the four ships. And finally, the last ship in transition would have to get within targeting range of their prey while still close enough to get accurate navigation and targeting data from her nearest comrade. Given that *Cinesstar* had sustained serious damages and was probably unable to put out full power, they had a good chance of catching her. But they'd have to do so within eight to twelve light-years. And it was Add'kas'adanna's job to wait, and wonder which of those two ships out there was *Cinesstar*, and pray they made no mistakes, though the only gods she believed in were the gods of war, and they were never terribly receptive to prayer.

••••

"Captain, you'd better get up here right away."

York nodded, cut the circuit and headed straight for the bridge. His yeoman barked, "Captain on the bridge," as he floated in zero-G out of the lift.

York strapped in at the command console, keyed his implants into the bridge circuit and scanned his instruments in a matter of seconds. Nothing imminent!

"What is it?" he demanded.

"I've been analyzing our orbit," Gant said, and from her navigational console she threw a plot of their orbit on one of his screens, "and that of our friends out there." Another set of elliptical lines appeared on the same screen. York looked at them closely.

They'd been orbiting Sarasan for the last fifteen hours while Cappik completed the repairs, doing everything possible to keep all detectable radiation to a minimum. And from that vantage they'd watched the feddies transit into the system, investigate the station, certainly interrogate the prisoners there, all of whom had been carefully misled to believe *Cinesstar* was transition worthy when she departed.

The feddies had fallen for it, gone after the other transition wakes driving away from the system. York wasn't terribly disappointed when they left two ships behind. It only meant they'd have to wait them out.

"What a stroke of bad luck," Gant said.

The two feddies that had stayed behind had gone into a forced orbit at about the same diameter as *Cinesstar*, but using power to swing them around the planet in well under an hour, while *Cinesstar*'s static orbital period was more like twenty days. The feddies' orbit was elliptical, and precessing, while *Cinesstar*'s was circular and stable.

Gant sounded tired as she told York what he could already see from the scan data. "The two orbits are considerably different, but eventually, if we or they don't change anything, their precession is going to bring them into fairly close contact."

"When?" York asked. "And how close?"

"Twenty-eight hours. Ten thousand kilometers."

"Shit," someone cursed. "That's almost a collision course."

The feddies were undoubtedly running close-range scans out to that radius, if for no other reason than to spot debris. That close, *Cinesstar* would stand out like a beacon. If York had been smarter, done his job, thought ahead and played it safe, put *Cinesstar* into an unusually large and eccentric orbit, they'd be safe now. He didn't bother to tell them he'd fucked up.

The next several hours were hardest on Cappik and his crew. To repair the transition drive and the power plant they'd had to strip the entire section. Before they'd left Sarasan Station they'd completed the heavy work on the drive and remounted the chambers. But most of the peripheral instrumentation needed a complete refit, and getting everything in place, and doing it right, was a monumental task, and there'd be no time for any testing beyond computer simulations.

The port chamber was a complete loss, Centerline was cold, with Starboard idling at a trickle. But when that feddie came within range they'd need both Starboard and Centerline hot and ready to defend themselves. If they really pushed it, that would take at least a half hour of slow warm-up, a process their friends out there could spot from half way across the System. And a half hour would be plenty of time to take *Cinesstar* apart piece by piece. Again, it was the normally uncreative Cappik who came up with the only idea that might work.

"What about this, Captain?" the engineer asked. "Centerline's in the center of the ship, which ought to provide some coverage, and I'll add so much shielding nothing'll leak through, as long as we don't push it too hard. And we're sitting right in the middle of all this hot debris from those platforms. With the added shielding we could probably bring Centerline up to maybe five percent. Now that ain't much, but it's enough to get her warm so she don't take any damage if we bring her up from there real fast. The only danger is we'll have to bring her up and hold her at five percent for a couple of hours."

Two hours during which the feddies had that much more chance to spot them.

Cappik's eyes met his, and he obviously shared the thought.

"Do it," York said.

Cappik had the makeshift shielding in place just in time, and once they started bringing the power up in Centerline York never left the bridge. Gant monitored every move the feddies made, ready to warn them if there was any change, for better or worse. And York sat staring at the data, trying to think what he was going to do with one marginally hot chamber. It wasn't enough to fight a battle, to power shields, gravity, drive, life-support, weapons. Just not enough. They'd have one shot. Then all they could do was run, and *Cinesstar* wasn't in any condition to do that very well.

"Fifty minutes and counting, sir."

"Eldinow, reposition us for a stern shot. I want the aft launch room lined up on their approach vector."

"Mister Jakobee. We'll launch two salvos, back-to-back. For the first, arm two one-megatonne warheads. Fuse them for contact detonation, one targeted at each of those two warships."

Their only chance was a sucker-punch, try to get a good first shot in under the response time of the feddie detection systems, which would be slowed down by the need to analyze radiation signatures from all the debris. If the feddies were within ten thousand kilometers when *Cinesstar* launched her warheads, they'd cover the distance between the two ships in microseconds. But it would take precious seconds to bring the chamber up to enough power to launch the damn warheads. York chose to use the small one-megatonne warheads for the first salvo—the smaller warheads required less energy to punch them into transition. "When I give the order to power-up, Mister Jakobee, launch the first salvo as soon as you have enough power. Don't wait for a specific launch command."

"Yes, sir."

"Very good. Also arm two one-hundred megatonne warheads for the second salvo. Fuse them for proximity detonation, one thousand meters, one targeted at each of those two warships. And again, you'll not wait for a specific command. Just launch the second salvo as soon as you have enough power to do so."

The second salvo, with larger warheads, was insurance, though privately, if the first salvo didn't do the job, York didn't think the second would do them any good.

"Ten minutes, sir."

••••

Add'kas'adanna looked at the reports coming in from her chase ships. Her flagship and its escort had their drones out at extreme range to get the maximum baseline for tracking the *impers*, though they were close to their limit. In another hour or two it would be necessary for the first of her chase ships to down-transit and take the responsibility for tracking their prey. But until that time it was imperative her ships and their drones make no changes in their orbits. Simple, stable orbits, with well-defined parameters. If they wanted to catch that ship, they'd need every advantage they could squeeze out of their instruments.

••••

"Range—one hundred thousand kilometers, closing at two hundred kilometers per second. Convergence in five minutes."

"We've got a good targeting solution, sir."

"Hold your fire, Mister Jakobee," York said. "Steady as she goes." It was eerie, fighting a battle this close to an enemy, one approaching at a bare crawl.

"Range—eighty thousand kilometers, sir. Convergence in four minutes."

"Remember," he said. "We take no action until ten thousand kilometers."

It was a guess, ten thousand kilometers. He had to assume the two Directorate ships were devoting their resources to tracking the imperial ships. They had their drones out near the edge of the system for a wide baseline, even had the drones constantly moving to accumulate a larger statistical base of data on their targets. All that processing ate up resources, forced a commander to set priorities.

"Range—sixty thousand kilometers, sir. Convergence in three minutes."

With their drones so far out, the two enemy ships would have to do their own close-in scanning. No commander would be happy with such a situation, though if she were confident there were no enemy ships nearby, then it was a risk worth taking. But the close-in scans would be slower to gather and interpret data, with fine resolution limited to something like one thousand meters. They'd probably still run coarse scans at five and ten thousand meters to catch large debris that might be dangerous to the ship, and something the size of *Cinesstar* had a high probability of getting their attention. All guesswork, surmise this, assume that; in the end York had to take his best guess—ten thousand kilometers.

"Range—forty thousand kilometers, sir. Convergence in two minutes."

"Sir," Gant said. "I've got better data now. Closest fly-by will be forty-three hundred kilometers."

"Thank you, Miss Gant."

"Range—twenty thousand kilometers. Fifty seconds to the ten thousand kilometer mark."

A half minute. "Mister Jakobee, are those warheads armed?"

"Yes, sir. First salvo—two one-megatonne warheads fused for contact detonation. Second salvo—two one-hundred-megatonne warheads fused for proximity detonation, one thousand meters."

"Here they come, sir," Gant shouted. "Fifteen thousand kilometers."

Don't jump the gun.

"Fourteen thousand . . ."

"Stand by all stations," York said.

"Thirteen thousand . . ."

"Be prepared for full engagement after the first salvo."

"Twelve thousand . . ."

"All stations ready, sir," Jakobee said.

"Eleven thousand . . ."

Silence. York could hear his heart pounding.

"Ten thou—"

York didn't wait for her to finish. He barked into his pickup, "Full power, Mister Cappik."

York watched the gages for Centerline start to rise as the seconds ticked away.

"Nine thousand . . ."

"Remember," York said, trying to keep his voice down. "No gravity, no shields, no drive—all power to weapons."

"Eight thousand . . ."

The captain wasn't supposed to get nervous, but York didn't care about that. "Mister Jakobee, don't you have enough power for that first salvo yet?"

"Negative, sir."

"Seven thousand . . ."

York heard Jakobee's hand slap the console as he shouted into the intercom, "First salvo away."

At such close range there was no tracking the missiles, no real response time on a human scale. There was no time for York to take in data and issue commands.

"Two detonations," Gant shouted, "close range. We're blind, can't see through them."

"Second salvo away," Jakobee shouted.

"Shields up," York shouted. "Gravity and drive up. Helm, get us the hell out of here. Nav, I want data. Priority to shields and defensive weaponry."

"Two more detonations, sir. I can't see a fucking thing."

Centerline's power rose steadily, and even the damaged starboard chamber was coming online. York hadn't noticed the gravity come up, but *Cinesstar* was under power again, driving at less than a hundred gravities away from their targets.

"I'm getting nothing, sir," Gant pleaded. "All I can see is the two fireballs from those big warheads and nothing else. No incoming, no drive readings, no . . . wait a minute. I've got something. It's big—ship sized—bigger than *Cinesstar*. I think it's static. No drive readings, nothing hot like an active power plant. It's too small to be one of those feddies, but I'm sure it is . . . And no sign of the other feddie. Those fireballs are dissipating . . . I'm starting to get real data, though my error factor is high. And there's no sign of one of those ships."

"All stop," York ordered, and once again silence settled over the bridge.

Little by little the picture unfolded. Both feddies had had their shields up, but one of them had taken a direct hit from the first one-megatonne warhead, not enough to destroy the ship completely—not a healthy ship with her shields fully powered—but certainly enough to damage her badly. The second warhead—one-hundred-megatonnes—had slammed into a completely defenseless ship, disintegrating it almost entirely. There was some debris in the area, but only pieces of the most dense metal and plast.

The other ship had endured a little better. Her automatic systems must have detected and destroyed the first warhead, but the fireball blinded any ship's defenses, and the second warhead detonated close to the hull. Half the ship was blown away or vaporized.

"There may be survivors in that," York said. "Commander Rame, let's get a boarding party on her, evacuate any survivors, then let's get the hell out of here."

29

Again Treason

THERE WERE SOME survivors on what was left of the feddie cruiser, though not many. It took most of that night and the next morning to cut them out of the badly damaged ship. Many were close to death, and almost all were wounded in some way.

Shortly after transition, however, York got a call from Alsa Yan. She was rather mysterious, refused to say anything substantive, but was adamant that he come down to sickbay right away.

When he got there she pulled him into her office, then sat down at her terminal and dropped a card into one of its slots. A picture of one of the feddie survivors appeared on the screen, a woman, a Kinathin breed warrior; the deep olive hue of her skin, the bone-white hair, all easy giveaways. She lay prone on an examination table, so her exceptional height wasn't obvious. One of her arms was missing at the elbow, and she was naked except for bandages and a wholly insufficient sickbay gown. There were streaks of yellow in her white hair, which was a sign of age.

York shrugged. "A Kinathin. And an old one. So what?"

Alsa stood, reached into a desk drawer and retrieved a sealed plast-pack. "So this." She broke the seal on it and dumped the contents on her desk. "Her personal effects."

Mostly clothing. York grabbed a piece, caught a flash of color that made him hesitate. He gave it a good shake, unfolding it: a feddie officer's tunic.

One of the arms was missing; the foreshortened arm of the tunic ended in a bloody tear, and he realized the woman had lost her arm long before Alsa had gotten to her. And there were battle ribbons, lots of them. He looked at the rank on the remaining sleeve: lots of stripes and lots of stars. "I don't remember my feddie rank that well," he said, "but she must be pretty high up."

Alsa grinned. "I looked it up. She's a fucking Director. In fact, I think she's one of *the* Directors: Fleet Director."

York had read somewhere that the highest feddie naval officer was a Kinathin. "Is she going to live?"

"Ya, though she's banged up pretty bad. Load of shrapnel in her abdomen, lost the arm, but worst is a heavy dose of radiation. Would have been dead in a couple hours if I hadn't gotten to her, but she'll be fine now. Though it'll be a couple of days before she'll be in any shape to talk."

York returned to Alsa's terminal, stared for a moment at the picture of the woman there. He thought it odd that he didn't feel any hatred for her, could only wonder how he might use her to get him and his crew out of this mess.

"Let me know as soon as I can speak to her," he said. "And until then keep her isolated, and I don't want anyone to know about this."

It was early morning when York got back to his cabin. He'd been living on drugs and about two or three hours of sleep per night for the last three days. They were in transition with no one following them, so relatively safe. He gave orders not to be disturbed, took the antidote to the drugs and crashed hard.

York slept through most of that day, woke just after the dinner bell. For some reason he'd had a vivid dream of Maggie. He couldn't remember any details, but after waking he had a terrible feeling of loss, and there were traces of the dream skipping through his memories. He tried not to think about her; she was dead, and if Alsa wanted her on ice in the tanks, and if that was Maggie's last wish—well, it didn't really make any difference to Maggie. It just ate at him when he thought about it, and he knew the best thing he could do was put her out of his mind.

He called down to the galley and had a simple dinner sent up to his cabin—one of the privileges of rank. He ate quickly since he had an appointment and he didn't want to be late. But before leaving his quarters he checked in with the bridge. "Status," he demanded, speaking into the pickup at his office terminal.

"All systems are green, sir," someone said.

Down on C-deck he found the cabin he wanted, rapped politely on the hatch. It opened without preamble, revealing a softly lit interior. Sarra Fithwallen's rather large and able-bodied "associate," Jandeer Faiel, had opened the cabin door. Behind him Fithwallen and Brentin Omasin both sat in comfortable chairs. Faiel politely offered York a chair; York sat while Faiel remained standing by the door.

The scene reminded York of the first time they'd met, though then it had been in Cienyey's cabin. York needed Fithwallen and Omasin, needed their industrial wealth, power and connections.

"Can I offer you a drink, Captain," Omasin said pleasantly. "I'm going to have one." He stood and looked at Fithwallen. "Sarra?"

She nodded. "Thank you, Brentin."

Omasin turned to a small bar. "We have just about anything you might want, Captain," Omasin continued. "Commander Sierka, while not terribly competent as an officer, was kind enough to have the kitchen synthesize quite a number of luxuries."

"I'll have whatever you're having," York said.

After a few seconds of clinking glasses and other noises Omasin turned around with three glasses in his hands, handed one to Fithwallen, one to York, then returned to his seat. He lifted his glass and said, "To the future, Captain. Let's hope we all have one."

York looked at the amber liquid in his glass, then took a sip. It burned much like 'trate, though the taste was considerably different. It would take some getting used to if he were to drink it regularly.

"It's Skatche whiskey, Captain," Fithwallen said. York looked at her over the top of his glass. She continued, "It's supposed to be a replica of an ancient whiskey drunk by pre-space civilizations, though only the gods know if we've really got the synthesis right. But it's enjoyable, don't you think?"

"Quite good," York lied, and she grinned at him knowingly.

"Well now, Captain. What can we do for you?"

York took another sip, threw away his little rehearsed speech and said simply, "Our futures are somewhat bound together. If either the Empire or the Directorate have their way we'll all be dead shortly. And I assume you would like to stay alive as much as I."

She chuckled softly and smiled. "Of course. However, that may be the only thing we have in common."

"What do you mean?"

"I'm not interested in revenge. Vengeance often precludes survival."

"And you believe I am?"

She frowned. "I'm not exactly sure, but that possibility certainly exists."

York shrugged and gave her the most honest answer he could. "I'm not sure myself if I'm after revenge. For the time being, I haven't had the opportunity to think that far ahead, and I'm only interested right now in short-term survival. Can we agree that in the short term, at least, we both share a mutual interest in survival?"

"I'll grant you that. But tell me, is it true our next destination is Andyne-Borregga?"

"Yes."

"Why Andyne-Borregga? You don't strike me as the pirate type."

"It's the only place where I can get this ship repaired. Given our present circumstances, do you know of a better place?"

She shook her head. "No. But you do realize that in return for financing repair of your ship, the Mexak League will demand you apply for membership. You'll owe them all of the money they loan you for repair of the ship, and they'll require you to pay it back from the profits of raids on legitimate shipping. You'll also be required to augment your crew with a fair number of people whom they feel they can trust. You do realize this, don't you?"

York met her eyes and didn't look away. "I was not fully aware of the details, but I have no misconceptions about obtaining anything free. However, Borregga is more than just a pirate base, more than just the home of the Mexak League. From what I've heard it's a free port in the truest sense of the word. I assume if I can independently finance the repairs to my ship, then those repairs could be purchased freely in the shipyards at Borregga, without further obligation. Is that not true?"

He'd taken her by surprise, though she showed nothing as obvious as a visible start, just a frown. "Yes," she said, nodding cautiously, and grinning as she slowly began to realize what he was saying. "So you don't want to be a pirate after all, eh, Captain?"

York gave her a Palevi-like nasty grin. "I have other things to do first. Maybe later. Right now I need to finance the repairs to this ship. You once gave me reason to believe you could be grateful in a financial way if I got you out of this."

"And can you get us out of this?"

York shrugged and tossed down the rest of his drink. "Possibly. No guarantees. All I can offer you is this: pay for the repairs on this ship, so I'm not obligated to the Mexaks, and after we leave Borregga I'll take this ship wherever you desire, as long as the location does not place this ship or her crew in further jeopardy. And I'll allow the three of you to go your own way, though once we part, we'll have no further obligations to one another. You'll be on your own, and so will we."

She was silent for a moment, then asked, "We're out in the middle of nowhere. Where'll I get the funds to pay for these repairs?"

"You tell me," York said. "I've never been to Borregga, but the intelligence reports I've read say there are any number of legitimate interests there. I assume that if you can communicate with your subordinates you can have funds transferred to some sort of institution or representative there."

She nodded. "A logical assumption."

York continued, "I can stop this ship at any time and send a message to any location you desire, though the location and the message will have to be approved by me."

She looked at him for a moment, rock-still, expressionless, and York decided the best thing he could do was keep his mouth shut and let her think. She frowned, pursed her lips, glanced at Omasin, then looked at York. "Tentatively," she said, "I agree to your terms, though I'm not going to sign a blank check."

"Of course." York looked at his watch and stood. "Forgive me but I have to go; we've got a course correction shortly. But I'll have a complete set of the damage reports made available for you at your convenience. I'll also have one of my officers available to assist you and answer any questions you have. We have eight days before we reach Borregga, so there should be more than enough time for us to agree on an appropriate budget. Is there anything else I can provide?"

"That'll be sufficient, Captain. Thank you."

Faiel held the door for York and closed it on him when he was out in the corridor. That had worked out nicely.

It was late, fourth watch, and the corridor was empty, quiet. York caught a glimpse of movement out of the corner of his eye, a crewwoman walking away from him. He glanced her way, froze—Maggie! It was Maggie! His muscles tensed, but he checked the reaction instantly. No, just a hallucination. Not Maggie . . . not Maggie!

He turned in the opposite direction, shook his head angrily and marched up the corridor, unable to get her out of his mind. He turned down another corridor, headed for the lift and saw that same crewwoman up ahead, an odd sensation tickling at the back of his thoughts.

How did she get ahead of him, when only seconds ago he'd left her behind. She stood in the middle of the corridor, at the intersection of two corridors, facing him, standing there as if waiting for him. As he approached her he slowed and his heart started pounding. The closer he got the more she looked like Maggie, and while his vision blurred his recognition of her was clear and distinct.

It wasn't Maggie, but it was Maggie, Maggie as she was now, not the bright healthy Maggie he'd known but the Maggie in the tanks, even to the ghostly, white skin that came from the tank fluids. He was barely a step or two away from her, and she was standing there holding her hands out as if to stop him, saying something, though no sound came from her lips.

He closed his eyes, shook his head—too much time on combat drugs, too little sleep. He opened his eyes and she hadn't gone away. Just a hallucination. He took a step forward, thinking he'd better see Alsa about this.

In response she shook her head violently and mouthed the word, "No," though again without sound. She pushed out with her hands to stop him, and her hands passed through him like a good hallucination should.

Goddamned hallucination, he thought as she back stepped into the intersection of the two corridors, shaking her head. He ignored her and stepped forward into the intersection, caught a glimpse of movement far to the right, heard the unmistakable click of a gun safety—

His implants crashed, an odd sensation like sticking a finger in his ear, and he realized his implants were being jammed, cutting him off from shipnet.

It was reflex more than anything else; he let his knees buckle, using his forward momentum to carry him through the intersection, hoping to shoulder roll into the corridor beyond and out of sight of the gunman. But halfway there he heard the puff of a silenced grav gun, and a sledge hammer slammed him to one side where he glanced off the corner of the intersecting corridors. A second bullet grazed off the corridor wall nearby, splattered into a dozen pieces and peppered him with shrapnel as he thudded to the deck.

He'd sprawled in the main corridor out of sight of the assassin, his legs still in the intersection. He heard steps coming his way, tried to struggle to his feet ignoring the pain that washed over him, slipped in his own blood and fell again. A third bullet slammed into his ankle, spinning him about, blowing off the foot of his prosthetic leg in a shower of sparks and synthetic skin. Slipping and sliding in his own blood he scrambled forward out of the line of fire, curled into a sitting position, reached into the belt under his tunic and pulled the small palm gun he always carried. He had four shots, and he could hear the steps coming down the corridor toward him. He released the gun's safety, swung it around the corner of the intersection and blindly squeezed the trigger. The shot exploded up the corridor with a thunderclap. He squeezed off two more rounds blindly. He struggled to his feet, actually one foot and the stump of his prosthetic ankle ending in plast and wires and shredded skin. The whole corridor was smeared with his blood. He hesitated and listened: no steps coming up the corridor. He tried to key his implants: still jammed.

He ran, hampered by the shortened prosthetic stump, the pain in his chest when he tried to breathe, the way the deck tilted and swayed beneath him. Turn into a side corridor, stop, listen—he heard rapid steps coming after him. He was breathing hard, couldn't breathe deep, too much pain. He swung the gun around the intersection and fired one last blind shot, then turned and ran, remembering not to toss away the gun—no need to let his enemy know he was no longer armed.

He ran; he was in one of the outer corridors next to the hull and he used the curve of the corridor to keep him out of sight of the assassin. But that was a foot race, one he couldn't win.

He stopped at a maintenance hatch, slapped the transmit switch on the wall intercom next to it and barked, "Security—Ballin—I'm being hit—C-deck—code red."

He palmed the lock on the hatch, swung it open, crawled through and felt a gravity boundary tickle his skin. As he pulled the hatch closed a bullet splattered off the rim of the hatch. In zero-G he dogged the hatch awkwardly.

He was in the dark, unlit section between the inner and outer hulls. He pushed off into the zero-G darkness, trying to avoid a nasty collision with a beam or girder, came up against a bulkhead. A shaft of light shot through the darkness as his pursuer opened the hatch.

He hooked an arm around a beam, looked right and left for the telltales near an access hatch, spotted them twenty meters away. He pushed off, crawling from beam to beam. A bullet zinged off a bulkhead nearby, a blind shot in the darkness.

He reached the hatch, popped the seals on it, swung it open and the bright lights of the corridor beyond blinded him for a moment. He swung one leg through into the gravity field of the deck, hung there awkwardly for a moment as he tried to use his right arm and a stab of pain shot through his side. He knew the lights of the corridor made him a beautifully silhouetted target, and he had to move regardless of the pain. He swung his right arm up, ignoring the pain, and grabbed the lip of hatch.

What with all the racket he was making, it was amazing he was able to hear the faint puff of the grav gun. The bullet caught him diagonally in the chest, entered just under his right breast, blew him through the hatch and bounced him off the deck.

He struggled to his feet, hobbled down the corridor hunched over in pain. That wound was lethal, he knew. The small entrance wound on his chest was gushing blood; and though he couldn't see the exit wound on his back he had no doubt it was even worse.

He heard the assassin struggling through the hatch behind him just as he made it to an intersecting corridor. A bullet tore into the corridor wall near his head as he rounded the turn. The deck swayed so badly beneath him that he bounced from one wall to the next as he tried to make his way down the corridor, smearing blood everywhere.

Someone stood in his way—a marine—Palevi. York hovered at the edge of consciousness, but not so far-gone he couldn't feel dread and fear as Palevi dropped into a crouch and raised a gun, aiming it squarely at him. The marines—he should never have trusted them.

"Hit the deck, sir," Palevi shouted. "Yer in my line of fire."

It took a second for that to register, and then York let his knees buckle, didn't even try to cushion the fall, landed on the deck with a thud and lost consciousness.

••••

Aeya crawled out of bed, rubbing sleep from her eyes. Someone was going to pay for waking her, pay dearly.

She opened her cabin door, found a marine with a gun standing in the corridor. "Why are you making so much noise?" she demanded angrily.

The marine started, surprised by her sudden appearance, aimed the gun at her for a moment, then swung it back down the corridor. "Stacy," the marine bellowed.

Aeya glanced down the corridor, saw a blond, young marine standing there, also with a gun.

The first marine bellowed. "Get a team down here. Secure the deck."

Aeya's patience was gone. "I demand—" she started to say, but the marine had the audacity to actually reach out with one of those big, ugly paws of his and shove her. He shoved her so hard she stumbled back into her cabin and fell in a sprawl over her bed.

As she struggled to her feet, speechless, but trying to think of just the right reprimand, the marine, keeping the gun leveled down the corridor with one hand, reached down with the other and locked his fingers into the folds of a messy bundle lying at his feet. Before she could say anything he dragged the bundle into her cabin, leaving an ugly red smear on the deck.

Again, she tried to say something, "What do you think—"

"Shut up," the marine bellowed at her, then slammed the door of her cabin and locked it. He spoke in that detached way naval people did when they were speaking into their implants. "Palevi here. Someone tried to pop the captain. He's hit bad. Multiple chest wounds, splatter slugs. He's in full cardiac arrest. Get a med team down here on the double. I'm holed up in—"

As the marine spoke Aeya looked down at the bundle, and for the first time realized it was a man, and that the large red puddle forming around him was his own blood. He was lying on his side, his back oddly shaped, and with a start she suddenly understood she was looking at several ribs that had erupted outward, opening an enormous hole in the back of his chest. Panic started to set in as she stepped around the wounded man to see his face, while in the background the marine still droned on about something.

The man on the floor lay deathly still. His eyes were open, and while blood obscured his features, the chrome eye and the scars produced instant recognition. She hated Ballin, but still, she wouldn't wish this kind of fate on any man. She reached out to comfort him, decided against touching him and getting blood on her hands. Instead she said, "There, there, Captain. It'll be all right."

He didn't say anything, didn't move or give any indication he was alive. Both eyes stared blindly at some random point in space. The pupil of the real eye had dilated badly, while that of the chrome eye kept opening and shutting, opening and shutting, opening and shutting . . .

Aeya fainted.

30

Treason Upon Treason

YORK SLAMMED AWAKE, sat up in bed, ignored the sideways tug of the gravity field of his cabin deck as it interfered with that of his grav bunk. He hesitated for an instant, wondering how he'd gotten back to his cabin, wondering why everything seemed so normal. Then he tore frantically at his shirt until he could see his bare chest. The skin there was pink and healthy.

He threw back the covers, found to his great relief his right leg was still whole, with no indication it had ever been missing. He wiggled the toes, they felt fine.

It had all been a dream, he realized, an insane dream . . .

Alsa looked sadly at her handiwork. All that remained of York was a bit of tissue, a piece of bone, a smear of blood.

The technician held out the open body bag. "I'll scrape him into it."

Alsa looked at what was left of York, shook her head. "That's not him. There's nothing left of him." She reached out, scraped the bits of tissue into a pan, turned toward the disposal can . . .

York woke up screaming, struggled for long seconds while mentally he flipped back and forth between the two realities: it was a dream. No it wasn't . . . yes it was . . . no it wasn't . . . This time he wasn't going to be fooled. Not by any of them. It was real, the body bag dream was a dream, but this was real.

He started crying with relief. It wasn't a dream. He wasn't insane. No, he was insane, but that was all right, as long as it was real . . .

Alsa looked at what was left of York, shook her head. "That's not him. There's nothing left of him." She reached out, scraped the bits of tissue into a pan, turned toward the disposal can . . .

. . . And then Maggie was there. She was alive, and whole and healthy. And he was alive and whole and healthy, and he started to sob.

She wrapped her arms around him, held him tightly while he wept, held him until the tears subsided. It was all a dream, he knew . . . all a dream, but he no longer cared.

When he stopped crying she still held him, and then she kissed him, gently at first, softly, then more passionately. And they made love, and for a time they were free.

••••

Imperial Captain Bella Tzecharra looked at her screens in utter disbelief. Sarasan Prime was no more than a derelict—an Imperial Subsector Headquarters reduced to nothing more than a hazard to shipping.

"Captain," her first mate said. "There's not really enough debris in the system for it to have been a full scale assault, though we've picked up a hulk orbiting the planet. Radiation profile is too much of a mess to provide definitive identification, but best guess is a feddie cruiser that went out with all hands."

Tzecharra nodded. "This doesn't add up. Instruct all captains to proceed with extreme caution."

"Captain," her com officer blurted out suddenly. "I'm getting a transmission from Sarasan Prime. It's uncoded and contains no Imperial ID header."

Tzecharra looked at her screens. Her captains were all tied into her command circuit and knew what was going on as well as she. "Answer it," she barked at her com officer. "Find out who they are and what's going on."

Tzecharra waited patiently and watched her screens. "Captain, this is really weird. The guy at the other end says he's a feddie sublegion. Says he and a small detachment were left on the station to guard a bunch of imperial prisoners. Said the prisoners are all in good shape, been treated well, and he wants to surrender. Also said . . . Sarasan was burned by one of our own cruisers."

••••

Tzecharra looked at Sierka, was careful not to let her distaste show.

"I know him," Sierka said. "I know what he's going to do next."

"And what is that?" Tzecharra asked.

Sierka shook his head and spoke as if she were a subordinate. "That's highly secret information. I can divulge it only to Lord Abraxa. Take me to him immediately. That's an order."

Tzecharra was tempted to show Sierka how much his orders were worth by having him vented. But the situation was too unusual for rash decisions—maybe the idiot did know something. For the moment Tzecharra swallowed her pride. "I'm under direct orders from Fleet. I'll have to contact my superiors there before taking any such action."

Sierka stood as if dismissing her. "Very well, Captain. Please do so immediately. I'll be waiting in my cabin." Then he turned and left.

Her first officer next brought in Major Juessik. Juessik saluted crisply, then without preamble asked, "Forgive me, Captain, for appearing brash, but before we go on I should establish my identity. May I use your terminal?"

Tzecharra hadn't made captain without learning one was always cautious around an AI officer. She smiled, nodded toward the terminal on the far side of her office. It was a duplicate to the one recessed in the desk in front of her, though its circuits were slaved to the one at her fingertips and she could monitor everything Juessik did with it.

Juessik bent over the small terminal, started a log-in sequence. She watched every keystroke echoed to the screen in front of her, and her first clue came when her terminal didn't echo the password he entered. She sat up a bit straighter. Then a file appeared on her screen, one she didn't even know existed in the log of her ship, with an access code she'd never heard of. The file identified Juessik as an AI colonel—a damn bird colonel—the only damn full colonel in AI.

Tzecharra stood cautiously and greeted Juessik as an equal, perhaps a superior. Juessik sat down opposite her, seemed pleasant enough. "What can I do for you, Colonel?" Tzecharra asked.

"Tell me what Sierka told you."

Tzecharra lit a tobac and offered one to Juessik. "He said he knows Ballin well enough to predict what he'll do next."

Juessik declined the tobac. "And what is that?"

"He won't tell me, says it's a matter for Abraxa's ears alone."

"And what do you think?"

Tzecharra shrugged, blew a stream of blue smoke into the air. "He's an idiot. Probably doesn't know a damn thing."

Juessik grinned and nodded. "Yes. He's an idiot. And he's unstable, not fit to command a garbage shuttle. But he does seem to know Ballin fairly well—has a personal vendetta against the man—and he may actually have some idea what he'll do."

"We could get that information out of him without having to wait the nine days it'll take a fast ship to get him to Abraxa."

"I'm tempted," Juessik said, "but Sierka's unstable enough to actually hold out against that sort of thing. In fact, it might push him over the edge and we could lose the information he does have. Let's humor him, put him on a fast ship back to Luna. I'll send a message to Abraxa to expect him. Perhaps I'll go with him myself."

••••

York slammed awake, sat up in bed, ignored the sideways tug of the deck gravity as it tried to pull him out of his grav bunk. He tore frantically at his shirt while his mind flipped back and forth between the hallucination that he was hallucinating and the hallucination that he wasn't.

Suddenly he realized what he was doing, froze, cursed, forced his hands down to his sides, refused to succumb to the urge to see if there were any indications his injuries had been real. They were real—he knew that, just as he knew there would be no scars or any sign that an assassin's bullet had nearly cut him in two.

He tried to recall how long it had been since the assassination attempt, guessed something like four or five days, though it didn't matter. Each night he dreamt of body bags and hallucinations— and Maggie. An odd part of his hallucination was that he was beginning to wonder if perhaps the dreams were in some way connected to reality. And each day he woke up with his heart pounding, climbing up into his throat. And each day he struggled with reality, to find it, to reach out and purposefully take hold of it. Reality was no longer something he could take for granted, and all day long he worried constantly that he might have taken hold of the wrong reality.

They managed to keep the assassination attempt quiet. Palevi had gotten all the blood cleared away before first watch, and they'd made excuses for York's absence while Alsa worked frantically to put him back together. Apparently a fragment from one of the assassin's bullets had torn a large hole in the left ventricle of his heart. Alsa wasn't able to repair it in-situ, so she'd removed his heart, put in a temporary prosthetic, and was even now working in her laboratory, trying to regrow a new left ventricle on his damaged heart. She thought she could put it back in his chest in a couple of days.

It was important York be visible and healthy, important for morale and important for the crew. He understood that, and they'd gotten him up and walking about within a single day. He walked around, gave orders, pretended he was in command, was thankful the drive to Borregga had been routine.

Sitting in his bunk, York put his hand to his chest, felt the arrhythmic thumping of the prosthetic heart. It mimicked a human heart nicely, but between beats York was certain he could feel a very nonhuman, electro-mechanical hum. Probably just another hallucination.

York climbed down out of the grav bunk and threw on his clothes. He'd taken to sleeping in empty cabins in junior officers country—picking a cabin at random, telling no one but Palevi where he was. He knew he was developing some serious paranoia. Not only had the assassin crashed his implants, he'd jammed selected sections of shipnet so there were no vids they might use to identify him—or her. Bringing that kind of tech aboard ship without detection was impossible for anyone but a seriously connected professional.

He threw on yesterday's uniform, tucked his gun under his belt. He was no longer content with just a palm gun, and while he tucked this new, larger gun under the hem of his tunic, making an effort to hide it from casual observation, he no longer cared much if someone noticed the bulge.

When he stepped out into the corridor there was a marine waiting for him, leaning casually against a bulkhead some distance down the corridor, as if no one would take notice of a marine just casually hanging around. Since the assassination attempt there was always a bodyguard somewhere nearby, though they stayed discreetly in the background. But still, York was thankful Palevi took no chances.

Back in his own cabin he showered and shaved, had just finished putting on a fresh uniform when his intercom chimed. "Yes."

"Captain," his yeoman said. "The empress is here to see you."

"Tell her I'm not in."

"That won't work," the empress voice said over the intercom. "You've been avoiding me long enough."

York gave the yeoman orders to admit her.

Lady d'Hart accompanied her. They both refused to sit, so York also remained standing. He offered them 'trate, gulped at his own while they sipped at theirs nicely and looked over the rim of their glasses at him. They were obviously concerned, probably about the state of his mental health and his ability to captain this ship. Well, they should be.

He started the conversation, speaking in a way that precluded any small talk. "Having second thoughts about your decision to give me command?"

Cassandra laughed. "I've had second thoughts from the moment I made that decision, Captain. But until recently you've done nothing to make me think it was a mistake."

"And now . . ."

She looked at her drink. "And now there are rumors all over the ship."

"Such as?"

"We're headed for Borregga."

"That rumor is correct."

"You've awakened Red Richard from the tanks and are negotiating with him."

"Partially true," York said. "The negotiations are complete, and Richard is now acting in an advisory capacity."

Cassandra flinched, had expected him to deny or explain the rumors. Lady d'Hart, however, remained impassive. It was she who spoke next. "There is also a rumor you're going renegade, that you're going to join the Mexak League and become a pirate."

York nodded. "I've heard that rumor too. Richard certainly believes it. There's also a rumor I'm going to attack Borregga, take it like I took Sarasan, though I'd think there aren't too many people on this ship stupid enough to believe I'm that stupid. There's also a rumor I've been working undercover all this time for AI, and another that I've been working for the Directorate. Pick your rumor. There're enough of them going around you should be able to find one that's close to what you want to believe."

Cassandra shook her head. "I don't want to *pick a rumor.* I want to hear from you what you're going to do."

York shook his head. "That information is available only on a need-to-know basis, and you have no need."

"I'm afraid I must insist."

York continued to shake his head. "You're in no position to insist. I told you when you gave me command I'd do certain things you wouldn't like, and that you'd not be allowed to change your mind, and I'll not voluntarily relinquish command, and there's no one here who can take it from me."

She stood and shouted, "We had an agreement."

York nodded, and when he spoke he couldn't hide the bitterness in his voice. "Yes. We did. And I kept my end of the bargain. I delivered you to the safety of the empire, and my people and I were betrayed. Your precious empire murdered a third of my crew."

She closed her eyes, took a breath and seemed to age right in front of him. "Captain, I'm sorry about your crew. I told you before I had no idea that was going to happen, though I suppose I might have suspected. If it's any consolation, they died for a worthy cause."

York's anger welled up uncontrollably, "A worthy cause." He suddenly had a thought. "I'll make another bargain with you. You tell me your secret, and I'll tell you mine."

The two women glanced at each other, trying to decide silently between them whether or not they should lie to him. York gulped down the rest of his drink and poured another.

The empress shook her head sadly. "I can't. As you say, that's on a need-to-know basis. But your people did not die in vain. Believe me, if we succeed, it'll be worth any number of lives."

"Oh really!" He paused for a moment, then said, "Computer."

Acknowledged, the computer said.

"Retrieve observed warhead detonations on or about Dumark during the most recent enemy assault."

Retrieved.

York had run this simulation before, already knew the answers, had even noticed that a cluster of warheads had detonated directly over Janston, solving all of Maja and Toll's financial difficulties.

"Assume no further detonations after our up-transition out of Dumark nearspace and estimate casualty figures for Dumarkan population. Answer to two-digit accuracy."

York had purposely asked a wide open question. *Assuming midday population distribution is not markedly different from residential distribution, initial death toll would stand at twenty-one million. Within one week death toll would rise to thirty-three million. At one month, forty-eight million. After approximately three months, starvation and disease will bring the death toll to eighty million. The final toll—*

"Abort," York said.

Acknowledged.

York turned slowly to the two women. "You said it'll be worth any number of lives. Will it be worth eighty million lives? Do you spend lives that easily? Answer that for me."

Cassandra sat down slowly and buried her face in her hands. For several seconds York could hear her ragged breathing, then she lowered her hands and said, "Each and every year this war goes on we kill far more people than that. Do you know how long we've been fighting this war, Captain?"

"I've personally been fighting it for twenty-two years. Don't really care how long anyone else has been fighting it."

"Believe me, Captain, it's been going on a lot longer than that. And if it could be ended somehow, wouldn't that be worth eighty million lives?"

York tried to sympathize, couldn't really get there. "So you're both peacers, huh?"

Lady d'Hart shook her head tiredly. "No, Captain, we're not peacers. Our purpose is not that simple, nor that naive. But we need to know what your purpose is. Will you tell us?"

"As I said, you tell me your secret, and I'll tell you mine."

The empress stood. "Then we have nothing more to discuss."

••••

York's yeoman opened the door to his office hesitantly. "Sir. Director Add'kas'adanna."

Add'kas'adanna had to duck her head to step through the door, and as she straightened she looked at York without expression. Two marines followed and stepped to either side of her, their hands resting on their sidearms. She straightened and saluted York formally. He returned the salute, waved a hand at the chair in front of his desk. "Please."

She lowered herself into the chair, and while she was clearly older and probably well past her prime, she moved like a powerful and dangerous animal.

"Are your wounds healing well?" York asked, though he knew the answer.

She lifted a hand in front of her face, flexed the fingers of the prosthetic. "Nicely, Captain, thank you." She had an odd accent.

"I must apologize for the prosthetic," York said. "Our facilities are somewhat strained at the moment, and for the time being we can't offer you regrowth."

Again she flexed her fingers. "This is quite acceptable, Captain. In any case, how can I expect better treatment than the captain." She glanced at York's left arm.

"The medical orderly who gave you that information has been disciplined."

"Yes, I know," she said. "Since then it's been difficult to learn anything."

"All you need do is ask."

"And you'll tell me?"

York shrugged. "Perhaps."

She considered that for a moment. "There is one thing I am curious about. Was it through luck, or by design, that you were lying in wait for me?"

"Luck," York said. "Pure and simple. And tell me something. Why have you expended so much effort to find this ship?"

She cocked her head slightly, as if to say isn't it obvious. "You have the empress on board."

"Please. Don't insult my intelligence. She's not worth the resources you've diverted. Not worth having the Fleet Director herself personally leading the effort."

She nodded agreement. "Yes. That is curious, isn't it? There must be something else, mustn't there? But I confess I don't know what."

York believed her. Whatever was going on, it was a closely held secret. "There is something you could help me with." He stood, purposefully not explaining. She stood, and the two marines behind her stiffened. "Please come with me," he said.

He led them all to the brig, and even he was surprised at Sab'ach'ahn's appearance. She had, to a limited extent, obeyed his orders. The marines told him she ate when they told her to, bathed when they told her to, but still she painted her left eye lid with blood, and still she sat and stared at nothing.

Add'kas'adanna showed no reaction as they entered the cellblock. York stopped in front of Sab'ach'ahn's cell and motioned toward the sublegion. "Can you help me understand what's going on in this young woman's mind?"

Add'kas'adanna's eyes scanned the cell, then she turned to York and he sensed anger. "I see nothing," she said. "I see no one." Her eyes bored through York, defying him to argue with her.

York deliberately, and carefully, related the story of Sab'ach'ahn and Andleman on Anachron IV, though he edited his own suicidal tendencies out of the story. And as he did so, her anger dissipated.

For the first time, she looked at the young Kinathin in the cell, not through her as if she weren't there. "There is a concept in my culture we call *kith'ain*. The word translates to something like 'blood-honor,' though not exactly. It really has no parallel in your culture. It is more than honor . . . but it is less. It is also our word for 'soul,' but again the translation is not direct. If you kill your *kith'ain*, Captain, then you are nothing, you no longer exist. And if you kill your *kith'ain*, and at the same time your enemy shows that his *kith'ain* lives strongly and is untainted, and furthermore, your actions, or lack of action, damages or endangers his *kith'ain*, then your *kith'ain* is his, and you must await the death your enemy chooses for you."

For a moment, she looked on Sab'ach'ahn in an almost motherly way. "Sometimes, under stress, the young judge themselves more harshly than might you or I, we who have learned the art of compromise." She looked again at York. "And too, I think you have not told me all concerning your own actions."

"Are you telling me she's waiting for me to tell her how to die, and then she'll take her own life?"

Add'kas'adanna's eyes clouded over, and again she looked at him. "Tell whom, Captain. I see no one. I see nothing."

York tried again. "A hypothetical warrior then, who has killed her *kith'ain*, is supposed to wait for me to tell her how to die?"

"She must await the fate you choose for her. Whatever you choose, she must obey without question. You could choose to have her make a suicidal attack upon her own comrades, an ironic and not uncommon way of settling the matter, forcing her to kill some of them, and them to kill her. In fact, the more ironic the death you choose, the greater the possibility she can regain her *kith'ain* after death. Of course, I'm speaking of this . . . hypothetical warrior."

"She has to do whatever I tell her, huh?"

Add'kas'adanna nodded.

York had an idea, though he wasn't sure it would work. He turned to Sab'ach'ahn. "Sublegion. From now on you'll eat whatever is required to regain your health and strength. You'll bathe regularly, and you'll exercise with the marines daily. I want you in top physical condition, because I'm giving you the responsibility of protecting me and my ship. You must guard me against any and all danger, including . . ." York looked at Add'kas'adanna, and Sab'ach'ahn's eyes followed his, ". . . including protecting me and my ship from anything Director Add'kas'adanna might think of."

Add'kas'adanna frowned.

"You'll try to think like her, you'll watch her closely and try to anticipate any move she might make against me, and you'll report to me anything you suspect or learn. That's your *kith'ain*, whatever that means."

Add'kas'adanna looked at him with a mixture of what seemed anger and respect. "Captain, I could almost think you are Kinathin."

••••

"Not so much as a blink," Alsa said. "Nothing." She leaned forward and touched the controls on her console. The image on the screen froze.

York had asked Alsa to orchestrate a situation in which the servant/feddie spy found herself unexpectedly alone with Add'kas'adanna.

"Nothing," Alsa growled. "She played it stone-cold straight, the humble and ignorant servant."

York made sure Alsa erased all copies of the recording, and on the way back to his office he thought carefully about what he'd seen on the screen. Alsa had been right about the servant: she'd shown absolutely no reaction. But Alsa had been so intent on the servant she'd missed everything else, like Add'kas'adanna's reaction when the servant arrived. Not much of a reaction, but on a Kinathin it had been the equivalent of a startled jerk. No, the servant was no ordinary spy, perhaps wasn't even a spy at all, had to be someone Add'kas'adanna actually recognized. Just another feddie wasn't enough. In fact, she had to be someone the Kinathin recognized personally, recognized instantly, someone whose presence was so unexpected the Kinathin broke a discipline based on years of intensive training and instruction.

York considered that for a long time. Could it be possible he was giving passage to *two* of the most powerful feddies in the Directorate?

••••

"Forty-two lights and she wants to go, sir. We got gravitational instability on all decks."

A gravity wave rolled through the bridge. York tried to sound calm. "Steady as she goes, Mister Eldinow. She's not ready to go yet. Remember, Miss Votak's record was thirty-one lights. Hold her as long as you can, and let her go only when you have too. Let's try for thirty-five lights." York held Maggie's record over Eldinow and the other two rookies.

"Thirty-eight lights, sir . . . Thirty-seven . . . Thir . . . No, there she goes, sir."

"Hold on to as much sublight velocity as you can. Keep that flare to a minimum."

"Down-transition, sir."

"All stop," York barked. "Rig for silent running."

The wait . . . York had sat out the wait immediately after transition a thousand times, and it never got easier.

"Clear to a hundred thousand klicks, sir. Going to long range."

"I want a system map soonest, and a plot of all electronic activity."

York switched to the marine command channel. "Palevi, bring Red Richard up here."

While York waited for Richard he examined the data on the Borreggan system. Andyne-Borregga had long ago been a large space station, the remnants of which still circled the Borreggan primary. But a few centuries back the station had been abandoned in favor of the asteroid belt.

Andyne-Borregga was distributed throughout hundreds of large asteroids; several hundred more were defensive stations, and thousands more were nothing but electronic decoys. If anyone ever wanted to clean out Borregga, it would take a rather sizable armada, and they'd have to spend years fighting their way from asteroid to asteroid.

Richard was bleary-eyed when Palevi hustled him onto the bridge, and he had trouble handling zero-G. York had kept him isolated for the last two days, and as he hung on to York's console, looking over York's shoulder at his screens, he rubbed a three-day old growth of beard and asked, "What ya got there, Cap'm?"

"That's Andyne-Borregga. We're sitting about point-one light-year off nearspace, coasting in at point-nine-three lights, running silent. In about a month or so we'll just coast right through the system, if we don't do something else first."

Richard frowned, looked more closely at York's screens, hesitated for a moment, pushed himself over to the scan console and looked at Gant's screens, then came back to York with a deepening frown. "Nobody's chasin' ya," he said unhappily. Then he threw back his head and laughed loudly. "That be a damn good trick, Cap'm. How the hell'd you get so close without them seein' ya? One of them hunter-killer tricks of yers, I'll bet, eh?"

York nodded. "Yup. One of my hunter-killer tricks. Now, how do we get inside without getting our mutual ass shot off?"

Richard laughed again, rubbed his chin while looking once more at York's screens. "Well, Cap'm, I suppose we just knock on the door."

"And how do I do that?"

Richard shrugged. "Give Borreggan Traffic Control a call and tell them you're here."

York wasn't sure how much to trust Richard. "Okay," he said. "Miss McGeahn, please contact Borreggan TC and request docking clearance. And play it straight."

York handed Richard a headset so he could listen to the contact. "Borregga TC," McGeahn said calmly. "This is the Imperial Warship *Cinesstar*, Captain York Ballin commanding, requesting docking clearance."

They waited through a long pause, then McGeahn repeated the request. Another pause, and then finally an answer, "Say again, out there. We read you wrong. Sounded like you said you're an *imper*. Please identify."

McGeahn grinned and York could see it coming. "You read me right first time. I am an *imper*, and this is an *imper* cruiser with an *imper* crew. This is the Imperial Warship *Cinesstar*, Captain York Ballin commanding, requesting docking clearance."

Again a long pause while York noted an increase in electronic activity throughout the system. "Please identify your position, *Cinesstar*."

McGeahn glanced at York through the instrument clusters. He nodded and she broadcast their coordinates.

"*Cinesstar*, we see nothing at those coordinates. Please confirm."

McGeahn looked again at York, but this time he shook his head. Borregga wouldn't be happy until they could see something that agreed with what McGeahn was telling them. York touched a switch on his console. "Cappik. Full combat status. Gravity, shields, the works."

As the gravity came up and York settled under his own weight, the electronic activity around Borregga shot right off the scale.

"Yer crazy," the Borreggan tech shouted. "You can't attack us."

"Miss McGeahn," York said. "I'll take it from here."

He spoke carefully. "This is Captain York Ballin, commanding *H.M.S. Cinesstar*. We are not attacking you. Andyne-Borregga is a free port, and this ship wishes merely to avail itself of her facilities."

"You're nuts," the tech shouted back. "*Impers* don't come here. You can't—"

The link went silent, then a different, calmer voice took over. "This is Antolla Breaug, Yard Captain, Borregga Yard. I've heard of you, Ballin. What's the empire want here?"

York was walking a narrow legal line. "The empire wants nothing here," he said. "But my relationship with my superiors has deteriorated somewhat, and I'm told Borregga, as a free port, can provide facilities on an independent basis."

Richard leaned close to York's ear, "I know Breaug. Let me talk to 'im, Cap'm."

York nodded, switched Richard's headset into the connection. "Breaug. This here's Richard. Get hold of Dandra and Kruhl. Tell them we got us a new fish. And what a fish we got!"

"Richard?" Breaug demanded. "What the hell are you doing on an imperial warship? And why should I believe you anyway? You ran out on your docking fees again."

That set the tone of the conversation. Yarmin Dandra turned out to be the elected Governor General of Andyne-Borregga, while Sefath Kruhl was the Chairman of the Mexak League. Before all was said and done both men had joined the conversation, and while Richard's freewheeling style made it impossible to completely reach an agreement—which was exactly what York wanted—they did get some basic terms in place, and York learned quite a bit.

Kruhl was the number one pirate in the Mexak League, and a powerful man. Borregga was a large commercial concern, independent of the Mexak League, and Dandra was her duly elected governor. It became obvious his first concern was Borregga, and not the League, and after watching him face down Kruhl on a few points of contention, it was clear he was the man they had to satisfy.

Richard told them about the double-cross at Sarasan that had landed him in York's hands, which appeared to ease Dandra's concerns a bit. Richard also made a lot of noise about York applying for membership in the League, reminded them pointedly he was the infamous Butcher Ballin. That clearly pleased Kruhl, but not Dandra. For his part, York was careful to agree only to pay for docking fees and all services, and to abide by Borregga's regulations for a foreign ship in port—they transmitted a copy to York. He carefully avoided discussing or agreeing to apply for membership in the Mexaks, though Richard assumed he would and spoke of it often and loudly. Such talk generated a lot of strange, sidelong glances from York's crew.

Once Dandra was satisfied York's intentions were unofficial and purely commercial, they were given clearance for docking, and one day to establish some sort of credit. And then, with Eldinow at the helm, they spent the next several hours maneuvering through the asteroid belt to a zero-gravity berth in the main docks on one of the largest asteroids. They spotted several asteroids with considerable capability in the firepower department.

"Cappik," York said into his implants. "Don't power down. Maintain full combat status indefinitely and until further notice."

"Commander Rame, you have the bridge." York stood up from the captain's console. Rame saluted him and sat down in his place. York looked at him carefully. "Keep this ship on alert until you hear from me. No one on or off without my express permission."

York looked at Palevi and hooked a thumb over his shoulder. "Put Richard here back on ice, Sergeant."

Palevi grinned, grabbed Richard by an arm. "Aye, aye, sir."

Richard squawked, "But we had a deal, Captain."

York gave him a Palevi-style grin. "And I'll keep my end of it. But not until I'm absolutely sure you've kept yours. I assume it won't trouble you to wait another day or two while I make sure of that."

"Okay, Cap'm," Richard said, as if he had a choice in the matter. Then he grinned and nodded. "I think you and me understand each other real good, Cap'm."

Once Richard was out of ear shot, York turned to Rame again. "Olin, pick a couple of people you trust, smart ones. Send them out in civilian clothing, as if they're on leave from some ship. They ought to be able to find a bar or two, have a drink or two, buy a drink or two for someone with a big mouth, see what rumors are floating about, see what they can learn."

"Good idea," Rame said. "But why don't I send out three or four teams? They'll learn more, and they can track each other, back each other up if there's any trouble."

"Good idea."

••••

Fithwallen, Omasin and Faiel were waiting for him in Fithwallen's cabin. York told them, "We're docked in Borregga, but Dandra won't give us a spot in their repair yard until we establish some sort of credit. They're obviously assuming I'll do that by going straight to the Mexaks. And we have twenty hours to do otherwise."

"Why Captain," Fithwallen said, chuckling. "I'm impressed. I've always been given to believe career military personnel were incapable of creative thinking, especially creative lying."

York frowned at her, not sure how to take her remark. "Right now we're sitting at a loading dock running up fees. So what next?"

"I'll call my office here and order a shuttle to run us over to the bank. We can have this matter cleared up within the hour."

York found it rather interesting that she had an office in a pirate stronghold. "Where is this bank?"

"It's on one of the other asteroids."

York shook his head. "We'll take one of our . . ." York almost said *gunboats*, ". . . marine shuttles."

"Fine. But I should call ahead."

York keyed his implants. "Olin, this is York. Miss Fithwallen needs to make a call to her bank. Please arrange it for her." York didn't need to tell Rame to monitor the call closely.

To Fithwallen he said, "I'll meet you down on Hangar Deck in ten minutes. The marines outside your cabin will show you the way."

She smiled and he left. Out in the corridor he gave quick instructions to the two marines, then keyed his implants and spoke while walking. "Palevi, this is Ballin. I want an assault team of twenty marines ready on the double, in full combat armor. Put Yagell in charge of them, and make sure they've got whatever equipment might be necessary to break into a bank under fire."

"We gonna rob a bank, Cap'm?" Palevi asked with a certain amount of anticipation in his voice.

"No, I'm going into one. And if, for some reason, they decide not to let me out, I want your people ready to change their minds. But they're going to have to stay hidden in *Two* until and unless they're needed. I also need a visible escort, say ten more of your people in light kit—with visible sidearms but without armor. And make them your biggest and brawniest and ugliest, with you in charge."

"Am I big and brawny and ugly, Cap'm?"

"You do qualify for ugly, Sergeant. Next, I want Notay and four of your best people—smart ones—all armed to the teeth, but nothing that shows. And put them all in navy uniforms, brand new ones. And make Notay an officer. She's now Lieutenant Notay, my chief accountant, and the four with her are her staff. Try to pick people that look like accountants, whatever accountants look like. With me will be Sarra Fithwallen, Brentin Omasin, Jandeer Faiel, and Thomas Harshaw. Of the four marines, assign one to each of the four, with Notay assigned to me. None of them are to ever let their assignment out of their sight. And make sure whomever you assign to Faiel is good—Faiel's a pro. You got all that?"

"You bet ya, sir. Sounds like we're gonna have some fun."

"No, Sergeant, I doubt it. Probably won't be any fighting at all."

31

Andyne-Borregga

COUNCILOR ARD'DHA'SIT, PRIMARY seat of the Kinathin delegation to the Directorate General Council, waited impatiently for the shuttle to settle into its docking berth. He was tempted to reread the private communiqué from Add'kas'adanna, but he already knew its contents well, and doing so would only upset him further.

It had come to him in a most unusual fashion, carried by a young sublegion who had been personally instructed by Add'kas'adanna to hand-deliver the message. After dismissing the sublegion, Ard'dha'sit had opened the packet and found, to his surprise, an envelope and a message handwritten on paper, not coded onto a computer card. No one but Ard'dha'sit was to know of the envelope, and it was to be opened only in the event of Add'kas'adanna's death. And then, only a few days later, he had received word that she had been killed.

The true message contained within the envelope had upset and confused him terribly. Add'kas'adanna had invoked the kith'ain debt between her and Ard'dha'sit, and had written of her concern that Ninda was close to killing her kith'ain, which for any Kinathin would be an outcome far worse than mere physical death. There were implications of a devious political plot, and a request that Ard'dha'sit investigate her death carefully. And the circumstances of her death: her flagship torpedoed without a fight while orbiting a strategically unimportant imperial base in an apparent effort to search out and capture one, lone imperial ship. All under the orders of Ninda.

The hull of the shuttle echoed with the clang of the docking boom. Ard'dha'sit was on his feet immediately and headed for the air-lock, catching his aide off-guard. The crew of the shuttle sensed Ard'dha'sit's impatience, so they cleared the air-lock quickly.

A young, female DCO lieutenant met him on the other side of the air-lock, bowed deeply. "Councilor Ard'dha'sit. Director Ninda is awaiting your arrival. I'll escort you to him immediately." She glanced questioningly at Ard'dha'sit's personal bodyguard of six breeds.

"They will accompany me," Ard'dha'sit said, and she nodded.

Ard'dha'sit instructed the bodyguard to wait outside Ninda's office; he was not surprised to find Kaffair and Zort waiting with Ninda. They all rose and greeted him, smiles on their faces, but Ard'dha'sit could see the tension and fear hidden beneath the surface. Add'kas'adanna had told him about each of them: devious Director of Security Ninda; spineless Operations Director Zort; pragmatic Director General Kaffair. "And where's Director of State Theara?" Ard'dha'sit demanded, interrupting the pleasantries.

Kaffair spread his hands. "She's been missing for some time now, though we have no proof of her death so we haven't replaced her."

He was lying about something. Theara and Kaffair tended to think alike and vote as a bloc, while Zort didn't think at all, just did whatever Ninda told him to do.

Ninda smiled insincerely. "And now we are faced with the most untimely death of Director Add'kas'adanna." Somehow, even while stating the obvious, Ninda lied. Ard'dha'sit began to understand why Add'kas'adanna often found working with these people so distasteful. "But

Councilor, by withdrawing all Kinathin warships from DCO control you've seriously disrupted operations throughout the Directorate. And furthermore, by forming those ships into a single armada, and bringing them here with you, stationing them not half a light-year from this very facility . . . Well, I must protest."

Of course, you must, Ard'dha'sit thought. *Especially since my armada outnumbers the ships you have in this system ten to one.* But he didn't voice that thought. "Your protest is noted. However, the circumstances surrounding Fleet Director Add'kas'adanna's death are under question, and until the matter has been resolved, all Kinathin units will remain under the direct control of the Kinathin Delegation. Furthermore, the Kinathin Delegation has withdrawn from the General Council, also pending a satisfactory determination of the circumstances surrounding the death of Director Add'kas'adanna."

Zort's eyes darted from side to side. So far he'd said nothing, but he had guilt written all over his features. That, more than anything, decided Ard'dha'sit's hand. He touched the throat mic sewn into the collar of his councilor's robes, spoke three words in Kinathin *battlespeak.* Only a heartbeat later the door opened and one of his bodyguards entered, leveling her sidearm at the three Directors. In *battlespeak* she said, "We have secured the outer vestibule, My Lord. Marshal Sin'bos'menna reports she is transiting into the system now, and with the armada behind her she should have the system secure within the hour."

Ninda demanded, "What's going on here?"

At the tone in Ninda's voice the bodyguard tensed, but in *battlespeak* Ard'dha'sit cautioned her to remain calm. To Ninda he said, "I and the Kinathin Armada are going out to personally investigate Add'kas'adanna's death. And it is only appropriate the three of you accompany me. You will, of course, be allowed to bring your own retinue, and to maintain communication with your subordinates."

••••

Palevi had chosen his marines well. Yagell and her twenty in full armor were nicely hidden in the troop compartment behind the back bulkhead in *Two.* Palevi and his ten were appropriately big, and brawny, and ugly, and their sidearms were very visible, and there was no doubt they would do a good job of upholding the rather unpleasant reputation of imperial marines. And Notay turned out to be an actress of star quality. She'd tied her short hair back into a bun, managed to look strict and severe and accountant-like. The four with her did a pretty good job of acting also, though York wasn't sure if they fooled Faiel.

York wanted everything nice and legal, so Harshaw was his legal counsel. York had briefed Harshaw several days ago, and the man had spent the intervening time poring through *Cinesstar*'s library files on naval law. Oddly enough, York trusted the man more than any other civilian.

Somehow Harshaw had scrounged up a business suit and a brief case. "Have to look the part, Captain," he said in response to York's glance.

"How do we stand legally?"

"There's nothing that prohibits the commander of a ship from independently contracting for her repairs, nor any prohibitions regarding Borregga, nor any prohibition against independently financing said repairs, as long as you don't enter into any agreement that conflicts with your duties." Harshaw raised a questioning eyebrow at him.

York shook his head. "Don't worry about that. That's taken care of."

Fithwallen and Omasin and Faiel arrived in short order. They looked rather skeptically at Notay and her "accountants." Omasin frowned at Palevi and the escort of ten armed marines. "Is that necessary, Captain? Borregga is really quite civilized."

York looked at him and grimaced. "There's still a reward of one million crowns on my head."

"Ah! I had forgotten about that."

Fithwallen added, "I do have the resources to ensure your safety on Borregga."

"Thank you all the same, but I prefer to do my own ensuring."

Fithwallen smiled and looked at the marines. "You know, you're only going to enhance your image with such a retinue."

"What image?" he asked.

She shook her head sadly. "Don't be naive, Captain."

The short hop to the bank in *Two* was a bit strange. While the major hunks of rock in the asteroid belt were spaced thousands of kilometers apart, in astronomical terms it was a tight fit. York watched the screens all the way; saw a lot of small boats traveling back and forth between rocks. Borregga was indeed a thriving metropolis.

The bank was on an ovular rock about thirty kilometers in diameter named Gibraou. The president of the bank, Mr. Kaiya Danthor, met them at Gibraou's shuttle station. He was a small, rather officious man, who stopped just short of offering to act as Sarra Fithwallen's personal carpet. He was surprised by the size of York's retinue, but when Fithwallen introduced York as the "famous Captain Ballin," Danthor nodded, glanced at the ten armed marines and said, "Ah yes! There are rumors all over the rocks about you and your ship, Captain. I dare say that incident at Sarasan was a rather unpleasant business."

York looked at his watch. "How do they know about that? We've only been in Borreggan nearspace for ten hours."

"News travels fast, Captain, though in the finer details most of the rumors are somewhat incorrect. I, of course, have other, more reliable, sources of information."

Danthor ordered up a small fleet of electrically powered transports to drive them all to the Borreggan branch of Suin & Danthor, a bank apparently owned by a company owned by another company owned by Fithwallen. As they split up into the transports York pulled Notay aside. "Who have you got assigned to Faiel?"

Notay inclined her head toward a rather attractive, but small, female marine, the top of whose head barely reached Faiel's chest. At York's frown, Notay said, "Don't let Calla's size fool you, Captain."

The ride to the bank was about a kilometer through busy streets. At the bank they were escorted through a side entrance into a large, private reception area obviously not used by the general public. There, Danthor, looking at Fithwallen, said, "Shall we adjourn to my office?"

She nodded and looked at Faiel. "Jandeer. Why don't you and Brentin remain here? Captain Ballin and I have a few details to discuss with Mister Danthor."

York brought Notay and Harshaw. The two marines assigned to Fithwallen and Harshaw hesitated uncertainly until York said, "That's all right. You can stay here." Then he glanced at Palevi, keyed his implants and whispered, "No one in or out."

In Danthor's office the banker offered them all a drink. York and Fithwallen accepted while the rest declined. Harshaw and Danthor went to work immediately, while Fithwallen and York stayed in the background. Notay, staying in character, pretended to listen in on Harshaw and Danthor, though York noticed she constantly scanned the room.

"Your bodyguards are rather apparent, Captain," Fithwallen said with a smile as she and York waited.

"There are a lot of people who would like to see me dead."

She laughed. "Yes. That is the unpleasant truth." She played with her drink for a moment, had something on her mind. "Captain. I once offered you a job, though the circumstances were not right and you turned me down. If you get out of this alive, and you think you might be interested in making a career change, let me know."

"There's not much I know how to do, other than soldiering."

She smiled warmly. "We can discuss the possibilities at that time."

A few minutes later Harshaw approached York. "This all seems in order, Captain. Nothing terribly complicated really. In return for delivering Miss Fithwallen to Borregga, she funds all of the repairs to *Cinesstar*. And to protect you, the ownership of all repairs reverts to the empire upon completion."

He looked at Fithwallen and frowned. "Delivering you to Borregga?"

A side door to Danthor's office opened suddenly, and three civilian equivalents of Palevi's big, brawny uglies melted into the room. They were armed, guns drawn, but Notay was fast enough to step behind Danthor, draw a gun and aim it at Fithwallen. Danthor snapped, "Hold your fire, gentlemen," then looked at Fithwallen for further instructions, and as everyone froze York keyed his implants and whispered "Code blue."

Fithwallen raised her hands, palms out. "I won't be leaving with you, Captain."

At York's look, she added, "Don't worry. We had an agreement. Your end of the bargain was that you would deliver me to any location of my choice. Well, quite honestly, I don't believe your chances are very good once you leave Borregga, so this is the location of my choice. You have kept your end of the agreement, and I'll keep mine. And if you don't mind, I'd like you to leave Brentin and Jandeer here also."

Palevi's voice came over his implants. "Blue secured."

It was time to trust Fithwallen. "Okay," he said, leaving his implants keyed so he was broadcasting his words. "Sergeant Notay. Secure your weapon."

Notay complied, but Danthor hesitated to give the same order to his uglies.

"Kaiya," Fithwallen said. "Don't be foolish."

He nodded to his uglies and they holstered their guns.

Fithwallen looked at York. "Tell me, Captain. What is *code blue*?"

York kept his eyes on Danthor. "Sergeant Palevi and his marines have secured the outer corridor and are prepared for a firefight. An assault team is standing by, in full combat armor, with heavy assault equipment, ready to cut their way into the bank and pull me out."

Fithwallen smiled. "And I suppose the order for them to fight their way in here is code green, or red, or something like that?"

York grinned back at her and she nodded. "And knowing your marines, they would be unhappy to find you in anything but the healthiest condition."

She looked at Danthor. "You see, Kaiya, I've come to understand that Captain Ballin here is a thorough man."

In the reception area, Palevi's uglies were all waiting tensely with weapons drawn, though Notay's little "accountant" had Faiel face down on the floor with his hands cuffed behind his back. She was sitting on his back holding a small gun to the back of his head. York glanced at Notay and she gave him a smile and a wink.

The ride back to *Cinesstar* was uneventful, and contrary to York's paranoid fears, his ship was in no worse shape than when he'd left her. Rame had recalled his rumor teams, and debriefed them before York arrived. As York sat down at the captain's console Rame told him, "A lot of conflicting rumors floating about, though they do have it right about the double-cross at Sarasan. Some rumors that involve the empress' presence on this ship, but they're not consistent enough to worry about. Even rumors that she was among the dead at Sarasan."

York had an idea. "This place has to be loaded with spies and informers. Let's make up some rumors that could help us, then send out some new teams to spread a little misinformation."

Rame actually broke into a grin, but that disappeared. "We did get one piece of information that bothers me. Apparently, there isn't a single Mexak ship that comes even close to carrying the kind of firepower we have. And every pirate captain in the League is scheming to gain control of her, under the assumption we'll soon be heavily in debt for repairs. Some of them are going to be disappointed when they learn otherwise."

••••

York got in a short catnap of a few hours, was awakened by his yeoman. "There's a call for you, Captain, from Governor Dandra."

York took the call in his office. "Captain," Dandra began. "I've been notified by Suin & Danthor that you have rather substantial credit." Dandra's eyes narrowed suspiciously and he paused, but when York made no comment he continued. "You may move your ship to the yards and effect whatever repairs you need. You can make the arrangements with Yard Captain Breaug."

A few hours later *Cinesstar* settled into a low-gravity dock in the Borreggan shipyard on another big rock. The dock was completely enclosed, a fact York disliked intensely, but he had no choice. And as the giant gates swung slowly shut, sealing *Cinesstar* inside, he tried not to let his paranoia win out.

There was a lot of room in the dock, however, and he immediately stationed marines in full armor all around *Cinesstar*, cordoning her off from any unauthorized visitors. It took another day to get it clear to Breaug and the yard crews that none of them would touch his ship. The yard would provide parts and equipment, but Cappik and his people would do all the work.

Then York had to wrestle with Cappik for a few hours to get the chief to set his sights a bit lower. With their rather substantial credit, Cappik wanted to overhaul *Cinesstar* from stem to stern, which would only take about three months. York gave him one tenday.

"Captain, you can't be serious," Cappik pleaded. "We can't do shit in a tenday. Beggin' yer pardon, sir."

"Think about it, Chief," York said. "This place is full of spies and informers, and we've been here now for almost two days. You can bet both the empire and the Directorate now know we're here, in pretty good shape, and getting better. They've already scrambled an entire armada to burn us. Remember what they did to Dumark. A tenday probably leaves us some margin for error, but not much."

Cappik sat down and shook his head tiredly. He sat there quietly for a few long minutes, but York could see the wheels turning as he came to terms with their situation and made plans. "I guess we won't put any time in on the computer. We'll just load up on parts, then we can work on her later in transit. Have the department heads make shopping lists. We've got two places still need some serious structural work. We'll go after that first. We can easily replace turret seven. Her mountings are still intact so that won't take too long. Turret one and the bow are a different matter. No time to replace twenty meters of bow, but we can reinforce the structure beneath the surface, make sure the patch shielding we put there is fully effective, then mount a whole new turret. And of course we should go over the hull, patch any damage to the structure and shielding."

He looked at York, smiled unhappily. "The old girl's gonna have a bit of a funny shape, Captain, but she'll work just fine, and she'll fight good too. Power plant's the problem, though. We did a pretty good job on the centerline chamber at Sarasan, but it won't hurt to go over her one more time. We'll give priority to mounting a new port chamber. She won't be anything near functional when we leave, but we'll get the heavy work done in the yard, try and finish the rest later on our own."

"Thank you, Chief," York said. "Let me know if you need anything."

And then the waiting began.

••••

Seated comfortably in his office on Luna, Bargan Abraxa watched with considerable interest as Sierka entered the room. Sierka stopped in front of Abraxa's desk and saluted casually. "Your Grace," he said, with just a hint of informality, as if they were equals. "You wished to see me."

Juessik had warned him Sierka's over-inflated ego could be easily bruised, so Abraxa stood to greet him. "No need for the formalities, Mayhue. I'm told you have excellent insight regarding this renegade, Ballin."

Sierka lowered his hand carefully and smiled. "Yes, Your Grace. The traitor. He's a maniac, a fool. And he's dangerous."

Abraxa stood and motioned toward a chair. "Sit down, Mayhue. Can I offer you a drink? I have some of the finest Tithian brandy here."

Sierka sat down and beamed like a strutting rooster. "Why thank you, Your Grace."

Abraxa poured two glasses, handed one to Sierka, took a sip and gave Sierka a moment to do likewise. "Now," Abraxa prompted him. "You were saying about this traitorous bastard Ballin . . ."

"Yes," Sierka said, almost snarling. "Do you realize he had the gall to think he was capable of commanding that ship? And then the empress actually took command away from me and gave it to him. Somehow he fooled her."

Sierka went into a tirade that lasted for ten minutes. Abraxa helped him along a bit, realizing that before he could get to the crux of the matter Sierka needed to unload all of his hatred of Ballin. As Juessik had warned him, Sierka was quite unstable, and to flatter the fellow Abraxa was not above stooping to a bit of sanctimonious verbiage.

". . . He thinks he can fool me," Sierka snarled. "He thinks he's smarter than me. Well, he's not. I know exactly what he's going to do."

Abraxa interrupted him carefully. "And what is that?"

Sierka looked at him and beamed triumphantly. "He's coming here. What else? He's got to come here. That's the way he thinks."

••••

"Very interesting," Archcanon Bortha said. "Do you think he's right?"

Sierka was gone, and Abraxa had played a recording of the conversation for the churchman. "I don't know. It's possible, though I can't imagine Ballin is that much of a fool."

Bortha laughed and shook his head. "If that fool Sierka thinks Ballin's a fool, then young Ballin is quite probably a genius."

"Yes. Our Commander Sierka does not appear to be a good judge of character. However, I believe I have a means of evaluating his reliability."

Abraxa touched his intercom. "Send in Colonel Juessik."

Juessik, attired in a new uniform, stopped in front of Abraxa and bowed deeply. He turned to Bortha and repeated the bow.

"Good of you to join us, Colonel," Abraxa said.

"I'm at your command, Your Grace."

"Of course you are." Abraxa played the recording of his interview with Sierka. It was fascinating to watch it again, to see the man work himself up into a state of such hysterical rage. When it was done, he gave Juessik a moment to digest it, then asked, "How reliable is he?"

Juessik glanced at Bortha. At a slight nod from Abraxa he shook his head and said, "Not very. Sierka is incompetent, nearly got us all killed several times. I notice he managed to blame everything on Ballin, using what was often rather twisted logic, though it occurs to me when we get our hands on Ballin we can use that same logic ourselves to dispose of him via court-martial."

Abraxa nodded. "Good idea, Colonel. That may come in handy."

"As to Ballin," Juessik continued, "he knows how to run a ship, can be quite ruthless when he believes there's a need, and he's not afraid to take chances. But contrary to Sierka's opinion, Ballin is no fool."

Bortha leaned forward. "Then you don't think Ballin'll come here."

"I didn't mean that, Your Eminence. Sierka is an unmitigated fool, but he's so obsessed with Ballin there's a chance he does truly understand the man. It won't hurt to take a few precautions just in case Sierka is correct."

Abraxa watched Bortha nod, thinking he should have gotten rid of the whore's brat long ago. If Ballin did come to Luna, Abraxa would have to play a careful game. If the emperor got involved, or the nobility got wind of the situation, it could make things difficult. Abraxa could take precautions concerning Ballin, but as for the emperor, perhaps it was time to take tighter control of that situation.

It occurred to him that while Sierka was a fool, with careful manipulation he could still be useful. Abraxa decided not to have him killed, at least not until he knew to a certainty Ballin was dead.

••••

While Cappik was busy with the repairs York had nothing to do, so he spent a lot of hours sitting at his console on the bridge, reviewing every damage report as it was filed. It was Rame who approached him, leaned close and whispered, "Beggin yer pardon, sir, but you're making everyone nervous." York went to his cabin and hid.

At the end of the tenday Cappik wasn't ready. York hadn't really expected them to finish that quickly, but he wanted everyone to feel the pressure, so he grudgingly doled out the extra days watch by watch. After twelve days they were ready.

"Captain," Gant said. "There's something suspicious here."

York had called Breaug about an hour earlier, made arrangements to disembark. Then he'd released Richard, but as the pirate left the ship he said, "I thought we was gonna get along better'n this, Cap'm. We'd of made a good team, you an' me."

"What is it, Miss Gant?" York asked.

"I left a couple of drones outside before they locked us in this dock. Thought it might be good to have eyes out there, sir." A scan summary flashed on one of York's screens, a jumbled mess of dots scattered randomly. Gant highlighted one green. "That's this rock we're on, sir. The rest are other rocks around us. Except maybe these . . ."

She highlighted five more red dots, evenly spaced around the shipyard asteroid. "I'm getting some low level transition noise from these five, something like the stuff a ship emits if it's in a holding pattern."

York made a call to Cappik. "Looks like our pirate friends are going to try something funny."

Cappik grinned. They'd carefully discussed that possibility. "You got full combat status right now, sir."

"Thank you Mister Cappik. Mister Rame, sound General Quarters, Watch Condition Red."

The alert klaxon blared and the ship went through the well-rehearsed ritual. York waited until everyone was on station and Rame cut the alert klaxon, then he placed a call to Breaug, but Breaug didn't answer. Instead, Kruhl appeared on his screen, seated in the Yard control room, with Richard standing behind him. "Captain Kruhl," York said. "Where's Yard Captain Breaug?"

Kruhl grinned. "Well now, Captain. Breaug ain't available. But he asked me to fill in, help you complete your application to the Mexak League, so's you can leave."

"I don't intend to join the League. Open the gates."

Behind Kruhl, Richard also grinned. "I'm sorry, Captain, but the gates seem to be malfunctioning at the moment."

York grinned back at him. "Well, perhaps I can repair them.

"Mister Jakobee," York said calmly, leaving the channel open so the two pirates could hear him. "Open those gates."

York had instructed Jakobee carefully. *Cinesstar*'s turrets swung toward the gates. "Continuous fire," Jakobee ordered, and *Cinesstar* rocked under the impact of the barrage. The gates were only about fifty meters from the hull, and York watched the shielding draw power as the explosions splattered her with debris. When the debris settled, the hole in the gates was large enough for *Cinesstar* to maneuver through.

"Very impressive," Kruhl said, maintaining his grin, though it was now strained. "But as I said, it won't do you any good."

York grinned back at him. "Yes. I know. Your five ships."

Kruhl's grin disappeared and he looked angrily over his shoulder at Richard. Richard shrugged.

"Mr. Jakobee," York said, "stage two."

Jakobee said, "Warhead away," and touched a switch on his console. One wall of the Yard erupted in a fountain of debris and the entire rock shook as the warhead, launched almost at transition velocity, ground its way through the rock of the asteroid.

"You're insane," Kruhl shouted, his grin gone.

York didn't grin, just nodded. "You're not the first person who's told me that. That was a one-gigatonne warhead. We buried it in the center of this rock."

Kruhl looked over his shoulder at Richard. "I thought you said this would be easy."

"Mister Jakobee," York continued. "How's our warhead."

"She checks out just fine, sir, though I missed dead center by about a kilometer."

"Don't worry about it, Mister Jakobee. Go to stage three."

Kruhl demanded, "What the fuck is stage three?"

York kept his voice level and calm. "We've armed and fused that warhead remotely, and set it up on a deadman signal. That warhead should crack this rock into quite a number of pieces. It'll kill us all."

Kruhl screamed, "You're bluffing."

Richard leaned forward and growled into Kruhl's ear. "I don't think he is, Sefath. He's just fuckin' nuts."

Kruhl looked at York uncertainly. "It's your call," York told him plainly. "Tell those ships to power up and get out of here. Otherwise, I'll lift out of here, get as much distance as I can between us and this rock before your ships get to me, then I blow you to hell. We'll probably go with you, but I'm willing to take my chances, which are a lot better than yours."

Richard growled, "He ain't bluffin', Sefath."

"Oh shut up!" Kruhl shouted. He looked at York. "All right, Ballin. But how do I know you won't kill us anyway, after you're out of range."

"You'll just have to trust me. Besides, I don't want to kill Breaug and the Yard crews. I'm assuming they weren't part of this. Come to think of it, release Breaug now. I want to speak to him."

Breaug had an ugly bruise next to one eye. "What the hell have you done to my Yard," he screamed at York. "You're a madman."

York shook his head. "I accept no responsibility for the damage. We were forcibly detained, so I acted in self-defense."

Breaug turned slowly to Kruhl. "You fucking idiot. You're going to pay for every bit of damage out there, even if it means your ship." Richard was skulking quietly into the background. Breaug turned on him. "And you too, Richard."

Breaug turned back to York. "I didn't have anything to do with this."

••••

They had no trouble getting out of the Borreggan system. York had Gant set up a transition heading that led them off into uncharted space, and they followed that for one day, while all the time the crew were wondering what their captain had in mind.

Each day they down-transited so Cappik and his crew could work for a few hours with all systems shut down, then York gave Gant another seemingly random transition vector, though York did keep them heading in the general direction of their ultimate destination. Finally, after four days, Cappik had had time to complete his repairs.

Gant asked, "Where to now, Captain?"

Everything suddenly fell silent, and he knew they were all holding their breath.

"Luna," he said into the silence. "Set up a transition for Luna Prime, Miss Gant. We're going home."

32

Homecoming

BELLA TZECHARRA WATCHED Abraxa's image carefully as she spoke. "Yes, Your Grace, an armada, looks to be about one hundred ships. We were too heavily outnumbered so we had to withdraw from Sarasan a few light-years."

Abraxa didn't seem upset by that. "That was a wise decision, Captain."

Tzecharra held back a sigh of relief. "I did, however, station two fast ships just outside of nearspace so they can relay accurate information to me. The composition of the armada appears to be exclusively Kinathin. And they've done nothing more than occupy the system and set up a strong defensive perimeter."

Abraxa's eyes shifted to one of his other screens, then returned to her. "AI has gleaned no hint of such a marshaling of forces."

Tzecharra knew her career was riding on this. "That would seem to indicate, Your Grace, that this armada was assembled rather hastily, which correlates with the intelligence reports we've been getting of disruptions in Directorate operations all the way up and down the line." Tzecharra decided to take a chance. "I would guess a hundred ships is close to the full complement the Kinathins have fielded in support of DCO."

"And based on our intelligence reports, your guess would be correct. Continue."

"This wouldn't be the first time the Kinathins have veered off on a private crusade of their own."

"Yes," Abraxa said, and he smiled. "It may even be that we have a small civil war developing within the Directorate."

Abraxa suddenly focused his attention sharply on Tzecharra. "Captain, you've done well here. Please hold your position as long as you can and report to me directly if anything develops, though you have my permission to withdraw if you deem it appropriate."

Abraxa signed off, and Tzecharra relaxed, realizing with satisfaction this little situation may have vastly enhanced her career.

••••

The sound of the gunshot brought Edvard awake with a start. He'd fallen asleep at his desk, and was struggling groggily to his feet when he heard a short burst of automatic weapons fire, followed by several more gunshots.

He started for the door, but before he could cross the room the door opened and four of his household guard calmly entered, all carrying short, rather stubby looking rifles. His momentary relief disappeared quickly when he didn't recognize any of them. Then all four of them reached into their tunics and retrieved small cloth caps and stretched them over their heads, AI black caps with AI insignia.

"Secure the room," one of them told the others, and as they fanned out to check the exits he turned to Edvard with a wicked grin on his face. "Your Majesty," he said, holding the rifle casually, though Edvard noticed the muzzle slanted his way. The man reached into his kit and retrieved an injector, then, still grinning, said, "It would be best if you cooperated."

••••

York climbed groggily out of the grav bunk, realized he was running late. He threw on yesterday's uniform, stuffed his gun under his tunic, stepped through the cabin hatch and glanced quickly up and down the corridor. This early in the morning it was deserted. He turned and hurried quickly up the corridor.

He was heading for the lift when it hit him—*deserted!* He froze in his tracks, glanced over his shoulder. There should be two marines dogging his heels. He listened carefully, pulling the gun from under his tunic, heard a single, soft footstep down a side corridor, pressed his back against a bulkhead and waited for the assassin to show himself.

A hand cupped itself over his mouth, and another removed the gun from his hand with crushing force. With his heart pounding up into his throat he waited helplessly for a knife thrust into his back, or something else equally lethal. But then he noticed the deep olive hue of the skin on the hand cupped over his mouth, and as his captor leaned forward to say something, he caught a glimpse of bone-white hair.

"Captain," Sab'ach'ahn whispered. "The assassin is close by. Do not cry out." She released him and gave him back his gun. With her eyes scanning the corridor, she added without emotion, "Can you admit us to one of these cabins?"

He turned to the nearest cabin hatch, palmed the lock and growled at it, "Computer. Override. Captain's priority. Emergency access. Override, damn you!"

He heard the hatch mechanism cycling, watched as the hatch slowly started to swing inward, leaned his shoulder into it to help it, stumbled into the cabin and landed on the floor. A woman screamed and a man's voice demanded, "Who the hell are you?"

Sab'ach'ahn stepped in behind him, put her shoulder to the hatch and slammed it shut. As she cycled the lock the man ordered, "Computer, lights," and the cabin lights flared much too brightly.

A middle-aged woman in the lower grav bunk clutched the edge of a sheet to her throat in an attempt at modesty. The man was already out of the upper bunk, standing defiantly on the deck. He demanded, "Who do you think you are, barging—"

Sab'ach'ahn shoved the muzzle of her gun under his nose and said softly, "Be silent."

The man paled, and wisely shut up.

"Palevi," York barked into his implants. "This is Ballin. Code red. I'm being hit again."

In moments, armed marines swarmed the deck. Palevi had figured there could be no better bodyguard than a Kinathin, so he'd given Sab'ach'ahn free reign of the ship.

The two marines Palevi had assigned as York's bodyguards were dead. They'd each been shot in the face at close range with a small-caliber weapon—quiet, clean, fast—an assassin's weapon. Then they'd been stuffed into a maintenance closet with a couple of service bots for company. "They were a couple of my best people, Captain," Palevi said, shaking his head. "That's why they were on this job. Whoever popped them like this—so clean, without a fight—he's gotta be good." Palevi shook his head worriedly.

••••

Ninda finished his report with an air of smug satisfaction. "One of our agents on Andyne-Borregga broke deep cover to file this report."

"And what of the agent?" Ard'dha'sit demanded.

"Another agent whose cover is still intact reported that shortly thereafter, agents of Admiralty Intelligence attempted to capture him and he was killed in the ensuing fight."

Ard'dha'sit considered the information carefully. "So she's alive, and apparently healthy, and a captive of the imperials. And Theara as well?"

"Yes." Ninda added, "I knew you'd be pleased to hear Add'kas'adanna hadn't been killed."

Ard'dha'sit choked back an angry retort, but he'd been choking back angry retorts for days now as he'd gotten to know these three men. Kaffair had some redeeming qualities, and seemed basically honest, though like anyone in such a position he was rarely entirely truthful. But Zort was a cowardly snipe, and Ninda—Ard'dha'sit had had to struggle often to restrain from having the man throttled. Add'kas'adanna had told him of these men and their games, had warned him the Central Committee was even more devious than the General Council. And Ard'dha'sit realized that to get any answers he would have to use every bit of his training.

Careful to allow none of his preparations to show, he slowed his pulse and lowered his body temperature. He concentrated on the disciplines of thought construct, built the logical sub-mind carefully, then experienced the odd, schizophrenic sensation as he released the separate consciousness.

The question he would now ask had been very carefully chosen. He probably wouldn't get a straight answer, but the question was really meant to elicit a response at a subconscious level. "How did Theara come into their hands?"

In the fraction of a second immediately following the question he obtained several answers. Kaffair's eyes shifted and glanced at Ninda. Ninda blinked, and pretended to be calm, though Ard'dha'sit's hearing picked up a rise in his pulse rate. Zort's body temperature actually rose slightly, while Kaffair's dropped.

Ninda was saying something about investigating the disappearance, and as Ard'dha'sit watched Kaffair and Zort listen to him he gained more answers. Kaffair was in some way involved in Theara's disappearance, though not because he was her enemy, but more likely because they were co-conspirators. Ninda was apparently aware of everything they'd done, and was confident he had thwarted their plot. And Kaffair, aware that Ninda had uncovered their plot, was apparently backed into a corner.

Ard'dha'sit interrupted Ninda in mid-sentence. "And how was it Add'kas'adanna was in a position to be captured."

"The matter was of such importance . . ." Ninda answered, ". . . that she chose to lead the search for the imperial ship herself. We can only guess . . ."

Ard'dha'sit's sub-mind allowed his formal mind to argue with Ninda, while carefully observing the responses of all three.

More answers. Ninda had clearly used Add'kas'adanna in some way, regarded her as no more than his personal lackey, discounted her altogether. Kaffair considered her an opponent, perhaps even an enemy. And Zort sought only to align himself with whoever might win, though since he didn't know who that might be he wanted to keep his options open. Yes, this was a matter of Add'kas'adanna's *kith'ain*, and her *kith'ain* was in danger, grave danger.

Ard'dha'sit relaxed, released control of his pulse, respiration and body temperature, experienced a moment of disorientation as his formal mind absorbed the sub-mind and became aware of the knowledge it had gained. He would pay a high price later for the energy expended, but it was well worth the knowledge.

He stood and silenced them all with a look. "It is time we dealt with this directly. We go to Luna."

••••

After two days of total isolation in a small cell, Edvard was close to complete despair. It had been the longest two days of his life. He'd struggled with the thugs posing as his household guard, but they'd been careful to subdue him without hurting him. He'd awakened in the cell, and since then he'd had no human contact.

There was a clock on the wall, a small terminal for ordering food, a receptacle where the food appeared after he placed his order, and a plain cot. There was also a door with a small wall-com next to it. The door was locked, and would not open in response to his commands, and he got no response from the wall-com, no matter how loud or long he shouted into it. He'd discovered the environmental comp was still active since he could control the lights and temperature and humidity with a word or two. But no contact with the outside world. No news, no information.

On the third day, the door suddenly cycled open and Abraxa stepped into the cell, saying, "Please forgive me, Your Majesty, for keeping you waiting so long. I had a few difficulties consolidating my control—but that's over now and we can breathe easier. Have you been comfortable?"

Edvard shook his head. "You're behind all this?"

"Of course. Who else is powerful enough to stage a coup, and make it look like Admiralty Intelligence valiantly foiled an assassination attempt? Why, on the vids this morning you even awarded several of them medals. And of course you're keeping a low profile until we've finished rounding up the traitors involved and executed them all."

Abraxa looked around the cell. "I do apologize for the accommodations. We'll have you moved to something more comfortable shortly."

At the look of astonishment on Edvard's face Abraxa shrugged. "There's no need to be barbaric about this; you are the king and emperor, after all. Now, there's going to be a press conference tomorrow morning, and we need to review what you're going to say."

"No we don't," Edvard shouted, standing and approaching Abraxa. As he did so two AI thugs stepped through the open door, crossed the room and held Edvard immobile between them. Again they were careful not to hurt him.

"Now, now!" Abraxa said. "If you don't cooperate, then we may have to get barbaric. Cassandra and Aeya are still alive, you know."

That piece of information was like a slap in the face; Edvard recoiled and almost staggered.

Abraxa glanced around the cell again. "But I think that can wait. Let's do something about your accommodations first."

••••

Bella Tzecharra was barking orders into allship when her yeoman interrupted her. "Captain, His Grace is waiting."

Tzecharra slapped a switch on her console, and when Abraxa's image appeared she spoke breathlessly. "Your Grace, forgive me for being abrupt, but I have very little time. I'll probably be forced to cut this contact prematurely.

"The Kinathins have transited out of the Sarasan system en mass, and they're headed this way. Now I may be paranoid, but that also means they're headed toward Luna."

Abraxa's eyes sharpened as he considered her words. "That's still quite a distance. There's no reason to believe they won't change course long before they get here."

"Let's hope."

"And if they don't," Abraxa asked, "Can you divert them?"

"I doubt it. After Aagerbanne, then the mutinies at Sarasan, I have fewer than twenty undamaged ships. And even those are operating with limited reserves."

Abraxa shook his head thoughtfully. "I'll pull Seventh Fleet in from the third quadrant. They may be able to intercept."

"What about Home Fleet, Your Grace? With their . . ."

The alert klaxon interrupted her, and allship blared, "Watch Condition Red. Battle stations. This is not a drill . . ."

Tzecharra looked at Abraxa pleadingly. "Forgive me, Your Grace. I must cut transmission."

Abraxa nodded and waved a hand at her. "Of course."

••••

"Two light-months out, sir. Holding at forty lights." Gant's voice held a metallic edge.

York knew they all thought he was crazy, perhaps even suicidal—ordering them to Luna like this, right into the heart of the empire. He could see the doubt in their eyes, hear it in their voices, and all he could do was pretend that he didn't notice.

When the empress had heard what he planned she'd stormed into his office. "You're insane."

He'd looked up from the reports he was reviewing. "I think we've already established that."

"Don't be flippant with me. Abraxa will destroy this ship on sight."

York shook his head. "I hadn't intended to ask his permission."

"He's no fool. No doubt he's got every ship in the empire searching for you."

"No doubt," York agreed. "But not at Luna. And will he oppose you openly? Would he murder the empress in front of everyone? If we can sneak into the system quietly, then tell everyone we're there, loudly, with you personally broadcasting some sort of message on every channel *Cinesstar* can tap, will the Admiralty Council just burn us out-of-hand?"

"No," she said hesitantly. She sat down and frowned as she considered that. "Much of Fleet would oppose such an open power grab."

"That's what I'm counting on. I'll get us to Luna, in one piece, and it's your show from there."

She shook her head worriedly. "It'll never work. The odds are stacked against us."

"The odds are worse out here in the fringes. Abraxa and his buddies can burn us and make up whatever they want."

York sat at the captain's console, kept hearing his own words again and again: *I'll get us to Luna, in one piece.*

They could sneak in like a hunter-killer. When approaching an enemy installation, all he had to do was make some educated guesses about his target: but this was Luna, so he didn't have to guess. With a lot of number crunching he could produce an optimum deceleration curve—if he decelerated too quickly, it took forever to get there, too slowly, and the outer pickets would spot them and they'd eat a warhead.

The final trick for a hunter-killer captain was to keep his transition flare to a bare minimum—reduce transition velocity as much as possible before transition, and retain as much sublight velocity as possible after transition. In any case, he needed all that sublight velocity to drift slowly into range.

A hunter-killer might take a month to set up such a shot, but they didn't have a month. So he'd had to come up with something better than that. He'd sweated over that for days, and eventually the answer lay in the very thing that caused the problem. Luna Prime closely monitored all incoming traffic, but there was so much of it York decided to use the traffic density to his advantage.

"Two light-months out, sir. Holding at forty lights."

"Start easing her back, try for a new record."

"Thirty-eight lights, sir . . . Thirty-seven . . ." A gravity wave rolled ponderously through the bridge and Eldinow held at thirty-seven lights for a few minutes while he and Gant and Cappik worked feverishly to stabilize *Cinesstar*'s systems. "Thirty-four . . . Thirty-two . . . Twenty-nine . . . Twenty-eight . . . Twenty-seven . . ." Eldinow's voice suddenly jumped an octave. "There she goes . . . Down-transition, sir."

"All stop," York barked. "Cut all power. Rig for silent running."

And again the wait . . . always the wait. "That's a new record, Mister Eldinow," York said, trying to break the tension. "Congratulations."

"Clear to a hundred thousand klicks, sir. Going to long-range."

They were all operating on a sort of personal auto-pilot, too numb and frightened to think about what they were doing. York had drilled them for months to just that purpose, so that when the pressure was really on, they could find comfort in routine. Sometimes that was all that separated a professional soldier from an amateur. "Start an electronic activity map. Keep it fully updated at all times."

"Clear to a million klicks, sir," Gant said. "And nothing on passive long-range."

York looked at his console, at their sublight velocity and range. "Now we wait. Miss Gant, start looking for any hint of radiation somewhere between us and nearspace, anything that might indicate where they've stationed their pickets. Also watch for the picket tender. If they make rounds to change crews on the weapons platforms, we can see where they stop. And monitor all incoming traffic. Anyone incoming is going to be challenged, and we have a chance of spotting any transmitter splash if they're at all sloppy. And start looking for that freighter, a big one, coming in a little too fast. We need that baby, now."

He was repeating his earlier instructions because of his own nervousness. Gant and Rame and the bridge crew were at it before he'd even stopped talking. He hung around for an hour, reviewed the early data on the system and electronic activity maps. The back-scans showed all the incoming and outgoing traffic he'd expected.

He put in a call to the empress. She had insisted he brief her on a daily basis. As always, Lady d'Hart was with Cassandra when York arrived. York bowed, "Your Majesty."

"I'm told the maneuver was successful, Captain."

York gave a cautious nod of his head. "As successful as we can expect at this stage."

"Your ever-present caution is beginning to wear thin."

Lady d'Hart interjected, "But that may be what's kept us alive, Your Majesty."

Cassandra asked, "Are we in danger?"

"The danger at this stage is slight. If we're spotted now we're still far enough out to make a run for it. At worst, we could end up back where we started, with a whole train of pursuers on our tail."

"So where do we go from here?"

York stepped to a terminal and brought up a display of the developing system map. Even as they looked on, Gant and her people added more detail. "We're about two light-months out, coasting in at point-eight lights. Since we can't wait two and a half months to coast into the system, we're going to hitch a ride on the transition wake of an incoming ship passing close to us. We need something large, like a freighter, and coming in too fast, so she'll have to start braking hard before down-transition. Her speed and tonnage will all add to the size and intensity of her transition wake, and when she starts braking like that, she'll make a lot of transition noise. And when she's close enough we'll give ourselves a little boost with our transition drive. With that, I believe her transition wake might pull us into up-transition, and all the noise she's making will hopefully mask any flaring we do. We'll have to accelerate hard so we can stay on top of her. Then when she down-transits we down-transit with her, which should be somewhere inside of nearspace. And from there we can coast into Lunan nearspace in something on the order of a day or two."

Lady d'Hart asked, "How long might we have to wait for such an opportunity. I wouldn't think freighters would make such mistakes often."

"Actually they do," York said. As an academy cadet, York had stood apprentice watches in every conceivable function in the system, including a short stint in traffic control on Luna Prime. "Freighter captains often come in fast like that to shave time off their trips, especially if they're running behind schedule and their contract calls for late-delivery penalties. Their contract may even specify an early delivery bonus. They'll usually jimmy some of their equipment, so even if later they're boarded and inspected, they can claim faulty equipment. It's tolerated as long as they don't push it too far, and we can count on one of them coming in like that every few days." York didn't add that his own stint in TC was almost twenty years ago, and no one else on board had ever served such a stint, at least not on Luna Prime.

"Excellent, Captain," Cassandra beamed. "Excellent. Is this another one of those hunter-killer tricks?"

York hesitated. "Sort of . . ."

"What do you mean by that?"

"Well . . . It's the kind of trick a hunter-killer captain might use. But it depends on a large freighter coming in too fast right over the top of us. And the probability of that happening is pretty slim unless you're going into an important, busy system and you place yourself right in the middle of one of their major approach patterns." York hesitated, and both Cassandra and Lady d'Hart eyed him warily. "Hunter-killers don't usually try to set up sneak shots on systems that are so heavily guarded, especially since once you're in, you're not going to get out."

Lady d'Hart asked, "So no one has ever done this before?"

"To my knowledge, it hasn't been tried before. Or, if it has, and it was unsuccessful, then that's why we've never heard about it. There are any number of things that might go wrong."

York braced for an onslaught of angry words, but Cassandra threw her head back and laughed. "I guess if it's never been done before, they won't know to guard against it, and our chances are even better."

York had barely left her cabin when Gant's voice came over his implants. "Captain, I think we've got our ride coming in fast."

York rushed up to the bridge, but it was a false alarm. As he looked at the scan reports, and the details of the incoming transition wake, he shook his head. "Negative. That's a military vessel, probably a cruiser."

"But she's big, sir, and coming in too fast. She'll have to start braking pretty soon and throwing noise all over the place."

"Yes. And her scanning equipment is a hundred times better than that of any freighter, and her scan operators are used to watching for sneaky little tricks, for anything out of the ordinary. We try to hitch a ride in her wake and she'll spot us for sure. So batten down all hatches and sit tight. We'll wait for a big, fat, dumb freighter."

••••

"It's an ore freighter, sir, lot of mass, and coming in fast. She's about two hours out, and hasn't begun braking yet. Looks like she's the one."

It was the middle of the night, and York was standing over the terminal in his cabin, doing a poor job of waking up quickly. "I'll be right up."

On the bridge, York confirmed Gant's assessment. "Yes, she's our ride in, as long as we can intercept. How close?"

She shrugged and hunched her shoulders. "Not good, not bad. She'll pass within about ten million kilometers, close by astronomical standards, marginal if we want to intercept her wake."

Leaning over Gant's shoulder, York scanned her screens quickly. "What if we give ourselves a little nudge, minimum possible drive power now, a little more as she gets closer and begins to mask our noise?"

"We'll be taking a chance, sir."

"Add it to all the other chances we're taking. Let's do it."

"Shall I sound General Quarters, sir?"

"Negative. Wake everyone up easy, tell them to get some breakfast, and I want them on station in an hour and a half."

York had sandwiches brought up to the bridge, and lots of hot, black caff. They were chewing on the sandwiches and trying to estimate what their transition vector would have to be when, an hour later, the freighter got an angry message from Luna Traffic Control, and began braking. Her captain pleaded a fault in their auto-pilot.

An hour later, York placed a call to Cappik. "You know what I need?"

"Yes, sir. Full combat status, gravity and drive, all switched on fast at your command."

"Right. Eldinow, any questions?"

Eldinow was nervous. Much of this depended on him. "Just before she gets to us I start pushing a little drive, try to adjust our vector for intercept and hover just under transition, let her pull us into transition when she goes over the top of us. Then when we're in transition, give *Cinesstar* everything we've got and try to keep up with her."

"Jakobee?"

Jakobee started reciting his role, though York didn't really pay attention to him. They'd drilled this routine in sims repeatedly for days and he knew his part. He was just giving them all something to do other than sit and wait.

"Captain," Gant said, "You asked me to give you a quarter-minute warning. We're there."

"Thank you Miss Gant." York switched to allship. "Stand by all stations. Hold your discipline. Shoot at nothing unless you're given a target by your station commander."

"Ten seconds and counting, sir . . . nine . . . eight . . . seven . . ."

York scanned his screens one last time.

". . . zero," Gant barked. The freighter was still several seconds behind them, overtaking them rapidly as York's screens showed Cappik bringing up the power. Eldinow started to apply sublight drive gingerly.

"Hit it hard, Mister Eldinow," York growled. "This is no time for a soft touch."

Eldinow obeyed instantly, but sublight drive was nothing compared to the transition velocity of the freighter overtaking them. "Here she comes, sir," Gant said. "Eight hundred million kilometers and closing . . . Five hundred million . . . Two hundred . . . She's going to pass to within . . . forty thousand klicks. Here she comes."

They could all feel the leading edge of the freighter's transition wake as it interfered with *Cinesstar*'s internal gravity. York's stomach did a somersault and a wash of static surged through the air as the freighter passed over them. "Shit!" Eldinow squeaked. "Up-transition, sir."

"All ahead full, Mister Eldinow," York shouted, swallowing to keep the sandwiches down. "Don't let us down-transit. Not now."

Cinesstar's hull groaned as the freighter's transition wake twisted and warped her gravity. The readings on York's screens shot upscale as her transition drive struggled with the mess in local space created by the nearness of a large ship in transition. Wave after wave of gravity rolled through the decks, and the computer started diverting power into *Cinesstar*'s structure to hold her together. "Mister Eldinow," York shouted above the noise. "To starboard, minimum drive power, one second burst."

He couldn't hear Eldinow's reply but he saw the response on his screens, and as *Cinesstar* slid farther out toward the edge of the freighter's transition wake, the warring pressures on the hull eased slightly. But not enough for a young tech at Gant's scan console. York had to give him credit though. He had the presence of mind to turn his head and blow his breakfast all over the deck rather than on his console. And then he had the further presence of mind to wipe his chin and turn back to his work as if nothing had happened, vomit staining his tunic.

York watched his screens, held on tight, tried to ignore the noise as the hull of the ship complained loudly. He was close to vomiting himself, but he was certain no ship's captain had ever puked on his own bridge, and he would accept utter damnation before being the first in the history of Fleet to do so.

He held on, watched his screens, kept his mouth shut, monitored the freighter's velocity and *Cinesstar*'s relative proximity. He had only one order to give in this situation. His crew knew what they had to do, but it was up to him to tell them when to stop doing it. The freighter was slowing steadily, dumping inordinate amounts of power to kill her velocity. Then she appeared to hesitate, almost to pause as if waiting for something. York hadn't been sure what he should be watching for, but that was it. "Down-transition," he shouted, "All stop."

"Down . . . transition," Eldinow groaned.

The change was so sudden he almost did lose his breakfast. One moment he was hanging on while *Cinesstar*'s hull screamed at them, and the next a frightening, intense silence settled throughout the ship.

York swallowed hard. "Miss Gant?"

"Nothing yet, sir."

The freighter down-transited just in front of them.

"Where the hell are we?"

"Beggin' yer pardon, sir. One minute, sir."

They waited while Gant tried to assess their situation. York switched to the command channel. "All station commanders, this is the captain. If you had the same kind of trouble we did, you've got some fairly sick people on your hands. Don't assign cleanup details yet. We may be under fire momentarily."

"We're two-point-one light-days out, sir," Gant interrupted him. "Coasting in at point-five-six lights . . . We're well within the rear picket line . . . None of the pickets we identified are turning toward us . . . None are powering up. No signs of any abnormal activity in our vicinity . . . Wait a minute!"

Gant worked at her console frantically, and York kept his mouth shut. "There's one ship ten AUs off our port bow, another fourteen off our stern, but we were tracking their vectors before we made transition and they haven't changed course. No signs of anyone else suddenly powering up."

"McGeahn," York growled. "What's on the com?"

She hesitated. "Well, there's lots of stuff, sir. We're in Luna system, you know."

York lost his patience. "Yes, Miss McGeahn. And if anyone picked up an unauthorized transition, or anything out of place, there'd be a system-wide intruder alert on every channel, and all hell would be breaking loose."

"Oh, sir. Sorry, sir. Didn't think of that, sir."

McGeahn switched channels several times, listened to each carefully. "Nothing, sir. Just a lot of chatter, and the usual traffic. Though the Watch Commander at Luna TC is giving that freighter captain hell. Nothing else, sir."

York looked at his screens. Traffic flowed in front of them, behind them, over them, under them, everywhere, some military and some civilian. York looked up from his screens and glanced around the bridge.

They were all looking at him, waiting. "We . . . made it. Yes, we made it."

They waited for several seconds, then suddenly McGeahn let out a yelp, and they all cheered.

••••

"We coast for another day or two," York told Cassandra and Lady d'Hart. "Get right into the heart of the system. We're still in danger here, but the closer in we get, the better chance we have."

Cassandra frowned. "Why not just announce ourselves now? I have a grand speech all written up. We can saturate the media with my face and a wonderfully happy report of our successful escape from the clutches of the evil DCO. Surely they wouldn't try anything now."

York shook his head. "We're still out far enough they can jam our signal. We've got two rings of picket ships behind us, an inner ring of orbital weapons platforms in front of us. I'd like to get within that, get inside nearspace. It'll then be difficult for anyone to make an accurate transition toward us, and impossible for them to use their transition batteries with any accuracy unless they're right on top of us. Less chance for them to jam us, more time for you to broadcast."

Cassandra smiled. "You're the expert, Captain. At least let me congratulate you, and thank you."

"Don't thank me yet. We're now in the most dangerous part of this. We're at a good targeting distance for them, and we're too close to run."

Cassandra waved the comment off, but when York left he remembered that Lady d'Hart had frowned, as if that were terribly upsetting news.

••••

". . . I don't know where I am, but I'm all right."

Sylissa d'Hart watched the screen on her terminal go blank, had to force herself not to cry. She'd watched the recording of her son a dozen times, had struggled almost continuously with the choice before her. They had Andrew. They had her son and there was nothing she could do to help him.

She reached out to play the card again, realized she was only torturing herself. Juessik had said she would know the right moment. They had Andrew, and now she must choose.

33

Honor Abandoned

BELLA TZECHARRA TRIED to conceal her uneasiness. Five admirals—Bargan Abraxa, Andralla Schessa, Johan Soladin, Katrine d'Avollo and Shinton Diego; respectively the Dukes and Duchesses de Maris, de Vena, de Satarna, de Tarris and de Uranna—were awaiting her response. One slip and Tzecharra's career would end. "We've confirmed their course, Your Grace. If the Kinathin armada continues on its present course they'll transit into Lunan nearspace in just under eight days."

Andralla Schessa leaned forward pensively. Next to Abraxa, Tzecharra feared her more than any of the others. "You say *if*. Where else would they go?"

"The Kinathins are not fools, and they have no way of knowing the chaos that has resulted here in Third Fleet. After the defeat at Aagerbanne they could guess that Third Fleet is not strong enough to engage them directly, but they would still expect fairly strong resistance. So I can't believe they intend to just transit directly to Luna."

Schessa nodded her approval. "Very good reasoning."

Diego interrupted her. "But we all know the rebellion of Leonavich's officers has rendered Third Fleet incapable of any resistance. So that leaves Home Fleet as the only formidable battle force we have between Luna and an armada of a hundred Kinathin warships. And I doubt if any of us wants to trust our lives to Home Fleet."

Tzecharra couldn't hide her confusion. "But, Your Grace, Home Fleet has more than two hundred battle-ready ships. Surely they can . . ."

d'Avollo interrupted her. "Captain Tzecharra, please don't be naive. The average combat experience among the officers of Home Fleet is a few months at most. Home Fleet itself has not been in a serious engagement for more than a century." d'Avollo's eyes drifted downward, as if embarrassed by what she was about to say. "Home Fleet is the repository for our children, the children of the wealthy and the privileged. The more foolhardy among them get some real experience, but no more than a year or two. And then we bring them back here where we can ensure their safety." d'Avollo looked up and met Tzecharra's eyes. "I'm afraid if Home Fleet must face that armada it'll be a rout."

Tzecharra struggled to hide her shock and dismay. "There are some things we in Third Fleet can do, have been doing already." She shrugged uncomfortably. "A few."

Soladin demanded, "Such as?"

Tzecharra shook her head and tried to think. "I've been using the few ships I have that are battle worthy to strike quickly, then retreat before anything serious starts. We can position those that aren't battle worthy as if they're ready to engage. The Kinathins won't drive suicidally into that; they'll stop, engage at long range and we'll withdraw. It'll buy us a few days. Then maybe we can lay down a gauntlet of mines. It won't defeat them, but it'll slow them."

Schessa smiled at her warmly. "As I said before, very good reasoning. Buy us what time you can, though we don't expect anything foolish. Seventh Fleet is in transit now, but they'll be hard-pressed to get here before the Kinathins. Buy us time, Captain. Buy us time."

••••

It was the alert klaxon!

York struggled out of bed, realized it wasn't the alert klaxon, just the emergency buzzer on his terminal. "Lights," he told the computer as he floated across the deck and hit the receive switch. Rame's face appeared. "What is it?" York demanded.

"Unauthorized transmission," Rame said. "Lower decks. It's broadcasting continuously, some sort of scrambled transmission. Not as visible as a transition wake, but someone's damn well going to home in on it. I've got the marines sweeping G through K decks now, but I think it's too late."

York didn't have time to react, to think about who or what or why. "Sound General Quarters. Tell Cappik to stand by for full status immediately. I'll be right up."

York floated onto the bridge half dressed, and by the time he strapped down at the captain's console two patrol boats were already changing their orbits to intercept and investigate, and Luna TC was broadcasting a *stand-to and be boarded* warning. *Cinesstar*'s stations were still checking in so York sent a call down to the empress. The staid Major Dewar answered. "No time for explanations," York snapped. "We've been double-crossed. Get Her Majesty up here on the double. Tell her to wear something nice, look real calm, and be ready to give her speech. Our only chance is to make a run for it, now."

He cut the circuit just as the alert klaxon went silent. "All stations standing by, sir," McGeahn said, an edge of fear giving her voice an overly mechanical sound. "Turret three has a minor malfunction . . ."

York listened with one ear, while he scanned his screens and tried to let part of his mind think ahead. The two patrol boats were moving quickly. They had transition capability, though they couldn't maintain that long enough for interstellar transit, but soon they'd be on top of *Cinesstar*, and they'd give the weapons platforms the information that an armed intruder was deep within Luna's defenses.

"Cappik," York ordered. "Gravity, shields, drive, now—full status. Mister Eldinow, all ahead full. Force us into transition, soonest. Miss Gant, I want a course for Luna herself."

Eldinow kicked in the sublight drive. They were quickly approaching one of the big weapons platforms. "Jakobee, arm a one hundred-megatonne warhead. Fuse it for detonation one million kilometers in front of us while it's still in transition. And stand by."

York felt it before Eldinow said it. "Up-transition, sir."

York had to fly by instinct. They were in transition now and their data had to be extrapolated from what they'd acquired earlier. On York's screens the weapons platform was only a few AUs distant. "Hard a'port, Mister Eldinow."

"Hard a'port, sir."

York waited a few seconds for the maneuver to change their vector, then ordered, "Down-transition, now."

"Down-transition, sir."

A large warhead flared in front of them at a safe distance. "Up-transition, Mister Eldinow. Mister Jakobee, on my commend I want you to launch that warhead and blow it between us and that platform to obscure their targeting data."

"Up-transition, sir."

The hull thrummed, and the computer said, *Warhead detonation at eighty-three kilometers—yield strength, eight megatonnes.*

"Mister Jakobee, fire! Mister Eldinow, hard a'starboard."

York ignored the acknowledgments they shouted out, saw the empress stagger onto the bridge with a marine helping her. He watched the warhead blow to one side of them, filling the entire transition spectrum with noise. They were now past the weapons platforms. "Mister Jakobee, another warhead behind us and one in front of us. Blow them in transition at a range of twenty AUs. Launch them as soon as they're ready. Miss Gant, where the hell are we?"

"Warheads away, sir."

"We're thirty-eight AUs from Luna, sir, closing at one hundred twenty-seven lights and accelerating. ETA Luna nearspace in two-point-eight minutes."

"Evasive maneuvering, Mister Eldinow."

They couldn't really target at anything, not while they were in transition and too blind to compute accurate solutions. *Cinesstar* groaned as a big transition pulse slammed through her hull, and York watched damage reports flashing on one of his screens.

"Mister Jakobee, stand by all stations. I need a—"

The gravity on the bridge suddenly shifted, and York's restraints were the only thing that kept him from sprawling over his console. The power drain to the shields red-lined momentarily and he felt *Cinesstar* down-transit. The computer droned, *Near hit, heavy damage amidships.*

"Up-transition, Mister Eldinow. Hard a'starboard."

"Sorry, sir. Transition drive is not responding."

There was no time to think and plan. York had to react on instinct. "All stop. Shields down, gravity down. Rig for silent running."

It was a testimony to his crew's discipline. A month ago, with every targeting computer in the heart of the empire trying to shove a warhead down their throat, at such an unusual command, someone would have questioned it, and he would have had to waste valuable seconds giving the order a second time. But not now, not this time. Suddenly he floated up in his restraints.

Without a transition drive they were finished, but with all the warheads blowing around them making a horrendous racket in the transition spectrum, it was possible they could just disappear right off the scan reports of Luna's targeting computers. It wouldn't work for long—a minute, two, maybe more—but that was precious time they needed.

"Mister Jakobee, have all stations standing by.

"Miss McGeahn, put Her Majesty on every channel you can access, especially civilian and commercial—uncoded, unscrambled. And make sure you broadcast both visual and audio."

Cassandra was seated at the com console in the apprentice's couch, completely hidden from York's view. "Your Majesty," he said, hoping someone had remembered to give her a headset. "Do you hear me?"

There was a second's hesitation. "Quite well, Captain."

"Good. Forget any rehearsed speech. We only have a minute or two before they get enough data to compute a solution on us."

"Very good, Captain."

McGeahn said, "Your Majesty, you're now live."

York heard her take a deep breath, perhaps to compose herself, then she said, "I am Cassandra, Empress and Queen of the Nine Beasts. I am here aboard the ship *Cinesstar*, and . . ."

York would have liked to listen to what she said. He heard a word here and there, but he, Rame, Gant and Jakobee went into a hurried conference on what they could do to defend themselves.

"Make no mistake," Cassandra continued. "If this ship is destroyed and we with it, it will not be . . ."

York and his officers tried desperately to come up with some sort of solution, but they'd run out of luck. Rame said, "The defensive stations might buy us a little time."

"Captain." It was the empress. "I can't locate His Majesty. No one will let me speak to him directly. They tell me he's being held in protective custody, something about an assassination attempt."

"Who's holding him? Who's doing this protecting?"

"AI."

"Keep talking. See if you can get one of those cruiser captains, maybe even an admiral. If they know you're on board this ship we stand some chance we can buy more time. McGeahn, help her out."

York scanned his screens. There were no warheads in transition at the moment, but York could count at least thirty ships converging on them.

"Captain." It was the empress again. "Abraxa wants to speak to you."

"Did you speak to anyone beside him?"

"Yes. The captain of a destroyer, the commander of a weapons platform, and a number of their subordinate officers."

"McGeahn," York said. "How is Abraxa's signal coming in?"

"It's on a standard military channel, sir, normal encryption and coding."

"Connect him to me on a low-clearance circuit so you can monitor the conversation. Then rebroadcast both sides of the conversation unscrambled and uncoded on all channels accessible."

Abraxa's image appeared on one of York's screens. He was overweight, well past middle-age, with grayish-brown hair. But his most outstanding feature was his confidence, the supreme confidence of absolute power.

"Well, Lieutenant," Abraxa said. "You've certainly proven to be difficult. What made you think you could attack Luna herself?"

"Your Grace," York said with a slight bow of his head. He had to get the empress' name into this. "I'm not here to attack anyone. I'm here by orders of Her Majesty, the empress, who is one of my passengers. She has ordered me to deliver her safely to His Majesty, the emperor. I am merely trying to do that."

Someone in an AI uniform suddenly stepped into the view of Abraxa's pickup, whispered in Abraxa's ear. Abraxa's eyes lit up, and York guessed he'd just been told they were retransmitting the conversation uncoded. Abraxa spoke more warily. "The question still remains: why are you attacking the heart of the empire? That's treason. That's mutiny."

York scanned his screens to be sure Abraxa wasn't trying to distract him while they slipped something nasty in. He also scanned *Cinesstar*'s damage schematic on one screen: serious damage amidships, minor damage to the transition drive, easily repairable, though not in the short time they had.

"If you look closely at the log of this incident, you'll see that every warhead we launched detonated harmlessly in space as a defensive tactic. And you'll see that we used no offensive weaponry. We are not here to attack anyone. And as an act of good faith, I'm prepared to surrender myself and my ship to you immediately."

Abraxa grinned. "Really! Then depower your shields."

York grinned back at him. "I already have, Your Grace." He didn't bother to mention he had no choice, that *Cinesstar* was helpless. And he couldn't stop thinking of Sarasan.

"Very well, Mister Ballin. Stand by to be boarded."

York leaned toward his pickup in the equivalent of a bow. "As you command, Your Grace."

York cut the circuit, ordered gravity up and minimum power, told Rame to be certain not to power the shields, then he made three quick calls. He asked the empress to join him in the captain's conference room. Then he asked Palevi to round up Lady d'Hart, and the empress' servant and bring them there also. Last he called Alsa Yan. "Alsa. I need an injector loaded with three doses of something painless, fast and lethal. Bring it to the captain's conference room." He cut the circuit before she could argue or ask questions.

York stood. "Commander Rame, you have the bridge."

Lady d'Hart, the empress, her servant and Palevi were waiting for him. Alsa was only a few seconds behind him. York held out his hand without saying a word, and she reluctantly put the injector in it. She started to say something and he shook his head. "Not now. You're dismissed."

She turned angrily and left. York looked at Palevi, and without a word the marine turned and left. When they were alone, by the looks on their faces the three women did not miss the significance of the fact that they, and no one else, were present. York didn't give them a chance to say anything.

"In a few minutes we're going to be boarded by AI troops. From what Her Majesty tells me, AI is holding the emperor in protective custody, which sounds suspiciously like a coup. They aren't going to kill us out of hand, or burn us and say I was a renegade, but I wouldn't count on much more than that."

He let that sink in. The servant, without asking permission, sat down and sighed deeply, sounding on the edge of tears.

"Now I don't know what kind of conspiracy you three were hatching, but I do know you . . ." he nodded at the servant, and she looked him squarely in the eyes, ". . . are a feddie. I don't know if you're a spy or not—"

"I'm not," she said. "Not a spy. We—"

He cut her off with a wave of his hand. "It doesn't matter and you don't have time to explain. What I do know is that the three of you were up to something, and you each have a suicide device implanted at the base of your skull."

All three started at that. "I don't know how they're triggered, but I had them deactivated long ago. And since I took that option away from you, and now it appears you'll soon be Abraxa's captives, I'm prepared to offer you that option back."

He let that sink in, though it took several seconds. When Cassandra realized what he was saying she too sat down, while Lady d'Hart backed fearfully up to the bulkhead behind her.

York lifted the injector, checked the charge. The display listed three dosages of some chemical with a long name. "There are three dosages of a lethal, but painless, drug in here. You don't have to administer it to yourself—I'll do that for you, if you wish. They're going to hang me anyway. But you have to make the decision, each of you, for yourself. All I can do is carry out your wishes."

That too he let sink in. He let it hang there because there was nothing else to say. They had come to defeat, and not knowing what he had done by having their last option removed, he felt obligated to return it to them.

"Tell me, Captain," the empress said calmly. "What'll you do? Will you commit suicide with us?"

York didn't have to think about that. "No. I still have to worry about my crew. And in any case, that's not my way."

"Nor is it mine," the empress said.

"Nor mine," Lady d'Hart said with as much conviction.

They all looked at the servant, the feddie. She had buried her face in her hands, and several seconds passed before she looked up and slowly looked each of them in the face. "Nor mine, of course."

York keyed his implants. "Rame, Ballin here. When's that boarding party due?"

"Seven minutes, sir."

"Where?"

"Hangar Deck, bay four."

"I'm going down. You remain on the bridge. And whatever happens, don't start anything."

York tucked the injector under his belt like a gun, looked at Lady d'Hart and the servant. "You two had best return to your cabins." He turned to the empress. "Would you like to join me, Your Majesty?"

She sighed. "It's probably best."

The servant/feddie looked up. "I just want to know who betrayed us."

Lady d'Hart drew in a breath, stepped back but ran into the bulkhead behind her.

The empress turned on her. "You, Sylissa? No. Tell me it's not true. Please!"

For one instant, York was tempted to pull the injector and give the woman all three doses. But then he saw in her eyes that her betrayal already haunted her. A lethal but painless poison would be the easy way out for her, and he didn't want to give her that.

He turned, walked out of the room, leaving the angry voices of the empress and her "servant" behind.

••••

Hangar Deck, bay four, was the extra service bay used for shuttles not belonging to *Cinesstar* herself. It was empty now. York stopped in Hangar Control to glance at some screens. A cruiser and three destroyers were already standing a million kilometers off, easy targeting range, and more ships were arriving every minute, slowly englobing them. He made a call to the bridge, told Jakobee to comp-lock the main weapons console and shut down all weapons stations. He told Rame to put them on green status, to put Jakobee in charge and join him. Then he told McGeahn to put him on allship.

"This is your captain," he said slowly. "You've been a good crew, an excellent crew, and I'm proud of you. I could not have asked for better. But now we've come home, and our mission is done.

"I'm yielding command of this ship to the proper authorities, and I'm sure they'll deal with you fairly." He wasn't sure he believed that part, but there was nothing else he could say. "You're all ordered to comp-lock your weapons, and return to your quarters and wait there until you hear otherwise. Ballin out."

When he looked up, Rame and the empress were standing behind him. Rame glanced at his watch. "Less than two minutes, sir."

York leaned over a console and switched one of its screens to a view of the interior of bay four, another to an exterior view. The deck crew had already opened bay four to space, and only a black void was visible beyond the hatch. Another screen showed a short-range scan of an approaching shuttle. York watched it on the scan until it was close enough to see on exterior view, and he was not surprised to see the AI emblem painted on its side.

"Olin," York said. "Remember, you were only obeying my orders. Nothing more. And I think it would be best if you returned to your cabin."

"I'm sorry, sir. I can't obey that order. My place is beside you."

"You're a damn fool."

Rame grinned at him and said nothing.

The shuttle settled into bay four, and the deck crew sealed and began pressurizing the bay. York waited until the green light over the bay's hatch flashed, then he cycled the lock and stepped into the bay with Rame and the empress behind him just as the shuttle hatch opened.

An AI captain stepped out and a troop of armed AI soldiers fanned out behind him. He walked up to York arrogantly and asked, "I take it you're Ballin?"

York nodded.

"You're under arrest by order of the Admiralty Council. You're charged with high-treason, murder, mutiny, espionage—"

The empress interrupted him. "That's not right. You can't do that."

He nodded to her carefully and looked at her without expression. "My orders have come directly from His Grace, Lord Abraxa, and the Admiralty Council. His Majesty has confirmed those orders by sealed warrant." He snapped his fingers, and two female AI goons took up positions on either side of the empress. He flashed her a sharp grin. "I have been instructed to take you into protective custody, Your Majesty, so we may ensure your safety."

The empress looked right through the man as if he wasn't there. "And I'm sure you will."

The AI captain asked York, "Have you locked and sealed your weapons?"

"Yes, and I've instructed my crew to wait in their quarters for further orders. Skeleton crew assignments only."

The AI captain spun about, walked back to the open shuttle hatch, looked in and said, "It's safe, Your Lordship."

Not even York was ready for what came next. Sierka stepped out of the shuttle, a big, toothy smile plastered across his face. He carried a baton about half the length of his arm and he approached York with a swagger. He stopped with his nose only inches from York's. "Well, Ballin. I told them you would come. I know you better than you realize. And that's why I'll always win."

Sierka stepped back, smacked the baton into the palm of his hand, and York noticed then it had a power grip, and he realized it was a nerve prod. York actually saw the blow coming, but with fifty armed AI goons surrounding him it was better to take it. The nerve prod struck him across the side of his face, though thankfully Sierka hadn't activated it.

The nerve prod, even without power, was a formidable club. York staggered backward and fell to his knees. Rame stepped forward crying out, "You bastard," and reaching for Sierka. A shot rang out and Rame dropped to the deck, a small hole in the side of his temple. York struggled to his feet, wanted to do something, wanted to kill Sierka with his bare hands, but the deck reeled beneath him and all he could manage was a stagger.

Sierka grinned again, twisted the handle on the prod. The empress shouted, "Stop that." Sierka ignored her, jammed the muzzle of the prod into York's groin.

For York it was as if someone had stuck the bare leads of an electrical conductor in his crotch. Sierka shoved the prod harder into his groin, and all York could do was scream and twitch, clutching the prod as everything from his waist down spasmed with pain. Sierka growled something at him, but York couldn't really hear the words. He could hear the hum of the nerve prod, felt the pain slowly climbing up into his gut as Sierka turned the intensity up. The pain eventually reached York's chest, then his arms, and by that time all he could do was lay on the deck and twitch while Sierka turned the intensity to maximum . . .

••••

Tzecharra looked at Abraxa's image, reminded herself to show no visible trace of the anger she felt. "We lost seventy-four ships, Your Grace."

"A terrible price," Abraxa said, "but it bought us needed time."

You bastard, she wanted to shout. She had positioned the remnants of Third Fleet as if it were ready to engage the Kinathin armada, all in accordance with the plan of delaying the Kinathins with a bluff. It had worked. The Kinathins had pulled up short, paused for a full day to examine the situation and prepare a strategy. Then yesterday they'd moved to engage. And Tzecharra, according to plan, had prepared to withdraw, content with the small delay they'd purchased. But Abraxa had intervened at the last moment, ordered her to engage. She had actually shouted at him, and he had threatened her with court-martial to silence her. In the end, he gave the orders and she obeyed them.

"It only bought us a few hours, Your Grace. I told you those ships weren't battle ready. Many had no ordnance reserves, were completely out of ammunition within the first minutes of engagement. They massacred us. I think even the Kinathins were surprised."

"Yes," Abraxa said insincerely. "A high price, but the time we purchased was invaluable."

"*We* didn't purchase it, Your Grace. Please don't include yourself among those who paid the price."

Abraxa frowned. "Don't be insubordinate, Captain. I hope you're not going to give me more trouble. You and your ships still have work to do out there."

She shook her head. "No, Your Grace. I'll be no more trouble. I'm resigning my commission, effective immediately. And so are all of the other officers of command rank here in Third Fleet, at least those who are still alive." She leaned forward and pressed a switch on her console. "I'm transmitting our resignations en mass as we speak."

"You can't do that," he shouted. "I won't allow it."

"It's done," she said emotionlessly, then leaned forward and cut the circuit.

34

More Illusions

YORK DIDN'T WANT to wake up. It was easier to remain comatose, and a lot less painful. But they'd turned the lights up to maximum. And the cold, they'd dropped the temperature of his cell to somewhere between uncomfortable and damn cold.

He opened his eyes—correction, only one eye opened; the other was caked shut with dried blood. He wasn't even sure if it was the real eye or the steel eye. And he wasn't sure if the blood had come from his broken nose, or the deep gash on the bridge of his nose, or the cut over his eye, or who knew what else. He tried to get oriented. He was lying on his side on the deck of his cell somewhere in Luna Prime. They'd left him there after the last beating, how many days—hours— ago, he didn't know.

Sierka had certainly had his fun. Time and again he'd shown up at random intervals with a couple of AI thugs, and usually playing some sort of game they beat York senseless. The guards in the cell block had gotten into the act too: heating and cooling his cell to random extremes at random times; changing his gravity, sometimes cutting it off completely, at other times pinning him to the deck, or a wall, or the ceiling, with four or five gees; switching the lights on and off; feeding him food sometimes too cold, sometimes too hot, all at random.

Sierka never asked any questions, never made any demands. This wasn't an effort to extract information, just a plain and simple death sentence, an execution. York understood that, understood he was going to die, understood they were going to make his death take as long as they could, and he no longer cared. He just wanted them to get it over with, though if the opportunity presented itself, he sure wouldn't mind taking Sierka with him to hell. But that was wishful thinking since they'd stripped, cavity-searched and scanned him thoroughly, and made sure he had nothing he might use against the asshole.

York's face had stuck in a puddle of dried blood, and when he peeled it off the deck he reopened several gashes. He remembered just in time not to lean on his broken arm, but he forgot about the torn ligaments in his knee and he made the mistake of putting weight on it, which dumped him back on his butt on the deck. He sat there for a while letting the pain recede. Eventually he managed to struggle onto his bunk, though he had to be careful to avoid getting tangled up in the wire-thin plast cables attached to his manacles. He'd lost control of his bladder while comatose and he stank.

He sat there for some indeterminate time, staring at the opposite bulkhead, and then the cables started retracting into the bulkhead behind him, another of the guard's tricks. The thin plast cables attached to the manacles on his wrists could be retracted into the bulkhead under control of the guards. And if he wasn't careful, and let a limb tangle in one of the cables, they'd retract anyway, and those thin cables of plast would cut right through flesh and bone—slice an arm or leg off rather cleanly.

An agony of pain shot through his broken arm as the cables lifted him off his bunk, retracted fully into the bulkhead and left him hanging by his wrists. He tried to take all his weight in his good arm, to relieve some of the pain in the broken arm, but he was too weak, and he just hung there screaming, until, mercifully, he passed out.

••••

"Wake up."

A loud crack sounded in York's ear. He hung there for a moment between shock and consciousness, then the crack sounded again and he realized he was hearing the sound of a flattened hand striking his face. He opened his eyes—correction, eye.

"Well, Ballin," Sierka said, leering at him. "You don't look so smart now." He looked at someone and commanded, "Let him down."

The cables began to reel out of the bulkhead, lowering York slowly to his bunk where he collapsed in a heap. He wondered what creative little trick Sierka had come up with this time. One of his favorites was to turn out the lights so York couldn't see, then wearing night vision helmets he and the guards could have their fun, and York couldn't even react to the next blow.

A shock of pain ran up his broken leg; he flinched, screamed, realized he'd passed out for a moment. "Stand up."

York ignored him. It wouldn't make any difference; whether he obeyed or not, they'd still have their fun.

"You're nothing, Ballin. A tramp. A drunk. The lowest form of scum in the empire." Sierka leaned over him. "You're finally getting what you deserve, getting what you should have gotten long ago . . ." Sierka emphasized the statement with a kick to York's ribs, then leaned down, working himself into a real tirade, leaned down so far his nose was only inches from York's. "You and your ilk . . ."

York thought about his *ilk*: Maggie, Frank, Paris, Olin; all dead. And Maggie, hanging in a tank, not even given a decent burial in space. Sierka started ranting, shouting and kicking, then leaning close and shouting more. By now it was a familiar pattern, but this time York suddenly had an idea. He waited until Sierka leaned close one time, then lunged out and clamped his hands about Sierka's throat.

Sierka gasped, croaked, "Get him off me."

The two guards grabbed at York's arms, tried to pry his fingers loose, and when that didn't work they started beating him. But York had an advantage: he didn't care. He focused his entire existence on his hands, on crushing Sierka's throat, ignoring the pain in his broken arm, ignoring the desperate blows from the guards. Sierka was starting to turn blue, his eyes bulging outward in panic, and then one of the guards shouted, "Retract the manacles," and the fear left Sierka's face, was replaced with a grin. But Sierka didn't realize that was exactly what York wanted.

He kept his grip on Sierka's throat, let the cables retract until he felt a tug on one manacle, then he suddenly rolled over, let go of Sierka's throat, quickly looped one of the cables about Sierka's neck, then resumed his grip. Sierka didn't realize what he'd done, grinned at him, thinking the cables would pull York off him, would save Sierka and pin York helplessly to the bulkhead. It wasn't until the cables began lifting them both, and the noose around Sierka's neck tightened, that he realized the trap York had sprung. "Stop!" Sierka croaked, and York squeezed tighter. "Stop the cables."

Sierka started to turn blue again as the cables dragged them both up the wall, and only then did the guards realize His Lordship was about to be beheaded. One cable had looped badly around York's arm. But he didn't mind losing the arm since Sierka was going to lose his head.

They were almost all the way up now, and the cable was tightening around Sierka's throat. Sierka thrashed about in blind panic, and while York was close to passing out, he held on to consciousness so he could watch the asshole die. He heard a crunch as the cable crushed Sierka's voice box, then blood ran down his arms as the cable actually began to cut into his throat. All York wanted to see before he died was Sierka's head rolling across the deck.

And then the cables suddenly stopped, and one of the guards produced a power knife, cut the cables, and both Sierka and York dropped to the deck. The guards pulled them apart just as a medical team arrived, and while the medical team worked on Sierka, the guards beat York into unconsciousness.

••••

"You think you're clever, don't you?" Sierka's voice was a grinding croak, and the scar that circled his neck was a livid pink. Clearly, the medics hadn't been able to fully repair the damage to his voice box, and York took some satisfaction in that.

Sierka's boot caught him in the cheek, but he was past caring. He just wanted them to get it over with. But then Sierka had no intention of being that kind.

••••

Someone was dragging York—two someones—dragging him by the cable connecting his leg manacles, dragging him on his back down some corridor. The lights in the deck above flashed by him as if the lights were moving and he was stationary. But then a jolt reminded him of his broken legs, and he tried to forget the splintered bone jutting out through his thigh. He was getting close. Soon he would die no matter how hard they tried to keep him alive, and he prayed he wouldn't have to wait long for that. He passed out again . . .

. . . He came to when they dropped him into a chair and his face slammed painfully down on the table in front of him. He passed out for a time, came to again with someone sounding official saying, "This court will come to order. Mister prosecutor. Read the charges into the log."

Someone else, also sounding official, read out a long list of crimes. Then the first official asked, "How does the prisoner plead?"

Someone nudged York and growled in his ear, "Stand up and say 'Not Guilty.' "

Both his arms were broken so he couldn't lean on them to climb to his feet, and even if he could, both his legs were broken so he couldn't stand, and even if he could his jaw was broken so he couldn't speak. He managed to grunt something like, *Uzusshuhhbuhh*, then someone swatted him in the ribs—broken ribs—and he was too weak to even scream.

"Cut," someone shouted, a very unofficial voice. "That's enough. This just isn't working."

The voice was so out of place York made an attempt to open his eyes, got one opened, though he left his face resting on one cheek on the table. He was in a military court, very official, very correct, very proper, but this civilian in fashionable, but improper, attire marched right through the middle of it up to the justices, waving his hands. "This isn't working at all. His Grace wants the empire to see a dangerously mad megalomaniac. And look at him. Whose idea was it to beat the poor fool into something resembling chopped protein cake? All we're going to get on camera is *pathetic*, and that's the last thing . . ."

York saw Alsa standing to one side and their eyes met. There were tears in her eyes. He lifted his face off the table, couldn't really do more than make a quick scan of the room before his vision blurred; he closed his eyes and lowered his face back to the table.

He replayed the image in the darkness of his mind. Most of his officers were there, those still alive, standing silently in the prisoner's box. And the empress was there, looking frightened; and the emperor, also frightened; and the d'Hart woman—more horrified and disgusted than frightened—

York felt unconsciousness coming on. He watched it approach and he welcomed it, hoping he wouldn't have to return to the living.

••••

York slammed awake as a wave of intense hatred washed through him, and he almost vomited. He stood up, stood amazingly on healthy and whole legs, bellowed at the top of his lungs a curse that frightened even him.

There was a face in front of him. He reached out, put his fingers around the throat, fingers that only moments ago had been broken and disfigured and were now whole and strong, and he squeezed with maniacal, vice-like strength. He felt the man's voice box crush, the neck snap, and he kept screaming and squeezing, and everyone around him was screaming also. Then all his strength left him, and so did the anger, and he collapsed back into the chair.

"You'll have to control him better than that," that unofficial voice said into the stillness that followed.

York lay there, not paralyzed, but so overcome with a deep lethargy that he couldn't move. But his eyes were open; he was conscious, and basically alert.

"Sorry," someone answered. "I'm having trouble getting the signals calibrated. All the speed-healing and regrowth have really screwed up his neurotransmitters."

Implants, he realized. They were controlling him through his implants and a neural probe. He couldn't move but he could feel the weight of the small transceiver remote clipped behind his ear where it wouldn't show on the cameras. Using it they could transmit signals directly into his cerebral cortex. He guessed it was also controlling an injector pack buried somewhere beneath his skin. With the right combination of neural signals and drugs they could control him nicely.

An AI security guard bent down over the fellow whose neck York had just broken, examined him carefully and stood up shaking his head.

"Damn it," the first voice said. "Good vid-techs are expensive, and the insurance is going to run us way over budget."

As two guards dragged the body away, a woman stepped into view in front of York holding a small control unit in both hands. "Let me try again." She made a few adjustments to her control unit, glanced at York and hesitated suspiciously, took a cautious step back, then pointed the unit at York and did something.

He was prepared in a way, had a vague idea of what to expect. Anger, hatred, fear, nausea, terror, lust—they all flushed through him. He was up out of the chair and already over the table screaming, "You fucking whooorrreeeeeeee!" reaching for her with only one thought in mind.

She casually flicked a switch on the control unit, and dropped him in his tracks in a state of complete lethargy, managed to control him so precisely he didn't hit the floor hard, just quietly sat down. He didn't move while she fiddled at her control box. "All right," she said. "Let's try *calm reason*."

York felt control return and he looked around. They were all there again: his officers, the empress, the emperor, the d'Hart woman, staring at him like some freak. He stood, brushed dust off his uniform, noticed they'd given him a nice new uniform. The vid-director pointed to York's chair and said, "Please take a seat, Lieutenant Ballin."

York realized it was a lot easier to just play along, so he sat down. The vid-director looked at the technician with the control box. "Very good. Now let me see solid anger, slightly out of control, but none of this berserk stuff."

That was enough, York thought. He stood. "Now wait a minute," he argued. "You have no right to treat anyone this way."

"More anger," the vid-director said.

That made York really angry. "God damn it," he shouted. "Listen to me."

"Excellent," the vid-director said. "That's enough. Shut him down."

The lethargy returned and York sat down, no longer caring.

The next couple of hours were really quite fascinating. York was able to observe the whole thing in a schizophrenic sort of way. They all play-acted their way through his court-martial. The Admiralty Court charged him with just about every heinous crime a mutineer-renegade-rapist-sociopath-pirate could commit. The vid-director regularly stopped the proceedings to adjust camera angles, to coach the justices—which York learned were really just actors—to give instructions to the med-tech controlling the neural probe behind York's ear. They played York like a finely tuned instrument. They didn't have to give him any script, didn't have to depend on his cooperation. When they wanted him to explode at the justices or some poor witness, they'd give him a nice little cocktail laced heavily with frustration, building it to a crescendo, then tossing in a dose of aggression at the last moment. He would end up ranting with just the right degree of demagoguery, and then they'd turn him off like a light.

All in all, the schizophrenic half of York that had retreated into some depth of his mind to observe the whole thing was quite impressed. At the end, the director even instructed the justices to find him innocent on a few charges. "It'll look much more believable," he said. "Find him guilty on the really nasty ones, of course, so we've got a reason to execute him. But let him off on a couple of the lesser ones."

Yes, it was quite impressive. And when they were done, they just switched him off.

••••

York slammed awake, sat up in bed with a scream, threw the blankets off and stumbled across the floor. Vertigo hit him like a bullet and he staggered back toward the bed, sat down there and waited for the nausea and fear to pass. He was sitting there with his face buried in his hands, trying to recall the dream that had frightened him so, when it hit him: *bed, blankets?*

He opened his eyes carefully. The room was dark, though someone had programmed the lights for a dim nightglow. "Lights," he said. "Slow ramp." The computer brought the lights up slowly.

He looked first at his hands. They were whole and healthy; the fingers weren't broken and bloody. Then he remembered the court-martial. They'd fixed him up so he could look appropriately sinister, must have had to overdose the hell out of him on accelerated-healing to fix him up so quickly. But he wasn't back in his cell, nor was he drugged into the next century.

He looked around. He was in a fairly normal bedroom, much like that in a good hotel. A clock on the wall showed midmorning. He was sitting on a dirtside bed, not a grav bunk. To his left there appeared to be a large curtained window, and to his right an open set of double doors. He stood again, pulled open the curtains and stared for some moments at what he saw.

He was looking out a real window—not a projection or a screen—at a landscape of green and brown vegetation, with rolling hills and a small river in the distance. There was no sign of man or habitation or civilization anywhere, just those beautiful rolling hills.

He turned about, went through the open doorway into a small sitting room with a vid recessed into one wall, a comfortable looking couch, a small desk with a card viewer and a computer terminal on it. There was another door on the far side of the room, closed, and, as he quickly discovered, locked. It refused to respond to any effort he made to open it, nor to any commands he gave the computer. He set about exploring the limits of his jail: four rooms—roughly the equivalent of an expensive hotel suite. He found fresh uniforms in the closet, all sorts of toilet articles in the fresher—everything nicely stocked, ready for occupancy.

He tried the computer first, had access to all sorts of functions and information, but nothing of any consequence. He could call up books to read, vids to view; he could program his environmental controls, schedule meals and laundry service; basically he had full civilian access to all unclassified information. But he could send no messages; make no contact with the outside world, whatever world this might be.

He shaved, showered, had just put on a fresh uniform when the door opened suddenly and a servant entered the room carrying a large tray. The servant was dressed in a white coat and black slacks, with a white shirt and black tie—a uniform that had changed little in centuries. "Good morning, sir," the servant said and put the tray down on the table. "The monitors indicated you were up and about so I took the liberty of preparing your breakfast."

York revised his opinion. The servant was military all the way, probably a noncom, a twenty-year man, probably AI. He placed York's breakfast on the table with meticulous care, then turned to leave.

"Wait," York said, and the man turned and hesitated. "Where am I? What is this place?"

"I'm sorry, sir. I'm not allowed to answer questions. If you have any physical needs, you can call me through your terminal." With that, he turned and left.

Suddenly, York realized, none of it was worth it. It was all a big waste, and he just didn't have the energy to keep on trying. They would do with him what they would, and there was nothing he could do about it.

He sat down to the breakfast and turned on the vid, scanned the channels for news, found a station broadcasting his court-martial. He ate a little, and watched his own court-martial with rapt fascination. It seemed to take longer than he remembered. The defense council and the prosecutor objected to everything each other did, and the York on the screen frequently burst out with maniacal threats to the justices, the prosecutor, even his own defense counsel and his own crew. They'd cleaned him up nicely, made him look healthy, though they'd left the chrome-steel eye and the scars on his face. A nice touch, he realized, made him look even more fanatical. They even managed to use the shots of him breaking the vid-tech's neck, at which point the courtroom burst into pandemonium while three AI guards restrained York. The chief justice called a recess, and a vid announcer's face appeared. "We now return to our regularly scheduled programming. Stay tuned for continued live coverage of the court-martial of the renegade ship captain, York Ballin."

"Masterful, isn't it?"

It took York a moment to realize the voice had not come from the vid. He started, turned toward the door to find a tall, rather distinguished looking man, wearing a uniform with admiral's stripes on the sleeves; he stood just within the open door. York looked at the stripes, the bearing of the man, the way he stood, realized he had to be one of the nine Grand Dukes of the empire. "Your Grace," York said, standing slowly, then bowing.

"They said you were quick on the uptake," the man said, crossing the distance between them and extending his hand as if he and York were old friends. He shook York's hand eagerly. "I've wanted to meet you for some time now, Lieutenant. I'm Johan de Satarna."

Johan Soladin, Duke de Satarna. Perra Soladin's father, probably second only to Abraxa on the Admiralty Council. York nodded and said again, "Your Grace."

Soladin voiced a quick command to the room's computer to blank the vid, then turned back to York. "Those vid people are quite impressive, aren't they? Amazing what they can do with a few properly staged scenes. They're going to draw this out for several days before convicting you."

York walked over to the window and looked out on the landscape below. "Where are we?"

Soladin joined him at the window. "Beautiful, isn't she. We're on Terr, the large planet that's Luna's primary. It's not all wilderness like this. There are the ruins of a rather large civilization spread all over the planet, though the archaeologists need shielded radiation suits to get near them. Apparently the civilization was well in to space when they were burned off by some fairly extensive bombing about two or three thousand years ago. In fact, many of the scientists believe this was the cradle of our own civilization."

"What are we doing here?"

Soladin raised an eyebrow. "To the point, aren't you?" He shrugged. "I suppose you deserve a straight answer."

York decided he liked Soladin far more than his son.

"This is a private reserve," Soladin continued. "I keep it stocked with game for hunting, and there's a wonderful countryside out there for all sorts of activities, though you have to stay away from the contaminated areas. We felt it would be a good place to hold you incognito during your court-martial."

York couldn't hide a skeptical frown. "I'd think you could just stuff me back in a cell on Luna Prime, let Sierka finish the job he started."

"Yes, that," Soladin said uncomfortably. "Listen Ballin, I do apologize for that. We had no idea Sierka would resort to such barbaric tactics when we asked him to interrogate you. We felt that since he'd been able to predict your return here, he must know you well enough to learn whatever else you knew. But we're not cruel, and while I confess I have no qualms about brutality if it serves a purpose, I don't condone it purely to satisfy the sadistic whims of a fool like Sierka. Your life may be forfeit, Lieutenant, but there is no need for plain and simple barbarism."

"Nice speech," York said. "Knowing all that will greatly ease my mind when you execute me."

"Yes," Soladin sighed. "Nice speech. Tell me something, Lieutenant. You don't strike me as a fanatic, but only such a man could have withstood Sierka's brutality without cracking. And yet you refused to answer a single question."

York looked carefully at Soladin, was on the verge of telling him Sierka hadn't asked any questions, but bit back the comment, realizing that Sierka had been sent to interrogate him, hadn't done so, had merely sought his own form of revenge. But when faced with providing answers to his superiors, he'd had to lie to save his own neck. He'd told them York was a maniacal fanatic, when in fact York had broken, would have answered any question he asked, if only he'd asked one. Well, as long as they were misinformed, there was no sense in setting them straight. "I don't think I could explain it to you."

Soladin nodded. "You know, Lieutenant. At another time, had our paths not crossed as enemies, I would have valued a man like you in my personal service. Perhaps you could have taught my son a few things, turned him into something other than a fop."

York looked out over the beautiful green landscape. "But it's not another time. And our paths crossed the way they crossed."

••••

"Let me see him," Sylissa shouted.

"I'm sorry, Your Ladyship," the receptionist said mechanically, looking crisp and neat in her black AI uniform. "Colonel Juessik is a busy man, and without an appointment—"

"Then give me an appointment and I'll come back."

The receptionist turned to her computer screen, touched a few keys. "We could schedule you in next month—"

"Next month! He's been putting me off for more than a tenday now. You tell Juessik I want to see him right now. Tell him I'm going to sit down right here until I do. Tell him—"

Suddenly the receptionist glanced down at her console, touched a key and said, "Yes, sir." Sylissa decided to wait. The receptionist listened intently for a moment, nodded, then said, "Yes, sir. Right away, sir." She looked up and smiled. "Colonel Juessik will see you now."

Once in Juessik's office, Sylissa waited only for the door to close behind her before she demanded, "Where is my son? I did your dirty work for you. Now give me back my son. You promised."

Juessik stood from behind his desk and stepped around it casually. "Calm down, Lady d'Hart. May I offer you a drink?"

"To hell with your drink. I want my son, and I want him now."

"Now you'll have to be patient—"

"I've been patient. We had a deal."

She let that hang, let the silence draw out and watched Juessik's face as he considered his next words. He was uncharacteristically uncomfortable, and that made her heart sink.

"He's hurt," she shouted. "You've done something to him, haven't you? What? What is it?"

Juessik spread his hands, and her heart dropped into the pit of her stomach. "I'm sorry," he said. "One of my people was a bit over-zealous, overstepped his orders . . ."

She waited for more, realized there wasn't more. Her words barely escaped her lips. "He's dead, isn't he?"

Juessik nodded, pretending sorrow. "I assure you, the man has been punished most severely."

Sylissa didn't remember attacking Juessik, didn't remember crossing the few paces between them and going for his eyes. But she found herself on top of him on the floor, tearing at his face while he struck back at her frantically. She didn't see the fist that caught her on the side of the head.

••••

Rear Admiral Lord Stephan Tarkoff looked carefully at Abraxa's image. "We're still four days out, Your Grace . . ."

"And the Kinathin armada is only three days out, Stephan." Abraxa was frightened, and doing a poor job of hiding it.

"I don't know what else we can do, Your Grace. I'm pushing the fleet at maximum drive now."

"Maximum drive for your slowest ships. You do have ships that can go faster."

"Yes, Your Grace. But that would string Seventh Fleet out over several parsecs. We'd be easy pickings for a united force like the Kinathin armada. Have Home Fleet hold them off for just one day, then we'll be there in full strength."

"No." Abraxa dismissed the idea without even considering it, and that made Tarkoff mad, though he wasn't foolish enough to say anything. "Get your fastest ships here soonest so they can support Home Fleet."

There were rumors everywhere of the *Cinesstar* affair, and the mutinies in Third Fleet. Tarkoff hadn't understood it until he'd received a coded transmission from Tzecharra only seven days ago. Third Fleet was disbanded, not by royal or Admiralty edict, but because there was no Third Fleet left. Her officers were all either dead or mutineers. And with good reason, after the way the Admiralty Council had betrayed them. Tarkoff wondered if he were about to be betrayed in a similar fashion.

••••

Over the next two days, York spent many hours at that window, looking at the strangely beautiful landscape. At night, the bright orb of Luna floating above the horizon lit up the landscape. And during the days it was green and clean and healthy. He spent hours glued to the vid watching his own trial, which proceeded in fits and starts due to constant interruptions. Sometimes he'd call up a book from the library, sit down at the reader, though he often found he let his mind wander, and after reading for several hours he could remember nothing of what he'd read, not even the title of the book.

Sometimes he became so wrapped up in his trial, he watched the latest development intently as if he didn't already know the outcome. A secret little part of him hoped it would turn out differently, that somehow, somewhere, there was a great surprise waiting to happen, perhaps a last minute reprieve due to new evidence. When they did finally convict him, it deeply disappointed him. The court decided to show him no mercy for all his crimes, and sentenced him to slow death in a low-gravity gallows.

He slept very little, slept between sessions of his court-martial, between hours standing at the window, between the nightmares. Sometimes he slept on the bed, sometimes seated at the reader, sometimes seated in a comfortable chair at the window. The nightmares never let him sleep for long, so he slept at random, whenever he could, and he always woke screaming, though he could never remember the dream itself.

He felt empty, though he brightened a little after the chief justice pronounced sentence, for after that he felt oddly refreshed, and free of the responsibility for this whole mess. They would execute him, and there was nothing he could do about it. They probably wouldn't even give him the traditional spacer's burial at space, probably just cremate him. He thought about it a lot, and he just wanted to get it over with.

35

The Fruits of Betrayal

SYLISSA FOLLOWED THE AI guard up the corridor, marveling at the deathly stillness of the immense ship. The silence was eerie, and she realized why these people thought of their ships as if they were alive, almost sentient beings in and of themselves.

The guard stopped abruptly and Sylissa nearly ran into him. He turned into an open room, large for a ship, though small by planetary standards. She recognized the room, had visited it in the company of Martin Andow, what felt like an eternity ago. It seemed wrong that there was no marine standing guard just within the entrance, no group of marines off to one side cleaning some sort of weapon, no one doing whatever it was these marines were always doing. Like everything else about *Cinesstar*, the room felt dead.

The guard marched up to a door, pulled his sidearm, pressed the small portable terminal he carried against the lock and stepped back warily as the door cycled open. Keeping one eye on the door he stepped aside and nodded with his head. "He's in there. Go on in. I'll lock it behind you, then you got one hour, and all the bribes in the universe won't buy you a minute longer."

He waited. She stepped past him, stepped into the small cabin and clamped her hands together to keep them from trembling visibly as the door closed behind her.

The cabin was empty. The guard had lied to her. He'd taken her money and lied—

"And what can I do for Yer Ladyship?"

She gasped, jumped back and came up against the closed door. She looked up, saw Palevi lying in his grav bunk like a fly sleeping on the wall. The bunk was several feet off the floor, and he was laying there casually, with both hands behind his head as if he had not a care in the universe. He looked down at her, suddenly spun his legs downward, slapped at a switch with his hand and, with practiced ease, landed on his feet on the deck. "Well?" he asked.

"I want you to look at something," she said, reaching into a pocket, retrieving a small card and holding it out to him.

He didn't move, stood there looking at her. Not so much as a muscle twitched. Finally, he said, "I ought to just kill you right here. I've got a whole hour to do it, right?"

Her hand, holding the card out to him, trembled. "Yes. You ought to. But as you say, you do have a whole hour. So first you should look at this. You'll still have plenty of time to kill me afterward."

Again he regarded her, his face lifeless and unmoving. Then he reached out, opened a hand palm up, made her cross the small room and hand him the card. He closed his fingers over it, but didn't lower his hand and continued to stare at her. Then he turned the card over in his hand and examined it as if he'd never seen one before. Finally, he turned, crossed the room in one step, pulled a seat and a small shelf-of-a-desk out of the wall and sat down behind the desk. He reached out, swung a reader into place, inserted the card into it and pulled on the earphones. He positioned the reader between them so he could look at it and watch her at the same time, then he touched a switch.

He watched in silence, no sound from the reader escaping the confines of the earphones. While he watched and listened, she stepped backward slowly until her back pressed against the plast of the bulkhead behind her. She relished its coolness, closed her eyes, tried to forget so many things, tried to forget everything.

After what seemed like far too long she opened her eyes again, realized he'd already finished playing the card, had been sitting there in silence staring at her. "So it's another double-cross," he said. "So they're going to kill us all, make it neat and convenient." He shrugged. "The whole thing's been a double-cross from the beginning, and you were the biggest double-crosser of the bunch. So?" He let that question hang in the air.

She said, "We can save him. I can help you, so you can save him. There are rumors all over Luna about a coup, about a revolt in the Fleets; some of the rumors are absolutely ridiculous, some, perhaps, factual. There's enough confusion that we could succeed."

"And do what with him?"

"Free him. Get him away from here. Thwart them in that if nothing else."

"Why?" he said, though she could swear his lips didn't move; nothing moved.

"So at least he doesn't have to die. So someone doesn't have to die."

For the first time since he'd started reading the card he moved, shook his head. "I meant, why would you help us? Why double-cross your friends?"

She chose her words carefully. "Let's just say they're not my friends, never have been. Let's just say I was myself double-crossed."

••••

That morning, York didn't recognize the servant who brought his breakfast tray, but the man's face did seem vaguely familiar. There were three or four different people who regularly brought his meals. And every few days, about the time he would get to the point where he could recognize them, the powers-that-be rotated them out and brought in a new group. Today was one of those days.

As usual, the tray contained his meal, utensils, condiments and other items, and a news card. And as usual, York only lightly touched the meal and ignored the news card completely. He no longer cared what they had to say about him.

The servant that brought his lunch was a woman, though like all the rest she was clearly military. She put the tray down on the table, arranged the setting carefully, but before leaving held up the news card and asked, "Beggin' your pardon, sir. But would the cap'm like me to put this in the reader?"

Odd question, York thought. But he just shook his head and she left.

He didn't touch lunch, spent the time at the window. He spent most of his day now just staring out that window, replaying bits and pieces of his life, trying to avoid too much analysis of the meaningless events contained therein.

She had said *cap'm*, he realized. The AI guard had called him *cap'm*. AI didn't use that term. No AI guard would ever have called him that, not even as an insult. Only a marine would have done so. He tried to remember what she had said as he turned slowly back to the untouched meal. He stared at the plates and utensils and food for a long moment, then reached out and picked up the news card. He walked over to the reader, sat down and switched it on, pulled on the earphones and inserted the card.

It was just the usual stuff. He sat there for a while not really listening to the recorded news broadcast. His eyes were drooping, and he was close to falling asleep, his face buried in his hands, when a familiar voice brought him up short: ". . . thought you might want to see this, Cap'm."

He looked at the screen of the reader; it showed a large room with a conference table in its center and a number of individuals seated around it. There were nine of them, all wearing admiral's stripes.

York hit the backtrack key on the reader for a few seconds. Now the scene showed an ordinary news caster describing the events of the day, until suddenly his voice shifted and his lips no longer matched the words in York's ears, ". . . Thought you might want to see this, Cap'm."

Palevi!

A few seconds later the picture fluttered, and again he was looking into the conference room with the nine admirals—six men, three women. York recognized Soladin, Abraxa, Andralla Schessa and Sergai Leonavich, guessed who the other five had to be. Soladin was standing, speaking to the others and referring to a piece of paper held in his hands. ". . . Ballin was apparently resistant to mild dosages of the normal interrogation drugs. And because he had recently been seriously injured and gone through extensive speed healing treatments—apparently more than once—analysis of his blood chemistry indicated heavier dosages would probably kill him, something we need to avoid, at least until after his trial. So we resorted to more traditional techniques. But he still refused to answer any questions."

Abraxa asked, "How intensive was the interrogation?"

Soladin shrugged. "See for yourselves." He reached down to the console built into the conference table in front of him, touched a switch, and a small square near the top of York's screen showed a separate image of an earlier recording, evidently a copy of what was replayed on the screens in front of each admiral.

The recording showed York lying unconscious on the deck of his cell, though so much dried and caked blood covered him he was hardly recognizable. The camera panned around him as Soladin spoke. "Most of the bones in his hands and feet and arms and legs have been broken, one by one. He has several broken ribs and torn ligaments—the list goes on and on. This was all administered slowly, over a period of several days."

An admiral York didn't recognize leaned forward. "And yet he refused to tell us anything."

Soladin shook his head. "The interrogator has provided us with a recording of one of the sessions that nicely illustrates the man's defiance."

Soladin touched another switch, and the small split screen showed Sierka going carefully through one of his interrogation sessions. Sierka evidently knew this one was being recorded, remained calm and impersonal through the whole thing, though no less brutal.

York couldn't actually remember that specific session, but from the vivid scar on Sierka's neck and the way his voice croaked when he spoke, it was sometime after York had tried to kill him, which meant it was long past the time York had broken psychologically. Sierka and his AI thugs worked him over and pretended to ask questions. York just lay there and ignored them, and he could see why anyone watching might take it as a sign of defiance, when in fact he had just plain given up.

"Amazing!" one of the admirals commented.

"In fact," Soladin emphasized, "some of you may have noticed the scars on the interrogator's neck; they're from an attempt Ballin made on the interrogator's life during an earlier session. An attempt, I might add, that almost succeeded."

"This man is a maniac," one of the men said. "He's a renegade, a traitor, a mutineer—"

"Oh shut up, Karltine," Leonavich shouted, identifying the man as Karltine Degaas, Duke de Mercus. Leonavich stood, leaned forward angrily and glared across the table at Degaas. "That bullshit is for the masses. Don't start believing your own goddamned propaganda. Ballin was just obeying the orders we gave him."

"Nonsense," Degaas shouted back. "He's a danger to us all, and can't be allowed to live."

"Gentlemen," Andralla Schessa said calmly. "Please!"

Both of them looked at her, bit back whatever they'd been about to say. Leonavich sat down and Schessa continued. "I agree with you Karltine. Ballin is a danger to us all and can't be allowed to live. But Sergai is also correct when he reminds us we mustn't start believing our own propaganda—Lieutenant Ballin is not the cause of the mess we're in. In fact, if the circumstances were a bit different, we'd probably give him a promotion and a medal. I almost wish he were working for us."

That brought a few laughs and eased the tension a bit. "That's interesting you should say that, Andralla," Soladin said. "In looking into Ballin's past I discovered he *was* apparently working for one of us, though he didn't know it."

The admirals seated around the table reacted with dead silence for several seconds, until Schessa asked, "Are you telling us this Ballin was in the employ of one of us? That one of us has betrayed the others?"

Soladin lifted a single eyebrow. "In a manner of speaking. But why don't you judge for yourselves." He looked at his papers for a moment, then began reciting facts. "Ballin is thirty-four years old. We know he was brought to the planet Dumark when only an infant, and arrangements were made for him to be raised by foster parents. However, payments to the foster parents stopped when Ballin was six years old. And while his foster parents continued to raise him, they put little effort into it. Ballin was arrested at the age of twelve after mugging an old woman. And it appears someone powerful intervened with the courts on Dumark to get him turned over to the press gangs, rather than serving a prison sentence he might not survive."

Schessa interrupted him. "That's rather slim evidence, Johan."

Soladin smiled knowingly. "There's more. At the age of eighteen, Ballin was sent to the Royal Military Academy at Mare Crisia on Luna, auspiciously because he was the youngest survivor of the *Andor Vincent*. Now tell me, in the history of the Empire, how many juvenile-delinquent, lower-deck pod gunners have been admitted to the Royal Military Academy?"

A heavy silence answered Soladin. He continued. "It's also of interest that Ballin is a lifer. Now lifers are an interesting phenomena. For some reason no one quite understands, every assignment the Fleet computers give them is combat duty. They never get a rotation back to a non-combat assignment. They never get a few years off like everyone else, just perpetual combat. In fact, with the exception of his few years at the Academy, Lieutenant Ballin has been in combat almost continuously for twenty-two years. Furthermore, he's fought in most of the great battles of our time: Trefallin, Sirius Night Star, Arman'Tigh, Shamrock Alley, Turnham's Cluster, Tsairmegan—the list goes on and on, names that are legend."

Soladin nodded his head quietly, apparently lost for a moment in thought. "There's another interesting thing about lifers: they're extremely rare. I've done a little research, and while we've all heard of the phenomena, it turns out that with the exception of Mister Ballin, none of us have ever actually met one. In fact, they're so rare, there has actually only ever been one: our Mister Ballin."

A chorus of hushed whispers answered that. Soladin continued. "Someone carefully inserted that legend about lifers into the common military myth. And that same someone intervened every time Ballin was about to be reassigned, intervened to ensure he would always be held at a safe distance, always far out on the front lines; intervened sometimes to keep him alive, undoubtedly, but always to insure he was never too close."

"Too close to what?" someone demanded.

Soladin shook his head. "Not too close to *what*," he said. "Too close to *whom*. In fact, too close to us."

Schessa said, "I'm assuming you can verify all this with hard data. But you haven't yet told us why. Why go to all this trouble for, as you put it, a *juvenile-delinquent, lower-deck pod gunner*? Why?"

Soladin looked at each of them carefully, and the answer he gave seemed completely odd and out of context to York. "The man who brought the infant child York Ballin to Dumark, the man who arranged for the foster care, the man who arranged for regular payments to the foster parents, the man who visited yearly until the boy was six years old—that man was Collier Maczek."

Again silence answered Soladin, and for several seconds everyone sat in complete stillness. Schessa was the first to move: she punched something up on the screen in front of her. Several of the others followed her lead, one or two scratching hurriedly on pieces of paper. It was the strangest sort of reaction, beginning with that long moment of silence and no reaction, moving to a stage of almost frantic activity, then dawning comprehension on several of their faces, and then sudden pandemonium. They all stood, shouting, demanding to know who had betrayed the rest, trying to shout above the others. Soladin let it go on for a few seconds, then held up the paper he was holding and waved it at them carefully. "Yes," he said as they quieted down. "We all knew Ballinov had a brat hidden away somewhere. And with a little arithmetic anyone can see the payments to the foster parents ended when the whore and her servant were killed in the palace revolt. And with a little more arithmetic we know who she was bedding at the time Ballin was born. And we know the old man was quite smitten with her."

More shouts and angry demands. "Yes," Soladin shouted above them. "We have the illegitimate son of the late emperor, and the younger half-brother of the present emperor. We have a prince of the royal blood in a cellblock on Luna Prime. And any one of us might have kept him in the wings, out of the way, waiting for some opportunity to use him. For if he were legitimized somehow, we also have a potential pretender to the throne."

"So Ballin was part of all this?" a woman demanded. "Is this some sort of move to take the throne?"

"No, no, no, no, no," Soladin shouted above the uproar that followed. "Not at all. Ballin was, and is, an innocent dupe. He knew nothing of this, still knows nothing of his own lineage. In fact, as Andralla pointed out, Ballin was just obeying orders, and his only crime was that he's too damn good at what he does, and he managed to carry out his orders with a bit too much success. It's a shame. Beyond a few faults, none of which seem to get in his way, he's a capable officer."

"That he is," Schessa added. "He managed to single-handedly capture and destroy our sub-sector headquarters at Sarasan. And with both the Directorate and the empire trying to destroy both him and his ship, he got her into Andyne-Borregga, got her repaired, and got her out again. And we're still trying to figure out how he brought a full sized cruiser into Lunan nearspace without detection. And finally, thanks to him, we now have in our possession two members of the Directorate Central Committee."

A large muscular man, who until that moment had remained silent, leaned forward and asked carefully, "What did you just say, Andralla?"

Schessa smiled. "It's just a little secret, Marko," she said, identifying him as Marko Simma, Duke de Jupttar. She looked at Abraxa. "Another one of Bargan's little secrets."

It was clear now that Schessa and Soladin had carefully orchestrated the meeting. Simma demanded in a hard, angry voice, "What is she talking about, Bargan?"

Abraxa shrugged and recovered quickly. "It's no secret, at least not beyond these walls. In fact, I had prepared a briefing for all of you. If you'll all look to your screens . . ." The split screen on York's reader showed a picture of Add'kas'adanna. She looked better, though that streak of Kinathin pride glared out at them like a new sun in the galaxy. "Let me introduce Fleet Director Add'kas'adanna. Ballin captured her off Sarasan when he destroyed her ship. Of course, we've no hope of interrogating her. Like us, her neural core has been carefully programmed, and she'd die quickly should we attempt to extract any information from her by force.

"Next . . ." The picture shifted suddenly to the empress' servant, though she was attired much more expensively than before. "Let me introduce Director of State Theara. Ballin didn't exactly capture her. Apparently she was traveling in Her Majesty's retinue disguised as a personal servant. That was the reason, by the way, for the trip to Trinivan—to meet up with Theara and have her join Sylissa d'Hart's retinue, and then later that of Cassandra. And of course, we can no more interrogate Theara than we can Add'kas'adanna. But from other sources we know she was involved in a little conspiracy with Edvard and Cassandra, and she brought with her a proposal for a cease-fire, and a possible peace treaty."

The shouting started again, and it was clear none of the nine admirals wanted to see their personal empires suddenly stricken with peace. There was no real argument, no disagreement, just an obvious and clear understanding among them all that, at any cost, peace could not be allowed to break out. But with his revelations Abraxa had effectively deflected their attention from his own little conspiracies. However, Soladin moved quickly to deflect them back. "At the moment," he said, "I'm far more concerned about Ballin. He's more dangerous to us than a few Directors of the Central Committee. Even more dangerous than that Kinathin fleet that's bearing down on us. But there are some answers to be had. I think the foremost question on all our minds is, *Who is responsible for Ballin's existence?* And that question wasn't terribly difficult to answer. Remember, one of us had to intervene to save the young boy from a prison sentence. And again to get him into the Academy, and again every time he was reassigned, and again for any number of reasons. Now each intervention was carefully and subtly covered up, but each did leave a slight trace. And when you isolate them and put them together, they form a rather complete picture. Though, there is one question I still have." He looked pointedly at Abraxa. "Tell me, Bargan. Who, or what, is *Wildflower?*"

Everyone looked at Abraxa, who sat back in his chair and let a sly smile form on his lips. "Very good, Johan," Abraxa said. "Very good. Not just the detective work, the presentation was also quite impressive. How long have you known?"

Again angry shouts, demands and general chaos. "Silence," Schessa shouted, raising her voice for the first time. York had heard that, next to Abraxa, Schessa was a power to contend with all her own. And the obedient silence that answered her spoke volumes for the respect, or awe, or more likely fear, with which the others regarded her. "Bargan," she said, "Have you betrayed us?"

"Come now, Andralla," Abraxa said, shaking his head impatiently. "Let's not overreact here. Many years ago I came across an opportunity and I took it. I've done nothing with the whore's brat other than keep him alive and out of the way, waiting to see if some opportunity presented itself. I did no more, nor no less, than any of you would have done." Abraxa looked slyly at Soladin. "In fact, it's obvious Johan has known about this for some time. So why didn't he reveal it when he first learned of it—because like me he was waiting for an opportune moment to make use of it. And apparently he's found it."

"And the result," Schessa continued, "is that you've put us all in danger. There's no telling how the public would react to this information, or the military, or the senate. At least we have the royal family under our control at the moment . . ." As she spoke she reached out and closed a fist tightly in front of her, as if crushing something within her palm. ". . . but if this news were to get out there's no telling what could happen."

"My people know we betrayed Ballin at Sarasan," Leonavich added, "and I'm having trouble with my junior officers."

Degaas said, "Having trouble with your senior officers too, if we gauge by the mutiny you had to put down."

"Nevertheless," Leonavich growled angrily, "there's a lot of potential for popular support for this man in the officer corps, if the truth got out."

Soladin spoke up. "Might I make a suggestion?"

York got the feeling that there was a constant power struggle for supremacy over the Admiralty Council between Schessa and Abraxa, At this moment, Schessa was temporarily top dog, and trying to consolidate her position. She nodded at Soladin.

"First," Soladin said. "Let's try Ballin in a military court, broadcast it and make it public. We'll make sure Ballin completely discredits himself, comes off as a megalomaniac, a half-mad renegade with a renegade crew. Ballin gets the death sentence, then after the trial he escapes, takes his ship and makes a run for it. In fact, we'll keep his entire crew on *Cinesstar* under lock and key, use our own skeleton crew to stage the escape and do something a little spectacular. We'll drive the ship out a few light-years from here, put a big warhead into it, then turn the propaganda people loose with a story about a pitched battle between our loyal troops and the mad renegade."

They answered him with a long silence, which Abraxa finally broke. "It's trite, sounds like a story on the vids."

Soladin nodded and smiled. "But it'll work."

Again silence, this time broken by Leonavich. "Ballin and his crew deserve better than this."

There was only a little more discussion, then the nine admirals voted, and unanimously sentenced York and his crew to death.

The scene on the reader card flickered suddenly, then switched to the courtroom, to York's court-martial. But this wasn't the prepared, edited, carefully massaged vid that had been broadcast to the public as a live trial. This was the raw footage. York watched them drag him into the courtroom, a beaten, broken man. Seeing it clearly now, even he was surprised at how brutal they'd been. He watched their first attempts at orchestrating the trial, watched the vid director interrupt and give orders to have him cleaned up. There were a few scenes of witnesses being called, scenes showing the vid director instructing them in the lies they were supposed to tell, instructing them in the punishment they would receive if they didn't lie convincingly. Then there were the scenes when they brought York back, all cleaned up and healthy. York watched as he broke the vid-tech's neck, watched the med-tech trying to calibrate the neural probe under the vid director's instructions. And then there were scenes where they played him like a marionette, made him angry, made him sad, turned him on, turned him off.

The reader finished with more words from Palevi. "You just give the word, Cap'm, and we'll get you out of there. Just let the next marine you see know, and we'll take it from there."

York withdrew the card from the reader, put it in a pocket, stood, went to the window and looked out at the lush, green countryside. That was clever of them. What a clever way to orchestrate the escape attempt Soladin wanted! Make him think he was escaping from the orchestrated escape attempt, escaping for real. If he gave Palevi the word he'd play right into their hands.

They'd won. He knew that now. He just wasn't good enough at this game, and he didn't want to play any longer. All he wanted now was to get some sleep, sleep with no nightmares.

36

Party Time

YORK WATCHED THE sun rise outside the window. He'd been up for some hours, awakened by one of his nightmares, could still remember the visions of body bags and body parts. It was a beautiful day, with a clear, blue sky like nothing he'd ever seen.

One of the AI goons brought his breakfast, did a good job of pretending to be a marine and asked him, "If there's anything else the cap'm wants, anything at all, just let me know, sir."

He had more of an appetite that morning, managed to eat something, then spent the morning staring out the window.

The AI goon that brought his lunch was rather transparent, picked up another reader card she'd brought with the food, shook the card at him and told him, "Real interesting news this morning, Cap'm."

York was curious enough to take a look at the card. Like the other it was a normal vid broadcast, and at a certain point Palevi's voice overrode the vid announcer's. "Shit, Cap'm. Beggin' yer pardon, sir, but we can't keep these people in place forever. We got to move quick. Just give us the word."

After lunch, York returned to the window. He didn't know how long he stood there when there came a knock at the door.

No one ever knocked, they just came in, so he crossed the room and opened the door, found Andralla Schessa standing there.

It occurred to him that a condemned man didn't have to bow to anyone, but there was no reason to be uncivil. "Your Grace," he said, bowing and stepping aside. "Come in, please. I doubt I can go out."

She smiled at that as she stepped past him. "Thank you, Captain. Or should I call you Lieutenant, or . . . Cap'm."

"Does it really matter?"

She lifted an eyebrow. "No, I suppose it doesn't."

York looked down the corridor outside before closing the door, saw no one, saw only wood paneling and carpet and other doors. He wondered for a moment if he should try to make a break for it, realized everything here was an illusion so he closed the door carefully. When he turned around Schessa stood there studying him. "Why didn't you try for it?" she asked.

He thought about admitting he was beaten, decided he'd rather keep her misled. "I doubt I'd have been allowed to open the door if the appropriate precautions hadn't been taken."

She lifted an eyebrow. "You're a smart man, Captain. For a man who's kept alive all these years, how did you get yourself into this mess?"

He almost said, *It was Abraxa who kept me alive all these years*, but he wasn't supposed to know about that. "Just in the wrong place at the wrong time."

"No loyalties?" she asked. "No bitterness?"

He shook his head, walked past her to the bar, poured a strong drink and offered it to her. She took it, so he poured himself another. He looked at the drink, realized he hadn't drunk anything for several days. "The loyalties I had are gone, and I can't be bitter at anyone because I was the fool." He tossed the drink down in a gulp.

She hesitated for a moment. "You know . . . there is a way out."

He walked over to the window, looked out at the green countryside and took the bait. "And that is?"

She joined him at the window. "Join me. Come to work for me. I'll make you one of my closest advisors."

York looked at her carefully—she was serious. "I assume your colleagues on the Admiralty Council wouldn't approve of my continued existence."

She wrinkled her nose and shook her head at him. "A new face, a new name, a new identity, a carefully staged death, a body with your face and build, and a properly altered DNA report—these things can be arranged."

"And my crew?"

"What crew?"

"*Cinesstar.*"

"Oh, that crew. I'm sorry, Captain. You must be realistic. We can't save everyone."

York nodded, continued to stare out the window and realized she was trying to do the same thing to him Abraxa had done for so many years, keep a prince of the royal blood on ice and wait for an opportune moment to make use of him. He thought of the pretty, young spacer he'd sat next to at *gunner's blood*. She had looked at him with such admiration, expected so much of him. She was probably still on *Cinesstar*, waiting for him to do something miraculous, if she was still alive. "Let me think about it," he lied.

"Very well, Captain. But don't take too long."

He didn't escort her to the door, continued to stare out the window and heard the door close softly as she left.

No, he wouldn't take Schessa's offer. But unfortunately for that pretty, young gunner, he didn't know any miracles either.

••••

Another polite knock on the door. York answered it, ready to tell Schessa he couldn't be her pawn, but found Palevi standing there dressed in an AI sergeant's uniform. Palevi stepped quickly into the room; four of his people followed him, also in AI uniforms. He closed the door and said nervously, "Cap'm. We gotta move, now. We got the vids and monitors covered, and that'll hold for maybe two hours, then they'll know you're gone."

York shook his head. "We can't. It's what they want us to do, make a break for it like this."

Palevi frowned and looked at him oddly. Then he grinned that grin. "Right, Cap'm." He turned, scanned the room and barked orders at his people. Two of them started pulling at York's clothes, undressing him, while the medic Kalee pulled out her kit and went to work on the scars on his face. She sprayed something on the skin there, did something with some chemicals, then peeled back his eyelid and said, "Try not to blink, sir." She inserted a large lens over the face of the chrome eyeball while someone else guided his legs into a new set of pants. It was much like the drill they'd rehearsed to get him into his armor in a hurry. But this time, when they stood him up in front of a mirror, the man who looked back at him was a middle aged, lower rank AI noncom with no chrome eye and scars.

"Hustle it up, boys and girls," Palevi barked. They stepped into the corridor, and Palevi set a careful pace. They were just a group of AI going somewhere on some business, two noncoms and four enlisted, not likely to be questioned by anyone except other AI. And York didn't doubt Palevi's people were ready for a nasty fight, if it came to that.

There were few military personnel present, though they passed quite a number of servants and civilians, all of whom avoided eye-contact with the group of AI. Palevi led them through a large kitchen, then out into the open air across a wide, grassy lawn and into a garage where a number of vehicles were parked. He chose one, and the six of them climbed into it, then Palevi lifted it up on its grav fields and arced them slowly up into the sky.

It was that simple, too simple, York realized. They had to be playing right into the Admiralty Council's hands, giving them exactly what they wanted. But why not, he thought. They were going to execute them all anyway. At least this way they could all go out clean, go out thinking they were doing something, rather than just sitting there waiting for the inevitable.

Palevi drove the grav car to a small, but well equipped, shuttle port. They parked the car in a neat row of other vehicles, walked openly into the shuttle terminal, where Yagell and three other marines, also in AI uniforms, waited for them. York recognized Stacy and Dakkart among them. Security waved them right through.

"How'd you manage this?" York asked Palevi.

"Lady d'Hart set it up, passed around some rather hefty bribes, though the people she paid off don't realize what we're really doing. But she got us legit AI credentials with reasonably high-level clearances, so for a few hours we got quite a bit of freedom."

York couldn't hide his anger. "And why's Lady d'Hart want to help us?"

"Apparently they double-crossed her some way, Cap'm. She was the one who gave us that recording you viewed. I guess they always record Admiralty Council meetings, and some officer on the admiralty staff thought she'd find it interesting, for a price."

They hustled York into a shuttle where Lady d'Hart waited. "Good day, Captain," she said.

York nodded politely, turned away from her and found a seat, sat down and closed his eyes tiredly. The Council had thought of everything, even to having her keep a close eye on them while they acted out this little charade.

"My personal yacht is waiting for us up at Luna Prime, Captain. It's small, but transition worthy, and fast, and quite comfortable. We should be able to have you well out of reach before the day is out."

York opened his eyes and looked at her closely. There was something hidden behind her eyes, some kind of pain, or sorrow, not the right emotion for someone so faithless. He wondered then if she knew how much of a pawn she was. He closed his eyes and tried to sleep.

••••

The young AI lieutenant on the screen was quite nervous. She was pretty, and Juessik wondered how much she might want to advance her career. "Lady d'Hart's shuttle lifted off Terr about an hour ago, sir. It should be docking with Prime shortly. Shall I issue an intercept order?"

Juessik shook his head. "No. This is the fun part. Let's watch them run a little. They'll squirm even harder when we close the trap."

She nodded respectfully. "As you wish, Colonel. Shall I notify the Admiralty Council?"

"Not yet." Juessik didn't want that fat old fart Abraxa stealing his fun. "There'll be time for that later. Just keep me informed."

Juessik cut the circuit.

"What was that, Torrin?" Dulell asked, stepping into the bedroom with two cold drinks.

"Nothing really," Juessik said. "A little surprise for the Admiralty Council, when they find out their little bastard prince has escaped."

Juessik took his drink from Dulell, pulled Dulell close, kissed him on the cheek. "I like surprises," he said. "Especially when I get to give them."

••••

The shuttle docked in a small service bay on Luna Prime without incident. Lady d'Hart led them through busy corridors, with York and Palevi and the marines an apparent AI escort. York just coasted and let them lead him where they chose. It was easier that way, simpler not to think about what was coming.

There was some sort of snag gaining access to her yacht, some problem with their clearances. She told the ten of them to wait up in the Service Controller's office while she made a call to clear the matter up, then left them waiting for the lift. When the lift doors opened Palevi grabbed York's arm, held him back as his people stepped into it. He said to them, "The cap'm and me, we'll follow in a second."

Standing in the open lift Yagell looked at him oddly, then shrugged, voiced commands at the lift and the doors cycled shut, leaving York and Palevi standing alone in the corridor.

Palevi grabbed York by the lapels of his AI uniform and slammed him up against the corridor wall. "God damn it, Cap'm," he growled, his nose only inches from York's. Palevi was shaking as he spit words in York's face. "Don't give up on us like this. We'll follow you to hell and back, as long as you lead us. God damn it, we'll follow you to hell even if we don't get back. Just don't give up like this. You're a marine, damn it, so act like one."

On the tip of York's tongue were the words, *I ain't no fuckin' marine,* but he let it go, just stared into Palevi's eyes.

"Damn it, Cap'm. You once asked me to make sure you went out clean, no tanks. Well, that's what I'm askin' you now. We want to go out clean, and you're the only one who can give us that."

York opened his mouth to say something, but he couldn't give Palevi what he wanted so he shut his mouth carefully.

"Shit," Palevi cursed as the lift doors opened again.

The Service Controller wasn't at all happy to have ten AI troopers using his office as a waiting room. He was busy, tried to ignore them, concentrated on his screens and his work.

There was a large transparent, plast window in one wall of the Controller's office. York stepped up to it and looked out at an unobstructed view of the main Navy Yard on Prime. It was a large open bay, more than a kilometer across, and in the distance he could see the entrance open to space, a few stars twinkling in the beyond. There were a number of ships in dock, ranging in size from small personal vessels like Lady d'Hart's yacht, to *Cinesstar* herself, battered, damaged, looking more like a derelict than a man-of-war. The Yard operated under vacuum in one-tenth gravity, making it easier on service crews. There was one now crawling over the skin of *Cinesstar.* York counted seven or eight techs in vac suits, wondered what they were up to, probably had to ensure she was worthy to make a run for it and play her role in the little charade the Council was orchestrating.

Don't give up on us . . . Palevi had said. Those words hurt. York tried to forget them and just stared at his ship, wondered if that pretty, young pod gunner was still alive.

"Hello, Cap'm," Yagell said, planting herself beside York at the window. She followed his gaze and looked at *Cinesstar.* "She's kind of sorry lookin', ain't she, sir?"

Don't give up on us . . . Palevi had said. But what else could York do? The Admiralty Council had all moves covered, were one step ahead of him, knew what he was doing before he did. He couldn't fight that kind of power. "*. . . we'll follow you to hell even if we don't get back . . .*"

York chuckled. Pretty simple logic. Maybe that was the answer; keep it simple. "Ya know, Cap'm," Yagell said. "Everyone's still aboard her. It's a shame we can't do nothin' for them."

"Yeah," York said. The words came out hard. "A real shame." But as he said them, he knew he had to do something. He couldn't win, but he'd lost so long ago winning was no longer important. Maybe he could screw things up for the bastards. And maybe he could give his people a clean end. He owed them that, at least, owed Maggie and Frank and Paris and Olin, and all the others.

"Sergeant," he said to Yagell, though he continued to look at *Cinesstar*.

"Ya, Cap'm," she said tiredly, "Whaddaya want?"

That was sloppy. Yagell was often unpleasant, but never sloppy. York realized she'd given up on him. He turned his head slowly toward her, let his eyes settle on her and stared her down hard. She looked at him for a moment defiantly but he didn't flinch; he looked through her as he'd seen Palevi do with a recalcitrant recruit, until she lowered her eyes and mumbled, "Sorry, sir."

He looked back at *Cinesstar*. "Everyone's still aboard her, huh?"

"Yes, sir."

"What kind of shape is she in?"

"They repaired the damage amidships, sir. I think they fixed the transition drive, so we could make our escape attempt, and get burned."

"How many actives do we have here?"

"Nine, sir."

York turned slowly about. There were ten of them in total; she hadn't counted York as an active. "Guards on board the ship?"

"Yeah," she said. "But no more'n twenty or thirty. They don't need them, not with everyone comp-locked in their cabins or bunk rooms."

"We're going to need some vac suits," he said, turning back toward the window and nodding at the service crew crawling over *Cinesstar*'s hull. "Standard maintenance issue, like the ones that crew are wearing. And I assume you're armed."

She held out a small gun. He looked at it and shook his head. "You'll need something heavier than that. Tell everyone here to upgrade their weapons . . . now."

Yagell turned to York slowly and squinted at him. Then, without taking her eyes off him, she cocked her chin to one side and bellowed, "Sarge. Sarge, you better come over here."

"What is it?" Palevi yelled back at her. "I got my hands full."

"This here's more important, Sarge."

"I said I'm busy. What the fuck is so important?"

She paused for several long heartbeats, then said, "I think the cap'm here wants to party, Sarge. Party big time."

The marines went suddenly silent. Still looking at *Cinesstar*, York heard Palevi march up behind him and demand angrily, "What's that?"

"I said the cap'm here—"

York cut her off. "Sergeant Palevi, we're going to need some vac suits, and heavier weaponry than you people are presently carrying. And of course, I'll need a weapon." York turned about and looked past Palevi at the Service Controller. "And we're going to need his help."

Palevi stared angrily at him for a moment, then his lips curled slowly upward into a big, cheesy grin, the grin that York hated. "We goin' to a party, Cap'm?"

York grinned back at him, with that same grin. "More like we're gonna crash a party a bunch of admirals got planned, make sure they don't enjoy it that much."

"Told ya, Sarge," Yagell said. "It's party time."

••••

The Service Controller decided it was his duty to resist any cooperation with the maniacs who had suddenly taken him hostage. "You people'll have to do whatever you're going to do on your own. I'm not helping you."

One of the marines jerked on his collar, but the man wasn't easily intimidated. It was then that Lady d'Hart returned. "What's going on here?" she demanded.

"Change of plans," York told her. "I'm taking my ship back."

"You're insane. You can't fight them. They're prepared for any move you make . . ." As she looked in his eyes her voice trailed off. She put a hand to her mouth and stepped back from him.

He turned to the Service Controller, stepped up close to the man, realized the man didn't know who he was, couldn't see past Kalee's makeup, so he hooked a thumbnail under the edge of the synth-skin and slowly peeled away the patch. He needed Kalee's help to remove the lens, but when he turned back to the Controller the man gulped and blanched. "Yer Butcher Ballin."

"Good," York said. "You know who I am. That'll save us a lot of time."

"Sergeant," he growled over his shoulder without taking his eyes from the Controller's. "How long do you think it'll take this man to die?"

"How long you want it to take, Cap'm?"

The Service Controller literally stuttered and stumbled in his desire to please York.

37

Return

"WHAT DO YOU mean *you've lost them?*" Juessik shouted.

The young AI lieutenant squirmed noticeably. "Someone put a security lock on the d'Hart woman's yacht, and by the time we got that cleared up they'd all disappeared. I've ordered a sweep of all decks—"

"What!" Juessik screamed, and she cringed. "Cancel that order, you idiot. Immediately. You start running sweeps and Ballin'll know we're watching him."

"Yes, sir." While she contacted her subordinates and canceled her previous orders, he looked her over carefully, decided she might be a bit of fun, if handled properly. They'd find Ballin; Juessik was confident of that. But in the meantime it wouldn't hurt to let this young woman think the present difficulty was her fault. Later, when he forgave her, and offered her some wise and fatherly advice, she'd be all the more grateful.

She turned back to him and lowered her eyes. "It's done, sir."

"Good," he said, holding on to a hint of anger. "Find Ballin and his ilk, immediately. Then call me." Juessik cut the circuit.

Staring at the blank screen he pondered the situation for a moment. Ballin was loose somewhere on Prime, which could be a problem. But Juessik had a carefully prepared little trap with just the right bait. No matter where Ballin went he would eventually come after this bait and, unknowingly, walk right into Juessik's hands.

He placed a call to the Hospital Deck to check on the bait, was answered by a large and beefy AI sergeant dressed as a medical orderly. "Sir."

"How is Miss Votak, Sergeant?"

"She's unchanged, sir. I checked on her myself not five minutes ago."

"Our people are all in place?"

"Yes, sir. I checked on them too."

"Good. Stand ready. Your guests should be arriving sometime in the next few hours."

"Very good, sir."

Juessik cut the circuit.

••••

The docks were crammed with AI carefully checking identities, so they couldn't just walk aboard *Cinesstar*. York and several of the marines stuffed themselves into some ill-fitting, standard issue maintenance vac suits—just battery packs, no armor and no weaponry. At least the tool harness hid the gun Yagell had given him.

They raided a supply closet for the equipment they'd need, then left Yagell and two of her people with the Service Controller to ensure his continued loyalty, and to keep an eye on Lady d'Hart. York and the rest crammed themselves into a service airlock. The lock cycled and they stumbled out into the vastness of Prime's Navy Yard.

In the low one-tenth gravity York had to control his reflexes carefully. Low grav was sometimes more difficult to work in than zero-G, and as they crossed the breadth of the Yard on foot, *Cinesstar* loomed in the distance. The shadow of her bulk grew with each carefully placed step.

In twenty odd years York had never seen a ship-of-the-line from that angle before. He'd done repair work on the outer skin of ships in deep space, but it was odd to stand in her shadow, to look up at her battered and scarred undercarriage. He could almost count the individual wounds in her skin, could almost recall each damage report as it had flashed across one of his screens.

York keyed his com. "We need a maintenance sled down here."

Yagell answered him. "Ya know, Cap'm. I can see the Controller just wants to please."

"Cut the chatter," York growled. They were using their own private encryption key so they couldn't be monitored, but it was stupid to push their luck.

One of the maintenance crew, working high above on *Cinesstar's* outer hull, stepped onto a plast framework of rods and girders, did something with its controls and it floated off the ship's hull, then descended slowly to the floor of the Yard.

The sled driver grumbled and growled under his breath as he helped them load the equipment on the sled. The ride up was quick and without incident. York directed him to land the sled on *Cinesstar's* hull close to a maintenance airlock that opened into engineering.

York keyed his com. "Yagell, go."

The airlock cycled, and as the outer hatch popped open a new voice demanded, "What's going on out there?"

York tried to sound surly and overworked. "Who wants to know?"

"Lieutenant Jessup, AI. I'm in charge of security on this ship."

Now time to act appropriately contrite. "Uh, sorry, Lieutenant. Didn't know it was you. We just got our orders, supposed to repair some damaged circuits in engineering."

"You're not on the maintenance schedule."

"I ain't had any sleep in forty hours either. They suddenly got us working triple shifts."

"Well, you're not authorized to work on that section of the ship, so clear out, now."

"Sorry, Lieutenant. I got a work order says otherwise. If you want us gone you gotta speak to my Controller, get this work order rescinded. I'll be in a mess of trouble if I just walk away from it. You know regulations."

"Damn," Jessup swore, and switched out of the circuit.

York switched to the marine channel. "Yagell, tell that Controller to call Lieutenant Jessup and make this good."

Jessup was waiting for them when they stepped through the inner hatch into engineering, and even before they'd begun pulling off their vac suits he snapped angrily, "Ok, you're cleared. But don't leave engineering without checking with me." He turned and stormed out.

They stripped off their vac suits, opened up an instrument panel so it'd look like they were working on something. And while the marines spread a lot of tools and equipment on the deck, York watched a marine carefully examining a hatch that gave access to the core of the ship.

AI had clamped down on all access rights, with comp-locks on all cabin doors to imprison the crew in their quarters, and security alarms programmed on just about every hatch in the ship. The marine delicately opened a maintenance panel above the hatch, working as if he were defusing a bomb, then went to work on the wiring within. It took him several minutes, but then he stepped back and said, "She's clear, sir."

York palmed the lock and the mechanism cycled. The hatch popped and he shoved his shoulder into it, followed it into the dim lighting of *Cinesstar's* core as he forced it open. Behind him he heard Palevi growling, "Move it, Dakkart, you shit-for-brains, go, go, go."

York recalled using the shaft once before, recalled thinking then that he could use it to sneak onto the bridge if needed. He took the rungs one at a time, moved carefully in the zero-G shaft, conscious the slightest noise could echo through the hull of the ship for a good distance.

The hatch that opened onto the bridge was a different matter; the maintenance panel was on the other side. York looked at the stenciled letters above it, keyed his com, "Yagell, hatch A-oh-two."

"Give us a minute, Cap'm."

York waited . . . waited . . . waited . . .

"Go," Yagell snarled.

York triggered the lock on the hatch and shouldered it open. The Service Controller had scheduled maintenance access through the hatch so they wouldn't blow an alarm. But the newly scheduled maintenance would appear on a screen down in security, and if one of the AI troops happened to be looking at just that screen—

York and Dakkart scrambled through the hatch, Dakkart muscled it shut, and locked it. York keyed his com, "Yagell, we're clear."

He waited, listening for an alarm as the Service Controller rescinded the order, which cleared it from the screen in security.

"Who's there? What do you want? Can't you see I'm busy?"

York couldn't believe his ears: Sierka. The lights on the bridge were dim, and he and Dakkart had emerged behind Fire Control, which hid them nicely from the rest of the bridge.

"Who's there? I said I'm busy."

From the direction of his voice he had to be seated at the Captain's Console, which would have him facing away from them. York stood up a little and scanned the bridge quickly; apparently he and Dakkart and Sierka were alone. They stepped out from behind Fire Control, and as they approached Sierka he didn't look up and remained hunched over one of the screens at the console.

York pressed the muzzle of his gun against the back of Sierka's head, Sierka stiffened and York said, "It's me, Sierka. Don't even twitch."

Sierka raised his hands up off the console and grinned. "I should have known you'd try something. I'm just surprised you got this far."

York looked over his shoulder at the screen. Sierka had been in the midst of a log-on procedure, though it looked rather abnormal. "You're trying to get ring-zero access, aren't you?"

Sierka said nothing. York grabbed him by his tunic collar, hustled him away from the console, half dragged him across the width of the bridge, stood him up against Nav and left him there.

Sierka snarled at him, "You're a fool."

Dakkart asked, "Want me to kill 'im, Cap'm?"

York shook his head. "No. Just keep an eye on him. I've got work to do. But if he pulls anything, shoot him."

Dakkart grinned happily. "Happy to, sir."

York sat down at the Captain's Console, blanked the screen, then pulled on a headset and lowered his voice to a whisper so Sierka couldn't hear him. "Computer."

Acknowledge, it replied.

"Log on. Access Three-Charlie-Two-Niner-One-Niner-Alpha."

The computer hesitated for what seemed an interminable second. *Please confirm access Three-Charlie-Two-Niner-One-Niner-Alpha.*

"Access Three-Charlie-Two-Niner-One-Niner-Alpha confirmed."

Again the computer hesitated. *Access Three-Charlie-Two-Niner-One-Niner-Alpha confirmed. Access denied.*

Sierka threw back his head and laughed. Dakkart tensed, but York waved her down. "I told you you're a fool, Ballin. Don't you think we're smart enough to have thought of that? Your little ring-zero access code has been changed. All access codes have been changed. You're locked out, Ballin."

York turned back to the console. Without some sort of high-level access—at least command level—Sierka was right.

"And we found your little virus too," Sierka sneered. "We flushed the entire system, and reprogrammed it with a new OS master."

York looked at Sierka, and defeat must have shown visibly on his face, for Sierka laughed triumphantly. The Admiralty was always one step ahead of him, almost as if he was programmed like one of their computers. But there was one other chance, though it depended on where they'd gotten the new OS master.

He'd created another virus and infected the Sarasan operating system while Cappik was repairing *Cinesstar*. But now it depended on how badly damaged the Station had been, on whether they'd allowed it to make contact with any other component of Fleet before shutting it down for repairs, and on how far the virus had propagated through Fleet during the intervening time. Had a ship, any ship, taken something as simple as a contact packet from Sarasan and passed it on to other ships? Had York's program made it halfway across the empire?

"Computer."

Acknowledge, it replied.

"Log on. Access Ballinov-Francesca-Francesca-Ballinov."

Leaning against the Nav console Sierka frowned while the computer hesitated. York waited, and nothing happened. He waited longer and still nothing.

"Computer."

Acknowledge, it replied.

"Confirm access."

Access denied.

Sierka chuckled.

York closed his eyes, tried to think. What had he forgotten? Maybe he hadn't forgotten anything. Maybe he'd just failed completely. If he couldn't get access he and Dakkart were stuck on the bridge, Palevi and his marines were stuck in the maintenance closet below, and AI could just sweep them up like a minor nuisance.

So much had happened, it was hard to remember. But he knew he'd forgotten something and he had to try one more time.

"Computer."

Acknowledge, it replied.

"Log on. Access equals vocal print confirmation plus Ballinov-Francesca-Francesca-Ballinov."

Again the computer hesitated, and again York waited and nothing happened. And again the computer was unresponsive, neither granting nor denying access.

"Computer."

Acknowledge, it replied.

"Confirm access."

Access is incomplete. Complete access sequence.

York's heart pounded its way up into his throat. "Log on continuation," he said carefully. "Access concatenation Three-Charlie-Two-Niner-One-Niner-Alpha."

This time there was an even longer wait, and a bead of sweat rolled slowly down York's cheek. He jumped when the computer said, *Please confirm access Three-Charlie-Two-Niner-One-Niner-Alpha.*

York almost shouted, "Access Three-Charlie-Two-Niner-One-Niner-Alpha confirmed."

No hesitation this time. *Access Three-Charlie-Two-Niner-One-Niner-Alpha granted. Access priority is ring-zero.*

38

Prisoner No More

IT TOOK YORK several minutes to dig his way into *Cinesstar*'s system without alerting AI. He also had to be absolutely certain nothing he did showed up on any screen outside *Cinesstar*. Next he had to override the screens the security team was monitoring, make sure they got what appeared to be normal updates, when in fact they were seeing none of his activity. Then he took a careful look at the telemetry link with Luna Prime.

Comp Central was monitoring a massive amount of data, and setting up dummy data feeds for every element would take days. He pondered that for a few minutes, then decided to use *Cinesstar*'s combat simulation computer. It was designed to feed simulated data, in infinite detail, to every function of the ship, data so real, and in such detail, that no crewmember on station could tell the difference.

He scanned *Cinesstar*'s telemetry recordings for the last twenty hours, looking for any major changes in routine that might bring the wrong kind of attention. It wouldn't do to have a repair crew called back to repair something they'd already repaired. There had been a site calibration on the telemetry feed about four hours ago, but since then it had all been routine.

York made a copy of the last four hours of the full telemetry record, fed it as a standard program to the combat simulation computer, diverted the output of the simulation computer to Prime's telemetry feed, and, holding his breath, activated the simulation.

Nothing . . . He cleared the access locks on the access shaft he and Dakkart had just used. Again, no response. He took a tally of the AI guards on *Cinesstar*—forty-two.

"Dakkart," he called. "Get over here and take a look at this."

She squeezed her way past the navigation console and appeared behind York, looking over his shoulder.

Twenty of the AI were spread out among ten watch stations at various sites on ship, eight more were split into two teams making the rounds of the various watch stations, and fourteen were in the marine ready-room. York nodded toward the screen. "Crawl back down that shaft and brief Palevi on this. Tell him to go for the ready-room first—if he gets there fast he's only got fourteen to worry about at the moment. Then he can wait for the eight on patrol to return and take them when they do. Then we'll take the rest one station at a time."

"Yes, sir," she said happily, spun and disappeared behind fire control. He'd turned off the sensors in the access shaft, heard the hatch grind open, then creak shut—no alarms; nothing on the telemetry feed to Luna Prime, nothing on the security feed to the AI Watch Commander, nothing.

He watched the screens intently for any sign of discovery. He couldn't follow Dakkart's progress, but he could guess when she reached Palevi, and still there came no alarm. He had to guess further about the time it would take them to crawl down the shaft to the ready-room, to surprise the AI squad down there, to take command of the ready-room, hopefully without alerting anyone.

Suddenly a red light flashed on his screen—someone in the ready-room had manually activated an alarm. But York's combat simulation program continued to feed routine telemetry to Prime, and after desperately scanning all the information feeds in *Cinesstar*'s systems, York was confident the alert had gone no farther than his console.

Later, he would think back on that moment and realize how stupid he'd been. He could use the excuse that he was tired, that he'd been tortured, that he'd been blown apart and put back together so many times he just wasn't thinking clearly. But inside he would always know it was just plain careless to concentrate so intently on that screen, to forget everything else around him.

He never did identify what hit him, but it was something heavy and blunt. The only thing that saved his life was that Sierka's throw wasn't very accurate. But it did strike him a glancing blow along the side of his head, knocked him into a sprawl on the deck and sent his senses spinning near the edge of consciousness. Dizzily he scrambled halfway back to his feet, only to catch Sierka's boot in his ribs.

He bounced off the navigation console, staggered away from it with the deck swaying crazily beneath his feet. Close to blacking out, struggling desperately to hold onto consciousness, he wasn't even sure where Sierka was, so he swung wildly and tried to pull his sidearm. York got his hand on the butt of his pistol, but Sierka tackled him. He got hold of York's gun hand, while York wrapped his free hand around Sierka's throat and tried to bite his ear. Locked together they both rolled off the fire-control console onto the deck. Sierka landed on top of him, trying to knee him in the groin . . .

"Fuckin' asshole." There was a nasty thud and Sierka groaned and rolled off him. Dakkart stood over them both and snarled, "You've just had your last chance, Sierka."

York scrambled to his hands and knees. His head was still spinning, but he could see clearly enough.

Sierka was on his face on the deck. Dakkart had one knee buried in the small of his back, had put her sidearm away and pulled out a power knife. Her thumb twitched and York heard the power knife hum to life. With her free hand she grabbed Sierka by the hair, pulled hard and lifted his chin off the deck, arching his back so she could cut his throat.

"As you were," York shouted.

She hesitated, looked over her shoulder at York defiantly. "That's an order," York growled. "We may need him."

She still hesitated. "You can cut his throat later," York added. "When we know we don't."

She let go of Sierka's hair, thumbed off the power knife. She stood slowly, gave Sierka a final kick in the ribs and turned to York. "Ready-room's secure, sir. Palevi says if you can give him access codes he can monitor those AI patrols from the Security Console and wrap the whole ship up in half an hour."

York's ribs complained painfully as he climbed to his feet. He pointed at Sierka. "Get him on his feet and ready to travel."

As he sat down at the Captain's Console he noticed Stacy, Dakkart's partner, had joined them. From the Captain's Console he opened up the Security Console, got hold of Palevi, set up access codes for him. "I want those AI goons buttoned up tight. While you're doing that I'm going to set up access codes for the rest of the crew."

"Aye, aye, sir." Palevi winked and grinned. "We're gonna have us a real party, ain't we, Cap'm."

York nodded. "Ya. A real loud and noisy party, Sergeant."

York cleared access on the main lift, then shut down access to it for the rest of the ship. It wouldn't do to have one of the loose AI patrols blunder into their operations. He called to Dakkart, hooked a thumb over his shoulder. "Get Sierka down to the brig. You can use the lift, but no side trips until the entire ship is secure."

"Aye, aye, sir," Dakkart said. She dragged Sierka to the lift, palmed the doors open and tossed him ungently into it.

As the doors cycled shut, Stacy stood uncertainly nearby. He was just a kid and wasn't sure what to do. York nodded toward the lift. "Just stand by. No one on or off the bridge without my permission."

"Yes, sir," he said, wide eyed.

Feeling a little paranoid York pulled his sidearm, laid it on top of the command console close at hand. He slaved one of his screens to Palevi's Security Console so he could follow the progress as they rounded up the rest of the AI. Then he began reprogramming *Cinesstar*'s access codes. It wasn't a difficult task, just time-consuming, and it required concentration. Occasionally he glanced at the screen showing Palevi's progress, but Palevi knew what he was doing and needed no help from York. York wouldn't have looked up from his work for quite some time had it not been for that odd sound, a familiar click that registered on his subconscious, the hammer being drawn back on a gun. Not an energy weapon, but the kind of old-fashioned, chemically powered slug thrower favored by some marines, and most assassins.

York opened his eyes carefully as Stacy stepped into his field of view. The kid had put his rifle down somewhere, was holding a small black pistol with the muzzle pointed at York's chest. York opened his mouth to ask him what the hell he was doing, but any question he had died on the tip of his tongue as his eyes met Stacy's, and right then the kid became something more. His features didn't really alter, didn't actually shift, but Stacy went from being a fresh-faced kid to someone who could have been anywhere between sixteen and forty. His eyes now showed a certain hardness, a subtle indication of age and experience not there before. York was oddly impressed at the control the man had exhibited. Not one of them had ever guessed he was anything more than just *the kid*.

"It was you," York said. "All along, it was you."

Stacy nodded, though there seemed no malice in him. "Sorry, Cap'm. Sorry it's gotta be this way. I like you, and if it was up to me I'd let you live. But I'm a professional."

York thought of his gun, sitting in plain sight close at hand. But he knew he wasn't fast enough. "Abraxa hired you, didn't he?"

Stacy shrugged. "I don't know who hired me, Cap'm. They don't know who I am, and I don't know who they are. It's better that way."

York shook his head. "It was Abraxa. I know that now." York had to keep Stacy talking, stall for time. If *the kid* was really a pro, and York had no reason to doubt his word on that, then he was certainly faster and better than York. Just stall, and try to think of something. "He hired you to kill me."

Stacy shook his head. "Not exactly, Cap'm. Whoever hired me sent me here with orders to keep an eye on you, to protect you if necessary, to report regularly on you. Nothing more."

York thought he saw a shadow flow cat-like behind Stacy from one console to another. But he dare not take his eyes off Stacy's face, dare not look that way. "Then why are you doing this?"

"There was a contingency plan in my instructions. If I received a certain coded message, I was to terminate you as soon as possible." Stacy shrugged. "I'm real sorry about this, Cap'm."

"I assume your name isn't really Stacy."

Stacy shrugged. "No. But then I haven't used my real name in years. Just call me Wildflower."

York glanced at his gun lying on the console. Stacy looked at it also, shook his head. "Don't, Cap'm. I'm going to make this easy on you, no pain, quick, clean, neat. Don't mess it up."

At that moment a soft click sounded behind Stacy, the lock on the hatch to the access shaft. Stacy stepped forward quickly, retrieved York's gun off the console in front of him and hissed, "No sound, Cap'm, no warning," then he disappeared into the shadows behind fire-control.

Whoever stepped out of the shaft did rather well, hardly made a sound. If York had been tapping away at his console that would have easily masked the faint hiss of a foot sliding carefully across the deck. Then Dakkart peeked around the side of Navigation with a gun in her hand, frowned at York and mouthed words silently, *Where's Stacy?*

Stacy appeared in back of her, pressed the muzzle of his gun behind her ear and she froze. "I'm here, Dakkart."

"Why you little twerp," she growled. "I knew it was you, you little asshole. I should of—"

Stacy swatted her on the back of the head with his gun and she crumpled over the navigation console, then slid to the deck. Again York thought he saw a shadow flow a step closer to Stacy. Then Stacy stepped forward, and standing over Dakkart he glanced at York. "It's time to end this, Captain." With a cold-blooded lack of expression he jammed the muzzle of his gun against the back of Dakkart's head, but behind him York saw a flash of white hair, and an olive colored hand settled silently on the nape of Stacy's neck. York heard a snapping crunch and Stacy slumped to the deck next to Dakkart.

Sab'ach'ahn stepped into the light. "My apologies, Captain. I had to wait until his weapon was diverted from you."

York asked, "Is he dead?"

Sab'ach'ahn's look said, *Need you ask?*

Dakkart groaned, crawled slowly to her feet rubbing the back of her head. She looked at Sab'ach'ahn, then down at Stacy's body and growled, "Little twerp!" and gave him one last kick. "Thought you could fool me. But I knew there was something wrong with you all along." She gave him another kick.

York would have liked to question Stacy further. "Get him out of here," he snarled. "Real soon he's going to get in the way."

As Dakkart threw Stacy's body over her shoulder the Command Console started bleeping at York. It was Palevi. "Captain. We got most of the AI in the brig. There's a squad of about fifteen holed up on G deck, but we've got them isolated and bottled up tight. It may take us a while to dig them out, though."

Cinesstar's hull echoed with the distant thump of a concussion grenade. Palevi shrugged. "May have to kill a few too."

York checked the telemetry feed to Prime. He then dug into the system, pulled up the access codes for the comp locks imprisoning his crew in their quarters. "You've got the comp-lock codes on your screen. Release my crew."

York had to wait about five minutes.

"It's done, sir."

Well, York thought, *here goes.*

He keyed his implants and spoke carefully. "Watch Condition Red."

In his implants the computer demanded, "Confirm Watch Condition Red."

"Red confirmed," York said. The status horn burped once and the alert klaxon started blaring. York switched his pickup into allship. "Watch Condition Red. Battle stations. This is not a drill. Repeat: this is not a drill." He repeated the message once more, recording it, then put it on continuous replay and sat back to watch the combat status summary on one of his screens.

Palevi and the marines green-lighted first, though their time was terrible. He could forgive them that under the circumstances. He waited, watching his screen for more green—and he waited. At about two minutes a defensive pod checked in. At four minutes one of the transition launchers yellow-lighted.

York cut the recording of his voice, left the alert klaxon blaring and switched into allship. "This is Captain Ballin. I'm sitting here on the bridge, and more than four minutes have passed, and most of you have yet to check in. Get off your fucking asses and get to your stations." He shouted the last word, "Now!"

The first station green-lighted one minute twenty-one seconds later—an entire station, not just an isolated pod or launcher. Then he heard the lift open and McGeahn took a tentative step onto the bridge. York didn't give her a chance. "What the hell are you waiting for?" he shouted.

She jumped, shot across the bridge and practically fell into her couch. Eldinow was right behind her, and the lift door cycled shut. Only seconds later it cycled open again and Gant and Jakobee stumbled over one another as York shouted them to their stations. It wasn't a full bridge crew, but it was all he had left, and it was enough.

York blanked the combat status summary from his screen. "McGeahn," he growled. "Check all actives on board ship. If anyone is still in their quarters and not sure what to do, please instruct them personally. And no communications outside this ship. And don't touch that combat sim I'm running. That's what's feeding phony telemetry to Prime so we can maybe get away with this."

Cappik was on station in Engineering. "Check out our drives and power plant," York ordered him. "We're going to have to make a run for it, and we'll probably need full combat status."

Nemkov checked in on Hangar Deck. "Forget Hangar Deck," York told him. "I need bridge crew. Get up here, on the double. Wait. On second thought, first get Hangar Deck organized, put someone you trust in charge, then get up here.

"Jakobee. I want an ordnance inventory soonest, and a status summary on all offensive and defensive stations. And review your crew assignments. We may have to restation some of them to get even coverage."

39

Bait

YORK SAT AT his console and drummed his fingers nervously. They needed hours, days, but all they had was minutes. Something would eventually focus Prime Central's attention on *Cinesstar*.

York tapped in to Prime's command grid. The Admiralty had deployed Home Fleet out near the edge of the system, just beyond nearspace. They were too far out to hinder *Cinesstar* if she made a run for it. There were a few AI ships in system, and Seventh Fleet was a good day out, driving in hard, though the idiot in command of her had strung her out over several light-years.

There was something odd and wrong with the deployment of Home Fleet, something equally wrong with the way Seventh Fleet was strung out. He stared at his console for a long moment, realized some piece of data was missing from the equation, then recalled that Soladin, during the meeting of the Admiralty Council, had said something about a Kinathin fleet.

York considered carefully that he was looking at a standard system-wide situation map, accessible by any Fleet officer. There had to be other data available—and he did have ring-zero access, but only within the confines of *Cinesstar*'s operating system. He needed to extend that access beyond the hull of the ship.

"Computer," he said. "Confirm access."

Access ring-zero confirmed.

"Computer. Access patch—*Cinesstar* main to Luna Prime main. Execute."

He waited for a long moment, then the computer said, *Confirm access level.*

He spoke quietly. "Access ring-zero."

Confirm access code.

"Access Three-Charlie-Two-Niner-One-Niner-Alpha confirmed."

*Access patch—*Cinesstar *main to Luna Prime main complete. Access ring-zero.*

York let out a long, slow breath. Given several hours to set up and debug the proper programming, with ring-zero access he could take complete control of Luna Prime, but there were too many system-level fail-safes, so to attempt to do so in the few minutes he had would prove disastrous. Cautiously, using this near godlike access, he dug deeper into Fleet's information structure, checking every step before taking it, conscious that he could easily trigger some alarm. He dug into the private Admiralty Council files, and after several minutes of exploration he found it, a special limited-access situation map. It was tracking a good-sized Directorate Fleet, information hidden from all but members of the Admiralty Council. Home Fleet was deployed to intercept, with elements of Seventh Fleet driving hard to support her. Sometime in the next day all hell was going to break loose.

"Cap'm," his implants bleeped. "Palevi here. Down in sickbay. Uh . . . you better come down here, sir."

"What is it?" York demanded angrily. "I don't have time."

"I can't describe it, Cap'm. You better come down yourself."

Something had shocked Palevi. "I'll be right down."

••••

"He's escaped," Abraxa screamed.

Soladin nodded. "He had help, a few bribes generously distributed, a shuttle waiting in just the right place at just the right time."

"But who?" Schessa asked. The three of them were meeting separately from the rest of the Admiralty Council.

Soladin speculated, "Sylissa d'Hart?"

Abraxa shook his head. "No. She's Juessik's. He's a devious little twerp, and he has some hold over her."

"For the time being it doesn't matter," Schessa said. "We'll find out and deal with whomever it was later. Right now we have to find Ballin. We can't let a potential pretender to the throne escape."

Abraxa shook his head worriedly. "But we have no track on him. It was cleanly done, no trace, no trail, and those guards who took bribes have long since disappeared."

"But we do have a track on him," Soladin said carefully, his lips curling up into a satisfied grin. Both Schessa and Abraxa looked at him and waited. "He'll go to his ship. He won't just run, not him—that ship'll pull at him like drugs to an addict. All we have to do is wait for him."

"Of course," Schessa added. "We'll alert the AI squad aboard *Cinesstar*. And we'll post an additional guard on the docks around her. He'll come to us."

••••

Palevi was waiting for him at the entrance to sickbay, but even before the sergeant showed him into the small surgery at the rear he could smell it. The unmistakable scent of burnt flesh clung to everything, accented with the equally unmistakable scent of decay. York had seen many atrocities in his time, but nothing had prepared him for what he found in the small surgery.

There were two examination tables in the surgery, cold impersonal things used for any number of purposes. On one, a female marine lay on her back, naked, strapped down, her hands and legs restrained by cuffs, her eyes staring fixedly at the deck overhead, her teeth clenched in the rictus of the agony she'd experienced during the throes of death. Most of her pelvis and abdomen had been burned away some time ago, and lying in the middle of the scorched mess was a badly damaged nerve prod. There were also dozens of small, round, puckered burns covering her body. It was all too clear what had happened. The nerve prod had been modified so it could inflict damage rather than mere pain, then used to torture her little by little, until finally it had been inserted into her vagina, and, either by design or accident, it had shorted badly, and burned away her midsection from the inside out.

Someone was crying, a soft, suppressed whimper. York saw Tathit huddled in a corner seated on the deck, curled up in a fetal position. A blanket had been thrown over her, though an exposed bare shoulder, with a small, round, puckered burn on it, made it clear she was naked beneath the blanket, and had been subjected to the same treatment as the young woman on the table.

York walked over to Tathit and crouched down beside her. Mec Notay said, "We found her strapped to the other table."

"What kind of shape is she in?"

A medic said, "Probably okay, but she won't let us examine her."

York reached out to her but she cringed away from his touch and continued to whimper. "Corporal," he said quietly, carefully, though he gave the word the familiar inflection of command.

She stopped whimpering, her eyes focused and she blinked several times, then looked at him out of the corners of her eyes.

"Who did this to you?"

She took a deep, stuttering breath, continued to stare at him and let it out shakily.

"Corporal," he said again. "I asked you who did this to you, and I want an answer. That's an order." Somehow he knew she needed to hear that.

Again she took a ragged breath, then slowly, carefully, she said, "Sierka." Her eyes started to retreat back to that blank, unfocused state of a few moments ago.

"Corporal," he growled at her, and again the familiarity of command brought her back. "The medics are going to examine you. You will allow them to, and you will cooperate with them. That's an order."

She said nothing. "I said, that's an order."

"Yes, sir," she whispered. "Very good, sir."

York stood up. Palevi stepped in his way and growled, "He's mine, sir."

"No he isn't," York said, shaking his head. "He's mine, and I want him kept alive, unharmed and unhurt. We may need him, and until I'm done with him, I want you to see to it personally he's kept well."

A low, feral growl escaped Palevi's lips, but he said, "Aye, aye, sir."

"But when I'm done with him," York continued, "then he's yours . . . my word on that, Sergeant, one marine to another."

Palevi grinned, and York knew he would obey.

"Captain," his implants barked. "McGeahn here. Luna Prime security is trying to establish contact with us."

"Ah shit!" York said. He looked at Palevi. "Did you hear that?" The sergeant nodded. "Get someone into an AI uniform, NCO rank, someone who can act. Tell them to answer that call, act stupid and stall for time."

••••

"They've disappeared?" Juessik screamed at the image of the pretty AI lieutenant. "They've disappeared completely, you say? Luna Prime is a closed, sealed environment, and you have all of Admiralty Intelligence at your disposal, and you can't find them?"

She cringed, refused to meet his eyes. "I'm sorry, sir. Somewhere along the line they deviated from the plan you outlined. The d'Hart woman went to some effort to get the security hold on her yacht cleared, and then she, along with Ballin and his marines, just disappeared. The yacht is empty. No one has boarded her, or even approached her, and we've been watching her closely."

"All right. We'll try to correct for your incompetence. Any vessel, regardless of how large or small, is to be delayed and examined for any possibility they may be aboard her. Do you understand?"

"Yes, sir."

He slapped a switch on the console and her image disappeared.

"What are you doing with Captain Ballin?"

Juessik spun at the sound of the voice behind him, realized as he calmed his heart it was only Dulell. "Nothing, Arkan. Nothing for you to worry about."

"No," Dulell said heatedly. "It's not *nothing*. You're playing some game with him, aren't you? You won't even execute him cleanly. You have to torment him. Don't you see how cruel you are?"

"Oh, Arkan," Juessik said, rolling his eyes. "Not that argument again."

Dulell spun on his heel and stormed away.

••••

York dropped into the Captain's Console and growled orders at McGeahn to show him the conversation between Luna Prime Security and whomever Palevi had chosen to act the part of an AI goon. It was Mec Notay. "Lieutenant Jessup is making his rounds right now," Notay said, addressing an AI major, "but I'll relay your message to him immediately. We have forty-two actives here, fully armed and kitted. We'll cover every entrance, and with the troops you're placing on the docks, I doubt we'll need additional support, though Lieutenant Jessup will have to be the judge of that."

"Very good, Sergeant," the AI major said. "If Jessup needs anything, have him call me immediately." He cut the circuit.

York demanded, "What was that about?"

Notay grinned. "Well, sir, apparently you've escaped, and they believe you're headed straight for this ship. They want us to take you into custody as soon as you get here, though they don't think we'll have to worry about it since the AI troops on the docks will intercept you first. They're scared, but they think they got the situation in hand."

York breathed a sigh of relief. "Keep that AI uniform on."

Using ring-zero access, York set up a small program to scramble some of the communications port codes for ships docked on Luna Prime. At random intervals it would scramble a couple of port addresses, then a few minutes later unscramble them. Anyone placing a call to a ship on Prime might find themselves talking to the wrong ship. He told McGeahn, "The next time someone calls this ship, answer it yourself and claim to be some other ship, complain that they'd better not screw up our port fees—stuff like that."

McGeahn grinned. "You're pretty sneaky, Captain."

York scanned the intelligence reports on the Directorate force approaching Luna. The fact that it was wholly Kinathin must have something to do with Add'kas'adanna. He checked carefully, found her presence was as much a secret as the approaching Kinathin armada, though with ring-zero access he learned she was being held incognito at the navy base at Mare Crisia on Luna. On impulse he checked on the location of the other feddie Director, Theara. She too was at Mare Crisia.

"McGeahn," he barked. "Where's Sab'ach'ahn?"

"I don't know, sir. Do you want me to find her?"

"I'm here, Captain," a ghostly voice said from somewhere behind York, and the Kinathin stepped forward to stand beside York's console. She still wore the reddish-brown patch of dried blood painted on one eyelid. It made her pale blue eyes stand out even more.

York pointed to the screens on his console. "Do you know how to read an imperial situation map?"

"I do, Captain."

"That approaching Directorate fleet is wholly Kinathin, and we have reports the Kinathins have withdrawn all their ships from Directorate operations. What do you make of that? Is this a *kith'ain* thing? Something to do with Add'kas'adanna?"

She stared at his screens for a long moment, then turned her head slowly and stared at him. "You understand more than you profess."

She turned her attention back to the screen. "Where is Add'kas'adanna Kith'at'annan?"

"She's being held incognito at the Mare Crisia Navy Base on Luna."

Sab'ach'ahn nodded slowly, as if that confirmed her thoughts. "They're not approaching in a Kinathin attack formation, though apparently your commanding officers do not realize that."

"And if we fire upon them first?"

"It will mean battle to the death."

"And if we don't."

"I do not know, Captain."

"But it's a *kith'ain* thing?"

Sab'ach'ahn nodded.

"What was that other word you used—Kith'at'annan?"

"A title. An honorific." Again she turned those blue eyes on him. "The Kith are the highest caste in the Kinathin class structure. Kith'at'annan . . ." She hesitated. "There is no word for it in your language, or even the concept. It translates loosely to *lone warrior*, but that too is inadequate. There are only three living Kith'at'annan, and they are honored above all others."

"And Add'kas'adanna is one of them." How could he use that to *Cinesstar*'s advantage?

"Captain . . ." Sab'ach'ahn continued. "The word Kith'at'annan has another meaning. It is also our word for enemy, traitor, or betrayer, and when used with the proper tone and inflection, it is often a challenge, as well as an insult. Entire planets have been devastated in reply to such an affront."

York looked at her carefully. "Thank you, and please stay close at hand."

She bowed slightly, stepped back and disappeared into the shadows of the bridge.

York's immediate concern was escape, and to that end he had to know what ships were within range to intercept them when they made their run for it. There was an AI cruiser docked in the Yard on Prime, two berths down from *Cinesstar*. There were two AI destroyers in orbit around Luna, another in orbit around Terr, and a dozen AI patrol boats dodging around the Luna-Terr system. But, with the exception of a light destroyer in orbit around Terr, waiting for a berth in Prime's Yard for needed repairs, there were no regular naval vessels within nearspace. Now that was curious, very curious indeed.

Prime herself was their biggest danger. She had enough weapons to do a lot of damage to *Cinesstar* during the time it would take them to get out of range. And there were the large orbital weapons platforms orbiting Terr, all controlled by Prime Central. He'd prefer to sneak out quietly, but he didn't have that option. That meant he'd have to take control of Prime Central, scramble the command grid long enough get out of Lunan nearspace.

York keyed his implants. "Kalee, this is Ballin. Get up here and bring that makeup kit of yours. I'm going to need a good eye again."

York checked on the location of his former passengers. The empress, her daughter, the old queen mother and Martin Andow were all listed with a location of *insufficient access priority*. York went to ring-zero and learned they were all being held incognito at Mare Crisia. "McGeahn. Get Lady d'Hart up here, on the double."

Kalee showed up and started to disguise his chrome eye and scars.

When Sylissa d'Hart arrived York told her of his unusual find, that the VIP's who'd been aboard were all now at Mare Crisia. "Where's the emperor?" she asked.

York checked. "Incognito, Mare Crisia, being held in protective custody because of an assassination attempt."

She pursed her lips. "Check on Senator Tycho Marin."

"Incognito, Mare Crisia."

She threw several more names at him, and each was the same: Mare Crisia. "That's the leadership of the imperial senate." She looked at him carefully. "There are rumors of a coup."

"Who's involved?"

"It would have to be the Admiralty Council."

York stared hard at his screens, an idea beginning to form. But then he squashed it and refused to let it mature.

"What'll you do?"

"Nothing I can do, just escape with my life."

She stepped around in front of him. "There is something you can do; I saw it a moment ago in your face."

"No. There's nothing I can do."

"You're lying."

"Enough," he shouted, standing. "Get out. You're not my conscience. Sab'ach'ahn."

The Kinathin appeared beside him. "Sir."

"Escort Lady d'Hart off the bridge."

She pursed her lips at him angrily, then turned carefully and left, with Sab'ach'ahn behind her. In her absence the bridge was strangely silent, with York's officers frozen at their stations staring at him. "Get back to work," he shouted and sat down.

He called Alsa Yan. "The wounded are still aboard, right?" He didn't want to abandon any of them.

Yan didn't try to hide her anger. "They left them all here to rot in the tanks. All but Maggie."

A cold lump formed in the pit of his stomach. "Maggie?"

"Ya. I don't know why, but those AI goons took her away from me. Don't know where she is."

It took him several minutes to locate her: *Magdelena Votak, hospital sector, Luna Prime, room 3G9. Condition: catatonic and nonresponsive, with brief and infrequent moments of semi-coherence.*

York stood, his heart pounding in his ears, and for several seconds he couldn't breathe.

"Captain?" It was McGeahn. "Are you all right. You don't look well."

"I'm okay," he shouted. "Pay attention to your station."

She flinched and mumbled, "Aye, aye, sir."

He sat back down, forced an artificial calm. "McGeahn," he barked.

"Sir."

"Have Palevi, Yagell, Tathit, Jakobee, Nemkov, Gant and Cappik join me in the captain's office in ten minutes. Until then I'll be in my cabin. Sab'ach'ahn. Come with me."

He stood and walked off the bridge.

••••

He sent Sab'ach'ahn to his office to wait for the others, then he sat down at the console in his cabin. He put in a call to one of the major media services, though he blanked his picture so they wouldn't recognize him and flagged the call as Imperial Security. That would indicate to anyone the call was coming from someone with unusually high access rights. It worked, and in seconds he was speaking to the general manager of the service, a Mister Thoring.

"Who am I speaking with?" Thoring demanded.

"If I were going to give you that information," York said patiently, "this call would have a very different flavor."

Thoring nodded. His access rights were not sufficient to blank his picture. "Very well. What do you want?"

"I'm going to transmit the contents of a recording to you, and some other information. Are you ready to receive and record?"

"One moment." Thoring leaned out of the view of his pickup, there were a few noises in the background, then he leaned back. "I'm ready."

York pulled the card Palevi had given him out of a pocket, inserted it into his console and started transmitting it. He gave Thoring the whole thing, the recording of the meeting of the Admiralty Council, the out-takes from his staged court martial. Then, as an afterthought, he added a copy of the special situation map that showed the approaching Kinathin fleet.

"What is it you've sent me?" Thoring demanded.

"Look it over. It's self-explanatory. I'd like you to broadcast it, but don't waste any time getting to it. I'm going to begin distributing it rather widely. You're the first, so you've got a real scoop on your hands. But if you delay, someone else'll beat you to it."

York cut the circuit.

He then addressed a copy of the card to every officer in Fleet, and transmitted it immediately, and again he made sure the origin of the transmission was anonymous.

Sab'ach'ahn stepped into his office. "They're waiting for you, Captain."

••••

Bella Tzecharra looked at her screens with a deep sadness. She had served the Empire for so many years, served it faithfully, honorably, but she was at a loss now. She and the other officers of Third Fleet had been forced to betray Ballin and the crew of *Cinesstar*, and while she had obeyed her orders then, it had been hard to remain loyal. And then Abraxa had in turn betrayed her, and she'd barely escaped with her life, and her ship and her crew. Her fellow officers, the remnants of Third Fleet, no doubt felt the same. Their sense of outrage, of betrayal, united them and they could no longer serve the empire as they once had. But neither could they betray her by going renegade. They'd met long and hard, had argued heatedly, and had finally decided to appeal directly to the emperor.

There were few of them left, only twenty-three ships, several badly mauled, all with some damage. Those that could, a mere sixteen, had driven ahead of the approaching Kinathin fleet, down-transited well outside of nearspace at the edge of the Lunan system. But there was no emperor upon the throne to whom they could appeal, and with a major battle imminent, they'd decided to stand aside, to watch and wait.

Never before had she been faced with such indecision.

••••

York began the briefing to his senior officers by playing the card for them, simultaneously broadcasting it to every station on ship—the meeting of the Admiralty Council, the out-takes from his trial. He then addressed the crew on allship. "I'm going to keep this simple. Our leaders betrayed us. At Sarasan our comrades did not die in battle, they were murdered, and our leaders have betrayed us again and again. And even now they intend to betray us one last time. Our purpose now is not noble, nor honorable, it is merely to escape. I don't know what we'll do after that—I'm not going to think about that now. I'm going to think only that I must do whatever is necessary to escape, and that I have the right to do that. I recommend you think the same. You're a good crew, and you deserved better than this."

He cut allship, turned to his officers. Certainly some of them were wondering why Tathit was present, leaning against a bulkhead in the back of the group, her complexion pale, her expression distant and detached. He ignored that, continued the briefing by giving them the entire situation, held back only that he had ring-zero access. When he finished he let them think on it for a moment, then he said, "Our biggest problem is the orbital weapons platforms and the weapons stations on the outer hull of Luna Prime, all controlled through Prime's command center, and dependent upon her for target allocation and fire coordination. With surprise we can shoot our way out of the Yard easily, and there aren't enough fighting ships near enough to stop us, but those weapons platforms can shoot the hell out of us before we get out of range. So we're going to take Prime Central and disable her. To do that I'm assembling a small assault team, to be led by myself and Sergeants Palevi and Yagell. Right now this ship is sealed up tight, since they think we're still out there somewhere trying to get aboard her. Commander Sierka is going to leave, and we'll leave with him, wearing AI uniforms, auspiciously as his escort."

He looked at Tathit. "Corporal, you're going to be Commander Sierka's personal bodyguard."

Suddenly Tathit's expression focused sharply on York. She stood up straight and grinned, though York saw something in her eyes that made him shudder. "I'll personally give you your instructions later."

"Captain." It was Yagell. "I'm familiar with the security around Prime Central, and the main checkpoint is a blast-proof bulkhead that's constantly sealed and power reinforced. We won't be able to carry enough explosives to blow through her without being obvious."

"I have a trick up my sleeve," York said. "I can open the entrance to that last checkpoint. But as soon as they realize what's happened they'll manually override and shut it again. So when I open it you'll have to be in place, and you'll have only seconds to shoot your way inside and keep it open long enough for all of you to get in, then shut it, trash the place, shut everything down, and get back to this ship. However, when I use my little trick, that'll alert Prime's operating system to my presence, though not my location. So we have to have everything in place then. Jakobee."

He turned his attention to the former first officer of the hunter-killer they'd rescued. "You'll be in command of this ship while I'm gone, and if for some reason I don't get back, then you'll have to shoot your way out."

He turned to Palevi. "Sergeant. Assemble the assault team down on Hangar Deck. Use your own discretion as to number, makeup and weaponry. And get Sierka down there. Make sure he looks unruffled."

They filed out obediently, and only Jakobee and Palevi remained. When the rest were gone Jakobee spoke, "Beggin' yer pardon, sir. But you shouldn't be leaving the ship. As CO you should command from the bridge, and let the rest of us do the doing."

Jakobee was right. Palevi stood behind him, expressionless, saying nothing. York owed them some explanation. "I have something personal to take care of. And I won't discuss it." To Palevi he said, "I'll meet you on Hangar Deck in a few minutes. Have Kalee come up here. Tell him to bring me an AI uniform that fits, and also his med kit."

Once they were gone York started programming. Using ring-zero access he dug into Prime's security network, set up a special scramble code no one on Prime could monitor. Next he set up high-level access rights for Palevi, under an alias. York had no identity card, but when Palevi used his, the computer would show him as having the highest level of clearance possible—with an AI flag. It was the kind of thing that would open up a lot of doors for them without any questions asked. He did the same for Yagell. The last thing he did was set up the program to open the last checkpoint at Prime Central. He keyed it to his vocal signature, and set it to activate on the words whore's brat.

Kalee showed up with his AI uniform. While York was putting it on he made Kalee give him an injector loaded with a massive overdose of pain killer, quick, lethal, painless. He shoved it into a pocket and headed for Hangar Deck.

40

Payback Time

PALEVI AND YAGELL had ten marines waiting for him on Hangar Deck, all in AI uniforms. York pulled the two sergeants aside, told them about their identity cards. "You now have level-one security access, and you're flagged as high-priority AI. Act like AI assholes, and don't let them scan anyone else's card."

"I'm impressed, Captain," Yagell said.

"Don't be," York growled at her. "You're in charge of the squad going for Prime Central. Palevi, I need you to volunteer to help me on a personal matter."

Palevi had stood there with his usual grin, but now it disappeared. "We going to help Miss Votak?" he asked.

"Ya," York said. "I know she's navy, but for me this is no different than leaving a marine behind."

Both Yagell and Palevi nodded. Palevi asked, "Are we gonna make it back, Cap'm? You and me?"

"Probably not."

"I'm good with that, sir."

"Thank you." York keyed his implants. "McGeahn, get Jakobee, Notay and Hyer in circuit. You four, me, Palevi and Yagell."

"Here, sir," McGeahn acknowledged. Jakobee, Notay and Hyer were only a moment behind her.

"I've set up a special scramble code that no one can monitor. But it's tied to *Cinesstar*'s marine frequency, so stay on that channel for all off-ship communications. Notay, Hyer, I want all actives in full combat kit, full combat armor, heavy assault weapons with the addition of nonlethal anti-personnel gas. Yagell, just as you reach the last checkpoint I'll give the computer the command to execute whore's brat. That'll get that checkpoint open, and that'll be the signal for all of us to move.

"Notay and Hyer, there's only about forty AI out there, lightly armed, and no armor. When Yagell hits Prime Central, you and your people take the docks, then send a squad of fifty double-time to pull her and her people out. When they're back, withdraw into *Cinesstar* and use her to shoot your way out of here." York realized he was speaking as if he wouldn't make it back.

"Don't kill unless you have to, but if you have to, kill. Remember, when I give the computer the command to execute whore's brat, we move. Is that clear?"

Each of them acknowledged his instructions in turn, but it was McGeahn who said, "Yes, Your Highness."

"Fuck that shit, McGeahn," he growled at her, then cut the circuit.

Tathit showed up with Sierka, who moved with his usual arrogance. "What little plot are you hatching now, Ballin?" Sierka didn't recognize Tathit, and clearly hadn't looked in her eyes.

"Commander Sierka," York said calmly, looking from Sierka to Tathit. "Let me introduce Corporal Larwa Tathit. We're leaving the ship, and you're going to be our excuse for doing so, and she'll be your bodyguard."

Sierka rolled his eyes and turned a bored look on Tathit. Recognition still didn't come. But then Tathit grinned and carefully unfastened the top button of her tunic, slid one collar down past a shoulder, exposing one of the round, puckered burns.

Sierka gasped, looked from the burn to her face. His eyes widened, and finally he looked into her eyes. What he saw there forced him to take an involuntary step back, but one of Tathit's comrades standing behind him prevented him from backing away from her.

"Ah!" York said. "I see you do know each other."

"You can't do this," Sierka cried. "She's not sane."

"No," York said. "She probably isn't. And that's what you should keep in mind. Right now she has orders not to harm you, and she'll obey them. But if you don't do what I say, when I say, how I say, then I'm going to give you to her."

York looked at a couple of marines behind Sierka and hooked a thumb over his shoulder. "Get him out of here."

They hustled Sierka away quickly, leaving York alone with Tathit. "You know," he said to her, "I'm using you. When it's all done you may not get him."

She shrugged. "You do what you gotta do, Cap'm. I never had no problem taking orders from you." With that, she turned and joined her comrades.

With Sierka as their excuse, getting off the ship was actually quite simple. Apparently he had already proved such a nuisance the AI lieutenant in charge of the squad on the docks understood fully when Yagell silently rolled her eyes at him.

They entered a large causeway filled with commercial establishments. Those closest to the docks were primarily bars and whorehouses, while farther down the quality of the shops and clientele rose considerably. There, they split up, Palevi and York heading for the hospital sector, Yagell and the rest for Prime Central.

••••

"You were right, sir," the young AI lieutenant said. "He and a marine sergeant named Palevi, both wearing AI uniforms, just checked in at the main desk in hospital sector."

"He swallowed the bait," Juessik crowed. "I knew he'd come back for the Votak whore. Stay out of his way, and let him in to see her. I'll be there shortly, and we'll handle it then."

"I can't let you do it."

Juessik turned slowly, knowing what to expect. Dulell stood there, holding a small grav gun.

"He's an innocent man. They're innocent people. All they want to do is escape. Let them go."

Juessik shook his head scornfully. "No."

"Then I'll have to stop you."

"You can't."

Dulell raised the gun higher. "I have this, though you probably think I won't use it."

"No, Arkan," Juessik said. "I know you'll use it. But I also know you, so I damaged the trigger. It won't work."

Dulell frowned, looked at the gun, looked again at Juessik. "You care nothing for anyone, do you? You said you loved me, but that was just another lie, wasn't it? Everything about you is a lie. You care only about manipulating us for your twisted ends."

He raised the gun higher and squeezed the trigger. Nothing happened.

"Arkan, you've become quite tiresome," Juessik said as he reached into his pocket and pulled out a gun of his own. Without hesitation he shot Dulell in the chest.

Dulell staggered backward, fell to the floor, lay there gasping desperately. Juessik stood over him, finished him off with a bullet in the forehead.

York could not put aside the fear that someone would recognize him. His face had been plastered on the vids for days, so he was prepared to fend off any curiosity by acting the arrogant AI officer. But the public had seen a man with a chrome-steel eye, and a shell-burst pattern of scars radiating outward from the eye socket. Few people saw beyond the chrome eye and the scars, and with those hidden by Kalee's makeup, no one recognized him.

The AI uniforms and Palevi's identity card helped. People tended to look away from an AI uniform, and the higher the rank, the greater the desire to be somewhere else. Even other AI grew cautious. AI with that kind of security clearance were probably high-level field operatives. It was best to ask no questions and stay out of their way.

A young nurse showed them into Maggie's room. It was a Spartan room, classic hospital decor: a bed, a stand beside the bed, a chair in one corner with a small table beside it. Maggie sat in the chair, a blanket thrown over her lap. She was whole again, with arms and legs, probably clonal transplants, but still she was whole, and for just an instant York thought she might have recovered, she might be the old Maggie again. But then he saw her sallow complexion, her face expressionless, her eyes lifeless, her mouth open, her lips moving slightly, perhaps saying something—though nothing audible—or perhaps just trembling.

The nurse said, "She's been like that since she regained consciousness. She'll walk with us if one of us supports her and leads her around. But the rest of the time she just sits there in silence, though I'd swear she's trying to say something sometimes."

With the arrogance typical of AI York said, "Leave us."

The nurse nodded silently and left.

"I'll wait outside," Palevi said.

York heard the door close quietly. He knelt on one knee in front of Maggie's chair, took her hands in his. "Look what they've done to you, girl." He shook his head. "No, it's not *they*, it's me. I did this to you, and to Frank and Paris and Olin and all the others. I knew there was something wrong with this whole setup, but I didn't listen to my instincts."

For a long moment he held her hands, looked into her eyes, and in them he saw what he hoped was some sort of distant recognition. He remembered the good times she and Frank and he had had. There weren't many things in this universe he would have given his life for, but to see her and Frank get away from it all, escape to someplace and *go make babies*—for that he would have given his life a hundred times over.

She was holding on to him now with a strong grip, but he managed to extract his right hand, and reaching into his pocket he retrieved the injector. He looked at it for a moment, then looked at her.

She knew what was in the tanks. She had seen them, just as he had seen them all those years ago, and he knew that troubled her now. They haunted you, awake and asleep they haunted you. He and the survivors of the *Andor Vincent* had seen them, and now she too had seen them, and like him they haunted her. She had escaped from the tanks briefly when she'd warned him of the assassin in the corridor. He was certain it had been her, not some hallucination dredged up from the depths of a warped psyche, though he would never admit as much to a psych-tech. In appearance she had been like the rest in the tanks, but they'd been screaming and tearing at themselves, struggling to escape the torment and pain.

All he had to do was press the muzzle of the injector against the side of her throat and pull the trigger. There would be a soft puff, she would feel only a slight sting, nothing really unpleasant, and in a few seconds it would all be over, a quick, painless, easy death. And she would be free of them, in much the same way most of the survivors of the *Vincent* had freed themselves.

He lifted the injector, but as he did so she lifted her hand and rested it carefully on his wrist, as if trying to help him, or trying to stop him, he couldn't tell. He looked into her face and now he was certain he saw recognition there.

"Why," she said softly, her voice barely a whisper.

He said, "Because I can't leave you like this, Maggie."

She ignored him, looked right through him. "Why?" she pleaded. "Why did they do it?"

"Do what?" he asked.

Still she ignored him. "Why did they have to take everything from us? They killed us all, Frankie and Paris and you and me, and now that we're all dead even that's not enough. They want everything. They want it all." Suddenly her eyes did focus, though in them York saw nothing close to sanity. "You have to stop them, York. You must."

"I can't," he pleaded, thinking of the d'Hart woman's words. "I can't stop them. They're too powerful."

"We've nothing to lose," she said. "We're already dead; we have no dignity left, no pride. You have to stop them—"

A loud thud against the door of the room interrupted her. There was a scuffle, York heard a grunt, then the door slammed open and the room filled with AI uniforms. Instinctively he shoved the injector under the blanket in Maggie's lap. And then the muzzle of a gun pressed against the back of his head and he froze.

"Ballin," a familiar voice said only inches from his ear. "You're so predictable." Then the gun struck him on the side of the head and he dropped to the floor at Maggie's feet. He struggled to hold onto consciousness while someone rifled his uniform, removed the small sidearm Palevi had given him. He was on his side on the floor, and he decided to lie still for a few seconds, let the room stop spinning. But hands hoisted him to his feet by his armpits, and turned him to face Juess-ik.

There were four of them: Juessik, a muscular AI private holding a pistol to the side of Palevi's head, and the two holding York up. The one on York's right was a medium-height female AI lieu-tenant. York outweighed her by forty kilos, so he decided to play up his dizziness, leaned on her more than he had to.

Juessik stepped up to him, punched him in the ribs; York grunted and doubled over. The thug on York's left grabbed York's hair, pulled his head up until his chin pointed at the ceiling. They repeated the process several times, then they let York drop to the floor where he curled up, came close to vomiting, to losing consciousness.

They hoisted him back to his feet. Juessik leaned forward, grabbed York by the hair, lifted York's chin and put his nose only inches from York's. "For a short while you did have us a bit concerned, Ballin. A few of my people panicked when you didn't show up at Lady d'Hart's yacht. But I knew you couldn't leave the Votak whore behind. She was my hole card. If we lost you, all we had to do was wait and watch. I am curious where the rest of your little entourage is holed up. But we'll get that out of you shortly."

York had almost begun to believe Juessik knew everything, that AI knew everything, that, as before, they were one step ahead of him. But with Juessik's words he realized they didn't know about *Cinesstar*, or about Yagell's assault team headed for Prime Central. He met Palevi's eyes and saw that the sergeant had caught the same message.

Juessik let go of York's hair and turned toward Maggie, who remained unchanged. He stepped behind her chair so he could face York. He reached down, touched her cheek lightly, almost a lov-er's caress. "Quite poignant, actually, that you came back for her. But not practical." Juessik leaned down, touched his cheek to hers. "She's actually quite lovely. Perhaps I'll find some use for her after all. Perhaps . . ."

It was not a quick or rapid motion, not the kind of motion one would make in desperation. It was sudden, but it had the calm, deliberate movement of unpanicked motion. Maggie's hands had been resting beneath the blanket on her lap, and as Juessik spoke her right hand emerged holding the injector. In a single, efficient motion she raised it, pressed the muzzle against his throat and pulled the trigger. York heard a faint puff. Juessik stopped in mid-sentence, straightened, touched his throat and looked at Maggie. "What have you done?"

The thugs holding him and Palevi were focused on Juessik, so York brought his elbow up into the larynx of the thug on his left, heard a satisfying crunch. He was vaguely conscious of Palevi across the room erupting like a madman. York brought his right elbow around, but the element of surprise was gone and he only caught the young lieutenant in the chest. It was enough to stun her, but she had her gun out. York grabbed at the gun, got hold of her wrist and they both went down. She squeezed off a few shots wildly as they rolled over together, the gun emitting the soft *phutt* of a silenced weapon. York heard another *phutt* and his side lit up with fire, but the young lieutenant went limp in his arms. Someone had shot at him, shot through him and hit her. He tore the gun out of her hands, rolled over pulling her on top of him, using her as a shield just as the thug with the crushed larynx squeezed off another wild shot. The man was clutching at his throat, shooting wildly at anything that moved. York leveled her gun at him and pulled the trigger twice. The bullets slammed into him and he slid to the floor in a heap.

York tried to stand, fell onto his side. Palevi knelt over him. "You hit, Captain?"

A faint, distant voice pleaded, "Help me." They both looked up to find Juessik, seated on the floor with his back against the wall, his head bobbing as consciousness slowly faded away. York looked Maggie's way. She was slumped forward in her chair, the front of her blouse soaked in blood. "I'm okay," York grimaced. "Check Maggie."

"Please help me," Juessik pleaded weakly, his words beginning to slur.

Palevi jumped to his feet and crossed the room to Maggie. York pulled open his tunic, checked his own wound. The bullet had punched a shallow hole through his side, just above the waistline. Both entrance and exit wounds were visible. "How is she?" he demanded as he climbed unsteadily to his feet and staggered across the room.

"Not good, Captain. Chest wound."

Juessik said, "Ahh sha . . . hafff . . ."

"We're in a goddamn hospital. Get a doctor."

Palevi was gone in an instant. York lifted Maggie out of her chair and laid her gently on her bed. He took her hand, felt her grip his hand strongly. Her eyes fluttered open. "York . . ."

"Don't talk," he said. "We're getting a doctor."

Blood spilled out of her mouth. "You . . . have to . . . stop them."

He shook his head. "I can't, girl. I can't."

Her eyes closed and her grip went slack.

••••

"Yagell," Terk's implants growled in the familiar voice of the captain. "Ballin here. Where are you?"

She keyed her implants. "Not far now, Captain. Another hundred meters of corridor, a couple turns here and there."

"Change of plans. We need to stall for a bit. Find a place to hole up, then get back to me."

Yagell glanced up and down the corridor. They were in a well-lit, heavily used section of Prime, close to the center of operations. She walked down the corridor looking at the labels stenciled on the doors, found one that read *Accounts Payable*. She looked over her shoulder at her squad. "Stay with me."

She opened the door and walked in like she owned the place, walked up to the startled receptionist and handed her the identity card. "Scan this," she said.

The receptionist did so, and though she was already startled and intimidated by the AI uniforms, what she saw on her screen had the desired effect. "Yes, ma'am," she said. "What can I do for you?"

"We need an empty office for a few minutes," Yagell growled arrogantly. "I need a good comp terminal urgently. And I need privacy."

"Certainly," she said. "Mister Loring isn't in today. You can use his office."

She led them down a narrow corridor to a large, well-furnished office. Loring was obviously a big shot. "This'll do fine," Yagell said. "Now don't disturb us."

"Yes, ma'am," the receptionist said, and backed out of the room.

Yagell keyed her implants. "Captain, Yagell here. We're holed up. Not sure how long we can sit tight, but we're out of the way for the moment."

"Good. McGeahn, get Jakobee, Notay and Hyer in circuit with me, Palevi and Yagell."

"They're already in, sir."

"Good. Listen carefully. There's been a change of plans. Yagell, when you take Central, instead of trashing her take control of her. I want full control of Prime. Notay and Hyer, after you take the docks Hyer leads a squad of one hundred to reinforce Yagell. Terk, Bad, we're going to leave you behind in control of Prime while we go dig the emperor out of Mare Crisia. I will come back for you, though, or die trying. My word, one marine to another."

••••

Palevi brought back a doctor and two nurses, none of whom were terribly willing. They were even less so when they saw the carnage in Maggie's room. Palevi pointed the doctor and one nurse at Maggie. "Help her," he said. He dragged the other nurse to York and said, "Help him. Forget the rest. They're already dead."

"How'd this happen?" the doctor demanded as he started cutting away Maggie's blouse.

"You know who she is?" York asked as the nurse worked on him.

"Ya," the doctor said. "She was one of Ballin's officers."

"Field prep it," York barked at the nurse working on him. "I have to move." To the doctor he said, "Ballin escaped, tried to break her out of here. Keep her alive, god damn it, or I'll have your balls."

"I'm trying," the doctor pleaded. "I have to get her down to surgery."

"Then do it," York shouted.

The doctor hesitated. "I have to report this."

York glanced at his own uniform, an AI uniform. "It's already been reported."

"Is it true?" the nurse asked York.

Whatever she was doing to him hurt like hell. "Is what true?"

"There're rumors everywhere. There's even a vidcast showing he isn't guilty, that it was all a setup by the Admiralty Council. Is it true? Is he really the son of the old emperor?"

"Ow!" York grimaced. "Yes, it's true. A bastard son."

"Is he going to take over the empire?"

Now that was something York had never considered, not even in his wildest thoughts. York looked across the room at Palevi, and he saw the same question in the sergeant's eyes. "No," he said, and he felt an odd sort of calm descend upon him. "He doesn't want to run the empire. He wouldn't know how."

••••

Tathit's implants spoke in Ballin's voice. "Palevi and I are headed for a bar just off the docks, name of *Down Time Charlie's*. We'll hole up there. Notay, when we execute you're going to have to fish us out of there . . ."

Tathit listened to the captain's instructions with only half an ear, enough to satisfy herself she was no longer needed. Then it was time to wait. She was a marine, and marines were used to waiting. She'd learned long ago how to kill time without taking the edge off.

"Palevi and I are in place," her implants said. "Everyone check in."

The squad leaders all checked in quickly, then Ballin gave the command, "Okay, Yagell. Move out."

Yagell acknowledged him, and quietly they filed out of the office. Tathit held back, held Sierka back too. The son-of-a-bitch cooperated, thinking that staying toward the back was the safest place for him. But as the last of her comrades stepped through the office door, Tathit pulled Sierka back and closed it carefully.

"What are you doing?" he demanded.

Saying nothing, she locked the door from the inside and turned to face him. She grinned at him. His eyes widened, he lifted his hands and stepped back. "No. Please no."

She remembered begging him for mercy. She remembered Jainnie begging him for mercy. She just grinned back at him. He opened his mouth to scream, but she shut him up by kicking him in the groin. He grunted and doubled over. Using a plast tether, she tied his hands behind his back, tied his feet together, then cinched his hands to his feet. She tore off a piece of her tunic, jammed it into his mouth and covered his mouth with a strip of heavy maintenance tape. She'd come prepared.

He lay on the floor on his side, pleading with his eyes and mumbling through the gag. She reached into her pocket, pulled out a small power knife, touched the switch on its side and it hummed to life. His eyes widened even further, and he pissed himself. She grinned and said, "It's payback time, Commander."

••••

Yagell marched directly down the center of the corridor and mumbled under her breath, "Thirty meters, Captain." Directly in front of her the corridor ended at the blast reinforced shields of the last checkpoint. Two bored AI guards stood casually on either side, rifles slung over their backs. To right and left were two security stations, each protected behind transparent plast shields broken only by gun ports. The only access to the security stations was from within Central, so their only objective was to get into Central. The corridor widened suddenly, allowing a better line of fire for both security stations. "Twenty meters, Captain."

"Computer," her implants said in Ballin's voice. "Load, but do not execute, whore's brat."

The emotionless voice of the computer answered him. *Loaded and standing by.*

The two guards in the corridor looked her way, but seeing more AI uniforms they remained bored. "Fifteen meters, Captain."

She decided to take the one on the right first. "Ten meters, Captain."

The two guards were turning toward her as her implants said, "Computer, execute whore's brat."

She completed two more strides before it happened, and then suddenly the blast-reinforced shields slid aside with a loud *whoosh*. Startled, both guards looked back toward the shields, then back at her, but she already had her gun out. She fired as she dove toward the opening behind them, saw the one on the right crumple and fall. A bullet whizzed past her ear as she hit the deck sliding, and the one on the left went down. She slid into Prime Central on her side, caught movement out of the corner of her eye coming from the open hatchway to the security station. She popped the pin on a grenade, slid it along the floor into the security station. She was too close when it blew, too close.

41

Loyalties Shift

PRIME WAS CONSTRUCTED with acoustic baffling in its bulkheads, but it was still just a big hunk of metal and plast that transmitted sound like a kettledrum regardless of the efforts of her designers. Yagell's grenade was too far distant to be heard inside *Down Time Charlie's*, but *Cinesstar's* guns, a ship's guns, were a different matter altogether. York had ordered Jakobee to disable any weapon on any ship that might be turned on *Cinesstar*, specifically the AI cruiser docked in Prime's Yard. Jakobee wasn't using *Cinesstar's* main batteries, which, from the inside would punch massive holes in Prime's hull, but the secondaries and defensive stations were taking the cruiser apart piece by piece, and with *Down Time Charlie's* close proximity to the docks, the resulting din was frightening. Everyone inside the dimly lit bar looked up from whatever they were doing and froze, for in all the centuries that Prime had been orbiting Terr a ship's guns had never before been fired *inside* the station.

"Captain, Simorka here. Three dead, plus Yagell's in bad shape, probably won't make it. I've got six actives, we've got Prime Central, and we're sealed up tight."

York looked across the table at Palevi, silently mouthed the question, "Simorka?"

"The green second looey off *Irriahm*," Palevi said. "The redhead. She's learned a bit."

York keyed his implants. "Keep telemetry and com traffic normal. I don't want anyone to know we've done this. Hyer, Simorka needs you."

"Docks were a pushover, Captain. We're on our way now, double-time, experiencing no resistance. Ten minutes."

York was about to ask where Notay was, but he got his answer when twenty marines in full combat kit burst through the establishment's entrance and fanned out, weapon's at ready. The patrons and employees of *Down Time Charlie's* hit the deck, leaving York and Palevi the only two above table level. As York stood a sharp pain shot up his side, the room tilted crazily and he staggered. Palevi caught him and braced him against a wall. "You don't look so good, Captain."

The sergeant turned his head. "Medic," he shouted in that drill-sergeant voice.

They laid York out on a table, and the medic cut away his tunic and removed the dressing they'd applied in the hospital. The medic frowned and shook his head. "This wound ain't bad enough to cause this much bleeding."

York gritted his teeth and growled through the pain, "Can you stop it?"

"Sure, Cap'm. Just take a minute, but it bothers me."

"And give me a kikker."

The medic pressed the muzzle of an injector against his throat and pulled the trigger. York felt a slight sting, then a wave of nausea washed over him followed by intense anger. "Ahhh!" he shouted. "I hate that shit."

But it did the job. The medic stopped the bleeding and York could stand on his own. The pain didn't go away, but it became a distant thing. The marines formed a phalanx around him and Palevi, and they headed for *Cinesstar*.

••••

"Captain on the bridge."

York started barking orders before he was seated at his console. "Prepare to cast off. Cappik, what's our status?"

"Full combat status, sir. Use her and abuse her."

"Captain, Hyer here. We've secured Prime Central. When they want her back they're gonna have one hell of a firefight on their hands."

Move, move, don't stop, don't think, just move.

York surveyed the carnage in the navy yard. The AI cruiser was a mess; taken by surprise, with no shield power and at close-range, even *Cinesstar*'s secondaries had been devastating. Jakobee, thinking on his own, had disabled every craft in the yard on the chance someone might try ramming *Cinesstar*. Shell craters from stray fire pocked the rest of the Yard with debris scattered everywhere, but for now the yard was silent and still.

Eldinow gingerly applied power to *Cinesstar*'s drive and eased her away from the dock. He turned her nose toward the star-filled entrance to the yard and nudged her gently forward.

"Captain, Simorka here. Prime's engineering section got a message off to Fleet, told them we've taken over Prime Central. They think we're feddie saboteurs. Now they're trying to isolate the command center's operations access. I don't think they can, in fact we have more control than they do, but the weapons stations on Prime got the word and won't take orders from us. I've managed to keep the orbital weapons platforms isolated, so we still control them, but I don't know how long that'll last."

York put the sit-map on one of his screens. The two AI destroyers in orbit around Luna and the other in orbit around Terr were powering up, coming into the command grid. No doubt they had orders to converge on Prime and take her back. The AI patrol boats were already converging, and more were lifting off Luna and Terr. The navy light destroyer in orbit around Terr was showing no signs of life.

Simorka was looking at the same situation map. "Captain, I can try allocating those AI destroyers and patrol boats as targets for the platforms."

The platforms wouldn't knowingly fire on friendly forces. "You'll have to delete them first from the grid, then reassign them as Kinathin warships and allocate them as hostile targets. Don't worry about the patrol boats. We'll handle them. And try deleting us from the command grid entirely."

Move, move, don't stop, don't think, just move.

Cinesstar's bow was just edging out of the yard into open space. As yet, no one knew she was anything but another friendly ship. "Full shield power," York ordered. "Eldinow, keep us in close to Prime's hull. We're going to be under fire from her stations shortly, and the closer we are the fewer can target on us. Jakobee, target on Prime's weapons stations, concentrating our main batteries on her primaries. Simorka, cut all power to Prime's shields."

It was an incredible sight, a heavy cruiser almost hull-to-hull with the giant station. Fighting at distances of a hundred thousand kilometers was close-in fighting, and here there were no more than a hundred meters separating them. "All stations," York said, feeling a certain calm wash over him. "Commence firing."

It was an all too familiar din, the pounding of *Cinesstar*'s guns as she spit death at her enemy. Without shield power, Prime's weapons stations were fodder. York's crew disabled the secondaries and defensive pods easily, but as Eldinow eased the ship around the curve of Prime's hull and the first of her main batteries came into view, *Cinesstar*'s power plant redlined twice before the big gun turret blossomed into a plume of fire and escaping gas. They continued that way, easing slowly around the curve of Prime's hull, taking on the big turrets one at a time. Prime's main batteries were far more powerful than *Cinesstar*'s, but with no shield power and no coordination from Prime Central, and against the combined might of all of *Cinesstar*'s guns, caused the ship only a little damage.

York was more interested in those AI destroyers. The one in orbit around Terr was dead in space, with enough nearby debris to indicate serious damage, while another was engaging one of the platforms. The third had apparently sustained some damage and was now hiding behind the targeting shadow of Luna.

"All stations, cease fire."

Jakobee's command pulled York's attention away from the sit-map. Prime was still intact, but her outer hull was a ruin of shell craters and escaping gasses, and she had no functional weapons station. For an instant York was tempted to redock, pull Simorka and her team out, then run for it and leave the empire to its own fucked up mess.

Move, move, don't stop, don't think, just move.

"Mister Eldinow. Set course for Luna, maximum sublight drive. Execute."

Cinesstar's hull groaned as Eldinow firewalled her sublight drive. They were about four hundred thousand kilometers from Luna. At ten thousand gravities it would take them one hundred forty-eight seconds, almost a minute and a half, to reach the halfway point. They'd cut drive, flip her over and begin decelerating just as hard.

"Mister Jakobee, target the naval base at Mare Crisia. All stations, full saturation barrage."

"Targeted and standing by, sir."

"Commence firing at turnover."

York turned to the computer. "Computer. Confirm access."

Access ring-zero confirmed.

"One hundred seconds to turnover," Gant said.

"Computer," York continued. "Access patch—*Cinesstar* main-zero to Mare Crisia main-zero. Execute."

"Ninety seconds to turnover," Gant said while York waited for a response from the computer. "Eighty seconds . . . seventy seconds . . . sixty seconds . . ."

The computer said, *Confirm access level.*

". . . fifty seconds . . ."

He dropped his voice to a whisper. "Access ring-zero."

". . . forty seconds . . ."

Confirm access code.

". . . thirty seconds . . ."

"Access Three-Charlie-Two-Niner-One-Niner-Alpha."

". . . twenty seconds . . ."

*Access patch—*Cinesstar *main-zero to Mare Crisia main-zero complete. Access ring-zero.*

". . . ten . . . nine . . . eight . . . seven . . . six . . . five . . . four . . . three . . . two . . . one . . ."

Eldinow cut the drive and simultaneously flipped *Cinesstar* over. As he firewalled the drive again Jakobee gave the order to commence firing.

It was an impressive display. Every weapon on *Cinesstar* was throwing ordnance at Mare Crisia, a rain of fire and death that streamed down toward the surface of Luna as if the heavens had opened up with the fires of hell. But Mare Crisia was the largest navy base in the empire, and her defensive capabilities were massive. They intercepted most of the heavy ordnance long before it touched the surface, had recovered from the initial onslaught and were firing back.

Cinesstar's defensive pods now turned their efforts to intercepting the incoming ordnance, and York watched the power drain to the hull-shielding flare and jump.

"Mister Jakobee. Arm twenty one-megatonne warheads for contact detonation, and launch at two second intervals."

Cinesstar's launch crews started slamming warheads into transition, while damage reports appeared on York's screens. They were thirty seconds out from the surface of Luna when they took serious damage aft and lost some sublight drive capability. Eldinow could only get seven thousand gravities out of her. "Veer north of the terminator, Mister Eldinow, we'll have to overshoot.

"Mister Jakobee. Arm a one-gigatonne warhead for detonation at an altitude of one hundred kilometers over Mare Crisia, and stand by for launch."

"Armed and standing by, sir."

Jakobee had just launched the twelfth one-megatonne warhead, and like the others it was intercepted and detonated in space about a thousand kilometers above Mare Crisia. The resulting transition noise was phenomenal, and targeting on both sides was becoming difficult.

"Computer," York said. "Access Mare Crisia comp-operations, shield power, targeting control and ordnance control."

Warning! Access at ring-zero to such sensitive operations is extremely dangerous. Please confirm access request.

"Computer," York said. "Confirming access request to Mare Crisia comp-operations, shield power, targeting control and ordnance control."

Access confirmed.

A shell from one of Mare Crisia's primaries slammed into *Cinesstar*'s bow; damage warnings flashed across York's screens. Jakobee had just launched the nineteenth one-megatonne warhead. "Computer," York said. "Execute to Mare Crisia comp-operations, shield power, targeting control and ordnance control the following command . . ."

York hesitated as Jakobee launched the twentieth one-megatonne warhead, and like the others Mare Crisia's defenses intercepted it in space. ". . . Abort, abort, abort, terminate and deactivate . . ."

There was a delay of about one second, as if even the computer feared carrying out that order, and then Mare Crisia's shield power went down. Her weapons stations started firing wildly in all directions and the pressure was off *Cinesstar*. "Mister Jakobee. Launch that big warhead."

"Missile away, sir."

"Kill the saturation barrage and switch to surgical bombardment—take out their primaries."

They were only ten seconds off the surface of Luna when the horizon blossomed with a new sun, a one-gigatonne ball of expanding thermonuclear fire. The power to *Cinesstar*'s hull-shielding flared, and her sensors were momentarily blanked to protect them, but the transient York had thrown into Mare Crisia's operations would prevent her from protecting her own sensors that way. She would now be blind for several minutes, perhaps hours.

Because of the damage to *Cinesstar*'s drive her ability to decelerate was badly limited and they overshot Luna, swung around the backside in a long elliptical arc. The damaged AI destroyer hiding on the far side just turned and ran, so York ignored her.

They came back in low and slow, hugging the horizon line at an altitude of ten thousand meters and watching carefully for any weapons stations still active. There were a few north of Mare Crisia, but without shield power or coordination from Mare Crisia Central they were able to take them on one at a time.

Twenty minutes later York parked *Cinesstar* in a forced synchronous orbit ten thousand kilometers above Mare Crisia. "Miss McGeahn, broadcast our recognition code, identify us, and put me in contact with whoever's in charge down there.

"And tell Palevi to put together an extraction team. We're going to be bringing some VIPs up here."

••••

"Well, Ballin," Abraxa said, seemingly unperturbed by events. "Again you've proven yourself quite resourceful."

York had had to bully his way past a commodore and two rear-admirals to get to Abraxa; they tried to deny he was present. "I know the entire Admiralty Council is down there with you, along with Directors Theara and Add'kas'adanna, the royal family and the leaders of the imperial senate." They were holed up in shelters deep beneath the Mare Crisia base.

Abraxa smiled. "We do have a rather impressive list of guests down here."

"Guests? Or prisoners?"

"What do you want, Ballin?"

"I want all of you up here, on this ship, under my thumb."

Abraxa shook his head as if patiently instructing a naive child. "Don't be ridiculous. We're not even at stalemate. You can't dig us out, not quickly, so all we have to do is wait for reinforcements from Home Fleet to arrive and overwhelm you. It may take them several hours, but we can wait." Abraxa finished with a big, cheesy grin.

"You're right in that I can't dig you out, but I don't have to."

Palevi had taken a small squad of heavily armed marines in *Two* down to the surface. With ring-zero access patched through into Mare Crisia main, York could clear the locks on any hatch or door, or lock any hatch or door so completely no one could open it. With schematics of the base to guide them, overlaid with full details of the deployment of the base's marines, York opened a path for Palevi's squad to the security bunkers buried beneath the base. At the same time, he imprisoned most serious resistance behind a locked hatch or blast-proof shield, so Palevi's squad encountered little opposition.

York switched to the marine command frequency, though he let Abraxa hear his side of the conversation. "Sergeant, what's your status?"

"We're inside all blast-proof shielding, sir, down on the bunker level, two more hatches to go, and waiting for your command."

"Very good, Sergeant. Execute."

Abraxa's big, cheesy grin disappeared at the sound of a gunshot. His eyes widened and he looked to one side. Several more shots sounded as York cut the link.

Abraxa and the other members of the Admiralty Council had brought about thirty AI to control their royal and senatorial prisoners. But the AI were not armored, and armed only with sidearms and a few rifles, no match for Palevi and his marines in powered combat armor.

The fingers of York's left hand were going numb: his cybarm. "Get Kalee up here."

••••

Palevi commandeered a couple of gunboats from the hangar where they'd parked *Two*, and used the three boats to ferry their captives up to *Cinesstar*. York told him to be sure Theara, Cassandra and Add'kas'adanna were among the first aboard. "Put Theara and Cassandra in my office," he told Palevi, "then take Add'kas'adanna down to your office and brief her fully on the situation with Home Fleet and the Kinathin armada. And give Abraxa enough com access to warn everyone off this ship. Now that he's aboard her, I don't think he'll want anyone shootin' at us."

"Aye, aye, Captain."

When York joined Theara and Cassandra in his office, both women looked at him suspiciously. "Director Theara," he said formally. "Your Majesty, I'm told you have negotiated a cease-fire agreement and a peace treaty that's acceptable to the two of you. Is it acceptable to anyone else?"

Theara was hesitant, but Cassandra spoke boldly. "Director General Kaffair, the emperor, a few selected members of the senate and a few selected members of the Directorate General Council. We were going to sign it, try and use that as leverage to get more signatures."

"What about Add'kas'adanna?"

Theara shook her head. "She'll go with Ninda. She always does."

York wasn't so sure about that. "Where's this treaty?"

Theara spoke now. "I have a neural implant."

York turned to his terminal and reset it for limited access. "Can you download it now to my terminal?"

"And what'll you do with it?"

York looked her in the eyes. "I'm going to get the fucking thing signed."

••••

He left Theara and Cassandra in his office and marched down to Palevi's office where he found Add'kas'adanna looking at a sit-map on the screen of Palevi's terminal. The sergeant stood to one side, his back to a wall, his hand resting nervously on his sidearm. Sab'ach'ahn stood behind Add'kas'adanna like a predatory animal. York walked around Palevi's desk, stopped beside Add'kas'adanna and looked at the screen. Home Fleet had taken up a classic defensive formation, with support from portions of Seventh Fleet. The rest of Seventh was too far out to make a difference, and the Kinathins were driving inward at maximum transition velocity.

"They're not approaching in strike formation," York said.

"And how do you know that?" Add'kas'adanna asked.

"I have fought Kinathins before. And Sab'ach'ahn confirmed it."

She said nothing and continued to stare at the screen.

York continued. "Your people think we'll understand their approach, that we'll know they want to talk first, fight later only if there is no alternative. And my people don't know how to read a Kinathin approach formation. They'll fire upon your people, and then we'll battle to the death."

For the first time, she looked away from the screen, looked at him and waited.

He continued. "I'll give you access to a communications link, and I ask that you contact your people and explain to them the danger we all face from misunderstanding. And then extend an invitation for them to meet with the Imperial Senate, the Admiralty Council and the emperor aboard this ship."

It unnerved him the way she stared at him. "And how do I know you'll not betray us? You who know nothing of *kith'ain*."

Move, move, don't stop, don't think, just move.

York extended his hand out to one side, palm up. "Sergeant," he said calmly. "Your sidearm."

Palevi slapped the gun in his hand so hard it hurt. York checked the load, then reversed the gun, and holding it by the barrel in his right hand, he reached out with his left and took Add'kas'adanna's hand in his. He placed the butt of the gun in her hand, wrapped the fingers of her hand carefully around it, specifically positioned her index finger on the trigger, then raised the muzzle of the gun and put it beneath his own chin. Then carefully, audibly, he clicked the safety off, and lowered his own hands. He looked her in the eyes as he said, "I can betray no one if I'm dead."

She frowned and her eyes narrowed, then suddenly she laughed. "Are you certain you're not Kinathin, Captain Ballin?" She lowered the gun, clicked the safety on and tossed it across the room to Palevi.

"Kinatha will talk, Captain Ballin," she said. "But with you. Only with you."

"Captain," York's implants snapped. "Jakobee here. We've got the last of them on board. We're ready to depart."

York keyed his implants. "I'll be on the bridge momentarily."

••••

"Mister Eldinow, set course for that Kinathin armada, maximum sublight drive. Get us out of this gravity well and start building velocity so we can make transition. Miss Gant, compute a short transition hop to coordinates halfway between Home Fleet and the approaching Kinathins."

"Cap'm?"

He glanced over his shoulder; Kalee was standing there. "You got a problem with your cybarm?"

"Ya." He stuck out his left arm where the fingers were going numb. Kalee grabbed York's right arm, pressed one of his little instruments against it.

"Seems to be working fine, Cap'm."

York looked at his two hands. The cybarm felt so real he'd forgotten which was which. He decided not to mention the numb fingers. "Get lost," he growled at Kalee.

"Captain," McGeahn said. "I have a Captain Bella Tzecharra, commanding *H.M.S. Stargazer*, requesting permission to speak with you."

"What does she want?"

"She didn't say, sir, but she did identify *Stargazer* as, in her words, *late of Third Fleet*."

That was a curious way of putting it. "Okay. Put her on."

Tzecharra was an attractive, middle-aged woman with dark hair and a lean, angular face, and she was all navy. "You were at Aagerbanne," York asked, "and then at Sarasan?"

"Yes," she said. "I obeyed orders, though they didn't sit well with me and my fellow captains."

"Then you were one of the captains who mutinied?"

She shook her head slowly. "No. But later, like you, we were given a taste of the Admiralty Council's loyalty." She quickly described the events that led up to the short battle between the Kinathin armada and the remnants of Third Fleet. "I have sixteen battle-ready ships, Captain. We're in reasonably good condition, and our ordnance reserves are standing at fifty-two percent. We can fight, and now that we've seen the broadcast of what they did to you, we want to ask you a question. Are you trying to take over the empire by coup?"

"Hell no," York snarled. "I just stopped a coup. The emperor's trying to negotiate a treaty, and I intend to help him get it signed."

"Good," Tzecharra said. "We've taken a vote, and as long as you support the emperor, we're throwing our support behind you."

York leaned back in his seat, completely at a loss. "I've just assaulted Mare Crisia, killed I don't know how many of our comrades. I'm going to go down in history as one of the worst traitors that ever lived, and you'll take orders from me?"

"Yes."

"This is unanimous among your captains?"

"Yes."

York ran numb fingers through his hair. He couldn't trust her completely, would have to deploy her in such a way she could help him but not betray him, if that was her intent. "Okay, Captain," he said. "But there won't be any more voting. We're navy. I give orders, you take them."

"We understand that."

"Very good. Commander Gant is my navigator. Get the coordinates we're headed for from her and meet us there."

42

One Big Party

YORK STOPPED IN his cabin to change his uniform, but as he yanked off the AI uniform he noticed blood oozing through the bandages on his side. He put on his navy blacks to conceal any blood that might seep through the material, then popped a kikker in his mouth and washed it down with a gulp of 'trate. He also removed the contact lens hiding his chrome-steel eye and the plast skin covering the scars. For what he was about to do he had to look the part.

York had had the marines rig a makeshift conference table in empty *One Bay*, which was now badly crowded. At his instructions the marines seated the emperor and the Admiralty Council at the conference table. Around them were ringed about twenty members of the imperial senate, along with the empress, Aeya, Add'kas'adanna, Theara, Rhijn, Thring, and an old churchman York didn't recognize. About them all Palevi had placed twenty marines with visible sidearms. York had given them copies of Theara's treaty more than an hour ago, and copies had been transmitted to the Kinathins through Add'kas'adanna.

As the lift doors opened York confronted absolute chaos and the sound of several dozen voices shouting angrily. He saw one middle-aged man waving a copy of the treaty over his head while shouting at a younger woman, his face red and flushed. Among the nine admirals two were out of their seats, leaning across the table, arguing heatedly with Soladin. But amidst the tumult Abraxa sat calmly, a faint smile marking his otherwise placid features. When York stepped from the lift with Harshaw and Sab'ach'ahn in tow, Abraxa was the first to notice him. His smile deepened, and he nodded almost imperceptibly.

Palevi bellowed, "Captain on deck," though even his parade-ground best didn't carry above the din. But as York, ringed by marines, marched toward the table, the crowd parted and the voices died.

Edvard stood to confront him, suspicion and distrust written in every line of his face. Cassandra stood supportively behind him. With York's marines forming a ring about the three of them York bowed carefully. "Your Majesty."

Edvard spoke softly, though there was steel in his voice. "If you're after my throne I'll fight you for it. With my dying breath I'll fight you for it."

York shook his head. "I don't want your throne, wouldn't make much of a king in any case."

"Then what do you want?"

"I don't know. Maybe I want justice."

Edvard shook his head. "Justice is a rare commodity, Captain, and often expensive."

"Then again, maybe I just want revenge for my murdered crew. Maybe I just want to kill a lot of goddamn senators and admirals and a king or two."

Edvard paled. Cassandra stepped between them and spoke softly. "Captain, I know you're not the blood thirsty maniac your reputation purports." She turned to Edvard. "And you, Edvard. When you get to know him you'll trust him as I do. For now, you must trust him through me." Again she looked at York. "They've kept him in solitary confinement, given him no news or information. He knows only what I've been able to tell him in the last few minutes. What do you need?"

York met Edvard's eyes and lowered his voice. "I'm told, Your Majesty, that as Duke de Lunis, the tenth duke, you're officially a member of the Admiralty Council, though you don't customarily attend their meetings. But you can call for and convene such a meeting. Will you do so now?"

"Why?" Edvard demanded.

York held up a copy of the treaty. "Before this day is out, every member of the Admiralty Council is going to sign this . . ." Edvard lifted a skeptical eyebrow, and York grinned at him. ". . . at lease every member that's still alive."

Edvard frowned, then his lips slowly curled up into a grin that matched York's. "I begin to think they just might." He turned to the table, pulled a chair out, pulled another out next to it and looked at York. "Won't you join me, Captain?"

Cinesstar's hull drummed as a grenade exploded on G deck. Soladin demanded, "What was that?"

York smiled at him. "We still have some AI to kill."

Captain, his implants said in Jakobee's voice. *Fourteen ships have broken away from Home Fleet. They're headed this way and we're still too far inside heliopause for up-transition.*

York keyed his implants. "Stand by all main batteries. And tell Tzecharra to do what she can to help us. I'll be on the bridge momentarily. And get ready to force us into up-transition if I give the order."

He turned to the empress. "Your Majesty, will you come with me?"

As he and the empress stood, Add'kas'adanna stood with them. They left everyone in a stunned silence.

••••

Jakobee was ready for him, had a full sit-map on one of his screens. Home Fleet was sitting on the edge of nearspace, between *Cinesstar* and the safety of Tzecharra's ships. Tzecharra was already in position halfway between Home Fleet and the Kinathin Armada, but not in a position where she could help *Cinesstar*.

"Gant, compute a transition hop. We'll have to run through Home Fleet.

"McGeahn, put Her Majesty on an open channel to Home Fleet.

"Your Majesty, please tell them who's on this ship, who they'll be killing if they burn us. Tell them I'm taking orders from the emperor, and that we're about to make a transition jump out past them. If they want to know why, make up whatever you want."

The empress sat down next to McGeahn. In just a few seconds she was looking at a screen and talking heatedly into a pickup.

Gant said, "It's going to be sloppy, sir, but I'm ready."

"Your Majesty?" York asked.

She looked at him, frowned and said, "They know, but I don't know if they believe."

"Power priority to shields," York ordered, then he gave the order for up-transition. *Cinesstar*'s hull groaned, and he felt the familiar tickle in the back of his mind as she fought her way into transition.

"Down-transition in six seconds . . . five . . ."

York watched the power drain jump as a warhead detonated somewhere nearby.

". . . four . . . three . . . two . . ."

The shield power suddenly redlined and a nasty gravity wave rolled through the ship. *Cinesstar* down-transited prematurely with every reading on York's screens overloaded.

"Gant, I want a scan on our nearspace. McGeahn, get me—"

"Incoming," Gant shouted, and before York could react Jakobee dumped all *Cinesstar*'s power to her shields. The hull kettle-drummed as a large warhead detonated just astern and the power drain to the shields redlined.

"Drive, all ahead full," York demanded. "And what the hell was that?"

"Sir, Captain Tzecharra on three."

McGeahn had already put Tzecharra on one of York's screens. Tzecharra didn't wait for York to ask. "Six more ships have broken away from Home Fleet—that's a total of twenty—and they're fighting among themselves. From what I can tell, eight of them are attempting to burn you and the rest are trying to intercept what they throw at you. You're out past Home Fleet, but still short of where I can protect you. Keep headed this way while I try to put more ships between you and them."

York was absorbing the scan summary on his screens while listening to Tzecharra's words. The ships that had broken away from Home Fleet were spread out in a free-for-all. He watched three of them go out under big warhead flares, wasn't sure whose side they were on, didn't really care at that point. "Keep a close eye on all those ships," he told Tzecharra. "Try to identify those that are helping us, finish off those that aren't. But don't trust any of them."

He turned back to his screens. "Cappik, status."

The engineer's face appeared on a screen. "Starboard's finally shot, Captain, Centerline's running well though a little ragged, and Port is fully operational. I can still give you full combat status. Only limitation will be reduced drive capability in both sublight and transition."

"Jakobee?"

"We took very little hull damage, sir, and weapons stations are ninety-two percent operational. Ordnance reserves stand at thirty-three percent, sir."

"Gant?"

"It was sloppy, sir, but we're just outside of nearspace, and just outside of Home Fleet's defensive perimeter, though still within their targeting range. And the Kinathins have down-transited at one thousand AUs, well out of anyone's targeting range. More ships have broken away from Home Fleet and joined the free-for-all, though no one's throwing anything at us at the moment. We're still on the edge of nearspace, but we're far enough out that I can give you a much more accurate transition vector."

"Good. Set it up."

Tzecharra sent four of her ships into short transition hops. The system's gravity-well perturbed their vectors and they down-transited in a random spread around *Cinesstar*. But one of them was nicely positioned between her and any danger from Home Fleet. Tzecharra knew what she was doing.

"Captain," McGeahn said. "I have a Commander Barrett, commanding *H.M.S. New Hope* of Home Fleet. He says he's placing his ship under your command."

"Tell him to take his orders from Tzecharra."

"Captain Ballin." Tzecharra spoke from one of his screens. "One of those Kinathin warships just up-transited and it's coming our way."

"Hold your fire," he told her. "Fire only if fired upon." He glanced quickly at Add'kas'adanna. She stood impassively in the background, seemed to understand his doubts and nodded at him as if to say, *Yes, you can trust us.* He wondered if he could.

He stood. "I'll be down on Hangar Deck with our royal guests. Keep me informed of everything. Mister Jakobee, you have the bridge."

••••

York eased his way quietly into the crowd surrounding the conference table. It wasn't hard to remain anonymous, with senators and admirals competing in a continuous shouting match. A grayhaired fellow, with unkempt hair and wearing a sloppy, rumpled suit and old-fashioned spectacles, gained the upper hand in the contest of voices. "Damn it," he shouted. "This treaty is an opportunity that no sane person would pass up. Two hundred years. We've been fighting this war for two hundred years and we have an opportunity to end it. Finally, we can . . ."

York stopped listening to the words, paid more attention to the man. Senator Tycho Marin had an orator's voice, with a simple home-spun style, though his delivery was clearly practiced and quite polished.

Captain. Jakobee's voice in his implants. *That Kinathin matched velocity, cut drive and dropped shield power one hundred thousand kilometers off our bow.*

York keyed his implants. "Do likewise, Mister Jakobee. Then use sublight drive only, ease forward slowly, drive to a position fifty thousand kilometers off that Kinathin's bow. Then stand by. And tell all stations to maintain full combat status and readiness. And tell Cappik those shields could be needed on a moment's notice."

An eerie stillness had descended up Hangar Deck. A small circle of space had opened about him as if he was dangerously radioactive, and everyone stared at him silently. Slowly they edged further away from him, opening a clear pathway to the conference table and Senator Marin.

Captain, we're in position, and as soon as we got here that Kinathin started forward, coming slow, shield power down.

York keyed his implants again, and with his eyes locked to Senator Marin's he said, "Steady as she goes. Don't alter our position, course or status. Keep those shields unpowered but ready, and do not fire unless fired upon. I'll be on the bridge shortly."

Aye, aye, sir.

He turned to leave. A path to the lift suddenly opened in front of him and he started forward. "Captain."

York stopped at the sound of Marin's voice, turned to face him and nodded politely.

"As I was saying," Marin said, "we've been fighting this war for two hundred years. Don't you think you could spare a little time to help us end it?"

York looked around the room carefully before answering. "*We* have not been fighting this war, Senator. I and my crew, and people like us, have been fighting this war. And it's we who have been dying for people like you and those I see around me here. And I think we are no longer prepared to do that. So, if, as you say, you have an opportunity to end it, then I suggest you do so. Because I intend to end it one way or another before this day is out, and in my rather naive view of life, I wonder if I might do so simply by venting all of you to space . . ."

The silence that followed York's words was complete and unbroken. "If you'll excuse me, I have to go continue fighting your war." He turned, and with Add'kas'adanna, Sab'ach'ahn and Palevi in tow he headed for the lift.

••••

In the lift the deck seemed to tilt crazily beneath York's feet. Add'kas'adanna caught his elbow and steadied him against a bulkhead. When it was clear he wouldn't collapse she released him, stepped back and looked at her hand, at a bright, red smear of blood on her fingers. "You must take better care of yourself, Captain."

His vision had started to constrict, and she stood at the center of a halo of diminishing sight. "Treason is a dangerous business."

She nodded. "*Kith'ain* is the most dangerous business of all. But when it calls we must answer."

"I don't know anything about *kith'ain,*" York growled, and he took a moment to catch his breath and let the pain recede. "By the way. You're not a prisoner here. You and Director Theara are my guests. You're not allowed free rein of the ship, and you'll be escorted at all times, but you're free to go, though at the moment I don't have alternate transportation to offer you."

He looked at Palevi. "You understand me, Sergeant?"

"Yes, sir."

Add'kas'adanna looked at him carefully and grinned, a rare gesture for her. "Did you know, Captain, that *kith'ain* is much more than honor and reputation. It is often a challenge that can mean life and death, and sometimes a contest in which the players struggle to acquire obligation. It is a game, Captain, of debt and indebtedness, and for one who claims to know nothing of *kith'ain*, you appear to play the game quite well."

The lift doors opened. The marine standing guard on the bridge glanced in, frowned. "You okay, Cap'm?"

Palevi turned on him. "Get a medic up here for the captain."

York added, "Make it Kalee, and tell him I need a kikker. And get out of my way."

The marines ducked aside as he strode onto the bridge, trying to hide the fact he was ready to collapse. The bridge was unnaturally silent as he dropped into the couch at the Command Console. "What the hell's going on? Pay attention to your duty assignments. And Jondee, put Director Add'kas'adanna at a console and open up a channel to that Kinathin."

"Uhhh . . . Captain . . . sir . . . uhhh, Mister Jondee is dead."

York took a deep breath and let it out slowly, tried to make sure he held onto reality.

"Captain." It was McGeahn. "That Kinathin is hailing us, uncoded transmission."

"Put him through to me, and copy both sides of the conversation to Director Add'kas'adanna's console."

The Kinathin that appeared on York's screen showed about as much expression as a block of stone. "I am Councilor Ard'dha'sit. And you are?"

"York Ballin. Captain, commanding *H.M.S. Cinesstar*."

The Kinathin nodded. "You are holding Director Add'kas'adanna as a prisoner on your ship."

It was time to gamble. Add'kas'adanna and Sab'ach'ahn had given him hints, but any understanding of the Kinathin psyche was guesswork. "You have lost Director Add'kas'adanna? Have you also lost Director Theara?"

The Kinathin's face hardened. He looked ready to spit nails into transition. "There is *kith'ain* debt—"

York cut him off. "Not I, nor any of my people, owe you, or Director Add'kas'adanna, or any Kinathin, *kith'ain* debt. So don't speak to me of *kith'ain* debt. Add'kas'adanna and I are enemies. We've fought, and I have been victorious. But she's not a prisoner here, she's my guest, and free to leave when she chooses."

York thought if Ard'dha'sit grew any angrier he might sprout gun turrets in place of ears. York continued. "If you wish to discuss the matter, you're invited to join me aboard my ship. The articles of truce will pertain. You may bring whatever retinue you wish, though no armed troops will be allowed. Your safety and that of your retinue is guaranteed by me, and will be my responsibility."

Ard'dha'sit nodded coldly. "I will have my shuttle prepared."

"No," York barked. "My gunboats are already prepared. One of them will pick you up immediately."

Again Ard'dha'sit nodded coldly. "Very well, Captain." He cut the transmission.

"Jakobee," York said. "Send *Two*, with two marines, sidearms only, as security. And clear *Three Bay*. We're going to need the room. Set up a conference table like in *One Bay*."

Add'kas'adanna met him at the lift. "You play well, Captain."

When the lift doors cycled open, Kalee and Alsa Yan were in the lift, and Alsa looked no happier than Ard'dha'sit. She grabbed York, pulled him into the lift and barked, "Computer, seal this lift and hold static."

She ignored the computer's acknowledgment and turned on York. "Kalee tells me you're wounded."

"It's a minor wound," York pleaded. "We don't have time for this."

She spun him about and lifted the side of his tunic. "Shit," she said.

"See what I mean, ma'am," Kalee said. "He's bleeding like all hell, but the wound don't justify that."

She probed, poked, let her instruments bleat at her for a few seconds. "You're experiencing regrowth rejection, and some clonal implant failure. We've done too much work on you lately, haven't given your body a chance to absorb and adjust to all the repairs. Any other wounds?"

York decided not to tell her about the broken ribs. "No."

"Any other symptoms? Numbness? Anything out of the ordinary?"

Again he lied. "No."

"All right," Alsa said unhappily. "I'll stop the bleeding, but you get your ass to sickbay as soon as this is over."

"Yes, ma'am," York said. Kalee grinned.

••••

Councilor Ard'dha'sit stepped off the gunboat in *Two Bay* accompanied only by six unarmed Kinathin bodyguards, and three middle-aged men. He was the first male Kinathin York had ever met in person, and while York had become accustomed to the height of the two female Kinathins, Ard'dha'sit stood a head taller than them, and he towered over York.

Sab'ach'ahn, whom York had instructed to stay close at hand, stood behind him, though she seemed not to exist for Ard'dha'sit. If any Kinathin words were spoken, she was to quietly translate them into her throat mike so he could pick them up in his implants. Add'kas'adanna was conspicuously absent, and York had no idea where she'd gone. Ard'dha'sit made it clear he would rather just chew York up along with the mouth full of nails he was enjoying. When Ard'dha'sit turned and introduced the three middle-aged men with him, it was York's turn to stand open-mouthed and dumbfounded: Directors Kaffair, Ninda and Zort. Through some strange quirk of fate he now had in his possession all five members of the Central Committee of the Federal Directorate of the Republic of Syndon.

York was starting to recover his composure when his implants said, "Cap'm, Mec Notay here. I'm with the empress and Directors Theara and Add'kas'adanna in Hangar Control. They want to talk to you."

He keyed his implants. "I'll be right there." To Ard'dha'sit he said, "Sergeant Palevi will show you to a place where we can talk."

Ard'dha'sit demanded, "Where is Add'kas'adanna?"

York said, "Add'kas'adanna is where Add'kas'adanna chooses to be, though I do hope she'll join us shortly."

••••

"Captain," Cassandra said as he stepped into Hangar Control. "This isn't working."

Theara and Add'kas'adanna stood beside her as if to protect her from him. He ignored her, sat down at a console and keyed his implants. "Jakobee, I'm in Hangar Control. Give me a sit-map."

A full situation map appeared on the screen in front of him. Half of Home Fleet had fragmented into a dozen small free-for-alls. Another forty ships from Home Fleet appeared to have joined Tzecharra. She had positioned them into a defensive line between the fighting and *Cinesstar*, with her sixteen original ships providing a second buffer behind them where she could intercept anything that might get through. The Kinathin armada had not moved. "What's the situation, Jakobee?"

"You can see for yourself it's a mess, and unstable as all hell. Tzecharra says she'll try to give us plenty of warning if it starts to go bad on us."

York ran his fingers through his hair. "I suppose that's all we can hope for. Let me know if anything breaks."

York stood and almost bumped in to the empress. She and the other two women had been looking over his shoulder at the sit-map. "I didn't realize the situation was so unstable."

Theara added, "All the more reason to get the treaty signed as soon as possible."

Cassandra shook her head sadly. "That's the problem. Abraxa, Soladin and Schessa are holding out. Ordinarily the three of them are at each other's throats, and if we could get just one of them to break it might be enough to sway the other six. But with all three of them aligned the Council won't budge."

York looked at Add'kas'adanna. "How'll you vote on this treaty?"

Theara looked at her sharply. "She always votes with Ninda."

Add'kas'adanna shrugged. "When I return to the Directorate I will do as *kith'ain* dictates."

York grinned. "You don't have to wait until you return to the Directorate. Ard'dha'sit brought Ninda, Zort and Kaffair with him."

Even the stoic Add'kas'adanna lost her composure for a moment. Into the silence York said, "We have aboard this ship the ruling bodies of both the Directorate and the Empire, so let's see what we can do with that."

43

The Final Treason

IN *THREE BAY* Ninda and Kaffair were already arguing over the treaty while Zort looked on. When York stepped out of Hangar Control with Theara, Add'kas'adanna and Cassandra, Ninda turned on Theara, his voice dripping with sarcasm. "I knew it had to be something like this. You and our esteemed Director General have always been naive."

Theara held up a copy of the treaty. "It's time for this, Ninda. And it's long overdue."

Ard'dha'sit silenced them both. "Stop this petty squabbling." He turned to Add'kas'adanna and spoke in Kinathin.

He is saying nothing more than a polite greeting, Captain, York's implants said in Sab'ach'ahn's voice.

Ninda turned to York. "Now what, Captain?"

"No one is a prisoner here," York said. "You're free to go, all of you, including Directors Add'kas'adanna and Theara."

"Then we will go," Ard'dha'sit said.

Add'kas'adanna spoke barely above a whisper. "I will stay."

Ard'dha'sit rounded on her, locked eyes with her for a moment then nodded. "Then we too will stay." He turned carefully to the other Directors. "And that includes you."

York hastily introduced Cassandra then gestured to the conference table, "Shall we be seated?"

Ard'dha'sit stiffened. "In Kinatha we do not sit while confronting our enemy."

York pulled out a chair, sat down, leaned back casually and spoke harshly, "First, Councilor Ard'dha'sit, we are not in Kinatha. We are within sovereign imperial space. Second, we are not on a Kinathin vessel, we are on an imperial vessel. Third, you're my guest. And fourth," York softened his voice. "I think I'm no longer your enemy."

Ard'dha'sit frowned, considered him for a moment, then pulled out a chair and sat. Cassandra and the five feddie Directors did likewise. The hull echoed with the distant, muted sound of automatic weapons as Palevi's marines continued digging out the last of the AI holed up on G-deck.

"We have a treaty here," Kaffair said. "It's not perfect, but it's better than anything we could hope for."

"And what will it buy us?" Ninda demanded.

Theara answered him, but York didn't listen. Ard'dha'sit's attention briefly appeared elsewhere as he obviously used his implants to speak with his subordinates. He was paying no more attention than York to the argument raging about them.

York was tired, and he could see this was an old argument they'd gone through many times. He keyed his own implants and spoke softly, "Jakobee, what's the status on G-deck?"

I'll put you directly in contact with the corporal in charge down there.

There was a brief pause, then, *Cap'm, Cleaver here.*

"What's the status down there, Meat?"

There's only about five of them left, Cap'm, and we got them bottled up tight. I tell you, we could end this fast if you'd just let me blow vacuum in this section. They don't got no vac suits.

"Negative, Corporal. As long as you've got the situation under control I'm not desperate enough to try that. You do have the situation under control, don't you?"

Yes, sir. They don't have any more heavy stuff, so it's just a matter of time.

"Very good. Ballin out."

". . . and so I call for a vote," Ninda shouted.

Kaffair argued, "You're calling for a vote only because you know you'll win."

"Nevertheless, I'm calling for a vote."

Kaffair nodded sadly, obviously resigned to defeat. "Very well. As Director General it's my duty to administer a vote. It will be a voice vote. Those in favor of signing vote aye, those opposed, nay." Kaffair spoke mechanically. He sounded tired and lost. "We'll vote in order of precedence, and so I'll vote first. I vote aye."

That was expected. Kaffair and Theara were in favor, Ninda and Add'kas'adanna opposed. Zort was the wild card.

Kaffair looked at Ninda, who reveled in what he and everyone perceived as a forgone conclusion. "Nay," he barked triumphantly.

Kaffair turned to Theara. She looked around the table sadly. It was clear she too thought Ninda's victory was complete. She shook her head and closed her eyes, spoke as if she were on the verge of tears, spoke barely above a whisper. "Aye."

Zort was next. Theara had told him Zort occasionally went his own way, whereas Add'kas'adanna had never done other than rubber-stamp Ninda's wishes.

Zort looked at Ninda and spoke hesitantly. "Nay."

Kaffair buried his face in his hands. "Add'kas'adanna," he said through his fingers.

Add'kas'adanna looked at York and, as if by way of apology, said, "*Kith'ain*, Captain. *Kith'ain.*"

York nodded back at her. He had come to like her, wanted to say he understood.

She looked at Ninda. "I vote aye."

It took them all a moment to realize what she'd said. Kaffair was the first. He dropped his hands from his face and his head snapped toward Add'kas'adanna, his eyes wide.

Zort cringed. "What's this mean?"

"It means," Theara said, "we've won. We've won."

"No," Ninda shouted and stood. He leaned across the table. "You have not won. I invoke the right of executive veto."

Theara closed her eyes and her shoulders slumped. Cassandra turned to Kaffair, demanded, "What is he talking about?"

Kaffair took a long, tired breath and spoke calmly. "All votes in the Central Committee are carried by simple majority. But any Director may veto any vote by invoking executive veto, in which case the vote will be carried only if the other four unanimously override the veto."

Kaffair looked at Zort. "The vote was carried properly. Help us."

Zort looked from Kaffair to Ninda and shook his head. "No. I can't change."

Ninda grinned. "The veto stands."

Captain, Jakobee here. Jakobee's voice in York's implants was excited, almost shrill. *We've got three transition wakes bearing down on us from the vicinity of Luna, ETA eight seconds.*

York noticed Ard'dha'sit had cocked his head, listening to his own implants, probably getting the same message. York keyed his implants. "Take evasive action, and tell Tzecharra to take them out. We'll ask questions later. Stand by for—"

York was completely unprepared for the hand that suddenly gripped his throat, lifted him out of his chair and slammed him against a bulkhead. His head cracked hard against the plast and he almost lost consciousness. He struggled weakly, but he was pinned against the bulkhead with his feet several inches off the deck, and in the background he heard Palevi shouting, "Hold your fire. Hold your fire. Stand to, marines."

The grip on York's throat was like a steel vice. Ard'dha'sit leaned in close to him, their noses almost touching. He spit a single word in York's face, "Kith'at'annan." Sab'ach'ahn had told him Kith'at'annan could mean either supreme warrior or hated enemy. There was no doubt which form of the word Ard'dha'sit meant.

Palevi stood behind Ard'dha'sit, his sidearm aimed at the back of the councilor's head, and behind him Ard'dha'sit's Kinathin body guards had all dropped into a crouch, while Palevi's marines had drawn their weapons. York caught Palevi's eye, managed to squeak out, "Hold." Ard'dha'sit's grip tightened around his throat, the blood pounding in his head. If he lost consciousness a blood bath would follow.

Through it all, Add'kas'adanna strode calmly across the deck, stopped just to one side of the enraged Ard'dha'sit. She said something to him calmly in Kinathin, and in the middle of it York recognized the words ". . . Ballin Kith'at'annan . . . ," though the tone and inflection of her use of the word was far different than Ard'dha'sit's.

Through a growing haze of unconsciousness, York heard Sab'ach'ahn's words. *Captain, she told him she bears you* kith'ain *debt, and she has acknowledged you Kith'at'annan.*

The vice-like grip suddenly disappeared from York's throat and he dropped to the deck in a heap. He tried to stand, then decided against it as a wave of pain shot through his wounded side. To hell with it, he thought, and decided to stay there, maybe just sleep for a century or two. He was so very tired.

"Cap'm." York opened his eyes. Palevi was leaning over him. "You all right?"

He growled, "Help me up, god damn it."

Palevi lifted him to his feet, steadied him against a bulkhead. "You sure you okay, Cap'm?"

"I'm as okay as I have to be. Where's Cassandra?"

The empress sat at the makeshift conference table, her face buried in her hands. York fell into the seat beside her. She looked into his eyes, and he could see the tracks of the tears that had streamed down her cheeks. "We've lost," she said calmly. "It's over."

York was reminded of his own thoughts. *Move, move, don't stop, don't think, just move.*

"Let's throw them all together," York said. He didn't wait for Cassandra's reply. "Palevi," he bellowed.

"Sir," the sergeant bellowed back at him.

"Bring them all with me. Anyone doesn't want to come, drag them. They become too much of a problem, shoot them."

"Sir. Yes, sir."

As York stood Ard'dha'sit caught his arm, demanded politely, "What do you want, Ballin Kith'at'annan?" There was a clear difference in the way Ard'dha'sit now said the word.

"Bring your people with me. Everyone."

York staggered toward the hatch to *One Bay.*

••••

When they stepped into *One Bay* they must have seemed an odd assortment of Kinathins, Federals and Imperials. York let Cassandra make the introductions, which were sufficiently startling on both sides. As she did so, he scanned the faces on the deck, saw that everyone was exhausted. They'd also decided that Abraxa and Ninda had won. Some were ebullient, some clearly disappointed.

A wave of nausea washed through York. He closed his eyes, reached out, clutched at the nearest thing to him. When he opened his eyes he found he'd grabbed Ard'dha'sit's arm. York would have expected Ard'dha'sit to pull away, but instead the Kinathin merely said, "What next?"

York grimaced, swallowed the nausea. "Get your directors seated around that table with our admirals."

York realized then that he'd been wrong in assuming the other Kinathins were Ard'dha'sit's bodyguards, that in fact two were assigned to each of the three Directors, and they acted more like babysitters than bodyguards. It didn't take long to get everyone seated at the table.

York sat down next to the emperor, facing Abraxa. Ard'dha'sit remained standing. Ninda, Zort and Kaffair were at the far end of the table, with Theara and Add'kas'adanna seated on York's right, and the rest of the admirals scattered among them. Tycho Marin stood solidly behind Soladin, polishing his old-fashioned spectacles with the cuff of his shirt. There was a long moment of silence broken only by a lot of fidgeting and shuffling of papers, though Abraxa didn't move, didn't so much as twitch, and Ninda seemed wrapped in smug certainty. Then someone tried to speak, but was quickly drowned out as everyone tried to speak.

Captain, Jakobee here. We've got a make on those three transition wakes that made a run at us, an AI cruiser and two destroyers. It was a stupid move. They didn't make it past Tzecharra and her defensive perimeter.

York keyed his implants. "Thank you, Mister Jakobee."

Amidst all the voices it was the emperor who managed to restore order. He shouted, "Silence. All of you."

York had never heard a voice carry such command. It was not just authority but a sense of empowerment and the assumption that everyone would obey without question: probably the kind of thing one learned when raised from birth to be an emperor. It startled all of them into momentary silence.

Edvard seized the moment. "A little while ago I told Captain Ballin that I would fight him if he intended to take my throne, and he assured me he had no such ambitions. There are some things many of us will fight and die for. For me, my throne is one of them, and the end of this war is another."

He looked slowly around the table. "I don't need to point out that we have a unique opportunity here. We've spent generations wasting millions of lives, and it's time to end it. And to accomplish that I would even give up that for which I would die. I would give up my throne."

He looked pointedly at York. "Captain Ballin?"

York said, "That won't be necessary. Perhaps it'll be more productive if we go directly to the issue at hand."

Andralla Schessa recovered first, leaned across the table at York. "The issue at hand is the legality of this meeting. You kidnap us, force us to sit here in a clearly contrived attempt at getting this bogus treaty signed."

Tycho Marin struck back at her. "Perhaps we should discuss the legality of the recent attempted coup, Your Grace, as well as the kidnapping of quite a number of imperial senators and the imperial family."

Soladin came to her defense. "You were not kidnapped, senator. You were taken into protective custody because of . . ."

Marin interrupted him. "Oh come now, Your Grace. We're not children here. The legality of this meeting will stand on its own. We still have a treaty to consider."

The chaos erupted again. York's implants said, *Captain, Jakobee here. The situation here is still as unstable as hell. Captain Tzecharra and I have been talking it over and we think we can gain an extra margin of safety if we redeploy.*

York keyed his implants. "If you and Tzecharra are in agreement then do what you think is best. But brief Ard'dha'sit first so we don't have a load of Kinathin warships thinking we're pulling a double-cross."

Across the room, York saw Palevi perk up for a moment, then he eased his way through the crowd to Ard'dha'sit, politely pulled the Kinathin aside.

Sergai Leonavich caught York off guard and demanded, "Since we're cutting the bullshit, let's get all the issues on the table here. This is really your show, Captain. So what's your game?"

York stared at Leonavich, and after a moment the admiral looked away as if shamed. If the man still felt guilt for the betrayal at Sarasan, York wasn't above using that. "It's not just me. There are a lot of us who are no longer willing to fight this war for you. I could die this instant and that won't change what's going to happen. Have you read this treaty?"

Leonavich nodded wearily.

"And is it so unacceptable?"

The admiral looked tired and beaten. "By and large, it's okay, though there are some fine points I might argue."

York decided to kick him while he was down. "Home Fleet is, as we speak, breaking up into factions, and they're all fighting one another. The ships of Seventh Fleet, as they arrive in-system, are joining the fray. A number of ships have already been destroyed, along with the crews aboard them. If you don't sign this treaty now we'll have civil war. If you do, maybe you'll still have an empire."

That shook Leonavich, shook a lot of them, senators and admirals alike. Leonavich demanded, "And you'll help us hold this empire together."

There it was. Leonavich wanted York to commit to an empire he'd just as soon abandon. "I'll do what I can. But I'll not guarantee the status-quo."

The silence in the room drew out as York and Leonavich held each other's eyes across the table. If only one of the admirals broke, then the rest might follow, and York was counting on Leonavich, on the obvious guilt the man wore like a shroud.

Leonavich blinked first, closed his eyes fully and lowered his head, drew in a slow, deep breath, then let it out in a long sigh. "Yes, I'll sign."

The entire power structure in the room shifted in York's favor. It was a palpable, manifest sensation, and York could see that others felt it also. Before Leonavich's words, York had been the center of attention, but after, he had, in some indefinable way, become the center of power. It was tenuous, delicately balanced, and could be easily broken.

Abraxa shattered it. "And I'll sign nothing." Again the power structure shifted, but now to Abraxa. The fat, old admiral had known when to strike, and had done so decisively. "This document is nothing more than the foolish whim of a naive child who plays at empire. Empire is strength, not compromise and treaty."

Abraxa understood power in a way that York never would, and York realized that now. Abraxa had watched and grasped the shifts in power that had occurred, had waited carefully like a predator stalking its next meal, then had pounced at just the right moment. He had regained the power of the moment, had also regained ascendancy over Schessa and Soladin's scheming, all in one, single stroke. York had to admire him for that, but now Abraxa had made himself the key. Earlier, capitulation by one of the weaker admirals like Leonavich might have stampeded the rest, but now they would all follow Abraxa's lead. If he did not sign, then no one would.

There was a hesitant moment of silence, which Cassandra broke. "Just over one hundred days ago eighty million people died on Dumark. Is that the strength of empire you speak of?" She held up a copy of the treaty. "And this treaty, this attempt to end such mindless slaughter, is this the foolish whim of a naive child?"

Abraxa waved a hand, dismissing all those lives with a single gesture. "Eighty million is nothing. We rule an empire of more than a hundred billion. We cannot concern ourselves with a few million when the greater good of all is at stake."

Ninda chimed in. "And the same is true in the Directorate. I agree with you wholeheartedly, Bargan."

York was not the only one present who caught the slip, the use of the first name, a rather strange level of familiarity between two men who purportedly had never met. York watched

Ard'dha'sit's head swivel slowly on its base like a gun turret until it came to rest with his eyes pointed at Ninda, as if he could see into the heart of the man. Then his head turned toward Abraxa, and his eyes bore into the admiral in the same, eerie way.

Edvard asked, "And continuing the slaughter is in the greater good of all? Or is it merely in the greater good of those in power?"

Soladin joined the fray. "That's an old saw, Your Majesty. We regret the loss of lives on Dumark, and other planets, but we cannot let that deter us from the proper course of action. We have too long . . ."

Captain, Jakobee here. We're redeployed. About half of Home Fleet has now voluntarily placed themselves under your command, though they've made it clear they're doing so only as long as you support the emperor.

Soladin was still speaking. ". . . and for these reasons I too cannot sign this document." Soladin was in a push-pull contest with Abraxa.

"I'll sign it." Everyone looked down the length of the table to Karltine Degaas, surprised to see the duke stand forth so decisively. Next to him, Shinton Diego opened his mouth hesitantly, seemed about to agree, but Abraxa cut him off.

"No you will not. I forbid it." There it was, out in the open. True equality among the nine was a thing far in the past.

A dangerous stillness settled over the room. Abraxa looked at York and spoke more calmly. "Stalemate, Captain. We'll not sign it, and there is nothing you can do to make us sign it."

It was York's move, and everyone there paused, waiting for him to make it. He reached for a copy of the treaty, found that his entire left hand had gone numb, that his fingers wouldn't cooperate, wouldn't pick the damn thing up. He quickly disguised the motion, pretended he was merely gesturing toward the document. He wanted to choose his words carefully, but his anger got the best of him. "Before we are through here, I will have the signatures of all nine members of the Admiralty Council on this document. What remains to be seen is whether or not you'll still be members of the Admiralty Council."

Abraxa grinned, almost a snarl. "There is no legal premise for removing any of us from the Council."

York didn't look at Harshaw as he asked, "Mister Harshaw?"

"New members of the Admiralty Council are appointed by the emperor," Harshaw said, "and ratified by the Council. All appointments are for life, unless a member chooses to voluntarily abdicate."

"There," Abraxa said triumphantly. "You see, Captain. Abdication is the only means by which we can be removed, and of course none of us will abdicate."

York wanted to take back his words, replay the scene and return to the point where he had some options. But it was too late for that. "Mister Harshaw mentioned another means of removal. Appointment to the Council is for life. What's your life expectancy right now, Admiral?"

"Are you threatening me?"

York stood, leaned across the table and looked into Abraxa's eyes. "All my friends are dead, Admiral. Everyone I cherished and loved. You killed them. You betrayed them . . ." Suddenly the deck beneath him seemed to shift and he was forced to sit back down. A wave of nausea washed over him as he growled, "I will have this document signed."

Abraxa threw back his head and laughed. "You're bluffing."

There it was. Abraxa, confident he could steer the Council in the direction he chose, confident York was powerless to force the matter. There was no question in Abraxa's mind that he had won, that York could not carry out his threat. York stared at the surface of the table in front of him, was unsure of how far he would go. His heart thundered in his chest as he looked up at the faces around him, saw nothing but doubt. The power had shifted to Abraxa completely now. The senate, the Council, the church, would all follow Abraxa, out of fear if for no other reason. They too believed York was powerless, that he could not summarily displace the man, even a man so lacking of innocence, so guilty of crime, sitting there confidently with the blood of so many innocent people on his hands.

Paris Jondee came to mind, the handsome, rakish womanizer. And Olin Rame, cold and impersonal on the surface, but he'd proven a loyal friend in the end. And Frank, steady, reliable Frank. And of course Maggie, Maggie who'd had her chance at happiness with Frank. All dead, all gone. But when York finally made up his mind, it wasn't eighty million lost lives, nor the lives of his crew, nor even the lives of Paris and Olin and Frank and Maggie. It was the lost happiness, the lost chance for joy, for hope. It was those things that brought York to his decision.

His eyes suddenly came to focus. He looked up, spotted Palevi across the deck standing at ease with his back to a bulkhead. "Sergeant," he barked, trying to imitate Palevi's drill-sergeant bellow.

Palevi snapped to attention, then with parade-ground style marched across the deck, stopped and came to attention behind Abraxa. He stood there rigidly, almost quivering like a rod of steel struck by a hammer. "Sir," he bellowed.

York looked at Abraxa, who grinned confidently. He scanned the faces in the room, saw that they too believed he was bluffing. He looked again at Abraxa, but he spoke to Palevi. "Sergeant . . . vent him. Now. That's an order."

Palevi's answer was earsplitting. "Sir. Yes, sir." He reached down with a meaty paw, grabbed the back of Abraxa's collar.

Abraxa was still grinning as Palevi lifted him out of his chair, stood him on his feet. He snarled at York, "You wouldn't dare." Then Palevi yanked him toward the personnel lock at the back of *One Bay*. Given no choice, Abraxa stumbled awkwardly in Palevi's wake. He shouted, "Stop this charade. You're fooling no one, Ballin."

Everyone in the room stood immobile, frozen, watching Palevi drag Abraxa toward the lock, glancing at York uncertainly. But their uncertainty only mirrored York's own, because he didn't know if he could go through with this.

Halfway to the lock Abraxa's tone changed. "You can't do this," he screamed. "I'm the most powerful man in the empire. Stop this. Stop." He finally started to resist, swung a fist at Palevi. The marine didn't even flinch as the blow glanced off his shoulder. Abraxa tried to dig his heels in, but Palevi gave him a hard yank, pulled him off his feet and dragged him on his butt across the deck.

At the airlock, Palevi slapped the latch on the hatch and it cycled open. "Please," Abraxa screamed as Palevi tossed him into the lock.

Palevi put his shoulder to the hatch, was about to close it when Ard'dha'sit shouted "Stop," with such deafening force it froze everyone in their tracks.

Ard'dha'sit stood next to Ninda, and he looked down at the Director carefully. "I think the admiral should not take this journey without his dear friend to accompany him." And then, mimicking Palevi's movements, he reached down, grabbed a handful of Ninda's collar, lifted him out of his seat and dragged him toward the airlock.

Ninda broke immediately. "No. No. You can't do this. This is insane . . ." He fought and kicked, but against the strength of a Kinathin his struggles meant nothing and his feet hardly touched the deck.

Abraxa had recovered inside the open airlock. He was standing, about to step out of the airlock when Ard'dha'sit threw Ninda into his arms. Both of them tumbled into a heap. Ard'dha'sit joined Palevi as they both put their shoulders to the hatch, closed it and cycled it shut.

Palevi touched the intercom next to the lock's control mechanism. "Computer," he said. "Emergency override on all safety constraints for lock . . ." he looked at the label next to the lock mechanism, ". . . 15289. Override, override, override, and stand by for emergency blowdown."

Override confirmed, the computer said. *Standing by for emergency blow-down.* A light above the lock flashed from red to green. Palevi looked at York, his hand poised above the switch. Ard'dha'sit shook his head, edged him gently aside, put his own hand over the switch and paused. He looked to York for the final command.

Every eye in the room turned to York. No one spoke or moved in the stillness that descended, and the only sound present was a faint metallic ping as Abraxa and Ninda beat their fists desperately against the inside of the lock.

Again York scanned the faces about him. He looked at the senators, the churchmen, the nobility, even his crew, and on all their faces he saw uncertainty. Only in Cassandra's face did he see something else: horror. Apparently she believed he was capable of doing it, while the others were uncertain, as he was uncertain. He looked in Schessa's eyes, and Soladin's. Those two were on the fence, waiting to see which way the power would shift. He realized then that Abraxa was finished as a power within the empire, that York could let him live and Abraxa would no longer be a threat. But if he did, then Schessa and Soladin would be the threat. Abraxa would sign, but they would not, and all would be lost. In the end it was they who condemned York to murder.

York's vision compressed as he looked at Ard'dha'sit. York nodded.

Ard'dha'sit slammed his fist down on the switch, the metallic ping of the two men's struggles disappeared, was replaced by the muffled explosion and whoosh of the emergency blow-down cycle, a sound that clung to the hull of the ship, a sound that refused to die as if it had a life of its own, but instead diminished with an agonizing lethargy until finally absolute silence fell upon them all with oppressive clarity.

York sat transfixed, and like everyone about him he was paralyzed and unable to move—they with fear, he with doubt. Abraxa had driven him to become the one thing he dreaded most, a cold-blooded murderer, the worst kind of traitor. But now they would sign—that, at least, he could be certain of. And he could also be certain that he had lost. A treaty signed under such duress was no treaty at all.

It was the emperor who broke the silence. He whispered, "We need to replace him."

Moved by sudden paranoia, York keyed his implants. "Jakobee, Ballin here. I just vented two bodies out the aft personnel lock in *One Bay.* Track them, make sure nothing gets close to them. If anything does, put a warhead into it."

Aye, aye, sir.

York scanned the faces about him again. Once more the power structure had shifted to him, but this time irrevocably. He said, "Let the record show that Fleet Admiral Bargan Abraxa died honorably in the service of his emperor and the empire. That he and Director Ninda died struggling to make this treaty a reality."

In the ensuing silence York scanned the faces at the table and looked into the eyes of each of the four remaining Directors, the eight remaining Admirals. "Now get this damn treaty signed. Anyone doesn't want to sign joins Ninda and Abraxa."

He turned and started walking to the lift. His left arm had gone completely numb to the shoulder. The right side of his trousers was plastered to the skin of his leg with blood from hip to ankle, and he made an odd sloshing sound as he walked. His legs were getting rubbery as he reached the lift and hit the call button. Someone was using it and he had to wait, wasn't sure he could remain on his feet much longer. He leaned against the lift doors as a painless lethargy settled over him.

••••

"Doctor Yan."

Alsa looked up from the patient on the surgical table at the med tech who had just burst into her surgery.

"Captain Ballin's implant sensors just went nuts. Massive internal bleeding. Full cardiac arrest is imminent."

Alsa looked at her assistant, nodded at the patient. "Can you finish this?"

She knew he could, didn't wait for an answer and tore off her surgical gown as she sprinted out of the surgery barking orders. "Full CGIC unit, Hangar Deck, stat. And get a tank ready."

She grabbed her portable kit on the run, skidded to a halt in front of the lift, hit the call button. "Computer."

The lift cycled open and she stepped in. "Hangar Deck. Medical priority. Stat."

It took only an instant for the gravity compensated lift to travel the distance, then the lift cycled open and York fell into her arms. He gasped, "Don't let them see me."

She laid him on the deck of the lift as it cycled shut. "Sickbay. Med emergency priority," she shouted as she started tearing open his tunic.

She slapped a small monitor on his chest, which told her he was in full arrest. She reached into her kit, pulled out an injector, slammed a load of oxyline into the grip, pressed the muzzle against his carotid artery, pulled the trigger three times. She yanked out the oxyline clip, tossed it aside, jammed in a clip loaded with a mix of stimulants, dialed the gun for direct inter-cardiac insertion, pressed the muzzle against his chest and pulled the trigger once.

She watched the monitor on his chest carefully. His heart beat once, then again, then a third time, and that was it. No more.

The lift cycled open to a crowd of med techs with a portable cart. "Forget that," she growled. "We aren't getting anything more out of his heart, but I got enough oxyline into his brain to buy us about ten minutes. Get him on a table now, and get a tank ready."

••••

York felt good. In fact he felt wonderful. He was curious why Alsa and her people were working so frantically on that fellow on the table. But then that no longer mattered to him. He felt good, and he felt free, and nothing like that really mattered any more.

He turned to leave, surprised to find that he was floating, rather than walking. But that didn't matter either. He was free to go.

Maggie was waiting for him, though he didn't see her as much as he just sensed that she was there. And she didn't want him to go. He kept getting the message that it wasn't his time, but he didn't care. He wanted to go so badly, wanted the freedom, the lack of pain. But he sensed Maggie didn't think he should go yet, though he wanted to, so very badly he wanted to.

Epilogue:
Options

YORK SLAMMED AWAKE, sat up in bed, started to tear at the dressings on his chest.

"Wait," he shouted, forced his hands away from the dressings, medical dressings. They were real. It wasn't a dream.

He took in his surroundings. He was in a private cabin in sickbay. He closed his eyes—*Cinesstar* was silent, deathly so, lacking even the hum of her engines.

He eased slowly off the bed, was grateful that he hurt in every joint. He should hurt, that was right, and his knees were a bit weak. That too was right, but everything about *Cinesstar* was wrong. He needed a weapon, searched around painfully, though quietly, through cabinets and drawers, until he found some sort of plast medical instrument that was heavy enough to serve as a club. He found disposable jumpsuits sealed in sterile packages in a drawer. It took some effort to pull one on, but he managed. As he moved he felt stronger, and that heartened him, though he was constantly glad that he hurt everywhere, because that was as it should be.

A marine guard was stationed outside the door to the corridor, but York didn't recognize him. He stumbled clumsily to one knee in front of York, and before he could do anything else York clubbed him in the back of the head and he slumped to the deck, not completely out but badly dazed. Before he recovered York took his sidearm, then staggered toward the lift.

As the lift cycled open someone behind him shouted, "Wait."

York stepped into the lift, spun and raised the gun. A young med-tech froze in the middle of the corridor in York's sights. York knew he should kill him, buy more time, but the kid was so scared he just couldn't do it. The lift doors cycled shut, freeing them both of the need to decide what to do.

A skeleton crew of three techs manned *Cinesstar*'s bridge, none of whom York recognized. He waved the gun at them. "Get out. Now." They left quickly.

The lighting was dim, cut way back to conserve power. York eased his way around the instrument clusters, dropped down at the nav console.

Cinesstar was in a parking orbit around Luna, englobed by four destroyers. No sign of the Kinathin armada, no fighting going on anywhere, and home Fleet had been dispersed. Then York looked at the clock on the console and he was stunned to realize he'd been out for eight days.

"What the hell do you think you're doing?" Alsa Yan said calmly. She sat down at the console next to him, slapped a portable monitor on his chest where it stuck. "That marine you clubbed has a nice concussion. You should still be in bed. You weren't supposed to wake up for another hour or two, but then your system's so screwed up it'll be months before I can predict any timing on you."

She stared at the monitor for a bit. "You're doing all right."

"I hurt all over."

"Well, you should. No more artificial regrowth for you, no more speed healing, no more clonal implants. At least not for a while. We're going to get you well the old-fashioned way."

"How is he?" York looked up. Edvard stood over them both.

Alsa jumped to her feet, performed a rather clumsy bow. "Your Majesty."

"Please, Doctor Yan," Edvard said, waving a hand at York. "I think our patient is more important than court etiquette. Continue. Please continue."

Alsa leaned over York, took one more look at the monitor on his chest. "I think he just might be all right, though I don't like surprises like this."

York demanded, "Will someone tell me what's going on?"

Alsa pulled the monitor off York's chest. "I'm through here. If you'll excuse me," she bowed again. "I'll leave you two to talk."

After she was gone the emperor sat down in her place. He and York stared at one another for a long moment, then Edvard asked, "Do you know who your mother was?"

York nodded.

"And your father?"

York nodded again.

"I've never had a brother before," Edvard said. "Not even a half-brother. And Mother wishes you didn't exist at all. And by the way, she tried to correct that while you were unconscious, though the assassin she hired didn't get far, and your marines weren't kind to him. I've told her not to do it again, and she promised not to, but she only keeps promises that suit her, and I don't think this suits her. We'll just have to keep a close eye on the situation."

He paused for a moment to consider his words. "You know our father never really loved my mother. She's not a lovable person, and it was just a marriage of state. He loved me as his son, loved me dearly—I never doubted that—but it was your mother he loved as a wife. And when she was killed the life seemed to go out of him. He was never the same after that."

"Where's my crew?" York asked.

Edvard looked at him carefully. "A lot of them have been sent to hospital sector on Luna Prime. There were an amazing number of them wounded. The rest are still on this ship, though she's not in very good shape either. We'd like to start repairing her, but we can't do much of anything until we get your permission."

"My permission?"

Edvard looked at York carefully. "The empire has been split into a lot of factions. There are those who support me, those who support the senate, those who support the church, those who support you, those who support the old status-quo—though they are, by and large, a rather small minority—the list is endless. Interestingly enough, though, in every faction there are a lot of people who will support you, as long as you don't make a grab for power. Though, to be honest, you probably could take the throne if you wanted to. It wouldn't be much of a throne if you did, and you'd have a difficult time holding it together . . ."

Clearly Edvard needed some response from York. "I told you once I don't want your throne. I wouldn't know how to be a good emperor if I did."

"I thought you'd say that. In fact, that's the reason you're the one man in the empire who can pull together a coalition large enough to hold the empire together. There are a lot of people in almost every faction who believe you're driven by higher motives than the rest of us. It's ironic; as long as you don't make a grab for power, you are, at this moment, and probably for some time to come, the single most powerful person in the empire. Even the Kinathins support you. They're ready to join us against the Directorate, if the Directorate doesn't hold up its end of the treaty."

"The treaty was signed then?"

Edvard nodded. "Oh yes. Unanimously, on both sides, though there is some question as to its legality. But such questions will dissipate with time. And then there are a lot of details to work out and we need your help. We need the Kinathins, and they'll negotiate only with you."

"Where are the Kinathins?" York demanded.

"They've removed the armada from sovereign imperial space, though they left behind three cruisers, Add'kas'adanna and Ard'dha'sit as ambassadors." Edvard frowned for a moment, and chuckled.

"What's so funny?"

"Ard'dha'sit! Who would have ever believed he'd toss Ninda into that airlock with Abraxa?" Edvard shook his head and grinned. "We're going to have to be careful how we write the history books. We can't have it recorded that the old Duke de Maris was executed by the new."

York didn't like that. "What do you mean by that?"

Edvard suddenly looked quite guilty. "The situation is much too delicate to have it wholly dependent upon a mere captain, and one whose promotion was never approved by either me or the Admiralty Council. And you're going to have to represent the empire in negotiations with the Directorate and the Kinathins, and you'll need the appropriate rank and position to—"

York interrupted him. "Get to the fucking point."

Edvard grimaced. "You're not going to be happy with me, Admiral, but Abraxa had no heir, and his properties were originally in our family anyway, until they were taken illegally—"

"Damn it," York shouted. "What the fuck do you mean by *Admiral?*"

Edvard took another breath. "By royal edict, and with unanimous approval of both the imperial senate and the Admiralty Council—I should add that both were concerned that if they didn't approve it, they'd join Ninda and Abraxa breathing vacuum—we've ceded all of Abraxa's properties and titles to you. I regret to inform you that you are now His Grace, York, Duke de Maris, Admiral of the Fleet Ballinov."

Edvard let that hang while York came to the slow realization he could do nothing about it. "You've trapped me, you know. I don't want this, don't even know how to do it."

York closed his eyes, rubbed his temples, and thankfully Edvard didn't break the silence. A thought came to York. "A moment ago you said you couldn't do anything with this ship without my permission. What did you mean by that?"

Edvard grinned at him. "Your people are rather protective of you, and distrustful of the rest of us. They won't let us take you off this ship, won't even let us repair her. We can bring in supplies, and your people will do the repairs, but until you say otherwise we can't move one way or the other."

York couldn't help chuckling. "Good for them."

"I don't think you realize," Edvard said, "how close we came to having the empire destroyed. After the treaty was signed everyone wanted to speak with you, especially your subordinates, who wanted you to give them orders. But then we found you were close to death, and many officers like Captain Tzecharra thought it due to foul play. We came close to a free-for-all civil war. But Commander Jakobee put Doctor Yan on a system-wide broadcast, and after she explained the situation calmer heads prevailed. For all intents and purposes a small coalition of your subordinate officers is running this empire right now."

York couldn't help but laugh and shake his head.

"We have to hold this empire together, Admiral, in a delicate peace. And to do that we have to move forward, and we can't do so until you pull out the stops. By the way, Miss Votak has been asking about you. You two were close, weren't you?"

York started. "Maggie? She's alive?"

"Very much so, and doing quite well, actually better than you. She was able to take a lot of the treatments we can't yet give you. We—"

York was on his feet. "Can we go see her?"

Edvard stood. "Of course. But your people won't let you off this ship without a rather sizable, armed escort."

Edvard leaned over the console, touched a switch. A speaker answered him, "Ready-room, Palevi here."

"Sergeant," Edvard said. "Admiral Ballinov will be leaving shortly to see Miss Votak in hospital sector, Luna Prime. I assume you'll want to escort him."

"Who?" Palevi demanded, obviously unaware he was speaking to the emperor.

"Admiral Ballinov," Edvard repeated.

"Like I said, who the hell is that?"

"Sergeant," York said. "It's me."

"Cap'm, that you?"

"Yes, Sergeant, it's me. We're going to see Miss Votak, and I'll need an escort."

"Damn, it's good to hear you, sir. We're ready when you are. Uh, by the way, sir, they're gonna make me an officer, a cap'm. It ain't right, me bein' an officer. Can you do something about that?"

"We'll talk about it later," York said. "For now, we'll be down shortly."

"Aye, aye, sir. Palevi out."

York looked at the emperor. "If I have to be a fucking admiral, then he has to be a fucking officer."

Edvard laughed and shook his head.

York motioned to the lift. "After you, Your Majesty."

The emperor nodded, turned toward the lift and wove his way through the instrument clusters. York let him go until he was out of sight, then whispered into his implants, "Computer. Confirm access Three-Charlie-Two-Niner-One-Niner-Alpha."

Access Three-Charlie-Two-Niner-One-Niner-Alpha confirmed at access ring-zero.

York nodded slowly and grinned a little.

"Are you coming, Admiral?"

He turned toward the lift. "Yes, Your Majesty, I'm coming."

Appendix: Some Notes on Time

THE LUNAN EMPIRE and the Republic of Syndon operate on decimal (base-10) not duodecimal (base-12) time. The standard Lunan day, which is derived from our Terran day, is divided up into 20 hours, not 24. Each hour is divided up into 100 minutes, and each minute into 100 seconds. Hence, in our present-day duodecimal time, the day is divided up into 24 x 60 x 60 seconds—we'll call them Terran seconds, or ts—whereas in York's time and place that same day is divided up into 20 x 100 x 100 seconds—for clarity we'll call them Lunan seconds, or ls. So 86,400 (24 x 60 x 60) Terran seconds is equal to 200,000 (20 x 100 x 100) Lunan seconds, which means: 1 ls = 0.4320 ts. Or, one Lunan second is a little less than half a Terran second. The table below compares hours, minutes and seconds for the two timing systems.

Measure	Terran	Lunan
hour	1	0.83
minute	1	1.38
second	1	2.31

This is why there appear to be some unusual statements in the story. For example, Captain Te-lyekev said, "You made it on station in ninety-three seconds, almost a full minute." He said that because, for him and his shipmates, a minute is 100 seconds.

Author's Note

IN PREPARATION FOR publication of *A Choice of Treasons* by Open Road Integrated Media, it was necessary to make some revisions to the manuscript. When I self-published the original edition of the novel, I employed a contract copy editor to ferret out typos and errors, but once Open Road editor Betsy Mitchell got her hands on it, I was amazed at the number of little things she uncovered. In addition to typos, dotted t's, and crossed i's, she found a couple of real inconsistencies. The changes were all minor, so the original story and characters remain intact, but the final version is now considerably improved.

Furthermore, during the writing of *Of Treasons Born*—the prequel to this novel—it was necessary to make a few minor changes to ensure consistency between references to York's past in the later book, which was written first, and the events that took place during his youth in *Of Treasons Born*. Again, none of the changes affected the story, but it would be exceedingly poor form to ignore minor errors or allow inconsistencies to propagate.

Thanks, Betsy.

Acknowledgements

I'D LIKE TO thank Karen for supporting my dream and being my most valuable critic, Betsy Mitchell for fixing all my dotted t's and crossed i's and for believing in an indie, Steve Himes and the team at Telemachus for their support for the last several years, and all the people at Open Road Integrated Media for making this happen.

Books by J. L. Doty

Series: The Treasons Cycle
Of Treasons Born
A Choice of Treasons

Stand Alone Novel
The Thirteenth Man

Series: The Gods Within
Child of the Sword
The SteelMaster of Indwallin
The Heart of the Sands
The Name of the Sword

Series: The Dead Among Us
When Dead Ain't Dead Enough
Still Not Dead Enough
Never Dead Enough

Series: The Blacksword Regiment
A Hymn for the Dying
A Dirge for the Damned
A Prayer for the Fallen
A Requiem for the Forsaken

Series: Commonwealth Re-contact Novellas
Tranquility Lost

About the Author

JIM IS A full-time SF&F writer, scientist and laser geek (Ph.D. Electrical Engineering, specialty laser physics), and former running-dog-lackey for the bourgeois capitalist establishment. He's been writing for over 30 years, with 15 published books. His first success came through self-publishing when his books went word-of-mouth viral, and sold enough that he was able to quit his day-job, start working for himself and write full time—his new boss is a real jerk. That led to contracts with traditional publishers like Open Road Media and Harper Collins Voyager, and his books are now a mix of traditional and self-published.

The four novels in his new hard science fiction series, *The Blacksword Regiment*, are scheduled for release in July 2020. Right now he's fleshing out ideas for the next book in *The Dead Among Us*, he's writing another episode in *The Treasons Cycle*, and he's working on a new fantasy series *The Deck of Chaos*.

Jim was born in Seattle, but he's lived most of his life in California, though he did live on the east coast and in Europe for a while. He now resides in Arizona with his wife Karen and three little beings who claim to be cats: Tilda, Julia and Natasha. But Jim is certain they're really extra-terrestrial aliens in disguise.

Visit the author's website at http://www.jldoty.com
Contact the author at jld@jldoty.com